ROGER STEVENSON
JULY, 1995

# THE
# ELEMENTALS

# THE ELEMENTALS

# Morgan Llywelyn

**TOR**

A TOM DOHERTY ASSOCIATES BOOK  NEW YORK

THE ELEMENTALS

Copyright © 1993 by MORGAN LLYWELYN

This book is printed on acid-free paper.

A Tor Book
Published by Tom Doherty Associates, Inc.
175 Fifth Avenue
New York, N.Y. 10010

Tor® is a registered trademark of Tom Doherty Associates, Inc.

Book design by Maura Fadden Rosenthal

Library of Congress Cataloging-in-Publication Data

Llywelyn, Morgan.
   The elementals/Morgan Llywelyn.
      p.    cm.
   ISBN 0-312-85568-0
   I. Title.
PS3562.L94E4 1993
813′.54—dc20                          93-12760
                                       CIP

First edition: June 1993

Printed in the United States of America

0  9  8  7  6  5  4  3  2  1

*For Jack Snyder*

*The earth does not belong to Man.*
*We are merely tolerated.*
*For now.*

*We are the sea.*

*We are the planet's dual-purpose organ of reproduction and reverence. The trinity of sun, moon, and earth exchange their sacred energies through the linkage we provide.*

*We acknowledge no limits, merely impediments that we continually whittle away. We are a prism through whose liquid lens the colorful diversity of the planet is refracted. We contain the images of Atlantis and Lemuria and Mu, of transoceanic Pheonician trading vessels and the Titanic and the five lost planes of Flight 19.*

*Aswarm with life, we think trillions of versions of thought. Our sentience is in your blood, in everything that contains water.*

*We are the sea.*

*We do not see humans as humans perceive themselves. The creature called Man appears to us as a core of heat giving off radiance in the warm spectrum. Man is a seeker of solid surface, a self-replenishing organism capable of creating toxic wastes.*

*Man is a cancer that crawled from our womb.*

*We are watching. We are aware. We are the sea.*

1

*As the ice cap melted, the seas rose.*

*When they realized the land mass would be*

*inundated, people reacted in various ways. Some*

*planned, some panicked. Some did nothing, retreat-*

*ing into apathy until it was too late.*

A colony of craftspeople that had established itself on the western shore of a forested peninsula built a boat. They equipped it with oars and a square sail, and painted it a defiant crimson. They worked night and day on their project while the sea crept higher with each incoming tide.

Soon they found themselves having to fight to defend their boat from others who had not been wise enough to build one. The attacks grew progressively more desperate and savage. By the time the boat was completed only three men of the colony survived. Three men, and fifty females.

The woman called Kesair was big-boned and tawny-colored, with angry eyes. When the others gave way to despair, she climbed onto a stump left by the timbering and shouted at them. "Get ready to board and set sail! We must leave here before we are attacked again and lose the boat!"

"How can we," asked a grieving widow, "with no men?"

"We still have three," Kesair reminded her, "and our own strong backs. Don't just sit there! Let's get going!"

The surviving men, exhausted by their labors and battered by battle, gazed numbly at Kesair.

Fintan had broad shoulders and a noble head, but his face was grey with fatigue and blood was seeping from his bandaged arm. "She makes sense," he said hoarsely. "Let's do as she says."

"I don't like taking orders from a woman," Ladra growled.

"Then why didn't you get up on the stump and give the orders yourself?" asked Byth, the third man, who was slumped on the earth as if he had grown to it.

Ladra said defensively, "I was busy tarring the ropes."

"That's an excuse."

"Take the livestock from their pens and get them into the boat," Kesair ordered. After a brief hesitation, the others began complying. Fintan and Byth joined the women in the work, but Ladra stood off to one side, scowling, until so many people glanced at him contemptuously that he was forced to join them, muttering to himself.

They loaded a few small black cattle, a few long-legged sheep, a trio of yellow-eyed goats. The animals resisted but not very much. They could sense the sea, waiting to swallow them. They clambered up the ramp into the boat and stood shivering, with no control over their fate.

The humans felt the same.

When the moment arrived, they were sick with fear.

"We can go inland and wait a while longer," Ladra urged. "Perhaps the water will stop rising. We'd feel like fools then, if we had panicked unnecessarily. It would be better to be safe on dry land than on that boat somewhere. What if it leaks? What if it sinks?"

Kesair looked at the sea, heaving and muscular and alive. Then she looked down at her feet, where the first wavelets of the inrushing tide were already lapping her toes. "The peninsula will be inundated today," she predicted, "and I had rather be on the boat when that happens."

Turning her back on the others, she marched up the ramp.

They followed her. Timorously, casting anxious glances at the water and the land as if there was a choice, they followed her. Even Ladra, in the end, boarded the boat.

They pulled up the ramp, secured their vessel, and settled down to wait for the sea to float the boat.

The water hissed around its timbers as the tide swept in, rising past all previous high-tide marks. Rising and rising. There was a gentle bump; the boat shifted slightly. Its occupants tensed but nothing happened. Then it rocked again and they heard a grating sound down below.

At that moment men came over the horizon, running hard, yelling, waving weapons.

"We're trapped here!" Ladra cried. "They'll kill us and take the boat!"

The running men drew closer, shouting threats and demands. Byth, who was a grandfather, regretted his age. Fintan regretted his wound. Ladra shook his fist at Kesair. The women drew together in the center of the boat as the sea, testing, tentative, gave a tug at the vessel.

Then it wrenched the boat free from its blocks and swung it into the tide with a creak and a groan and a mighty rolling motion.

Kesair gasped and caught hold of the nearest support. A cow bellowed, a goat bleated. The waves pounded in, devouring the shore, hurling the boat forward like a battering ram. Its attackers broke ranks and ran, making for the rapidly shrinking surface of the dry land. The sea pursued them, driven by a power beyond all understanding. Reclaiming the earth.

The boat was hurled across a shallow sand spit and into deeper, roiling water that swept it away like a leaf on a river.

At first its occupants were too dazed to do more than hang on and stare back at the land as it fell away from them. They were dazed by the rapidity with which they were launched. The square sail was still furled at the mast, the oars lay untouched in their oarlocks. No one was doing anything, except the sea with its unexpected tidal surge.

"Can't we steer this thing?" Kesair cried.

Fintan shook off his shock and hurled himself toward the tiller. His wounded arm was the left; his right arm was undamaged, and strong enough to grasp the tiller and begin trying to bring some direction to the boat's gyrations. When she saw what he was doing, Kesair made her way to him and crouched down beside him, adding her strength to his on the tiller.

Through the wooden shaft and up into their straining arms came a sense of the boat and the water beneath it. Their efforts seemed hopelessly minuscule, compared to the forces with which they struggled, yet a faint response shuddered through the boat timbers. Out of sight, the rudder moved, making a statement against the tide.

The prow of the boat edged northward.

"Yes," Kesair said. "Yes!"

"We can't do anything with the tiller alone," Fintan told her. "We need the oars and the sail."

She repeated his words in a shout of command, addressing them to whoever would respond. Byth and Ladra were the first. It was hard work and they were awkward, being carpenters rather than sailors. Those who knew how to manage the boat had died defending it.

Some of the women began trying to help them. Confusion mounted. Men and women got in each other's way, stumbled, lost their tempers. An oar was somehow broken, snapped like a twig.

Fintan groaned in despair. "We have to do something," he said through clenched teeth. But he did not say what.

Kesair knew no more about boats than the rest of them. She was a weaver. But she was familiar with lines, leverage, spatial relationships. They were part of her craft. She squinted at the sail, which was now half-raised and flapping. "Take hold of that rope, that one there, and pull it toward you hard! No, toward *you!*" she shouted at Byth. Then, to one of the women, "And you there, take an oar and sit there, And you, next to her . . ."

They gaped at her, but did as she commanded. Hers was the only commanding voice in a great din of sea and snapping sail.

The sail tautened, the boat bounded forward.

Then the wind failed. The boat hung in the water. The inexperienced rowers flailed the oars to no purpose.

"Someone needs to set a beat for the oarsmen to follow, I think," said Fintan.

Kesair caught the eye of the oldest woman, Nanno, who had no useful strength, but had always been musical. "Nanno!" she shouted. "Pick up that broken oar and beat it against one of the kegs in a steady rhythm. The rest of you, follow the beat, row together!"

After a bit of trial and error and some ludicrous mistakes, the amateur crew began a rough approximation of rowing. The boat moved forward, slowly but with a sense of purpose.

"You don't know any more about boats than I do," Ladra said resentfully to Kesair. He was among the rowers, but had soon learned he did not enjoy the feeling of blistered hands.

She did not bother to answer him. The intensity of the task at hand—molding a crew out of people with no training, when she had no training in seamanship herself—took all her concentration. She paid no more attention to Ladra than to the bleating of the goats.

When the wind filled the sail, Kesair let the crew rest on their oars. When the wind fell off, they rowed again at her command. She began to feel an unfamiliar, and pleasant, sensation of power, as if the boat itself were consciously obeying her order.

The vessel was not easy to handle. It had been hastily built, wide in the beam to carry livestock, but with a draft too shallow and a rudder inadequate for the size of the boat. A rough sea would have swamped them.

But the sea was not rough. Once they passed beyond sight of land it subsided into vast grey-blue swells that heaved slowly, almost titanically, carrying the boat gently along. Toward sunset it grew even calmer, a huge beast settling itself for the night.

Fewer people were vomiting over the rails.

Byth leaned on his forearms on one of the barrels lashed to the deck, watching as the sail was lowered at Kesair's command. He felt shrunken by the immensity of sea and sky. "What will happen to us?"

"Did you say something?" Her task finished, Kesair turned toward him. She was hoarse from shouting orders.

"Just talking to myself. I . . . did you ever really believe the ice was melting?" he asked abruptly.

"I didn't pay much attention one way or the other, not for a long time. We were always being threatened with something, weren't we? Failing economy, disease, war; one after the other. That's why we moved to the peninsula. At least, that's why I did. To escape all the gloom and doom and live a constructive life in some sort of peace."

"Once it began, the disaster came upon us so fast," Byth said wonderingly.

She nodded. "What do you suppose has happened to the others?"

"Which others?"

"Everyone."

Byth drew a deep breath. "I don't know. It depends on where they were, I suppose. And how soon they realized the danger and began preparing for it."

"We didn't start soon enough, ourselves."

"No," Kesair agreed, "but at least we started. We didn't sit around waiting for someone else to save us. Those who waited are—"

"—probably dead now."

"Yes," she said sadly. "When I was a child, there were always strange men who wandered around prophesying the end of the world. My mother said we should feel sorry for them because they were mad."

"When I was a boy we threw stones at such men," said Byth. "If I had one of them here now, I would apologize to him."

"So would I."

Byth looked at Kesair out of the corner of his eye. He liked her. He wondered what she thought of him. He ran his fingers through the tight curls of his close-cropped, grizzled hair. You are an old man, he reminded himself.

Aloud, he said, "We have fifty females and only three men."

"What of it? There were always more women than men in the group anyway."

"But not such a disparity. Wherever we land, if we do land, it could be a problem."

"What are you talking about?"

"I am saying there is a possibility we may be the only people left alive. We haven't seen any other boats, not one. If you are going to be the leader, you have to think about these things."

"I never said I wanted to be the leader."

"No, but no one has challenged you for it."

"That's because they're dazed by everything that's happened."

"You were less dazed than the rest of us, it seems," Byth pointed out. "You could still think and act when action was most needed. That's what leadership is, I suppose. You have the title whether you sought it or not, and I suspect it will be very hard to put down."

Nightfall necessitated assigning people to stand watch. Kesair chose the most alert to take turns. Ladra was among them, grumbling, but he served his time when it came.

Kesair the leader had been created where only a weaver existed before.

When the last light faded from the sky it seemed to linger in the sea, a dark green luminosity lurking in the depths. Then it too faded. A velvety darkness, more intense and tangible than they had ever known, clamped down on the occupants of the red boat. Its weight pressed them into their weariness and they fell asleep thankfully, except for the few who had duties, or tried to stay awake long enough to search for familiar stars in the sky.

There were no stars. The night was overcast.

The wind ceased. The air was still.

The ocean surrounded them like a dark universe, oily-smooth, boundless. The brooding, merciless, destroying sea.

Empty except for themselves.

The boat drifted on the surface of the sea like a child's forgotten toy.

Trying to follow her mental image of a leader's behavior, Kesair had taken a place in the prow. There she spread her blankets for the night. She meant to sleep but lightly, just enough to restore a measure of energy.

The sail was lowered, the oars were in their locks. She had decided there was no point in trying to make more headway. They might as well drift during the night.

Tomorrow would be soon enough to decide on a course and begin a serious search for land.

But in which direction?

Kesair closed her eyes, but she could not sleep. Her eyeballs felt grainy against her lids. She opened them again and stared into the darkness.

The sides of the prow rose, curving, above her, like walls looming over her. Like waves about to crash down on top of her. She felt suffocated. She sat up abruptly and bunched her blankets behind her back, so she could lean against them without lying down.

Time passed without definition. Kesair tried to fight back the fears that kept surfacing in her mind. Her fists clenched with the effort.

A delicate, questing touch drifted across her face.

"What?" She glanced around, startled. She could make out only faint shapes in the darkness, but no one was anywhere near her.

There was no wind to have blown a strand of hair across her face.

Her mouth went dry. Don't panic! she told herself sharply. You're tired, that's all. You're imagining things.

She was touched again. This time the pressure was more pronounced.

Gooseflesh rose on her arms. Her frantically groping fingers found nothing in the air around her face.

She started to get up and was touched a third time. She froze, knees bent, one hand outstretched. The touch trailed lingeringly down her cheek, explored her lips, cupped her chin, then circled around below her ear, crawled up her hair, across the top of her head, down over her forehead, pressed her eyelids closed.

The thudding of Kesair's heart shook her entire body.

The pressure on her eyelids eased; she opened them. She was aware of a presence, unseen but palpable, beside her. The nearest human lay sleeping several paces away.

Something else was with Kesair in the night.

*The night seemed endless. Byth's*

*years weighed heavily on him. He stayed awake*

*during his turn at watch with the greatest difficulty,*

*and gladly surrendered his post to Kerish when she*

*came to relieve him.*

"What should I watch for?" she asked him.

"I don't know," he replied honestly. He shot a look in the direction of Kesair but she was only a shadowy shape in the prow, unmoving and unspeaking.

Byth was asleep before his head was pillowed on his arm.

Kerish shivered in the night and wrapped her cape more snugly around herself. She wished Kesair would come back and talk to her. Kesair was always so practical, so reassuringly full of common sense. But she seemed oblivious, sitting up there in the prow alone.

The night lasted for an eternity or two, then faded into a dull grey day. The sun never penetrated the clouds. The sea looked cold and sullen. And terribly, terribly vast.

Kesair came awake abruptly, surprised to find she had been asleep. Her muscles were stiff, her joints locked. When she tried to move she felt like a plant that had been frozen and would break rather than bend. She got to her feet slowly, holding on to the side of the boat.

When she stood and looked back at the others, she saw their faces turn toward her as flowers turn toward the sun. They sat waiting for her to tell them what to do next.

Seeing them waiting like that was a bit of a shock. I have to say something positive, she thought. They need it. *I* need it.

"We've passed safely through the night." She sounded pleased. "Perhaps we should offer a prayer now."

"A prayer?" They stared at her. Kesair had not been known as a fanatic before. Religion was unfashionable, an outmoded superstition. They believed Man was supreme in the cosmos, a belief Kesair had seemed to share. Before the catastrophe.

"I wouldn't care to pray to any deity who would let this happen to us!" the woman called Barra said angrily.

A murmur of agreement rose from the others. On their faces, Kesair read a threat to her newfound authority. If she tried to force the issue they might reject her.

She shrugged, and changed the topic to the distribution of food and assignment of tasks. After an uncertain pause, the group reverted to obedience. It was already becoming a comfortable habit. They were silently relieved that the embarrassing suggestion of prayer had been dropped.

Day wore on, became night, became day again. And again. They sailed this way and that, found no land, no people. Nothing. More and more, they simply drifted. It did not matter.

Social conventions were abandoned. Men and women openly relieved themselves over the side. Quarrels sprang up. The people were nervous, irritable, and apathetic by turns. Friendships were formed one day and broken the next.

Their food stores dwindled. The sea waited.

Byth droned on and on, listing an increasing catalog of physical complaints. The formerly brisk and bustling woman called Leel began sleeping the day away like a creature in hibernation.

Staring morosely at the sea, Ladra swore at the water bitterly, continually. He was inventive with profanity. Against her will, Kesair found herself listening to him. Once she laughed aloud.

He turned toward her, scowling darkly. "What are you laughing at?"

"Not at you. I was just enjoying your use of the language, that's all. You're very original."

He gazed at her for a long moment, then went back to cursing the sea. But after that he seemed more kindly disposed toward Kesair. That night when the food was distributed, he ate sitting beside her.

From his place opposite them, Fintan noticed the change in Ladra's attitude. He realized he was looking at Kesair differently himself. Before the catastrophe, he had paid her no attention. Women outnumbered men in the colony and he had always had his choice, which did not include Kesair. She was too tall, too fair, and he liked small dark women. More damning still, she was a loner. She did not seem to need a man. Fintan, who liked his women dependent, had ignored her. She was an exceptionally good weaver and did her share of the work, and beyond that he had no interest in her.

Before.

But now . . . he could hardly ignore the one person who had been able to take charge when he and the other surviving men were weary and defeated.

Surreptitiously, Fintan eyed the other female occupants of the boat. Old Nanno, two prepubescent daughters of a man who had been killed, an infant girl in her mother's arms. And forty-six women of childbearing age, including Kesair. Kesair, to whom the others deferred.

This gave Kesair an attractiveness Fintan had never noticed before.

Under his breath, he said to Byth, "Look at Ladra over there, trying to curry favor. Can't she see through him?"

"You sound jealous." Once Byth would not have commented on another man's emotions. But everything had been changed by the catastrophe. Byth stroked his chin, wondering when he had last shaved. None of the men shaved now.

"Jealous?" Fintan snorted. "Don't be ridiculous."

"Under the circumstances," Byth warned, "it wouldn't be a good idea to get too fond of any one woman. Think about it."

Fintan ignored him.

Byth shrugged. Arthritis bit deep into his shoulder and he rubbed the joint automatically, wondering how much damage the sea air was doing to him.

The color of the sea gradually changed. From slate-blue it became a warm, dark green. Kesair was the first to notice. She lifted her head and sniffed the wind.

"What is it?" Elisbut asked. Elisbut was a cheerful, chubby woman who made pottery and talked incessantly. "What do you smell?"

"Change in the wind," Kesair said succinctly. She did not want to encourage a flood of conversation.

Anything was enough to set Elisbut off, however. "I don't smell anything unusual, Kesair. Perhaps you're imagining things. I used to do that all the time. My mother—you would have liked her—my mother used to tell me I had too much imagination. Now I never thought a good imagination was such a liability in an artistic person like myself, but . . ."

Kesair was not listening. "We're going to change course," she shouted abruptly to her crew.

Within half a day they caught sight of a thin dark line on the horizon and knew they had found land.

Sailing in from the northwest, they made landfall on the rocky coast of what seemed to be a vast island. It was hard to be certain; most of the land was shrouded in mist. The boat ground ashore on a beach of white sand studded with black boulders. After dragging their vessel as far up the beach as they could, they secured it and set about exploring the immediate area.

"No sign of people," Ladra reported after scrambling up the nearest cliff and back down again. "But there is a sort of wiry grass up there, and I'd say we could find fresh water if we go in just a little way. We've been lucky. So far," he added darkly. "This could be a bad place. I wouldn't be surprised."

Kesair assigned armed scouting parties to explore the area more thoroughly. All brought back similar reports. Thin soil, unsuitable for farming, but a lushness of wild vegetation. A pervasive mist that rolled over the land, blew away, returned with a will of its own. Glimpses of distant grassland bordered by forest. Outlines of mountains beyond.

"If we have to start life over," Fintan said, "I would say we've found a good place for it."

They built a bonfire of driftwood that night on the headland above the beach. When Kesair found some of the women throwing the refuse from the boat into the sea, she ordered them to put it on the fire instead.

"What difference does it make?" they challenged. They did not want to carry armloads of rubbish up the slope to the fire. "One load of garbage in an empty ocean, what difference?"

But this time Kesair was adamant. Grumblingly, they obeyed. The tongues of the fire licked at the rubbish and a dark smoke rose from it, stinking of the old life.

Blue twilight settled over them. Down on the shore, the red boat gleamed dully in the last rays of the setting sun, then turned grey, like a beached whale dying at the edge of the sea.

As they ate their first meal on dry land, some people talked compulsively about their recent experience, retelling the boat-building and the battles and the flood, incidents which were already taking on a mythic quality in their minds. Others sat silently, simply trying to comprehend. Trying to realize that they were safe at last.

Kesair was not so certain of their safety. Any sort of danger might await them on dry land, on what seemed to be a very large and unknown island. They could die a more horrible death in the jaws of wild beasts than they would have suffered by drowning in the sea.

The next morning, Kesair organized work parties to build huts for the people and pens for the livestock. The men and women were to be housed separately, for the time being, and as leader she ordered a hut built for herself alone.

"Why don't we go farther inland?" Byth suggested.

"Not yet. We don't know what may be waiting for us. It's better we stay here for a while until we are established and used to the place."

The truth was, she was reluctant to leave the sea. But she did not say this.

They worked hard, bringing timber from the distant forest. They met no savage beasts, but twice they reported hearing a howling in the distance, as of wolves, and they were overjoyed to sight a herd of deer beyond the trees.

The group settled into a domestic routine not unlike the one they had known before the catastrophe. "We're lucky," she told Byth, who had become the closest thing she had to a confidant. "Among us we have most of the skills we shall need. We can make our own tools and clothing, we can build and repair."

She set up her big loom in the lee of her hut, where the morning sun supplied a clear yellow light.

Not everyone was ready to settle down. Some seemed devoted to grieving over what they had lost, hampering the work of the colony. Kesair learned she could rely on Elisbut, Fintan, Kerish, and the women called Ayn and Ramé to do what must be done, and enlisted them to help her encourage the others.

On a chill, damp afternoon when rain blew in from the sea in curtains of silver, Fintan came to Kesair's hut. He paused in the doorway, stooping, peering in, waiting for his eyes to adjust to the gloom. "Are you in here?" he asked uncertainly.

"I am," she said from a bed made of piled blankets. "I was just resting, listening to the rain."

Without waiting for an invitation, Fintan entered the hut. He gave off a smell of wind and water. "We need to talk."

"Sit there." The thought skittered across Kesair's mind that she should offer him food, or drink, but she was a solitary creature by nature and had never practiced the skills of hospitality. "Help yourself to whatever you want," she said lamely, making a vague gesture in the direction of her stores.

"Talk is what I want, some sort of plan. We can't just stay like this, Kesair. Winter is coming on, we probably need to go farther inland to avoid the worst of the weather. We don't even know how bad winter gets in this place."

"So how do we know it might be milder inland?"

"It stands to reason. And there's another thing . . ." His eyes were used to the dimness now. He could see her leaning on one elbow, watching him, her long legs stretched out beneath a blanket. Suddenly the hut seemed very small and intimate.

"What?" she said.

He swallowed. "We need to get on with our lives. We've been tiptoeing around this for weeks, but we must face the fact. As far as we know, we may be all that remains of the human race. If we don't reproduce ourselves, it could be the end of mankind.

"Of course, it could be too late already, I know that. But I feel an obligation to try . . ." He ground to a halt. She was looking at him intently, with an unreadable expression.

He picked up the threads of his thought. "People look up to you, Kesair. The other women follow you. If you were to urge them to, ah . . ."

"Mate," she said.

He had not expected her to put it so baldly. "Ah, yes. Mate. Have children, a lot more children . . ."

Kesair sat up, clasping her knees with her square, blunt-fingered hands. She locked his eyes with hers. "Fifty women alone on a large island with three men," she said in an expressionless voice. "Just imagine. Every man's fantasy."

He said huffily, "I'm not proposing an orgy, Kesair! You're an intelligent woman, you know exactly what I'm saying. You understand that—"

"—that you hope to use my mind to get at my body," she said flatly. "If you can. If I let you."

Stung by the truth in her accusation, Fintan retorted, "You don't have a very good opinion of men, do you?"

Kesair did not answer. He could have enjoyed an argument, but he had no coping skills for female silence.

Fintan tried to recall what he knew about her, seeking some sort of leverage. She was a latecomer to the crafts colony, having arrived with neither man nor child, only her loom and her skill, but she had proved to be an exceptionally creative weaver. Soon her work had been in great demand among the colony's customers, becoming a mainstay of their economy. No one had been willing to risk offending her by prying into her private life.

Very little was known about Kesair, Fintan realized. She was something of a mystery.

A most intriguing mystery.

He must get her to trust him. "I don't much care for the company of men myself," he told her confidingly. "I really prefer women, always have. I think women are the best of us." He favored her with his most winning smile, knowing his teeth were white and even and his eyes crinkled boyishly.

Kesair stared right through him, unimpressed.

Fintan choked back his annoyance. Did she not understand that men were now at a premium? That he could have his choice of any woman he wanted? He could walk out right now and it would be her loss, not his. He had forty-five others to choose from.

But he did not walk out. There were forty-five others, but Kesair was the leader. She was not beautiful, like Kerish, but she was special, she had an indefinable something extra. And he was Fintan, whose pride demanded he go for the best.

Wiping his smile from his face, he replaced it with a studiedly serious expression he thought she might like better. "What we need to do, Kesair, is to divide the women into three groups. Each man will take responsibility for one third of the women, do you see?" He paused. "Well, not Byth, perhaps. He may be a little old. But he can at least take a few and Ladra and I can handle the rest."

"Responsibility? What sort of responsibility? There is already a leader. Myself."

She is pretending to be stupid to irritate me, Fintan thought. She wants to be blunt; very well. I can be blunt. "Responsibility for them sexually. For getting them pregnant," he elaborated, trying to stare her down.

To his astonishment, she laughed. "Is that all? Fine. Pick out your—how many would you say, twenty each for you and Ladra, and ten for Byth?—pick out your twenty and get on with it. Just don't impregnate all the sturdiest ones at the same time, we need to keep an able work force. And wait for the younger girls to grow a few more years before you start with them."

Fintan's jaw sagged with dismay. What had happened to the titillating mating games a woman was supposed to play? He had imagined a very different sort of afternoon in Kesair's hut, listening to the rain on the roof, talking first impersonally and then very personally of sexual matters, advancing, holding back, weighing selected phrases with double meanings, gradually offering more intimate caresses. The mounting excitement, the thrill of the chase . . .

"Which women do you want?" Kesair drawled with supreme indifference. She twisted her upper body to put back a piece of chinking that had fallen from between the timbers of the hut wall beside her. The repair had her total attention.

Fintan got to his feet. "Not you, anyway!" he told her. He stomped furiously from the hut into slanting silver rain.

Kesair turned her head to watch him go. A light flickered in her eyes. He's proud, she thought. I like that in a man.

Fintan sought Ladra, whom he found at the edge of the cliff, throwing rocks down at the sea as if he were pelting an enemy. There was hatred and anger in every throw.

The sea had swallowed the world he knew. Ladra hated the sea. From time to time he yelled curses at it.

"Come with me to the men's hut," Fintan said to him. "We need to talk."

Ladra squinted at him from beneath dark, tangled eyebrows. Ladra was slightly taller than Fintan, with long arms but disproportionately short legs. He looked as if he had been made from the parts of several men. "Is it important?"

"I think so," Fintan replied.

Ladra hurled one last stone, then shrugged and followed Fintan. "I'm tired of being wet anyway," he said.

The men's hut was empty. Byth was elsewhere. Fintan and Ladra went in out of the rain. The hut was small and dark and smelled of mud and freshly cut logs.

"It's time we organized our social structure for the future," Fintan began earnestly. "I've been giving it a lot of thought and I've come up with a workable, sensible plan."

Ladra listened, frowning, as Fintan outlined his idea. Then Ladra said, "I don't much care for all this organizing. It smacks of a desire to control. And I think the desire to control has caused a lot of mankind's problems, Fintan."

"There will be more problems if we don't agree on a plan soon and start to follow it. You can't put this many people together in this sort of situation without trouble, sooner or later. I'm just making the most intelligent suggestion. People need to know what to expect."

"But Kesair wants us to use our energies for getting dug in here for the winter, making more tools and weapons, setting up some sort of defensive perimeter in case—"

"We can do all that too," Fintan interrupted impatiently.

"What does Kesair say to your plan? You did discuss it with her, didn't you? She and I should be—"

"You're making assumptions. You can't just appropriate a woman for yourself, Kesair or anybody else. We have to be sensible about our, ah, breeding arrangements. We have to use our heads."

"Our *heads?*" Ladra said with a grin. "That's not how I do it."

Fintan had the grace to laugh. "You know what I mean."

"I know what you mean all right." The other man sobered. "I suppose you expect the best women for yourself?"

"To avoid arguments I thought we might, well, draw lots for them."

Ladra shook his head. "I can imagine you trying to convince those women out there that it's all right for us to draw lots for them. Good luck. I don't want to be around when you try to sell the idea."

"You always criticize," Fintan complained, "but you never have a better suggestion."

Ladra said smugly, "As it happens, this time I do. The other women accept Kesair as leader. So have her make the assignments, just as she assigns work. If she's willing to accept this plan of yours at all, that is. I'm not sure she is, I'd like to hear what she thinks."

"She said we should get on with it," Fintan said with perfect honesty.

"Did she now? Ah. Well then." Ladra seemed satisfied.

He thinks Kesair will give herself to him, Fintan thought darkly.

When Byth returned to the hut and was told of Fintan's plan another problem arose. Byth was insulted at the suggestion that he take fewer women than the other men.

"But you're always complaining about your age and your infirmities," Ladra reminded him. "You even call yourself Grandfather!"

"And so I am, which is just my point. Before my wife died I sired seven children on the dear woman, all of whom grew up to have more children. They went out on their own long ago, but let me assure you I am patriarch of a large brood of extremely healthy . . ." A shadow crossed his face. "At least, they were healthy. Strong, intelligent. Exactly the sort of people we need. I can give the colony many more like them. Divide the women equally and I can take care of mine, never fear."

Later, Fintan said privately to Ladra, "How many women are going to want to go with an old man?"

"That will be Kesair's problem, won't it?"

Kesair. As he lay wrapped in his blankets that night, listening to Byth snore like pebbles rattled in a bucket, and Ladra toss restlessly in his own bed, Fintan thought of Kesair and brooded on the choices she might make.

The perpetually moist air of the land they had found lay lightly on his skin; permeated his lungs; surrounded and contained him. A damp, penetrating cold seeped into his bones.

Fintan pulled his blankets more tightly around his shoulders. He was uneasy.

He did not sleep well.

3

*When he emerged from the hut in*

*the morning, the rain had passed and a radiant*

*autumn sunshine was gilding Kesair's face as she*

*came toward him. She was returning from a dawn*

*visit to the*

seashore, a strange habit she had adopted. Beckoning her aside, Fintan told her of his discussion with the other men, and Ladra's suggestion.

"So Ladra thought of that, did he?" She smiled, which irritated Fintan. "Good for him. Of course I'll divide the women among you. They will see the necessity for it; I'll talk to them and explain. Some of them may not like it, however. It's a pity we don't have a better choice of men."

Fintan bristled. "What do you mean by that?"

"I mean, I assume I shall have to select one of the three of you for myself, and it's not a particularly appealing thought."

There! she thought. See how you like that!

Fintan bit back an angry response. The thought briefly crossed his mind that Kesair might prefer women, but he discarded the idea. There was something in the back of her eyes that told him otherwise, he was sure of it.

Perhaps she just was not interested in sex. But he did not believe that either.

When Kesair talked to the other women, she got mixed responses. Some were plainly horrified. "It sounds like dividing a herd of cows among three bulls," Leel complained.

"I don't see what else there is to do," Kesair said flatly. "There aren't enough men to go around, and we have to think of the future. If this island has enough resources to allow us to survive, we must start planning for the next generation here."

"I refuse to be a breeding animal!"

"That's your prerogative, no one's going to force you. You'll simply be left out." Kesair folded her arms, waiting.

Left out. Leel hesitated, considering the ramifications. Kesair had chosen the phrase deliberately, and it carried weight. In a more subdued tone, Leel said, "Can't we at least choose our men?"

"If we tried, there would surely be quarrels and resentment. And the distribution would probably be uneven. No, I think it's better we make an unemotional assignment and abide by it. We can do that, I know we can," she added with a confidence she did not feel.

Some of them accepted. Others refused for a while. But in the end they agreed. Kesair had been thinking about the matter for longer than they had, and had her arguments skillfully prepared.

The night before Kesair was to announce her decisions, she walked alone by the sea. Without even bothering to eat an evening meal, she had gone to the beach, drawn by the hissing of the foam. The white sand glimmered in the moonlight. A cold wind blew off the ocean. Kesair shivered, then wrapped her woolen cloak more tightly around her shoulders.

After tomorrow, she thought, our lives will be changed in ways we cannot yet imagine.

She had counseled a pragmatic, unemotional approach to the situation, but she was too wise to believe it possible. By its very nature sex involved passion, and when human passions were aroused anything might happen.

Like someone exploring a sore tooth with just the tip of the tongue, Kesair let her thoughts skim the surface of her personal history. She thought for one brief moment of the man who had hurt her more than she would have believed possible. She had thought her emotions were cauterized by the experience.

Now she knew they were not. She could feel. She could be hurt again. She did not want to be hurt again.

In sharply delineated footprints the soft sand recorded every step she took at the ocean's edge. A blurred area showed where she finally halted and stood gazing outward, lost in thought, then started forward as if to enter the water, hesitated, scuttled backward, stopped again, stood at last immobile. Caught. Held.

She breathed shallowly. She did not want the sound of her own breath to interfere with the voice of the sea. She listened, and that voice built, became a great rolling thunder resonating through her bones, a massive muffled booming as if some mighty heart were beating there, out beyond the breakers. A long sigh . . .

"What?" Kesair asked eagerly. "What?"

The new day dawned cold and crisp. As the people assembled in the open space around which they had built the huts and pens, Kesair studied their faces. The men looked more anxious than the women. In their faces was a tension, a wary watchfulness of one another.

By contrast the women stood quietly, looking from one male face to the other with a glance both dispassionate and measuring.

"The sooner we get this over the better," Kesair announced. "There is no way to divide fifty evenly, so I've decided that two men will take seventeen women each, and the other man will have sixteen. Fintan and Byth have seventeen." She saw the look of surprised anger on Ladra's face but went on smoothly, "Byth's group will include Nanno and the girl children, because I am sure Nanno would prefer being with a man of her generation and the children already consider Byth as a grandfather."

Ladra's expression eased slightly. "Fintan still has more women than I do," he pointed out. "Shouldn't I get the best ones, to make up for that?"

"'Best' women?" Leel challenged. "Do you think it's your place to grade us on merit? Are you asking for the prettiest as if the others were inferior?" Her eyes were blazing. Leel was thin and dark and very intense, with a temper like the crack of a whip.

Kesair smiled to herself. She meant Leel for Ladra; let the two of them blunt their bad tempers on one another.

"Silence, both of you," she commanded.

Smoothly, without pausing for comment or reaction, she called out the names as she had mentally arranged them the day before. Ramé, who was calm and steady, was assigned to Ladra. The reliable Ayn, who had nursing skills, was paired with Byth. Kesair wanted to have at least one woman whose common sense she trusted in each group. Elisbut she assigned to Fintan. Velabro for Ladra. Barra for Byth. Salmé for Fintan. Murra for Ladra.

When she paired Kerish with Byth an astonished light leaped in the old man's eyes.

"Kerish will warm your blood," Kesair told him, smiling.

So the beauty of the colony went to a grandfather. To their credit, neither Ladra nor Fintan voiced an objection. Each grudgingly admitted to himself the wisdom of the choice, and was thankful that at least his rival would not have Kerish. She was ideal for stimulating an old man's virility.

As the number of unassigned women dwindled, Ladra kept trying to catch Kesair's eye. Fintan did not look at her. He accepted the assignments impassively, with a brief nod to each woman who was named for him. He might have been accepting a portion of food, or clothing, for all the emotion he showed.

He does not want to be hurt, so he pretends not to care, Kesair thought.

The day before, she had decided to assign herself to Byth's group. Byth in the role of father figure was appealing to her. Her own father had been loved, but was long dead. Besides, Byth would probably not make much in the way of sexual demands on her, not when he had Kerish.

The naming went on.

Kesair had given so much thought to her choices that she could recite them automatically, allowing her tongue to follow the grooves she had worn in her mind. she hardly had to think, merely to say, "Ashti to Ladra, Datseba to Byth, Kesair to Fintan . . ."

The words flashed through the air before she realized what she had said. Her tongue had betrayed her. She drew in a startled breath, as if she could unsay the words by inhaling them.

Fintan was looking at her now.

She dare not contradict herself and say she meant Byth instead. She would look like a fool.

She made herself go on. "Leel to Ladra . . ." But her heart was pounding as it had pounded the night before, when, all her choices made, she had gone for a walk by the sea.

Fintan's grey eyes were gazing at her fixedly. Ladra was flushed with anger.

She swallowed hard, trying to steady herself. Listening to her own words, she realized she had almost completed the list of names. The mother with the baby she must now give to Byth, to make the numbers come out right.

When the woman smiled with relief Kesair felt a stab of jealousy.

Once the divisions were made, people were curiously uncomfortable with each other. No one seemed to know what to do next until Byth said, "Come to me, all my chicks. This occasion deserves to be celebrated."

After a momentary hesitation, his women joined him. The littlest girl, Datseba, stood close beside him and slipped her small hand into his.

Byth grinned. Ignoring the arthritic twinge in his shoulder, he made an all-encompassing gesture with his free arm. "Follow me, please."

He led them to the men's hut, where he kept his small hoard of personal effects. Each female was given something. Datseba received a tiny carved figurine he had once meant for his own granddaughter, but not sent to her before the flood separated them forever. Old Nanno beamed toothlessly when Byth wrapped his favorite woolen scarf around her neck. Kerish was awarded the only gold ornament Byth possessed. He presented it with a gallant speech. "This dims by comparison with your beauty," he said.

The others watched from a distance as Byth won the hearts of each of his women in turn.

"An old man can get away with that," Ladra muttered. He began calling the names of his own assigned women. They stepped forward, some willingly, several reluctantly. When they were gathered around him he turned toward Kesair. "Am I expected to build individual homes for them or what? How are we going to do this?"

Kesair gave him a blank look, suddenly embarrassed to realize her careful planning had not foreseen the next step.

Fintan spoke up, and she was silently grateful. "We should stay as we are through the winter, until we know what winters are like on this island. In the spring we can go out and let each group find a different location for itself, some place with good soil for farming.

"This winter will give us time to get used to the new, ah, arrangements, and to plan for the future. Plus we will have the security of being together through the hard season."

Ladra cleared his throat. "What are we going to do about beds? As it is, the women sleep in several huts, the men sleep in another, it's awkward, considering."

In spite of himself, Fintan glanced at Kesair. She met his eyes unflinchingly but said nothing.

He scratched his jaw reflectively, wondering why she was leaving it to him to answer. "I don't think we should rush things," he said at last. "This isn't the way relationships were . . . before. We're all going to have to get used to the idea. Allow some time, and I suspect it will sort itself out. We might build a few, ah, private huts, where couples can be alone together. When they want to. But it's up to you, of course."

Fintan's words relieved some of the tension. As if saved from some disaster, the people threw themselves into their day's tasks with excessive enthusiasm, talking about everything but the change in the social order. Yet Kesair noticed the way Velabro kept glancing at Ladra. The way Elisbut winked at Fintan.

Kesair said nothing to Fintan beyond the requirements of their tasks. She was more formal with him than she had ever been. He showed the same attitude toward her. There was a new brittleness in their voices when they spoke to each other.

If she is so indifferent to me, Fintan was thinking, why did she burden me with herself?

Is he angry? Kesair wondered. He said he didn't want me, but I didn't think he meant it. What if he did?

They had other things to worry about. Winter was rushing in upon them. Every day seemed perceptibly shorter than the one before, and an awareness of night and dark and cold permeated everyone's thought. Almost daily, Kesair examined their supplies, watching with alarm as they dwindled. She organized hunting parties. The men went after the red deer with limited success; they were unused to hunting for the sake of survival. The deer, who were accustomed to avoiding predators, usually escaped them. Two does and a half-grown buck were all the men could bring down in a fortnight of hard effort. Then the deer took to the mountains and were seen no more, hiding successfully in enshrouding mist.

"You've led us to this place to starve," Ladra accused Kesair.

She read the same accusation in other eyes. They were already cold, and growing increasingly fearful of hunger. They had found a good harvest of autumn nuts and berries, but these would not see them through the winter.

In an effort to cheer them, Kesair ordered a huge fire built in the center of the compound and kept burning night and day, so its warmth was constantly available and its light could challenge the increasingly gloomy atmosphere. There were numerous cloud-muffled days when the sun never broke through the heavy overcast and the people were trapped in a perpetual twilight.

Kesair fought their depression with the fire. They huddled around it gratefully.

In its light, however, she could see their faces growing thinner. She cut back rations again and yet again, ruthlessly, in an effort to make them last. But last until what?

Instinct drove her to the sea at last. Buffeted by a gale, she walked along the wind-whipped shore, watching great crested white dragons rise out of the surf and fall back, snarling. The ocean wore a savage face. Yet she stayed beside it, numb with cold. She remained until the icy wisdom of the sea seeped into the marrow of her bones.

With chattering teeth she returned to the compound.

The fire was a warm orange god, shedding beneficent heat and light on its worshipers.

But there were other gods.

"Extinguish that blaze," Kesair ordered.

Shocked faces turned to stare at her. "What are you saying?" Byth cried.

"We are spending all our strength gathering wood for the fire. Then we crouch beside it until it's time to go get more wood. We are doing nothing else, and we're wasting wood. If we moved around more briskly we wouldn't be as cold. Bring buckets of water, dig earth and throw it over, to extinguish the fire. Then let's start seriously finding food for ourselves. We can't afford to pamper ourselves any longer."

It was the least popular order she had issued. People whined, protested, argued bitterly. Byth the kindly, the avuncular, called her a fool to her face. Salmé accused her of being callous. Datseba began to cry. Byth put a protective arm around the girl and glared over her head at Kesair. He looked like an eagle defending its nestling.

Unexpectedly, Ladra got to his feet with a grunt and began kicking dirt on the fire. "She's right," he said. "Everyone has to be right sometime. Let's go hunting."

Fintan raised his eyebrows in surprise. Ladra had been the first to be disheartened by their lack of success as hunters and abandon the effort. "The deer are long gone," he pointed out.

"We weren't good at catching deer anyway," Ladra replied. "But we've seen lots of birds, and there are any number of small animals in the woods. I've heard them even if I haven't seen them."

No one had any experience of building traps or setting snares. They had never required such primitive skills. But the weapons they had tried to use on the deer were not suitable for birds and small game, so they had to discover new techniques.

Working together, Murra and Ladra invented a clumsy trap that was nevertheless capable of catching hares and stoats, and minuscule voles. Stoat and vole were only edible if one were starving, but Kesair ordered that they be cooked anyway, and the people try to acquire a taste for them. Hare, roasted or boiled with root vegetables, became a staple of their diet.

As a weaver, Kesair was the one to construct snares to hide in woodland undergrowth. These produced a constant supply of small birds to augment the diet, even in the worst weather. Particularly in the worst weather, when birds took shelter in cover.

They would not have to eat their few livestock. The land was supporting them. Cow and goat and sheep would live to see the spring and reproduce themselves, guaranteeing herds and flocks.

When they were sure they could make it through the winter, people's attention began to turn to other matters. Kesair had rewarded their diligence by allowing a fire in the compound at night, but smaller than before, not so lavishly wasteful of timber. Sitting around the campfire, eating their evening meal, men and women glanced at one another meaningfully.

Ladra and Murra were the first to go off together and make use of the private huts built on the far side of the compound. The others pretended not to notice. Since they shared quarters on the crowded boat, they had learned to erect invisible screens of privacy for the most personal functions.

The night Ladra took the first of his women to a private hut, Byth could not eat his meal. He sat staring at the food. Then he looked at Kerish, sitting cross-legged several paces from him, glowing from the heat of the fire, tearing meat from bones with her strong young teeth.

"Ah . . . Kerish," he said softly.

She glanced up.

"It's going to be cold tonight. I think I smell ice on the wind."

"Do you?" Kerish did not seem particularly interested. She was warm by the fire, as a cat is warm, languorous and easy in her body. She took another bite of meat.

Byth tried again. "I don't sleep well when it's very cold."

Ah, thought Kerish. Yes. She looked at him in the firelight. An old man, a ruin of a man. But the ruin of a man who had once been handsome. A woman with a little imagination could, in a dim light, see him as still handsome. And he was kind.

Ah, thought Kerish again. I might as well get it over with. It won't be so bad, not if I set myself to enjoying.

She rose and went to sit beside Byth. Close beside him. "There are three private huts," she said in a low voice. "One is occupied, but . . . perhaps you might sleep better in one of the others? If you had company?"

Watching them, Kesair felt the sea singing in her blood. Answering the tug of the tides. She glanced covertly at Fintan.

If he felt her eyes on him he gave no sign. He was talking to Elisbut. The potter was responding vivaciously, with smiles and expansive gestures and occasional laughter, obviously enjoying herself.

I don't care, Kesair thought. I'm only with him because I meant one name but said another.

I wish I were with Byth.

She rose and walked restlessly to the edge of the compound. They had established themselves on the headland. Below, no distance away, was the sea.

Out of the corner of his eye, Fintan watched her. He smiled and nodded to Elisbut, paying superficial attention, which was all she needed to encourage her flow of words. But his true focus was Kesair. He knew where she stood, how she stood—straight-backed, almost leaning forward, her arms folded across her chest for warmth.

He knew everything but what she thought and felt. Did she care about anything?

Below her was the sea. Kesair could see the luster of the water, far out. Its power was so immense, its presence so demanding, that her awareness of Fintan fell from her. The sea absorbed her thoughts as it had absorbed the existence of millions.

All those lives destroyed, she thought. Or were they? Do they still exist in some way, as part of the sea? Can life be destroyed? Or merely transmuted?

She had never thought such thoughts before. Where did they come from?

# 4

*Once the mating dance had begun,*

*it continued throughout the winter. Mindful of the*

*injunction not to get all the strong women pregnant*

*at the same time, each man concentrated on only a*

*portion of his*

group. Fintan spent time in the private hut with Elisbut and with dark-haired Surcha. But never with Kesair.

The little girls were very curious. Covering giggling mouths with their hands, they crept as close to the private huts as they dared and tried to hear what was happening inside. They made wild guesses. "I think the men and women go in there to fight!" little Datseba said. "They grunt and squeal, don't they?"

As the group waited for spring, there was a subtle shift in its dynamic. Kesair was the acknowledged leader, but as one woman and then another conceived, the pregnant women became the focal point of the community and their men strutted proudly.

Elisbut and Murra announced their pregnancies within days of one another. But it was Kerish who caused the most excitement. When she told Byth he had sired a child, his joy overflowed.

"What do you think of this old man now, eh?" he kept asking people. "This old man? Eh?" He could not stop grinning. He treated Kerish as if she were made of spun glass, and found tiny presents to give her. He wrapped her in his warmest blanket and quoted everything she said, no matter how banal.

The little girls laughed and giggled and watched with wide eyes.

More and more, Kesair spent her time alone on the beach. The susurration of the sea was her companion's voice. The incoming tide laid gifts at her feet. She found pieces of flint, bits of colored glass, twisted fragments of forged metal. Once a human thigh bone, sand-scoured to ivory.

What the sea had taken it gave back transformed.

She tried to get others to share and appreciate her growing awareness, but she could not adequately articulate her discoveries, and the others were too busy or preoccupied to listen.

"You're in danger of becoming a fanatic," Ladra warned her, "and nobody likes a fanatic. We've been through a lot, but you mustn't give in to these wild notions of yours, Kesair. You'll lose everyone's respect if you do. What has the sea done for us but flooded the land and killed people? I'll tell you what I think about the sea. I piss in it!"

Ayn put it more delicately. "I would like to stop and listen to what you're trying to tell me, Kesair, honestly I would. But you know yourself there is work to be done. You assigned it. You can't expect us to abandon our chores now, when we need every pair of hands, to come and listen to you talk about, well, about something no one understands. I'm sure you mean well, but it's really just superstition, isn't it? Worshiping the invisible, so to speak?

"We don't have time for that sort of nonsense anymore, Kesair. As a race we've long since grown beyond it. Come now, come away from the sea, back to the huts and the fire. And your loom, that's where you're needed. We need your talents and your strength and your energy more than you need to be staring out at the sea all the time."

Kesair began to feel a sort of pity for them. They were blinded by daily routines. They were deaf to the voices she heard.

Alone, she began collecting shells and stones, secreting them in a tiny cove sheltered by dark boulders. Almost every day she went there. Only the most bitter weather could keep her away. Answering some deep need beyond the design of rational thought, she began assembling her stones and shells into a tower, a conical symbol rising from the sand. On the rare days of pale winter sun and deceptive warmth she could spend a whole morning there, frowning at her handiwork, perhaps moving just one shell a fraction to the left.

At night she dreamed of the cove and the tower.

The days were growing longer, misty and mild.

The people began to talk of leaving the compound and seeking land to farm. As their infants grew inside them, Elisbut and Kerish and Murra and Surcha turned their thoughts inward, but their companions began looking outward.

Ladra became the spokesman for those who were anxious to find their own place and build new lives. Approaching Kesair, he said, "We've waited long enough. I want our share of the livestock and those sacks of seed we brought. My women and I are going farther inland, where there is land that will grow grain."

"What do you know of growing grain?" Kesair asked him.

He bristled. "Leel comes from a farming family, she knows. And we'll learn."

"You didn't used to be such an optimist."

"That was before. This is now. This is a new world, we can do as we like here and that makes everything different."

"Are your women able to travel?"

"The pregnant ones? Murra can, she's not too big yet. And Velabro. She doesn't expect to give birth until early summer, so we should leave as soon as we can in order to be settled in new homes by then. The winter's over, Kesair. Or hadn't you noticed? This is a good land with a mild climate. We're going to enjoy ourselves here."

"Is that what it's about?"

Ladra frowned at her. "You're aren't going to try to keep us all here, are you?"

"Why would I do that?"

"You enjoy being in charge. You're like Fintan, you want to tell other people what to do. I don't mind it, coming from you, but I have to go my own way."

"I never said otherwise," Kesair reminded him. "I agreed that the groups should split up, remember. When the time is right. But . . ."

"But what?" he asked with sudden suspicion.

"But don't you think you should make an effort to . . . to placate . . . to ask for . . . before you go, shouldn't you . . ." The words dried on her tongue.

"Are you trying to get us to pray again, Kesair? Forget it. You're getting tiresome, you know."

Preparations began for the departure of Ladra's group. Kesair supervised the meticulous division of provisions into three equal parts, counted almost to the last seed. She knew how Ladra would complain if he thought he was being cheated.

Then she went for her usual walk by the sea—and returned with a new suggestion.

"We're all going to need to find land we can raise crops on," she said. "and we can't predict what dangers may lie inland. I say the three groups should leave together now, and stay together until we have some idea what to expect in the interior of the island. When we're certain it's safe to divide our numbers, we can split up and each group can choose its own land."

Fintan said, "I'm surprised at you. I thought you would want us, at least, to stay here by the sea you're so fond of."

"I can leave the sea," she told him, adding cryptically, "as long as I stay near water."

The others approved of her suggestion. "Kesair makes good sense, as usual," Surcha remarked to Murra.

"She's strange, that one. Nothing like the rest of us. But you have to admire her," Murra replied. "Where would we be if not for her?"

Excitedly, the entire colony prepared for departure. Even old Nanno had spots of color on her seamed cheeks. The young girls were giddy, and Byth, bemused by approaching fatherhood, spoke dreamily of "the warm valley I'll find for me and my chicks."

Kesair paid one last visit to the sea. The water was deep green, streaked with foam. Their abandoned boat was a forlorn splash of fading ruby against the emerald water.

Slowly, thoughtfully, Kesair dismantled her tower. She put the stones and shells back where she had originally found them, except for one particular shell that she held to her ear, then tucked for safekeeping in the bosom of her gown.

Returning to her people, she assigned herders for the livestock and supervised the final departure arrangements. The soon-to-be-deserted compound presented a forlorn sight. "We can't leave it like this," Kesair said. "We must clear away the midden heaps, burn our garbage and those broken timbers, and . . ."

"Forget it," Ladra said. "Let them rot where they are. No one wants to waste time building up another fire."

The others echoed his words. Their future was tugging at them, they were impatient to go. If Kesair held them back a moment longer they might turn on her.

Reluctantly, she gave the order to leave. But the mess they left behind remained like a dark stain at the back of her mind. She could not stop feeling guilty about it.

Traveling inland, they used the watercourses to make their way through a chain of low mountains carpeted with heather and bracken. Because their pace was adjusted to that of the slowest among them, they had ample time to appreciate the beauty of the land they were crossing. Green, lush, misty.

It took Fintan's breath away. He frequently stopped to stare.

Once, captivated by a spectacular view of a series of lakes nestled among hauntingly lovely hills, he lingered to admire until the others were long out of sight. He did not realize Kesair had come back, worried, to look for him. But when he started forward again he caught a glimpse of her looking toward him from atop an outcropping of rock. Her figure was a dark column silhouetted against the sky, holding up the dome of heaven.

Fintan's breath was suddenly harsh in his throat.

Daily, the air grew warmer. A scent of green, as thick as moss, hung in the air. Soft, moist air. The pregnant women ripened. Their flesh took on the luster of pearls.

A sort of madness infected Ladra. Losing all restraint, he insisted on sleeping with every one of his women as often as he could. Soon he would not even wait until nightfall, but would pull the nearest woman behind a tree or a boulder and take her without ceremony, like a rutting goat.

Byth was appalled. "What's wrong with you?"

"Nothing's wrong with me, and my women aren't complaining."

"They are. To my women."

"They're boasting, because they know you aren't satisfying your women," Ladra said spitefully.

The old man's eyes blazed. "I'm not mauling them every chance I get, if that's what you mean. You act like a man demented, Ladra, and it's making the rest of us uncomfortable."

"You're just jealous!"

Hornetlike, anger hummed in the air between the two men. Kesair became aware of it. She stepped between them. "We can't afford to quarrel," she said. "Walk on now, you're holding us up."

At her urging they resumed the march. But like Byth, Kesair was worried by Ladra's behavior.

He could not control his passions. The very air he breathed was saturated with the impulse to life. The cells of his body responded. They combusted independently of his reasoning mind, burning him with lust. He could concentrate on nothing but the sweet heavy pressure in his groin, driving him, demanding, insatiable.

"I think Ladra's sick," Kesair remarked to Fintan. They were following a thread of water leading eastward from the mountains.

"What makes you think so?"

"Look at his eyes. They're glassy, wild, and he's sweating heavily. It isn't that warm yet. His face is ashen, too, as if the color's being leached out of it."

Fintan grinned. "I'd say everything's leached out of him by now."

"I'm serious. I'm worried about him."

"What am I supposed to do about it? I don't know anything about illness. If he is ill, and I'm not so sure."

But Kesair was sure.

Feeling her concerned gaze upon him, Ladra intepreted it as something else. He began watching for his chance.

Kesair did not always walk with Fintan and his other women. She preferred to find a path of her own, a little distance from anyone else. She would stroll along lost in her own thoughts, aware of the location of the others but not with them.

Ladra made it his business to know where she was. Even when with another woman, he knew where Kesair was; how near to him, how close to some place where he could cut her off from the others and take her the way she wanted. The way they all wanted. They all wanted him, wanted Ladra. Wanted, wanted, needed, had to . . .

His eyes glittered in his pasty face like broken glass.

On a morning of soft rain, they were late in leaving the camp they had made for themselves in a glade in an oak forest. Moving inland, they had found vast expanses of forest land, huge primordial oaks, elm, trees whose leaf and bark they could not identify mingling with more familiar species, all surging upward in search of the sun.

There was no sun this morning. The air was saturated with the mist that oozed from every pore of the land, bearing the scent of earth and water. The day had a curious languor. Kesair, lying in her blankets, reluctant to get up, had a fanciful half-dream of floating in her mother's womb. When she did arise her eyes were still brimming with the dream. Her lips curved in a private smile.

Watching her covertly, Ladra noticed.

Today, he thought.

They set off once more. Water oozed into the footprints they left behind in the mossy soil.

As they walked together, Byth confided to Kerish, "If there is a good valley beyond this forest we're going to stop there. I see no need to go farther, nor have we met any real dangers. Aside from game, this entire island is uninhabited. We could settle anywhere, don't you agree? So why keep on?"

Kerish, heavily pregnant, nodded. "We must stop soon." She smoothed her hands down the bulging moon of her belly. "We will have to stop," she added meaningfully.

The baby inside her shifted, made groping motions with its unseen hands, wriggled down toward the tunnel that led Out.

The forest was increasingly dense. They were following a

winding stream that offered the only open pathway, though its banks were slippery with moss and studded with frequent clumps of vegetation. Once Kerish slipped and cried out. Byth tried to catch her, but he was not quick enough. She saved herself by a desperate grab at a holly bush. The prickles tore her hands, making them bleed.

She caught her breath with a sob. "I have to stop soon," she said to Byth. "I can't go much farther."

He wondered if they should simply turn back. It would be a long journey to the last night's camping place. Better they go on. Or stop here, though the forest was damp and gloomy, an uninviting haven. It was hard to know what to do. He felt his responsibilities pressing down on him. My chicks. I must do what is right for my chicks.

Walking in the lead, Fintan suddenly called back over his shoulder, "I see a wedge of brightness up ahead. I think we'll be out of this forest in a little while."

Ladra grunted deep in his throat. He was walking a few paces behind Kesair, who as usual was eschewing the common path and treading her own way among the trees. She had taken off her cloak and stuffed it into the pack on her back, for it was warm in the forest. Warm and close.

Warm and wet. Ladra's eyes followed the clench-and-relax of her buttocks, clearly visible beneath the fabric of her gown.

Off to their left yawned the mouth of a small cave, almost hidden by moss and shrubbery as it backed into a hill. Ladra's darting eyes observed the cave; returned to Kesair.

"Kesair," he said. Very softly. "Kesair."

She heard him the second time and glanced back. "What is it?"

"Did you see that?"

"What?"

"Something just moved inside that cave. Something large. I think it's watching us."

"Are you sure?" Kesair stopped walking and turned to face the cave. "I don't see anything. Should we call Fintan?"

"I can do anything Fintan can do," Ladra said petulantly. "If there's any danger, you're safe enough with me. But I think we should take a look. Just because we haven't seen any large predators yet doesn't mean there are none. If one is in that cave, I want to know."

She nodded agreement and came back toward him. "Be ready," she warned. Her own long knife was already in her hand, taken in one smooth motion from the scabbard on her belt.

I am ready, Ladra assured her silently.

They advanced with cautious tread toward the cave. Its mouth was narrow, but it could be of any size within, burrowed into the tree-covered hill. Ladra held out one hand, signaling Kesair to move slowly.

The longer it took them to reach the cave, the farther away the others would get. If she should cry out, he did not want them to hear her.

When they had crept almost to the cave's mouth, he faked a stumble and dropped his own knife into the thickest undergrowth. "I've lost my knife," he hissed. "Quick, give me yours." He reached for it so suddenly and imperiously Kesair surrendered her weapon before thinking.

One slow step at a time, Ladra entered the cave. He had to duck his head under the low overhang, but once he was inside it was more spacious and he could stand. He was aware of Kesair behind him.

"What do you see?" she whispered. "Be careful, don't go any farther!"

"I see . . . I see . . . it's all right, but come in here, look at this. Just look!" he said in a voice of feigned excitement, as if he had found some treasure.

Kesair entered behind him. She stood so close to him he could feel her breasts against the back of his upper arm. "What? I don't see anything." Her breathing was light and quick.

She wants it, Ladra assured himself. She knows why we're here.

Turning, he dropped his knife to the floor of the cave to free his hands. He caught her by the shoulders and pulled her against him.

"What are you doing?" She struggled to get her hands between their bodies and push him away, but Ladra held tight.

"Don't fight me, Kesair. This is what you're meant for." He bent his face to hers but she twisted aside, denying him her mouth.

"Let me go!"

"You're just saying that. Why don't you relax? We're all alone here, no one will bother us. It won't take long, I promise you, I never take long." He gave a wild laugh.

Kesair tried to get her knee up but he had her clamped so tightly against him that she could not. She had never thought Ladra was so strong. The fight between them became desperate; silent. She saved her breath for the struggle.

He pushed her toward the unseen back of the cave. She fought him every step, feeling a mounting panic beat like a pulse at the base of her throat. What difference does it make? a coolly rational part of her mind asked. Him or another. But the rest of her mind screamed silently, Not him! Not this one! It had nothing to do with rationality and everything to do with the integrity of her free will.

She redoubled her efforts and managed to break the hold of one of his hands. He grabbed for her again but she flung herself sideways, falling onto one knee on the cave floor, scrabbling with her free hand for purchase on the gritty stone.

Ladra did not give her a chance to get up but flung himself down onto her, knocking her flat beneath him. He gave a grunt of triumph and began tearing at her clothes.

His fingers closed on the shell tucked in the bosom of her gown. A small spiral shell, with a sharply fluted edge at its aperture.

The feeling of it was so unexpected Ladra snatched his hand back, thinking he had been grazed by unseen teeth. "Something bit me!" he cried in disbelief. "Something in your gown!" His fevered mind imagined a giant insect, some alien life form attacking him in the dark cave.

He half lifted his body off hers, trying to look at his hand in the dim light filtering in from outside. He thought he saw the ooze of blood.

Taking advantage of his distraction, Kesair gave a mighty heave and threw his body aside so she could roll out from under him. He reached for her again but she was too quick. She was on her feet as his hand closed on her gown. She strained; he held on. The fabric tore with an audible ripping sound and she was free. Kesair took the two paces to the mouth of the cave in one bound and was outside. With a great gasp, she drew the wet air of freedom into her lungs. She ran a few steps; slowed; looked back.

Ladra was not following her.

There was no sound from the cave.

He thinks I'll be curious and go back, she told herself. It's a trick.

Anger sizzled in her. She bent swiftly, pawed through the undergrowth until she found the knife he had dropped, and put it in her own scabbard. Then she hurried after the others.

She had almost caught up with them when her steps slowed of their own volition.

I am the leader, she thought grimly. I can't go off and leave him, even if I'd like to see him dead. And I would. I would!

She drew in a breath to call Fintan and ask him to go back with her, but never made the call. She did not want to give Ladra the satisfaction of thinking she was so afraid of him she had to ask Fintan for help.

I can handle Ladra myself, she thought. I'll control my fear and my anger too. I can do it. I *can*.

She gritted her teeth, biting down with all her strength on her seething emotions. Knife firmly in hand, she went back alone.

# 5

*No sooner did Kerish see the light*

*ahead that meant the end of the forest, than the*

*vague disquiet that had troubled her belly all day*

*became something more defined. A spasm like a giant*

*cramp doubled her*

over. She tried to call Byth's name but could not get her breath.

He was aware at once, however, and bent over her. "What is it? Are you all right?"

Old fool, she thought. You can see I'm not all right, do something! But she could not speak. The cramp was crushing her insides.

Byth straightened and looked around wildly for help. Some of his women were ahead of them, some behind. Fintan was still back among the trees somewhere. He did not see Kesair at all, though hers was the face he would have welcomed.

"Help!" he cried at random. He croaked like a frog, his voice breaking.

People hurried to them. The solicitous hands of other women touched Kerish, understood at once. A place was swiftly found for her and her bulky body eased down onto a mossy bed. The women crowded around her. There were hasty consultations. The young ones were frightened. The older women, particularly those who had given birth themselves, were calmer, insisting that everything was normal, there was no need to worry. They would care for her. With swift efficiency they divided themselves into groups to stay with Kerish and comfort her, and other groups to bring fresh water, gather clean moss, search through the packs for items that might be needed.

Ayn thoughtfully assigned herself to Byth and led him some distance away. "She'll be fine, they'll tend to her. You come with me now. You'd only be in the way and make her anxious. That's it, come along. We'll find a nice place where you can wait."

Had he been a younger man, Ayn might have encouraged him to stay with the woman. But Byth was paler than Kerish, and she was worried about him. With difficulty, she got him seated on a fallen tree near the stream, and tried to make distracting conversation with him.

When Kerish screamed the first time, though, he jumped to his feet and hurried back to her in spite of all Ayn could do.

By then Fintan had arrived, assessed the situation, understood he was less than useless, and gone looking for something to hunt while he waited. Most of the women, aside from those looking after

Kerish, were taking advantage of the halt to bathe themselves in the stream, or gather the shiny brown nuts that strewed the earth beneath some of the trees.

Fintan had not noticed that Kesair was not with the other women. Her absence did not cry out for his attention. She was inclined to go her own way. He assumed she was nearby, without giving it any specific thought.

A small furry animal sprang up almost under his feet and ran toward the light at the rim of the forest. Fintan ran after it.

When Kerish screamed a second time one of the women gave her a piece of cloth to hold between her teeth, and another gave her a piece of rope tied to a tree to pull on. They kneaded her belly to locate the infant. It had entered the birth canal.

There would not be long to wait.

Barra and Salmé supported Kerish in a squatting position. Old Nanno had put herself in charge. Her cracked voice guided their efforts. When Byth hovered too close she snapped, "Take him away, somebody!"

Hands tugged Byth a few paces from the scene of action. He protested every step of the way. "You're hurting her! Be careful! Can't you see she wants me?"

No one paid any attention to him.

Leel said in an awed whisper, "This will be the first child of the new world."

A sense of occasion overtook them. The women exchanged glances. Their eyes gleamed. Kerish, sweating, torn in half, struggled to bring forth life.

Her two screams had coincided with the struggle in the cave, so Kesair did not know. She only knew that she could not in good conscience go off and leave Ladra. He was sick; sick in his mind, of that she was convinced. His body had given off a sour, unhealthy smell that still clung to her clothing.

She fumbled at the bosom of her gown. The shell was missing. It must still be in the cave then.

For that reason alone she had to go back.

The dark cave mouth waited for her. She approached slowly. "Ladra?"

There was no answer. Nothing appeared to stir inside the cave.

"Ladra? You'll be left so far behind you can't find us if you don't come now." Kesair waited tensely, ready to run if he made any threatening moves toward her. But only silence greeted her words.

She stepped almost to the mouth of the cave and cupped her hands around her eyes, peering into the darkness. "Ladra?"

Then she saw him. He was lying on the floor, far back in the cave, with his knees drawn up against his chest. His face was turned toward her, a pale blur in the dimness. His mouth worked but no sound came out.

It's a trick, Kesair warned herself. "Come now," she said sternly.

He made no move to get up. Instead there was a whimper like an animal in pain, and his body thrashed weakly on the floor.

Kesair held out the knife so he could see she had it. Step by cautious step she advanced, ducking under the low overhang. She did not get within grabbing distance of him, but went close enough to see his face more clearly.

Ladra's face was bloated, twisted. "Annnhh," he moaned. "Aaaannnnhhhh." His eyes pleaded with her.

"What happened?" she asked in a shocked whisper. Suddenly she knew it was no trick.

"I'm . . ." His mouth struggled to frame words. "I'm . . . poi . . . soned. Poisoned. You poisoned me."

Kesair almost dropped the knife. "I did what!"

"That thing. Hidden. In your breasts. I . . ." His voice failed, but still his eyes pleaded for help.

"No poison could act that fast," Kesair protested. "I wasn't carrying any poison. Just a shell from the sea."

"Poisoned teeth," Ladra insisted. "Bit me. You . . . tried to kill me . . . why?" The last question was a piteous sob.

Kesair thrust the knife into her scabbard and bent down to try to help the man to his feet. But Ladra had no strength. Even with her aid, he could not stand. He was in undeniable pain.

Beside him on the floor she saw the pale gleam of the seashell.

Kesair picked it up. She turned it over, wonderingly, in her hand, then put it back into the bosom of her gown.

Ladra's eyes widened. "It will kill you!"

He is out of his head, Kesair thought. Aloud she said, "I'll go get help. But you're not poisoned, you couldn't be. It's a seizure of some sort. Don't worry, I'll get help." She was backing away from him as she spoke. She could not wait to leave the cave, to be in open air that did not choke her with the sour smell of him.

Once outside, she ran.

She came upon the others soon enough, although she had expected they would be far ahead by now. Instead she found them gathered beside the stream shortly before it emerged from the forest. In the center of the group was a figure that held their attention; they did not even notice her come running up to them.

"Ladra's ill," she called out. "I need someone to help with him. He can't walk."

Faces turned toward her. "Kerish is having her baby," Murra said.

"Oh!" Kesair hesitated. "Is she all right?"

"Seems to be."

"Then . . . can't we spare some people to come help me with Ladra? Where's Fintan? And what about Byth? Surely he's no use to Kerish right now."

Murra chuckled. "I don't think you could drag Byth away with a team of horses. But Fintan's around here somewhere, I think." She looked around, searching. Then she cupped her hands around her mouth and called, "Fintan? Where are you?"

"Be quiet," someone hissed. "You're disturbing Kerish."

The admonition was unnecessary, actually. Kerish was not disturbed. She was lost in the throes of birth, all her attention centered on the cataclysm within herself.

"I don't know just where Fintan is," Murra admitted to Kesair. "How ill is Ladra? Is it urgent? And where is he?"

"Back there." Kesair waved a hand vaguely. "I don't know if it's urgent, but I'm worried. He thinks he's been poisoned."

Murra's brow furrowed. "Did he eat some berries? What did they look like?"

"Not berries, and I don't really think he's poisoned. It's something else, but I need help. Stay there, I'll go find Fintan myself. I suspect he's gone on ahead to see what's there." She started toward the light beyond the forest.

She met Fintan coming back with a limp furry body in his hand. "Ho, Kesair," he called, brandishing his kill, "look at this!"

She averted her eyes. She was uncomfortable with death while life was beginning so close behind her. "Can you come help me get Ladra?"

Fintan's eyes dimmed with disappointment. He had expected praise; he had killed the creature with his first effort, a lovely clean kill. "What's wrong with Ladra?"

"He . . . ah . . ." Kesair pawed among the available words in her mind. She did not want to tell Fintan everything. "He caught hold of a seashell I was keeping and he thinks it's poisoned him. It couldn't have, but something has made him very sick. He's in a cave back along the trail, and he can't walk."

"What about the baby, is it born yet?"

"Not yet. But Ladra needs help now."

Fintan fell in step beside her. They made their way past the cluster of women around Kerish and on down the stream, deeper into the forest, until Kesair was able to point out the cave. "He's in there."

Fintan followed her to the cave mouth. She stepped aside and let him go in first.

Ladra lay as she had left him, knees drawn up against his belly. He was breathing shallowly but he was conscious. He said something unintelligible to Fintan.

"He's sick all right," Fintan affirmed. "But if we can get him on his feet with an arm around our necks, between us we can get him out of here."

Kesair did not really want to touch Ladra, but she forced herself. Between them, she and Fintan got him unsteadily to his feet and walked him out of the cave. He smelled worse than ever, a nauseating stench like something going rotten.

But his face was not as bloated Kesair noticed once they had him out in the leaf-filtered light of the forest. The illness, whatever it was, was abating. He stumbled but he could walk, and when he spoke again his voice sounded minimally stronger. "Thought I was going to die in there," he told them.

He did not mention his attack on Kesair. Nor did she.

Moving slowly, they rejoined the group. Ladra kept his eyes closed and let them guide him while he hung between them almost as limply as the furry creature had dangled from Fintan's hand.

They reached the others just as Kerish let out a great cry and a wet, bloody mass slid from her into old Nanno's waiting arms.

Within moments a boy baby was filling the forest with lusty cries.

In the excitement, no one paid much attention to Ladra.

Kesair and Fintan let him sit down, propped against a tree, and went to congratulate Kerish. It was Byth who was garnering the congratulations, however, his face shining like the risen sun. Kerish lay exhausted, watching the baby on her breast.

"Doesn't anyone care if I live or die?" Ladra's peevish voice asked at last.

When she was satisfied that Kerish and her baby were well, Ayn went to Ladra. She had the most experience among them in dealing with illness, but she could not explain his fading symptoms. "I don't think it's poison," she told Kesair, "but I couldn't be certain. It might be a kind I've never seen. Whatever it is, it's passing off anyway. I'd say he'll be all right. He'll have a day to rest. We won't expect Kerish and the new baby to move until tomorrow."

Instead of being reassured, Ladra took exception to Ayn's words. "She doesn't know what she's talking about. I almost died. I could still die. It's obviously something rare and dangerous, and no one knows what to do about it."

Kesair, making sure no one else was listening, said to him, "It was just a seashell I've carried in my gown all this way, with no harm to me. It couldn't hurt you. Your own guilt is making you sick, Ladra."

"Guilt? Guilt for what?"

"You know," she said in a low voice.

"I didn't do anything wrong. I didn't do anything you didn't want me to do."

"Did I act as if I wanted you to do it?"

"The fighting, you mean? That's just your way, I'd say. Some women like to pretend to resist."

"I wasn't pretending. And if you ever try that again, I'll fight harder. I'll kill you if I have to."

He gave her a shocked look. "You wouldn't! Consider! There are only three men now!"

"I'd rather there were no men, than to have to put up with you," she told him coldly.

Camp was set up around Kerish and her baby. The day of relative leisure was welcome. Fintan went back to his hunting, taking with him some of the women who had shown skills at catching small game. Nanno and Ayn looked after the new mother, a task that primarily consisted of keeping Byth from pestering them too much. He wanted to hold the baby, he wanted to ask Kerish how she felt, he wanted to do something for them. Anything.

He drove the others mad.

At last Nanno snapped, "If you want to help, gather more moss for diapering!"

Byth scurried away importantly. He spent the better part of the afternoon selecting, grading, and discarding bits of moss as if life or death might depend on them.

Ladra sat propped against his tree for a long time. The color slowly returned to his cheeks and the light to his eyes. Kesair was aware that those eyes followed her as she moved around the encampment. She began planning her paths so that trees interposed between herself and Ladra, blocking his vision.

Her warning had meant nothing to him. He did not take it seriously because it interfered with his fixed idea of reality.

She began to wonder if she would actually have to kill him eventually—kill him, or submit.

But it was not in her to submit.

That night they built a fire in a glade in the forest and roasted the game Fintan and his fellow hunters provided. Byth insisted the best parts, such as the liver, be given to Kerish. He forced more meat on her than she could possibly eat.

"Was he always like that, do you suppose?" Kerish asked Nanno.

The old woman's eyes were lost in wrinkles, but a smile lurked in their depths. "I knew him as a young man with his wife, and I assure you, he paid very little attention to his children then. Nor to the wife either. He had a wife and children because it was expected of him, and once he had them settled in his house he got on with his life. Oh, I'm sure he was fond of them in an absentminded way. But he took them for granted.

"Now he is no longer young, Kerish, and he has realized how fragile existence is. He is a different man."

"We are all of us different people," Kerish said. "I never imagined I would give birth in a forest and diaper my baby with moss. Me, who used to spend hours buffing my fingernails!"

"That was in another world," Nanno reminded her.

"Do you miss it? Do you wish we could go back?"

"Of course I do. But that's like wishing you could be young

again. We only travel in one direction, Kerish. Forward. Remember that, and waste no time regretting."

The baby at Kerish's breast whimpered and began seeking the teat again. His mother gazed down at him, then bent her neck to kiss the downy crown of his head.

Sitting opposite them, Kesair looked at mother and infant in the firelight. The picture they made was creating maternal stirrings in many of the women. She could not help noticing how they drew closer to their men, so that the three groups became more clearly delineated than usual. Even Ladra's women gathered around him, though of late they had been avoiding him whenever they could.

But it was Kesair his eyes sought.

She edged closer to Fintan. Salmé, sitting on his right, glared at her and refused to give ground. If Fintan was aware of the silent duel between the two women he gave no sign; he went on eating his food, his face impassive. With no word spoken, Kesair realized he would sleep with Salmé that night.

But she must talk to him. "Fintan," she said in a low, urgent voice, "there is something I must discuss with you. Tonight. It's a serious problem. I need you."

Salmé's lips tightened over her teeth and she moved still closer to Fintan.

Kesair reached past her, putting a hand on the man's arm. Immediately Salmé put her own hand on the arm, pinning it down. Her eyes were hot with challenge.

Kesair tried to make Fintan look at her but he would not. Nor did he respond to her touch. He sat immobilized, letting the women fight it out. Enjoying it, no doubt.

In that moment Kesair hated him.

She drew her dignity around her like an invisible cloak and relinquished her hold on his arm. "Very well. I shall handle the problem myself." Her voice was cold. She stood up and left them, walking with a straight back and high head into the sheltering darkness of the trees.

She knew that Ladra was following her with his eyes. But he did not come after her.

He was still feeling weakened, so he remained where he was, biding his time. There would be other chances. Tomorrow. Or the day after.

He had a score to settle.

The next morning Kerish insisted she could get up and walk if they did not walk too fast or too far without resting. So they pitched camp and set out. A doting Byth carried the baby, refusing to surrender it to any of the women. He only gave it back to Kerish for feeding.

"What if he drops my baby?" she complained to Ramé.

"He won't. Just look at him. He would rather die than let anything happen to that child."

They were soon out of the forest. Beyond lay a rolling meadowland that stretched to the horizon. "I'd say it's a central plain, if this really is an island as we think it is," Fintan remarked.

Leel paused, squatted on her heels, dug in the earth with her fingers. It was loamy and dark. "Rich soil," she said.

The plain was crisscrossed with watercourses, to which Kesair was inevitably drawn. They could not lose their way if they followed the water.

They were on open grassland under an open sky. Making sure there were others close by, she fell into step with Ladra. "This is good farmland, I'd say," she told him. "Fertile. And since we've met no serious danger, you might want to claim this region for yourself while the rest of us look farther."

"I'm in no hurry to leave you," Ladra drawled, enjoying the discomfiture in her eyes. "I'll stay with you a while longer. You can never tell what we may discover up ahead. Better land, perhaps. Or something . . . wonderful," he added meaningfully. He ran his eyes over her body like impertinent hands.

Kesair edged away from him, repelled.

But Ladra made no move to pursue her. He seemed content to watch her and make her uncomfortable.

He had never toyed with a woman in that way before, and he found he enjoyed it. It gave him a sense of power. It also was a form of revenge, and revenge was power too.

Ladra speculated as to whether Kesair might have told Fintan about the attack. Probably not, or Fintan would have done something. Or perhaps he was just waiting for Ladra to try it again, and catch him in the act. Then there would be a fight between them.

I am bigger, Ladra told himself. I would win.

He imagined bludgeoning the other man to the earth. The idea gave him an almost sensual pleasure. He strolled along with a tiny smile playing around the corners of his mouth, dreaming with his eyes open.

But Kesair had not told Fintan. After the scene with Salmé, she spoke to him no more than she must. His use of the other woman's body did not upset her, that was inevitable. But she could not forget how meekly he had submitted to Salmé and rejected Kesair when she needed him.

Crossing the central plain, they came to a valley of abundance at the confluence of three rivers. When they pitched camp for the night Kesair spoke to Ladra again. "This would be a fine place for you and your women."

"There is something I have to settle before we separate from the rest of you, Kesair," he replied. "I think we'll just stay with you a while longer. Until."

That night, wrapped in her blankets, Kesair fingered the knife she had taken to bed with her and wondered what it would be like to kill a man. Could she make herself do it? And what would the others do to her if she diminished the adult male population by a third?

I should discuss this with someone, she thought. But ever since she first joined the crafts colony, she had kept a certain distance between herself and the other women. Their talk seemed superficial to her, their interests were rarely her interests. And men had represented an area of life she had chosen to ignore.

Old Byth, fond as she was of him, would be little help to her in the present situation. And Fintan had rejected her.

Lying alone on the yielding earth, Kesair fingered the knife and thought of past and future. She was suspended between them.

We thought we were so highly developed, she mused. We believed humankind masters of the universe.

Now we are fifty-three people on an island. And I am contemplating murder.

Why can you not give in to Ladra? her rational mind demanded to know. Any one of the three would do as well as any other for the purpose of procreation. Surely it is not worth destroying what little civilization we have left, just to deny yourself to him.

But she could not submit to Ladra. Rationality had no power over elemental emotion. She had once been terribly hurt by a man, and she had been hurt again by Fintan's recent rejection. Some quality in him had begun the slow process of thawing her frozen passions, but that was now reversed. All she had left was the integrity of her inmost self, and she would rather die than surrender it to any man on demand.

Dying, killing, repeated her rational mind. After all that has happened, still you think these thoughts. Are you not revolted by the unquenchable darkness of the human soul?

I am, she answered. Yet she ran her finger down the knife blade again, testing its sharpness. She felt balanced on a knife blade between the old world and the new.

The blade was killing-sharp.

Close to her head, something crackled.

Kesair stiffened. Someone was creeping toward her in the darkness.

Her fingers closed on the hilt of the knife, easing it out from under the blankets. Suddenly she felt more alive than she could remember feeling. Every cell in her body tingled.

Whoever it was came closer.

The night was very still. The air was damp and heavy, and brought her an ominous, sour scent.

Ladra was stealthily approaching her bed.

Kesair felt a shock of surprise that he would risk such a move in the open, where one cry would alert the others. She was ten paces from the nearest sleeper.

Now she regretted even that distance, though keeping space between herself and the others was a well-established habit. She wished she were lying pressed close against Elisbut or Sorcha or even Salmé.

Her straining eyes made out the dim outline of the approaching head and shoulders. Ladra was actually crawling toward her on his belly, she realized with revulsion. Her hand made a small, convulsive movement, eager to use the knife.

"Kesair." His whisper was so soft she would not have heard it if her senses had not become preternaturally sharp with tension. "Kesair."

"Get away from me," she said in a low voice. She was embarrassed; she did not want the others to know.

"I have to talk to you." He wriggled closer.

"Talk? Talk isn't what you want from me."

"Oh but it is. Just listen." Ladra lay down beside her. He made no effort to touch her. "You tried to kill me," he said in that same insidious whisper. "But I forgive you. I want you to know I forgive you."

His unctuous tone infuriated her. "You can't forgive me for something I didn't do. I never tried to kill you. But I promise you, if you try to lay a hand on me now, I will."

"You should be nicer to me, Kesair. I'm the only one who appreciates you."

"They follow me as their leader," she said proudly.

"It isn't the same thing. You are the leader because you're . . . different. I understand that, I'm different too, in my own way. I could show you. We could make something very special together." His voice was soft, insinuating.

"You're different because you're insane," she said bluntly.

To her surprise, he chuckled. "Is that what you think? I'm insane because I don't subscribe to the same behavior as the rest of you? I am the sanest person among us, Kesair. I'm the only one who realizes that everything is different now; none of the old laws and restrictions apply. We can do what we like here, don't you understand? Don't you know how wonderful that is? We are free. *Free.*" The word hissed between them.

"Take advantage of your freedom, Kesair. Don't limit yourself to that wretched Fintan. Come to me. Be with me. Together we can explore ourselves, each other, this island, the whole world. It's all ours to take and shape, don't you see?

"You're still tied to the past. You wanted to burn the rubbish, rather than simply walk away from it. You can walk away from everything now. No more responsibilities. Just pleasure. Pleasure . . ."

Now he reached for her. Now his fingertips brushed her cheek with a touch as light as cobwebs. A touch as light as the kiss of sea mist . . .

She drove the knife into him with all her strength.

# 6

### The tensile strength of living flesh

surprised Kesair. For a moment she was not

sure the knife had gone in.

Then she heard him gasp.

Some reflex made

her snatch her hand back as if to undo the deed. Too late, too late. The tug she had to give to remove the knife told her how deeply it had penetrated. She felt it grate against bone as she withdrew it.

Appalled, she lay frozen.

Ladra coughed. "You . . ."

"I warned you!" she said through clenched teeth. She was alternately hot and cold. Her entire body was shaken by the pounding of her heart.

"I . . ." Ladra stirred, gathered himself, struggled to his hands and knees. His head swung slowly back and forth.

Warm blood spattered onto Kesair's hand.

Ladra began crawling backward, away from her. She lay immobilized by horror. What to say? What to do? She could not think. Her paralysis of mind was more frightening than the menace of Ladra.

He somehow made his way back to his own bed without awakening anyone else. The wound was deep, his probing fingers discovered, but not close to the heart. Nor did it seem to have penetrated a lung. If he did not bleed to death he might survive.

Fighting waves of dizzying pain, he gathered moss to stuff into the wound. There was a roaring in his ears like the sound of the sea. He lay on his back, clinging desperately to consciousness. He was afraid he would never wake up if he let himself fall asleep.

The night was endless. The slightest sound was an assault on Ladra's raw nerve endings. All around him people slept, blissfully unaware that he might be dying. He hated them for their indifferent comfort.

This is me! he wanted to shout. This is my precious life seeping away!

But he did not shout. He lay in silence, fearing. Hating.

In the morning he was still alive.

Ladra was surprised to discover he was actually seeing the first flush of dawn. I am not going to die after all, he thought. His survival seemed almost anticlimactic.

With a great effort, he dragged himself to his feet and went to the stream to splash his face with cold water. It revived him a little. A close examination of the moss showed that blood was no longer seeping from the wound. He was weak, but he was alive.

Every movement hurt, however.

One-handed, he struggled to wrap his cloak around his body and fasten it so no one would see the bloody mess at his shoulder. Only then did he allow himself to make enough noise to awaken the others.

Kesair was already awake. She did not think she had slept at all. She heard him get up and go to the stream. She heard him return. He did not come anywhere near her.

At least she had not killed him.

She wondered how she felt about that.

She got up cautiously, surprised to find the world much the same as it had been the night before. Familiar forms surrounded her. Familiar sounds: coughing, farting, a groan of awakening, a muttered, sleepy conversation. The new baby's cry and Kerish's tender answer.

As Kesair bent over to pick up her blankets, the seashell fell from the neck of her gown.

She caught it in midair, instinctively. Holding it to her ear, she listened for a moment to the voice of the sea. Then she tucked the shell back between her breasts.

Though she watched him warily, Ladra gave no indication of what had happened between them. He moved stiffly as he gathered himself for the day, but he was able to walk. No one commented on his obvious discomfort. His women assumed it was a residue of his previous illness. The only one who reacted to it at all was Ramé, who trimmed a branch and gave it to him for a walking stick that he could lean upon.

When they left camp and got under way, however, Ladra moved so slowly even Kerish could outpace him. Eventually Ramé spoke to Kesair. "Ladra is in considerable pain," she said, "but he won't admit it and he won't let Ayn look at him."

"That's his right," Kesair said through stiff lips.

Ramé went to walk with Velabro. "Kesair is an unfeeling woman," she complained.

Velabro considered. "Aloof, perhaps. I wouldn't say unfeeling. And she may have her reasons," she added charitably. Velabro had a deep, slow, husky voice. Ramé liked to talk to her for the sake of hearing the music in her voice.

"Ladra's hurting, Velabro. Kesair should be more solicitous of him. She's the leader, after all. Our welfare is her concern."

"You weren't so solicitous of Ladra," Velabro pointed out, "after the last time he flung himself on you."

"That's different, I just got tired of him acting like a rutting stag. But I hate to see him suffer."

"Perhaps you should suggest to him that we stop, then. He might be willing, if he really is in pain. Leel says this is fertile soil. We could settle here and let the others go on, and Ladra could rest and get well."

"You make it sound simple enough, but it isn't. Think, Velabro. What will it mean? A band of women alone in a strange place with just one man—and him ill? Aren't you afraid?"

Velabro shook her head. "I was afraid when the sea rose. When the others came and killed our men and tried to steal our boat, I was afraid. I was terribly afraid when we were alone on the ocean. But I wore out my capacity for fear, finally. Now I just want to stop walking and stay somewhere and get on with whatever happens next. I suspect the other women feel the same."

Ramé quietly canvassed Ladra's other women. She found that they all were willing, even eager, to stop and stay. The weather was mild, the sun was shining, there was fresh water and abundant grass. The women who were in charge of the livestock were the most ready to stop traveling. Getting the animals through the forest had been arduous enough, but on lush pasturage they almost had to be dragged to keep them moving forward, exhausting their herders. "Let's stay right here," Ramé was told. "Look at the animals, they know best."

The next time they stopped to rest and let Kerish nurse her baby, Ramé spoke to Ladra. "Your women want to stay here and go no farther," she told him. "Leel says we could farm this region successfully, our seed would grow here. And you could regain your strength and—"

"I . . . am . . . not . . . stopping . . . yet," Ladra said, forcing each word as if it cost him great effort. But even as he spoke he swayed and almost fell.

Ramé caught him in her arms. "This is as far as we go!" she called to Kesair. "Ladra's ill, he's fainting!"

"We'll stay with you," Fintan said.

Kesair cried sharply, "We won't! Ladra's women can take care of him."

Fintan rounded on her. "Do you mean to leave him when he's sick?"

"I'm not . . . sick," Ladra insisted, fighting to stand upright again, pushing away Ramé's arms.

"There, you hear him, he's not sick. They just want to stay here, Fintan. So we'll leave them and go on."

"I'm going . . . too . . ." Ladra tried to insist, but waves of weakness were breaking over him. He met Kesair's eyes. His ears began to ring, as if with the roar of the sea.

"You're not going anywhere," Ramé said gently, taking hold of him again. Velabro hurried to help her.

Leel remarked, "I don't think we could find any better place than this no matter where we go, so we might as well stay here."

"I think that's a good idea," agreed Kesair. "The rest of you, prepare yourselves and we'll move on now."

"We can't just go off and leave them like this!" Fintan protested.

But Kesair would not listen. She seemed almost indecently eager to put distance between herself and Ladra's group. Byth was anxious to move on as well, he kept talking about the valley he wanted to find.

Fintan gave in, realizing that Ladra had not endeared himself to the others and no one would be heartbroken about leaving him. Besides, that had been the plan.

Still . . . he sensed something of a mystery about Kesair's attitude. When they were under way again, and Ladra and his women were dots in the distance, setting up their camp and staking out their animals, Fintan fell into step beside Kesair.

"Was something wrong between you and Ladra?" he wanted to know.

"No."

"Then why were you so anxious to get rid of him?"

She spun around and glared at him. "You wouldn't know, would you?"

"That's why I'm asking you. If there is some sort of problem, you should share it with me."

"I tried. You weren't interested." Her voice shimmered with icicles. "Now I'm not interested in sharing anything with you. Just service your women and leave me alone."

Fintan was mystified. The incident with Salmé was trivial to him, already forgotten. He found Kesair's attitude inexplicable.

But then, he reasoned, who could ever understand women?

They traveled on until Byth found his valley. As always, Kesair was following a river. It led between two hills that rose in gentle curves from the plain. Within the sheltering arms of the hills, which blocked the wind and trapped the sun, the river spilled into a crystal lake. An ecstasy of birds was in full song, and the valley surrounding the lake was fragrant with flowers.

"Here we are!" Byth cried, flinging his arms wide and ignoring his arthritis. "I knew we would find this place. We're home, chicks."

Indeed, the valley was beautiful enough to bring a lump to Fintan's throat. Had Byth not already claimed it, Fintan would have wanted it for himself. But he could not deny the old man. "This is your land, then," he agreed, "and we shall go on and find someplace for ourselves."

"Stay with us until we get settled in," Ayn urged Kesair. "Byth is not as strong as he thinks he is, and we would be grateful for some help."

Kesair had no hesitation about staying to help this time.

It was fortunate, because that meant they were still there several days later, when Ladra's women caught up with them. Several were already thickening with pregnancy.

Ramé led the group. Her face was haggard, her eyelids swollen as if she had been crying. Ashti, the youngest of the party, was still sniffling and wiping her nose on her sleeve.

Kesair hurried forward to meet them. "What happened to you?"

"He died!" Ashti wailed. "He was just sitting there, propped against a stone, and then he gave a sort of gurgle and blood started coming out of his mouth and he . . . and he . . ."

"Died," Ramé finished. "There was nothing any of us could do."

"It was horrible!" Ashti was crying. "Horrible! He kept struggling, and his legs were running but he wasn't going anywhere, and . . ."

Kesair said to Velabro, "Take her over there, away from the others, and give her a drink, will you?

"Now, Ramé, tell me just what happened."

"That is what happened. At first we could hardly believe he was dead. You saw how he was, he wouldn't even admit to being ill. Then all at once he was gone."

Listening to the conversation, Ayn was obviously puzzled. "I don't understand this at all," she said. "He was sick, then he got better. Then he was weak again, then he bled at the mouth, convulsed, and died? What sort of illness is that?"

"And how did he get it?" Fintan questioned. "Something fatal like that . . . could we all be subject to it?"

Seeing the fear in their faces, Kesair wanted to tell them. But she could not. She dared not. "No one else feels sick," she pointed out, "so we must assume this is something that affected only Ladra. Maybe an illness he'd had for a long time that we didn't know about."

They wanted to believe her but they were obviously frightened. Even Velabro was frightened. She found herself trying to comfort Ashti with words she did not believe. "Everything will be all right, we're safe, it's all right."

There was no conviction in the words. Ashti continued to cry.

In their panic to rejoin the others, Ladra's women had left most of their supplies behind. The cattle and other livestock had been abandoned to graze and run wild. Ramé, knowing Kesair would cling to the river courses, had been able to guess which way to go and so had found them, but her practicality had not extended to taking time to pack up and bring everything. She had been too afraid of being left behind.

There was only one thing to be done. Kesair arbitrarily divided Ladra's women among the two surviving men. She was annoyed with Ramé for leaving the animals, but assigned her to Fintan.

The urgency had gone out of them. They spent most of the rest of the summer getting Byth and his flock comfortably settled in their valley. It was only when the first chill winds blew over the hills that Kesair recognized the approach of autumn, and decided Fintan's group must be on its way. The valley would not support all of them on a permanent basis, and they would need to find their own place before another winter set in.

Leavetaking was hard. Ladra's death had made them aware of possibilities they had not wanted to consider before. Some of the women clung to one another and cried. But at last the final goodbyes were acknowledged, and Fintan and his party left Byth's valley.

After its first chill herald, the autumn was mild, a long and golden season. Kesair's rivers eventually led her to a vast deep lake with a strange red cast to its waters on certain days, and mountains standing like sentinels on either side. The land beside the lake, though hilly, was composed of rich loam, and there were fertile valleys not far away.

It seemed a good place to end their wandering.

A river flowing from the north fed the lake at its upper end, and that same river emerged at the lower end of the lake, wider, stronger, flowing toward the distant sea.

Surely flowing toward the distant sea.

I could follow the river and find the sea again any time I wanted to, Kesair told herself.

"There is timber here," she said. "We can build permanent houses of wood and stone, and we shall always have fresh water. There is no life without water."

She often stood by the lake shore, as she had once stood by the seashore. The same sense of reverence enveloped her. Instead of white sand she gazed upon reedy shallows, yet she could feel the water's presence just as strongly. Fresh or salt, it did not matter. What mattered was the element itself. It might be endlessly transformed yet it was always the same.

Holy, Kesair thought. Holy.

She wished the others could feel what she felt. She tried to explain to them.

In time, some listened.

Some did not.

In late winter, the body of water Kesair named the Red Lake was bitterly cold. Fires were kept burning night and day in the snug, small houses of stone and timber on the western shore of the lake, where the nearby mountains cut the wind to some extent.

Even on the coldest day, however, Kesair left the warmth of her hearthfire to stand beside the lake. Her house was hers alone, unshared. The other women lived five or six to a small cabin; only Fintan also had a place to himself. He invited the woman of his choice to it each night.

Kesair invited no one to hers.

Sometimes, she saw Fintan look at her in a way which she interpreted to mean he was going to ask her to his bed. Her reaction was always the same. She said something cruel or cutting or cold, and he invited someone else instead.

One by one, his women ripened with child. Kesair remained barren, big-boned and tawny-colored and barren, with angry eyes.

Salmé was also barren, though Fintan slept with her repeatedly. On the mornings after Salmé had been with him, Kesair spent a very long time beside the lake, communing with the water. Scooping it up in her shell, pouring it back.

"What are you thinking?"

His voice startled her from her reverie, but she did not look around. She knew Fintan was standing behind her.

"Thoughts are private," she said.

He ignored the rebuff. "You looked lonely standing here by yourself."

"I'm never lonely."

"I don't believe you. Everyone is lonely sometimes."

"You aren't. You couldn't possibly be."

"Because there's usually some woman with me? Surely you understand why, Kesair."

"Oh yes, I understand." Her voice was flat.

He waited. She said nothing more. How did we become so distanced from each other? Fintan wondered. Of all the women, she is the most intriguing, the one I thought would be closest to me once we got settled. "Kesair, what have I done to turn you against me?" he asked bluntly.

"Nothing." She was annoyed at his lack of subtlety, and she let him hear the annoyance in her voice.

He would not give up. "To tell you the truth, I'm getting very tired," he said confidingly. "Of the demands made upon me, I mean. It takes a lot out of a man, being the only male for so many. Sometimes I wish I could just sit and talk with an intelligent woman. Like you."

"You and I have nothing to say to each other."

"I think we do. There's mystery about you, you know. Layers to you. You've had experiences you haven't shared with the rest of us, that have made you what you are. I think I could learn from you."

She turned toward him then. Her expression was guarded. "Do you?"

"Of course. I admire you more than you know. The others are pleasant enough, but . . . ." He smiled his winning, boyish smile, and gave a slight shrug.

Be careful, Kesair warned herself. His is a very practiced charm.

He's trying it on you simply because he can't bear to think any woman could resist him. "The others aren't stupid, you could talk to any one of them," she said aloud.

"Not the way I could talk with you. I need more than a warm body and someone to agree with me, Kesair. I'm not just a breeding animal. I need . . ."

He left the thought hanging unfinished on the cold air, like a cloud of vapor. She saw it there, hanging.

On the cold air, permeated with silvery light reflected from the cold lake.

Beyond the lake the mountains rose, each peak an icy solitude against the vast and empty sky. Cold. Cold.

The frozen liquid core of Kesair longed for the spring thaw.

Looking at Fintan, she saw heat in his eyes.

Turning from him, she looked at the water. Red Lake. Usually it was a deep, dark blue, but today it had taken on the strange red hue that occasionally resulted from the invasion of some unidentified life form.

The lake could not always maintain its integrity. Life intervened.

Byth is old, Kesair thought, and we have heard nothing from him since we came here. He might be dead by now. Fintan might be the last man I shall ever see.

The last man.

How precious is anger?

Abruptly she said, "I was thinking of Byth."

"Has anyone come with news of him?"

"No. I doubt if they could spare a messenger, and if they did, I doubt if a messenger could find us. We've come a long way from Byth's valley."

"I hope they're all right."

"This is a benevolent land, Fintan. We haven't seen any predators large enough to be a danger to us, and there are plenty of natural resources. Everyone is subject to illness and injury and age, but we all have a chance. We all have a chance," she repeated. "We've been very fortunate."

The day was still and cold. When a bird called in the distance, its voice carrying across the lake, the sound was like a spear of beauty lancing through the silence.

For once even the customarily busy human settlement on the lake shore was quiet. No sounds of human activity came from the huts. The women inside were resting, sleeping, mending their garments, tending their fires.

An ineffable and timeless peace hung over the Red Lake. Kesair and Fintan might have been the only two people in the world.

"Are we the only survivors, do you think?" Fintan asked in a low voice.

"We who made it to this island?"

"Yes."

"No. There are others."

She spoke with such certainty he looked at her in astonishment. "How can you say that? How can you know?"

"I know."

"You mean, you want to believe. So do I, Kesair; I very much want to believe that other people reached dry land somewhere, and life goes on. But I don't know."

"The sea knows."

"What are you talking about?"

Gazing fixedly at the lake, she replied, "Did you ever enter a room that was totally dark, yet you were aware someone else was already in it?"

"I suppose so." He thought for a moment, remembering. "Yes, I have."

"Your senses told you of that other person through some faint disturbance in the air."

"Perhaps. But that was an enclosed room. You can't expect me to believe you somehow sense survivors on the other side of the ocean . . ."

"I don't. I told you. The sea does, the sea is aware of them and if you listen to it . . ."

He was beginning to lose patience. This was more of that wild mystical talk of hers that some of the others had complained of before. "We aren't anywhere near the sea, Kesair."

"We're near a lake. And all water is one water."

How tranquil her voice was; how at peace she sounded. Was she mad? Fintan wondered. If so, was she more comfortable in her madness than he in his sanity?

"Do you expect me to believe you talk to the *water?*"

She shook her tawny head. In the cold blue light of winter her face was pale, her eyes large and luminous.

"I don't talk *to* water. What could I possibly say of any

importance to a force so much greater than myself? I merely listen. I am quiet, and I listen."

Mad, Fintan decided. Yet there was an allure in her tranquillity, in the knowledge and conviction she contained deep within herself. He was inexorably drawn. "What does the water tell you?"

"Whatever it wishes to tell me. Tales of other times. Ideas from the stars." She paused meaningfully. "How to survive, if we but listen and learn.

"The water brought us this far, across the sea, along the rivers and streams. It has forgiven us the damage we have done and allowed us to start afresh. But we must not make the same mistakes again, Fintan. No god is endlessly forgiving."

"No god . . . are you saying you worship the water?"

For the first time, she took her gaze from the lake and fixed it on him. The radiance in her eyes took his breath away. "We have not worshiped anything, Fintan, except ourselves and our own puny achievements. And see what has happened to us. We are reduced to abject helplessness. We are forced to admit our total dependence on that which is beyond our control. Earth and air, fire and water. The fine trappings and comforts we prided ourselves on having are stripped from us. The way of life we knew is gone forever.

"But some things remain because they are immortal. And is not the immortal, holy?

"In the future, if we are to continue to survive, we must revere the holy, the essential, the powers above our own. We must not put our faith in temporary things. We must listen to the immortal voices of sea and lake, river and stream. They have great powers, Fintan. We must listen and obey."

"Create new gods, you mean? We put that behind us long ago. We've outgrown superstition."

"By 'we' you mean humankind? And where is humankind now?" Kesair made a show of looking first in one direction, then another. "Gone, most of them," she concluded. "But the water remains."

He could not find a way to refute her. He was aware that a few of the women had begun to listen to her, during the long winter nights when there was little to do but sit around the fires. A few of them now joined her each dawn beside the lake, to dip up water in a jug and pour it over their hands into a basin, then empty the basin back into the lake. He had thought the ritual harmless, women's foolishness.

Perhaps it was.

Perhaps it was homage to a power that should be placated by people in a situation of tenuous survival.

Kesair believed this, and her belief carried its own power. Standing face to face with her in the silvery loneliness, he could feel the power.

What had she said? Water sustains life?

It does, Fintan thought. I cannot deny it.

She was looking at him intently.

"The water remains," he echoed.

The tension in her face eased. "That is the beginning of understanding. We are starting over, Fintan." She reached into the neck of her gown.

To his disappointment, she withdrew a simple seashell. She held it up. "Look, Fintan."

He looked, puzzled as to what she wanted.

The shell was white with the faintest rosy tinge that darkened to a deeper color within its fluted lip. Round at one end, it spiraled to a pointed tip at the other. When he looked more closely he realized how beautiful it was.

We share a love of beauty, he thought. I could make something of that . . .

"Listen, Fintan."

Kesair held the shell to his ear, pressing the fluted edge against the curled ear flap that was so like the curve of a shell.

Obediently, Fintan listened, keeping his eyes on hers.

She waited.

At first he heard nothing but a sound that might be the muffled beating of his own heart.

Then, faintly, he became aware of something else. He began to listen with his whole being.

The sound grew in intensity. Became a roar. A roar of ancient power, the roar of a billion voices held within the shell, muted to softness, but immortal.

Fintan's eyes widened with delight.

"I hear the sea," he said.

Fire. Fire! Firefirefirefirefirefire.
Let there be fire.
Hot hotter hottest singeing singing soaring burning
blazing conflagration inferno holocaust.
Let there be light.
Sparking flashing flaring flaming illuminating glow-
ing gleaming glaring dazzling radiant.
Let there be life.
Vigor ardor intensity vehemence fervor passion fury
magic inspiration genius brilliance.
Thoughtless explosion of power giving birth to all
thought, all awareness. Vast outgoing surge of creative
passion studding the universe with stars, smoldering in
the souls of planets.
Simmering scorching scalding sizzling bubbling boil-
ing molten inflaming energizing consuming.
Firefirefirefirefirefire.
Fire is. Fire was. Fire will be.
Mindless.
Allmind.
Fire.
Fire.
Fire!

# 7

*Meriones awoke with a sense of*

*guarded expectation. It felt like a day when*

*something good just might happen.*

*He opened his eyes to the light of the*

*Mediterranean reflecting from*

the plastered walls of the second-story sleeping chamber. Beyond the window, the dawn glowed rose and gold. The music of the waking city was a harmony of voices and bustle, carts creaking, neighbors calling out to one another, shutters being thrown back.

Meriones stretched lazily beneath the linen sheet. The other half of the bed was empty. Tulipa had been up since before dawn, pouring a bowl of milk for the house snake that guarded their spirits when they slept, building a fire in the bake oven in the courtyard, setting up the small folding table beneath their one olive tree for their morning meal. As usual, she talked to herself as she worked, pitching her voice so it was certain to carry through the open window to Meriones.

Tulipa had lost interest in spending the early morning in bed with her husband. When he tried to lure her back she was quick to point out it was his fault she must leave him. "Who will milk the goat if I do not?" she would ask. "Who will cook our food or sweep our share of the street? There are no slaves here such as are to be found in the houses of more famous musicians. The wife of The Minos' favorite says she doesn't even know how to use a broom, can you imagine? But I do. I'm just Meriones' wife. I know how to do all manner of tiresome tasks. I have to get up right now and empty our night jar, so the whole house doesn't stink of it. I have no time to loll in bed with you."

As soon as she began, Meriones would shrug and smile his shy smile, offering little tokens of peace between the flying arrows of her words. "I am sorry . . . of course, you're quite right . . . you do work very hard, I know . . . yes, yes . . ."

But she had to run on to the end, always. And loudly, so others heard. In the city the houses huddled close together.

"She will be different when the children start to come," Meriones had once said apologetically to Phrixus, who lived next door.

"I doubt it," commented Phrixus, who was older. "Sometimes the marriage rites bring forward the worst in a woman. Your Tulipa told my Dendria that she had married beneath herself and regretted it."

Meriones had hung his head at these words. "Tulipa's uncle was Keeper of the Bulls. I'm just one of the countless musicians at the palace, with no royal blood to give me status."

"How did you come to play the lyre?"

Meriones had hesitated before answering. When he spoke his voice was low with embarrassment. "My grandmother was brought here as a slave from the Islands of the Mist. Are you surprised? Not many know; Tulipa would rather die than tell anyone. My grandmother taught me to play a small stringed instrument that had belonged to her father. It was the only possession she had been allowed to bring with her."

"You don't have to be ashamed, Meriones," Phrixus had said. "Almost everyone on Crete has ancestors who came from somewhere else, and a lot of them were slaves. After all, the commerce of the world goes through our harbor. Slaves are treated well here and their descendants can prosper, you are proof of that yourself. So be proud—and start siring some descendants of your own. They will keep Tulipa too busy to scold you."

But although Meriones and his wife prayed daily to the Good Goddess and observed her rituals, and Tulipa made several pilgrimages to the cave of the deity of childbirth, her belly remained flat while her tongue grew sharper.

Now as Meriones emerged, blinking and yawning, from the windowless ground floor of his house into the brilliant sunlight of the courtyard, she began on him at once. "That thief at the oil merchant's shop sold me a whole pithos of rancid oil, husband. It was delivered yesterday. I just unstoppered it and the vile smell turned my stomach over. What will I boil tonight's meat in? Why does everyone think they can take advantage of us? It's your fault, Meriones. Because you are unimportant we are sold rancid oil and we live on a crowded back street with no view of the harbor."

"We have a nice house," Meriones replied. "You seemed to like it well enough when we married, and you said nothing about the view then." Trying to hold on to the good mood he had awakened with, he looked admiringly at his little house of stone and plaster. Its exterior walls were painted the cheerful yellow of field flowers. As was the custom in Knōsos, the ground floor was windowless to insure privacy, but the upper story was windowed front and back to catch the light and draw the salty breezes from the harbor.

A man's status in the community could be judged from the view he commanded, and in the ninety cities of Crete there was intense competition for a panorama of the mountains or the dark glittering sea. The day room and sleeping chambers were at the top of the house, so their occupants could enjoy the scenery and be removed from domestic activities taking place at ground level in the megaron, or hearth room.

Meriones' house boasted no view more lofty than that of the paved street in front and its own tiny courtyard behind, but the building itself was bright and comfortable. Privately, Meriones thought it a fine achievement for the grandson of a slave. Yet many of his class lived as well or better, for the wealth of the sea kings lapped like a tidal wave over the inhabitants of the island of Crete.

Tulipa was not really dissatisfied with the house. It was her life and her husband that displeased her. She sat tapping her foot while Meriones ate, then sent him on his way with a negligible pat on the cheek, her mind already casting about for some way to avoid the chores waiting for her. She felt they were making her old before her time. Perhaps she could put off airing the bed until tomorrow— "Meriones will never notice anyway" she muttered to herself—and spend the morning with her friends Lydda and Dendria, gossiping over bowls of spiced fruit juice and comparing the faults of their husbands.

"Men are all alike," one of them would say with a sigh, and the other two would readily agree.

Meriones swung around the corner and set off up the main street of Knōsos, heading south, inland. He blended immediately into the crowd, one more slender, almond-eyed young man in a throng of chattering townspeople. He walked with his chest thrust out and his back arched, swinging his arms freely and flexing the arches of his feet to produce the exaggerated, jaunty gait that identified a Minoan of Crete anywhere in the known world. It was a walk that had taken him years to perfect. A strain of rogue blood in his veins resisted the effort, but had at last been overcome.

Now anyone seeing him would have thought him pure Minoan. The dazzling sunshine of Crete had tanned his skin to copper. His black hair was folded and knotted at the nape, with oiled curls hanging over his ears in the latest fashion. Around his waist he wore a linen apron embroidered in gold thread, emblem of one who had access to the palace of The Minos, the greatest sea king of all, Lord of Knōsos, god-king of the Minoan empire.

Meriones' waist was tightly girdled to accent its abnormal smallness, the result of wearing the heavy copper girdle that was fastened on children of both sexes almost from birth. "The tinier the waist, the more elegant the person," was a Minoan axiom.

Meriones was considered elegant indeed.

A stray hound trotted out of a narrow alleyway and came to a halt at Meriones' feet, looking up at him hopefully. He stopped and returned the dog's gaze. "I'd be glad of a companion as far as the Sun Gate," he told the white hound, "but they won't let you come into the palace." When he began walking again the dog trotted at his heels, its feathery white tail waving like a plume.

They threaded their way through a polyglot of lean dark Egyptians and ebony-skinned Nubians, Syrian traders and Cycladic purchasing agents, Libyans and Amorites and Hittites, porters and sailors and laborers who jostled one another and laughed or swore as the occasion dictated. Nobles in sedan chairs claimed right of way. Small donkeys, overburdened and uncomplaining, picked their way over the paving stones and ignored the impatient hands jerking their headcollars.

As Meriones moved inland toward the great sprawling palace known as the House of the Double Axes, the shops and small businesses that lined the main street began to give way to public areas furnished with fountains and flowers. Curving walkways led to luxurious villas set well back from the road. The tang of the sea was replaced by the heady aroma of flowering trees. Behind walls painted in blue and yellow and coral, caged birds could be heard singing, their music mingling with the laughter of children.

The land lifted, the houses climbing with it in a series of steps, bright blocks of color forming a random mosaic across the hills. Had he looked back, Meriones would have seen the cobalt sea and the mass of lateen-rigged ships crowding the harbor. Instead he gazed steadfastly ahead, contemplating immortality. Beyond Knōsos great Zeus himself lay sleeping, pretending to be a mountain.

Meriones and the dog passed a small stone shrine by the side of the road, heaped with floral offerings and containing a glazed jar of seawater with a realistically painted octopus curling its tentacles around the vessel.

Meriones paused. The hound flopped down in the dusty road beside him and scratched behind one ear with an audible sigh of relief.

A vendor carrying a wickerwork tray stepped out from behind the shrine. "An offering for the god of the shaking earth?" he suggested.

Meriones considered. The sun was warm. The ground felt stable beneath his feet. The flower-bedecked shrine to Poseidon gave no hint of the unstable temper of the god. Still . . .

"It never hurts to be cautious," the vendor urged. "Only last year, at Phaistos . . ."

"Yes, yes, I remember." Meriones quickly selected a sprig of mint from the man's tray and added his offering to the heap, though he was embarrassed to see how small one sprig looked amid the piles of gaudy, more expensive flowers. The vendor was looking at him with contempt, like Tulipa. He pressed a coin into the man's hand, whistled to the dog, and hurried away.

The sunbaked road broadened into the Royal Avenue as it led into the valley that sheltered the palace of The Minos from the greedy gaze of sea pirates. Not that there was any real danger of invasion, not anymore. For several centuries Crete had ruled secure and unchallenged at the heart of the world's seaways.

And sometimes the god who ruled those seas reminded man of his ultimate power by shaking the earth.

With the white hound at his heels, Meriones crossed the stone bridge that spanned the stream east of the palace. The House of the Double Axes, called Labrys in the court language, spread out before him as if a bag of jewels had been spilled from a giant's hand, tumbling down the valley in gay profusion.

No huge perimeter wall protected Labrys. Its guardian was the power of the sea's mightiest fleet, defending not only Knōsos but the other cities of the Cretan sea kings. Instead of a fortress, the palace of The Minos consisted of a number of elegant villas surrounding a central core of chambers and halls. Some of these villas, which served as homes for the vast array of officials and functionaries required by The Minos, rivaled the king's own quarters in splendor. But none could compete with the royal residence in terms of sheer size.

"There it is," Meriones said to the dog. "I spend every day of my life there—except feast days, of course. The palace is a city in itself, you know. There's a maze of passages and storerooms and private chambers inside. It took me years to learn my way, but I did," he added with shy pride.

The dog wagged its tail and grinned up at Meriones.

Labrys had been built from the heart outward, as a tree grows, until it sprawled in giant tiers like a child's blocks. The heart itself was the Great Central Court through and around which all life flowed. Four main gates led into the complex. The westernmost, called the Bull Gate, was the ceremonial entryway, with a pillared portico fronting on a broad paved courtyard. The south gate was the Zeus Gate, facing the mountains. To the north was the Sea Gate. Meriones approached by the eastern Sun Gate, following a walkway through flowered gardens. He wove his way among increasing crowds of gaily dressed men and women in animated conversation, hands fluttering, voices trilling. In addition to the customary courtiers there was the usual scattering of long-haired folk from Boeotia and Attica and Euboea, travelers from Pylos and Lerna, even a few flint-eyed warriors from Mycenae and Tiryns.

Everyone came to the House of the Double Axes.

Meriones, like most citizens of Knōsos, was fluent in several languages. He smiled from time to time at some overheard witticism, and translated for the dog's benefit.

As he climbed the broad stone steps that led to the Sun Gate itself, the giant Nubian warrior at the top of the stairs looked down at him. His usually impassive face cracked into a smile.

"Not another dog, musician?"

Meriones glanced ruefully at his companion. "I'm afraid so. They follow me and I can't help encouraging them. I would like to have a dog of my own but my wife says they make her sneeze." He gave the white hound a last fond pat, then handed it over to the Nubian, who held it by the scruff of the neck until Meriones disappeared inside the palace, and then gave it a shove, not unkindly, and sent it on its way.

Meriones made his way through the corridors and service rooms that lay between the Sun Gate and the residential quarter. Like all public areas of Labrys, the royal apartments featured spacious open rooms, often divided by the same dark red columns that were used to support the exterior porticoes. The columns tapered downward in the distinctive Cretan style, and were as integral a part of palace design as the painted frescoes glowing on every wall. The famous Grand Staircase was renowned throughout the Mediterranean world for its scenes of cavorting sea creatures, blooming lilies, and elegant court life. Numerous light wells provided adequate illumination for the appreciation of such beauty, even in the inner recesses of Labrys.

But Meriones did not reach the Grand Staircase. His progress was interrupted by Santhos, Master of Musicians. "You have a new assignment," the round-faced Santhos announced. "You won't be playing in the royal apartments for a while. The queen is very dissatisfied with the quality of work being done by the goldsmiths these days, and wants a musician sent to play in their workrooms and inspire them."

Meriones' erect posture slumped. The workrooms of the royal craftsmen were in the northeast quarter of the palace, a comparatively dreary place where a musician himself might despair of inspiration. But there was no point in arguing.

Meriones forced a smile, straightened his spine and saluted Santhos. He strode off jauntily, springing upward from the balls of his feet, looking as if the prospect of days spent in gloomy workrooms was the thing he most desired.

Watching him go, Santhos said to himself, "Thank Zeus for men like Meriones. Musicians are so temperamental. Most would have refused."

The craftsmens' workrooms were on the ground floor beneath the Great Eastern Hall. In separate cubicles, men fashioned furniture, fabrics, tableware, jewelry, the myriad items required by the huge community above them. The chamber of the goldsmiths was in a favored position, with a light well and freshly painted walls, but Meriones' heart sank when he entered. It was hot and cramped and utilitarian rather than elegant. Tulipa would be angry if she learned of this.

Half a dozen men were working at benches and tables. They all looked up as he entered.

"I am a musician of The Minos," he began formally. His words dropped like stones into a sudden silence. "I have been sent to make music for you while you work. Is there, ah, a bench, a stool . . . ?"

They stared at him unresponsively. Meriones felt his ears reddening. Why couldn't someone else have been sent? Why did these things always happen to him?

Then one of the goldsmiths, a ruddy, thickset man with bloodshot eyes and an uncut mane of sandy hair, stepped forward and guided Meriones to a stool. "Here, musician, perch on this. And play quietly, don't distract us."

The man's voice was harsh with the accents of distant Thrace, but Meriones felt a sudden warmth toward him and smiled gratefully. "I'm called Meriones," he offered.

"Hmmm." The other turned back to his table. Then he said "Hokar" over his shoulder as an afterthought before forgetting Meriones entirely and returning to his work.

Meriones sat on the edge of the stool, trying simultaneously to be inspiring and inconspicuous. He was a success at one of the two, for the goldsmiths paid no further attention to him.

In mid-afternoon two slaves arrived, bringing watered wine and a tray of bread and cheese. Hokar put down the gold plate he was working on and stood up, stretching. "I need to walk," he said casually to Meriones. "Do you know your way around this place?"

"Yes, absolutely."

"Come, then." Hokar headed for the door, massaging the muscles of his shoulder with one hand. Glad of the break, Meriones followed him.

"Working with gold is like working with the sun, isn't it?" he said, to make conversation. "I mean, molten gold looks like liquid sunlight, doesn't it? I envy you, really. It must be wonderful to be able to make beautiful things . . ." His voice trailed off. Hokar did not appear to be listening.

They sauntered along hallways that wound a baffling route toward the Great Central Court. Once, when Hokar was about to make a turn that would take him into a warren of storerooms, Meriones corrected him with a gentle hand on his arm. Nothing more was said until they reached the colonnaded walkway overlooking the Court. There they stood shoulder to shoulder, watching the constant crowd swirling across the mosaic tiles.

"I've never known a day so hot," Hokar remarked. Sweat was pouring down his face.

"It is hot," Meriones agreed, "hotter than usual. And so still." That seemed to exhaust the fund of conversation. The two men were quiet for a time.

Then Meriones volunteered, "The women of Knōsos are the most beautiful in the world, don't you think?"

"You haven't seen the women of Thrace," Hokar replied. But his eyes were following a Cretan priestess of the Snake as she minced past. Like all women in the House of the Double Axes she was fashionably pale, her powdered complexion a marked contrast to the glossy black of her hair. Kohl rimmed her dark eyes, accentuating their almond shape. Her slender body was clad in a flounced skirt of multicolored layers that swung beguilingly above her bare feet and dainty rouged toes. A gem-studded belt defined the impossible smallness of her waist. Above it her breasts bloomed, pushed upward by a tight saffron-colored bodice that clung to her shoulders and upper arms but left her bosom bare. Her erect nipples were sprinkled with gold dust.

Meriones saluted the priestess and made flattering gestures with his hands, to which she responded with a few softly lisped syllables.

"You understand her?" Hokar queried.

"Of course. That is the court language, the Old Tongue still favored by the nobility and the priestly class. One could not be long in Labrys without learning at least a few words of it."

"I'll be the exception. If I have to learn to sound like a dove cooing I prefer to be speechless."

Meriones chuckled. "It's a difficult language," he agreed. "You never hear it now, outside of the palace. Crete speaks the New Tongue, the language of the markets. You're quite good at that, I notice, which proves you have a gift for language as well as for creating beautiful objects. I also have a gift for language. I speak several, even one I learned from my grandmother, who spoke the tongue of the Islands of Mist."

"You talk a lot," Hokar observed. "all Cretans talk a lot, don't they?"

"We enjoy the arts, including that of conversation."

"There is a lot to enjoy here," Hokar remarked. His eyes were now following a graceful woman dressed in a vivid shade of orange, her fingers and toes weighted with jewels, her nipples painted a brilliant blue. She returned his frank stare with an amused smile.

"You'd never see anything like that on the mainland," Hokar said. "My cousin Tereus would consider it an invitation to rape."

Meriones was shocked. "She is merely sharing her beauty! To ignore her would be rude, but it would be ruder still to abuse her as a result of her generosity."

"Hmmm." Hokar dug his unpolished fingernails into his beard, scratching. "I suppose it's this Cretan worship of beauty that creates such a good climate for artisans, so I shouldn't joke about it. We're given opportunities here we would receive nowhere else. I devoted years of my life to obtaining an invitation to come to Crete just as an apprentice goldsmith, whereas in Thrace I was already considered a master."

"What is Thrace like?"

"Rugged country. Breeds rugged people. We have no patience with effeminate manners in Thrace."

"We are not effeminate," Meriones protested, stung at last by the other's patronizing tone. "We are an *elegant* people. You mainlanders don't understand elegance."

Hokar grinned. "Not in our heads, perhaps. But watch me at work and then tell me my hands don't understand elegance."

That night over their meal Meriones spoke to his wife about Hokar. "He's a gruff sort of fellow, devoted to his work. He keeps to himself, mostly. But I know he has a kind heart, and he's a brilliant artisan. It's a treat to watch him, it truly is. I wish you could see him take those big paws of his and move them this way and that—and then something delicate and exquisite emerges. I could watch him for hours."

Sundown had marked the beginning of a feast day, and Tulipa had purchased a small kid in the marketplace. The remnants of the meal, still redolent of spice and honey, lay on their plates. She picked idly among the bones. "You are always trying to make friends with the most unlikely people, Meriones. If you must attach yourself to someone, why not to someone important who can do you some good?"

"But I like Hokar. He was nice to me, in his way, and I take it as an honor. Did I tell you he used to make sword hilts for the warrior princes on the mainland?"

Tulipa sniffed and wiped her greasy fingers on her forearm, working the grease into the skin to keep it soft. It was a habit of the lower classes, one no court lady would have allowed herself. But Meriones made no judgment. After all, as she so often reminded him, her uncle had been a person of importance.

"You fasten yourself onto someone who doesn't care if you're alive or dead," she continued in an aggrieved voice, "while I sit home alone, fading away for lack of entertainment. If you made some really important friends perhaps you could get me invited to the palace."

"If we had children you wouldn't be bored," he ventured. "Shall we . . . go upstairs now?"

"No. I don't want to. Listening to you rave on and on about some common Thracian has given me a headache. You are so thoughtless, Meriones."

"I'm so sorry! I didn't realize." Meriones jumped to his feet. "I'll go dip a cloth in cool water and vinegar to put on your head," he promised, hurrying away.

As the days passed, Meriones continued to play in the chamber of the goldsmiths. Hokar gradually accepted his patiently proffered friendship. They began taking a daily stroll together in the gardens, though as long as the heat wave continued even Meriones, who dearly loved sunshine, had to make a conscious effort to keep his step fashionably brisk.

"No one can remember it being so hot for so long," he once commented. "I used to think it could never be too sunny, but now I wonder. Is it hot in Thrace, Hokar?"

"In the summers it is. But we pay no attention."

Hokar enjoyed talking about his homeland, so Meriones constantly plied him for details. The Thracian spoke glowingly of the mountains of his boyhood, and of things he had seen in his travels as an apprentice goldsmith. He alluded to the growing power of the citadels of Mycenae, and described chariot races so vividly Meriones could almost see them. Inflamed by his own words, Hokar embossed a scene of chariots and charioteers into the rim of a platter he was making for The Minos' table.

At last the heat broke. The brief Cretan winter arrived, bringing raw damp air that bit into a man's bones. It was the Season of the Dying God. In the House of the Double Axes the chambers were divided into smaller, more heatable rooms by means of sliding wooden panels. These rooms were heated by bronze braziers. Fires were built in the central hearths of the megaron. Meriones enjoyed staring at the bright tongues of flame, children of the sun. His grandmother, who remembered the Islands of Mist as being always cold, had taught him an appreciation of fire.

Meriones personally tended the fire in the brazier in the goldsmiths' chamber.

He never tired of watching his friend at work. Once Hokar had begun on a piece he tolerated no distractions and would lash out at anyone foolish enough to disturb his concentration. Meriones learned to time his music to the rhythm of the Thracian's work pattern.

Melding with the music, Hokar so lost himself in his art that it seemed no man was involved, just a pair of skilled hands taming the molten gold, the melted sun, turning it into exquisite jewelry and tableware and ornaments for the palace.

To Meriones, Hokar's gift seemed like magic.

"The queen is very pleased with the work coming from the goldsmiths now," Santhos reported to Meriones. "You may become a permanent fixture here."

In the Season of the Borning God Meriones invited Hokar to come to his house for dinner, to celebrate the arrival of spring.

"Will I be able to get home afterward before dark?" the Thracian inquired.

"Where do you live?"

"In a little house at Arkhanes, in the shadow of the Hill of Tombs."

Meriones whistled. "It depends on what time you leave my house, then. That's a goodly distance. We can loan you a lamp. Or you can spend the night with us. My wife will make up a pallet."

As they talked, the two men were standing side by side in one of the gardens, eating their bread and cheese and watching a pretty girl play with a chained monkey. "Do you have a nice place?" Hokar asked.

Meriones beamed. "I think so. It was a great piece of luck, getting it. For some reason the old Minos—the one before this, that is—took a fancy to my music toward the end of his reign. He had grown quiet, and I think he liked me for playing softly. He chose me alone to play for him on Last Day, so for a brief time I was very important at Labrys. My reward was enough to buy my house, and Tulipa married me."

"Tell me about Last Day, Meriones. What was that like? We have no such custom in Thrace."

"It's the sight of a lifetime! The final day of the Nine Years' King must be more spectacular than any that has gone before, to show our gratitude to him for a prosperous reign. The Bull Dances are better than ever. Outstanding teams of Bull Leapers compete with each other for the honor of performing on Last Day, and the bull who proves to be bravest and most agile in the Bull Dance is sacrificed to Poseidon at the end of the day."

"You always offer a bull to Poseidon?"

"We make many offerings to the sea god, but it is the gift of the mightiest creature on earth that pleases him most and keeps him from shaking the land."

Hokar nodded. "I've heard that Poseidon Ennosigaion ripples Crete from time to time, though I've yet to experience a bad earthquake here."

"Ah well, they do happen," Meriones admitted. "But we build to allow for them, and we do those things that keep us in good favor with the gods. And with a joyous spirit!" he added quickly. "That is the Cretan way—with a joyous spirit!"

"Tell me about the sacrifice. Would it make a good scene to depict on a gold bowl?"

Meriones hesitated. "I don't like to talk about sacrifices, really. I never enjoy seeing blood spilled. But if you want the details . . . the priest of the Double Ax, the two-faced ax that faces both toward this world and the netherworld, sacrificed a huge pied bull in the Central Court, and its head was brought to this very chamber, to have the horns gilded."

"Was the old Minos sacrificed too?"

Merioned recoiled. "Of course not! What a ghastly idea!"

"I just wondered. It is the custom in some lands, sacrificing the king at the end of his reign. It's supposed to restore fertility to the soil."

Meriones was quite pale. "How grim." He swallowed, hard. "No, we don't practice human sacrifice on Crete. It is unbearable to imagine."

"Yet the sign of the Double Ax is everywhere in this place," Hokar pointed out. "It must have some significance beyond the killing of bulls."

"Ah, well, er . . . I suppose it is a symbol from the olden times. Long ago . . . but surely not now . . ."

"This is a huge place. There could be rites carried out in Labrys that you would know nothing about, Meriones."

"Oh, I hardly think so, not the way people love to talk. You are very bloodthirsty, Hokar."

"I'm not, I'm realistic. We Thracians are earthy people, that's all. But if this bothers you, tell me instead about what happened to the old Minos."

"Ah, yes." Meriones looked relieved. "I stayed with him until the end, playing the music he liked. Then the priestesses took him to the Chamber of Robes and removed all his finery, sending him out naked to his women. How they sobbed, his queen and concubines! But that was just part of the ritual, there was nothing to be sad about, really. They wrapped him in a simple robe and led him away. I stopped playing just as the priest brought forward the new Minos, a young man at the peak of his strength, naked, freshly bathed, and took him into the Chamber of Robes. There he was dressed in the royal clothes, still warm from his predecessor. That's important, the warm part," he added.

"And the former king?"

"I saw them bringing a covered sedan chair from the Zeus Gate to take him away. I believe he was taken to a distant palace such as Phaistos to live out his life in luxury, for he had been a good king and we prospered during his reign."

"But do you know for certain if he's still alive? Has he ever been seen since?"

"Oh no. At the end of his nine years a Minos must disappear from the sight of his people forever."

"I see." Hokar nodded. His eyes were on the omnipresent sign of the Double Axes, depicted over the nearest doorway.

**8**

*On a languid blue evening when*

*the rusty voices of the gulls had ceased and bronze*

*lamps of welcome burned in residential windows,*

*Hokar dined with Meriones. At the*

*conclusion of*

the meal he wiped the crumbs from his beard and belched appreciatively.

Tulipa sniffed. The man was crude. His hairy face offended her. Men should be clean-shaven and polish their nails. But at least he had brought her a present. For the sake of the silver bracelet he had given her, she would try to overlook his rough edges.

Now the two men lolled at their ease beside the table in the courtyard, watching idly as Tulipa cleared away and brought a fresh pitcher of wine.

"Your wife is a good cook," Hokar remarked when she had gone back into the house. "I never had birds stuffed with barley before, or those little shellfish."

"And raisins soaked in fruit juice," Meriones said. "They were especially good. Did you like them?"

"Mmmmm. Does she always cook like this?"

"Always," Meriones was proud to say. There was no faulting Tulipa's cooking, even if she hated domestic duties otherwise. "Have you never married, Hokar?"

"Never. Though at a time like this, I can see some of its advantages. But I've always been devoted to my work. That takes my energy, I have no time left over for women. My art is my life. My only passion."

"Ah now. Ah now." Meriones smiled a sly smile and waggled a forefinger in front of Hokar's eyes. "That isn't true. I've seen how you look at the girls in the palace, particularly those young ones, the new Bull Leapers."

"Any man would look at them, but looking is all I want to do. Can you imagine trying to catch hold of one? They are all muscle, those girls. And they have hardly any breasts. They look like the boys."

"They have to be slim and strong. It's a very hard thing to do, the Bull Dance, and demands the greatest athleticism. Bull Leapers are recruited from every land, you know. It is a high honor to appear in the Bull Court."

"Recruited? Kidnapped, you mean. In Thrace we heard of young people who were seized and taken aboard Cretan ships and never heard of again. Rumor was, they disappeared into the bowels of Labrys."

"You make it sound as if something awful happened to them,"

Meriones protested. "But they were taught a high art instead. Dancing with the bulls, leaping over their horns, somersaulting in teams through the air while a bull charges beneath you . . . it is not only beautiful to watch but it tests the courage of both human and bull. The best Bull Leapers become famous."

"If they live long enough," Hokar commented. "What about the ones who are killed learning this 'art'?"

"Killed?" Meriones raised his eyebrows. "I've heard of no one being killed."

"I suppose you wouldn't," said Hokar. "I suspect it's kept very quiet. Like the old Minos."

A shiver ran down Meriones' spine. "You're just saying that."

Hokar relented. "I enjoy teasing you," he said. "I mean no harm by it, forget I said anything."

The rest of the evening went well. At one stage, Meriones went next door to bring Phrixus over to meet the goldsmith. "He's very important at Labrys, you know," the musician said under his breath to his neighbor.

"I hear you had an important visitor from the palace yesterday," Dendria said with barely concealed envy when she met Tulipa at the well the next morning.

Tulipa affected nonchalance. She yawned, she patted her hair, she studied her nails. "Oh, yes? My Meriones knows everyone who matters." Balancing her filled water jug on her head, she walked away, swaying her hips.

Several days later, Hokar mentioned that his cousin Tereus, who was captain of a sizable trading vessel, should be arriving in the Cretan harbor soon. "You would enjoy meeting him, I think. He's very full of life, is Tereus; he's been everywhere and seen everything and he tells great stories."

"We'll invite him to my house for dinner," Meriones decided, flushed with his recent social success.

Tulipa was not hard to convince. She was wearing Hokar's silver bracelet, which she had shown several times to Dendria and Lydda. This Tereus might bring her something even better.

On the appointed evening, Hokar came straight from the palace with Meriones, and the two settled in the courtyard to await Tereus. They did not wait for long. A brawny man with a jutting jaw pounded on the outer door. When Tulipa opened to him, he scarcely noticed her. Looking past her into the interior of the house, he bellowed, "Hokar! Where are you?" At an answering shout from the courtyard, he pushed past Tulipa and found his own way to the rear of the house.

She trotted after him, wide-eyed with indignation.

Hokar got to his feet as Tereus appeared in the doorway. "Meriones, this is my cousin Tereus, captain of the *Qatil* out of Byblos," he said.

Tereus filled the doorframe with his broad shoulders. Vitality radiated from him like heat from a brazier. He made Meriones feel insignificant, and when his brilliant blue eyes swept over her household Tulipa received a distinct impression of contempt. This was a man who demanded much. Whatever life was lived in the house of Meriones, the musician was insufficient for his appetites.

He was polite enough in his unpolished way, however, and thanked Meriones—though not Tulipa—for receiving him. As the three men sat at the table Tereus had great tales to tell of ocean voyages and sea monsters and terrifying storms. His stories were so vivid Meriones often forgot to eat, sitting with his mouth agape and the food congealing on his plate.

When Tulipa finished serving the men she drew up a chair to the table for herself, so she could listen to Tereus. His accent was no thicker than Hokar's, and she understood most of what he said.

She understood very clearly when he remarked, "Only on Crete do women dare sit at the table with the men. Elsewhere they know their place and keep it."

Tulipa's cheeks burned. She looked to Meriones, expecting him to defend their customs, but he only stared at his plate and toyed with his uneaten food.

Snatching up her husband's plate, Tulipa strode furiously into the house.

"That's better," said Tereus. "Women get in the way of serious conversation. Meriones, my cousin tells me you have served in the house of The Minos for a long time."

"Since I was old enough to take off my waist-shaper."

"Then you have good knowledge of the place, of its staffing, the habits of its purchasing agents, and so forth?"

Meriones had been surprised, and secretly, guiltily pleased at

Tereus' handling of Tulipa. And he was flattered at the way the ship's captain made him feel important, privy to the inner workings of the House of the Double Axes. "Oh yes," he said, waving his hands. "I know all the stewards, the keepers of the stores, everyone."

"Hokar said he thought you might. You are the very man I need, then." Tereus leaned forward, folding his thick arms on the tabletop. His voice dropped to a more confidential tone. "I have a very special cargo from my last voyage and I would like to sell it here, to the household of The Minos. A sea king can afford the kind of price which would give me enough money to buy my own ship at last, and not have to bow my head to some Syrian owner who never sets foot on deck."

There was something about the emphasis Tereus put on his words that made Meriones nervous. "If you have a valuable cargo I suppose the quartermaster already suggested the best market when you cleared it through him? And the ship's owner—a Syrian, you said—will he not get the profit?"

Tereus and Hokar exchanged glances. The goldsmith gave a barely perceptible nod. "Meriones is all right," he said softly.

Tereus dropped his eyelids halfway over his eyes so their expression was veiled. "I have not discussed this particular cargo with the harbormaster, Meriones. Do you understand? Nor will it be reported at Byblos. There is a bit of profit in it for you, too, if you keep your mouth shut and put me in contact with the right buyer. Would you not like to have a bit of wealth to impress your wife?"

Meriones felt his mouth go dry. "What is your cargo?"

Tereus smiled lazily and leaned back, resting his broad shoulders against the plastered wall behind his chair. "My last voyage was through the Pillars of Herakles and then north, following the coast," he said. "A dangerous trip into unpredictable waters. Not many are willing to make it. Our final destination was to be the lands at the edge of winter, where people collect lumps of raw amber on the seashore after storms. To trade for amber, we took flint from the Islands of Mist."

"You have been to the Islands of Mist?" Meriones asked in an awed whisper.

"Of course. We started from Byblos with timber and jade, and pearls from Dilmun. These we traded along the way for obsidian, for copper, then for Nubian ivory, and that in turn went for textiles and bronze which we traded in the Islands of Mist for tin and flint and, on the westernmost island, gold."

Meriones' existence was circumscribed by the luxurious, enclosed atmosphere of palace life. But Crete was the land of the sea kings, so he had heard tales of the far places beyond the horizon, tales of Ugarit and Mitanni and Assyria, of wild Iberia and fabled Babylon. Now he was looking at a man who had personally sailed to the very kingdom of winter, where blond giants farmed steep fields and amber lay free for the taking on rocky beaches. Meriones strained to envision a land of deep fjords and long blue silences.

But he was more interested in the Islands of Mist. "My grandmother came from the Islands of Mist," he said.

Tereus lifted his eyebrows. "As a slave? Then you understand what sort of cargo I brought this time. I hope you won't be offended when I say the best slaves are from those rainy islands. Their skin is very white and they are highly prized throughout the Mediterranean. I try to pick up a few good ones each voyage, to sell privately."

Meriones suffered confused emotions. Slavery was very much a part of life, and central to Cretan economy, as it was everywhere in the Mediterranean. Thousands were traded each year at places like Kythera, where men dealt in nothing else. But, remembering his grandmother, he found it hard to think of people like her as if they were merely cargo, so many cattle to buy and sell. "Is that this special, valuable cargo, then?" he asked Tereus. "Captives taken from the Islands of Mist?"

"Yes. Five of them, three females and two males. The females are young, very pretty. They would be valuable anywhere. But the men . . . that is, one of them . . . ah, this one is something very special.

"If your grandmother came from those islands, what do you know about them?" Tereus asked Meriones.

"Only a little. How green they were, how mild the climate. How many lakes and rivers they had."

"It is the inhabitants who are interesting," Tereus said. "They are strong and brave and are ruled by warrior princes. In some ways they remind me of Thracians. But they live intimately with gods I do not know: water gods, weather gods, gods of the wild places. And they build stone ritual centers with as much engineering skill as the Egyptians, though in a very different style. I have seen nothing anywhere that raises my hackles like the great stone circles in the Islands of Mist.

"One of the slaves I brought back with me this time is some sort of priest. Not such a priest as you have here. I believe theirs is a fading race, though once it may have been very powerful. Their sorcerers can still do things to freeze a man's marrow. This old fellow should be worth a fortune as a worker of magic, or at least a royal diviner. For all I know the old man can predict the shaking of the earth, which would make him beyond price, eh? And even if he fails in that he can do a lot of other tricks."

Meriones was shocked. "You would take a priest and sell him as an *entertainer?*"

"I would sell the woman who bore me if she were still alive and the sale would enable me to buy my own ship and be answerable to no man."

"Your mother would cheerfully cut your throat if you tried such a thing," Hokar interjected.

"My mother was a proud woman and a warrior in her own right. She would have understood my desire to be my own master."

Meriones was frowning. "I just don't like the idea of selling priests as slaves. Angering the gods is dangerous."

Tereus said, "His gods aren't our gods, I told you that. Besides, if I can turn over a cargo twelve times in a voyage and avoid the pirates of Mycenae, I fear nothing."

"But—"

"Never mind, just do as I tell you and fortune will smile on us. The gods of whatever land support the successful, have you not noticed? Put me in contact with someone at the palace who is empowered to purchase slaves—expensive, unusual slaves, by private treaty—and I will present my treasures for his inspection. Here, at your house."

Meriones was startled. "Why at my house? Why not take them direct to Labrys?"

"They are, shall we say, unpredictable. Especially the old man. Hokar tells me you know a little of the language they speak, so I want you present throughout the negotiations to persuade them to be cooperative. It will all go more smoothly here, in a private house."

Watching Meriones closely, Tereus assessed his exact degree of resistance. He immediately poured another bowl of wine for Meriones, saying, "And of course I will pay you extra for the use of your house. Agreed? Good, good!"

When Tereus left them for a few moments to go and relieve himself behind the wall, Meriones said to Hokar, "I always seem to be letting people talk me into things. I can never say no when I should. I admire your cousin. I doubt if he has that problem."

"He has others," Hokar replied. "Is there any more wine?"

Meriones gazed solemnly into the pitcher Tulipa had left on the table. "It's empty," he reported with regret. "But I think we have some milk flavored with kinnamon."

"Milk!" Tereus guffawed as he returned to them. "Men don't drink milk, even flavored with spices! Once this deal is concluded, my wasp-waisted friend, you'll be able to afford amphorae of wine, one for every day of the week." He clapped Meriones heartily on the back.

Much later, in the privacy of their bed, Meriones made the mistake of telling Tulipa about Tereus' offer.

"You certainly are going to help that big Thracian sell his slaves!" she insisted, sitting bolt upright in the bed. "If you don't, I'll go back and live with my mother!"

For a moment—only for a moment—Meriones was tempted.

After several false starts when his courage deserted him, Meriones spoke to Carambis, Master of Slaves, and a meeting was arranged. Carambis had been party to such deals before and knew exactly how much padding could be concealed within the price he would ultimately collect from the palace treasurer. A nice little profit would be made all around, if the slaves lived up to their description. The new Minos was known to have a taste for exotics.

Tereus' men were to bring the slaves from the ship to Meriones' house before dawn on the appointed day, and hold them there until Carambis arrived for the inspection. Tulipa disliked having so many strangers under her roof, but the promised commission placated her.

Meriones had less easily dismissed reservations.

When he heard the muffled knocking at the street door in the predawn darkness, he thought for the tenth time, I wish I had not agreed to this. Tulipa burrowed more deeply into the bed and pretended not to hear, so it was Meriones who padded downstairs on bare feet and opened the door.

Four husky seamen pushed past him into the small passage opening onto the megaron. The area was filled with the stench of their unwashed bodies. Meriones was aware of huddled forms being dragged and shoved with them, and the thump of a fist on someone's back. He lifted his bronze night-lantern in an effort to make out faces, but only succeeded in casting distorted menacing shadows on the walls, figures that gesticulated like dark frescoes come to life.

Tulipa joined them in the megaron. She shrank against the wall and rolled her eyes at Meriones.

"It's all right," he assured her with a total lack of conviction. "These men are from Tereus, with the, ah, guests, we talked about."

One of the seamen grinned, a flash of broken yellow teeth in a swarthy face. "Guests, is it?" he mimicked. "Look at this one." He thrust one of the bound, cloaked figures into the lantern light and uncovered its head. "You have strange tastes if you invite people like this to be your guests."

A thin old man stood blinking before them. He was taller than either Meriones or Tulipa, as tall as any of Tereus' men. His gaunt face looked like wrinkled parchment stretched tight over a skull. A fringe of white beard edged his jawbone, then slanted upward to meet the tangle of his uncut hair. His eyes were set deep in cavernous sockets. When they accepted the light and were able to focus he turned their full glare on Meriones. Strange eyes, colorless, burning with a life more intense than any other in the room.

Meriones involuntarily took a step backward.

The old man murmured something and struggled to free his hands. Instantly his captor pulled the cloak over his face and spun him around to face the wall. "Here, that's enough of that," he warned. To Meriones he said, "You don't want to let him look at you too long, or make those signs with his hands."

Tulipa asked in a harsh whisper, "Why not?"

"It's just better if you don't," the man replied. "I am Jaha Fe, third officer on the *Qatil*. My men and I will stay here and guard these guests of yours. Is there anything to eat while we wait?"

Without complaints for once, Tulipa hurried away to prepare food. When she was gone, Jaha Fe winked at Meriones. "Now these women, they could be guests in my pallet any time. Want to see?"

Meriones nodded, though his eyes kept straying to the cloaked figure of the old man. Jaha Fe unwrapped the nearest woman and pushed her toward the light.

She was beautiful, even by Cretan standards. Her skin was as luminous as seafoam.

"I think she's the daughter of the old man," Jaha Fe said. "Or granddaughter, could be."

Her frightened glance skittered about the room until she met Meriones' eyes. He offered a shy smile. She said something in reply.

Meriones struggled with the scattered fragments of childhood memories, put together a few words, discarded them and tried again. A sound emerged that might have been the sighing of wind in the cypresses of Knōsos, a confusion of sibilants and aspirants that startled him as much as anyone else. But the girl flashed a grin of acknowledgment and replied in the same tongue.

"What's she saying?" Jaha Fe demanded to know. "Get her to tell you her name."

Sweating, for the heat had returned to Crete, Meriones struggled with the forgotten language of his grandmother. His words came haltingly, but his understanding of the language improved as he listened to the girl. "She is called Ebisha," he translated at last, pleased with himself. "It means something like . . . Green Eyes."

"And she does have them!" Jaha Fe exclaimed. A roll of laughter relieved the tension in the room.

Meriones did not go to the palace that day. Even if he had not been instructed to wait for Carambis to come and inspect the slaves, he would have been unwilling to leave his wife alone in the house with the Thracian seamen.

He spent his time in conversation with Ebisha, who was pitifully eager to talk now that she had someone who could understand. She spoke with longing of her lost land, a land of many tribes, ruled by warrior chieftains who were very much under the influence of the priests. According to Ebisha, the inhabitants of the Islands of Mist were obsessed with the supernatural. They envisioned a community of spirits freely mingling with the living, interacting with them as if both seen and unseen were members of one ongoing community. This concept was inexplicable to the Cretan mind, whose vision of the netherworld was a simplistic paradise.

Ebisha told Meriones of priests who manipulated the power in the standing stones that dotted the islands, drawing down that power in some extraordinary fashion to make crops grow and heal the sick and control the weather to their advantage. This was not magic, she insisted, when Meriones tried to apply that term to the priests' actions.

"Not magic," Ebisha said. "Priests use . . . what is. Earth, fire, water, stone. They know how to use. They . . . shape. Make happen by shaping. My grandsire"—she nodded toward the old man—"he makes happen."

Meriones looked toward the tall, gaunt figure that was still standing immobile, facing the wall. He shuddered. It was as if something alien, cold beyond cold, had come into his warm little house.

Tereus arrived before Carambis. There was no mistaking the way Ebisha's face lit up when she saw him, though the other slaves turned their faces away from him. "He is like a chieftain of my own people," she told Meriones. "As soon as I saw him I wanted him to put his hands on me. I knew he wanted it too."

"Did he . . . on the ship?" Meriones asked, surprised to find the thought angered him.

"No. But he will, he will." She looked past Meriones to Tereus and smiled.

Tereus was paying no attention to her. Instead he had the old priest brought before him and asked Meriones his opinion of the man's saleability. The priest stood silently, glaring out of his skull-like face, eyes blazing with a light that might have been madness or even the manifestation of a god. Once, perhaps, they had been as green as Ebisha's, but all color had long since been burnt out of them by the heat of the spirit within.

"Tell him he will go to the king of Knōsos," Tereus instructed Meriones. "Tell him that if he pleases the king, he will have a good life and be treated well."

Meriones repeated the message. The old man's only response was a contemptuous flicker of his eyelids. "I don't know if he will cooperate," Meriones said doubtfully.

"He must," Tereus grated. "I didn't haul this ugly old weed all the way here just to have him turn obstinate when the time came to prove his value. He's worth more than the rest of them put together, and I mean to make a lot of money with him."

"Shall I ask him to do a feat of sorcery that would impress Carambis?"

"He had better; a damned impressive one."

"What can your grandfather do?" Meriones asked Ebisha.

The girl cast a wary glance at the old man. "He is a servant of the sun. He can ask the sun to hide his face and darken the land. He can summon the wind."

Meriones said he was vastly impressed, but he doubted those acts would be suitable for performing in a small house. Besides, thinking about them made him nervous. "Can he cause a lump of glass to change color?" he asked Ebisha. "Or charm a snake? Those are the sort of tricks The Minos enjoys."

Ebisha's eyes were cold. "You mock him."

"No! I did not mean—" His apologies were interrupted by Tulipa's entry with a tray of food. Meriones was too tense to eat, but Ebisha showed an appetite that outstripped even that of Tereus and his crewmen. She and the other captives—with the exception of the old man, who ate nothing—stuffed food into their mouths as if they had been starving for days.

"Didn't you ever feed them?" Meriones asked Tereus.

"I offered them what I feed my crew. They didn't seem to think it was food."

One of the crewmen laughed.

The old man behaved with a dignity that never deserted him. His hands had been untied to allow him to eat, though the guards watched him closely every moment. He lifted the bowl Tulipa offered him and carefully examined its contents without touching them. Then he placed his bunched fingers against the bottom of the bowl in its exact center and chanted something under his breath. The ritual completed, he put the bowl down, the food uneaten, and sat back, withdrawing into some private place beyond their reach.

Carambis arrived in a painted sedan chair befitting his station.

He was a bulky man, obese by Cretan standards, with a jowly face and a voice that gurgled upward from deep in his belly. The glitter of his eyes betokened a lustful nature, and Tereus shrewdly presented Ebisha to him first.

"Ah, this is a gem," Carambis agreed. "She looks like something from a lapidary's workbench. Silver skin, jade eyes."

Tereus said, "I understand the wife of The Minos collects exotic handmaidens? Think how she would prize this one!"

Carambis circled Ebisha, then signaled for her to be stripped. She stood with her head up, watching not Carambis, but Tereus. Aside from faded briar scratches on her legs and rope burns on her wrists, her body was unflawed.

But Tereus did not see her beauty. He saw instead a proud wooden galley, fresh from the boatbuilders, and felt the deck beneath his feet. One of those new ribbed coasters, with space for thirty oarmen and a square sail for long-distance voyaging.

The bargaining for Ebisha was so intense it made Meriones uncomfortable. He left the room, joining Tulipa in the courtyard. "What will our share be?" she asked him at once.

"I don't know. It depends on how much Tereus makes, I suppose."

"Didn't you agree to a sum in advance?"

"How could I?"

Tulipa's lips formed a thin line. "You are an idiot."

But Meriones was not thinking of profit. He was feeling guilty, as if he had somehow betrayed the girl with green eyes and the others. The blood in their veins flowed, to a small extent, in his. He heard its voice crying out.

In time the negotiations for Ebisha were concluded, and one by one the others were examined, argued over, sold. The day grew stiflingly hot. When Tereus noticed how heavily Carambis was sweating, he insisted they conclude their business in the courtyard and ordered Tulipa to bring them cool drinks.

"I'm not his slave," Tulipa muttered. But she brought the drinks.

By this time there was only one captive left to sell. Tereus had saved his prize until last.

"Look at this creature!" he enthused. "Is there not a divine madness in his eyes? This man is a high priest among his own kind, a sorcerer without equal."

Carambis looked skeptically at the old man. "What is this? Do you think we have any use at the House of the Double Axes for skinny old sticks like this one? It is you who are mad, Tereus."

"You don't understand, Carambis. I have with my own eyes seen the priests of the Islands of Mist exhibit abilities beyond the range of mortal men. The female pharoah in Egypt would pay any price I asked for this creature, but I . . . ah, have no authority to take the *Qatil* to Egypt."

Carambis smiled an oily smile. "I understand your situation perfectly. But I never buy fruit without taking a bite of it first." He folded his arms across his ample chest. "If he is as good as you say he is, have him do something right now. Prove your claim."

The scene that ensued was painful to all concerned. Tereus gave orders, Meriones translated them to the best of his ability, and the seamen struck the old priest when he stood immobile, indifferent, turned to stone.

"I think you're trying to sell me a deaf-mute by pretending he's something else," Carambis accused Tereus. "This deal begins to stink in my nostrils. Do not try to swindle me, or you will find no safe harbor in Knōsos."

"But this priest is worth a fortune!" Tereus protested, feeling the decks of his own ship fading away beneath his feet. "Meriones here says he can make the sun stop shining just by casting some sort of spell."

Carambis curled his lip. "If that's true he's too dangerous to have at the palace, and if you lie he's not worth a sack of meal. Either way, I want nothing to do with him. He's your problem; you brought him, you dispose of him. But not to the House of the Double Axes. As for the rest of this lot, I'll send men to collect them before dark and you'll be paid for them once they're in our custody."

Tereus simmered with anger. He bit back the words he wanted to say, however. It would be foolish to make an enemy of Carambis if he ever hoped to sell slaves to the palace again.

When the Master of Slaves had departed in his sedan chair, Tereus rounded on Meriones. "Why did you fail me? Why didn't you make that wretched old fool perform!"

Meriones held his hands palm upward in a placating gesture. "I did my best."

"Your best is no good, then. And I've lost a lot of money. That old man is of no value except as a diviner or sorcerer for a king's household. I might be able to sell him to one of the princes of Mallia—though I doubt it. I can't waste time trying, I'm due at Byblos."

"What will become of him, then?"

Tereus shrugged. "We'll throw him overboard," he said casually. "As soon as we're at sea again."

"No! You mustn't! I mean . . . I did my best . . . he is an intractable old man . . . but you mustn't kill him because I failed . . ." His words somersaulted over each other. Then he stopped. He drew in a sharp breath, his eyes lighting with inspiration. "There is a Cretan colony on the island of Thera."

"What of it? It's not even on my usual route," Tereus said. "My owner avoids them, they have a nasty reputation."

"But they're very wealthy," Meriones argued, "and their number includes scholars and wizards and all sorts of strange people who are reputed to do remarkable things. Why not take the old priest to Thera and try to sell him to them? It is the one place that might value him. I'm almost certain of it."

"What do you know about anything?" the Thracian sneered. "You're a bumbling fool, Meriones, and I'd be another to take any advice from you."

Meriones replied, miserably, "I never wanted to be involved in this anyway. I was only doing a favor for a friend."

"Then you can't expect much recompense in return," the Thracian said abruptly. "I'm willing to pay you for the food and the use of your house, but that's all."

Meriones felt his heart sink. What would Tulipa say?

Tereus gave Jaha Fe and his men orders to stay with the captives until they were collected, then bring the payment to the ship. This done, he stalked out of the house, dragging the old priest with him like a goat to the slaughter.

Meriones watched with a pained expression. At the last moment, Tereus relented enough to call back, "Oh, all right, if I get something for this old fool on the island of Thera, I'll see that you receive a share. But I don't expect to make a fortune for him in Atlantis."

# 9

Meriones went to the palace next

day without his usual jaunty gait. The white hound

ran out to meet him, recognized his depression, and

sat down in the road, whining.

"I'm sorry, Meriones,"

Hokar said when he had heard the entire story. "I thought it would be a good opportunity, I didn't know it would turn out badly."

"My wife isn't speaking to me. and that old man will be killed unless the Atlanteans buy him."

"They will," Hokar said confidently. "Those Cretans on Thera will buy anything that's truly unusual."

"They won't know he's unusual unless he shows them."

"Ah, they'll make him show them. They have ways, in Atlantis," Hokar added mysteriously.

"What ways?"

"I don't actually know. I've just heard whispers."

Meriones nodded. "We've all heard whispers. But no one knows very much about what they do over there."

"I for one don't want to know," Hokar told him. "I'm more interested in that girl you mentioned. Tell me about her."

Meriones tried to describe Ebisha, but his words could not bring her to life. "I'll play her for you instead," he told Hokar, taking up his lyre.

He stroked a delicate melody with a recurring throb like a beating heart. The music was as lovely as any he had ever played, with the exception of the songs he had composed for Tulipa in their first days together.

Craftsmen wandered in from other chambers and stood in rapt silence, listening.

When Meriones finished playing, Hokar said, "If that is Ebisha, I want to see her."

But no one saw Ebisha for a while. She had vanished into a perfumed opulence where even slaves lived lives of comparative luxury, and would not reappear until she had been refined and polished into a work of art worthy of the queen's service.

Knowing her destiny, Meriones did not worry about her. But sometimes at night as he lay sleepless, with Tulipa's rigid back like a wall turned to him, he thought of the old man. He did not know the old man's name, even. Ebisha had refused to tell it, saying, "Names of holy men belong to the tribe. Not for use by strangers."

An old man stolen from his home, his dignity assaulted, his scrawny body lashed by some slavemaster's whip . . .

Then Meriones remembered the priest's eyes, and he shivered and pulled the bedclothes over his head, though the night was hot.

Meanwhile word of his newly lyrical music reached the ears of Santhos, and he found himself reassigned to the royal apartments. He hated leaving Hokar. They promised to meet from time to time in the mazes of Labrys.

One scorching morning when the perfumed air lay heavy in the halls and even the liveliest courtiers were lethargic, Meriones was sent to the queen's megaron, the pillared "public room" in the center of her suite.

There he saw Ebisha again.

She knelt beside the queen, holding open an olivewood casket inlaid with ivory, from which the wife of The Minos was selecting jewelry. The queen pointed to a rope of pearls spaced with carnelian and lapis lazuli. The pearls were the perfect accompaniment to the bodice the wife of The Minos wore, an exquisite garment dyed in royal Tyrian purple. To obtain that dye a thousand tiny sea creatures had been crushed in their shells. The bodice might be worn only once; the queen rarely repeated her costumes.

But Meriones was not looking at the queen. He was staring in admiration at Ebisha, who was very changed.

The briar scratches and rope burns were healed. Her nails were smoothed, shaped, painted carmine. Her oiled hair was twisted and curled into a fanciful sculpture, revealing the elegance of her skull shape. She was dressed in the height of Cretan fashion. An ankle-length skirt of pleated tiers in contrasting colors fell from a tight belt, while her upper body was naked except for a short-sleeved, tight-fitting bodice that encircled her bare breasts like a frame.

Feeling Meriones' eyes on her she turned toward him, recognized him, smiled.

The queen signaled to Meriones to play. When he responded with his latest composition she clapped her hands with pleasure. "What a lovely song! I have not heard it before, it is like water tinkling." She rippled her fingers descriptively through the air. "Is it your own creation?" she asked Meriones.

"Yes, lady. I call it 'Green-Eyed Girl.'" Glancing at Ebisha, Meriones saw her smile again, pleased.

The queen followed his glance. "Well done," she commented. "Green is my favorite color, as that scoundrel Carambis knows. He found this green-eyed girl for me and paid a pretty price, I suspect.

But we are well pleased with her. Play us some more of your music now."

During the long, hot day, Meriones found several opportunities for snatches of conversation with Ebisha. He was surprised to discover she had already acquired a rudimentary understanding of the New Tongue. She insisted on using it with him, trying to improve herself. It was hard not to laugh at her grammar, but her eagerness impressed him.

Once she said, "I hear from my grandsire."

Meriones stiffened. "How?"

"He has ways. He gets word to me."

"Where is he?"

"On an island called Thera."

Meriones was relieved. "That's good, he's safe, then."

The girl frowned. "Not safe. They hurt him when he does not give them his gift. But he cannot give it to them. It is his, you see? It is not theirs. His, for his people."

Meriones did not see. But he hated the thought of men on Thera abusing the old man. "What about you?" he asked Ebisha the next time they could talk together. "Are you happy here?"

"Happy?" She puzzled over the word. "I am not free. So I am not happy. But I am not cold, or wet, or hungry. So is good. Some good. Is wonderful place, here. Is magic here."

"Magic?" Meriones thought she misunderstood the meaning of the word.

"Oh yes. The queen walks through that doorway to her water closet, she calls it. She sits on stone there. Her droppings are carried away by water poured through drains. Is magic, yes?" Ebisha smiled her radiant smile at Meriones.

"Yes," he echoed, chuckling.

When he was with Ebisha, Meriones' normally buoyant spirits returned.

Although he missed Hokar and the goldsmiths' chambers, he could not deny that he was infinitely more comfortable in the royal apartments. The queen's megaron was exquisitely furnished with gilded benches, tiled floors, mosaics on every wall. The ceiling was decorated with spirals of plaster as perfectly formed as seashells. Ebisha commented many times on their beauty.

By prior arrangement, Meriones and Hokar met in the palace gardens one twilit evening as both were on their way home. The goldsmith related what little gossip he knew; Meriones told him of life in the queen's megaron, and of Ebisha.

"I'd still like to see her," Hokar confided. "That music you used to describe her has haunted me ever since."

His opportunity came soon enough. An ambassador presented the queen with a delicate gold pectoral, a gift from one royal family to another. Somehow it was dropped and the shape of the soft gold was distorted on the hard floor. The queen ordered a goldsmith sent quickly to her apartments, to repair the pectoral before the ambassador should see it.

The task fell to Hokar. He entered the megaron in the company of the Master of Craftsmen, rehearsing the words of thanks he would say to the queen if the opportunity arose.

Then he saw Ebisha, and all words went out of his head.

There was discussion about the pectoral. ". . . A tap with the hammer, here, and perhaps the slightest twist just there . . ." and Hokar nodded his head and set his hands to their task, but they worked without a conscious thought to guide them. Hokar's true attention was concentrated on the girl.

When the pectoral was repaired to the queen's satisfaction, he forgot to thank her humbly for the honor. He left the megaron with his eyes filled with Ebisha.

Hokar sought out Meriones every chance he got, always to talk about Ebisha. "How is she? Did she notice me, do you think? What is she like?"

Meriones ransacked his memory for tidbits about the girl. When he mentioned her admiration for the plaster spirals on the ceiling of the megaron, Hokar was excited. "I shall make a piece of jewelry for her! And you will give it to her, Meriones. And tell her it comes from me."

Another favor. Meriones wriggled uncomfortably. "It isn't really appropriate, Hokar. To give gifts to slaves, I mean. Nor for me to be the carrier either. You see—"

"Nonsense, it's just a small token, who could object? In a way you're responsible for her being here, Meriones. You should want her to be happy. And a gift will make her happy. How can you refuse?"

How indeed? Meriones asked himself gloomily as he walked home later, through a stifling heat so intense it threatened to press the air from his lungs.

It was worse than the heat wave last year. It was worse than any weather he could ever remember.

When he reached his house he entered eagerly, longing for its cool darkness. But the air inside was stuffy and still, hardly less unpleasant than outside. Passing through to the courtyard, he found Tulipa lying on a pallet under the olive tree with a cloth dipped in cool water pressed to her forehead.

"The heat gives me a headache," she greeted him. "Be quiet."

"I wasn't going to say anything. Is there something I can do for you?"

"Make the heat stop," she replied petulantly.

But no one could make the heat stop. Day by day it mounted, fraying nerves, spoiling food. Tulipa's headache had become so constant he no longer questioned its reality. It was not a device she used to make him feel guilty. She was in real pain. Dark circles appeared under her eyes and she could not eat. She did not even have the energy to scold him.

He grew increasingly worried about her. She was losing all her pretty roundness; her bones showed through the skin of her face, strangely reminding Meriones of the skull-like visage of the old priest from the Islands of Mist.

The more ill Tulipa became, the more Meriones recalled how dear she had been to him in their early days together, when he had been as enchanted by her as Hokar was by Ebisha.

He went to every physician in Knōsos, and every herbalist, seeking help for his wife. But nothing stopped her headaches.

When he played his lyre in the queen's megaron he was distracted and it showed in his performance.

"What is wrong with you?" Ebisha whispered to him. "The queen frowns when you play. Does not sound the same now."

"My wife is sick and I'm worried about her."

"She has a pain?"

"In her head."

"Ah." Ebisha nodded. "My grandsire could heal."

"Much good that does me!" Meriones burst out before he could stop himself. The heat was getting to everyone.

Next day, Hokar met him at the Sun Gate and pressed an object wrapped in linen into his hands. "Give this to Ebisha, and tell her it's from me."

He had to wait for his chance. At last came a time when the megaron was briefly all but deserted, its usual throng of chattering, chirping courtiers gone to bathe in the pools or lie panting on their beds. Ebisha remained, and Meriones beckoned her to join him behind one of the pillars. "I have a gift for you from Hokar the goldsmith."

"Who?" But she took the parcel and unwrapped it.

Then she gasped. "Look!" She held up a necklace as fine as spiderweb, made of tiny gold links. Spaced along the chain at regular intervals were six miniature gold nautilus shells, repeating the spiral design in the ceiling of the queen's megaron.

The gold flashed in Ebisha's fingers. "It is the metal of the sun!" she cried.

"This is too elaborate and costly for a slave," Meriones tried to tell her. "You won't be allowed to keep it. Give it back and I'll return it to Hokar and explain."

Ebisha's eyes brimmed with tears. "I cannot keep?" But she handed the necklace back to Meriones without protest.

Tulipa would have held on to it and argued vehemently, he thought. Aloud he said, "It would make trouble. Hokar should have known this." He turned away, unable to bear the look of disappointment on her face.

When he could, he returned the necklace to Hokar in the goldsmiths' chamber. Hokar looked as disappointed as Ebisha had been. "But it's not anything lavish," he protested, "just a trial piece I made that didn't work out. I thought no one would mind."

Meriones turned the glittering trinket over in his fingers, studying it. "Are you saying it's not perfect?"

"Yes."

"Then you lie," Meriones replied softly. "It's the best thing I've ever seen you do. This is no trial piece at all, and if the queen had caught Ebisha wearing it I don't know what would have happened. The queen herself has nothing finer. More elaborate, but not finer."

Hokar was crestfallen. "But I want her to have something to

remind her of me. I wish I were a painter. I'd reproduce her face and form on every wall in Labrys."

Meriones was beginning to lose patience with his friend. "If you care for this girl you have to be quiet about it, Hokar. The courtiers and servants of the palace aren't encouraged to . . . well, you know . . ."

"I know. And I don't need any encouragement. Just one look from those green eyes would do it. Meriones, you have to arrange for me to see her again."

"Aren't you listening? She's a slave. We are not supposed to have anything to do with slaves."

"Then I'll buy her!"

"How could you? Carambis paid a high price for her, more than you make in a season, I'd guess."

"I'll think of something," Hokar said. His mouth became a grim, determined line.

When he left the palace that evening, Meriones did not stride out with his usual arched-back, arm-swinging ebullience. He trudged with his head down, his thoughts alternating between Tulipa at home and Hokar and Ebisha in the palace. A presentiment lay like a cloud on his spirit.

He walked through heat so thick as to be palpable, even though the sun was setting. The omnipresent sea, nibbling at the northern coastline, had lost its luster and turned dull and sullen.

The music of Meriones had also lost its brightness. Santhos spoke sharply to him the next day. "What's wrong with you? Your music sounds more like a dirge, and that is not the sort of music we like in the palace. The queen is displeased."

"I have worries."

"Everyone has worries! But our personal concerns must not dim the color of the royal apartments. Now Orene is playing your songs, and he sounds better than you do. Correct yourself or you will be playing for the cooks in the kitchens!"

Meriones struggled to throw off his melancholy. He could not bear to think of reporting another demotion to Tulipa.

Day after day she lay in the sleeping chamber, or under the olive tree. The olive tree was better, she said, because it was not quite as hot in the courtyard as it was in the upper rooms of the house. But there was no escaping the heat anywhere.

She had grown very thin. On her behalf Meriones offered gifts of food and wine and faience beads at the shrine of every god who might have any connection with good health and healing. But the sacrifices were wasted. Almost every day, Tulipa suffered a savage headache.

"Sometimes I wish you would plunge a knife into my skull and let my brains spill out," she told Meriones. "That would ease the pressure."

Her pain tortured him. His early tenderness came flooding back and he sat on the edge of the bed, stroking her hand, fighting back tears.

He spoke privately to Ebisha in the queen's megaron. "You said your grandsire could heal?"

"He can."

"You said you have ways of getting word to him?"

She gave Meriones a guarded look. "Why?"

"I need . . . I mean, my wife needs, really . . . she is very ill, you see, and nothing anyone does seems to help. I have grown desperate, Ebisha. I thought perhaps . . . your grandsire . . ." He ran out of words. His dark eyes pleaded.

"Meriones, I—" Ebisha clamped her mouth shut suddenly. Looking up, Meriones saw the queen watching them.

"We'll talk later," he said under his breath.

But that same day Santhos came to escort Meriones to the palace kitchens.

"This is your last chance," Santhos said. "Do well here, and you will stay in the House of the Double Axes. Fail here, and you will go."

But how can I play when my heart is a lump of lead in my breast? Meriones wanted to ask.

He sat on a bench; he strummed his lyre. No one listened. The kitchens bustled like a hive of bees from before dawn until long after dark. Everyone was hot, bothered, in a hurry. They brushed past Meriones, cursed at him if he was in the way, shouted at one another over the constant clatter of cooking utensils.

Worst of all, he was not allowed to leave until all work was done in the kitchens for the day, which meant very late at night. He had to make his way home in the dark when most of Knōsos was long since asleep. He could not meet Hokar anymore; the goldsmith was also snoring in his bed by the time Meriones made his weary way through the Sun Gate and headed for home.

He barely had time to prepare a sketchy meal which Tulipa usually could not eat, fall on his bed for a troubled, brief sleep, and arise still in the dark to go to the well for the day's water. Then he must be on his way back to the palace, leaving his suffering wife behind him physically but carrying her every step of the way on his conscience.

He arranged with Phrixus and Dendria to look in on her and do what they could for her, but it was not enough. Nothing was enough.

Meriones began to fear his wife might die.

A different man might, perhaps, have welcomed freedom from a scold. But Meriones had a gentle heart. Long ago, he had given that heart to Tulipa. It would go into the grave with her. A girl like Ebisha might stir lust in him, or even tenderness, but he had given his wife a part of himself he could not take back, and thus would never have to give again to any woman.

The music would die with Tulipa, Meriones thought.

He was desperate to find help for her. When he could slip away from the kitchens he haunted the passageways leading to the royal apartments, hoping to see Ebisha. At last his patience was re-warded. He managed to signal her with his eyes as she walked past at the end of a procession of slaves, carrying bales of fabric to the queen's seamstresses.

From the citadels of Mycenae and Tiryns a huge tribute was sent each year to The Minos of Knōsos—cattle and oil and wine and every manner of merchandise. Goods were stored in the vast warehouses beneath the palace, but only briefly, for most were used as soon as they arrived. The royal family indulged in an orgy of consumption meant to impress the Mediterranean world with the unrivaled wealth and power of Crete.

Within the last few days a shipload of rare and costly fabrics had arrived in the harbor. The goods were immediately transported to Labrys, where the royal family would make their selections from the best of the best. When their choices were made, complete new wardrobes would be sewn not only for The Minos and his family, but also for every member of their court.

The minions of The Minos would bloom like fresh flowers.

The Minos had recently decreed that each season's clothing was to be burned at the end of the season, a ceremonial destruction of the old and celebration of the new. This unprecedentedly lavish gesture could not fail to impress the other sea kings.

Ebisha could barely see over the folds of shimmering cloth she carried, but she nodded to Meriones as best she could. When the procession of slaves passed an open doorway she slipped inside and Meriones quickly joined her.

They found themselves in one of the many bathing chambers scattered throughout the palace. Its walls were lined with alabaster decorated with frescoes, and the terra cotta bathing tub stood in a recess ornamented by columns. A brazier burned continually, casting flickering shadows.

As she talked with him, Ebisha rested her burden on a marble shelf meant to hold sponges and bath oils. Meriones was saying, "My wife is very ill and no one can heal her."

"I am no healer."

"But your grandsire is a magician. Tereus said so. And you are in touch with him. Is there some sort of magic he might do, perhaps? I could find a way to send payment to him, I would gladly . . ."

Her eyes filled with pity. "Meriones, I tried to explain before. I can't talk to him, not the way you think. We exchange our . . ."—she struggled with words—"our feelings. I know his emotions. No more than that."

"You couldn't ask him to help Tulipa?"

"No. I am sorry. Nor do I think he would," Ebisha added honestly. "He is very angry. They treat him badly in this place where he is; they hurt him. He is . . ."—she sought for the right word again—"he is *simmering* with anger. He would not want to help. He wants to strike out." Her eyes were very large. "His feelings frighten me, Meriones."

"I'm sorry about all this, Ebisha."

"Is not your fault."

"I was involved."

"If not you, Tereus would have used another person. You at least were kind to us. You tried to help, you argued for my grandsire's life.

"Perhaps it would have been better if he died," she added in a low voice.

Meriones put a hand on her arm, trying to comfort her in spite of his own pain. Then he saw the slender gold arm ring she wore, half concealed by the sleeve of her tight-fitting bodice.

The arm ring was gold.

"Where did you get that?"

Ebisha's lashes lowered over her green eyes. "A gift from a friend."

"Hokar the goldsmith? You've been seeing him?"

"We meet sometimes," she admitted.

"And you're taking presents from him? Don't you know how dangerous it is?"

"He wants me to have them."

"But what about Tereus?"

"I will not see Tereus again," Ebisha said with female practicality. "I know that. Hokar I see every day. He is good to me. He says he will buy me out of the palace and give me my freedom."

Hokar was obviously telling the girl a pleasant little lie. "He can't buy you," Meriones said. He did not want her to be deceived, even by his friend. "Hokar is well rewarded for his work, but a master craftsman does not make enough to buy a favorite of the queen."

Ebisha lifted her head. In the flickering light her green eyes blazed. "I was born free," she said.

"I know, but look at you now. You have beautiful clothes and all you can eat. And I know the queen doesn't beat you. What more could you want? You are fortunate, really."

When she spoke, Ebisha's voice rang in the alabaster chamber in a way that curiously reminded Meriones of his long-dead grandmother's voice. "I come from a race of free people," she said. "I was born free, and even if Hokar has to steal to get me out of here, I shall die free!"

Her words made a chill run up Meriones' spine.

# 10

*Several days passed, days of unre-*

*lenting heat. The House of the Double Axes lay*

*languid beneath a blazing white sun. People longed*

*in vain for the first cool breeze off the sea that would*

*hint at the Season of the Dying God.*

Tulipa was dying. But she did not die. It was as if she held death at arms' length, somehow, which made it even more painful for Meriones. It was agonizing to leave her in the mornings, yet equally painful to return at night, not knowing what he might find.

When he found her alive, he knew the agony would continue.

"There is a growth in her head," a physician finally told him. "It is the only explanation."

"Can't you do something?"

"The Egyptians have a technique for opening the skull and operating on the brain, but the only Egyptian physician on Crete is in the court of The Minos. He would not treat your wife."

Meriones knew that already. Early in Tulipa's illness he had tried to gain access to The Minos' private physician and been forcefully turned away.

I am no one. Just a minor musician. As Tulipa said, I am nobody.

Pain lapped in him like a rising tide.

Santhos caught him by the arm in a passageway of the palace. "There you are! I've been looking everywhere for you. Why aren't you in the kitchens, where you belong?"

"They never miss me," Meriones said truthfully.

"That's immaterial. You are supposed to be there. If you disobey, I shall be blamed. And I promise you I will pass on to you any punishment I receive!"

Santhos had caught him just as Meriones was about to attempt another visit to the royal apartments. In desperation, he was going to try to find and appeal to the royal physician himself. But Santhos took hold of his arm in a painful grip and dragged him back to the kitchens, where he proceeded to place a scullery boy on guard over Meriones with orders to report to Santhos immediately if the musician left his post even for a moment.

When the final meal of the day was cooked and Meriones was at last allowed to leave, he stepped from the perpetually lit halls of the palace into a Stygian darkness. The night was starless and oppressive. Leaving by the Sun Gate, he had to make his way down the stair very carefully to avoid losing his balance and falling. It would have been easy in the dark to step by mistake into one of the gutters that ran down beside the stair, part of the elaborate system of drains and baffles that slowed the flow of rain runoff and prevented the flooding of palace floors on the lower levels.

But there had been no rain in a long time. Meriones found himself longing for a storm to lighten the air.

When he reached Knōsos, and his own street, a dark shape rose before him. By the light of a lantern burning in a nearby window, Meriones recognized Hokar. The goldsmith's face was haggard and his eyes were sunk in dark hollows.

But it was not the heat that was affecting him.

"I'm in terrible trouble, Meriones. I need your help as my friend," Hokar said urgently, whispering as if afraid they would be overheard.

"You'd better come into my house and tell me about it." The musician longed to take off his sweaty clothing and sponge himself from the water barrel in the courtyard, but that would have to wait. Leaving Hokar in the megaron, he took time only to tiptoe upstairs and check on Tulipa.

She was awake. "I think I feel a little better, Meriones," she said to his vast relief. "Just a little. The headache is not as bad as it has been."

His heart pounded with hope. "Are you sure? Are you getting well?"

"I don't know about that, but I do feel somewhat stronger. Perhaps I could eat a little broth . . . ?"

Meriones plunged back down the stairs. Ignoring his guest, he busied himself with cooking pots until he had put together a concoction of leftovers that would, he prayed, do his wife some good. He carried a bowl up to her and watched with held breath while she sipped it. When she yawned and fell asleep again he returned to his guest.

Hokar was waiting patiently. "I have nothing else to do," he said.

"What's this trouble you're in?"

Hokar was reluctant to say outright. He came at the subject with uncharacteristic obliqueness. "There was a wrestling exhibition in the Great Central Court today, you know. Everyone who could went to see it."

"I know. The cooks made up countless platters of food to pass among the spectators. Fish, mostly. My clothes still reek of it. But what has the wrestling to do with your trouble?"

"The craftsmen were given permission to attend, and everyone in our chambers went. Except me. I stayed behind, crouched down behind my workbench so no one would notice."

Meriones felt a cold hand squeeze his heart. "Why?"

Hokar would not meet his eyes. "Ebisha." His shoulders slumped. Then he burst out, "I can think of nothing else, Meriones! She fills my mind the way my work used to!

"She said she would be my woman if she was free, but I know it would be very costly to buy her from the palace. So I stole what should be enough gold from our supplies. I buried it in the terraced gardens. They were deserted for once; everyone was at the wrestling. I did not dare keep it on me in case the loss was discovered and we were searched. Then I joined the others at the Great Central Court. No one noticed I had not been there all along.

"The theft was discovered almost as soon as we returned to our chambers. They thought someone might have come in from outside and taken the gold, but they couldn't be sure. They searched us, and I suspect they sent men to our homes to search us again when we arrived at the end of the day.

"That's why I didn't go home tonight. I couldn't face another search. My hands have begun shaking."

"I'm not surprised! I don't know how you managed to do it in the first place."

"It wasn't that difficult. The gold wasn't locked away."

I suppose not, Meriones thought. Theft had never been a problem in the palace. It was well known that anyone caught stealing simply vanished, and there were whispered rumors of some horrible fate that awaited them deep in the bowels of Labrys, lost forever amid its labyrinthine twistings and turnings. The fear of the unknown kept most people at the palace honest.

Unfortunately, the Thracian's desire for a woman had outweighed his fear—for a while. The fear appeared to be catching up with him now. He had gone very white around the eyes and his hands were, indeed, shaking.

"I don't know how I can help you," Meriones told the unfortunate man.

"Would you if you could?"

Without thinking, the musician nodded assent.

"You can," Hokar said eagerly, "because no one would have any reason to suspect you, you haven't been near our chambers for a while. I'll tell you just where I hid the gold. You watch for your chance and retrieve it for me and hide it in a safer place. The gardens were just a temporary solution. The gardeners might dig there any time and find it."

"But you can't take raw gold to Carambis and offer to buy Ebisha with it! Everyone will know exactly how you came by it!"

"I'm not going to approach Carambis at all. I've thought it out. We'll take the gold to Tereus the next time he puts in at Knōsos. I'll allow him a large cut of it, and he will use the rest to buy Ebisha himself. Once she's out of Labrys she and I will leave Crete on board the *Qatil* and make a new home for ourselves far away somewhere. An artisan can always find work."

"This is madness, Hokar," Meriones said flatly. "You have no right to ask me to get involved."

"I thought you were my friend," the other chided him. "In Thrace, friendship is sacred to the death. Is it not that way on Crete? Is it not that way with you?" Hokar knew when a metal lacked the tensile strength to hold firm under the hammer. Meriones would give in if pressed hard enough. "Think what I will lose if I am caught, Meriones! Would you have my death on your conscience?"

Meriones squirmed. "Don't put it that way."

"Then say you'll help me."

Meriones had a vision of the great bull being led in for sacrifice, its piebald hide washed and gleaming, flowers wreathing its neck. He remembered the way the bull had lifted its head and looked with sad eyes at the inevitability of the ax.

"I'll help you," he said at last. "But you'd better go home now. It's better if we're not seen as being too friendly from now on."

"I'm afraid to go home. If any of The Minos' men are there I might give myself away, coming in so late. So nervous."

"Drink enough of my wine to slur your speech and relax you," Meriones instructed, thinking fast. "If there are guards tell them you've been at a party. Laugh a lot. Seem carefree. You can do it, if you drink enough beforehand."

Hokar's beard split in a grin. "I knew I could rely on you, Meriones. The gods put you in my path."

"I wish the gods would put someone in my path to help me,"

Meriones muttered to himself. Hokar, intent on his own problems, paid no attention.

The musician fed the goldsmith wine until the man's speech slurred convincingly, then sent him on his way. "Now remember to act much drunker than you are," he instructed. "And cheerful. Unworried. That's the important part. You must act as if you have nothing at all to feel guilty about. You've just been having a wonderful time at a party."

He pushed Hokar out the door and watched, worrying, as his friend weaved his way up the narrow street and out of sight. Hokar was clutching the last jug of Meriones' wine in his fist.

The musician's inspiration saved the goldsmith. There were guards from the palace waiting at his house to search him again. When he arrived, however, he was so drunk and seemed so jovial they could not believe he was guilty of anything more than overindulgence. He even insisted they share his jug of wine with him.

"We've had a long wait for nothing," one of the men said. "It's the least we deserve." They leaned against Hokar's wall and drank the last of the wine before returning to Labrys.

Meanwhile Tulipa lay on her bed and dreamed. The pain's easing had left her prey to a curious hallucination. She thought it was the season of the Festival of the Snake, the time sacred to females.

The wombs of donkeys would be swelling with foals. New kids would soon be suckling the milk goats. It was the season, in her fevered mind, of fertility. Pilgrimages would be made to the inland mountains to conduct the rites sacred to the Good Goddess. Men were excluded as long lines of women snaked up the slopes, carrying torches and singing.

Tulipa imagined herself among them, begging the boon of motherhood. She thought she felt a cosmic response shudder through her barren belly.

In the darkness of predawn she became aware of Meriones lying beside her. "We're going to have a child," she murmured.

He was instantly awake. "What did you say?"

But she had sunk back into her dreams. When he tried to question her she muttered crossly, not remembering.

Could it be possible? Meriones felt a jolt of joy. A child!

Suddenly the future became very precious to him.

He bitterly regretted promising to help Hokar. What if they were caught?

He went to Phrixus' house to ask Dendria to stay with Tulipa for the day. "She might be with child," he explained. "I don't want her to be alone."

Dendria raised her plucked eyebrows. "Tulipa, with child? I shouldn't think so."

"I'm not certain. But she might be. And I'm very worried about her."

"If you're that worried you should stay with her yourself," retorted Dendria, who had better things to do.

But Meriones dared not stay home. He did not fear the wrath of Santhos as much as he feared doing something unusual that might cause suspicion.

To his relief, Dendria reluctantly agreed to keep an eye on Tulipa. Only a little late, Meriones hurried off toward the palace, forcing himself to his usual jaunty gait, even whistling a little, as if he had not a care in the world.

He had not gone very far before he encountered the white hound. The dog stood with its head cocked on one side, not completely fooled.

"Come on," Meriones coaxed. "Walk with me." He snapped his fingers and made cajoling noises.

The dog cocked its head on the other side, but then it came. The two walked on together. The dog was panting already, its red tongue lolling.

As they climbed up from the city toward the palace, Meriones glanced back as he often did to enjoy the view. Almost the entire Cretan fleet, largest in the Mediterranean, was in. The ships' captains were waiting for a freshening wind to blow along the northern coast.

But the air was leaden and still. There was a sullen haze to the north. The fleet which was Crete's pride and power would stay where it was until Poseidon showed a more amiable face.

Somewhere on the sea Tereus is heading for Crete, Meriones thought to himself. I'll need to retrieve the gold and have it ready for him when he arrives.

"My cousin's current trading voyage is just to the major ports of call in the Mediterranean and Aegean," Hokar had said. "He will return to Knōsos before long."

So they did not have much time.

"This is going to be dangerous," Meriones said under his breath to the dog.

The hound wagged his tail. With a last glance at the ships and the sea, Meriones set off again, springing upward from the soles of his feet as if he had not a care in the world.

No one could see the thoughts roiling in his head.

According to Hokar, the gold had been hastily buried in a shallow hole beneath a red-flowering bush that smelled of honey. The bush was to the left of the steps leading down to the largest of the many pools in the terraced gardens.

The gardens were popular with courtiers and visitors to the palace alike. As long as daylight lasted, there were usually a number of people wandering through them.

But as Hokar had pointed out, "Now that you are assigned to the cooks you arrive very early and leave very late. If you know a way to reach the kitchens by going through the gardens, you could actually be there when it's dark and no one else is around. I could never do that. We arrive later and leave earlier. And besides, they will be watching us. No one will be watching you. Get the gold for me, Meriones, and hide it in a safer place until Tereus gets here."

Meriones did indeed know how to reach the kitchens by way of the terraced gardens, but it was a highly circuitous route. One he might have to explain if he was questioned.

As he walked along, he had a flash of inspiration.

"I'll say I'm picking flowers to garnish the royal platters!" he told the dog.

By the time he reached the palace a sultry heat was already building up. With a casual salute to the guard, and a farewell pat to the white hound, Meriones entered the Sun Gate. But he did not follow his usual route. Instead he trotted briskly down endless passageways, up stairs, around corners, across courtyards, until at last he reached the garden.

To his disappointment, other people were already there. The time he had spent arranging for Dendria to stay with Tulipa had cost him; the sun had risen before he ever left Knōsos. He had no chance of getting the gold this morning. But he plucked flowers just the same and took them to the cooks, to establish his story.

The cooks were delighted. Garnishing food with flowers at once became the fashion in the House of the Double Axes.

That night Meriones left by the same route, but once again he found people still loitering in the gardens, trying to find a breath of air in the darkness.

To his dismay, when he reached home Tulipa was alone. "I sent Dendria away," she said in a petulant tone. "Her voice cuts into my head like a knife into a melon. I wish we could go away, Meriones. Really go away, I mean. To someplace cool. To the mountains . . ." She sighed.

"The heat will break soon, everyone says so. It can't go on much longer like this. The Minos has offered sacrifices to be made to Poseidon in exchange for cool winds from the sea."

"I think the gods are angry with us, Meriones," Tulipa replied. "It will take more than sacrifices to placate them. Look at me. You must have done something to make the gods angry and I am being punished." Weak tears of self-pity crept down Tulipa's sunken cheeks.

Meriones was frantic. He had done everything he could think of to help his wife; he was doing all he could to help his friend; neither situation was getting better. He felt caught, trapped, helpless.

He was exhausted, but he could not sleep. At last he left his wife alone in their sweat-soaked bed and went down to lie on the cool paving stones of the courtyard for a few hours, until the light of the false dawn summoned him back to the palace.

The stones were hard and unyielding, but they had already given up their heat. They soaked up his body heat instead, giving him a measure of relief.

Lying pressed against the ground in his courtyard. Meriones was one of the first to feel the rumbling deep in the earth that signaled the awakening of the gods.

11

*En route to Knōsos again in hopes*

*of exchanging a cargo of oil and spices for Cretan*

*pottery, Tereus was still dreaming of his own ship.*

*He had come to hate every plank of the* Qatil

*because it belonged to someone else.*

He considered his prospects. The men in the Cretan colony that called itself Atlantis had been willing to buy the old priest, so Tereus had left the man on the island of Thera with them. But they had not paid much for him. They said he was an unknown quantity whose worth would have to be proved.

By now, Tereus told himself, they should have found ways to force that old savage to reveal his talents.

And if he's as good as I think he is, they might now be willing to buy more like him. We could discuss their commissioning me to go back to the Islands of Mist and capture other sorcerers. It could be enormously profitable.

Yes indeed.

If the old man has proved himself.

Tereus made a decision.

"We're going to call in to Thera again before we go to Crete," he informed his helmsman. "I have some enquiries to make."

The helmsman did not like the sulfurous look of the sky toward Thera, but he knew better than to argue with Tereus. He changed course at once.

At first the blue sea hissed as always, running past the prow. Then it grew sluggish, almost oily. They were making slow headway in spite of their best efforts. But even when the air became gritty and his crew started coughing, Tereus insisted they hold to their course. If a man protested, he felt the lash of Jaha Fe's whip across his shoulders.

They began meeting other vessels coming out from Thera. Luxurious pleasure galleys as well as ordinary fishing boats, everyone of them packed with white-faced, staring people whose household goods were piled around them. It appeared to be a migration, as if the population of Thera had in some common madness decided to take to the sea.

Leaning on the rail of the *Qatil,* Tereus stared down at them. No one waved to him. No one called a greeting. Some of the women, he observed, were crying.

A larger vessel, a trader like the *Qatil,* approached. Its captain was an old acquaintance with whom Tereus had shared wenches and wine in many ports. He hailed the other ship and it drew alongside.

The *Qatil* put down a boat so Tereus could go over to the other ship.

Its captain wasted no time with pleasantries. "Everyone who can lay hands on a boat is leaving Thera," he told Tereus. "They would rather be at sea than wait on the island to face the wrath of the god."

"What god?"

"Ennosigaion. Earth-Shaker! For days he has been growling underground, and Zeus supports him with a rain of ashes from the sky. The air stinks like rotten eggs. Thera is unsafe, Tereus. I implore you, turn your ship about and come away with us before it gets any worse."

Tereus looked toward the island barely visible through the murky air. Its solitary peak thrust upward from the sea like a warning finger. For the first time he recognized a certain malevolence to the shape. Near the southern tip of Thera was the commercial town of Akrotiri, mercantile hub for the sprawling Atlantean colony that had expanded up the slopes to command sweeping views toward their native Crete.

Akrotiri; abandoned. Atlantis . . . a cold worm stirred in Tereus' belly.

"The gods cannot threaten me," he said to the other captain with too hearty a laugh. But as soon as he was on board the *Qatil* again Tereus gave the order to put about and make for Crete. The helmsman responded gladly.

There was not a breath of wind to stir the sail. Oars were their only power now. The sweating oarsmen labored, grunting, impelled by a nameless fear. Jaha Fe no longer needed to use the lash on them. In the sullen, lowering light, they were doing their best to leave Thera behind them.

On Crete, Meriones was also doing his best that morning. After several frustrating days when he had found someone in the gardens every time he passed through, today he found the gardens deserted. People were being kept under roofs by the persistent grit that fell like rain from the sky.

Meriones hurried to the bush Hokar had described. Crouching down, he dug with feverish fingers into the soft earth at the bush's roots. It was volcanic soil, friable and loose, and offered little resistance. He scrabbled hurriedly. In a moment more he had the package in his hands.

He glanced nervously around to see if anyone was watching. The gardens were still deserted.

Meriones stood up. The package was both bulky and heavy. But when he sucked in his belly as hard as he could, he was just able to thrust it down between his belt and his flesh, where it would be somewhat hidden by his embroidered apron.

If anyone looked closely his shape would have seemed very suspicious. But no one was paying any attention to Meriones that morning.

For several days the people of Crete had been living in a state of accelerating apprehension. Poseidon was flexing his muscles and rippling the earth from one end of the island to the other. Meriones had felt the first tremors as he tried to sleep in his courtyard. Since then, subterranean movement had become almost constant. From long experience, Cretans knew how to build to withstand the milder attacks of the Shaker's temper, but the continual rumblings were wearing everyone's nerves. Dogs howled. Goats went dry. Children awakened crying.

Tulipa's headache had returned, increasing to alarming proportions.

Householders along the northern coast were complaining of a greasy ash that settled on everything, ruining food and fabric. Men began wandering down to the harbor to talk to experienced seamen, then stand and stare at the ugly light in the north. On their way home they visited the various sacred shrines and left lavish offerings to Poseidon Earth-Shaker.

People invented excuses to visit the inland mountains, or relatives in the south. Then they gave up making excuses and began fleeing openly, running from the unnatural evil that hovered on the northern horizon.

First singly, then in families, they had descended on the palace to demand protection from their god-king. But as they pressed in upon him, The Minos had panicked. He gave orders that the guards were to admit no more outsiders.

The court concluded that expendables such as craftsmen and entertainers would be next. It looked as if only the royal family and the most influential officials would be granted sanctuary within Labrys.

Meriones had come this morning, against his better judgment, to make one final attempt to retrieve the gold for Hokar before access to the palace was denied him. He would have preferred to stay with

Tulipa. No one, he felt sure, would have noticed or cared. People were too preoccupied.

But his promise to his friend compelled him.

Now that he actually had the gold, his first thought was to turn around and go home. But that would look more suspicious than if he had not come at all. No, he decided, better to wait until after dark, then leave as usual.

Finding a hiding place in the meantime should not be too hard, really; not for a man who knew Labrys so well.

Entering the palace, Meriones made his way to the upper levels. There an antechamber had been set aside for the exclusive use of the musicians, who visited it when they needed to repair their instruments. Aside from that, the room was never visited.

Meriones slipped into the chamber and pulled the door closed after him. The room was empty. With a sigh of relief, he dug the bulky package out from his clothing.

He could not resist opening it for just one look.

When he folded back the last flap of cloth, Meriones drew in a sharp breath. Gold gleamed like fire, like chunks of stolen sunlight. Pure, raw, massy gold, in nuggets worth a fortune.

So much gold! No wonder it was heavy. He realized at once that he could not leave it here, no matter how well hidden. He had planned to secrete it at the back of a small cupboard crammed with bits of wood and wire and pots of fish-glue. But that would never do, not for such a treasure. It would surely be found. Questions would be asked, musicians come under suspicion . . .

He would have to take it with him. No one would pay any attention to him now, he reasoned, not with Labrys rocking on its foundations. There would be no better time to get the gold out of the palace.

He wedged it back between his apron and his loincloth, wincing as the bulky nuggets dug into his belly. He wasted valuable moments readjusting his leather girdle to hold the package in place. His waist was no longer elegantly slim, he noted ruefully.

Then he brushed his hands and stepped out into the corridor trying to look nonchalant.

The atmosphere was changing rapidly. People's expressions were tense, their movements frenetic. Officials scuttled up and down the passageways, exhorting others to remain at their posts. Until the last, the minions of The Minos would strive to keep order.

But it was rapidly becoming a lost cause.

The bellowing of a bull reverberated through the stone-walled chambers of Labrys. Meriones realized sacrifices were being offered in an attempt to placate Poseidon Ennosigaion. The Great Central Court would run red with blood.

Priestesses howled eerily. Incense thickened the air.

Men and women started running; directionless, panicky.

"I don't suppose anyone will be expecting me in the kitchens today," Meriones remarked to no one in particular. Then, hitching his apron to make certain the gold was secure, he set off in search of the nearest safe exit.

He was almost knocked down by a man who came bolting out of an antechamber. "Watch where you're going!" the fellow snarled, sweeping Meriones aside with a wave of his arm.

"I'm sorry, I didn't mean . . ." The musician waved his fingers apologetically. But the other had already run off.

The floors were shuddering violently, Meriones realized with a thrill of horror. Not only walls, but the foundations themselves might collapse under such an onslaught!

A bull broke free from the sacrificial pens and ran headlong through the palace, his frantic bellowing adding to the mounting hysteria. A madness seized the palace animals. Pet monkeys bit and clawed. A hound savaged a royal child.

Cracks appeared in the smiling faces on the frescoes. Tiles fell with a clatter in the bathing chambers. Something grated; something crashed. Cries of distress were coming from the royal apartments. Plaster crumbling added its dust to the already polluted air. An enormous spiral shell made of stucco fell from the ceiling of the queen's megaron and crashed at Ebisha's feet. With a shriek of terror, she ran from the room. No one tried to stop her.

Hokar also was running through the dust-choked hallways of Labrys. A rumor that the gates had already been closed and barred had reached the workrooms, stampeding the craftsmen. Each was determined to find some way out for himself.

Upset and disoriented, Hokar lost his way. He found himself at the head of the Grand Staircase just as Ebisha came running up it.

People swarmed over the stairs. Someone bumped into her and she fell to her knees. With an oath, Hokar plunged down the steps to help her. The face she lifted to him was blank with fear.

He caught hold of her arm. "We must get out of here. Can you stand?"

Ebisha jerked free of his grasp and shrank back.

"I'm Hokar," he said, "don't you know me?"

She shuddered like the trembling earth. "Hokar?" The syllables sounded meaningless on her lips.

"Yes, Hokar the goldsmith, remember? Stand up now, that's it. Here, this way . . . do you know how to get out of here?"

"Out of here?" She was mimicking his words without understanding.

The air was darkening perceptibly. Even the light wells failed to dispel the gloom. A cloud seemed to have blotted out the sun.

Hokar guided the dazed Ebisha back to the top of the Grand Staircase, where he tried to figure which way to go next. Broad corridors lay in either direction but gave no clue of their destinations. "Which way does that go?" he asked Ebisha, pointing along one.

She stared at him with wide green eyes.

He swore under his breath and started in the direction he had pointed, drawing her with him by putting one strong arm around her trembling shoulders. "I think this is the way toward the Zeus Gate," Hokar said to no one in particular. "It's the gate nearest Arkhanes."

The mention of Arkhanes made him think of his little house there with a sudden, fierce longing. Everything in that house was Thracian in style. Familiar. His own.

He would take Ebisha there.

Someone wearing the stiff formal headdress of an offical stumbled past. "Which way to the Zeus Gate?" Hokar shouted at him. But there was no answer. The goldsmith's voice was lost in the wordless scream that was becoming the voice of Labrys.

People were running everywhere. The press of bodies shoved Hokar and Ebisha until passing through a doorway, they found themselves on the colonnaded porch that overlooked the Great Central Court. Below them people scampered across the mosaic tiles like a nest of disturbed ants. "The Minos has deserted us!"

someone cried. "He has evacuated his family and left us here to die!"

The last restraint dissolved. Whether the rumor was true or not, it was enough to instill blind panic.

People began clubbing each other with their fists, fighting for space, for air, for access to an exit, or just to relieve their unbearable emotions. Meanwhile the floor beneath their feet heaved and buckled like a living thing.

Ebisha screamed and clung to Hokar. He could hear her gasping names—the names of gods, he supposed—but they were not names he recognized.

Everyone seemed to be crying some name aloud. Some called on their mothers, others cursed or prayed to The Minos. Or Poseidon. Or Zeus. Or any of a hundred other deities, large and small, the particular image of a particular belief to which one might cling when the world was collapsing.

Nothing stopped the collapse, however.

The crowd was a mob, a mindless sea that moved like a tide first in one direction, then another, sweeping Hokar and Ebisha along with them.

Ebisha had one frightening glimpse of a great dark hulk lying on the floor of the court below. It was the corpse of the last bull to have been sacrificed to Poseidon. Forgotten now. The sacrifice refused.

"Hokar!"

The goldsmith heard his name, but in the melee he could not tell who was calling him.

"Hokar! Over here!"

He craned his neck. Then he saw a slim arm waving frantically.

"Hokar! It's me, Meriones!"

The musician hurried toward them, twisting and weaving through the crowd. When he reached Hokar he managed a harried grin of relief. "What are you doing here?" he asked his friend.

"Trying to find a way out. I got lost. What are you doing here?"

"Trying to find a way out. I was in this part of the palace looking for a place to hide your, ah . . ."

"My gold? You have it?"

"I do. But we don't have time to worry about it now. After we get . . . Look out!" Meriones cried suddenly. He grabbed Ebisha and pulled her aside just in time to keep her from being trampled by a clot of running men.

"What are you doing with this woman?" Meriones asked Hokar while Ebisha stood, panting, flattened against a wall.

"Trying to get her out too. I want to take her with me to Arkhanes. But there's a rumor that the gates have all been barred."

"Possibly," Meriones conceded. "But even if they are, there are many ways out of a palace as big as Labrys. Not everyone goes in and out through a public gate, Hokar. I haven't been here all these years without discovering that. I was just trying to decide which exit to use myself. I don't think anyone will question us under the circumstances."

"You talk too much!" Hokar snapped. "Just get us out of here if you know a way!"

Meriones nodded. "Come on, then. And bring her," he added, nodding at Ebisha. "Let's leave before the ceiling falls on us."

Taking a deep breath, Meriones plunged into the swirl of the crowd like a bather diving into a cold sea. Hokar glanced up at the ceiling, turned pale, hooked Ebisha with his arm and ran after Meriones.

For a measureless eternity they struggled through packed passageways and crowded corridors. Meriones, who was shorter than Hokar, kept disappearing. Finally Hokar caught hold of the fold of hair at the nape of his friend's neck and held on with all his might, though the pull brought tears to Meriones' eyes. Hokar dared not let go. If they lost Meriones he and Ebisha would be truly lost.

They ran up some steps and down others, scuttled across audience chambers, dodged through counting rooms, sidled along narrow passages meant only for slaves, and eventually emerged from a steep stairwell to find themselves on the lowest level of the palace. The walls of unplastered stone smelled of niter. A pervasive gloom was relieved only occasionally by a few plain bronze lamps burning in small niches set into the walls.

They had left the maddened crowd behind, but its roar could still be heard, echoing through the labyrinthine corridors of the palace.

Meriones paused, looking around. "There is an entrance down here somewhere that gives porters coming up from the sea direct access to the main storerooms. If we can find—"

He was interrupted by a thundering crash almost directly above their heads. The walls around them vibrated, the huge blocks of stone ringing like gongs.

"It's going to fall on us!" Ebisha cried. "We'll be crushed!"

The goldsmith folded the woman in his arms and bowed his head over hers protectively, as if he meant to take the weight of the palace on his shoulders rather than let it touch Ebisha.

In that moment, Meriones envied his friend. "It won't fall on us if we can get outside," he said urgently. "Come on!" He began running again.

They followed him through unlit areas floored with bare earth and rubble; stumbling, their breath burning their throat, the world they knew disintegrating around them.

"Here we are!" Meriones whooped suddenly, plunging toward a common planked door standing ajar in the thick wall.

The trio emerged into a daylight they scarcely recognized as daylight. The sky was as dark as mid-winter dusk, but with an evil yellowish cast.

The porters' entrance was let into a north-facing wall in the foundations of the palace, and had been abandoned at the first tremor of the earth. A flagged pathway led away from the doorway, but Meriones did not follow the paving. Instead he hurried away from the palace at an acute angle, making for the open ground beyond. Here the land began to slope upward, out of the royal valley.

The trio climbed the slope in silence, trying not to hear the screams and crashes coming from Labrys behind them. Other people ran past them from time to time, their faces distorted with terror.

Meriones led the way to the rim of the valley. There he paused. "You said you wanted to take Ebisha to Arkhanes," he reminded Hokar. "You'll want to go that way." He pointed.

Hokar's jaw dropped. "Aren't you going with us?"

"I can't, I must go home to my wife. I should never have left her this morning. I wouldn't have, if I'd thought things were going to get so bad."

"And they may well get worse," Hokar warned. "If we're separated now, we might never see each other again. Stay with us, Meriones, let's all help each other. Don't try to go back to Knōsos now, you might not make it. Stay with us," he repeated, putting all the strength of his personality into his urging. "Please!"

Just for a moment, Hokar thought he could hold Meriones. Then the earth shuddered as if Poseidon Ennosigaion was stalking across the land on giant feet, rumbling destruction with every stride.

Ebisha flinched and gasped.

"I have to go home to Tulipa!" Meriones cried frantically.

Hokar unleashed his temper. "Go, then! Desert your friend. Be a coward, who cares? Who needs a wasp-waisted lyre player? I can take care of Ebisha without you!"

Meriones blinked. Then he gave a thin-lipped nod, turned on his heel, and hurried off in the direction of Knōsos.

Hokar stared after him with rising dismay. When the musician was almost out of earshot, he relented and called out, "Meriones? My friend? Be . . . careful!"

Meriones heard. He paused and turned around long enough to give Hokar a Cretan salute. Arching his back like a bow, he made a fist and pressed his knuckles to the Palace of the Brain. "My friend," he echoed. "Try to be . . . cheerful."

Then he spun around and ran for home.

He had run for some distance before he became aware that his movements were being hampered by a bulky object thrust between his loincloth and apron.

He had forgotten to give Hokar the stolen gold.

# 12

*A dead calm lay on the sea.*

*On board the Qatil, Tereus felt his hackles rise.*

*"Pull!" he yelled at his oarsmen. "PULL!!!"*

*But it was too late. A growling roar, far away at*

*first, swiftly came*

closer, increasing in volume until the ship's timbers vibrated and men clapped their hands over their ears. It sounded as if the ocean floor was being wrenched apart.

The roaring grew to unbearable intensity then doubled; trebled. A tremendous thunderclap reverberated throughout the Aegean Sea, slammed across the Ionian Sea, rang the waters of the Mediterranean like a giant bell.

While the world still shook with its force, a second thunderclap boomed with enough power to dwarf the first. Then, impossibly, there was a third, mightier and more terrifying than anything that had gone before. It was a sound to freeze the blood and stop the heart. It was a sound to announce the end of the world.

Geysers of steam shot upward, hot fountains jetting from the sea bed into the sky. Pumice and ash rained down to meet them. The air stank of strange gases released from the bowels of the earth. When horror had exceeded all limits, with one final gigantic blast the world exploded.

A volcanic eruption mightier than any within the memory of mankind tore the entire side out of the island of Thera and hurled it into the sky. A monstrous flower of incandescent light blossomed, burning white, hot beyond heat, setting the air ablaze and drawing all breath, all life into itself. An enormous pillar of boiling smoke, shot through with orange sparks like evil eyes and lit from within by a lurid glow, rose from the disemboweled island. The cloud mushroomed upward, billowing into a burning sky.

The first shock wave rapidly radiated outward. It hit the *Qatil* like a battering ram. Tereus fell face forward on the deck, clawing long splinters out of the wood with bloody fingers. He screamed and did not know he screamed.

Outraged, the sea rose on its hind legs to bellow fury at the heavens.

Meanwhile, Meriones was pounding down the familiar road that led to Knōsos, his house, his wife. He hardly noticed when the white hound darted out from somewhere to join him. The animal was whimpering with terror. Man and dog ran together, fear making them lightfooted.

They had gotten as far as the long hill commanding a view of the harbor when the voice of Poseidon thundered across the sea and knocked Meriones flat on the earth.

He lay dazed, then pulled himself to his hands and knees, spitting earth and pebbles. The god again cried aloud, with a great booming voice. Meriones wet himself in his terror and drew up into a ball, waiting to die.

The god roared with the greatest anger that had ever been unleashed in the world. Meriones knew he was dead. He thought his heart stopped.

But he did not die. He lay helpless while the tremendous explosions echoed and reechoed throughout Crete. Eventually, the musician realized that he was still alive. Probably. He got to his knees again, very shakily, and tried to find the courage to stand.

The ultimate blast slammed across the sea, threw him on his face once more as the whole world rocked on its foundations. The northern sky caught fire, became a sea of molten flame.

Meriones did not try again to stand. What was the use? He lay with a calmer mind than he expected, his head turned sideways, cheek pressed against the road. "This is the end," he heard himself say. No one contradicted him. But somewhere close by, a dog whined piteously.

Meriones shifted enough to be able to see the white hound lying in a heap beside him. He reached out and drew the dog against his body. It did not seem any more injured than he was. Merely scared to death.

Scared to death. The term had new meaning. It meant being so scared that fear itself was slain and one waited placidly, like a bull awaiting sacrifice. Looking at the ax.

Listening for the voice of the god.

Then the god fell silent. Seventy miles to the north, the sea was rushing in to form a seven-mile-wide lake of boiling water and steam embraced by the ruined crescent of lava cliffs that was all that remained of the island of Thera.

From the shock of that monstrous reforming a great wave spread out and moved across the sea. In deep water it was like a ripple traveling across a pond when a stone is dropped in. But as the giant ripple neared the land and the sea bed was shallower, the wave swelled upward, building into a mighty wall with a crest towering hundreds of feet into the shocked sky.

With the speed of the gods, the wall of water rushed toward Crete.

Meriones felt a certain disappointment that he was not dead. Instinct told him the dead might be the lucky ones. But he was unquestionably alive. Slowly, expecting to be knocked down again at any moment, he got to his feet and examined his bruises. They were numerous but not serious. Then he turned the same attention on the dog. It had no broken bones but whined continually, a thin, high-pitched moan that did not sound like a dog at all.

He picked it up and cradled it against his body. The feel of another warm and living being comforted them both.

Meriones' gaze moved along the road toward Knōsos, noting how the paving slabs had heaved. For the first time he realized there were a few other people on the road. He saw them as dark lumps illuminated by the hideous light of the flaming sky. Some of the lumps were stirring, groaning.

Others lay unmoving and silent.

Meriones thought suddenly of Hokar and Ebisha. What had happened to them? Should he go back? He looked over his shoulder, indecisive, then thought of Tulipa and whirled around again, gazing toward the city and the harbor . . .

. . . and stood transfixed.

The cloud that had been Thera was clearly visible on the horizon, glowing like a firebed. In the foreground of this horror were the residents of Knōsos, staggering away from a city reduced to rubble. They resembled the survivors of a destroyed army. Some wept, some cursed, some moaned in pain. Some whimpered like the white hound.

The foremost reached Meriones and passed him, unaware of him. They had no thought but horror and escape. They went on, leaving Meriones staring.

He saw the wave come up out of the sea. But it could not be a wave. It could not be anything known and familiar. It was a giant, malevolent entity from an underworld that spawned monsters. Irresistible, it sped toward the harbor where the masts of the fleet still rose like a forest of sticks.

The tidal wave slammed against Knōsos, smashing the glory of the world's largest fleet into splinters. In the blink of an eye the forest of ships was devoured by the ravenous sea. Its appetite unassuaged, the monster swallowed the shoreline and gobbled up the ruined city beyond, crushing everything beneath a mammoth wall of water.

Staring, unbelieving, Meriones waited, fully expecting the tidal wave to continue inland and cover Labrys in the valley, then rage up the slopes of the mountains themselves, putting an end to one insignificant musician and the brilliant world of Crete.

It came very close.

But the land had a strength of its own. As the tidal wave swept across it the earth robbed the waters of their energy. At last they fell back, exhausted by their own fury. The water drained off toward the sea with a ghastly sucking noise, leaving a spoor of dirty foam and piled mountains of unidentifiable debris.

Still Meriones stood, and stared.

He did not know how much time passed. It seemed eons. Surely he had been watching there since the birth of the world, witness to the contest between land and sea for supremacy.

Where a rich seaport had been was now nothing. The little yellow house was gone. Tulipa's goat was gone. The olive tree was gone.

Tulipa was gone; gone with Knōsos.

Its streets had disappeared beneath the mud and slime that frescoed the site. The stench of the sea bottom floated up to Meriones and he bent to one side to vomit, spewing out his horror without ever turning loose of the dog clasped tightly in his arms.

Knōsos was gone.

Tulipa was gone.

As if from a great distance, Meriones heard the shrieks and wails of the survivors.

But Tulipa was gone.

Knōsos was gone.

"I would be gone too, but for Hokar's gold," he heard himself say to the dog.

The sound of his voice stilled the hound's whining. It twisted in his arms and tried to lick his face with its wet tongue.

"How strange," Meriones said wonderingly. "I could be out under the sea with Tulipa. Isn't that strange?"

His voice sounded calm, unemotional. He might have been commenting on a minor event in an ordinary day.

He did not notice the tears running down his cheeks.

He stared at the sea and the burning sky, and the empty place where the city had been.

"Hokar's gold," he said after a while in the same uninflected voice.

His body turned itself around and began to walk in the direction of Arkhanes.

# 13

*Shortly after Meriones left them,*

*Ebisha's strength deserted her. Her legs felt like*

*water. She sat down abruptly on the unstable earth*

*and stared helplessly up at Hokar. "No more,"*

*she said.*

He gave a worried glance at the peculiar sky, then reluctantly sat down beside her. "Just for a little while," he said. "We can rest for a little while, then we have to go on."

"Where?"

"To my house, in the hills beyond this valley. It might be safer there."

"Can we breathe there, in the hills?" Ebisha coughed, shook her head, coughed again. "The air is so bad here. So thick."

"It will be better at Arkhanes," he assured her with a confidence he did not feel. He sat with her for a little while then tried to get her on her feet again. When he tugged at her arm she sat like a lump of soft clay, unwilling to move. "Come to my house now," he pleaded. "I have something for you there, something I've been keeping for you. It is the gold . . ." Suddenly he remembered. His stolen gold. Meriones said he had it, but Meriones was gone.

Gone off with my gold, Hokar thought. His mouth narrowed into a bitter line.

"What do you have for me?" Ebisha asked, pulling his attention back.

The words were ashes in his mouth. "The gold necklace I made for you, the seashells." It's all I have left, he was about to add, feeling the anger flame in him.

But at that moment the first blast struck.

Ebisha screamed and cowered against the earth. Hokar stood swaying, his ears ringing. Then the second great thunder drowned out all other sound and hurled him to the ground.

As the final explosion ignited the sky, he twisted violently to shield Ebisha's body with his. Wrapping his arms around her head, Hokar pressed his face down beside her and waited for death.

Waited in a ringing silence.

Slowly, astonished to find himself alive, Hokar began trying to disentangle from the woman. A white-hot pain lanced through his hip.

Ebisha was crying in soft little hiccups.

When Hokar tried to stand, his wrenched muscles screamed. He tugged at Ebisha. "You must help me," he told her through gritted teeth. "I'm hurt. I don't think I can get up alone."

With an effort, she controlled her sobbing and peered at him through a curtain of disheveled hair. "Hurt?"

"My hip." Waves of pain lapped at him. "But we cannot stay here. Help me."

Ebisha got to her feet. Then she bent and helped Hokar drape an arm across her shoulders. She wrapped both her arms around his chest.

Very slowly and very carefully, between them they got him upright, standing.

Hokar was briefly nauseated, but it passed.

"That's better," he breathed. He straightened his spine and lifted his head, moving out of her embrace to stand independently. "I'm all right now," he said with conviction.

But when he tried to walk he knew he was not all right. The injured hip could not be trusted, and every movement of his leg was a painful effort.

Ebisha, watching him through narrowed eyes, moved close again without being asked and draped his arm back across her shoulder. She could not afford weakness when he needed her strength.

They set off once more in the direction of Arkhanes.

People were streaming past them. A small child, bloody and naked, appeared in their path, shrieked unintelligibly, and fled like a mindless animal. Moments later they came to the collapsed house where the child's family lay crushed. One clenched fist protruded from the rubble.

There was nothing to be done. Hokar and Ebisha went on.

Once the goldsmith glanced back toward the north, but the sight of a monstrous tower of flame invading the heavens so appalled him that thereafter he kept his eyes fixed on the ground in front of him. The ground was cracked, broken, the familiar way to Arkhanes already altered beyond recognition. But better than fire in the sky.

Shielded by the contours of the hills, Hokar and Ebisha were spared the sight Meriones would never forget, the massive wall of water rushing down on the defenseless coast. The concussion of the tidal wave was, to them, indistinguishable from the other tremors running continually through the earth.

The tidal wave did not reach the House of the Double Axes. The valley rim that had shielded Labrys from the rapacious view of sea pirates in former times now sheltered the palace from the most savage pirate of all. Poseidon did not carry away the treasures of The Minos.

But Hokar and Ebisha heard a change in the quality of the distant screaming. An added wail of terror was carried to them on the wind from the northern coast.

Hokar forced himself to a shambling run, a sort of hobbling hop half supported by Ebisha trotting beside him. Surprisingly, the effort eased his pain as if he were forcing some misaligned portion of himself back into place.

The hot wind, the long overdue wind, was blowing more strongly every moment, bringing a cloud of pumice and ash. In time it would begin delivering the fragmented flesh of Thera.

Hokar and Ebisha journeyed through nightmare. For a while he stopped thinking of her as a woman. Getting-Ebisha-to-Arkhanes became a task he had set himself, like fashioning fine gold wire. His mind fixed on that as the only reality, rejecting the unreal surrounding them and the surreal horror of the situation.

Struggling, stumbling, cursing, he guided her—he the cripple and she the crutch—through an endless filthy darkness in which a thousand raging fires were springing up as blazing cinders began to rain from the sky.

Hardly a structure they saw was still intact. Homes and farm-steads, their stones scattered, littered the land with rubble. Dazed people wandered about as aimlessly as dazed livestock.

Some survivors, less dazed than others, had already begun looting.

As Hokar and Ebisha approached Arkhanes, several times they encountered small groups of men going from one ruined homestead to another, taking anything of value they could find. Snatching, grabbing, grinning, running.

"They are like the men who capture free people to make them slaves," Ebisha said with repugnance.

But the looters did not bother them. They were so ash-covered and begrimed they looked as if neither ever had anything worth stealing.

Arkhanes had been a small but important town. It was on one of the main roads leading from the south, and was also the site of the royal tombs of minor members of the ruling families of Knōsos. Generations of sisters and nephews and mothers-in-law slept there peacefully with their grave goods piled high around them, fearing no grave robbers, for graves were sacred in the land of the sea kings.

At least, they always had been. Before.

"My house is just up ahead," Hokar told Ebisha with obvious relief. "If it's still standing."

The goldsmith's house was at the end of a road leading to the Hill of Tombs. An ugly glow behind the hill might have been sunset—or sunrise—who could tell?

Hokar directed Ebisha to the familiar pathway. Now he was looking ahead. He could hardly believe his stinging eyes.

His house stood relatively unharmed, with just a slight cant to one side.

They hurried gratefully inside.

The door could not be closed behind them. The doorframe was out of alignment. Putting his shoulder behind it, Hokar forced the door as far as it would go, which was no more than halfway, then sat down, panting, on the nearest couch.

The pain in his hip had become only a memory of fire. But suddenly he was desperately tired. He just wanted to sit. Not think, not feel. Just sit. He hung his head and closed his eyes.

Ebisha stood indecisively for a moment, then began exploring the goldsmith's house.

It was nothing like the House of the Double Axes. Simple to the point of being stark, it was a utilitarian residence for a man usually occupied elsewhere. A few couches, one of which served as a bed; some low wooden tables; a couple of chests carved in designs she did not recognize. Coarse woolen rugs hung haphazardly on the walls—though with a sense of color, bright dyes enlivening the plain white stucco. On one of the tables was a pitcher with dying flowers.

Ebisha smiled to herself when she saw the flowers, and nodded, as if they carried a particular message.

"Is there any water?" she heard Hokar say behind her.

She took the flowers from the water and carried the pitcher to him. He drank gratefully. The water was flat and stale but it cleared the dust from his mouth.

When he ran his tongue over his teeth afterward, he could taste the dead flowers.

Gingerly, he stood up. His hip ached, but it was bearable. Crossing the room to an assortment of householders' tools leaning in one corner, he selected a heavy metal bar. With the bar he pried up a flagstone from the floor.

There was a hollow beneath the flagstone, and a small parcel wrapped in linen in the hollow.

Wordlessly, he handed the parcel to Ebisha.

When she unwrapped it her eyes widened. "The necklace!" She turned the thin links over in her hands, her eyes following the spiral design of the tiny nautilus shells.

Hokar said diffidently, "It's . . . ah . . . the best thing I've ever done. Not very heavy though. If I had more gold . . ." He broke off, scowling. The memory of the stolen gold burned in him.

"You have a very great gift," Ebisha said reverently. "I think the gold speaks to you."

Hokar was embarrassed. "That's not possible. I'm just, ah, good with my hands."

"You don't think gold can speak to a craftsman? I do. Everything has a voice. Not as powerful a voice, perhaps, as one of the immortals, but . . ."

"What do you mean by 'the immortals'? Are you talking about the gods?"

Ebisha's forehead pleated with the effort to explain. "Not like the gods you have here, Hokar. Not giant men and women or magical animals or some blend of the two. The immortals my people know and understand are alive, but in a different way. They are the very forces of life. They provide what we need for our existence as long as we treat them with respect, but they . . . they are not . . ." She broke off, coughing.

When the seizure passed she resumed, "Water is one of the immortals. Among my people are some to whom the water speaks. They can find it hidden far beneath the earth. They hear the voice of unknown springs and show others where to dig their wells. The water calls to them, and they listen.

"My grandsire has a different gift. He knows the soul of fire. Fire is another of the immortals. Something in the fire speaks to my grandsire and he listens. They . . . communicate. He can make sparks leap from his fingertips or set a tree afire with a glance. Do you understand?"

Baffled, Hokar shook his head. "It's magic. I know nothing of magic."

The lurid light of the flaming sky shone through the window, painting the interior of Hokar's house the color of blood.

A face peered around the half-open door. "Hokar?" someone inquired. "Is this your house? Are you in there?"

Hokar stiffened.

Ebisha gave a squeal of joy. "Musician!"

Meriones entered the house warily, as if expecting it might collapse at any time. Hokar wanted to hurry forward and welcome him, but something held him back. "Why are you here?" was all he could say. His tone was surly.

Meriones peered at him. "I had to bring your gold to you," he said. It was the only answer he could think of.

Hokar exhaled a great sigh of relief. "You brought it back."

"Of course I brought it back, did you think I—you did! You thought I'd stolen it for myself!"

"Of course not," Hokar said, too heartily. "It never entered my mind!"

"It never entered my mind either," Meriones told him in a soft, sad voice.

Abashed, Hokar hurried tardily forward and clasped Meriones by both hands. "What about your wife? Did you reach Knōsos?"

"Knōsos is gone. Tulipa is gone."

"Gone? What do you mean, gone?"

"Gone. The sea took them." Meriones' tone was flat and dead.

Hokar and Ebisha exchanged shocked glances.

Something whined at the door. A very lean, very dirty white hound crouched there, wagging its tail to placate its god for the sin of having followed him.

The faintest spark of life crept back into Meriones' voice as he said, "It's all right, this is my friend's house." He did not think Hokar was the sort of person who would object to a dog in the house. He snapped his fingers and the hound ran to him.

"What's happening out there?" Hokar wanted to know.

"It's very bad. The air is thicker than water and cinders and other things are falling out of it. Fires are springing up everywhere. And looters," he added, relieved that Hokar had asked no more about Knōsos and Tulipa. "You should bar your door, Hokar."

"I can't, it won't close. The frame is twisted. But we'll be all right here."

Meriones was not so sure. The atmosphere in the house was only slightly less foul than outside. The wind blowing across Crete from destroyed Thera was bringing not only volcanic ash and debris but poisonous gases.

Ebisha coughed again, and again, more harshly each time.

The three sat on Hokar's couch, the woman in the middle and the dog crouching at their feet. They sat and waited. There was nothing else to do.

Sounds drifted in from outside. Crashes, shouts. Then long sullen silences broken only by the howl of the wind. Then different crashes, other voices shouting.

It might have been day or night.

"My throat is so dry," Ebisha gasped, reaching for the water pitcher on the table beside the couch. But the pitcher was empty. She clawed at her throat beneath the gold necklace she had slipped over her head.

"Where's your well?" Meriones asked Hokar. "I can go for more water."

"It's a good trot down the road, in a little square half hidden by shrubbery. Not easy to find unless you know just where it is."

Ebisha coughed again, violently. Her eyes pleaded.

"You go then, Hokar," said Meriones.

Suddenly Ebisha said, "Both of you go!"

"But I want to be with you," Hokar protested.

"I shall be all right for the time it takes you to fetch water," she insisted. "Just go now. The dog will watch over me."

She had grown accustomed to palace habits. At Labrys, men and women insisted on privacy when they relieved themselves. Bodily functions were circumscribed with rituals. It had been a long time since she last emptied her bladder and it was aching dreadfully, but she was reluctant to say this aloud. If the two men would just leave her alone for a little time she could take care of herself in private.

The more Hokar argued to stay with her, the more she urged him to go. And each time she spoke made her cough.

At last he gave in. "But we'll be back very soon," he assured her as he walked, somewhat stiffly, toward the door.

It would be good to do something other than sitting passively, he suddenly realized.

Meriones had a last word for the dog. "Guard her well!" he ordered the hound.

The white dog, which had started to follow him, sank back on its haunches with a disappointed whine, but stayed with Ebisha.

Outside the house the unnatural twilight closed in upon them at once.

There were other people at the well. A nervous scuffle had broken out. Everyone was in a hurry to fill the various water vessels they had brought. Once people waited politely at the well, each taking their turn. Not now. The eerie light, the quivering earth, the stinking air combined to strip away the patina of civilization and reveal frightened animals snarling at one another over water rights.

One man shoved another hard. The second man staggered back against an elderly woman. She dropped the vessel she carried. It crashed on the paving stones. Glancing down, Meriones saw that it had been a finely made piece of pottery formed to resembled a leather bag with a lip, with pottery handles simulating twisted rope. Rose in color, it was decorated with a repetitive double ax motif common to Cretan ware.

Smashed.

As Cretan pottery was ceremoniously smashed every year in an ostentatious display of wealth intended to give employment to more potters and enhance the economy still more.

Holding his own water pitcher against his chest, Hokar managed to edge closer to the well. Then a fight broke out in earnest. One burly man hit another in the face with his fist. In seconds, the area boiled with fury. People relieved their pent-up emotions by hitting out at whoever was nearest, for no reason at all.

Meriones had never liked fighting. He tried to stay out of the melee, but when he saw Hokar being pummeled by a pair of men he swallowed hard and plunged forward to try to help his friend. "You leave him alone!" he yelled.

The crowd swallowed him.

Meriones was, however, tougher than he looked. His was a wiry and agile strength and his reflexes were quick. He gave as good as he got and found, to his surprise, that it felt good to be hitting something.

Yelling wildly, he began to hit harder.

The crowd at the well was so intent on their impromptu war that they did not hear other voices crying out in the town, warning of the arrival of the looters.

Someone hit Hokar a thundering blow to the side of the head and the red world turned black. He slid down and away, into a ringing silence.

But consciousness did not totally desert him. He could still feel the pain in his hip, and he somehow knew he was in a sitting position with his back against the cold stone of the well-curb. Confusion swirled around him like spirits swirling through the netherworld.

His mind wandered off in a dream of its own. He envisioned the long, satisfying afternoons in the goldsmiths' chamber at Labrys. He fancied he heard the sound of the lyre, and he smiled to himself. Sitting dazed on the shaken earth of Crete, his ears temporarily deaf to the funeral laments of a shattered civilization, he lived again at his workbench. His fists uncurled and reshaped themselves as if holding his tools. He reveled in the rich satiety of designs running through his mind, waiting for his art to give them substance.

He thought he was watching his hands shape the gold necklace for Ebisha. He saw the shells . . .

"Ebisha," he groaned, clawing his way back to the here and now.

Meriones was bending over him. "Hokar? Are you all right?"

"No. Not. No."

"Can you get up?"

"I don't want to," Hokar said with conviction even as he reached for the hand Meriones was extending.

The pain in his hip woke afresh, but somehow he got to his feet. "What happened?"

"The fight's over. I think we all won. Everyone got their water and went home. I've been trying to get you to open your eyes for ever so long."

"Ebisha!"

"We'd better get back to her," Meriones said. "I don't want to worry you, but I heard someone say there's been looting not far from here."

"Why didn't you leave me and go to her right away, then?"

Meriones looked shocked. "You're my friend. How could I leave you here with men fighting all around you? And I couldn't carry you, you're too big."

"Ebisha," Hokar said again. This time it came out as a groan.

He leaned on Meriones' shoulder and reverted to the hobbling hop that was the nearest he could come to a run. The two men hurried up the road toward Hokar's house, neither speaking. They sped through a smoky, permanent dusk. Beneath the cloud of volcanic debris no daylight could survive.

Other survivors were still picking their way through the streets, not only of Arkhanes, but of the other cities and towns of Crete that had suffered the volcanic fury and its aftermath. They were digging at the collapsed walls, seeking friends and family, trying to identify landmarks, talking to one another—or at one another—in fragmented, disjointed snatches. Words drifted to Hokar and Meriones: ". . . the entire fleet . . . six generations to rebuild . . . collapsed on top of them, and no one . . . have you seen her? A little girl, only this high . . . burning, still burning . . ."

As they neared the house with the gaping door, Hokar and Meriones slowed by mutual unspoken accord. Nothing looked any different than when they had left it.

And yet.

"Don't go in there," Meriones said suddenly. "Let me look first." He pushed Hokar's arm from his shoulder and advanced toward the house alone. Hokar made no move to follow him.

Meriones was not afraid. As far as he was concerned, the worst possible thing had already happened. Nothing he might find in Hokar's house could be as bad as seeing the tidal wave that took Tulipa.

But Hokar was afraid. He stood frozen with anticipatory anguish.

Meriones edged his body around the door and peered into the gloom. At first he could not see anything. Then his eyes began to make out details.

An overturned table.

A couch hurled halfway across the room.

Meriones flinched in spite of himself. "Ebisha?" he whispered hesitantly.

A voice answered him. Not a human voice. The faint whimper came from beneath an overturned table.

Meriones flung himself down beside it. The hound lay there, thin ribs heaving, a bloody slash along them showing where the dog had been attacked with a knife. The hound tried to lick Meriones' hand.

"Did you fight for her?" he asked it. "Did you try to save her?" The dog whimpered again. Meriones' heart sank.

He knew what had happened as surely as if he had been there. Looters had stumbled across Hokar's house and seen the gleaming necklace Ebisha wore. He glanced to one side. The flagstone with the hollow beneath it was still in place. Meriones and Hokar had hidden the gold nuggets there before they went for water, and it appeared undisturbed.

But even in the gloom, looters would have seen Ebisha's necklace.

Gold. Deadly gold. Meriones stood up. "Ebisha?"

"Is she there? Is she all right?" Hokar called anxiously from the doorway.

Meriones knew he was not thinking clearly. He was too tired, and his brain was numbed by grief. Yet he must try to shield his friend, if he could, from an awful discovery.

"You stay there, Hokar!" he ordered sharply. "I'll find her, just a moment now . . ."

He fumbled about the room, stumbling over furniture. The dog tried to crawl after him, then sank back and lay panting.

Meriones came to the couch lying on the floor like a slain animal, feet upward.

Not lying flat.

There was something beneath it.

Meriones took hold of two of the legs and eased the couch onto its side.

Ebisha, a lifeless heap, had been underneath the couch.

Meriones held his breath for one agonized moment before calling out to Hokar. Let Hokar think, for that moment longer, that she might be alive. It was a small gift to give.

Meriones touched the dead girl's shoulder with gentle, regretful fingers . . . and felt her stir beneath his touch.

"Hokar!" he cried. "She's here, she's alive, come quick!"

Hokar flung himself into the room as if he had never been injured.

Between them they righted the couch and lifted Ebisha onto it. Some random part of Meriones' mind noted that she was heavier than Tulipa. Bigger-boned, from a bigger race.

Tulipa. Don't think about her.

Ebisha coughed and opened her eyes. "Aaannh?" she asked uncertainly.

Meriones told her, "You're alive, we're here. It's all right."

"Aaannh." Her eyes closed again, satisfied.

A hasty examination showed her to be stunned, but uninjured. Only the dog was injured. It whined pitifully, begging for Meriones' attention.

They had brought no water after all. Meriones had to run back to the well to fetch some. Every step of the way he expected to be attacked, but he was unchallenged.

He filled the pitcher and ran back to Hokar's house. Some water sloshed from the pitcher as he ran, but he arrived with most of it.

Ebisha was awake. She lay cradled in the goldsmith's arms. With one hand Hokar kept stroking her hair as if to assure himself she was real.

She was coughing when Meriones entered the house. She reached eagerly for the pitcher and gulped down half its contents. She choked, spluttered, drank the rest.

The coughing eased. She managed a wan smile. "The dog saved me. Strangers came. They saw the necklace and tried to take it from me, but the dog attacked them and fought them. They had knives, though. They would have killed us both. But then the necklace broke and they took it and ran because the dog was growling so savagely. They hurt him, but he never stopped growling!"

Meriones went to the dog and knelt down beside it. He stroked the animal's head tenderly. "You're going to be all right," he said. "We'll take care of you. You're safe now." The dog thumped its tail weakly against the flagstones.

"You're my dog now," Meriones added.

The feathery tail wagged harder. He could have sworn the hound understood.

He made another trip to the well, and got enough water to drink and to bathe the dog's wound. He was as gentle with the hound as he had been with Tulipa, pouring all his care and concern into his task, venting his amputated love.

They stayed in the house, waiting, but they did not know what they were waiting for. No one else bothered them. Hokar retrieved the gold nuggets from their hiding place, then seemed to lose interest in them. He sat with the package held loosely in his hands as he stared off into space.

Meriones eyed it. A thought occurred to him. "Hokar?"

"Mmmm?"

"Where did you get the gold for Ebisha's necklace?"

There was no answer. Meriones persisted. "Did you get it the same way you got those chunks of raw gold?"

Hokar looked down.

"Ah." Intuition moved through Meriones, forming a mosaic in his mind. "You stole it. And because you had stolen, you thought I would steal too."

Hokar said nothing.

Meriones carried his thoughts a step further. "Tereus stole Ebisha and the others from the Islands of Mist. They were free people, but he made them slaves. There has been too much stealing. We've made the gods angry, that's why this disaster has befallen us."

Ebisha looked intently at Meriones. "Do you think your gods did this? Do you think they are powerful enough to do this?"

Meriones ran his hands through his hair. "They must be, how else could it happen? So we must find a way to placate them. We have to give back what was stolen."

"Not my gold," Hokar said abruptly. His fingers clamped on the package in his lap. "I need this to buy Ebisha's freedom."

Ebisha said in a wondering voice, "I think I'm free already. Who at the palace cares now what has become of me?"

"She's right," Meriones agreed. "The pair of you could vanish completely and no one would ever ask questions. So many have vanished . . ." He paused, swallowed hard, went on. "If there are any ships left—and there must be—in time you could even make your way to the Islands of Mist. Take Ebisha home, return something that was stolen."

At the word "home" a great light dawned in Ebisha's green eyes.

Hokar responded to its blaze. "I suppose we could go down to the coast and ask about Tereus and the *Qatil;* they were due in. If we can't find them, there will surely be other ships taking refugees out. Everyone will want to leave Crete after this."

"Not everyone, but many," Meriones agreed. "I would like to leave myself. There's nothing left for me here," he added in a low voice.

Ebisha clapped her hands. "Then come with us to the Islands of Mist!"

Meriones looked at Hokar, who had believed him capable of theft. "I don't know . . ."

Hokar rightfully interpreted the musician's dubious expression. "You must come with us," he said. "You're my friend. My friend forever, beyond any doubt."

Meriones slanted his gaze sideways, to the injured hound lying nearby. "And my dog?"

Hokar laughed. "Bring him. We owe a debt to that dog."

"Hear that?" Meriones asked the hound. "We're going to the Islands of Mist!"

The dog lifted its head, wagged its tail, and grinned.

They gathered what food they could find and a waterskin, then made a bundle of these using one of Hokar's blankets. In the bottom of the bundle were the gold nuggets. Ebisha was assigned to carry the bundle, while Hokar leaned on her shoulder.

Meriones carried his injured dog.

Their waiting over, and firm in their resolve for a new beginning, the trio set out for the coast.

They traveled through an alien landscape. In places the hot ash was knee-deep and getting deeper. Great cracks had opened in the earth. Some of these revealed fire raging in their depths, devouring debris. Scorched, singed, and shaken, the Minoan empire was in ruins.

"The Mycenaean warlords have been waiting for an opportunity like this," Meriones remarked, unable to walk long in silence. "When they realize what's happened here, they'll probably attack Crete and take over the Mediterranean."

Hokar was not listening. He was not interested in politics or military adventurism. His eye was drawn to a burned tree standing alone against the sky. Its twiggy, blackened branches formed an elegant pattern, like freehand filigree by a master craftsman.

I could copy that, Hokar was thinking.

He was so intent he did not notice the fissure in front of him until he lost his balance and swayed precariously on its brink.

With a shriek, Ebisha grabbed for him.

At the bottom of the fissure a roaring fire waited.

Hokar tumbled forward.

Ebisha caught him at the last possible moment. But she had to drop her bundle to do it.

The bundle fell into the heart of the flames.

"My gold!" Hokar cried in dismay, reaching toward it.

Simultaneously, Meriones felt a stirring inside himself, like intuition. Like inspiration. His voice boomed above the roar of the fire. "Let it go!" he commanded.

As if in response, a red-gold belch of flame soared upward, driving Hokar and Ebisha back. Meriones stood alone on the edge of the fissure. Alone with the fire.

As it scorched his skin, awe bubbled through his blood. An ancient heritage came alive in him. His grandmother's voice sang to him in the hiss of the flames.

"Yes," Meriones whispered. "Yes."

Suddenly he *knew,* beyond thought, beyond question, what elemental power had been unleashed when Thera exploded. In the flames he saw, for one heart-stopping instant, the face of the old priest who was Ebisha's grandsire.

"Yes," Meriones said a third and final time. He arched his back and pressed his knuckles to the Palace of the Brain in salute. Then he stepped back to safety.

"The gold is gone," he told his companions. "We have given it to the fire."

*The stone sat on its hillside and thought. Its thoughts were not cerebral. It had no cerebral cortex. Nor were they visceral. Stones do not need viscera. The thoughts of stone are the thoughts of earth, compacted, weighed down by the eons, thrust upward by cataclysm, encased in ice. Immobile for millennia. Then pushed, shoved, dragged, dropped.*

*The stone sat where the glacier had abandoned it. The surrounding landscape slowly changed. Vegetation appeared, softly mantling the ice-scraped soil. Trees grew. Great lizards came. And disappeared. Mammals rubbed their itching sides on the stone to rid themselves of parasites.*

*Rain poured over the stone; rain from its cousins the mountains, who helped shape the weather, controlling wind currents and influencing the amount of precipitation.*

*Sun shone.*

*Change followed change.*

*Two-legged mammals arrived. They recognized the stone as fearsome and holy and bowed in worship before it. In what served as its consciousness, the stone thought this behavior just and proper. It was part of the sacred earth.*

*Then different, paler, bifurcated beings arrived, and began slaughtering the worshipers of the stone.*

# 14

Annie Murphy sat in the twilight of

her fine frame house with the book on her lap. It had

grown too dark to read unless she lit a lamp, and

Annie did not like to waste oil. There would be

God's daylight tomorrow

and she could read more. Meanwhile, her thin fingers stroked the leather cover of the book. The smell of new leather drifted up to her. Her fingers caressed the gold stamping on the cover. It read: NEW HAMPSHIRE AS IT IS. A GAZETTEER. And the date, brand-new, gleaming gold: 1855.

Annie Murphy sighed a contented sigh. She was a wealthy woman, by her reckoning. She had a fine new book to read that would last her through the hard New England winter to come and well into spring.

"No bigger than a bar of laundry soap after a hard day's wash," was the way she described herself. Tiny, meticulous, she ruled the Murphy household with an iron hand. There was only one way—her way, and nothing less than perfection would suffice. But her eyes twinkled as easily as they snapped, and her fine-boned face and slim little body radiated good humor.

She had peculiar eyes for a descendant of Irish immigrants, almost almond in shape, dark, exotic.

"My Annie's family had someone born on the wrong side of the blanket sometime," her husband said to his cronies down at the feed store. He, Liam Murphy, was as Irish as they came, there could be no doubting his pedigree. His blazing red hair and freckles were indisputable proof. "I come from the Murphys of Wexford," he loved to boast. "The Boys of Ninety-eight."

But the heroes of the most recent doomed Irish rising against English oppression meant nothing to hard-bitten New Hampshire farmers gathered around a potbellied stove in the feed store at Conway. What mattered was the oppression of the oncoming winter and the anticipated depth and duration of the snow it would bring, which would shape all their lives for the next six months.

"You reckon it's gonna be next May again, afore mud season?" Benjamin Osgood was asking Daniel Foster.

"Don't know yet," the other replied. "Ask me next week."

Daniel Foster was the local weather prognosticator. He had an uncanny record for accuracy, as well as owning Conway Feed and Grain. The two combined to make him an important personage indeed.

Ben Osgood sighed and tugged at his lower lip. A balding farmer, he had courted Annie McDonnell, as she was then, before Liam

Murphy married her. Annie's forebears had emigrated from the glens of Antrim in the north of Ireland back in 1719, seeking religious freedom. As good Presbyterians they had been welcomed into strongly Protestant New Hampshire.

But Annie had a blot on her escutcheon. One afternoon she had entertained her new beau by reading to him from her family Bible and Ben had discovered, to his dismay, that her mother came from a long line of Donegal Catholics.

The religious tolerance of the Osgood family did not extend to Papists. Ben married someone else, and Annie eventually married Liam Murphy, who adored her and was clearly happier with her than Ben Osgood ever was with his wife, a repressed and judgmental Freewill Baptist.

When Ben was in Liam Murphy's company, he was inclined to suppress an envious sigh from time to time.

Liam was saying, "My wife Annie'd sure like to know how you predict the weather, Dan'l. She 'lows as how it'd be a right valuable skill for me to have for my ownself. Lord knows it's hard enough to make a livin' when the weather's with you. When it's agin you, a man can starve to death."

Daniel Foster smiled thinly. "Weather prediction is a valuable skill," he agreed, "and I make too much money sellin' my predictions to farmers like you, to start givin' away the secret. But that's just like Miz Murphy; alluz thinkin', ain't she?"

Liam glowed with pride. "She's got a good head on her. Reckon it comes from all those books she reads. I fetched her home a new one when I was down to Moultonborough. Thing called a Gazetteer. Tells about soils and crops and towns and history. Annie's interested in all that."

"Cain't think why," Ben Osgood interjected. "Woman oughta be interested in her house and her children."

"Annie is interested in 'em," Liam told him. "She plans to teach our children outta them books. But she says this here Gazetteer has a lotta information in it that'd be useful to a farmer. She'll read those parts out to me in th' evenin's. She'll read every word in that there book. She loves to read anything about New Hampshire and the mountains. She purely loves this part of the country."

Ben Osgood snorted. "Don't set much store by bookish women, myself," he said contemptuously. "My wife now, she's a good

Christian woman and she puts up good preserves. That's what a man needs." He tilted his cane-seated chair back and laced his fingers over his belly as if he were the final authority on women.

To himself, however, he was thinking, I wonder what it would be like to be married to Annie McDonnell? That busy little way of walkin' she has. And the quick smile on her. She's alluz thinkin' of somethin' to help Liam. Liam Murphy's not much of a farmer. Never been much of a farmer. He couldn't grow rocks in a field if Annie didn't keep a fire lit under him.

Bet she lights a fire under him in bed too.

His mind far away, Ben tilted his chair back farther, crucially misjudging the weight-to-angle ratio. The back of the chair grated against the wall, then the legs shot forward and deposited Ben Osgood, chair and all, on the sawdust-covered planks of the feed-store floor.

The other two men guffawed.

Ben, red-faced, scrambled to his feet. "There's a devil in that thing!" he said of the chair.

"Ain't no devil," Foster retorted. "You lean back too far, you fall. It's a natural law, and cain't no one go agin natural law."

With a sullen scowl, Osgood shrugged into his coat and stomped from the store.

"Man ain't got no sense of humor," Daniel Foster remarked.

Liam Murphy gave a lazy grin. "You ain't exackly famous for your sense o' humor either," he told Foster. "My Annie says you're as mean as a ruptured goose."

Lean and irascible, Foster was not inclined to take an insult from any man. But he was not offended by Annie Murphy's statement. Everyone knew she had a twist to her tongue. She also had exotic dark eyes that tilted up at the corners, and a ready laugh. Foster was perversely pleased to think she had spoken of him at all.

"Mean as a ruptured goose," he repeated, mouthing the words to get their full flavor. "Happens I am, I reckon. To them as gits crosswise of me." He sounded proud.

Unconcerned, Liam Murphy yawned and ran his thumbs under his suspenders, easing the pressure they were bringing to bear on his flannel shirt. Liam was easily the tallest, strongest man for twenty miles in any direction, and another man's temper didn't worry him much.

Nothing worried him much, as long as he had Annie. She did the thinking and the worrying for both of them.

"Reckon I better get on home myself," he remarked. "Days're closin' in. I like to be with the wife when the light's gone."

Such open acknowledgment of fondness for one's spouse was rare among Conway people. Privately, Foster thought Murphy was tied to his wife's apron strings. But just as no one wanted to make an enemy of the man who owned the feed store and predicted the weather, so no one would make fun of big Liam Murphy.

"Give the missus my regards," Foster said.

Liam got to his feet, stretched, scratched himself in both armpits, retrieved his heavy coat from its peg, then vocalized the all-purpose New England "A-yuh" and left the store.

Murphy had been the last man in the feed store that evening, aside from the proprietor himself. When he had been gone a suitable time, Foster ambled over to the front door. He looked up and down the dirt road that was called, rather grandly, Main Street.

No one was approaching from either direction. Lamplight glowed from the windows of the false-fronted hotel across from the store. Off in the hills, a hound bayed at the cloud-shrouded moon.

The darkness crouched among the mountains, waiting.

Foster shivered, crossed his forearms over his chest, and rubbed his upper arms to warm them. Then he stepped off the porch and walked around the store, fastening the heavy wooden shutters, known as Indian shutters, tightly over the windows. He went back into the store, shut and bolted the door, and barred the Indian shutters from the inside. A second set of interior shutters was then also closed and barred.

He took his rifle down from the rack behind the stove and lovingly cleaned it, squinting down the barrel, wiping the highly polished stock with a soft cloth, working the mechanism to be certain it was in firing order. Overhead he heard the creak of the floor that told him his wife was moving about in their apartment over the store. She would be putting his supper on the table. It was time to go.

He made a final round of the store, checking both shutters and door again.

Then he shouldered his rifle and climbed the stairs.

Meanwhile, Liam Murphy reached home. Home was a cabin that

had been built by his neighbors, according to custom, the week after Annie agreed to marry him. Not a town house, it was constructed of pine logs, well chinked, with two rooms and a sleeping loft. The house was connected to the much larger barn by an enclosed dogtrot. The barn had been raised first, of course, being the more important structure.

Liam lifted the latch, pushed the door open, and called a cheerful, "Annie! Where's my girl?"

"Ssshhh, you great ox, you'll wake the children."

"They abed already?"

"Of course they are. I put the baby to bed before the sun goes down. She's fretful without lots of sleep."

"I thought Johnny might still be up," Liam said hopefully. Seven-year-old Johnny was his father's pride and joy.

Annie bent to the fireplace, lowering the cast-iron pot on its chain to heat up stew for Liam's meal. "I couldn't keep that boy up forever, waiting for you." Her voice was brittle.

"Aw now, Annie, I was just down to the feed store, talkin'. No harm in it."

"No harm? Sometimes menfolk stay talking at Foster's till all hours."

"Not me," he assured her. He tried to put his arms around her. She pretended to avoid him, then yielded, letting him pull her tight against his chest. The bottom of his red beard brushed the top of her head, where the glossy dark hair was sleeked back into a bun.

With her nose pressed against Liam's body, Annie inhaled the familiar, beloved smell of him, the smell of male sweat and wool flannel and, on a deeper level, the fragrance of the stony soil he worked, permanently absorbed into his flesh.

Her voice muffled against his chest, she asked, "What way did you come home?" and immediately bit her lip.

"Same as I alluz do," he replied with the infinite patience of one who has been asked a question too many times. "Up the orchard road to Mason's top field, then 'cross Dalrymple's meadow."

"You didn't see any Indians? You didn't go near the rock?"

Liam laughed, a comforting earthquake of a laugh that rumbled out of his chest and into Annie's bones. "'Course not. I told you afore, I ain't scared of Injuns but I know better than to go near their sacred rock."

"That's good," Annie murmured.

But she knew her man. She knew Liam Murphy would not let anything dissuade him if he ever took it into his had to come home by way of Pine Hill. And he might just do it sometime, to prove he was not afraid.

As he sopped up the last of the stew with the last of Annie's buttermilk biscuits, Liam remarked, "Mason got a mighty fine lot o' hay outta his top field this year. He had a good barley crop too. Got the rain just right, and a dry spell for harvest. That man has all the luck. Wish I was him this year," he added wistfully.

Annie shook her head. "If everyone had to hang their troubles on a clothesline for the world to see, and you were told to pick one, you'd pick your own."

"Meanin' what?" Liam asked, amused as ever by his wife's sayings.

"Meaning Susan Mason told me in town last market day that her husband has a tumor in his belly Dr. Smith can't fix," Annie said. "She sat right there in her nice shiny new cut-under buggy, with me sitting waiting for you in our old spring wagon, and told me with tears in her eyes. So don't ever wish to change places with anyone else, Liam. You don't know what you might get."

When they lay in bed later, Liam's healthy snores shook the rope supports that held the ticking mattress. Annie lay open-eyed beside him, but it was not his snoring that kept her awake.

She was reproaching herself for mentioning the stone. If she kept on reminding him of it, sooner or later he would be perversely tempted.

"Keep your mouth shut, Annie Murphy," she whispered angrily to herself, drawing the patchwork quilt up under her chin. "You just keep your mouth shut."

But she was afraid she could not, any more than Liam could stop snoring.

# 15

*In the morning, Liam went off to*

help the Burbanks mend a section of their fence.

Johnny dutifully recited his letters for her, then

Annie set him to work sorting strips of rag to be

woven into rag

rugs. Each pile of strips was a different color, and he had to study the colors and match pale blue with dark blue, bright red with dull red. She gave Mary a sugar-tit and settled the little girl at a safe distance from the fire to play. Then she opened her book again.

Annie sat close to the window, letting the dull light of a grey autumn day fall across the page as she read: "During the long and distressing war with the Indians it required all the energy of the people of New Hampshire to save themselves from utter destruction. But the glad return of peace brought with it a desire to develop the resources of the infant state."

"Return of peace," Annie muttered to herself, glancing out the window to a stand of pitch pine beyond the house. Pitch pine was a valuable commodity; tar and turpentine were manufactured from such trees. But Conway people did not cut pitch pines. According to local legend they were protected by the Indians, who would be angry. The Indians supposedly made some sort of medicine from them.

Annie stared at the trees and thought of the income they could bring, an income that would enable her to enroll Johnny in one of the new academies springing up farther south. "Learning is power," had been one of Annie's father's axioms.

His words came back to her. She returned to the book. Perhaps within its pages she might find some sort of power to use against the persistent menace that—in spite of boasts to the contrary—continued to influence life in parts of New England.

She had intended to read the book straight through, as was her custom. Books were scarce and expensive and each one a joy to be savored and prolonged. But now she found herself skimming through the pages, looking for something . . . something . . .

Her eye was caught by an entry on page 172 and she stopped to read: "CONWAY, Carroll County." Annie's eyes danced. "That's us," she murmured to herself. "Right here in this book." She read on, learning that Conway was 72 miles from Concord, and the Saco River in this region was about 12 rods wide and an average of two feet deep, though it had been known to rise 27 feet, and in a few instances 30 feet, in 24 hours. The largest collections of water were Walker's Pond and Pequawkett Pond, the latter being 360 rods in circumference. Pine, Rattlesnake, and Green Hills were the most considerable elevations in the town, situated on the northeastern side of the river.

Then Annie tensed. She put her finger to the exact line and read more slowly, her lips shaping the words. "On the southern side of Pine Hill is a detached block of granite, or bowlder, which is probably the largest in the state—an immense fragment, but which doubtless owes its present position to some violent action of Nature."

There it is, she thought to herself. There's the rock.

But the Gazetteer gave no further information, none of the strange and bloodstained history of the stone.

Annie's shoulders slumped in disappointment. But she read on. "Considerable quantities of magnesia and fuller's earth have been found in various localities. The soil is interval, plain, and upland. The plain land, when well cultivated, produces crops of corn and rye. The upland is rocky and uneven, and to cultivate it with success requires long and patient labor."

Annie nodded. Indeed it does. A mn must be out from dawn till dusk, breaking his back with a mule and a plow and a sledge for the stones. And even then you can't be certain anything will grow. What if the spring is too cold or the summer too hot or the rains don't come? What if your crops survive, only to be destroyed before you can harvest them by an early frost or an early snow?

How did the Indians manage to do so well here? Annie wondered. They prospered effortlessly, compared to our endless labors. And they begrudge us the land still. This would be a good place if the soil was more fertile and the fields weren't full of stones and the forests didn't conceal lurking Indians.

"There are in this town 5 hotels, 10 stores, 1 lathe manufactory, and 1 paper mill," she read on. "The Congregational church was established here in 1778. The Baptist church was formed in 1796. There is also a society of Freewill Baptists.

"On the 1st of October, 1765, Daniel Foster obtained a grant of this township on condition that each grantee should pay a rent of one ear of Indian corn annually."

Annie shook her head. Daniel Foster's ancestor and namesake had been as tight with a penny as the current feed-store owner himself. One ear of Indian corn. Fine rent for a whole township.

"Number of legal voters in 1854, 458," the Gazetteer further informed her. "Value of lands, improved and unimproved, $171,597. Number of sheep, 1017. Domestic stock, 1660. Domestic horses, 267."

There ended the description of Conway. Annie gave a sarcastic snort. Five hotels, ten stores, and a paper mill sounded more impressive than it was. "It's easier to acquire a grand name than it is to keep freckles off it later," Annie said to herself. "People who read this book and come to Conway expecting to find a city are in for a shock."

She gazed out the window again, recalling how splendid the town had sounded when Liam described it to her during their courting days. But the hotel where they spent their honeymoon, which he had made sound like a palace, was cold and drafty and had one two-seated backhouse to accommodate all its patrons.

She had promised herself then that life would get better. She had dreams for herself and plans for the children she hoped to bear. "You'll have to push that young man of yours," her father had warned her. "Liam has a good heart, but he's too slow to catch snails."

Annie had pushed. She was still pushing. She urged Liam to consider new crops and new ways of planting them, she did her full share of farmwork and still found time to keep an immaculate house and braid bright rag rugs for the floors. She had persuaded her bemused husband to build an imposing pine bookcase for her growing collection of books.

She was not a woman to be intimidated by stony fields or lurking Indians. Or heathen idols disguised as boulders. No.

All at once, Annie was tired of worrying. She closed the book abruptly, stood up, and went to take her cloak from the peg.

"You, Johnny, mind your sister while I'm out. Keep her away from the hearth, and if she gets hungry give her a bit of buttered bread and some of that buttermilk."

Annie slung the cloak around her shoulders and gave a last look around her house, making sure everything was in order as she always did before going out the door.

"Where you goin', Ma?" the boy asked.

"I'm going to look a problem in the face, so I'll know it's not sneaking up behind my back. Now, you busy yourself counting the dried apples in those baskets while I'm gone. When I come home I expect you to tell me how many tens of apples we have."

The freckled lad nodded eagerly. He thought he was helping. Annie knew he was learning.

As she walked away from the cabin, she noticed the day was

relatively warm in spite of its overcast skies. "Almost like Indian summer," she remarked to herself. But the phrase brought a chill. It referred to a season of terror, the warm dry days that often followed harvest; days when hostile Indians swooped down to slaughter hapless farmers and steal their provisions.

"Such things wouldn't happen," Annie's father had firmly believed, "if the white men had tried to establish amicable relations with the Indians from the first. We treated them badly, though, so how could we expect them to respond except with savagery and hatred? Hatred is too often the result of knowing only one side of another person, Annie. Remember that, and be tolerant."

The only daughter of Jackson's only doctor, Annie had adored her father and taken his word as gospel. Then one spring day, two young men from the distant town of Conway arrived in the area to attend a wedding—and Annie met Liam Murphy and Ben Osgood. Within a year, she had left her father and Jackson behind.

How strange that such a trip, no more than a day's buggy ride, could make such a difference in one's life!

"Bad Injuns still come outta the forests to visit a big rock on Pine Hill," Foster's frowzy wife Tabitha had confided to Annie at her first Conway quilting bee. "They bow down to it like a heathen idol. Don't you never go near it, and when your children start to come, don't let them near it neither." She had dropped her voice to a whisper. *"That there rock eats babies."*

Annie had responded with a burst of disbelieving laughter, making an enemy of Tabitha Foster.

In the years since, however, Annie had realized just how thoroughly locals avoided the boulder on Pine Hill. In time an amorphous fear had begun to infect her, as if transmitted subliminally; fear of the rock she never saw, fear of the close-crowding forests, fear of the wind howling with an inhuman voice from atop distant, brooding Mount Washington.

In a way no one could express, Conway seemed haunted by some malign montane presence as the village of Jackson had never been, though Jackson was a remote community high in the mountains and Conway was a bustling farming town in the Saco River valley.

Annie had grown accustomed to the local paranoia, yet some part of her mind never ceased to question and resent it. Annie McDonnell Murphy had not been raised to be a fearful person.

On this grey autumn day she was at last marching resolutely to face what she perceived to be the source of the fear, and put it to rest. Her spine was ramrod straight with determination. She crossed two stubbled fields, climbed over a stile, then made her way along a meandering livestock trail winding through dense stands of brittle, dying sumac.

Pine Hill lay between the Murphy farmstead and Conway town. Deliberately avoiding the vicinity of the stone made the journey to and from town longer.

With the loving attention of one who is delighted by scenery, Annie had explored most of the area beyond the farm before her babies had started coming. But she had never visited Pine Hill. Still, she knew where it was: a short distance above the Portland road.

The path she was following disappeared in a trampled mire of dried mud and cow dung. She paused and cocked her head, relying on an inborn sense of direction that was her pride. "This way," she decided, and set off again, briskly, whistling to herself.

Right where she expected it, Pine Hill rose above her, its slope crested with a mane of dark pines. She climbed the north side, picking her way through briars, and looked down from the top.

The boulder waited below. Its identity was unmistakable.

Annie stared down at it, impressed in spite of herself. The solitary stone had a presence. It appeared to be as tall as two men and as big around as a very large haystack. She started down toward it. She had stopped whistling.

The closer she got, the bigger it looked.

The boulder was as dull as the sky. Its weathered surface was grey and harsh, though as Annie picked her way toward it through clumps of sumac, she thought she glimpsed a lightning streak of quartz or mica, glittering.

"Nothing to be afraid of," Annie said aloud in a no-nonsense voice. "Just a granite boulder, like the book says. New Hampshire's full of granite. What makes you special?"

But the question had been asked for the sake of hearing a human voice speak. Anyone, looking at that particular boulder, would think it was special.

The boulder stood in solitary splendor. No granite outcropping supported it. The earth at its base was beaten flat, devoid of rocks or even pebbles.

What had the Gazetteer said? ". . . doubtless owes its present position to some violent action of Nature."

Not God, no. Nature. "Heathen idol," Annie said scathingly. "God had nothing to do with you. Sitting there like Mount Washington itself, glowering at me. Ignorant savages might think you're special, but I know you're just a rock, and a rock can't do anything *but* sit."

Emboldened by her own words she ventured closer, until she was standing beside the stone. The nearer she got, the larger it seemed to be. The surface of the boulder was abraded and pitted like an incredibly ancient face, but it was clearly inanimate. Harmless. Just, as Annie said, a rock.

Her lips quirked at the corners. "If that isn't like Conway people," she remarked, as her father would have done. "Scared silly of a rock." She could almost feel Dr. McDonnell standing beside her, though he'd been dead for five years. She could almost hear his practical, no-nonsense scoffing at pagan superstition.

Her mother, however—her mother with her Donegal-blue eyes and her fey sensitivity, her mother who secretly put a bowl of milk outside the door on All Hallows' Eve, for the "good people"—her mother would not have scoffed at the stone. Her mother would have signed the Cross the moment she saw the thing, something older than Protestantism rising in her. She would have known the stone for what it was: angry, aware. Malign . . .

Annie gave herself a furious shake. "Foolish woman! Anyone would think I didn't have the sense the good Lord gave me. I'm as bad as the Conway people, believing wild stories." She glared at the boulder. "You're nothing but a rock. A great big ugly dead-forever rock. Now that I see you, I can stop worrying about you. Be shut of you. I can tell Liam to come home this way any time he pleases, he'll just be under our roof that much sooner." She fixed the stone with a determined look. "Indians indeed. For good measure, we might just cut that stand of pitch pine and make some money out of it!"

To emphasize her words she gave the stone a defiant slap.

When her palm touched the rock, a jolt went through her body from her head to her heels.

Annie reeled backward.

Dazed, she struggled to keep her balance. She threw up her

hands, palm outward, toward the rock, as if to ward off . . . A wave of force hit her like an invisible wind, and she found herself hurled through the air to fall heavily into a clump of sumac some yards from the boulder.

She lay facedown in the sumac, smelling its drying, dying dustiness. Lights were flashing behind her eyes.

I've been struck by lightning, was her first thought. But there was no storm. The day was characterized by a soft grey overcast like mountain mist sinking into the valleys.

Annie swallowed hard. If not lightning, what . . .

Then she heard, or felt through the earth, approaching footsteps. Someone was coming toward the rock from its southern side, climbing the gentle slope of Pine Hill, pushing his way through the undergrowth.

The clump of sumac and the boulder itself concealed Annie from whoever was approaching. She could hear him, though. She heard the masculine grunt with which he deposited some burden at the base of the stone.

"Selah," she heard Daniel Foster's voice say, enunciating the Indian word clearly. It was a word Annie knew. It was both a greeting and a term of respect.

There was a pause, then Foster's footsteps moved away again, back down the hill, toward Conway.

She had been shocked, perhaps injured. Surely any woman in such a circumstance would have called out for help to a man she knew. But Annie Murphy did not call out. She lay as still as she could, hardly daring to breathe for fear he might discover her. She could not have said why. But she waited until he was long gone before she cautiously gathered herself and got to her feet.

Emerging from the sumac, she felt herself for bruises or broken bones, but there were none. She had been stunned but not hurt.

Stunned by what?

She advanced a few wary feet toward the stone. Nothing happened. It was as inert as it had first appeared to be.

She did not want to go any closer, but she walked around it in a wide, wary circle, watching it every step of the way.

On the downhill side she found the burden Foster had put down there. A bulky bundle wrapped in burlap lay at the foot of the stone.

She started to reach toward it. Then she drew back. Her curiosity was not strong enough to make her go close to the stone again, not now, not with her body still bruised and tingling from whatever it had done to her.

It had done.

The stone did it, she thought, not wanting to believe.

Believing.

She stared at its weathered face. "But I meant you no harm," she heard herself say in an aggrieved voice like a little girl's.

The stone watched her.

She knew, now, that it was watching her.

Her feet began backing away.

When they had carried her beyond a certain point, she whirled around and ran for home.

She did not stop running until she had almost reached the porch of the cabin. Then she slowed, stopped, stood half bent over with her hands on her knees and her heart hammering against her ribs, trying to catch her breath.

I can't believe I ran away from a rock, she thought.

I can't believe that rock flung me through the air either.

But it did.

It did.

Annie straightened slowly and squared her shoulders. Let whoever . . . whatever . . . was watching, see that she was in control of herself again.

With steady tread, she mounted the porch and went into the cabin.

Johnny lay curled up on a rag rug in front of the fire, sound asleep.

But there was no sign of baby Mary.

Annie saw again the burlap-wrapped bundle at the foot of the boulder.

*That there rock eats babies.*

# 16

*Tabitha Foster looked up eagerly*

when her husband entered the feed store.

*"Anything?"* she asked.

*"Nothing."* He shook his head.

**She came out**

from behind the counter, wiping her hands on a none-too-clean apron. "Did you see anybody?"

"I told you. Nobody."

"But people keep askin'!"

"Don't you think I know that?" he snarled at her. "I'm doing all I can. If you think you can do better, you try it."

"Ah, no." She shrank back. "No, Dan'l, don't say that."

"Then shet your mouth and don't criticize me." He shrugged out of his heavy jacket and went to take Tabitha's place behind the counter. "Anyone come while I was out?" he asked her.

She stood timidly in the middle of the room, looking as if she would dodge behind the nearest barrel at any moment. "Only Zeb Bigelow."

"What'd he want?"

"Same as the rest of 'em. He wants to know how bad the winter's gonna be, should he be orderin' . . ."

"What'd you tell him?" Foster interrupted.

"To wait till you got back and ask you."

"You tell him where I'd gone?"

"'Course not!"

Foster sighed tiredly. "Long trip for nothing." He adjusted the suspenders that held up his heavy woolen trousers, then looked down, frowning. He stooped to brush bits of dead stem and leaf from his lower legs. "I'm tired, Tabby. Fetch me a cup of coffee."

She scampered away, relieved to be out of his immediate presence.

Foster sat staring into the dark shadows in the corner of the feed store. His thoughts were far away. He did not even notice when Tabitha came back and set a cup of steaming coffee down beside him.

"Here, Dan'l," she said, waiting for him to become aware of her and dismiss her. She did not like to be around him when he came back from the boulder. Trouble sat on him then like a blackbird on a fence.

Tabitha knew her husband feared and hated the Pine Hill boulder. All local people did. It was not merely a focus of superstition. A real and bloody history was attached to it.

When Daniel's and Tabitha's parents were small children,

growing up in the Foster and Gray households a mile from one another, local men had fought off a band of marauding Indians. They had chased the savages to Pine Hill and the great boulder. There the white men had killed the Indians, every one. And scalped them for good measure, some claimed.

It was common knowledge that ever since, vengeful descendants of those Indians lurked in the wilderness beyond the town, never forgetting, never forgiving. A danger even when most other Indians in New Hampshire were long since pacified. Sometimes, it was rumored, they even returned to their sacred stone on Pine Hill to conduct blasphemous heathen rites.

People did not talk about it very much, not openly, anyway. Only Daniel Foster had the courage to drive his chestnut mare and his buggy out to Pine Hill on a regular basis.

Conway, as everyone knew, was the Fosters' town. Always had been. Even the massacre that had taken place on Pine Hill was not sufficient to make a Foster give up what was his, something his father and grandfather had claimed before him: the right to visit the stone and have prophetic visions of the weather.

So Tabitha's husband made his trips to the boulder, and from time to time returned with valuable knowledge. But it cost him. It cost him dear.

Tabitha gazed sorrowfully at his withdrawn, haggard face, then went back upstairs, unable to bear his presence any longer. When he had been to Pine Hill it seemed as if he came back poisoned, she thought to herself.

Foster continued to stare into the shadows. The cup of coffee cooled unnoticed beside him.

Meanwhile, at the Murphy cabin Annie's shriek of horror had awakened her son abruptly. He sat up on the rag rug, knuckling his eyes. "Mama?" he said fuzzily.

"Where's the baby!"

"Baby?" The boy gazed vacantly around the room. Then awareness returned. "The baby. Oh! I got sleepy, so I took her cradle up into the loft where it's warm and put her in it up there. Even if she got outta the cradle I knew she wouldn't try to come down those steps and get too close to the fire. She cried a while, then she went to sleep. I guess I did too."

But Annie did not wait for the end of his explanation. She was already scrambling up the steep steps to the loft.

As Johnny had said, the loft was the warmest part of the house due to the nature of heat rising. And there was baby Mary, sleeping peacefully in her pine cradle.

Annie stood looking down at her, waiting for her heart to stop pounding. Now why, she asked herself, did I think . . . ?

That bundle. That bundle Daniel Foster left at the rock. It was the right size to hold a baby.

A cold finger of fear traced up her spine.

For the rest of the day, she could not make herself settle to any task. She could not even read. She paced the floor, picked up her sewing and put it down again, half swept the floor and then propped the broom in the corner. Every sound from outside brought her to the door, looking out anxiously.

When at last Liam returned she hugged him even harder than usual.

"I don't smell dinner cookin'," he complained.

Annie made an impatient gesture. "I'll start it in a minute but I have to talk to you first." She glanced around to make sure Johnny wasn't listening. "Liam, you've lived here all your life; do you know of any children, any babies, who've disappeared in Conway?"

"What are you talkin' about?"

"Babies. Have any just . . . disappeared?"

Liam scratched his head. He suspected Annie was going to have to scrub his scalp again with yellow soap. Nits were in his hair, he could feel them. "Ever' now an' then some child wanders off an' ain't never found," he said slowly, remembering. "They fall in the river. Or perhaps the Injuns gits 'em. It happens. Why?"

"What about babies? Babies like our Mary?"

"Mary's old enough to toddle. I reckon she could wander off iff'n you didn't watch after her so good. But you never leave her alone, so I'd say she's safe, Annie."

I don't dare tell him I left Mary alone today, Annie thought. And I'll never do it again!

But what about those other children? God help us, what about the other little ones who have disappeared over the years?

Every rural community, as Annie knew, had its share of disappearances. Liam was correct when he said children wandered off and were never found. It had happened in Jackson too. And perhaps Indians occasionally did steal an unwatched baby.

But . . . but . . .

Annie's mother had loved to tell stories. In her soft, low Irish voice, she had recounted the tales her grandmother told her: Donegal stories, filled with rebel princes and magical women who could assume the shapes of seals. And one tale that had never failed to give Annie a delicious tingle of fear.

Crom Cruach, the terrible pagan stone of Ireland to whom infants had been sacrificed before the coming of Christianity.

Were there such stones everywhere in the world? Annie wondered. Were they thrust up by some violent action of Nature to serve as its avatars? Nature. Pagan, pantheist, Nature.

The same Nature New England farmers struggled with every day of their lives, trying to wrest a living from the grudging land.

"What're you askin' about this fer now?" Liam was inquiring. "You seem all het up."

With a mighty effort, Annie laughed. "Just my never-ending curiosity," she replied. "Seems like I heard Charity Allen say something at the last quilting bee about some baby that had disappeared, and I got to wondering."

"I don't recall no baby disappearin'. 'Course, one coulda got lost way out in the country and we might never hear about it. Lotsa folks live in the hills and don't come inta town from one summer till the next. It's even a right smart journey for us," he added.

Annie had expected to be able to tell him he could cut distance off that journey. But she said nothing.

Tardily she busied herself preparing a meal. If Liam was surprised to find his wife uncharacteristically unprepared, he did not say so. He settled happily into his chair and watched her hips as she bent over her pots and saucepans at the hearth.

Might be she's gettin' fretful, he thought. Women are mysterious. They take all sorts of vapors. Might be a good idea for Annie to have another baby, give her something more to think about.

Liam smiled to himself, watching his wife's hips.

For several days, Annie never got beyond shouting distance of the cabin. She even moved the hen boxes from the barn to the dogtrot, so she could gather her eggs without being away from the baby more than a couple of minutes.

But the fear rankled her. At night, when Liam took her in his arms and pressed his mouth on hers, she tried to respond. But her thoughts kept skittering off. Even when he sucked her breast like a hungry baby, his crisp beard brushing her flesh in a way that had always heightened her pleasure, she could not totally surrender to him and forget everything else. Some part of her mind insisted on picturing the boulder on Pine Hill.

"What's wrong with you?" Liam finally asked one night. He had returned to earth from his usual thundering, cataclysmic climax, only to find Annie lying wide-eyed beneath him, not sharing. She who had always shared, whose sensuality was his greatest joy.

"Nothing's wrong with me," she said quickly.

But he knew there was.

It can't go on like this, Annie decided. She felt as if the stone had moved into their house and was lying between them like a rock in the bed. Its shadow seemed to fall over everything she did.

Then the first snowflakes fell. A scattering like freckles in buttermilk, but a precursor of the blizzards to come.

"Reckon I better get on inta town and talk to Dan'l," Liam announced the morning of that first snow. "Find out how deep it's gonna be and how long it's gonna last. Might want to lay up more vittles in the root cellar. Ain't too late to buy more apples an' turnips if we need 'em."

"Don't go to Foster!" Annie exclaimed without thinking.

"What?" Her husband stared at her. "Not go to Dån'l? What're you talkin' about?"

But she could not tell him. The complicated layers of imaginings in her mind could not be peeled apart and exposed like the layers of an onion. And without a satisfactory explanation to give, she refused to hang on to Liam irrationally like a whining woman. She had too much pride.

After he had gone, she berated herself. Surely there were ways she could have described what had happened to her, and how she felt about it, without sounding like a fool.

I have to go back to the rock, she thought. I have to know if I imagined all that. Perhaps I did. I'll know, when I see the rock again.

But she desperately wanted not to go.

"Character is the sum of the choices we make in life," had been one of her father's favorite axioms.

She would go, she knew it. She would make the choice and go, rather than cowering at home.

This time, however, she did not leave Mary in Johnny's care. She dressed both children warmly and took them in the opposite direction from the rock, across fields to the Baldwin farm which lay northwest of the Murphy property. She asked May Baldwin to keep the pair for the day.

"You goin' inta town, Annie? If you are, I'd 'preciate if you'd get me a quarter bolt a' calico."

"I'm not going into town."

"You ain't?" May's slack jaw showed her surprise. For what other reason would a woman leave her children in someone else's care? "You goin' visitin' downcountry, then?"

Annie nodded. "That's it, I'm going visiting downcountry. I'll be back afore dark and fetch the children. Obliged to you, May."

"Say nuthin'," the other woman responded automatically. She stood in her open doorway, listening to the crescendo of noise rising behind her in her cabin as the Murphy children joined into the daylong riot of the Baldwin seven. Her eyes followed Annie back down the path toward the Murphy farm.

"Somethin' not right about her today," May said to herself. "Seems like she's poorly, somehow."

But Annie was as strong as three cups of hastily drunk strong black coffee could make her. She had been tempted to take a swig from Liam's jug of hard cider, but decided against it. She might need all her wits about her.

The sky was white with unshed snow. It would start falling again soon, she knew, and not stop. Not stop until the drifts reached the eaves of the house and yard-long icicles hung from the porch roof. Not stop until people huddled inside their houses like a race besieged, listening to the wind howl from distant Mount Washington.

How long? How deep? How cold?

Daniel Foster knew.

How?

Did the stone do things to him, as it had to Annie?

She had to make herself keep going toward it. At every bend, she was tempted to turn and run back. When she climbed the stile between two fields she teetered at the top, a breath away from going back down the steps she had just come up.

But she was Henry McDonnell's daughter and she kept going.

At last she saw the grim grey stone on the slope of Pine Hill, waiting for her.

But this time the stone was not alone.

Daniel Foster glanced up guiltily when Annie Murphy materialized on the crest of the hill above him. "What're you doin' here?" he called out, knowing she could see him.

She hesitated before answering. She must be very careful. She could not simply turn and run away; that would make him very suspicious. But she was dismayed to discover him there, and more dismayed by the fact that he carried yet another burlap bundle.

Foster was equally astonished. No local had surprised him here in all the years he had visited the place.

Of course, Annie Murphy was not really a local. Perhaps that was why she had not been sufficiently intimidated by the legends that kept others away and allowed Foster sole use of the stone.

She angled down the slope toward him. "I have as much right to be here as you. This isn't your land."

"Ain't yours neither," he pointed out. "And folks don't usually come here nohow."

Annie assumed a wide-eyed innocence. "Oh? Why not?"

"You know. You've heard the stories."

"You mean the local superstitions? My father raised me to pay no mind to superstition." She did not add that her mother had been a most superstitious woman.

"Ain't superstition," Foster insisted. "S'truth. There's a lotta death happened at this rock. Band o' dirty savages was killed here when my pa was a boy. That's why the Injuns in these parts are still hostile. Conway men killed a pack of 'em here, same as some men down in Albany once killed an Injun chief called Chocurua. Chased ole Chocurua to the top of his tribe's sacred mountain and killed him dead," Foster added with relish.

"I know that story," Annie interjected. "Chocurua was a gentle man who'd done the white settlers no harm, but a band of hunters killed him for the sport of it. As he was dying he pronounced a curse on his killers and their descendants. That was long ago, but my father still used to go all the way to Albany to treat people down there. They suffered from a strange complaint of the abdomen that eventually killed them. He used to make a long journey down there in his buggy, once or twice a year. The malady intrigued him. But he refused to credit it to the curse of Chocorua."

"Then your pa wasn't as smart as he shoulda been."

Annie bristled. "He was the smartest man I ever knew! He would have been smart enough to wonder why you're here, Daniel Foster. And just what sort of offering you bring to this pagan stone!" she burst out, too incensed to guard her tongue.

Foster hugged the burlap bundle against his chest. "None o' your business," he said sharply.

There was a recklessness in Annie Murphy. Side by side with her studied sensibility was a wild recklessness that had once made her thrust her hand into Liam Murphy's trousers as they sat courting in her father's parlor. In all his life, Liam had never imagined a woman would do such a thing. Not a nice woman. He had caught fire from Annie's fingers.

Now the fire was in Annie. As always, it surfaced when she least expected it. This time it made her grab for the burlap bundle.

Shocked, Foster tried to fight her off. But her small body concealed a wiry strength he did not expect, and an agility abetted by desperation. She wrenched the burlap out of his grasp and dropped to her knees with the bundle cradled in her arms, almost at the foot of the boulder.

Before Foster could stop her, she unwrapped the package.

Then she sat back on her heels and stared.

# 17

"Maize?"

*"Corn. Injun corn," Foster verified,*

*bending to rewrap the bundle.*

*"But . . . I don't understand . . ."*

*"'Course not. Ain't*

none of your business." As Annie stared up at him, Foster tucked the end flaps of the burlap neatly under the lengthwise fold until the package was secure again. Then he carried it a step or two, and set it down against the base of the stone.

"Selah," he said.

Annie was still sitting on her heels, watching him in bewilderment. "You give corn? To a rock?"

"A bowl of milk to the good people, the fairies, to keep them from doing us harm," her mother had once explained. Her mind made the leap from milk to maize.

"I think I understand," she said slowly.

"No you don't. And like I told you, 'tain't none of your business."

"But it is. I mean, I thought . . ."

Foster's eyes narrowed. "What did you think?"

"I thought . . . your wife said the stone eats babies."

To her embarrassment, Daniel Foster laughed. "'Course she did! I tell her to say that, same as my ma said it, and her ma afore her. Keeps people away. But you thought . . ." He glanced at the burlap. It was Daniel Foster's turn to be shocked. "Lordy, you thought I was bringin' *babies* to this thing . . . ?"

Confounded, Annie dropped her eyes.

"Well, I never," the man muttered. "Is that all you think of me, Annie Murphy? And I've alluz had admiration for you, with your book learnin' and your hard work and all. Now I come to find out you think I steal babies and give them to the Injun rock."

"I'm sorry," Annie said in a strangled voice. "I don't know what got into me, thinking something like that. I don't know how to apologize." She had made a dreadful mistake, she knew. Daniel Foster was the most important man in Conway. Directly or indirectly, almost everyone depended on him in some way, including her Liam.

Conway Feed & Grain was the only such store within twenty miles. If he refused service to anyone, they were effectively ruined. And if Annie Murphy was any judge of character, Foster was mean enough to refuse service to someone who insulted him as badly as she had just done.

How am I going to explain this to Liam? she wondered, sitting there with her head down and mortification burning through her body.

Daniel Foster was equally uncomfortable. He had spoken the truth; he had always admired Annie Murphy. Every man in Conway admired Annie Murphy. She was a breath of fresh air, a bright and laughing spirit. A sharp tongue, but a light foot and a twinkling eye that a man could not help responding to. Foster was horrified to think she believed him capable of so monstrous a crime.

"Ain't necessary to apologize," he muttered. "I can see how you thought what you thought, I suppose."

"But if it isn't true . . . I mean, why the corn?"

"You've found out my secret," Foster admitted. "The weather. You alluz wanted to know, didn't you? Well, now you do."

"The weather?" Annie was baffled.

Leaving the burlap bundle where it was, Foster came back and sat down beside Annie on the cold ground. He did not feel the cold. It was a warming experience, sitting close to little Annie Murphy. From this distance he could see the way her dark hair pulled loose of its bun and clung in tiny tendrils to the pink shell-shape of her ear. For the pleasure of sitting beside her—alone in the country, far away from prying eyes and wagging tongues—he would trade his secret. For that pleasure and more, perhaps.

"It started with my grandfather's grandfather. He was granted the township in return for—"

"One ear of Indian corn annually!" Annie interrupted. "I read it in my Gazetteer."

"A-yuh, that's it. But it was a funny sort of rental. The corn was to be paid here, at the Injun rock. Brought here and left."

Annie raised her eyebrows. She was aware of Daniel Foster's intense gaze on her, but his words were more interesting. "Paid to the Indians, is that what you're saying? But I thought the rental was paid to the local authorities, or—"

"Paid to the true owners of the land," Foster said. "We took their land, y'see, and we give 'em their own back for it. It was somethin' worked out in Conway long ago, and as long as my family abided by it, the Injuns never attacked us the way they did other places. But then there come a day when we forgot or the man who was supposed to deliver the corn to the rock got waylaid, or somethin'. Nobody knows what. Anyway, the rental wasn't paid. And the Injuns come outta the forest and attacked the town.

"The men got muskets and drove 'em off, finally. Chased 'em all the way back to this rock. And killed 'em here. Legend has it that the redskins' blood splashed on this stone.

"After that there were no more Injun attacks, but people didn't forget about the corn rental again either. In fact, my grandfather started bringin' more than just one ear, to be sure. And one day, after he delivered the rental, he came back sayin' he knew what the weather was goin' to do. He warned of a great storm fixin' to blow in on us. He begged people to get all their stock into their barns and prepare themselves, though there wasn't a cloud in the sky at the time.

"And he was right, Annie. A terrible wind blew up. Took roofs off cabins, blew down the front of the hotel, did all kinds of damage. But no one was killed, 'cause he'd warned people to hide in their root cellars and the storm blew over 'em.

"After that, people started comin' to him reg'lar to learn what the weather was likely to do. They were willing to pay money for it, and he was willing to take their money. But afore he could give a prediction he alluz had to visit this rock, and he alluz had to bring a gift of Indian corn."

Annie's eyes were fixed on his face. They were as bright as two stars. "Well, I never," she breathed. "And you still do it. You come here and leave the corn, and then . . . then what? How do you learn about the weather? Do the Indians meet you here and tell you?"

"Mebbe I ain't willin' to say," he replied. "Man should keep some of his business to himself, if he's anyway smart."

But she had to know. How could she bear it if she didn't know?

"I won't tell anyone," she promised.

"What'll you give me for it?" he countered with heavyhanded playfulness.

There was no mistaking his intention. Annie stiffened. "My thanks," she said coolly. "And the gratitude of my husband, who, as you surely remember, is a very large and powerful man."

Foster understood well enough. Her sudden icy dignity, combined with the implied threat, meant he had got all he was going to get from her unless he forced her.

Had she been a different woman in a different setting, he might. But the proximity of the rock restrained him. Its presence, glowering over them, drained his audacity. The thing always had scared him, he thought resentfully. And not because of the wild stories Foster womenfolk circulated about it either.

The situation called for caution. Liam Murphy would beat any man to a pulp for molesting his wife. Foster did not want Annie carrying a tale back to her husband. He bargained with what he had. "If it'll make you happy," he said ruefully, "I'll tell you about the weather. But remember you promised not to let it go any further."

Annie nodded agreement. But she stood up and put a bit of distance between herself and him, just in case.

Foster observed without comment. "The Injuns held this rock sacred because they said it talked to them," he related. "It was part of the earth, which in their way of believing things was also part of the sky and the weather, everything all mixed together. I don't understand it, heathen gibberish. But they believed it for centuries. They came here to touch that rock and have visions. In those visions, they saw what the weather was going to be like, and they arranged their lives accordingly. Bad winter comin', they went south. Mild winter, they stayed put. That sorta thing.

"My grandfather discovered by accident that when he touched the stone he had visions too. Sometimes, not all the time. He was afraid to tell anybody, afraid he'd be accused o' witchcraft. So he passed the secret down only to his eldest son, my pa, and he passed it on to me."

Annie asked, "Is it witchcraft?"

Daniel Foster shook his head. "I'm no witch, Annie. I can't do no magic. All I can do—sometimes, like I said—is see a vision. Kinda cloudy and far away, hard to see, but when it comes to me it shows me . . . it's hard to explain. It just shows me. In return for the corn."

"The Indians don't tell you about the weather?" she asked, unsure what he was saying.

"Not the Injuns. It's the rock, their sacred rock. My pa figgered bein' able to see visions from the rock was something passed on in the blood. Like inheritin' a good singin' voice. He figgered mebbe it came easier to Injuns than to whites, but us Fosters had a little bit of it. The visions ain't clear, but we can see 'em. Sometimes."

"Did you see a vision the last time you came to the rock?"

Annie's question surprised him. "Ah . . . no. I laid my hand on the rock but I couldn't feel nothin'. Like it was empty, somehow."

"Empty? What did you expect to feel?"

"What there alluz is afore a vision comes. A sort o' hum. You can feel it more'n hear it."

"Can you feel it now?" Annie wanted to know.

"I ain't touched the rock yet. I was just fixin' to when you come over the hill."

Annie gave the man a penetrating look. She would have dismissed his tale as foolishness, had she not received a mighty jolt from that same boulder. "I don't believe a word of it," she said emphatically, knowing how he would respond. "You're storyin' me, Dan'l Foster."

"I am not!"

"Then show me. Show me now."

"I cain't do it with you here," he muttered.

"Why not? Are you afraid it won't work? Are you afraid I'll know it's a lie?" she taunted.

Beads of sweat formed on his forehead. "It ain't meant for any but the Foster men, it's our secret."

Your profitable secret, Annie thought to herself. Maybe it is witchcraft. A lie is a poor substitute for the truth, but it's the only one anybody's found so far. If it is witchcraft, of course you'd lie about it to save your skin.

Memories of witchcraft lingered in New England, even in enlightened 1855. Annie was not certain she believed in witches— there was too much of her father in her for that—but she was not certain she disbelieved either.

Her mother would have believed.

And there was *something*. That boulder had thrown Annie through the air as if she were a piece of chaff.

Annie had to know.

"You've told me so much already," she said to Foster, "you might as well show me the rest. I promised you I wouldn't tell, and I won't. My word is as good as my husband's. What is it you do, Dan'l? Do you put your hand on the stone like this . . ."

She reached out as if to touch the boulder, encouraging him. She had no intention of making actual contact, however. The memory of the last time she touched that rock was sharp within her.

But Foster did not know she was only pretending. The stone was his, his secret, his family heritage though dark and filled with mystery. He would not share. With an inarticulate cry, he grabbed for her hand to stop her from touching the boulder.

Foster's sudden move startled Annie, causing her to dodge to one side. She slightly lost her balance, and inadvertently put out a hand to save herself.

Her hand touched the stone.

Later, thinking back, she would be able to recall the very peculiar sensation she had felt in that fraction of a second before her skin made contact with the boulder's surface. This time there was no jolt, no shock. Instead, she had felt her hand being irresistibly drawn as if by a powerful magnetic force.

Then the world as she knew it disappeared.

# 18

*She was in a high cold place.*

*Mountains rolled away from her. Peaks seemed*

*to be* below *her. She had a sense of vast distances,*

*as if she could gaze south to Massachusetts, east to*

*Maine, west to*

Vermont . . . yet she could not gaze. She had no eyes.

She did not need eyes.

Her entire being was a sensory organ.

She was aware of weight, mass, heat, fragility, temperature, color—an incredible spectrum of unimaginable colors!—texture, movement, upheaval, solidity, somnolence, energy.

Her awareness was total and generally unresponsive. She observed. She partook.

But she could respond; she knew that.

If there was a threat, she could respond.

She observed the vast mountain chain sprawled around her. It was rather like lying on a bed, looking down along one's own body. But she knew it was not Annie Murphy's body. It was not even female. Gender had become an irrelevant abstraction.

Many things had become irrelevant. Others had acquired all-consuming importance.

She partook of the passage of time as if it were the workings of heart and lungs and intestines within the body; building, repairing, altering, tearing down, redesigning, replacing, removing, a constant process of change that was necessary because existence itself was a constant process of change. But change could be a positive, or negative, force.

With an effort beyond comprehension, the tiny, stubborn seed of Annie Murphy's individual consciousness resisted absorption and struggled to assert itself; struggled to question and know.

What is this?

What am I?

I am in a high cold place.

No.

I *am* a high cold place.

Yes.

Partly.

She redoubled her efforts. With senses that were not mortal senses, she reached out and explored. She could not see, hear, touch, taste, smell. Yet she saw wind. She heard ice. She touched light. She tasted energy. She smelled time.

She was the massive patriarch settlers had named Mount Washington, and simultaneously she was the granite boulder, the glacial erratic Indians had worshiped on Pine Hill. She was Mount

Katahdin and chunks of amethyst in the hills above Kearsarge and grains of sand in the bed of the Saco River.

She was earth, she was stone.

Positive and negative forces coursed through her being, forming a circuit between earth and sky, connecting with clouds, streaking the air with lightning, striking into the silt of eons like the finger of God touching Adam's clay and bringing forth life.

She saw the solar wind and felt its song.

The seasons were hers. She knew, intimately, snow and sun, wind and rain. The least flake of snow was important to her because in its minute way the snowflake, frozen child of Water, would have an incalculably small but irreversible impact.

Every drop of moisture brought change, adding its impetus to the rivers that carved and recarved the face of the planet, swelling the seas that gave birth to the glaciers and gnawed away the land.

Every wind that blew drifted sand, eroded rock, resculptured the surface. Made a difference. Was felt. Must be endured.

The entity in which Annie Murphy's consciousness was suspended was like a flayed giant. It had no layer of toughened skin to protect its raw nerve endings. Those nerve endings were bared afresh by every breeze and raindrop. Earth felt everything done to its body. The shifting of a single particle of soil was measured on the same scale as the shifting of the continental plates. Both affected the being of Earth.

Earth was aware and vulnerable. Every cell of its being was aware of its vulnerability to the forces that acted upon it.

Annie, linked with it, was aware.

The planet knew what winds would blow and what precipitation would fall. In its own self-interest, the massive totality of Earth was continually observing every weather pattern, assessing with the experience of eons what each change would mean for itself. Every change mattered. Every change altered the fabric of its existence.

Earth contained an instinct for survival proportionate to its mass.

That which was still Annie Murphy felt a thrill of terror. She realized she was somehow partaking of the consciousness of something infinitely larger than herself. At the same time, she also seemed to be trapped within various separate aspects of that entity. She was a mountain; she was a grain of sand.

Her terror mounted. In a few moments her identity must surely be stripped from her by sheer force. What had been Annie would be irretrievably fragmented, dispersed among a trillion particles of soil and stone. She would be lost in the ponderous indifference of a planet.

She knew the fear the dead might feel if their brains continued to function while their bodies disintegrated. The fear of being absorbed into the earth, made one with the darkness. Spinning away into infinity. Lost. Lost to life as she knew it. Lost forever.

She grew as cold as all the glaciers that had ever glittered beneath a polar sky. She was frozen with a fear no human could imagine, yet her consciousness had expanded enough to imagine it.

I am a cold high place, she thought with resounding horror. And I shall be here forever.

Then, bubbling up through her fear like a spring of bright water, came an unexpected wash of sympathy. She felt a huge and tender pity for the flayed giant that was so beautiful, and so vulnerable. The massive peak rearing its head through ice and thunder. The grain of sand, enduring.

This is my land, she thought.

My land.

Oh, my lovely land!

The nerve endings of her spirit intuitively recognized kinship. Her flesh had been nourished by this soil, ingested with the crops she had eaten. She was not separate from Earth. She was one with Earth.

Yes.

As she should be.

Yes.

And it was both terrible and good.

The boulder on Pine Hill had recognized in her the innate devotion to and sympathy for the land that characterized both the Irish and the Indian. The love of place in Annie Murphy had spoken to the stone, and the stone had answered.

Invisible lightning had flashed and a circuit had closed.

When she touched the boulder a second time it had welcomed her in.

Now she was Mount Washington, brooding above the clouds, whipped by gales no human could withstand. Glorying in its strength, grim in its endurance.

Now she was the boulder on Pine Hill, fearsome and holy . . .

# 19

"*Gawdamighty! Annie? Can you*

*hear me? Gawdamighty! Miz Murphy? Miz Mur-*

*phy! Talk to me! Gawdamighty!*"

*Daniel Foster feverishly chafed Annie Murphy's*

*hands. She was*

aware of him as from a great distance. He was a puny being, less than an ant, a thing of no importance, and he labored frantically over another thing of no importance.

Annie observed.

The boulder observed.

The woman's body lay prone on the beaten earth in front of the stone, with Daniel Foster crouching over her. His face was pale, his eyes were wild. He kept repeating "Gawdamighty!" like a prayer as he struggled to restore her to consciousness.

Annie/boulder observed with a vast indifference. Why would any being wish to spend a few flickers of eternity in a parcel of flesh, isolated from similar fleshly beings by a total lack of communal consciousness, doomed to pain and disease and a swift extinction?

Boulder/Annie watched and pondered these things.

Once Foster shot a glance at the stone. Fear frosted his face.

His efforts were pathetic, but the human impulse behind them touched that which had been Annie Murphy. He had meant her no harm. He was a greedy, penurious man who forced his wife to live above the store when he could have built her a fine frame house with a dozen rooms, if she wanted—but he was not an evil man. Just flawed. As all humans were flawed in their various ways.

As stone was flawed. Boulder knew about fissures and cracks that would break open under pressure. Boulder knew about fire and heat and crushing weight, bearing down, solidifying.

Annie's thoughts were merged with boulder's thoughts.

Foster felt her hands growing colder in spite of his rubbing. He sat her unresisting body up, head propped against his shoulder, and began gently slapping her face with is free hand. "Annie! Miz Murphy! Gawdamighty, your husband will skin me alive . . . Annie!"

The mention of Liam reached Annie in some far place. With an effort, she reached out. But it was very hard to break free of boulder. Boulder wanted to keep her, incorporate her heat and light into its cold self. Boulder remembered glaciers, and bitter, grinding cold. Boulder remembered being dragged over the earth by the ice until it formed a great gouge in the soil, like the trail left by a huge animal . . .

No!

Annie made a terrible effort and wrenched herself free. It felt as if every cell of her body was being torn from every other cell.

She screamed with pain and opened her eyes. "Liam!" she gasped.

Daniel Foster's pale face hovered over hers. "Thank Gawd," he breathed. "Are you all right? Talk to me, Miz Murphy."

She swallowed, then moistened her lips with her tongue. She tried to remember how to shape lips and tongue. But the only shape they would take was to make the name of Liam.

"We better get you home, Miz Murphy," Foster said anxiously. "Gawdamighty, I never meant this to happen. I told you not to touch that rock. Didn't I say that? You tell your husband I said that. You tell him I never meant you no harm. But you wouldn't lissen to me. You wouldn't lissen."

Annie fought with her vocal cords and finally managed to say, brokenly, "Not your . . . fault."

"Thank Gawd you admit that! Well, come on now, let's see if we can get you on your feet and to home. Can you stand up?"

"I . . . think so." She was beginning to feel a little more at home in her body. But it was a strange sensation. Her body was so small. And so liquid!

It had the gift of movement, however. Movement was wonderful, miraculous! Just to be able to lift one part of oneself from the earth by the action of bone and muscle . . .

Annie gave a delighted laugh. The laugh shocked Foster almost more than anything else. It seemed so out of place.

Maybe her mind was hurt! Who knows what might have happened to her? One minute she seemed perfectly all right, then the next minute she was lying flat on the ground, not even seeming to breathe, her body as rigid as stone.

He watched, baffled, as she experimented with walking, taking her first steps with all the uncertainty and joyful discovery of a baby.

One foot and then the next foot, Annie thought to herself. Lift them, move them! Move forward!

Her face was split with a grin.

Foster hovered at her shoulder. When she was sure of her balance she reached out one hand and pushed him away. "I can manage by myself."

"Are you sure? That was awful, Miz Murphy." Thinking fast he added. "Like you had some kinda fit or somethin'. Are you given to fits?"

With every beat of her heart, her thoughts were growing clearer. "No, Dan'l," she said firmly. "I don't have fits. Not ever. No one in my family has ever had fits. This was something else. You know that."

He cringed visibly. "I don't know what you're talkin' about."

"Yes you do." She frowned at him. "Now you stand aside, Dan'l. I can get home under my own power, thank you very much." She bit off her words precisely and forcibly.

"Are you sure? I mean, what're you gonna say to your husband?"

"Why should I say anything to him?" Annie replied coolly. She almost laughed again at the relief on his face.

But she knew she could not tell Liam about this. She could not tell anyone. It was impossible to describe. Besides, she could well be accused of witchcraft, the accusation Daniel Foster feared. What other explanation could there be?

But for the first time in her life, she was not curious. She no longer sought answers. Answers seemed . . . irrelevant.

Turning her back on Daniel Foster, she began climbing the hill toward home.

The boulder watched her go.

Daniel Foster watched her go.

Then he shook his head, slowly.

His most recent offering of Indian corn still lay by the stone. He slouched over to it and stared down. Then, warily, he reached out and touched the stone himself.

Nothing.

A cold rough surface.

No hum.

No pictures, however cloudy, in his head.

Nothing.

He was a skinny, angry man, standing on the side of a bleak November hill with his hand on a huge boulder.

He stood there a long time. Then with a grunt, he put his hand down by his side again and turned away, heading back toward Conway. He left the corn, however. Just in case.

He always left the corn.

And when he came back the next time, it was always gone.

Meanwhile, Annie made her way toward home. As she walked, her head kept filling with unbidden images. They swarmed around her like a cloud of blackflies. Sometimes she even raised a hand and brushed at her face as if to brush them away. But they returned, or some variant of them returned.

She saw clouds above . . . and below her. Heard wind change its course. Sensed ice pellets high above, ready to fall. At the same time she felt heat, cold, compression, erosion. Was aware of warm blood trickling over a stony surface. Sounds of screaming.

She shook her head again and brushed at her face. When she moved her hand away, she saw her dear, familiar cabin, just across the next field, and broke into a run.

When Liam Murphy returned home for his dinner he found his wife making biscuits. There was nothing unusual about what she was doing. As she did every day, she kneaded the soft dough, cut it into circles with a round tin cutter, dredged the circles in a little melted lard, arranged them two deep on the metal biscuit tray, and set them close to the fire.

"Someday," she had always said, "we'll have one of those big cast-iron stoves with ovens in it, like my mother's."

Liam paused in the door as he sometimes did, watching her work while she was still unaware of him. In a moment the draft from the open door would make the fire leap up and she would turn around, and smile, and come into his arms.

The fire leaped up but Annie did not turn around. She went on working as if her thoughts were a million miles away.

Johnny and little Mary hurried to their father, however. The boy clung to Liam's arm with unusual tenacity; the baby lifted her own chubby little arms in a plea to be picked up.

"I'm home, Annie," Liam announced, surprised she had not already come to him as well.

She glanced around with a start. For one heartbeat her face was blank, as if she did not know him.

Then the moment passed and she was in his arms too, the four of them joined in one big hug.

Yet throughout the meal, Liam could not help noticing the nervous way the children, particularly Johnny, kept glancing at their mother.

While Annie was busy with the washing-up, the boy approached his father. "Somepin's wrong with Mama," he said in a confidential tone. "Ever since she went visitin' this mornin'."

Liam called across the room to his wife. "Annie, you go visitin' this mornin'?"

"Not that I recall," she said, her voice muffled because her back was turned toward him.

"Tarnation, sugar, you can't go visitin' an' not recall! It's a right smart walk from here to anywhere."

Annie's shoulders shrugged dismissively.

Baffled, Liam turned back to his son. "What's wrong with your mama, Johnny?"

The boy shuffled his feet. "I dunno," was all he could say.

For the rest of the evening Liam kept a watchful eye on his wife. Most of the time she was herself, merry and bustling. But occasionally she seemed to stop, almost in mid-motion, as if she saw something. Or heard something. Then her eyes held a faraway look, and if he spoke to her, he had to repeat himself more loudly before she would answer.

"Are you feelin' poorly?" he asked several times. But Annie always insisted she felt fine. And she had not gone visiting. "I just took the children over to May Baldwin's for the day to give myself a little rest," she said.

The mere idea of Annie saying she needed a little rest was so foreign to her nature it worried Liam more than anything else.

That night in bed, when he reached for her, she felt as rigid as stone. "Annie?" he said anxiously.

She softened at once beneath his touch and snuggled against him in the old familiar way. Yet nagging doubts continued to gnaw at the back of his mind.

Something was wrong. Johnny knew it, even if he couldn't identify the problem. Even the baby knew. She would not stay on Annie's lap anymore, but insisted on getting down almost as soon as her mother picked her up.

Liam Murphy was not a particularly sensitive man, but his family was his world. The subtle disruption in the atmosphere troubled him.

He would have been more troubled had he known that, sometime before dawn, Annie had awakened beside him sweating with fear.

The dream that was not a dream had intruded upon her sleep and dragged her into another time and place. A cold high place. A peak—not Mount Washington, she realized instinctively—whose slopes were fragrant with dark pines. At the foot of the mountain was a crystalline lake that reflected the trees as if they were warriors gathered around its shores.

There were warriors.

No.

A warrior.

No.

A chief. A strong, noble man in his middle years, dressed in deerskins, with soft moccasins on his feet. Feet that knew every step of the way up the mountain. Running feet.

Pursued.

The Indian's breath rasped in his throat.

He paused once and looked back. The sun, low in the sky, cast bloody reflections on the still water of the lake. Between himself and the lake, hurrying up the slope after him, was a band of men carrying long rifles and shouting encouragingly to one another. "There he goes!" "Up there!" "Lookit him run, the old fool! After him now, git 'em afore he goes to ground!"

Chocorua's moccasined feet ran lightly up the slope toward the summit, hardly disturbing a grain of soil. The air was thin and sweet, like pure water. Nestled amid stony outcroppings were beds of emerald moss, soft as down, upon which a weary man could sleep. But he dared not stop. He ran on.

He left the moss and rocks behind and began the steeper climb to the utmost peak of the mountain. The earth knew his feet; they had made this trip many times before. Since his young manhood Chocurua had climbed the sacred mountain to sing his tribe's greeting to the rising sun.

Now the sun was dying in the west.

A gunshot rang out from down below, echoing and reechoing among the mountains. Then another, sharper, closer. Lead spang and spattered against stone a man's length from the running Indian.

They were playing with him. He was a sharp silhouette against the skyline above them, and the best shot among the hunters could easily have picked him off. But it was more fun to chase him and shoot close to him, keeping him moving, adding to his fear.

He heard their laughter below him.

Chocurua knew some of those men. He had sold them otter skins and beaver pelts, and made them welcome among his people as was the custom of his tribe. In hard winters, he had taken some of his own provisions to the white settlers, who seemed to have little gift for providing for themselves from the natural bounty around them.

On this day he had encountered the party of hunters by the lake, as he was stalking a deer. Although the chief of his tribe and a man with grandchildren, he was proud that he could still bring down a deer quicker than any man of his age.

But the deer he had chosen for his arrow had a fine set of antlers. The white hunters had seen it, too, and were in hot pursuit. They fired their guns but did not hit the deer and it bounded safely out of range. Then, seeing Chocurua, in their frustration they accused him of driving their quarry off on purpose.

When he protested his innocence they turned on him and attacked him in place of the deer.

They would kill him. He had no doubt. He had seen it in their eyes, hot with baffled bloodlust.

Knowing they would kill him, he had fled up the sacred mountain. Perhaps he might have eluded them if he had set off in a different direction, but he did not think so. They were young, some of them mere boys, and they had stamina and speed. So he had chosen to come to the summit to die; to give his life's blood to the mountain his people recognized as holy. It would be Chocurua's last and greatest gift to the spirits.

He could go no farther. The hunters were coming up behind him, shouting their triumph. At bay, he turned to face them. He lifted his head and began to sing.

The first shot slammed into his body. He staggered with the impact. He kept on singing. His voice rose through the clear air, chanting the song of the mountain.

The second shot hit him. It took all his strength to stay on his feet. He swayed, then felt the reassuring solidity of stone at his back. Gratefully, he let himself lean against the stone.

The song continued.

The hunters gathered around him in a circle, jeering. "Crazy old fool, stop that godawful racket!" one shouted at him.

The guns spoke.

His right foot was shattered. At the same moment a sheet of white-hot pain enveloped his left leg.

The hunters laughed. They meant to kill him by inches.

Chocurua had reached the end of the chant for the stone. According to custom, he should have begun again, singing through a precise number of repetitions. Instead he drew a deep breath and turned his head slowly, from one side to the other, so he could look each man in the eyes.

In a voice that did not quaver—with the stone at his back supporting him—Chocurua pronounced his curse. Upon his killers, their posterity, their habitations, and even their possessions.

Then he closed his eyes and, with a calm face, resumed the song of the mountain.

The shot that killed Chocurua blew his belly open.

Annie Murphy, in the dream that was not a dream, felt the impact of the shot that had passed through him as it thundered into the stone.

She felt his hot blood splashed across her face.

She screamed.

"Wha'? Wha'?" Liam sat up in bed, befuddled by sleep but already fumbling for the rifle he, like all farmers, kept within reach at night. There was always a chance of some predator attacking the stock.

Annie grabbed Liam and clung to him. She was shaking.

"What is it?" he asked more clearly. "Annie?"

"A nightmare," she mumbled. "Just a nightmare."

Liam was surprised. His wife was not given to having nightmares. In fact, if one asked him, he would have said she was the least fearful of women.

"What kinda nightmare, sugar?"

She shook her head and would not answer. What can I say? she thought. Can I tell him I became a rock and an Indian was shot against me?

Can I tell him how I became that rock?

Annie was an intelligent woman. She knew, in the year 1855, there were only two explanations. Madness, or witchcraft.

Neither was acceptable.

"It's fading already," she lied. "I don't remember. I s'pose I was just too tired, Liam. Lie back now, let's sleep. I'm all right, truly."

He lay down beside her again, but he was still troubled. There was something wrong with his wife, no doubt about it.

But what?

For the rest of the night, Annie fought off sleep. She was terrified of finding herself in another of the dreams that were not dreams. The memories of stone.

The morning came at last. She got up, red-eyed, the inside of her head feeling scraped out by weariness, and took the bellows from the hearth to blow life into the banked embers and build up the day's fire.

Liam was unusually reluctant to leave the house that morning. He kept finding small chores to do that enabled him to keep a watchful eye on Annie. Aware of this, she went out of her way to make everything appear normal. She kept her emotions under iron control and showed him a cheerful surface.

At last he had no option but to go out and tend the stock, fetch the water, chop the firewood.

Annie stood listening to the reassuring sound of his ax as he split logs in the barnyard.

She was surrounded with familiarity. The fire crackled merrily. The smell of good cooking permeated the cabin. Her children's playful chatter was peaceful music.

Everything was normal. She was Annie Murphy, flesh and blood and bone.

And stone.

It came upon her so suddenly she had no time to prepare. One moment she was reaching for the broom to sweep the floor, the next moment she was a slab of rock on the floor of a riverbed scoured by the sand the rushing water drove across her surface. She lay in cold and darkness as she had lain for centuries; as she might lie for centuries more. Or forever. Cold. Still.

She was back in the warm bright cabin, paralyzed with horror.

Johnny was tugging at her arm. "I ast can we have some buttermilk?" he said in a tone that told her he had already asked the question several times, to no avail.

With a guilty start, Annie recovered herself enough to pour out buttermilk for the children.

She was appalled to realize this could happen to her at any time, with no warning and no protection.

Was it a curse put on her by the stone?

If so, why?

What had she done?

She tried to think of her possible crimes, but could find none that would merit such a punishment.

Perhaps it wasn't meant to be a punishment.

Perhaps it was something that just . . . happened. Like the Fosters being able to touch the stone and predict the weather. Perhaps she, too, had a gift for communicating with the stone. With stones.

Just a thing that happened.

Suddenly she recalled a madman who had lived in the tiny village of Bartlett when she was a child. Her father had occasionally driven over to Bartlett to care for him when he injured himself. Annie remembered Dr. McDonnell saying at the dinner table the night after one of those visits, "It's like he lives in another world. Some of the time he's with us, some of the time he's simply somewhere else."

Was that man mad? Annie wondered now.

Or did he, like herself, truly have a terrible and unwanted access to a world beyond ordinary human senses?

She gazed in horror at her children. Foster had claimed the gift of dealing with the stone was passed down through his family. If so, would Annie's children inherit the curse that had befallen her?

Suddenly she grabbed up the baby, who had been happily playing at her feet, and pressed little Mary to her breast with such hungry urgency that the child began to cry.

"Mama, you're hurtin' Mary!" Johnny protested.

Annie quickly set the child down. "I was just hugging her," she said. She could not meet her son's worried eyes.

For the rest of the day, nothing untoward happened, to her vast relief. There were no more of the flashes of altered consciousness she dreaded. She could—almost—convince herself they might have been dreams.

Almost.

For the evening meal she decided to open one of the jars of preserves she had put up the preceding year. Preserves were stored in a cupboard in the dogtrot, where they would stay cool but were protected enough to keep from freezing. Annie loved opening the cupboard doors and looking at row upon row of glass-encased fruit, ruby and purple and amber, gleaming like the jewels of summer.

She chose a jar of sweet mountain blueberries, Liam's favorite, and took it back into the cabin. When she had pried up the disc of paraffin wax that sealed the jar, she held the preserves under her nose and took a deep sniff. Her senses flooded with memories of hot summer days shrill with cicadas, and long dark shadows sleeping under leafy trees.

"Mama!" Johnny, who had watched her alertly throughout the day, was scandalized. "You told us never to smell our food!"

Embarrassed, Annie put down the jar. She had felt an irresistible desire to enjoy a human memory. Stones could not appreciate the fragrance of blueberries; could not reminisce about sunny afternoons spent berrying with a small, freckled boy who put more fruit into his mouth than he ever put into his basket.

That was an Annie Murphy memory.

While she was preparing the boiled mutton and potatoes that would be their meal, Liam appeared in the doorway, clapping his mittenless hands together. "It's jus' startin' to get cold," he reported. "Been mild for a mighty long time now. Reckon we might not see snow till after Thanksgiving, for a change. Might be able to order a little less feed, make up for it with grazin'."

Annie turned toward him. Her eyes did not seem to see him, however. "No," she said in a strangely hollow voice. "Order the feed. Order extra."

"What're you sayin'?"

"The snow will start by the end of the week and not stop. Blizzard after blizzard."

"Where'd you hear that?"

She did not answer.

The next morning, Liam left his chores undone and went into Conway. His first stop was the feed store. Money was tight; he did not want to order extra feed if he did not need to, but he would spend the required fee to get advice from Daniel Foster.

Foster, however, refused him. "Cain't tell you, Liam," he said succinctly.

"Tarnation, Dan'l, cain't you give me some idea?"

"Nope." Foster's face was as closed as a spring trap.

"Why not?"

"Don't know," was the unhappy reply.

Daniel Foster had been giving that same reply to other farmers for days. By this time of year, he was usually able to make a surprisingly accurate prediction of the winter to come. But since Annie Murphy's first visit to the boulder on Pine Hill he had had no prophetic visions.

"Waal . . ." Liam Murphy drawled, rocking back on his heels, "reckon I better listen to Annie, then. She says we're gonna have one helluva blizzard afore the week's out. Then another and another, right on up to April with no letup at all, hardly. She says I oughta get all our feed and supplies in now, and I should order extra corn, bran for mash, blackstrap molasses . . ."

He went on, ticking off the list on his fingers while Foster listened with growing alarm. The feed-store owner was glad of the order, but dismayed to hear that Annie Murphy was now predicting the weather.

He had a dark suspicion as to how she was doing it.

Three days later a monster blizzard hit, well in advance of its usual season. By that time Liam had his stock in the barn, his loft crammed with feed, his firewood cut, additional flour and salt and thread purchased, carrots and turnips and potatoes snugly bedded in fresh hay in the root cellar, and was just doing a final check of the shingles on his roof when the first flurry began.

By the time he had come down off the roof and put his ladder away in the barn, the howling wind was so full of snow it was impossible to see more than a few feet. He returned to the cabin through the dogtrot and settled down in front of the fire with a sigh of satisfaction.

"Just made it, Annie. Thanks to you," he said. If she had been acting strange lately, it was forgiven and forgotten in the relief of the moment.

Other farmers were not so fortunate.

**20**

*The exceptionally early blizzard*

*caught most people unprepared. Livestock was*

*trapped in the open and frozen. Great drifts blocked*

*roads. Supplies ran low. People huddled together in*

*snowy siege, measuring*

the level of oil in their lamps and food in their larders and worrying.

At last the snow abated, but only briefly. During that period men hurried into Conway from outlying districts, telling harrowing tales of blizzard losses and clamoring for supplies.

An angry band descended upon the Conway Feed Store. "Why didn't you warn us, Dan'l?" they demanded to know. "Any time afore this, when there was a major storm a-comin', you've let us know."

"I didn't know myself, this time," Foster protested. But they were in no mood to be lenient.

"You've cost me!" Nathan Nesbitt accused. "You've cost me a heap o' money in dead livestock, Foster, and I won't forget it! Any other man wants to set up a feed store in this area, he'll get my business afore you!"

There was a mutter of agreement.

Grudgingly, the men placed feed orders with Foster against the winter to come. But he could feel the resentment in them. Three generations of Fosters had prophesied local weather with uncanny accuracy. Until now.

They would not trust Daniel Foster again. That source of income had suddenly dried up.

Yet Annie Murphy had known about the blizzard.

"Annie Murphy robbed me," Foster growled to his wife.

"How'd she do that?" Tabitha wondered. "She ain't even been in town since harvest."

"She robbed me," he repeated stubbornly. "And I ain't one to forget."

Yet how could he prove it? he asked himself. How, without revealing his own involvement, could he accuse Annie Murphy of knowing the weather through ungodly means? Any mention of witchcraft on her part would bring the same accusation down on himself.

Besides, he was not certain it was witchcraft. His father had told him, "It's a curse, boy. A curse on the Fosters for what my pa helped do to them Injuns. That there stone calls us out to it from time to time to remind us o' what we done, and at the same time it makes us see things we got no business seein'.

"But when a man is faced with two evils, he'd be a pure fool not to try to make a profit outta at least one of 'em," the elder Foster had concluded.

Throughout his manhood Daniel Foster had made a good profit, indeed, from the visions the stone caused. Now that profit looked like it was being taken from him by a woman from another place entirely, a woman with no claim to it at all that he could see!

He raged silently, wondering how to get his own back. His wife, noticing that his mouth had become a thin, hard line, avoided him. She knew her man. As Annie Murphy had said, Daniel Foster could be mean.

He had a whole long, hard winter to brood on his loss. The weather was too unrelentingly savage, the roads too badly drifted to allow him to go out to the boulder on Pine Hill. But once mud season set in with the melting of the snow, he would. He vowed to return to the stone every chance he got, until he caught Annie Murphy there, stealing from him. Stealing his visions. Then he would . . . he would . . .

He was not sure what he would do. He had the whole long winter to brood about it, though. And if he forgot for a moment someone was bound to come into the store and remind him. "You sure messed up this time, Dan'l," some man would say with the ill-concealed pleasure people take in pointing out the failings of others. "Lookit that snow out there. Heaviest since '45. And the earliest. How come you didn't know, Dan'l? Eh? How come you didn't know?"

Then his questioner would laugh a sly laugh at his obvious discomfort. And Foster would promise himself anew to be revenged somehow on Annie Murphy, when the snow finally melted and he could catch her sneaking out to the stone.

But Annie had no intention of ever returning to the boulder on Pine Hill. There was no need. From day to day, she knew what the weather was going to do before she opened her eyes in the morning. Her bones knew. The message was carried through them by the same energy that hummed through the granite of New Hampshire.

With the knowledge, came the visions.

Days might pass without one. Then, horrifically, just when she had begun to relax a little, she would find herself bonded with stone. With a mountain or a pebble or, occasionally, with the entire chain of the White Mountains themselves. In and of and with the mountains, her soul unwilling witness to geologic history.

"Annie's got very strange," a worried Liam at last confessed to his nearest neighbor, Ezekial Baldwin.

"How so?"

"She goes off, like. Into some sorta daze. Don't seem to hear me when I speak to her, don't seem to know what's goin' on for the longest time. Then all at once she's back."

"She's broody," Baldwin declared with the authority of a man who had sired seven children.

But though Liam watched Annie's waist hopefully, it showed no sign of thickening.

The long winter passed, punctuated by Christmas and New Year and the first eager references to sugaring-off. "When the sap rises," Daniel told Johnny, "we'll sugar-off."

The prospect was almost more exciting than Christmas. The boy remembered from former years the sound of metal tubes being banged into the sugar maples, the clank of buckets as they were carried around and suspended from the protruding metal, the slow drip of the running sap into the buckets, the incredibly sweet fragrance of the boiling sap. And best of all, the thrill of dropping a ladle full of hot sap onto unmelted snow and then eating the confection thus formed.

"When, Papa?" the child asked almost every day. "When is sugarin'-off gonna be?"

"Not yet, boy, not yet. Not till the thaw starts and the trees begin warmin' up."

"When will that be?"

"It's in God's hands," Liam said.

But Annie knew. She knew almost to the exact moment. Liam returned to the cabin from the barn one morning to have her meet him at the door, with one word on her lips.

"Thaw," she said.

"Not yet, Annie. It's fixin' to blow up another blizzard out there!"

She shook her head. "Thaw," she repeated.

The blizzard the sky had threatened never developed. A wind blew up the spine of the mountains, driving the clouds before it like strayed sheep. In the wake of the wind's passage the sun shone, the earth warmed.

Water dripped steadily from the melting icicles along the eaves.

It was the earliest thaw in a decade.

Liam looked at his wife with wonder in his eyes.

"Go into town as soon as the road's passable," Annie told him.

"Order your seed, you'll be able to plant. Mud season's not going to last long this year."

She could feel it; could feel the heat in the stone underlying New Hampshire, knew the snow would melt and run off and the earth would dry early, ready for the seed.

When Liam entered the Conway Feed Store a surprised Foster greeted him with, "Didn't 'spect to see you for a while yet, Murphy."

"Wanna order seed now," Liam replied. "Brought the wagon. Gonna be plantin' soon."

The men gathered around the potbellied stove laughed. "You're soft in the head," one told him. "It's way too soon, we'll be wadin' in mud a while yet."

"Nope. Annie says get ready to plant."

Foster did not laugh. He sold Liam the seed. There was something cold and angry behind his eyes, however.

The viscous New Hampshire mud firmed, and in that brief but glorious season between the mud and the coming of the black flies and mosquitoes, Liam Murphy planted his crops before anyone else. His harvest would be the first to market, commanding the best prices.

No one would laugh at him anymore.

"I reckon I'm gonna be able to build a reg'lar second story on this house, 'stead of just a sleepin' loft," Liam told Annie proudly. "Have us a coupla bedrooms up there. Mebbe even put a pump inside so you can have runnin' water indoors for your cookin'."

She smiled wanly. "That'll be nice."

"Nice! It's what I alluz meant to do, give you as good a house as your pa had in Jackson. Better, even. Give you the finest house in the Saco Valley, you'll see."

"That's nice," she said again.

She was not the same Annie. The change was deeply troubling to Liam. Yet the change included an uncanny ability to predict the weather, an ability that was worth more than gold to any farmer.

The Lord giveth and the Lord taketh away, Liam concluded.

He never suspected his wife of witchcraft. She was Annie.

It was high summer before she visited the boulder on Pine Hill again. She did not want to; would have given almost anything not to go. But Liam's crops were in the ground and the rains had not come. With the passing of months, her tormenting vision had faded. Sometime around midsummer she had ceased to be certain of the weather.

Liam stood on the porch of the cabin and gazed out at the sky. Hot, blue, shimmering. Cloudless.

"You reckon we're gonna have rain soon, Annie?" he called over his shoulder to his wife. It was a question he was asking with increasing urgency. The dirt was powder dry. Crops were visibly wilting.

Annie stood behind him in the doorway. "I don't know."

"You've known all year, why don't you know now?" He turned to look back at her. For the first time, he noticed streaks of silver in her dark hair.

"I just don't." Annie went back into the cabin.

Liam took Johnny to the fields with him that day. As soon as he was out of sight, Annie bundled up the baby and carried her to the Baldwins' farm. "I need her tended for a while," she told May Baldwin, who responded with a lifted eyebrow but a willing nod. Folks did for one another. Raising barns or tending babies, folks did for one another.

Annie set out for Pine Hill with a pounding heart. I can't let Liam down, she thought.

Perhaps the stone would speak to her again, and in the speaking renew its gift.

Or it might kill her. She accepted the possibility. Anything with so much power might kill her. The journey on which it sent her might be enough to stop her heart—or leave her trapped forever this time, inside stone.

Yet Annie went on.

The stone eats babies.

Daniel Foster had said that was a lie.

But the stone had claimed victims; Indian victims. As the mountain in Albany had claimed Chocurua.

Maybe the stone will want my blood this time, Annie thought.

She tried to make her feet stop walking. But they were on the path now. They walked on in spite of her.

Up the hill that sang with summer. Toward the crest, then down. Toward the stone.

It waited for her.

It had no choice. No particle of earth, whether loose sand or compacted rock, could move by itself. An outside agency was required.

So the Pine Hill boulder must wait as the earth itself waited, for the action of wind and fire and water, for lightning and glacier and earthquake.

For Annie.

Annie Murphy was a better conductor for its petrified thought than Foster men had ever been. The aura of her energy was strong and clear, easily used to forge a connection with other cells of the earth. Mountains, rocks, pebbles, sand. Annie's energy could link the whole.

The stone, solitary, waited.

Annie stopped a few yards short of its weathered face. "I'm here," she said aloud as if to announce her presence to a sentient being. A sovereign being, with the power of life and death.

The stone waited. It could do nothing else.

Step by reluctant step, Annie moved closer. "Help me," she said.

The stone had no comparable concept for "help." To help implied physical action.

The stone could only wait.

"I should have brought you something, shouldn't I?" Annie said, tardily realizing. "Corn, maybe. But we don't have any crops yet. Be a while. Maybe not at all, if we don't get the rain. I need to know about the rain."

She took a last step forward, until she was close enough to touch the stone if she merely reached out her hand.

"I need to know about the rain!" she pleaded.

"I knew you were doin' this!" cried a triumphant voice.

Daniel Foster came running toward her. His face was as black as thunder.

"Stealin'!" he shouted. "that's what it is, Annie Murphy. You're stealin' money outta my pocket! The stone don't talk to me no more. It talks to you. You gotta make it stop, you gotta make it talk to me again. You don't need them visions!"

He skidded to a stop beside her—careful not to touch the stone.

She tried to give him a blank look, but Annie was not good at dissembling. "My husband needs to know the weather same as any farmer," she said.

"Give my gift back to me and I'll do his predictin' for free," Foster offered.

She looked at him sadly. "I don't know how to give it back."

"But you sure knew how to steal it, didn't you?" he accused.

"Not on purpose. Swear to God, I didn't do it on purpose. It just came to me. I touched the rock, and it came to me."

"'Twarn't meant for you. It's mine!" Blood suffused Foster's face. The cords in his neck stood out strongly above the open collar of his blue shirt. Annie was afraid he meant to hit her. She took a step back, away from him, away from the boulder.

He followed like a cat stalking a bird. "You give back what you stole from me."

"How?" At that moment Annie would have gladly given him the gift—the curse. To be rid of it forever!

A slow smile curled Foster's lips, though it never reached his eyes. His eyes were like two chips of flint.

"You don't never come to this stone empty-handed, that's what my pa taught me," he said. "Alluz bring an offering for the stone. If you want somethin', you gotta give somethin'."

Annie glanced around. She saw no burlap bundle. "What did you bring this time?"

His smile widened. "I didn't bring anything. You did."

"I didn't . . ."

"Yes you did. You brought yourself."

A shudder ran through Annie's body. I knew this all along, she thought with horror. I knew the stone would want my blood.

Abruptly, Foster dodged to his left, trapping her between himself and the boulder. "Come to me, pretty Annie," he said softly. He held out his hand. "Come to me. You owe me a debt. You're gonna pay it. We alluz pay our debts in Conway."

He's mad! she thought with horror.

Foster reached for her. She shrank back against the boulder, expecting a lightning flash, a monstrous jolt, a moment of unbelievable pain . . .

Nothing happened.

Annie Murphy stood with her back pressed against the rough surface of the granite and stared at Daniel Foster.

He hesitated, vaguely surprised. The length of the woman's torso was pressed against the stone, yet she showed no reaction.

"Don't you feel anything?" he asked.

"No."

"No hum?"

"No."

"Don't you . . . see somethin'? Anything? Kinda murky, like? Like clouds gatherin', and a sense of the weather about to change . . . ?"

"No," Annie told him a third time.

His face tightened with anger. "The stone's gone dead to you too, has it? You've damaged it somehow, that's what you've done. Fool woman, interferin' where you didn't belong. Outsider. I shoulda known, I shoulda . . ."

What he should have done, Daniel Foster never said. As he spoke, he reached for Annie's shoulder, and the moment his fingers closed on her the words froze in his mouth. He stood like a pillar of stone, mouth gaping, eyes bugging from his head.

Annie felt something run through her like a mighty river. Her body was covered with instant gooseflesh as her hair stirred and lifted. Vision dimmed. Foster's face was replaced by a silvery shimmer that flickered like the outer limits of consciousness. A vast nausea swept through her, followed by a sensation of cold as hot as fire; of heat as cold as ice. A diamond-lit memory of hurtling through the space between the stars . . .

She came back to herself.

She stood beside the Pine Hill boulder. The smell of sun-baked stone was in her nostrils. She could hear wind soughing in the pines on the crest of the hill. Somewhere a bird sang three crisp, sweet notes, paused, then followed them with an elaborate trill.

Daniel Foster stood unmoving. His face was the color of ashes.

Annie's mouth opened. But when she spoke, the voice was not hers. She felt incorporeal fingers fumbling through her mind, selecting words that then were spoken by her lips with a ghastly hollow resonance, as if emerging from some deep cavern.

"We," said the voice. "We."

Annie and Foster both stood rooted, unable to do anything but listen.

"We are . . . earth," the voice went on, gathering strength and certainty. "We are earth. You are only . . . the eyes and ears of the earth. But . . . you are think . . . ing, thinking, the earth's thoughts."

The voice fell silent. The silence swelled, occupying all space, holding Annie and Foster at its center like prisoners in a bubble.

"You . . ."—more fumbling with concepts in Annie's mind— "you presume. You must not presume."

The voice ceased. Annie had a sense of vast dark spaces and intense compaction; flickering fires; unbearable compression, unborn explosion. Whatever had spoken seemed to be moving away from her. Before it was gone, its mystery unexplained, she tried to probe its intellect as it had probed hers, seeking some common experience or emotion. She felt resistance. She pressed harder. The fire of her mind burned through the resistance. Something opened to her.

You are thinking the earth's thoughts.

There was no love, no hate. The entity was incapable of either, as neither was required for its survival. Likewise, it had no understanding of birth and death as humans understood those things.

But it did have a sense of justice. In the vast planetary scale all things must be kept in balance.

The entity was aware of construction and destruction. Of exhaustion and replenishment.

Of give and take.

It took. It gave accordingly, in kind, as it perceived with its nonhuman intellect.

What it gave might be accepted by humans as a gift or a curse, a bounty or a famine. But on the earth's scale, it was always a matter of maintaining the balance.

The earth did not care how humans were affected. They were specks on its surface, apparently unable to make a lasting impression.

Or could they?

Annie was dimly aware of some ancient memory, old even by the standards of the entity. Creatures, specks, long ago, striving, achieving, changing things . . . erecting crystalline forms that were . . . cities? Then catastrophe.

No. The idea was too far back, she could not grasp it. The

thoughts of the entity were slipping away from her altogether. She made a final effort to hold on. But all her focused curiosity could not prevail against the vast shifting of thought that was like a slipping of giant plates beneath the earth's unstable crust. The slightest echo of that shifting was enough to throw Annie to her knees, the link broken.

For a few moments her mind would not work at all. She was a body and nothing more. The heart beat, the lungs worked, but there was no conscious process to direct anything else.

She came to very slowly. Her eyeballs were painfully dry. She had not blinked for a long time. She was on her hands and knees, her vision fixed on the ground some eighteen inches from her eyes. The earth was beaten flat by generations of feet, but seen so close up it had a variety of textures. Annie was looking at individual grains of soil, minute threads of plant life, a tiny scurrying of black ants emerging from one hole and disappearing into another, a few crushed twigs, a pearly sliver of fossilized shell from some remotely distant past.

She blinked.

Her eyes watered profusely.

She swallowed, forcing saliva down her parched throat. With an effort, she lifted her head and looked around.

Daniel Foster was still standing in front of her, his own expression slowly clearing.

"Are you all right?" she said with a rusty voice that was at least her own.

The feed-store owner looked down at her in astonishment. "What you doin' here, Miz Murphy?"

"Don't you remember?"

He shook his head. "I don't remember nothin' since I got up this mornin'. Nothin'!" he repeated wonderingly.

He stared at the woman. She didn't look the same, somehow. He tried to remember how she should look, but his thoughts were cobwebbed.

Annie stood up. She was as stiff and sore as if she had been on hands and knees for hours. When she glanced at the sky and saw how far the sun had traveled, she gave a gasp of disbelief.

"I have to get home!" she cried. "I have to collect the baby and start dinner!"

Being able to say those words brought a peculiar relief to her, as if she were painting an image of normalcy over a window that opened onto an appalling vista.

Foster nodded, beginning to shift his weight from one foot to the other, trying to loosen locked joints. "A-yuh. You do that, Miz Murphy. I gotta get back to town myself. Cain't figger out what I'm doin' way out here anyway. Was I s'posed to go to Portland today? Where'd I leave my horse and buggy?" He turned and looked vaguely toward the road.

Annie glimpsed Foster's chestnut mare tied to a tree in the distance, waiting patiently in the shafts.

But there would be no buggy ride for her. She must walk across fields, and she would have to hurry if she was to be home before Liam and Johnny returned from the day's work, their bellies growling.

Wearing a baffled expression, Foster bade Annie goodbye and started toward the road. The blank in his mind was worrisome. But the more he tried to remember, the more solid his mental fog became. His brain was like a child's slate, wiped clean with one swipe of the cloth.

Everything pertaining to the boulder on Pine Hill was gone.

Annie could feel her own memories fading. She was aware that she had made a giant leap of understanding, but it was going from her as swiftly as the details of a dream fade with the coming of morning.

If I could tell it to Liam right now, maybe I could remember, she thought.

But Liam was not there. And Daniel Foster was hurrying away as if the hounds of hell were after him.

Annie circled around the boulder and began climbing the gentle slope of Pine Hill. Halfway to the top, she turned and looked back at the stone.

I wonder if it's lonely, she thought with a strange stir of sympathy.

No. Stones can't feel things like that.

Stones can't feel.

But they think. They are aware.

With an uncontrollable shudder she hurried on up the hill and through the pines, then began running for home.

I have to get home before it rains, she thought.

She ran under a blazing blue sky.

But by the time she was breathlessly mounting the Baldwins' porch to collect baby Mary, the first fat raindrops were splattering on the dry earth.

The creak of the porch floorboards brought May Baldwin to the door with Mary in her arms. Her jaw gaped open when she saw Annie.

"Lordy," she breathed.

Annie thought she was astonished by the rain.

"Much obliged," Annie said, taking the baby from the other woman's arms and turning quickly. "Gotta run or we'll get drenched," she called over her shoulder. "Much obliged, May!"

She sprang from the porch and pelted off toward the Murphy homestead.

May Baldwin stared after her in stunned disbelief.

Mary screamed and writhed in her mother's arms, making it hard to run. "Hush up now," Annie panted. "I know I scared you, grabbin' you like that, but we gotta hurry."

The baby kept on screaming.

When she reached the cabin, Annie let out a sigh of relief. As soon as she was inside she closed the door against the rising wind, and looked anxiously toward the banked fire. There was still a glow of coals; it would blaze up quickly once she got the bellows after it.

She set Mary down and the child, still screaming, scuttled away from her.

"Hush up, now!" Annie repeated. "A person would think you don't know your own mama!"

She busied herself with the fire, keeping one eye on the obviously distraught child. Raindrops were setting up a steady barrage on the roof. "Going to be a good soaking rain," Annie announced with satisfaction to the room at large. "Last all day and all night, most of tomorrow."

She could not say how she knew. It was in her bones, like her sense of direction.

The baby cried herself into a violent case of hiccups. Only then did she allow her mother to pick her up. Annie paced up and down the cabin floor, holding the child and crooning to her.

From time to time the child turned wondering eyes on her mother's face.

At last Annie put her down in the almost-outgrown cradle. For once Mary did not complain. She snuggled down gratefully as if returning to the security of the womb.

Annie busied herself preparing a meal. She went into the barn and used Liam's grindstone to put a fresh edge on her household ax. Then she went out into the yard and caught a hen that had grown too old to lay. She swiftly beheaded the bird, plucked and cleaned it, and had it in the pot in a matter of minutes. She was soon floured to the elbows as she made dumplings to go with the chicken.

"Sweet corn would be good with this," she decided. "And some green tomatoes, sliced thin and fried the way Liam likes them."

She whistled softly to herself as she worked. From the depths of the cradle Mary could not see her mother, but she heard the familiar, comforting sound, and relaxed. By the time her father and brother came home she was fast asleep.

Annie was putting the final touches on the meal. When she heard the thud of familiar footsteps on the porch, she called out, "There's dry towels there by the door. You men dry yourselves off before you come in my house, hear?"

The door creaked on its hinges. Annie turned around with a smile to welcome her menfolk.

There was a gasp of total horror.

Liam Murphy dropped the armload of firewood he was carrying in from the porch. The split logs fell to the floor with a clatter. At once Mary screamed from her cradle.

"What's wrong with you?" Annie demanded of Liam. "Listen to that, you've woken the baby when I just got her to sleep a while ago!"

Then she realized that both her husband and son were staring at her as if they had never seen her before. Johnny shrank back, putting his father's bulk between himself and his mother.

"What's wrong with you?" Annie asked again.

In a strangled voice, Liam replied, "What's wrong with you?"

"What do you mean?"

"Come over to the mirror, Annie." He took hold of her arm and led her across the room to her mother's oval mahogany-framed mirror, hanging in a place of honor between the two front windows.

"Look," Liam said.

Annie looked.

The rainy light coming through the windows fell softly on her face. But even its gentleness could not soften the image reflected in the mirror.

Bright, merry Annie Murphy was gone. In her place was a woman with the seamed and fissured face of a person twice her age. The eyes were ageless, and haunted.

Instead of sleek dark hair, the face peered from beneath hair as snowy as the peaks for which the White Mountains were named.

Annie's mind struggled to reconcile what she had expected to see with what she was actually seeing.

She raised a trembling hand to her head.

The figure in the glass did the same.

"My hair's gone white," Annie said in a disbelieving whisper. She turned toward Liam, seeking some sort of reassurance. "What happened?"

He could only stare at her. "I don't know! Don't you know? Good God almighty, woman, don't you know?"

Annie swung her incredulous gaze back to the mirror.

Her eyes locked with the haunted eyes in the glass.

In one dizzying moment she was sucked out of herself and plunged into a whirling vortex that spun her among a kaleidoscope of images. Incredible heat, the universe exploding, incredible cold, a sense of vast space, spinning, slowing, cooling, an infinity of time passing. A wrenching upheaval. Destruction, reformation. Great sheets of ice, grinding inexorably. Warming, melting. A swarm of motion on the surface. Crystalline shapes rising in clusters to sparkle in the sun.

Then cataclysm. Change.

Ice melting, seas rising. More motion, other construction. Volcanoes erupting like giant pustules. Lava flowing, seas boiling. Cataclysm. Change.

Faces! Faces that seemed to surface from somewhere deep inside Annie herself and imprint themselves over the images spinning past.

She saw, for one clear moment, a large tawny woman holding a seashell against a misty green background. Then she was gone. Countless other faces sped past, blurring. Hundreds, thousands.

Then another figure etched itself sharply on Annie's awareness. She saw a slim bronzed man with an abnormally small waist and almond-shaped, tilted eyes. He stood on the brink of a flaming abyss.

She wanted to shout a warning to him, but before she could he turned away, only to reappear against the misty green backdrop that had framed the tawny woman. Then he faded and was gone, to be replaced by another succession of figures rushing by in a measureless stream. Men, women. Faces. Faces with features Annie began to recognize. One had a familiar width of browbone. Another had a certain set to the shoulders. A third had, like herself, tilted eyes.

Family features, developing over the centuries.

Intuitively Annie understood. She was seeing connections. The people she was glimpsing as they were swept along by the river of time were her people. She was as much a part of them as sand and pebbles and boulders were part of the mountains.

The mountains! Suddenly they rose triumphant in her vision, brushing all else aside. Mount Washington, Mount Katahdin, Chocurua's mountain; vast and massive ranges whose names she did not know. The mighty mountains, enduring. Witnesses to the antediluvian past and the unimaginable future. Time viewed from the mountaintops. Eternity in stone.

"Some people worship mountains," Annie heard herself murmur in a faraway voice. "Some people see no difference between mountains and God."

Then she fainted in Liam's arms.

It was the first and only time in her life that Annie Murphy fainted.

Eight months later, when the Murphys' second son was born, people attributed the startling change in her to her pregnancy.

"Takes some women like that," Nellie Smith confided at the church's box supper. Nellie's husband was the local doctor. "My Zebediah says being in the family way changes a woman's whole system."

May Baldwin disagreed. "Not like that, it don't. It don't turn a woman's hair pure white between sunup and sundown."

"I don't think this is a proper conversation for a church social," Felicity Osgood said primly, pretending she was not listening avidly.

Ignoring her, Nellie went on, "Miz Murphy's doing fine now, my husband says. She's back on her feet and taking up her chores. Her hair's still white, but when he was out there the other day he said her wrinkles were softening. Nursing a baby softens a woman, you know. It was just such a big strong baby that having it was a shock to her body."

"I should think so!" Agatha Dalrymple exclaimed. "Having a sixteen-pound baby would be a shock to any woman!"

The Widow Mason giggled. "I alluz knew that Liam Murphy was a strappin' big man."

The others, except for Felicity Osgood, laughed outright.

Tabitha Foster commented, "The Murphys are gonna need a lot o' strong sons, the way things are goin' out to their place. That farm used to be piss poor, you know. Then last autumn Liam Murphy brought in the biggest harvest in these parts, and he's doubled his order for spring seed. Seems like he cain't put a foot wrong."

May Baldwin agreed. "That's true. He's alluz ahead o' the weather these days. How you reckon' he does that, Tabitha, when your husband ain't sellin' weather predictions no more?"

The question was asked with gleeful malice, as all present understood. Tabitha Foster kept her burning face lowered to her sewing as she replied in a low voice, "Don't know. Just lucky, I guess."

The others resumed their gossip. According to Elizabeth Wheeler, whose husband Matt owned the hardware store, "Liam Murphy's ordered a special new indoor pump all the way from Concord, to put by Annie's sink. Reckon there's gonna be more celebratin' when that comes."

"Take more than a new pump or a new baby to make a woman get over havin' her hair go white," Susan Mason said.

May Baldwin gathered spittle in her mouth and licked the ends of the thread she was trying to push through the eye of her needle. "I'd be right happy to see Annie perk up a mite," she told the others, when the thread was safely through. "She alluz used to be whistlin' or singin'. Sometimes when the wind was right we could even hear her over to our place. But ever since last summer—long afore she got big with that baby—she's gone quiet. Turned in on herself, like."

The other women continued sewing without comment.

Tabitha Foster did not think to remark that her husband's demeanor had changed at about the same time, as if some burden had been lifted from his shoulders.

The two had no connection in her mind.

*Everything that is, is alive.*

*Life did not come into this world. The life forms of the earth are a natural product of the earth, as the living planet is a natural product of the living universe.*

*Life in any form is part of life in every form. One, indivisible. The terrestrial spark is connected to the most distant star, just as the collective consciousness of the earth is one cell in the infinitely greater creative intelligence of the universe.*

*It is said, no one can know the mind of God.*

*Yet we are the mind of God.*

*And so we dance for joy.*

*We dance to the music of life, which ripples and shimmers across the universe. Even in the coldest depths of space, something is dancing the dance. Something is part of the music.*

*Every molecule of air on earth has its part to play in the whole. Myriad life forms dance in what appears, to human eyes, to be empty air.*

*Air is not empty.*

*Air is alive.*

*The angels of the air sing the songs of the spheres.*

# 21

**A *hot wind was blowing the White***

*People away. In the gathering silence, the Real*

*People met to dance the Ghost Dance and their dead*

*came alive again. Their land was repeopled*

*by ghosts.*

One of the ghosts was George Clement Burningfeather, who went to the reservation because he had no better place to go.

Throughout his life George had been suspended between two worlds. His name was indicative of his dilemma. His mother liked to claim that her paternal ancestors came over on the Mayflower, which was a lie. The Clements had been in New England for generations, however, as had her maternal ancestors, the Murphys. George's mother didn't talk about the Murphys very much. They were hard-working Irish farm folk and not suitably patrician from her point of view.

George's father was also a New Englander, but of considerably older stock. He was a relict of the all-but-extinguished tribe of Pennacook Indians, and when he had had too much to drink he claimed to be a prince of the tribe.

When she had had too much to drink at a cocktail party in Boston, Samantha Clement met him and believed him.

She thought he was exotic, and was soon showing him off to her friends in Manchester and Concord, expounding on the romance and hinting at the virility of the noble savage.

In point of fact, Harry Burningfeather was neither noble nor savage, and once his virility was blunted by familiarity, he tired of the white woman who had seduced him into marriage. He skipped out for parts unknown, leaving her pregnant with George.

Although the birth certificate said Burningfeather, Samantha raised her son to be George Clement. Period. She reverted to her maiden name and stripped the house of anything that could possibly remind her of her Indian interlude.

Except George.

Who had a questioning mind.

One look in a mirror was enough to assure the boy that his Amerindian features came from somewhere other than Mayflower stock. When he started going to school, other children who had listened to their parents' gossip were happy to tell him about his origins.

He came home crying, dirt-smeared, with a bloody nose and a black eye, and vehemently informed his mother, "I'm George Burningfeather and you shoulda told me!"

Samantha tried to spank it out of him. But there was a stubborn streak in the boy. The more she spanked, the more Indian he became. When her back was turned he sneaked into her room and used her lipstick to streak his face with warpaint.

From that point on, there was war between Samantha and her son. She provided him with a good education, smart clothes, a decent secondhand car when he entered college, and an icy reception whenever he was foolish enough to appear at home with his father's features stamped on his face.

Inevitably, he escaped as soon as he could.

George Clement Burningfeather attempted to escape to the stars.

Metaphorically speaking.

But by the time George graduated, the space program as such had run out of impulsion. With NASA as his goal, George had acquired a thorough grounding in the sciences, but no one was sending manned missions into space anymore. There were too many problems demanding attention on earth.

George had to settle for being an earthbound meteorologist, his only extraterrestrial explorations taking place among the wind currents and isobars in the atmosphere. His job was to try to figure out why the climate was going belly-up. Metaphorically speaking.

"We'll lick this thing, of course," his immediate superior assured him. George hated that term. It implied that he was T. Dosterschill's immediate inferior, which he was not. Except on payday.

"There's nothing science can't accomplish," Dosterschill frequently insisted with a bland arrogance that set George's teeth on edge. "Improved recycling techniques, improved substitutes for toxic chemicals. We'll get a handle on this. We have to. No one's willing to give up the way of life technology's made possible. Hell, I don't intend to start keeping my beer cold in a wooden icebox with a cake of ice either, know what I mean?"

George knew what he meant. What George did not know was how to make mankind's tardy efforts have any meaningful impact on a problem that was rapidly escalating. Recycling was not enough. Neither was cloud seeding nor improved methods of nuclear-waste disposal nor writing endless papers on the Greenhouse Effect.

Nothing science could do made an appreciable difference.

When the question was of academic interest only and there were very few academics left to ponder it, George went to the reservation.

It wasn't a Pennacook reservation. There weren't enough Pennacooks left to need one. It was simply the nearest Indian reservation George could discover through a cursory search in the deserted library, but it would do.

"Fuck you, Dosterschill," he said the day he hung up his identity badge for the last time in the echoing locker room. Dosterschill wasn't there to hear him. He had been one of the earliest casualties in their particular department.

The two black men, Hill and Webber, were still there, as was scrawny little Gerry Gomez, the one they called Whitesox. A couple of the women too—Mary Antonini and the blond with the long legs, the one the guys never believed was a natural blond. She was still at her desk when George walked for the last time toward the big glass double doors. "I won't be back," he called to her over his shoulder.

"Have a nice day," she said. The words sounded foolish but there was nothing else to say.

Given all the electronic information available, finding a reservation had been easy. Finding a bus that was still running in that direction was the hard part.

Finding any public transportation at all had become very hard indeed. But George didn't want to drive a car. He felt it would be curiously inappropriate to take a car with him in his flight to his chosen world.

All his life, George had had a strong sense of what was appropriate.

The bus rattled down an empty superhighway between expanses of parched earth. Heat waves shimmered on the pavement ahead. When George boarded the bus, there were two other passengers, but they soon got off. George moved up to sit behind the driver and stared over his shoulder at the mirages. If the driver saw them, he didn't say.

He didn't say much of anything, though George tried several times to start a conversation. At last the bus driver growled, "Look, fella, you got your troubles and I got mine, okay? I don't wanna hear yours, and I don't wanna talk about mine."

What happened to the friendly, courteous driver on the TV ads? George wondered.

For that matter, what happened to TV?

Not enough people around to produce television anymore. Not enough people to watch it, either, or buy the products it tried to cram down their throats, the glossy, elaborately packaged, outrageously trivial necessities that people had come to believe they could not live without.

Gone with the wind, George thought. The few of us who remain don't need the tube anymore.

The few who remain. Myself and the bus driver.

The great empty yawned beyond the smeared windows of the bus.

At last the vehicle shuddered to a halt. "Your stop," the driver said.

Shouldering his duffel bag, George got out. He hadn't brought much with him. A closetful of suits he would never need again had been left behind, along with the stereo and the CD and a superb collection of jazz. And an avalanche of polyethylene grocery sacks trapped between the refrigerator and the wall.

In George's duffel bag were two pair of clean jeans, T-shirts, socks, underwear, a Levi's jacket, a pair of cutoffs, a canteen, a compass from L. L. Bean, a Swiss army knife, matches, a dog-eared copy of *The Martian Chronicles* and another of *Tomorrow the Stars*, a small cache of emergency rations, a flashlight with spare batteries, a dop kit containing toiletries, and a string of rosary beads.

The rosary had been passed down through the generations of his mother's undiscussed Murphy ancestors, then buried at the bottom of Samantha Clement's cedar chest, out of sight and mind. When she died and George was going through her things, he found it and pocketed it on an obscure impulse.

He had briefly considering putting a packet of condoms in his duffel bag, then laughed ruefully.

How ironic, he thought. AIDS and contraception have both become irrelevant.

For a while he played a dark game with himself. Spot the Irrelevancies. Mink ranches. Renewal notices for magazine subscriptions. Sunlamps. Politicians' promises.

Insurance.

The broken line down the center of the highway.

When the game became too depressing, he stopped.

He stood on the heat-shimmered highway and watched the bus dwindle into nothingness. He doubted if the driver would bother to finish the run. For miles, the man had been driving with one hand and using the other to scratch furiously at the bleeding back of his neck.

George started walking. According to the directions, the reservation lay some two miles west of the highway. He squinted at the brassy sky. The glare was so pervasive he could not tell west from east. He paused long enough to take the compass out of his bag, consult it carefully, and clip it to his belt before starting off again.

He soon came to a road, of sorts; two deep ruts carved in the now hard-baked earth. The ruts were deep enough to break a man's ankle if he stepped wrong.

Sweat trickled down the back of George's neck.

He was thankful for his hat, a fine old silver-pearl Stetson from his college days, when he was a country-music fan. He had long since abandoned both hat and country music, but he had resurrected the hat again from the back of his closet. A Stetson kept a man's face and neck in the shade.

He shifted his duffel bag from one shoulder to the other, trying to remember if he'd put the Vaseline back in the bag. He'd smeared himself liberally with it before getting off the bus, covering all exposed skin . . . but had he left it on the seat when the driver called out his stop?

Feeling suddenly panicky, he threw down the duffel bag and began pawing through it. Must have done, must have done, must have put it back, wouldn't dare go out without it anymore . . . ah! There! He gave a great sigh of relief. The petroleum jelly was in his dop kit, with the white gunk for his lips and a bottle of aspirin in case he got too hot.

George put the white ointment on his lips and applied a second coat of Vaseline to his face and the backs of his hands. It wasn't as good as a real sun-block, but those had disappeared from drugstore shelves months ago.

When the reservation finally appeared on the horizon, it proved to be a disheartening straggle of ramshackle buildings with the dreary look of a place where dreams were born dead.

Well, what did you expect? George asked himself.

As he got closer he made out two rows of army-type wooden barracks sagging beneath unmended roofs. There was a store, of sorts, with rusted gas pumps in front, a porch, and a screen door permanently ajar, since the screen was too torn to be of any use anyway. Beside the store a few goats bleated in a barbed-wire pen, and some scrawny hens, half-denuded of feathers, scratched in the dust.

Beyond the barracks were some individual shacks with roofs of corrugated tin. The temperature under that tin must be enough to cook a roast, George thought. Surely no one tries to live in there, at least during the day.

So where is everybody?

His guts twisted. There might not be an "everybody." There might not be anybody.

He had just assumed this would be one place where . . .

George began to run forward in spite of the heat.

"Hallooo!" he shouted. He could hear the desperation in his voice.

There was a muffled response from inside the store. A tall, lean man came out onto the porch, shading his eyes with his hand. "What do you want?"

George squinted up at him. "My name's George Burning-feather."

"Burningfeather." The man came to the edge of the porch to get a better look. "Take off your hat."

George complied.

Instantly he was aware of the unshielded sun beating down on him like a weapon.

The man on the porch studied his features. "What tribe?"

"Pennacook. Well, half," George added, knowing dishonesty would be inappropriate at the end of the world.

"Half. Yeah. Well. I never heard of the Pennacooks."

"New England tribe. All gone now, or almost."

"'Cept you?"

"I'm the only one I know of."

"And you're just half."

"Yeah," George agreed, "but I'm alive. And I don't have any skin tumors."

The man said, "Then you better put your hat back on quick. At least until you get up here on the porch." He turned away and went back into the store.

George followed him with a profound sense of relief.

It took his eyes a few moments to adjust to the low interior light, after the fierce brightness of the day outside. Then he saw that the store was far from empty. A couple of dozen people sat, stood, leaned, lounged around its walls, occupying straight chairs, perching on boxes, propping their elbows against shelves. Men, women, children. A gawky teenaged boy. A little girl with huge black eyes and her thumb in her mouth.

The sight of the children gave George a jolt of joy.

The children had been the first to die. Out There.

Already he was thinking in terms of Out There and In Here.

"This here's George Burningfeather," the tall man told the others. "Says he's a Pennacook. New England tribe."

"How come he didn't go back north, then?" a man wanted to know.

"The database in our library didn't show any reservations in the part of New Hampshire I came from," George explained. "And since I was living down here, and this was the nearest one, I just sort of . . . gravitated here, I guess you'd say."

"Yeah," said the tall man. "We know. Getting pretty bad out there, is it?"

George shifted his duffel bag from one shoulder to the other, uncomfortably aware that no one had invited him to set it down. "Pretty bad," he confirmed grimly.

"Many left alive? We got a radio, but it's broke."

"Some. Not enough to keep the country running, though."

"How about the rest of the world?" another man asked. "White people dying everywhere?"

"*People* are dying everywhere," George corrected. "Caucasians are losing the highest numbers to malignant melanoma, but the various viral diseases are getting everybody."

"Africans and Orientals too?"

"Everybody," George said again. "There's more than enough death to go around, from a number of causes."

"What about survivors?" the tall man asked.

"The last reports I read said that aboriginal people like the

American Indians and the Maoris in New Zealand appeared to have the highest survival rate overall, but we don't know why. Could be genetic, could be pure accident. There aren't enough scientists left alive and working to find out."

"'We'?" said the tall man suspiciously. "You some kind of scientist too?"

"Not a biologist or a geneticist," George said quickly. "Just a meteorologist. I mean, I was. Out there."

"A specialist in the weather," one of the women said. "So you understand why it's gone so wrong."

"Nobody fully understands," George told her regretfully. "We only know some of the factors involved. Once the problems began multiplying exponentially, we—"

"Expo what?" someone interrupted. Indian eyes stared at George like polished stones.

"Faster and faster," he simplified, hoping he wasn't sounding condescending. "It all began going sour at once. Drastic changes in the climate, the expanding hole in the ozone layer, a decrease in breathable oxygen in the atmosphere—we think that might be partly the result of the huge number of trees cut down in the rain forests—it just piled up on us. Added to that there were so many pollution-related allergies. And the diseases. All those deadly new viruses, one after the other. People dying." George blinked as if to blink away a memory. "People dying," he repeated. "Most of the experts who might have come up with some answers died with the rest."

"Are you saying there's no one left alive who knows what to do about the heat?" a man asked, as if it was somehow George's fault.

"What to do about it? No. But we do believe it's an unnatural planetary warming caused by environmental damage."

"Caused by man," said the woman who knew what a meteorologist was.

"Yeah," George admitted. "It very much looks that way."

"But man doesn't know how to undo the damage." She was not asking, she was stating a fact.

"Yeah."

George looked at the woman with interest. Her speech indicated education. She was in her early thirties, perhaps, though he had no skill at assessing the age of an Indian face. Her features were unlike his, less rounded, more chiseled. A different tribe. One of the Plains Indians?

Sweeping his gaze around the room, he became aware of a variety of different types. This reservation was occupied not by one tribe, but by individuals from many.

As if reading his thoughts, the woman said, "We're all survivors, like you." Her face softened slightly, not enough to be a smile, but at least enough to mitigate the severity of her bone structure. "My name's Katherine," she said. "But people call me Kate. Kate-Who-Sings-Songs."

"And I'm Harry Delahunt," the tall man volunteered tardily. "That's Sandy Parkins over there, and Jerry Swimming Ducks and his wife Anne, and Will Westervelt—he's half Indian, like you and . . ." Harry continued around the room, introducing people. They variously nodded, raised one forefinger in token greeting, or just met George's eyes impassively. Their names were as diverse as their faces. Some used Indian names, others did not.

George rotated in the center of the room, acknowledging each person in turn. When the introductions were over he said, "Can I put this duffel bag down? I feel awkward standing here holding it as if I might have to leave again any minute."

Instead of replying, Harry Delahunt looked toward the far end of the store. Following his gaze, George saw someone he had not noticed before, sitting half hidden by shadows. It was an old, old man, with grey hair streaming over his shoulders like a waterfall, and a face fissured by age.

The face turned toward George.

He felt eyes looking him up and down.

The face nodded.

"Put 'er down," said Harry.

The duffel bag thudded onto the floor.

"You got any food in that thing?"

"Some candy bars. Beef jerky. Trail mix."

"Hunh!" Harry gave a contemptuous snort. "We don't eat that junk here. Kids might like the candy bars, though."

"Are you low on food?" George glanced at the well-filled grocery shelves.

"We got enough," Harry replied guardedly. "If we're careful."

Kate-Who-Sings-Songs said, "You're welcome to share what we

have." She looked toward the old man in the corner. He nodded. "If you're willing to eat what we eat," she added, smiling at George.

"That's kind of you," he said gratefully. He dug in the duffel bag and produced the candy bars. He offered them to the children. The gawky boy snatched his eagerly, but the little girl with the huge eyes stayed where she was, peering around her mother's skirts.

George went to her and hunkered down as low as he could get, holding out the candy bar. "It's real good," he said softly, slipping into the prevailing speech pattern. "But you don't have to eat it if you don't want to."

He continued to offer the candy bar. The little girl rolled her eyes up toward her mother, who gave a curt nod.

Slowly, shyly, one small brown hand was extended. Inch by inch, it reached toward George. He didn't move. He didn't even breathe.

The little fingers touched the shiny wrapper and stroked it. But she didn't take hold. Just stroked. Her eyes were huge.

"It's yours if you want it," George said.

All at once the fingers closed on the bar and snatched it away.

The people in the store laughed. Kind, fond laughter, the laughter of adults enjoying their children.

George felt a knot of tension loosen in his belly.

## 22

*The ice was broken. A man called*

*Bert Brigham offered George a can of beer.*

*"Ain't cold, of course," he said.*

*"I'm not used to refrigerated drinks anymore,"*

*George told him.*

He pulled off the tab and took a deep drink.

The others watched his throat muscles working.

When he had finished the beer, George put the tab back into the aluminum can and set it on the counter. "Thanks," he said. He could have drunk a second one, but he didn't ask. Nor did anyone offer. They had seen how he emptied the first can without stopping. They knew he was thirsty.

Everyone was thirsty.

The land was thirsty.

Parched.

George turned to Harry Delahunt. "You've told me everyone's name but his," he said, indicating the ancient figure in the corner.

Harry smiled enough to reveal tobacco-stained teeth. "He's Cloud-Being-Born. This is his reservation. Was. His family lived here. Most of 'em up and went off to the city to find jobs. Few came back, not many. His daughter, and then his granddaughter—that's her over there—stayed and took care of the old man. Reservation rotted around 'em. Then people began coming back. Not his tribe. Other people, like you, like me. He don't know where his tribe is. But this is his place, he was born here and he means to die here. So I guess he's the chief. And we're the Indians," Harry added with a humorless, eroded laugh.

"Cloud-Being-Born," George repeated. It was an evocative name. Poetic, he thought. He approached the old man respectfully.

The wrinkled face watched him.

He could not tell if the man was even breathing. He might have been carved from stone.

"How old is he?" George asked over his shoulder.

Cloud-Being-Born moved his lips almost imperceptibly. "A hundred and seven," said a voice like paper rustling.

George stared at him.

"A hundred and seven winters," the old man repeated. "You. Come close. Let me see you."

With a sense of awe, George moved closer, bending down so Cloud-Being-Born could see his face. Close up, he could also take a good look at the old man. He saw eyes sunken into deep sockets, a nose like an eagle's beak, rising proudly from between collapsed cheeks. A slash of a mouth, lipless. There was a smell of great age:

dusty, acidic yet not sour, not the sickly smell of the inmates of "convalescent homes" and "Golden Age nursing homes." Cloud-Being-Born's incredible antiquity was healthy.

"You," the old Indian said. "I see spirits in your eyes."

Harry Delahunt barked his strange laugh again. "Spirits is a right good idea," he said. "We got to welcome Burningfeather here properly!" Ducking behind the counter, he produced an assortment of smeared jelly glasses and a bottle with no label, containing what looked like water. A tiny portion was poured into the glasses, one for each woman. Then the bottle was passed among the men, starting with George.

He managed one cautious sniff at the bottle neck before he drank.

It smelled like nothing.

It smelled like rain, maybe. Or clouds.

He tilted the bottle back and took a swig.

His mouth filled with fire. Tears spurted from his eyes. Everyone laughed. Harry pounded him on the back. "Happens to everyone, the first time," he said. "That's the old man's firewater. It's some kinda powerful."

George felt as if his throat was being eaten by lye. But once the liquor hit bottom, a delicious glow began to spread through him, a sense of ease and well-being. He drew a gasping breath, coughed, wiped his eyes and looked around.

They smiled back at him.

These are my people, he thought.

"Dam' good stuff," he managed to say.

"Dam' right," Bert Brigham agreed. "Pass that bottle here."

The bottle was handed to each man in turn. No one took more than one swig before handing it on. Meanwhile, the women took tiny sips, glancing at one another with sparkling eyes. The little girl's mother hiccuped delicately.

The bottle reached Cloud-Being-Born. He accepted it with a grunt and took not one, but two swallows. Then he passed it back the way it had come.

Everyone, George included, took a second drink.

He was not quite as overwhelmed by the liquor the second time. "I'm glad I came," he said as he passed the bottle to Harry.

"Mmmm."

"I'm just not sure . . . why I did, though."

"Why you did what?"

"Came here. Why we all . . . came here," George elaborated.
No one replied.

The bottle was passed again. Then another bottle materialized
and at an unspoken signal from Cloud-Being-Born the second
bottle was emptied like the first. Heat faded; shadows lengthened.
George was vaguely aware of the sun setting, and someone—
Kate?—gave him some saltine crackers to eat with hunks of rat
cheese, strong and crumbly.

Later, he did not know how much later, he found himself sitting
on the porch in the dusk, dangling his legs in space. He was fuzzily
aware of people moving around him, coming and going. It did
not seem to have anything to do with him. From time to time a
bottle filled his hand. He drank. The roseate glow spread through
him.

He turned to the shadowy bulk of someone sitting beside him.
"Why?" he asked with the intensity of the very drunk.

"Why what?"

George struggled to remember the question, and why he had
asked it. "Why'd we come here?" he queried at last, peering
owlishly at his companion.

A voice answered from the far end of the porch. "The Ghost
Dance brought us."

That's important, George thought. That man is saying something
important. He half turned and tried to focus his eyes on the person
who had spoken, but he was having trouble with his eyes. They saw
double. Sometimes quadruple. He shook his head to clear it but
that set off a frightful clanging in his ears.

With a groan, George canted sideways until his cheek touched
the splintery planking of the porch floor. At least that stopped his
head from spinning. He stroked the planks with his fingertips.
Splinters . . .

Splinters of light dissolving behind his eyes, giving way to velvety
darkness. Darkness without stars.

Very much later, George awoke. He was totally disoriented. He
did not know where he was or even why he was. He lay in darkness.
He opened his eyes and it was still dark, but the thud of his
eyelashes striking his eyelids when he batted his eyes made him
flinch with pain.

He had the worst hangover of his life.

Something stirred nearby.

"I hope I'm dead," George muttered. "If I'm not, kill me, will you?"

"You'll be all right," said a voice. Female voice. George's bruised brain registered the fact without interest. Something hard touched his lips. "Drink this."

He sipped obediently, too weak to resist. The taste was like the way green grass smells.

George sank back into the starless night.

The next time he awoke, the dim grey light of dawn was streaming through a glassless window above his head. The air was almost cool. He was lying on a narrow cot, with a thin, worn cotton blanket pulled up under his chin.

His head did not hurt.

George sat up very slowly, waiting for the sledgehammer blow of pain that never came.

"Are you feeling better?"

Kate stood in the doorway, looking in at him. He realized he was in one of the shacks he had noticed the day before.

George turned his head gingerly, examining his surroundings. It was definitely one of the shacks; when he looked up, he saw the underside of a corrugated tin roof. Better get out of here before the sun hits that, he thought. Beside the cot on which he lay was a cane-bottomed chair. His Stetson hung from one of the chair posts. At the foot of the cot was a cheap pine dresser, decorated with a pitcher of freshly picked wildflowers.

Flowers?

Where did anyone find flowers still blooming?

"Where am I?" George asked, feeling like he was reading the lines from a corny old movie.

"Your house."

"*My* house?" George started to toss the blanket back and get up. Kate vanished from the doorway.

Air on his body warned him he was naked. Then he noticed his clothes folded neatly on the dresser beside the flowers. His duffel bag was on the floor at the foot of the cot.

"Hey, who undressed me?" he called out.

There was no answer.

Dressing thoughtfully, waiting for the hangover that never returned, George tried to recall the night before.

He remembered the bottle. Bottles. Oh yes, he remembered them all right. And somebody singing? Stories being told? Had he told some? About wanting to go to the stars, maybe.

He couldn't remember.

He found his wallet lying underneath his jeans. Citywise caution made him check its contents.

All there. Useless money, useless credit cards. Even the photographs. Someone had taken them out, probably to look at them, and put one back upside down. It was the snapshot of Stacey with her cloud of glorious red hair.

George blinked, trying not to remember the last time he'd seen Stacey. That was in the hospital ward, with her hair gone and her eyebrows and eyelashes gone and her face the color of old cheese. "Only family members," they'd said. But when he explained that he and Stacey had planned to marry as soon as she got her degree, a sympathetic nurse had relented and allowed him a few minutes. To say goodbye.

Hyden-Fischer Syndrome. One of the proliferating plague of viral diseases that had sprung up since the discovery of AIDS several decades back. When they first read about this newest one, Stacey had joked, "Looks like something's trying to exterminate the human race, George. AIDS, which we still haven't totally conquered, then NEEP, then AZ12, and now this Hyden-Fischer thing. What next, do you suppose?"

What next indeed.

He stared at the smiling face in his wallet, then folded the leather abruptly and jammed it into the hip pocket of his jeans.

He clapped the Stetson on his head and went outside.

Light and heat hit him simultaneously. Though the sun was barely clearing the horizon, it was already swimming in a sick yellow haze. The day promised to be another scorcher.

What next? George thought. I'll tell you, Stace, since you weren't here to see it. Lucky you. What next was a huge increase in skin cancer fatalities. The good old sun there did that, with the help of the hole in the ozone layer.

And if that isn't enough—if some few of us should manage to keep on living anyway—there's a joker in the deck.

We're running out of oxygen.

Bitterly, George surveyed the dreary landscape of the reservation before him. The earth was baked beige. The few straggling trees were dessicated. The only green remaining was in random clumps of weeds sheltered by the shade of fenceposts.

A lot of America looked like that, George knew.

A lot of the rest of the world was as bad or worse.

As his eyes accustomed themselves to the glare, however, he noticed a group of people on the far side of the barracks, moving around busily. Curious, he sauntered toward them. Then he stopped in astonishment.

They were tending a thriving vegetable plot. Hilled rows of well-worked soil alternated with narrow trenches. Men and women were hoeing weeds and staking up drooping plants. The children were bringing buckets of water to pour into the trenches.

Although he was no expert, George thought he recognized the feathery tops of carrots—he'd seen them in the supermarket—and heads of cabbage. Cauliflower, broccoli, pole beans.

Even a few flowers, like punctuation, at the end of each row.

Life was being coaxed from earth that was, elsewhere, refusing to nurture life.

George grinned. Trust the Indians, he thought. No machines, no fancy gadgets. Hand tools and sweat and kids to carry water.

He walked toward the nearest neat row. The woman called Kate, who was tying up bean runners, glanced up at him and smiled. "So you decided to come out for a constitutional."

"Yeah." He smiled back. "How the hell are you doing this?" He waved a hand to indicate the vegetables.

"The same way we've done it for thousands of years."

"No, I mean . . . seriously."

"I am being serious. We grow only what we need, and do as little damage to the earth as we can."

"That's all? You mean, like organic farming?"

"Even less sophisticated than that," she assured him. "This is purely subsistence level."

"You weren't born here," George said bluntly. "And you've had an education."

"Right on both counts. I'm Comanche, if you must know. Born in Oklahoma, educated in Chicago. Widowed in New Orleans," she added without inflection.

"I'm sorry."

"Why? You didn't know him."

"No, of course not, but . . . hell. I'm just sorry, that's all."

He felt his neck burning in spite of the Stetson. This woman made him uncomfortable. She was, he suspected, the one who had undressed him last night. The one who had left the flowers. And looked at his pictures.

"My fiancée died too," he said.

Kate nodded, her eyes on her work again. "White girl."

"Yes."

"Some white people are surviving."

"Not many."

"Not many people period," Kate said. She moved to the next bean pole, knelt beside it, her fingers working automatically, sure and deft. "You weren't telling us much we didn't already know, yesterday. Except when you said that aboriginal people seemed to be surviving better than anyone else. Is that true?"

"It's what I heard. Or read, rather. The report I saw named American Indians, Maoris, Inuit—"

"Alaska?"

"That's right. But I don't know how accurate it was, Kate. I read that report not long before I left, and we were hearing a lot of hysterical claims by then."

"Not long before you left," she repeated. "Do you think that's why you came here? Because you hoped you'd have a better chance for survival on an Indian reservation?"

"No," he told her honestly. Her dark eyes demanded honesty. "I've always thought of myself as an Indian, I suppose that's why I came. To be with my own at the end of the world, some romantic notion like that. Sounds silly, doesn't it?"

"No," she said shortly.

George went on, "Besides, if there is some gene-linked ability to survive our current disasters, it doesn't affect everyone. Indians and Maoris and Inuit are dying, we know that. Just not as large a percentage of them, perhaps. And I'm only half Indian anyway, so it might not do me any good at all."

Kate finished tying up the runners to the last bean pole and started to get to her feet. Without thinking, George reached out and took her hand. She gave him a swift, startled glance, then accepted, rising with a fluid grace.

He was concentrating on the way she moved when she said, "The diseases of civilization, like measles and chicken pox, killed vast numbers of aboriginal natives who had no immunities to them.

Wouldn't it be ironic now if the natives were the ones to survive the last, worst plagues of civilization?"

George forgot her grace and admired her mind. "Ironic indeed," he agreed. "Nice and neat and savage. But unfortunately, even they won't be able to survive the—" He bit off his word.

"The what?" Kate asked sharply. "They won't be able to survive the what? What didn't you tell us?"

"I told you. I said there was a decrease in breathable oxygen. I just didn't make a big point about it. There's no sense in scaring people when nothing can be done."

"Decreasing oxygen," Kate said slowly, her eyes widening as the message sunk home.

He nodded reluctantly. "Yes. We're running out of air we can breathe. Haven't you noticed that your lungs have to work harder than they used to? Don't you get tired easier, even over and above the heat? The people with weak lungs or emphysema or TB died quite a while ago, Kate. When the air is gone, we'll all go. End of story."

"When the air is gone," Kate said. He watched her draw a deep breath, tasting it with a sudden, desperate hunger. Her eyes met and locked with his.

"We won't die today," he told her. "Or even tomorrow. It'll just be a little harder to breathe tomorrow."

"But we will die. Everything that needs oxygen as we do will die." She searched his face for denial.

"Yes," he had to tell her. "Within the foreseeable future." The phrase had a new and awful meaning.

Kate stood still, breathing. Feeling the apparatus of her lungs work.

"Well then," she said at last. Turning from him, she walked down the row and picked up a hoe someone had dropped. "In that case, we don't have a lot of time, George. So we shouldn't be wasting what we do have. Here, take this and chop some weeds."

"After what I just told you, you still want to chop weeds?" he asked in disbelief.

"They won't chop themselves," she said briskly.

George shook his head and made an attempt at the weeds. But after a few efforts he admitted, "I'm afraid I can't tell a weed from a valuable plant."

Her lips twitched. "Some Indian you are. I'll bet you think milk comes out of cartons too. Here, give me that hoe before you do more harm than good. You might as well get a bucket and help the children carry water. Everyone who wants to eat has to work, and we need to finish tending the garden and doing the outside chores before the day gets any hotter."

So George Burningfeather found himself bustling between well and vegetable patch, carrying water. He watched Kate out of the corner of his eye. Stolidly pursuing an age-old task, she could have been any primitive female. Yet she had an air of confident self-possession that almost amounted to sophistication, as if her experience in the non-Indian world had altered her very genes, adding a new element. Yes, a new element. Kate was an amalgam. Earth and fire. And water—those liquid eyes.

Whoa, George, he told himself. Armageddon came and went and we lost, no contest. The world is ended, at least for the human race. There's no point in thinking the thoughts you're thinking. All that's left is to fall down and die, and that won't be very long.

Will it?

He looked at Kate again, calmly tending the vegetables.

And at the damned vegetables, green and growing. They did not have human lungs, they were a different life form.

Other life will inherit the planet we despoiled, George thought sadly. I wonder if they'll know, or care, how beautiful it was. Once.

His eyes stung. He blamed the pollution.

When the outdoor chores were completed, everyone gathered in the general store. It seemed to be a combination meeting place, day center, and dining room, with people willingly sharing a communal existence. Apparently other buildings were only used for sleeping.

I wonder where Kate sleeps? George asked himself.

Breakfast consisted of homemade bread, homemade jam, slabs of a peculiar substance Anne Swimming Ducks identified as goats'-milk butter, and instant coffee from a jar, the water boiled on a tiny camp stove.

"This is our second-last jar of coffee," Will Westervelt told George. "Don't suppose you brought some in that bag of yours?"

George said ruefully, "I didn't. I've been trying to give up caffeine."

Someone laughed.

"Why?" Harry asked. "Not good for your health?"

This time everyone laughed.

To keep the laughter going, George added, "I've given up smoking too."

They roared.

When the laughter died down, an ancient voice said, from the shadows at the end of the room, "No smoke. No pipe. How can you burn up your anger if you do not smoke it away?"

The people in the store met one another's eyes with brief, embarrassed glances, then looked away again.

"Cloud-Being-Born clings to the old traditions," Mary Ox-and-a-Burro, the mother of the little girl, explained to George. "The buffalo robe, the peace pipe, the Ghost Dance . . ."

Harry shot her a warning look. She fell silent.

"Ghost Dance," George said. "Someone mentioned that before. Last night?"

"Lotta things got mentioned last night," drawled a thickset man perversely known as Slim Sapling.

"And forgotten," added a man called Two Fingers.

But George persisted. "What is the Ghost Dance?"

Bert Brigham said, "Hell, I don't even like talkin' about this. Can't we just let it go?"

"We cannot forget the Ghost Dance," said the voice in the corner.

# 23

George felt Kate's light touch on his

arm. "Come out on the porch," she said in a low

voice, "and I'll try to explain it to you. There's no

point in upsetting people in here."

Feeling their eyes on him, he followed her out.

When he and Kate stood together under the sagging shingled roof of the porch, George asked, "Why did mentioning the Ghost Dance upset people?"

"It only bothers some of them, not all. But some people don't like being reminded that they were made to do something through magic."

"Magic? Come on now, Kate. I love Indian lore and tradition as much as the next person, but you can't really expect me to—"

"When things started to get really bad, Cloud-Being-Born was all but alone here," Kate interrupted smoothly. "Most of his family was scattered to the four winds. He had a daughter and a granddaughter and their husbands, that was about it. He wanted something more, so he worked with what he had. He taught the two men to dance the Ghost Dance. He danced it with them.

"It must have been very hard to make anything happen at first, with so few of them. But Cloud-Being-Born believed, and he made the others believe.

"The Ghost Dance is about communicating with the spirits of the ancestors. But Cloud-Being-Born used it to . . . to summon kindred spirits, I guess you'd say. Living kindred spirits. He used the magic of the Dance to reach out and call to Indians who'd left their ancestral homes and got lost in the white man's world.

"And it worked. People started coming to him here, seeking out this place. Two or three were his own relatives. The rest were just misplaced Indians. Like you, like me. Like Will and Harry and Slim and the rest. People who wandered in and didn't really know why they'd come.

"The old man turned some of them away. He never explained why. But the ones he wanted, he kept.

"A few weeks ago, when the radio broke past fixing, he told us we needed to dance the Ghost Dance again. I figured that with so many people dying, he wanted to save more while he could."

"Did you do it? Did you dance the Ghost Dance?"

Kate dropped her eyes. "The men did."

"What about you?"

"The Ghost Dance is for men. It uses their male power."

"Come on now! I'd say you're a pretty liberated woman, Comanche or not. Do you accept that six-steps-behind business?"

"No. But Cloud-Being-Born knows the Ghost Dance. I don't argue with him."

"If it ain't broke, don't fix it, eh?"

"Something like that," Kate said serenely. She gazed past him, sweeping her eyes across the drought-destroyed earth.

She looks at peace with this place and herself, George thought. Under the circumstances, that's damned near incredible. When did I last see anybody look that way?

Stacey for all her beauty had never looked at peace with herself. Like all their friends Out There, she had been charged with tension, anxious over her looks, her weight, her level of fitness, her achievements, her potential, even her ability to be multiorgasmic. Stacey had been many things, but never at peace with herself. Until she lay in her coffin, perhaps. But her family had kept the coffin closed at the funeral, so George would never know.

He dragged his thoughts back to the present. "So you're saying Cloud-Being-Born danced the Ghost Dance again, and I came as a result? Is that what you want me to believe?"

"Firstly, Cloud-Being-Born didn't do the dancing. He's too old. It must have been a terrific strain for him to do it that first time. Once he had a few more men gathered, he let them do the Dance under his supervision. But yes, you came as a result. I haven't a doubt."

"I do," George told her. "I certainly do. There's such a thing as free will, you know."

"I'm not denying that. I'm just telling you that some things override free will, or at least alter what we choose to do."

George was shaking his head. "I still can't buy it. And you haven't explained just how this Ghost Dance is done."

Kate crossed her legs and dropped effortlessly to a sitting position on the dusty porch. Mindful of splinters, George eased down less gracefully beside her.

"Since I didn't attend the Dance, I can't tell you the details," Kate told him. "But I do know there was fasting first and we built a sweat lodge out back. When the dancers were purified and ready, Cloud-Being-Born took them to a sacred place and had them go through the steps of a very ancient pattern, one his people have known for centuries. As I understand it, the pattern conforms to a pattern his tribe perceives in their own vision of the cosmos."

"Pattern." George screwed up his forehead. "You know, there was a time when I got interested in the Irish side of my family, just to irritate my mother, I suppose. I read a lot of books on Ireland. One of the things I remember was that the people used to do what they called 'a pattern' on religious feast days. It involved visiting some holy well, usually, and walking around it in a certain way."

Kate looked at him with light in her eyes. "Is the custom very old?"

"It predates Christianity, I think. The Christians just grafted their own saints and doctrines onto the pagan religion they found in Ireland. So the pattern may go back millennia, for all I know. There's been a civilization in Ireland for six thousand years."

"But in spite of an interest in Ireland, you chose to think of yourself as an Indian," she said. "Why, George?"

"Well, the way I look, for one thing. Black hair, bronze skin, features that aren't what you'd call Caucasian. But mostly I suppose I made that choice to irritate my mother even more than the Irish interest did."

"Did you dislike your mother so much?"

George considered the question. "Not dislike. I resented her because she resented me. It's a long story." He started to say, "I'll tell you some time," but then stopped. There might not be time for long stories. Time might have run out.

The sky was a hideous brassy color and the heat was intensifying. "Good thing we got your vegetables watered," he remarked.

"Yes." She smiled.

"But this Ghost Dance . . . what's the purpose of it, Kate? That's one thing you still haven't explained. You said old Cloud-Being-Born did it to draw people here, but why? Just to save them? And for what? It looks like we're all going to die anyway, of oxygen starvation if nothing else."

Kate's face sobered. "I honestly don't know. But I know the old man has a purpose. I have to be content with that."

There's her Indian passivity emerging, George thought. Then he checked himself. Are Indians passive? God knows I'm not. Are the Irish all drunkards? Of course not. When did we start accepting these stereotypes?

He thought again of Stacey, starving herself to be fashion-model lean because that was stereotypical beauty Out There.

Harry sauntered out onto the porch. "Well, old hoss, do you know all about the Ghost Dance now?" he asked George.

"Not really. It's still pretty much of a mystery."

"To all of us," Harry confided. "But the old man knows what he's doing. He's had a vision."

Suddenly George thought he understood. These people were sharing a common delusion brought on by stress. They were escaping an unbearable reality by putting their faith in the mystical visions of a senile old man. All over the planet, people were reacting to worldwide catastrophe in various ways. Plenty of them were losing themselves in religious mania, hyping up the adrenals, preparing to meet the end in a trance.

To meet the end. It all came back to that. To meet the end.

Why shouldn't American Indians prepare for the end by reverting to the faith of their fathers? It would do them no more or less good than any other.

George could not sit still any longer. He got up abruptly, clamped his Stetson more firmly on his head, and left the porch, seeking physical activity to ease his own tension.

Neither Kate nor Harry called after him to ask where he was going. They just placidly watched him leave.

He struck off aimlessly, not looking at anything in particular. Just moving. Using the body. Then he started watching the ground. The baked earth was scored with cracks caused by the heat, some of them wide enough for a man to put his foot into. They looked, to George's imagination, like mouths gaping for air.

Air. He looked up and saw the shimmer of a heat mirage in the distance. It floated, incorporeal, illusory, like a lake in the desert.

Desert, he thought sourly. The earth's turned into a desert.

The mirage sparkled ahead of him, as out of reach as a rainbow.

How long has it been since I saw a rainbow? George asked himself.

He could not remember.

He walked on, eyes fixed on the mirage. The sun beat down on his Stetson. He could smell his white cotton T-shirt, his sweat, his baking skin. I should have taken a couple of aspirin before I came outside, he thought tardily.

The sky was, as it had been for months, a flat-looking sheet of light with the blue long since leached out of it. It appeared to have no depth, no dimension. Yet when George looked at it more closely he discovered that the air was filled with tiny little squiggles, darts and flashes of color against that flat backdrop, minute figures liked coiled hairs wriggling and twisting in empty space.

What I'm seeing, George reminded himself, is really the imperfection of the human eye. Scratches on the eyeball, glitches in the optic nerve. Everyone has them.

Yet he kept on watching, with mounting curiosity. The longer he stared, the more convinced he became that he was seeing something of substance.

Dust motes?

Life forms?

Whoa, boy, the sun's getting to you! he cautioned himself.

But he was intrigued. The air looked alive.

It's full of angels, he thought fancifully.

That was the moment when he decided to turn back. Obviously the sun was getting to him.

When he reversed course he was startled to see how far away the buildings of the reservation were. They were only tiny dots in the distance. He extended his stride, anxious to be back in the shade again.

But the busy air kept pace with him, the tiny darting spiraling figures accompanying him, monopolizing his vision. It was like swimming through a school of . . . of . . . beings?

George stopped abruptly. He had a compelling sense that he was not alone. He turned around slowly, but in whatever direction he looked, he saw no human, no animal. Only the tiny images in the air. When he blinked his eyes, they were still there. Not on his eyeballs. Beyond. Outside. Around him.

Watching him.

An irrational fear overtook him and he began to run.

He pounded up onto the porch of the store, panting hard and dripping with sweat. The porch was empty. He stopped for only a moment, then went inside.

Cloud-Being-Born had come out of his corner. He was sitting on a stool just inside the door. He looked up as George entered.

"Come to me," the old Indian said.

George stood in front of him, still panting, feeling slightly foolish. What had he been running away from? *Air?*

"Let me look in your eyes," Cloud-Being-Born commanded.

George bent down. The old Indian's eyes met his for a long, searching look. Then the ancient man nodded, satisfied.

"This is the one," he said.

Straightening up, George looked beyond Cloud-Being-Born to the others in the store. Only half a dozen were there at the moment, the rest, presumably, being in their own quarters, in the barracks or the stifling tin-roofed shacks. There were no women in the store, George noted, automatically looking for Kate. But Harry Delahunt was there, and Two Fingers. And Jerry Swimming Ducks, and Slim Sapling, and the one called Westervelt whose first name George had forgotten, since it was not as memorable as an Indian name.

"What's he talking about?" George asked the men. "What does he mean, I'm the one?"

"He's been talking about doing another Dance," Harry said.

"Another Ghost Dance?" Maybe I'll learn what it is, George thought.

"Not this time," Two Fingers said. He was a short, swarthy man with only two fingers on each hand, obviously not the result of an accident but of some peculiarity of birth. "This one's going to be a new Dance. One we haven't done before."

"We were waiting for you," Cloud-Being-Born said.

George tensed. I don't want to be part of this, he thought. It's one thing to be an Indian, it's another to buy into all this religious ecstasy nonsense. I don't believe in it. I want a clear head when I go, it's going to be the last great adventure and I don't want to miss it.

"Count me out," he said to Cloud-Being-Born. Then he smiled, trying to mitigate the refusal. "I have two left feet when it comes to dancing," he added.

"It is not your feet we need," the old man replied.

George looked at the other men. Their faces were studiedly impassive. But he had an uncomfortable feeling that if he tried to make a break for it, they would stop him.

And where would he go anyway? Where was there, except this ratty, rundown reservation with its odd assortment of people loosely linked by heritage?

Very loosely linked, George thought.

"I'm only half Indian," he said lamely.

"You need not be Indian at all," Cloud-Being-Born replied to his surprise. "What we need is not your blood."

"Nor my feet?"

"Nor your feet."

"Then what?"

But Cloud-Being-Born said nothing else. The old man seemed to go off somewhere inside himself. Deep within the seams of his wrinkled face, his eyes filmed over. George was dismissed. The store and the other men in it were dismissed.

George stood, shifting from one foot to the other, feeling increasingly uncertain, until Jerry said kindly, "It's okay, he doesn't hear you anymore."

"Is there going to be another Dance?"

"Looks like it."

"What kind of Dance? When?"

"He hasn't told us yet. He will, when the time comes." Jerry seemed as oddly passive as the rest of them, accepting.

George felt a flash of anger. I can't do that, he thought.

But what choice do I have? I bought into this when I came here.

He was annoyed with himself.

He spun on his heel and left the store.

Since there was no place else to go, he headed for his shack. He kept his eyes on the ground, deliberately not looking at whatever might be swimming in the air.

Pollutant particles, he said to himself, trying to believe it.

The door of the shack was open, but the heat collected beneath the tin roof struck him in the face like a blow. He could not go in.

Turning aside, he headed for the only other possible sanctuary, the two rows of barracks. At least they were roofed with asphalt shingles, though in very bad repair. They should be marginally cooler.

As he approached the buildings he heard voices coming from inside. Someone was singing. He stopped for a moment to listen, recognizing Kate's voice.

She had been well named, Kate-Who-Sings-Songs. Her voice was a pure, clear contralto, deep and sweet as well water. She was singing a ballad George did not know, a song of loss and regret.

He opened the door and slipped inside.

Kate was standing in the center of the long room, singing with her eyes closed. All those who were not gathered in the store, including the children, were sitting in a circle around her.

A row of cots alternating with rusted iron beds ran down one wall. A few broken chairs were pushed against the other. At the end of the room was a single porcelain sink, with a run of rust down its backsplash, below the faucet. In one corner, a faded shower curtain half shielded a seatless toilet.

This is what they gave us to live in, George thought, an old anger rising in him. The people who seized our land and raped it for profit.

For a moment he forgot the other half of his family, the white half. Seeing the destitution of the reservation, he was pure Indian, as he had been pure Irish when he read the histories of colonial atrocities perpetrated on that race.

Kate finished the song she was singing and opened her eyes. She looked directly at him. "Hello," she said over the heads of the others.

"Hello," he replied with the same soft-spoken gravity.

She smiled then. "We have music every day," she explained. "Would you like to join us?"

Bert Brigham, who was seated nearest the door, moved over, beckoning to George to take the place beside him.

They were all sitting on the floor. No one was using the broken chairs.

George sat down. The air in the room was hot and still, but not as bad as it had been in his shack. And at least there was a roof to keep out the sun, though a few relentless rays made their way through the broken shingles and rotten boards beneath to illuminate dust motes dancing in the air.

George wanted to believe they were dust motes.

Someone suggested another song, another one George did not know, and Kate closed her eyes again and sang. George closed his eyes too, losing himself in the listening. Then the song ended and he heard her say, "This next one is for George."

Her smooth, supple contralto launched into a love song he had heard only once or twice in his life, in Irish pubs in Boston. "My Lagan Love." A song from Northern Ireland, incredibly difficult to sing. As he listened, George realized Kate must have been a professional singer . . . Out There.

He would ask her. He wanted to know more about her. He wanted to know all about her.

But there was no point. They would soon die.

The ballad flowed to its final, ineffably poignant lines:

". . . and hums in sad, sweet undertone
    The song of heart's desire."

George opened his eyes to find Kate looking at him. For a moment they were quite alone in the room.

Not now, George thought. Not now, at the end of the world.

He dropped his eyes, breaking the connection.

Someone else began to sing then, and one of the younger men produced a guitar and played an accompaniment. Kate moved from the center of the room to sit down with the others, though not by George. She listened with apparent keen interest, not looking in his direction again, and he felt a pang of regret.

The music session lasted for an hour or so. There were songs, some of them undeniably what George considered "Indian" music, others speaking of different cultures. Kate sang again after a while, this time a smoky rendition of "Walk on the Wild Side" in the best New Orleans tradition, affirming George's opinion that she had been a professional singer. He could just see her leaning against a piano in a top-dollar jazz club, carrying them away on the magical river of her voice.

By unspoken agreement, the group broke up after Kate's last song and began drifting away. Some of the women busied themselves sweeping the barracks and trying to make a presentable home of a place that could never be presentable. The children, denied the pleasure of playing outdoors, used the broken chairs to create a fort for themselves and began a rowdy game of Cowboys and Indians.

To George's amusement, it seemed they all wanted to be Cowboys.

"No takers for the role of Indian," he remarked to Kate as she walked past him.

She stopped. "Not exotic enough. Kids never want to be what they are."

"Did you?" he asked. Then, mildly embarrassed, he added, "We talked about me but not about you. I don't know anything about you, except that your husband died in New Orleans. Were you singing in a club down there?"

Her eyes twinkled with amusement. "You didn't have to be a genius to figure that out."

"Did you always want to be a singer?" he persisted.

Kate turned to face him squarely. "No," she said. "When I was a kid I wanted only one thing: to be rich. To have fancy clothes and more jewelry than any Indian woman ever possessed.

"So I grew up to become the highest-paid call girl in Tulsa."

# 24

*George's jaw dropped. "Excuse me?"*

*"You heard me. I was the highest-paid call girl*

*in Tulsa." Kate said the words matter-of-factly, as*

*someone else might say they had been a housewife—*

*or a meteorologist.*

"But . . . I thought you were a singer . . . I mean . . ." George fumbled, wishing he had never opened this particular can of worms. At the end of the world, why bother anyway?

Kate smiled. "I was a singer. Eventually. I made enough money on my back to buy some but not all the things I wanted. But I learned enough to realize I would have to change my life to get them. So I saved enough money to take myself off to Chicago and get a formal education, a bit of polish, so I could snag a rich husband who would give me the rest of the equation. The highest-priced hooker going can't afford to buy herself Rolls-Royces and villas in the Mediterranean."

"That's what you wanted?" George asked in amazement, gazing at her serene face, her smooth, plain hair, her simple slacks and shirt.

"It's what I thought I wanted. What the magazines and the TV had taught me to want ever since I was a little kid. In Chicago I got married, all right, but not to a millionaire. Like a fool, I fell in love with a saxophone player. Really fell hard, so hard I couldn't bring myself to tell him about my past. Until the day he died, Phil thought I was just a nice girl from the Southwest.

"He was the one who discovered I had a voice. He began calling me Kate-Who-Sings-Songs, using the Indian connection to make something unusual so he could get bookings for me.

"It turned out I was more successful than he was," she said softly. Sadly. "My career took off, his went downhill. We drifted apart, and then one day I learned he had died of an overdose of designer drugs. Designer drugs," she repeated with a world of contempt in her voice.

"You can't blame yourself for that," George said.

"I don't. Honestly. I did for a while, but then I realized everyone is ultimately responsible for themselves. And I had better start being responsible for myself. I cleaned up my act, you might say.

"Just in time to realize—" She broke off and shook her head as if she was angry.

"What?" George took hold of her elbow. "To realize what? Tell me."

Kate looked past him, toward the children. "Just in time to realize it was all too late. I was never going to be able to have . . . What's wrong with her?" she asked abruptly.

George followed her gaze. The tiny, big-eyed daughter of Mary Ox-and-a-Burro had stopped playing and was standing swaying, rubbing her forehead.

Her face was glazed with sweat.

Kate hurried to the child and crouched down beside her. George followed. "What's wrong, honey?" Kate was asking. "Don't you feel well?"

The little girl whimpered, "Hot. Hot."

Kate put her hand on the child's forehead and frowned. "Too hot. That feels like fever."

"I have some aspirin," George volunteered, but Kate was not listening. She gathered the child into her arms and called out to the room at large, "Does anyone know where Two Fingers is?"

"In the store," George said. "At least, he was."

Kate gave a brisk nod and headed for the door. Mary Ox-and-a-Burro bustled across the room to join her. "What's wrong with my baby?"

"I don't know," Kate said. "I think she has a fever."

Mary gasped. "Not . . . ?"

"I don't know," Kate said. "Don't start worrying before anything happens. We'll take her to Two Fingers."

"Is he a doctor?" George wanted to know.

"Better than that," said Kate. "He's a healer. It's his gift."

"How can a healer be better than a real doctor?" George wanted to know. He was having to trot to keep up with Kate who, with Mary at her shoulder, was sprinting across the open ground toward the store. But Kate did not answer him. All her attention was focused on the child, who was now very flushed.

Fortunately, Two Fingers was still in the store with Harry and the others. The two women took the child straight to him. "She's sick," Kate said, holding out the little girl.

But Two Fingers did not take her into his arms. Instead he gestured to Kate to put her on the floor. Kate and Mary sank down together, almost as one, with the child between them.

From his stool, Cloud-Being-Born watched.

Two Fingers held the palms of his deformed hands above the little girl's head, moving them slowly back and forth, as if he was smoothing a blanket. His face assumed a remote, listening expression.

The rest of the community came flooding in the door, talking worriedly among themselves. When they saw what Two Fingers was doing they fell silent and ranged around the walls, watching.

Two Fingers began to chant. The sound was eerie, hackle-raising, an echo from another time. The repetitive syllables sounded like gibberish, but he repeated them insistently, with rising and falling volume making a sort of music.

"You," said a voice behind George. "You, Burningfeather. No tobacco?"

George turned. Cloud-Being-Born was sitting right behind him.

"No, I'm sorry. I didn't bring any."

"Too bad," the old man said wistfully. "Tobacco draws evil spirits. Evil spirits like tobacco. Circle of tobacco would draw illness out of child."

Two Fingers continued to chant. His outstretched hands never touched the child. He reached out with one foot, however, and nudged the two women, urging them to move away from her. Kate complied at once but the girl's mother had to be nudged a second time.

When space was cleared around the child Two Fingers began to move in a circle around her, keeping his palms downward a precise distance above her head. As he circled he sometimes bent forward, sometimes straightened up, but he never lost the rhythm of the chant nor varied the distance of his hands from her head.

George was painfully reminded of the people he had seen contract disease and die. It often began like this, with a sudden fever. The deadly viruses announced their presence like a rattlesnake rattling, but they had already struck, and there was no antidote.

If the child's illness was the precursor of one of the viral diseases invading the reservation at last, the slim hope of some genetic immunity would die with her; with the rest of them.

I don't suppose it matters, George told himself. The whole planet's sick, it won't support us anymore anyway.

Then, as he watched with hopelessness spreading through him, he saw the flush fade from the child's face.

She smiled up at Two Fingers.

"You and you and you," Cloud-Being-Born said, stabbing the air with his fingers as he pointed at three of the men, "go build a medicine wheel. Quickly."

The three ran from the store.

Two Fingers kept on dancing and chanting.

The little girl sighed, curled herself into a ball on the floor, pillowed her cheek on her arm, and slept. To keep his hands the same distance from her head Two Fingers had to circle her in a crouch, but he never lost his rhythm.

The three men soon returned. "It's ready."

Two Fingers picked up the sleeping girl and carried her outside gently, so as not to awaken her. The rest of them followed. Even Cloud-Being-Born arose from his stool and paced after them, to George's astonishment. He had not imagined such an old man walking. Yet he not only walked, he walked with a relatively straight back, like a much younger person.

On the baked earth in front of the store was a circular arrangement of stones, resembling a wheel with spokes and a hub. Hastily assembled, it consisted of no more than the absolute minimum number of small rocks and pebbles to give the shape required, yet George counted a full twenty-eight spokes. Out of curiosity, he took the compass that was hooked to his belt and checked the alignment. As he had somehow known, one pair of spokes was perfectly aligned east-west, and another north-south. Perfectly. Yet none of the three men who had made the wheel was carrying a compass.

At George's shoulder, Harry Delahunt said, "Twenty-eight spokes for the days of the lunar month. We don't count the day when the moon is dark."

Carrying the little girl, Two Fingers stepped into the first wedge between the spokes, did an intricate little shuffle of his feet, stepped into the next wedge, and so on around the circle, still chanting. As he stepped over each spoke he lifted the child toward the sky, then lowered her to a comfortable carrying position again.

As he danced, the women, but not the men, stepped into the circle and followed him around the wheel. The men took up the chant, but the women repeated Two Finger's steps between the spokes.

"So women do dance," George muttered under his breath.

Harry Delahunt glanced at him. "Men do one thing, women do something else. Not the same thing at the same time, that'd be a waste of energy."

When the circle was completed and the last woman stepped outside the wheel, Two Fingers put the child back in her mother's arms.

George could not help himself. He stepped forward and touched the little girl's forehead.

It was no hotter than his own, and absolutely dry.

The people drifted away, most of them seeking the shade of the store. When Kate turned toward the barracks, however, George hurried after her and caught her by the arm.

"Is that child actually cured?"

"We hope so," she replied with equanimity.

"What is it? Laying on of hands, something like that?"

"Two Fingers is a healer, as I told you. A medicine man. More than that, he's a Sioux. The Sioux are best at using the medicine wheel."

"And Cloud-Being-Born, what is he? The chief?"

Kate paused and looked up at him, frowning slightly. "No. He's a, a sort of a medicine man too. But more than that. He's a . . . a . . . a shaman," she said, hitting on the word with relief.

"You mean a sorcerer?"

"A shaman," Kate reiterated firmly. "That's what aboriginal people called them, isn't it? Their holy men? People who could use earth magic and sky magic?"

"I don't know, I suppose so. I'm just a meteorologist. You'd have to have an anthropologist to explain all that."

"I don't have to have any of your modern scientists at all," Kate corrected him. "I have . . . we have . . . this." She extended her hands as if to indicate the reservation and everything it contained.

Sunbaked soil, dying trees, dilapidated buildings. Two Fingers. Cloud-Being-Born. And what else?

"What do you mean by 'this'?" George demanded to know.

Kate began walking again, hurrying toward the shelter of the barracks. The sun beat down on them like a fist. George kept step with her, subconsciously aware of the flex and swing of her legs in the cheap cotton slacks she wore.

She did not answer him until they were inside the building. Then, with a sigh of relief, she pulled a handkerchief out of her pocket and mopped her face and throat. When she handed it to him for the same purpose George noticed it was a handkerchief made of cotton, rather than a tissue of pulped paper.

"Now tell me," he said as he gave the damp cloth back to her. "Just what were you talking about out there?"

She sat down on the edge of a cot and looked up at him. "The people Cloud-Being-Born has gathered here are a very special group, George. No one told me that, it's just something I've observed for myself since I've been here. Each of us has a gift. No two have the same gift. Two Fingers is a healer, for example. I sing. Sandy is a Navajo and, though you'd never guess it to look at him, an exceptional artist. Mary is a water diviner. Don't smile; she can really find water anywhere. Each of us can do something. Cloud-Being-Born organizes us into various groups to achieve various results. You saw a Healing Dance just now. When we planted the vegetables we did a different Dance. And it worked. They came up."

"Vegetables do that. They come up."

"Do they? Are you so sure? The average temperature here is a lot hotter than it used to be just a few years ago. That's changed the growth habits of every plant. Just look at the trees, they're dying. But our vegetables are thriving."

"You give them a lot of tender loving care."

"We give them more than that, George. There's no way they should be alive under that sun out there. Nothing else is, even the mesquite trees are dying."

"Yeah. Well." George scratched his head, trying to think of some explanation his scientific mind could accept.

"Do you know of anyone else who can do what we're doing here?" Kate challenged.

"No," he said ruefully. "The radical change in the planetary climate was one of our biggest worries, for a while, because of crop failure on an international scale. We were predicting worldwide famine. But before that actually became a problem, it was overcome by even bigger problems. I doubt if anyone out there is obsessing about worldwide famine anymore.

"You know, Kate, it's like an old dog I read about someplace years ago. His owner said he died of everything at once. That's what's happening to this planet. It's dying of everything at once.

"No single factor is killing the planet, you understand. The ecology is being overwhelmed by dozens of assaults. The hole in the ozone layer is just one example. We didn't worry a helluva lot about that one, for a while. It was just a problem to the Australians, who had to start closing down their beaches during the hottest part of the day because too many people were getting skin cancers.

"But the problem didn't stay in Australia. Like the cancers themselves, it spread. Everything seemed to be connected to everything else in ways we hadn't fully perceived.

"Take Kazakhstan and Uzbekistan. Those countries needed a crop to boost their economies. So they diverted their major watercourses to irrigate fields and grow cotton on huge cotton plantations. They didn't realize they'd created a disaster until their climate was changed and drought set in. To combat the drought, they diverted rivers from Siberia, which in turn destroyed another ecosystem. Climatic change was spreading.

"That's symptomatic of what happened all over the globe. Famine in Ethiopia, rain forests destroyed in Brazil . . . in every case, someone was raping the land for the sake of jobs and profits and the balance of payments. All perfectly justifiable. We have to have jobs. And a man's entitled to a profit. And God knows we have to redress the balance of payments!

"But what we didn't seriously take into account was the amount of damage we were doing to the planet. Of course, along the way we've destroyed ourselves, because we've made the atmosphere unbreathable. But I suppose on the cosmic scale the destruction of earth's air-breathers is pretty small potatoes compared to the murder of a planet."

"Is that what's happening?" Kate asked. She shivered in spite of the heat. "The murder of this planet?"

"You might call it that. Oh, it isn't going to be blown up in an atomic explosion the way people feared fifty years ago. It'll still be here, circling the sun. But there won't be any life on it. Perhaps there'll only be water. The polar ice caps are melting as they've never melted before. If that doesn't stop—and we have no reason to think it will—then the continents as we know them will be inundated.

"Eventually the earth will cool again—far too late to do us any good, needless to say. Then the ice will come back. A great glittering ball of ice. Sterile. Dead."

"Everything that is, is alive," Kate said.

"Where'd you hear that?"

"It's a saying Cloud-Being-Born uses a lot."

"Meaning ice too? Well, maybe, according to his way of thinking. But as far as I'm concerned, a world covered in ice is totally damned dead." George's pent-up anger resonated in his voice.

Looking at him, Kate saw that his fists were clenched. "Did you know all this when you came here?" she asked him.

"Of course."

"Did you ever think of killing yourself?"

"Sure. Lots of people preferred suicide to sitting around waiting for the end. But somehow I couldn't do it."

"So you came to a reservation instead."

"Yeah. Home to die. Metaphorically speaking. It's what I get for being romantic about my Indian heritage. Funny thing about Indians, Kate. People did tend to romanticize them, same as they did the Irish. I've got Indian and Irish in me, so I guess that makes me doubly romantic, eh?" He essayed a halfhearted grin, trying to lighten the mood.

Kate replied seriously. "There's nothing wrong with being romantic. Maybe the Indians and the Irish still knew that when the rest of us forgot. Human beings have a real need to put a shine on things, to give them glow and glory.

"Why do you think I was so successful as a call girl? I'm no great beauty. But I could give my clients romance. I could give them soft music and low lights and intelligent conversation. I could even give them buckskin and beads and a real live Indian princess, if that's what they wanted. And they did. They loved it. The men who came to me were starved for some sort of romance.

"You and I grew up in an age that glorified what it called 'reality.' Ugliness was the fashion, everything else was sentimental crap. Garbage was art and noise was music. People's souls were starving, George, long before worldwide famine could kill them.

"No wonder our world turned so ugly. We made it that way. Maybe we all deserved to die."

"But you didn't kill yourself either," George reminded her. "You came here."

"Yes. I know now that Cloud-Being-Born called me here."

"You really believe that?"

She looked at him with enviable composure. "I know it," she said.

"Why?"

Instead of answering, Kate said, "Perhaps you should ask yourself why he called you here, George."

# 25

*During the days that followed,*

*George felt more and more a part of the community.*

*Sharing their isolated existence, he was able to forget*

*for hours, sometimes for half a day, the lurking*

*catastrophe.*

The Indians did not discuss it among themselves. Their only acknowledgment was to comment on the heat.

It was impossible to ignore the relentlessly increasing heat.

But they focused on other things, on the rituals of survival. Working together, they tended the vegetables and carried water from the well and milked the goats and made the repairs necessary to keep the dilapidated buildings from falling down. The men and women worked together. There was little division of labor according to gender. Everyone turned their hand at whatever needed to be done, according to their abilities. Mary Ox-and-a-Burro was the best carpenter on the reservation. Bert Brigham was the best cook.

George, somewhat to his surprise, discovered an unsuspected talent with needle and thread and was soon responsible for mending clothing in addition to his other chores.

Heat, sweat, dust, shabby things getting shabbier.

How strange it is, George thought, that a woman like Kate who sold her body to buy herself a better lifestyle is willing to settle for this. Indian fatalism, perhaps? He was not sure.

The influence Cloud-Being-Born exerted on the others was an ongoing source of fascination to George. The old man did not seem to do much of anything but sit around the store. Yet everyone deferred to him. On the rare occasions when he spoke, people held their breaths to listen.

Not that he said much. Mostly he just sat, dozing or ruminating, it was hard to tell which. Of all of them, Cloud-Being-Born was the only one who gave the impression of just . . . waiting.

George made several unsuccessful efforts to engage the old man in conversation. Finally Harry said, "I'd leave the old man alone, if I were you. When he has something important to say, he says it. Otherwise, he don't waste time in palaver."

Harry was beginning to get on George's nerves. There was the same arrogant I'm-in-charge-here-and-don't-you-forget-it air about him that T. J. Dosterschill had possessed. The irritant lay not so much in what they said, as in the way they said it. Both spoke as if contradiction was unthinkable.

"I'll talk to him if I want to," George replied. Only after the words were spoken did he realize he sounded like a sullen little boy talking back to his mother.

Harry shrugged. "Suit yourself. But it won't get you anywhere. Remember, I told you not to bother."

"Who put you in charge?"

Harry grinned. "Me? I ain't in charge, old hoss."

"Then what's your specific role here?"

" 'Specific role,' " Harry mimicked, still grinning. "My my, what fawncy language we do speak."

George snapped, "Cut the crap. You're no more an ignorant reservation Indian than I am."

"Mighty perceptive of you, old hoss. Point of fact, I used to be a supervisor for Con Ed, back East. Had practically the whole Long Island grid at one time."

"What tribe are you?"

"Mohawk. My dad was one of those structural steel workers who went up on the skyscrapers and walked around on exposed beams with nothing to lean against but the wind. That was phased out, though, by the time I came along. I had to find some other line of work."

"Until Cloud-Being-Born summoned you."

"Yeah. Now, he is a reservation Indian. But he sure as hell ain't ignorant, he's the smartest person here. Mescalero Apache, he is. He and my father had something in common. The Mescaleros used to say they 'lived in the sky.' All their rituals revolved around solar and lunar alignments, things like that. Very complicated people."

"I thought they were from the mountains in New Mexico," George said.

"Most of them. Cloud-Being-Born's people wound up here for some reason, on the flattest piece of desert for miles around. But at least he has a great view of the sky at night," Henry added. "When the rest of us are asleep, did you know he just sits on the porch steps and stares up at the stars? Don't even seem to sleep. Just sits there, staring up. Damndest thing you ever saw, old man like that."

Cloud-Being-Born and I have something in common too, George thought to himself. We're both displaced mountain men. The Mescaleros came from the White Mountains of New Mexico; my father came from the White Mountains of New Hampshire.

And here we are. In this godforsaken desert.

Here we are.

As he lay on his cot that night, with the door of his shack open in a vain effort to fight the heat, George could not sleep. He thought about the old Indian staring at the stars.

Then his thoughts slid sideways and circled around Kate. He folded his arms behind his head and thought about her until he could not stand it anymore, then got up and slipped on his cut-off Levi's and slipped out of the shack.

There were no lights on in the barracks. The community had a few kerosene lanterns and there were boxes of candles in the store, but generally daylight was the only illumination they sought.

In spite of the darkness, however, George felt sure Kate was awake too. He could sense it, as if the air between them was vibrating.

How to call her outside without looking like a fool? He stood lost in thought for a few moments, then the idea came to him.

Very softly, he began whistling "My Lagan Love."

As he had known she would, Kate came to him.

She was dressed in a thin cotton shift. Even in the light of a waning moon, he could see her body clearly through the fabric. She was barefoot, her glossy hair lying in a thick plait across one shoulder. She walked toward him without shyness, moving with a straightforward and sinuous grace.

No wonder the johns thought she was an Indian princess, George thought.

She is.

She stopped when she was so close to him he could reach out and put a hand behind her head and pull her mouth to his.

But he did not.

Not yet.

Instead he said something foolish, as people do. "How did you know it was me?"

She smiled. Even if the night had been pitch-black, he would have heard the smile in her voice. "Oh, George."

Suddenly it was George who was shy. "You don't have any other . . . I mean, there's no special man . . . ?"

"I know what you mean. And no, there's no man in my life now," Kate said calmly. "Have you anyone? Now?"

George made a gesture that took in the entire world beyond the reservation. "There isn't anyone," he said. "Almost literally."

"A few."

"Yes. A few. But none of them that care for me, or that I care about. That's an awful feeling at a time like this, Kate. I know we live and die alone in the strictest sense, but when you're faced with the end of the world, you should at least have someone to put your arms around, someone to cry with."

"Are you the kind of man who can cry?"

He had never given it much thought. But now, trying to be honest, he said, "Yes. yes, I guess I am." And to his surprise felt the tears just beneath the surface, burning in his throat.

The end of the world. All those people . . . all those lovely little things he had taken for granted . . . the laughter of children running across a schoolyard . . . the perfume of a strange woman lingering in an elevator . . . the roar of the crowd at a baseball game . . .

She knew. Kate felt the twist of agony in him, and knew. With one step she closed the distance between them and put her arms around him.

"Don't," she whispered, pressing her lips to the exact place at the base of his throat that was aching with the need to cry. "Ah, don't." Her lips moved on his skin. Moved slowly away from his throat, down his bare chest, brushing across his stiffened nipples, circling back up, up, seeking his mouth.

For just one terrible and shaming moment, he wondered if she was healthy. Then he almost laughed aloud. Irrelevant, irrelevant! He gathered her into his arms. She was a strong, solid woman, but he lifted her easily and carried her back to his shack; carried the captive princess home.

Neither of them was aware of the old man sitting on the steps of the porch in front of the store, watching them in the faint moonlight.

George had left his door open. He hated taking Kate into that small, stifling room, but it was better than lying her down on the rock-hard earth outside. At least he had a cot with a mattress on it.

He even had flowers. Since the first day, there had always been flowers in the pitcher on the dresser.

George did not put them there. But they were always there. Fresh ones every day.

He laid Kate on the bed and bent over her, wondering what were the appropriate words to say in such a situation. What phrases did you use with the highest-priced call girl in town?

The unbidden thought made him angry. He did not want to think of her that way. Indeed, it was impossible for him to imagine. She was Kate-Who-Sings-Songs, a lovely, grave Indian woman of grace and dignity. That was the true person. The call girl she had mentioned was an alien. He did not believe in her.

There was no room for her in what was left of the world.

If this is going to be the last time, George thought, let it be be beautiful.

They were gentle with each other, at first. Their shared hunger made them gentle, eager to prolong the pleasure. Kate had a superb sense of timing, George discovered. Whatever he needed, she kept him waiting until one heartbeat before unbearable, then she gave him more than he could have hoped. Her hands knew what his skin wanted.

"You're beautiful," he whispered to her, knowing the trite old words to be inadequate.

"So are you," she whispered back.

No one had ever called George Clement Burningfeather beautiful. It had never occurred to him that the term might be applied to a man. Yet he recognized it for what it was: a high honor. That clean, simple word, without all the euphemisms and evasions, was an accolade. A salute.

As her hands explored him he felt the male's ancient moment of concern, of insufficiency. Then its counterpoint, a sudden sure pride. He took her strongly, knowing himself capable and powerful.

"Yes!" cried Kate-Who-Sings-Songs.

Sitting on the splintery steps, looking at the stars, Cloud-Being-Born heard that cry. It was soft and low and muffled by the walls of the shack, yet he heard it. His keen ears would have heard if it had been much softer and much farther away.

He had been waiting for that sound.

The old man nodded to himself. Slowly, giving his ancient joints plenty of time, he got to his feet. He cast one more look at the stars.

Then, done with waiting at last, he went into the store and lay down contentedly on the pile of blankets in the corner that was his only bed.

Cloud-Being-Born had everything he needed now.

Before dawn, George and Kate lay pressed together on the narrow cot that smelled of sweat and love, and listened to the beating of their hearts. At last Kate made a move as if to get up, but he held her back.

"Where are you going?"

"Back to my own bed, before the others wake up."

"Don't you want them to know about this?"

"It isn't anyone else's business."

"Isn't it?" George wondered. "We're a mighty small group here. What one does could affect all. Stay with me, Kate. Let people see us together."

With a smile in her voice, she asked, "You want to boast?"

"Maybe," he admitted.

She snuggled against him.

They did not leave the shack until the red sun had begun to peep over the horizon. The sun was always red now, night and morning. It glared at the earth through an omnipresent dust haze. There seemed no moisture left in the world except the blood in their bodies. And that, too, would overheat, boil away, evaporate as the planet roasted and shriveled.

But there was a little life left. George resolved to enjoy what they had. He took Kate's hand in his own and gave it an encouraging squeeze.

"I don't suppose old Cloud-Being-Born is empowered to marry people," he said.

Kate glanced at him. "What?"

"Marry. You remember. Join for life, et cetera. I don't have that much to offer, I know. Slim prospects, you might say. But . . ."

She turned to face him. Her eyes were large and very solemn in the lurid dawn light. "I marry you," she said. "Here. Now. I, Kate, take thee, George."

"I, George, take thee, Kate," he responded, equally solemn.

The great hush of dawn lay around them. The dying land was witness.

The old man standing just inside the door of the general store, gazing out, was witness too. He said over his shoulder to Harry Delahunt, "Gather everyone. Here. Now."

The rising sun was a red and baleful eye.

Harry went first to the barracks, then to the individual shacks.

Some people had opted for communal life in the barracks but others had preferred to be alone, at least for part of the time. The community accommodated both.

Everyone was awake. Mary Ox-and-a-Burro's little girl was playing happily, the picture of health. Mary picked her up, gave her a loving hug, and followed Harry Delahunt outside.

The atmosphere was sultry and oppressive. Walking from their sleeping quarters to the store was enough to set people's lungs to laboring and their hearts to pounding. The little girl's good humor evaporated. She clung tightly to her mother's hand, with the thumb of her other hand firmly fixed in her mouth.

Harry did not need to summon George and Kate. To George it seemed somehow appropriate that they go to the hub of the reservation, following their exchange of vows. He felt a need to be at the center of the community; at the center of what life remained.

When they entered the store they found Cloud-Being-Born on his feet. The old man stood facing the door. He peered intently at the face of each person who entered, then gave a nod as if checking them off against a mental list.

George went up to him. The occasion required a formal announcement. "Kate and I . . . we've decided to marry," he said, feeling suddenly shy.

But Cloud-Being-Born hardly seemed to notice. He gave one of his brief nods, grunted, and looked past George to see who was entering the store next.

George went over to Kate, who was standing by the counter. "Bit of an anticlimax," he reported. "The old chief doesn't seem impressed by our marriage."

"Did you think he would be?"

"I thought he'd do something. Say something. Disapprove, maybe, I don't know. But I expected a reaction."

Kate patted his arm consolingly. "It doesn't matter. This only concerns us, really."

To her surprise, Cloud-Being-Born turned and looked straight at her, as if he had heard her words, though she had spoken very softly. Even more surprisingly, he smiled.

Then he raised his arms. "Strength of man, strength of woman, are joined!" he announced in a clear voice that belied his years. "It is a sign!"

The assembling group looked at him blankly.

"When everyone is here, we go outside," Cloud-Being-Born said. "Harry. You go, look. Be certain no one is left out." With an imperious gesture, he sent Harry out the door for one final head check. Then he just stood quietly, waiting.

"What's this all about?" George said out of the corner of his mouth to Will Westervelt.

"Beats me. Prayer meeting before breakfast?"

"I don't think so. You see anybody preparing food?"

Will glanced around. "I don't see anybody doing anything. Think I'll sit down." He started toward the nearest chair.

"Stay where you are." Cloud-Being-Born's voice cut the already overheated air like a stab of lightning.

Harry returned. "Got 'em all," he announced, shepherding the last of the group, a yawning Sandy Parkins, ahead of him.

"Good. We go now." Cloud-Being-Born headed for the door, obviously expecting everyone to follow him.

"Hey!" Anne Swimming Ducks protested. "No cup of coffee?"

"No time," said the old man.

Harry Delahunt advised, "We better go with him. That's what he wants."

"But the sun's up and it's already very hot outside," said Mary. "I don't want to take my child out again if I don't have to."

Harry shook his head. "You have to."

"Is that an order?"

"I guess so, yeah."

"By whose authority?" Will Westervelt wanted to know.

"His, of course." Harry pointed a thumb toward the old Indian, who by this time was out on the porch and on his slow, methodical way down the steps. "Someone go catch him and give him an arm to lean on," Harry added. He did not do it himself, however. He stayed in the store, bullying and cajoling to get the others out.

The teenaged boy caught up with Cloud-Being-Born and walked beside him, but the old man did not lean on the young one. He marched straight and sure across the dying earth with his head up.

The others, mystified, followed.

They were all too aware of the gathering heat; the baleful sun.

Cloud-Being-Born led his strange little parade for some hundred yards or so, to a withered clump of mesquite trees that slumped dejectedly at the edge of the rutted road.

The road led east.

Toward the sun.

Cloud-Being-Born stopped walking and drew a deep breath. For a moment he swayed; then he put one hand on the boy's shoulder and steadied himself.

When he spoke his voice was strong, however. "This place must do," he said. "We must do. We must hope there are others to do, also. You." He looked meaningfully at George. "You said there are others? Still alive?"

"Some, yes," George replied, puzzled.

"Like us?"

"I don't know what you . . . yes. Like us. At least there were. Amerindians, Maoris, Inuit, some African tribes . . ." George felt a growing sense of understanding.

"Ah." The old man took another deep breath. "Let us hope they know. Know what is needed. Know how to do." Cloud-Being-Born closed his eyes briefly, communing with himself. Then he opened them and looked toward each of his people in turn.

"You stand there," he began, beckoning to Harry and pointing to a bit of ground that seemed like any other bit of ground. Harry went over to it. "No," said Cloud-Being-Born. "One step back. There."

"Now you." He gestured to Mary Ox-and-a-Burro. "You, there."

But when Mary started forward holding her child's hand, the old man ordered, "Leave child! She has her own place."

Kate swiftly crouched down beside the little girl and comforted her as she watched her mother walk away from her.

Why don't any of them disobey him? George wondered. Or at least ask more questions?

But when his own turn came and the old man assigned him to a particular spot of earth, George felt his feet carrying him without hesitation.

It took a long time to get everyone arranged to Cloud-Being-Born's satisfaction. Meanwhile, the sun pounded on their heads. Not everyone was wearing a hat. Most of the women had straw hats, and the little girl was wearing a strange and faded garment that appeared to have once been a cotton sunbonnet. But the young boy was bareheaded, as was the old Indian's adult granddaughter.

Nor did Cloud-Being-Born himself have any kind of protection from the sun. It beat down mercilessly on his uncovered grey head.

George curiously studied the arrangement the old man had made using his people. There were thirty of them altogether, including himself and the children. They were spaced at irregular intervals to form a rough star shape with four points. The youngest children were at the outer edges. Cloud-Being-Born was at the center. He had very deliberately placed George and Kate on either side of him, so that they faced one another.

"Now," the old man said.

"Now we dance the Healing Dance."

"But there isn't a medicine wheel," George said.

Cloud-Being-Born replied, "Medicine wheel is not like medicine doctors give. Means something else. Means the moon. Means the seasons. Today we need to make medicine with the sky. Different."

He closed his eyes and began to chant.

The others stood, glancing uncertainly at one another. Are we supposed to do something? George wondered. If it's a dance, shouldn't we be moving around?

But no one else was moving. They had not been told to move. They stood. And waited.

The old Indian chanted.

Then Harry Delahunt began to move. His feet shuffled; his body began to turn in a series of abrupt, jerky movements. When he faced toward George, George could see that his eyes were open but were not looking at anything in particular. He held out one arm, however, rigid forefinger pointing.

At Two Fingers.

Something seemed to jump between them, like a spark of electricity. Two Fingers' body responded with the same sort of jerky movement that was animating Harry's. He began his own chant, almost sotto voce, very different from that of Cloud-Being-Born. As he rotated in place he held his hands palm upward, toward the sky.

Harry pointed at Kate.

Kate began to sing. A soft, wordless, plaintive air, rising and falling, strangely reminiscent of the sound of wind soughing in pines.

Harry continued to single out each member of the group in turn, as if he were turning on the power points of a . . .

. . . of a grid.

George felt gooseflesh rising on his shoulders.

Each person, when called upon, responded intuitively with something unique to that person. Their special gift. Their contribution to the dance.

The old man's granddaughter was a weaver, and when her turn came she began tracing patterns in the air with flying fingers, as if she were drawing invisible threads together.

Slim Sapling had been, in his former life and long ago, a professional boxer. When his time came he doubled his fists and began a simulated attack on the blazing sun, pummeling it furiously, darting and ducking, bobbing and weaving, defending the earth against its unshielded rays.

What will I do when my turn comes? George wondered. How will I know? How do *they* know?

The faces of the performers were trancelike. Perhaps they did not know what they were doing, or why.

Suddenly George realized that questioning was not relevant. Not appropriate. The thought processes of the human mind were not involved here. Each person in turn was submitting to the control of the old man's chanting, which in its turn was an intuitive response to something else.

Cloud-Being-Born wore the same trancelike expression as the others. The syllables he was chanting were not coming from him, but through him.

In the moment when George realized this, Harry Delahunt's finger pointed at him.

He felt a very definite electrical jolt. The sensation was unsettling but not unpleasant; curiously like the jolt of Cloud-Being-Born's firewater.

A tingling ran through his body. Harry's pointing finger moved on, seemingly making selections at random. Yet George felt that the connection remained, and as each new person was singled out, he was aware of an added force being joined to his own.

He was not unconscious. He did not even think he was in a trance. He was perfectly aware of who he was and where he was; he was also aware of a most curious phenomenon inside his skull. As if they were ranged around the perimeter of his brain, he could see the glowing computer banks and the charts showing wind currents and barometric readings, the plethora of scientific fact from which a meteorologist made his assessments.

George found himself studying them as if he were sitting in his air-conditioned office, forehead wrinkled in thought, fingers flying over the keyboard of his word processor as he made his notes. This and this and that, yes. Major depression here. Anticyclonic winds accelerating there. Yes. All in his head, clear to his inner eye.

Then something else came into his head. He became aware that he was listening to Cloud-Being-Born chant, but he was no longer hearing meaningless syllables. The old man was speaking directly to him, and the words made sense.

"Show me," said Cloud-Being-Born. "Show me where we are. Now."

And George scanned the maps and charts and pinpointed the exact location. "Here," he said in his head.

"And what is this?"

"That's an area of high pressure."

"What does it do?"

George tried to frame a simplistic explanation, but it was not necessary. He had only to open the door to his hard-won knowledge and the old man walked in.

He heard Cloud-Being-Born's distinctive grunt. "If high pressure moves this way, what happens?"

Again, George thought the answer—and the Indian knew it at once. In his head, standing with him in his head, surveying the technological miracles he could never in a thousand years have understood.

George had no way of measuring the amount of time that passed as Cloud-Being-Born sucked him dry of knowledge. He could feel that knowledge being disseminated through the group; through the network Harry had linked. Each person was receiving as much of it as they needed to incorporate with their own abilities.

Two Fingers ceased making smoothing motions with his palms toward the sky and began making great sweeping gestures with his arms.

Kate's song became less gentle and more insistent, as if a drum were beating in her, establishing a compelling rhythm.

The weaver bowed and bent and pulled and tugged, seizing invisible strands and crossing them over one another in an intricate pattern.

The boxer redoubled his symbolic attack on the sun.

Sandy Parkins, crouched on his haunches, was drawing designs in the sand.

Mary Ox-and-a-Burro, who could divine water, was rocking back and forth on her heels, turning her head from side to side like a blind person, sniffing the scorching air.

The teenaged boy began pulling hairs from his uncovered head. Wearing the communal entranced expression he began arranging the hairs on his bare chest, attaching each to his skin with a bit of saliva. When his mouth was too dry to furnish spit he paused, worked his lips, gnawed on his tongue, then at last found another drop of moisture and continued.

Everyone had something specific to do.

All the while the old man chanted.

All the while the sun blazed in the cloudless, killing sky.

All the while Cloud-Being-Born continued to demand access to the contents of George's head.

Through the Dance, George felt the others. He recognized the distinctive flavor of each mind; he observed and understood what they were doing. He knew, without having to think about it, why an awkward thirteen-year-old boy who knew nothing of metaphysics had precisely arranged a pattern of hairs on his skin to correspond to ley lines. He knew why Mary was searching for water. He knew why Bart Brigham was stamping his feet in an irregular rhythm.

A seemingly random assortment of human beings were performing together an incredibly intricate series of apparently unrelated actions that would make no sense at all to anyone else.

But it did make sense.

George felt the exact moment when the first faint sense of control touched the group. They all felt it simultaneously.

Control.

It was like the unforgettable moment when a child trying to learn to ride a bicycle wobbles, upright and unsupported, for a few revolutions of the wheels.

The balance was quickly lost but they tried again, tried harder, concentrated more.

The sense of being able to control returned.

Sweat poured from their bodies.

George was increasingly sensitive, in some new way, to the others. Kate in particular he perceived as he had never perceived a woman before. He felt her weaknesses, aspects of her persona that were incomplete, or misdirected, or in the process of being shed as a snake sheds its skin.

He felt her strengths, and knew what they had cost her.

He found the deep, calm pool at her center, and knew she had gone through an excruciating period of self-questioning and self-blame, to arrive at last at total, clear-eyed honesty.

He saw himself as Kate was seeing him. A man with the child still alive behind his eyes. A man who could cry, who could be romantic about being an Indian, even when he saw the reality of the reservation. A dichotomous human being . . .

Dichotomous . . . divided in two . . . consisting of two parts that need to be joined together again . . .

Joining.

Healing.

Cloud-Being-Born's voice rose above the sounds many of the others were making, a clarion command.

"Look!" he cried.

"Look up!"

# 26

*They could not stop the Dance.*

*They would not be allowed to stop the Dance until it succeeded in whatever its purpose might be—or until it killed them.*

But they were allowed enough autonomy to look up.

They were exhausted. George could feel it in himself and knew it must be worse for many of the others. Human flesh and blood could not sustain so intense an effort, in such terrible heat, for long. They needed a transfusion of motivation.

They were allowed to look up.

"Oh!" said a voice. The littlest girl, whose task had been to perform a pantomime with her own shadow, continued her pantomime but threw back her head and stared at the sky with huge eyes.

The blazing, brassy sky.

The yellow, superheated, poisoned sky that was burning away life.

For months that sky had been cloudless.

Now something interrupted its glaring expanse.

A tiny thread appeared, halfway between horizon and zenith. It could almost have been a hair on the eyeball.

But it was not.

As they watched, it grew. It drew unto itself, out of apparent nothingness, a visible wisp of matter as delicate as a feather. George had to squint to be certain he was seeing it. The heat and glare made his eyes water.

All the time the old man was in his head, busy.

The delicate tracery in the sky grew minimally larger. A tenuous swirl of vapor resolved itself into a tiny scrap of cloud.

In the mountains of New Hampshire, George had once watched as a mountain drew to its summit the moisture evaporating from the pine forests on its flanks. The moisture had coalesced into a silvery banner that blew from the highest peak, waiting for a montane wind to dislodge it and blow it across the land in the form of cloud.

Now he was seeing the same phenomenon take place above the desert. No trees. No mountains. Just polluted sky and pitiless sun. And the Dance.

"Damn," George said in an awestruck whisper.

Inside his head, the old man was working himself into a fever pitch. Like the conductor of a symphony he was trying to keep all the instruments in perfect harmony while building them toward an inevitable climax. George could feel the frenzy in him, and knew he could not continue for much longer. He was a very old man.

The cloud was expanding.

It grew from a wisp the apparent size of a fingernail to a mass the size of a half-dollar. Then the size of a bus. Then it multiplied itself into the sails of a galleon, full and billowing in breathtaking purity against the backdrop of dirty sky.

The clouds did not look polluted. They were as clean and white as fresh snow.

The armada set sail. It cast cool shadows on the land beneath as it headed for the northern horizon. There the clouds thickened, deepened, darkened. Became black-purple.

The first breath of cool air swept southward.

Cloud-Being-Born redoubled his efforts. Vision faded; George was not using human eyes any longer. He was being forced to a level of concentration he would not have thought possible, drawing on inherited gifts of strength and intuition and sensitivity.

At the old man's command he stretched his awareness. It was seized and woven by the Dancers into a net of consciousness that was then flung beyond the limits of the reservation and cast across the continent, seeking.

"Go farther!" cried the old man in George's head.

George had an impression of ocean, of water and weight.

Then he was deliciously buoyant, floating upward to follow the air currents he had once studied. Entering familiar territory seen from a new perspective, he began to examine the abused fabric of the atmosphere and guide the Healing Dance to its wounds.

He came to a vast gaping hole, like an immense burn. Its scorched, decaying edges extended for thousands of miles. The hole sickened him. It was a loathsome disease, a terrifyingly large ulcer that had somehow become malignant.

"Here!" George called to the Dance, summoning. "Here!"

Healing began to flow from earth to sky. George felt waves of comfort channeled through himself. The Dancers were mending the ozone layer. But the hole resisted. Its edges tore again.

"We need more help!" Cloud-Being-Born cried. "Can you find any others like us?"

George was totally consumed with his own efforts. He could not stretch any farther. But Kate responded.

Her song altered. Its syllables were incorporated into the structure of the Dance. Her song was no longer audible to human ears, but, amplified by the Dance, was radiating outward in sound waves capable of covering vast distances in microseconds.

Kate's song began reaching other minds. Elsewhere.

From such far-flung corners of the earth as the depths of the Amazonian jungle and the mountain peaks of Tibet, the response came. It came as a searing whiplash of energy that scorched through the Dance.

Harry Delahunt writhed, screaming with pain and clutching his head.

But the Dance must not stop.

Cloud-Being-Born was driving George mercilessly. George's knowledge was the guide. An increasing number were following the charts in his head. He could sense them joining in as Kate's song reached pockets of survivors in Australia. Alaska. A village in Wales. A community in Mongolia.

People who had never forgotten they were an integral part of the living planet.

Their mental strength was added to the Dance. Each had something unique to contribute as a result of that person's assortment of genes and experiences. No two were alike. Each was invaluable.

Summoned to the Dance, the last children of earth gathered into one consciousness. They had no sense of self.

There was only the Dance. The Dance, succeeding!

The Dance, cleansing and healing.

The Dance as an act of creation, making the earth whole again.

Feeding on powerful energies, the Dance was taking on a life of its own—and emotions of its own.

All the damage could not be corrected at once. Toxic wastes could not be made to vanish. They would have to be absorbed and purified, which in some cases would take eons.

Pollutants must be neutralized. They would have to be taken apart through natural action and reassembled into the basic, harmless substances from which man had constructed them. This, too, would take time.

Trees would have to grow from seedlings to replace the murdered forests.

Many generations would be required to restore the ecological balance of the seas.

The planet would be a long time healing.

The Dance had done all it could. The rest was up to the ages. But the Dance was not satisfied to wait; the freshening air began to crackle with the very human emotion of frustration.

Lightning laced the sky.

Thunder boomed its response.

Lightning stalked around the horizon on forked legs.

Thunder roared and rolled, reverberating like the cry of an angry god.

Lightning flamed in a dazzling sheet across the heavens, illuminating masses of boiling black cloud like dark armies on the march.

The air crackled and sizzled with anger.

Anger and energy and desire!

A minute fraction of George's commandeered consciousness sensed the gathering storm and recognized danger. He fought to clear his thoughts. He called out in his head to Cloud-Being-Born, "We've gone too far! We've unleashed forces we can't handle!"

He was trying to communicate with the old man, but instead he caught, just for an instant, the flavor of Kate's gentle irony, and heard her saying in his mind, "How like us."

Then she was gone. A massive storm howled around them, engulfing Dance and Dancers.

George felt the last shreds of their control being torn from them.

Ocean of air was convulsed by tidal wave of storm. Rain fell with murderous force, pelting down on the parched earth faster than it could be absorbed. Hurricanes roared into being, battering land and sea. Tornadoes spun out of nowhere in a deadly dance of their own, whirling cones of death darting down from the blackened sky.

The wind rose to an unbearable shriek.

George had an impression of incalculably mighty forces rushing in to fill a void. Their pressure kept building until he felt as if he was at the bottom of the sea, with its entire weight crushing down upon him. He fought desperately to keep his lungs working.

The old man in his head was silent.

But there was no other silence.

Above the tumult of storms that raked her from pole to pole, the earth screamed.

**27**

*George came back to himself very*

*slowly.*

*He felt as if every bone in his body was broken.*

*He lay without moving. Gradually he became*

*aware that he was lying in mud.*

Rain was pouring down on him with the force of a deluge.

The storm had passed, however.

He remembered the storm.

He remembered the terror of the storm.

But it was over. There was only rain. Cold rain falling from cold air.

George drew a deep but shaky breath. The air tasted sweet on his tongue.

His open eyes looked up into a sky banked with clouds. The clouds were no longer black, but a soft grey. Even as he looked they began to break up slightly. The deluge eased, became only a moderate downpour.

He sat up. His bones were not broken, but his entire body was bruised. His brain felt even more bruised. The inside of his skull was sore.

The old man!

He blinked rainwater out of his eyes and looked around.

He was sitting in the center of a circle of bodies. Sodden figures lay all about him in the mud, unmoving.

"Kate!"

She was some distance away. She lay flattened on the earth as if all the life had been pounded out of her. George threw himself toward her in a lurching, crawling run.

He cradled her head in his arms. Her eyes were closed. He could detect no sign of breathing.

He tried desperately to force his bruised brain to remember how to do mouth-to-mouth resuscitation.

Keep calm. Pinch the nostrils closed. Force air into the lungs through the mouth. Establish a rhythm. Keep calm!

Her jaw surrendered slackly to his probing fingers. Her mouth gaped open. George covered it with his own and began trying to blow life into her body.

There was no response.

In with the good, out with the bad, keep calm. Blow into her mouth, press down on her chest, maintain the rhythm. "Breathe, dammit!" Make her breathe.

Make her breathe!

Taking great gulps of cool, sweet air, he forced them deep into Kate's lungs.

After a frighteningly long time, her eyelids fluttered.

When she was actually able to open her eyes and look up at him, George felt weak with relief. "Hi there," he said inanely.

With an effort, she focused on his face. "You look awful. Water's dripping off your nose," she said in a faint voice.

"It's raining."

"Raining?" Her voice grew stronger.

"Yeah. And it's cool. Can you feel it?"

"Cool. Yes. Yes! I feel it!"

"You'll get a chill. We'll have to wrap you in something to keep you warm." George looked around, thinking vaguely that he might borrow a shirt from one of the others.

The others!

Puddles of people were scattered on the drenched earth. One was moving, feebly.

George got up and ran over to him. "Will! You okay? Say something!"

Will Westervelt groaned. "I don't have to get up until seven," he said clearly, eyes screwed shut.

"You have to get up right now, dammit. Get up and help me."

Will's eyes opened. "What happened?"

"We did it! We did something. I don't know exactly. But everyone's stunned. Or . . . get up, help me with them. We've got to get these people out of the rain. It's getting colder every minute."

"Colder?" said Will in astonishment. He scrambled to his feet and stood, swaying.

George went back to Kate and helped her to her own feet. "Move around," he advised, "warm yourself up."

"I'll be all right. What about the children?"

George found the little girl lying half under the body of Jerry Swimming Ducks. The child was awake and just starting to cry. George eased her out from under Jerry's unconscious form and looked around for her mother.

Mary Ox-and-a-Burro lay a few yards away. Dead.

Her body was not only lifeless but dessicated, as if every drop of moisture had been sucked out of it.

George stared down at her in horror. Then he turned and carried the child to Kate. "Look after her, and don't let her go anywhere near Mary if you can help it."

Harry Delahunt was dead too, his body blackened and burned, almost unrecognizable.

The young boy was alive. Dazed, almost incoherent at first, he responded when Will began talking to him and was soon on his feet. Will put him into Kate's care and went on, with George, separating the living from the dead.

Almost half of the Dancers were dead. Their resources had been totally exhausted.

Out of the corner of his eye, George kept glancing toward the silent form he knew was Cloud-Being-Born. He knew the old man must be dead. He had probably been the first to die. But he did not want to go to him and confirm the fact. It was as if the old Indian held a magic that would be broken once he was accepted as dead.

George still felt the influence of the magic. He saw its power in the falling rain and heard its voice in the north wind.

At last he could not put it off any longer. He went over to the old man's body and crouched down beside it.

Cloud-Being-Born lay on his back. His face was turned toward the sky. His dead eyes were open.

The sky was reflected in them.

George stared down.

As he watched, the clouds mirrored in the old man's eyes sped before the force of the wind. As they moved, they revealed the sky behind them.

The blue sky.

George twisted his neck and looked up.

The sky between the gaps in the cloud was azure-blue.

George blinked, then let the tears come.

It took a long time to get everyone, the living and the dead, back to the store. The dead were laid in a row on the porch, covered with blankets. The living huddled inside, wrapped in more blankets.

The cold was increasing.

Of the living, Two Fingers was the weakest. Even he did not seem to know if he would survive. Anne Swimming Ducks used the last of the coffee, liberally laced with firewater, to try to give him some strength. Then the straight firewater went the rounds. They drank it down like water. It seemed to have no effect.

Gazing out the door at the bodies on the porch, Slim Sapling remarked, "We need Cloud-Being-Born to conduct the burial ritual."

The teenaged boy spoke up. "I think we'll know what to do when the time comes."

"He's right," someone else agreed. "When it stops raining, we'll just know."

In spite of the patches of blue sky occasionally visible, there were still clouds and rain. No one was anxious to see the rain end, and the burying begin.

They waited.

While they waited, they talked among themselves.

There was a surprising lack of speculation about the Dance and its results. What one knew, everyone knew, though their minds were no longer linked in the Dance.

Their questions were about the future.

They felt confident there would be a future, now.

"Just think of it," said Will Westervelt. "Little groups of survivors like us scattered all across the globe. It's sort of like natural selection, when you think about it."

Kate knew what he meant. "It's as if," she said softly, "the planet left enough of us alive to save herself."

They sat in the cold and considered the thought.

Someone asked, "Think we should try to join up with the others?"

George shook his head. "Logistically impossible. There was an almost total breakdown of travel by the time I came here. I'd say it's worse now. Hopeless, internationally. No, it's better if we stay here and make the best of what we have. Get things going again in our little corner."

Kate managed a faint chuckle. "The announcement of the end of the world was slightly premature."

George grinned at her. "It was." He reached out and took her hand. Her fingers twined through his.

"It's not going to be easy," he warned. "The effects of what happened are going to be a long time working through the ecosystem. We'll have to face that and find ways to live with it. I suspect there will be a continued, and massive, climatic change on a planetary basis until some sort of natural balance is reestablished."

"What sort of change?" Jerry Swimming Ducks wanted to know. His speech was still slightly slurred, but he was otherwise recovered from a long period of unconsciousness.

George thought before answering. He felt the stirring of a powerful intuition. It might have been a remnant of his recent expanded awareness.

It might have been a genetic gift surfacing.

"The planet's had many recurring cycles of glaciation and warming," George told the others. "That's been the natural course of events. Something tells me we have another ice age coming now. A monster, I'd predict. To finish cleansing the surface and get the earth back into sync."

"Surely we won't live to see it?" someone said nervously.

"Probably not," George agreed. "Our descendants will, though. They'll have to learn how to survive it."

A tinge of coral crept into Kate's cheeks. Her fingers tightened on George's and squeezed hard. "Our descendants," she murmured, savoring the word. "Let's hope they appreciate what they inherit."

Keeping an optimistic smile on his face, George returned Kate's squeeze.

He did not say what he was thinking.

We might have it all to do again someday.

Humans are an arrogant species.

When the ice cap melted, the seas rose.

*When the ice cap melted, the seas rose.*

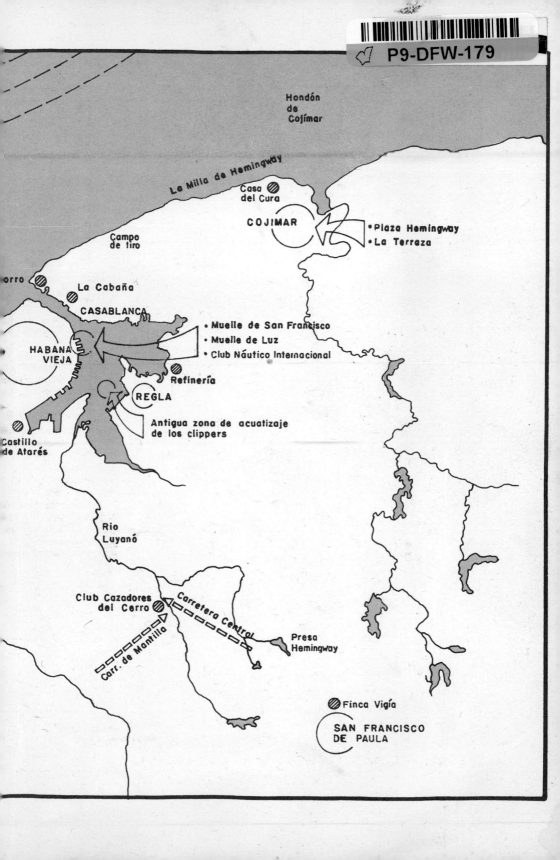

Hondón
de
Cojímar

La Milla de Hemingway

Casa
del Cura

COJIMAR

• Plaza Hemingway
• La Terraza

Campo
de tiro

orro

La Cabaña

CASABLANCA

• Muelle de San Francisco
• Muelle de Luz
• Club Náutico Internacional

HABANA
VIEJA

Refinería

REGLA

Castillo
de Atarés

Antigua zona de acuatizaje
de los clippers

Río
Luyanó

Club Cazadores
del Cerro

Carretera Central

Presa
Hemingway

Carr. de Mantilla

Finca Vigía

SAN FRANCISCO
DE PAULA

# Hemingway
in
Cuba

*Translated by Consuelo E. Corwin*
*Edited by Larry Alson*

# Hemingway
# in
# Cuba

by Norberto Fuentes

*with an Introduction by* Gabriel García Márquez

Lyle Stuart Inc.     Secaucus, New Jersey

FIRST EDITION

Copyright © 1984 by Norberto Fuentes

Translation copyright © 1984 by Lyle Stuart Inc.

*Hemingway—Our Own*, by Gabriel García Márquez,
copyright © by Gabriel García Márquez, 1982

Published by Lyle Stuart Inc.
Published simultaneously in Canada by
Musson Book Company,
A division of General Publishing Co. Limited
Don Mills, Ontario

Queries regarding rights and permissions should be
addressed to: Lyle Stuart, 120 Enterprise Avenue,
Secaucus, N.J. 07094.

Manufactured in the United States of America

Library of Congress Cataloging in Publication Data

Fuentes, Norberto.
    Hemingway in Cuba.

    Translation of: Hemingway en Cuba.
    Bibliography: p. 423
    Includes index.
    1.    Hemingway, Ernest, 1899-1961—Homes and haunts—
Cuba.    2. Authors, American—20th century—Biography.
3.    Cuba—Description and travel. 4.    Cuba in literature.
I.    Title.
PS3515.E37Z594513        1984        813'.52 [B]        84-2744
    ISBN 0-8184-0356-X

# Contents

# Acknowledgments

To Luis Pavón, who organized the work and for his friendship; to Estrella Cobas, who provided the necessary push; to Antonio La Guardia, for his help in every sense; to Luis Felipe Denys and Osvaldo Fleitas, for their collaboration in Camagüey; to Martha Arjona, Marilú Moré, Lyle Stuart, Raúl Rivero, Eliseo Alberto, Felipe Cunill, Raúl Torres, Eduardo Turguet, Luis García Guitar and Francisco Martínez Hinojosa, who participated from beginning to end; and to Lourdes Curbelo, who offered encouragement and love.

# Hemingway—Our Own

by GABRIEL GARCÍA MÁRQUEZ

Ernest Miller Hemingway arrived in Havana for the first time in April, 1928, on board an English boat, the *Orita*, which was taking him from La Rochelle to Key West in a two-week crossing. He was accompanied by his second wife, Pauline Pfeiffer, to whom he had been married a scant eleven months, and neither he nor she could have had any great interest in the Caribbean city other than as a two-day tropical stop after that vast ocean and the rough winter in France.

Hemingway was 29 years old; he had been a newspaper correspondent in Europe, an ambulance driver in the First World War, and had published his first novel, with some success.

He was far from being a famous writer, he still needed a second occupation to make ends meet, and did not have a permanent home anywhere in the world. Pauline, on the other hand, was what was then called "a society woman." Niece of an American cosmetics magnate who pampered her like a grandchild, she had everything in life, including the starlike beauty of the wife of Francis Macomber. But that was not her best April. She was pregnant and bored at sea, and their only wish was to get to Key West as fast as possible, where they would settle down so that Hemingway could finish his second novel, *A Farewell to Arms*.

Havana was then—and still is today—one of the most beautiful cities in the world. The dictator Gerardo Machado was at the height of his Pharaonic delirium, sustained by the last glow of a recent dazzling rise in the price of sugar, and by the patronage of the United States. He had broken the ties the previous governments had with Morgan banking and lived in public concubinage with the Rockefeller family's Chase National Bank, which denied him nothing in exchange for everything. The ravages of material progress were visible everywhere and Hemingway could not have seen them with indifference from the window of the Packard he rented in Parque Central.

The Malecón, the boulevard where beautification and security projects had been initiated in another time, was being extended to its present dimension, and new tree-lined avenues and millionaires' mansions appeared west of the old city. But the major work was to be the neo-classic absurdity of the Capitolio Nacional, copied stone by stone from the Capitol in Washington, and on whose construction worked a stonecutter by the name of Enrique Líster, who years later would be one of the legendary generals of the Spanish Civil War.

The frantic prostitution that would soon make of Havana the luxury brothel of the United States still hid behind the innocent mask of dancing schools. They were called Dance Academies and their cheerful girls—half virgins, half whores—earned one cent out of the five they charged for each dance, and were known by a name a writer couldn't have failed to notice: *académicas*. Over the orchestra seats of the very honorable Teatro Nacional, a wooden platform was built for public dancing, whose main event was the annual *danzón* contest. Machado's servility towards the United States reached the extreme of manipulating the jury so that the virtuoso dance contest in the most dance-oriented country in the world would be won by the American ambassador, Harry F. Guggenheim.

Of those first 48 hours of Hemingway in Havana there was not a trace in his works. It is true that in his articles he used to make intelligent observations about the places he visited and the people he met, but at that time he had imposed on himself a journalistic recess in order to devote himself completely to writing novels. However, six years later his first article as a recidivist was on a Cuban theme. From then on he wrote an additional half-dozen about his stay in Cuba, but in none of them did he make revelations that would be useful in the reconstruction of his private life, inasmuch as they referred in a general way to his dominant passion at that time: deep-sea fishing.

"This fishing," he wrote in 1956, "was what in other times brought us to Cuba." That phrase may permit the thought that at the moment he wrote it, when Hemingway had already lived in Havana 23 years, he had deeper or at least more varied reasons for his residence there than the simple pleasure of fishing.

It was not a case of love at first sight, but a slow, arduous process, whose intimacies appear scattered and in code throughout most of the work of his maturity. In 1932, on his second trip to Cuba to fish for marlin, he seemed convinced that he had at last found a stable home in Key West where his son had been born and where he had finished his second novel, and where no doubt he had planted a tree to become the complete man of the proverb. From that time on he made innumerable trips to and from Cuba, accompanied by his crony, Joe Russell, owner of Sloppy Joe's in Key West, who apparently used fishing as a screen behind which he carried on more productive occupations.

"He once carried from Cuba [to Key West] the biggest cargo of liquor ever known," wrote Hemingway. Contraband liquor, of course, at a time when drunks in the United States agonized with thirst under Prohibition. But those equivocal excursions, which were anything but literary, allowed Hemingway to come in contact with the good people of the sea who were to become his friends until he died, and who revealed to him a world that was to enrich his future writing.

In an article published in the July, 1949, issue of *Holiday*, Hemingway disclosed who were his Cuban friends at that time. "Lottery ticket sellers you have known for years, policemen you have given fish to and who have done favors in their turn, bumboatmen who lose their earnings standing shoulder to shoulder with you in the betting pit at a jai-alai frontón and friends passing in motorcars along the harbor and boulevard who wave and you wave to but cannot recognize at that distance." In other words, even then Hemingway thought of himself as a familiar character in the streets of Havana.

In those days he became acquainted as well with the Floridita, a seafood bar-restaurant established in the previous century that exists today with the same golden frieze and the same episcopal drapes. There the daiquiri cocktail was created, a happy combination of the diaphanous rum of the island, crushed ice and lemon juice, which Hemingway helped to make known throughout half the world. But as he was to write later, his main interest in the place was not so much its food and drink, but his desire to meet the tempestuous current of his countrymen who passed through the city.

"There are people there from all the states and from places

where you have lived," he wrote. "There are also Navy ships in, cruise ships, Customs and Immigration agents, gamblers, embassy characters, aspiring writers, firmly or poorly established writers, senators on the town, the physicians and surgeons who come for conventions, Lions, Elks, Moose, Shriners, American Legion members, Knights of Columbus, beauty contest winners, characters who have gotten into a little trouble and pass a note in by the doorman, characters who get killed next week, characters who will be killed next year, the F.B.I., former F.B.I., occasionally your bank manager and two other guys, not to mention your Cuban friends."

When Hemingway reminisced that way he had already won the Nobel Prize. More than a journalistic remembrance, it reads like nostalgia's telephone directory. It is difficult to reread his work now without recognizing many of the characters from that list, changed in time and place and transformed by the printed word, but hopelessly marked by the baptismal sin of the Floridita, where there is today a bust of Hemingway in a niche in the wall, and where an old bartender from his time never tires of showing tourists the bar stool where he used to sit.

Near the Floridita there is a hotel, Ambos Mundos, where Hemingway used to rent a room whenever he slept over on land. He ended up making it his permanent place to do his writing when he returned from the Spanish Civil War. It was always the same room: the one without a number on the fifth floor's northeast corner.

As Hemingway described it, "The rooms on the northeast corner of the Ambos Mundos in Havana look out, to the north, over the old cathedral, the entrance to the harbor, and the sea, and to the east to Casablanca peninsula, the roofs of all the houses in between and the width of the harbor."

I have never understood why Hemingway eliminated from that number the Palacio de los Capitanes Generales which was the most beautiful building that could be seen from his windows, and which is still one of the most beautiful in Havana. Years later in his historic interview with George Plimpton, Hemingway said: "The hotel Ambos Mundos was a good place to write." It is probable that that statement had already been tinged by nostalgia, for that room was not in the least the clean, bright place

Hemingway dreamed of for his writing. It was a gloomy room, 16 square meters, with a double bed made of ordinary wood, two night tables and a writing table with a chair. Today, the Ambos Mundos is a state hotel for teachers and functionaries of the Ministry of High Education, but the room on the northeast corner of the fifth floor, in memory of the illustrious guest, is kept locked and intact, including an old edition of *Don Quixote*, in Spanish, in two volumes, placed carelessly on the table.

When we think of how meticulous Hemingway was in his choice of places in which to do his writing, his preference for the Ambos Mundos could have only one explanation: without meaning to, perhaps without being aware of it, he was falling under the spell of Cuba's other charms, different and more difficult to understand than the great fish of September and more important to his troubled soul than the four walls of a room.

No woman, waiting for him to get through with his work so she could be his wife again, could tolerate that lifeless room. The beautiful Pauline Pfeiffer abandoned him in his most difficult moments. But Martha Gellhorn, whom Hemingway later married, found the intelligent solution, which was to find a house where her man could write in comfort and at the same time make her happy. And so she found the beautiful country place, Finca Vigía, in the classified ads of a newspaper. It was two and a half leagues from Havana. They rented it for $100 a month, and Hemingway later bought it for $18,500 cash.

Many writers who have homes in different places are often asked which is their principal residence and almost all of them answer that it's the one where they keep their books. In Finca Vigía Hemingway had nine thousand books, besides four dogs and 54 cats.

Hemingway lived in Cuba a total of 22 years. In an article published in 1949, he tried to answer the question about why he lived there such a long time, but he got lost in a maze of diverse and contradictory reasons. He talked about the fresh, caressing morning breeze on warm days, he talked about being able to breed fighting cocks, of the lizards that lived in the grape vines, of the 18 different kinds of mangoes in his courtyard, of the Sports Club just down the road where one could bet big money at pigeon-shooting matches and he spoke once more of the Gulf Stream which was only 45 minutes from his house and where he found the best and most abundant fishing he had ever seen in his life.

In the midst of so many justifications, rather elusive ones, he interpolated a revealing paragraph: "You live in Cuba because you can plug the bell in the party-line telephone with paper, so that you won't have to answer and that you work as well there in the cool early morning, as you ever have worked anywhere in the world." At the end of the paragraph, either as a diversion or coquetry, he adds: "But these are professional secrets." This comment was unnecessary, for as most everybody knows, the reason for the choice of the place where one writes is one of the insoluble mysteries of literary creation.

Havana in general and Finca Vigía in particular was the only really stable residence Hemingway had all his life. There he spent half his productive years as a writer, and wrote his major work: part of *For Whom the Bell Tolls*, *Across the River and into the Trees*, *A Moveable Feast*, *The Old Man and the Sea* and *Islands in the Stream*.

There he also wrote many articles for the press, including "The Dangerous Summer," and made innumerable attempts at writing the rare Proustian novel about the air, land and sea which he had always wanted to write. However, those are the least known years of his life, not only because they were the most intimate, but because his biographers have all glossed over them with suspicious haste.

As Hemingway built word by word the private world that was to nourish his glory, the project of national submission initiated by the dictator Gerardo Machado had reached its height, and was to be carried to an unhappy end by his successors. Political and moral corruption attained Babylonian dimensions. Submission to the United States, evident everywhere, acquired the appearance of a fantastic novel: the daily transport from Florida to Havana included a railroad car that was later hooked up to a local train to supply the island with items of prime need produced in the United States, including fresh fish taken from Cuba's own waters!

It has been too easily said that Hemingway was no more than a passive spectator, if not a quiet accomplice, of that gigantic undertaking of cultural denaturalization. His political thinking, which had been expressed in so unequivocal and passionate a manner in the Spanish Civil War, seemed to be an enigma when it faced the dramatic situation in Cuba.

There is no evidence that he ever tried to contact the intellectual and artistic community in Havana, which even in the midst of official vilification and public concupiscence continued to be one of the most intensely active on the continent. Such indifference on his part seemed to apply not only to the Caribbean area but to all Latin America as well, which he never knew and of which there is no serious reference in his work. The only Latin American countries he visited were Mexico in 1942 and Peru when he headed the expedition in search of a fish big enough for the film version of *The Old Man and the Sea*, but then he hardly touched land. Hemingway summed up that passionate adventure in this way: "For thirty days we fished from sunrise until the shadows of dusk made us stop taking pictures."

Another controversial aspect of Hemingway in his last years was his behavior during the Cuban Revolution. Although there is no recollection of his having expressed an opinion of public approval, neither is there one of disapproval, aside from the unreliable ones that some prejudiced biographers have attributed to him as having been said in private. Almost a year after the triumph of the revolution, at a time when the hostility of the United States was clearly established, the Argentine newspaperman Rodolfo Walsh carried on an instant interview with Hemingway among the pushing and yelling of the welcoming mob at Havana's airport. In that interview, which Walsh remembers as the shortest of his career, and which no doubt was the briefest and one of the last Hemingway gave, the writer managed to shout in his perfect Spanish, "We will win! We Cubans will win!" And then he added in English: "I'm not a Yankee, you know . . ." He couldn't finish the phrase because of the turmoil around him. A year and a half later he took his own life without finishing the phrase which has been subject to all kinds of interpretations from both sides.

Revolutionary Cuba, however, seems to have taken no part in this vicious polemic. No other writer—with the exception of José Martí—has been the object of so many Cuban tributes at so many different levels. From the first moment, Fidel Castro himself has been the sponsor of the most meaningful of them. It was he who took care of Hemingway's widow—Mary Welsh—on the two occasions in which she visited Havana after her husband's death. It was they who together agreed on the terms under which Finca Vigía would remain intact, as it is today, converted into a museum so true to life that at times one seems to feel the presence of the writer wandering through the rooms with his great dead-man shoes.

The only things the widow took away with her were the paintings from their stupendous private collection of the best contemporary artists. During her last visit in 1977, Fidel Castro declared before a group of American newspapermen that Hemingway was his favorite author. You have to know Fidel Castro to realize that he would never say such a thing as a simple courtesy, since he would have to go beyond some important political considerations to say it with such conviction.

The truth is that Fidel Castro has been for many years a constant reader of Hemingway, that he knows his work in depth, that he likes to talk about him, and knows how to defend him convincingly. On his long and frequent trips to the interior of the country, he always takes a confusing pile of government documents to study in his car. Among them one can often see the two volumes with red covers of the selected works of Ernest Hemingway.

In any case, it isn't easy now for someone to try to finish the phrase that Hemingway left unfinished at the Havana airport. The reality is that there were always two Hemingways, two distinct and often opposite ones. There was one for world consumption—half movie star, half adventurer—who would show off in the most visible parts of the world, who entered the Hotel Ritz in Paris with the vanguard of the troops of liberation, who gave lavish support to the fashionable bullfighters at the fairs in Spain, who had his picture taken with the most glamorous movie stars, with the bravest boxers, with the most sinister gunmen, and who killed first the lion, then the bison and then the rhinoceros in the meadows of Kenya, and still gave himself the luxury of crashing twice in two successive airplane flights.

That was the Hemingway of public spectacle, the one who

had never read a book or perhaps never loved anyone, and who couldn't leave any phrase unfinished. But there was another Hemingway in Havana, hiding himself in a house surrounded by enormous trees, in whose rooms accumulated the trophies of virile arts which the worldly Hemingway brought back from his travels. This was the insomniac artisan whom nobody really knew, overcome by the insatiable servitude of his vocation, who left not only one but many phrases unfinished.

What kind of man was this secret Hemingway, is the question Norberto Fuentes, the young Cuban journalist, asked himself in July, 1961, when his editor-in-chief sent him to Finca Vigía to write an article on the man who only the previous week had blown his head off with a rifle gunshot through the roof of his mouth.

Norberto Fuentes knew about Hemingway what little his father had told him one afternoon when they happened to run into him in the elevator of a hotel.

On another occasion, when Norberto was about ten years old, he saw Hemingway pass by in the back seat of a long black Plymouth and had the fantastic impression that he was going to be buried sitting up in that "hearse," the best known in the bars of the city.

From those brief memories Norberto Fuentes took on the colossal project of discovering what the Hemingway of Cuba was really like, the one whom some of his posthumous biographers seemed interested not only in hiding but in distorting. Fuentes needed many years of meticulous investigating, difficult interviews, and almost impossible recollections, until he succeeded in rescuing Hemingway from the memory of those anonymous Cubans who had really shared the writer's everyday anxieties: his personal physician, the crews of his fishing boats, his cronies from the cockfights, the cooks and the help in the bars, his rum-drinking companions on nights of revelry in San Francisco de Paula.

For many months Fuentes dug through the embers of Hemingway's life at Finca Vigía and discovered traces of his heart in the letters he never mailed, in regretted drafts, in half-written notes, in the fine navigation diary, aglow with Hemingway's bright style. Fuentes concluded that Hemingway had gone deeper into the soul of Cuba than the Cubans of his time had supposed, and that few writers have left so many imprints that testify to their presence in some of the most remote places on the island.

The final result is this hard-wrought and enlightening report that gives us back the living and slightly childish Hemingway that many of us thought we glimpsed between the lines of his masterful stories. Here is our own private Hemingway, a man troubled by the uncertainty and brevity of life, who never had more than one guest at his table, and who was able to decipher, as few have done in human history, the practical mysteries of the most solitary occupation in the world.

# Hemingway
## in
## Cuba

Finca Vigía today. The giant ceiba tree is on the right. (Enrique de la Uz)

# Sanctuary

[1]

Today only the objects remain. The hunting pieces and the small souvenirs that gave such pleasure to Ernest Hemingway are still in the places where he always kept them and are acquiring the look and patina of old and useless things. It would have upset him to see his size 11 shoes on exhibition, but the fact is that Finca Vigía—Watchtower Farm—seems to be frozen in time.

Laid out for everyone to see are not only his big shoes, but his infantry boots, his glasses with the round metal frames, his collection of Nazi daggers and his guns and fishing rods. Mary Welsh said it best on her last trip to Havana in July of 1977: "Everything is just where we left it in 1960. But the house is nothing without Ernest."

Visitors are allowed to view the house only through open windows as they walk around it. Access to the interior is forbidden by the authorities "to protect valuable museum-quality pieces." In the early days of the exhibit, a few objects were lost. There is an authentic story about a certain foreign government official who was seen taking one of the prized Second World War bullets from Hemingway's bureau. The situation was delicate. Nobody knew what to do at the moment. Does the diplomatic protocol prescribe a course of action in such cases? The piece of ammunition was returned only after much diplomacy.

Finca Vigía, due to that reverence Latins have for the dead and for "important people," has become a very popular museum. Visitors can see much of the house through the windows, with the exception of the kitchen, Miss Mary's room and the cellar.

Researchers, journalists and special guests are given authorization to visit the interior, although what is beyond the visual field through the windows is really of minor interest.

Only the cellar, where Hemingway kept his stock of wine casks and whiskey cases, is worth visiting. There one can view the five trunks covered with the hotel and steamship stickers that were seen so often in the photos of Hemingway arriving or leaving at airports or docks. In them, Hemingway took medicine, disinfectants, anesthetics and surgical equipment with which to open a dispensary in Masai territory and give minor surgical treatment during his second African safari. Next to the trunks there is an empty field glasses case. You'll also see a game bag and a man's sport corset, perhaps worn by Hemingway to relieve his back pain. The cellar is damp and dark.

Another secluded area which is worthwhile knowing lies near the dining room door. Hemingway called it "the cat cemetery." The gravestones bear the names of Blackie, Negrita, Machakos and Black Dog. The mortal remains of a literary character, Boise, are also buried here. Boise doesn't have the stature of Don Quixote's horse Rocinante, but he shares Thomas Hudson's life in *Islands in the Stream*.

Graham Greene, the British author, visited the house-museum more than once. It is clear that he did not share the affection for it that was felt by its late owner. Greene had a bone to pick with Hemingway ever since Ernest had referred to him in a mocking way in the *Paris Review* interview with George Plimpton.

Greene toured the house and in a loud voice told the journalist who accompanied him, referring to Hemingway's hunting trophies: "Don't know how a writer could write surrounded by so many dead animal heads." Later, when guide René Villarreal, who had worked for Hemingway for many years, mentioned the quantity of whiskey that normally found its way into Finca Vigía, Greene commented: "Now I understand for whom the bell tolls."

Gertrude Stein once remarked that Hemingway always had a good instinct for finding apartments or houses in strange but pleasant places, plus efficient *femmes de ménage* and good food. Aside from the nettles buried in her remark, Gertrude Stein was right.

Finca Vigía, a sprawling, breeze-swept farmhouse on a hill overlooking the small town of San Francisco de Paula, was Hemingway's most prolonged residence. It was a good place to live. It meant all the marvelous things that were happiness for Hemingway: writing in the cool of the morning, swimming, lounging in the sun with a drink in hand, plenty of well-stocked bookshelves, a big easy chair in which to read in the afternoon, a place to receive friends, breed cats, dogs and fighting cocks, a jumping-off place for big-game fishing.

In 1958, during his interview with Plimpton, Hemingway said: "This house is a splendid place . . . or was." His use of the past tense meant that by that time, particularly after receiving the Nobel Prize, and after the filming in Cuba of *The Old Man and the Sea*, his home had become the destination of too many pilgrimages.

Finca Vigía was by then an address well-known to bull-fighters, Hollywood magnates, prizefighters, soldiers, artists, journalists and many sorts of tourists who found their way to Havana and the house in the hills.

For this very reason, Hemingway had abandoned his first refuge in Cuba, the Hotel Ambos Mundos in Old Havana. The hotel had served as his base in the thirties, when he first started his big-game fishing expeditions in the Gulf Stream. But ten years later, when he returned from the Spanish Civil War with the novelist and journalist Martha Gellhorn, Hemingway needed a better place, a sanctuary in which to carry out his work and shelter his new-found love.

He bade farewell to Old Havana, which in other times had served as the background for *To Have and Have Not* and a half-dozen articles for *Esquire*, and moved to the country place Martha had found for them southeast of Havana. And just in time, for with the exception of Ambos Mundos, almost all the old places that served as the setting for Harry Morgan's adventures were soon to be transformed or demolished.

Martha Gellhorn located the country place through classified ads. Sometime in the middle of April, 1939, Martha, on her first trip to Cuba, took Ernest to see Finca Vigía, but he said it was too far from Havana, too much a ruin of flaking plaster and over-grown gardens, and that the rent—$100 a month—was too high.

Ernest left on a fishing trip. In his absence, Martha, with the help of masons and carpenters, hastened to fix up the house. When Ernest returned, she took him to see the place again. This time she was able to convince him. Finally, he was satisfied. Martha had her way and the couple had their refuge.

It was really Hemingway who needed a haven. He was halfway through the first draft of the big novel on the Spanish Civil War he had started in Ambos Mundos, which he'd fled to from Key West seeking the relative tranquility of the hotel room. Now, to finish it, he needed a quiet place, ideally that clean, well-lighted place on the hill. Martha and he rented it for a year and then bought it after the success of *For Whom the Bell Tolls*.

It would not be long, however, before Martha started to get restive and claustrophobic. Ironically, this happened just when Hemingway was getting fond of his Finca Vigía.

The place really captured his heart. In *Islands in the Stream*, Thomas Hudson compares his house in Bimini to a ship. That was the highest praise the writer could find. But Hemingway himself never found a permanent residence in Bimini. Through his alter ego, Thomas Hudson, his thoughts had been with Finca Vigía. Gazing at its white walls, he had said more than once: "It looks like an old ship."

The place was soon to acquire the fame that attaches to the close association of a home and writer. Somerset Maugham had his Villa Mauresque in Cap Ferrat on the French Riviera, Bernard Berenson had his I Tatti in Florence, Italy. Noël Coward had his Firefly Hill in Port Maria, Jamaica. Now Hemingway would have his Finca Vigía in San Francisco de Paula, Cuba. It too would become a famous home in the world of international letters.

At the end of 1943, however, immortality was far from the thoughts of Martha Gellhorn. She, who had discovered the Vigía, decided a short time later that the moment had come for her to leave. One day on the path that led to the house, she met Dr. José Luis Herrera Sotolongo, the personal physician and close friend of the Hemingways since the Spanish Civil War, and told him: "I'm saying goodbye to you, Doctor. I'm leaving for Europe and I won't come back to the *beast*," referring to Ernest.

"She's from St. Louis, Missouri," Ernest said cryptically when Dr. Herrera asked for an explanation of Martha's words. It was not long, however, before Ernest packed his own bags and went off to Europe. Some said that he was going to report on the invasion of Normandy. Others believed he was running after Martha. Whatever his reasons, the result was that he came back without Martha and with a new lady in tow: Mary Welsh.

Martha Gellhorn, a young, beautiful, independent woman

who wrote novels and covered the Spanish Civil War as a news-paperwoman, had many likable traits, but she was hardly the ideal woman for the Vigía. She was happy enough when it was the stage for her romance and honeymoon with Hemingway, but she couldn't abide it when it became solely the writer's refuge.

Martha had little interest in running a house. She spent much of her time with the sports she loved. While she lived at Vigía, she busied herself playing tennis and sunning at the swimming pool, delegating the domestic duties to such people as the gardener, Pichilo, and the carpenter, Francisco Castro. She spent a lot of time with her friends in Miramar, where very wealthy Cubans and Americans lived. And then one day she was gone, soon to be replaced by a more sympathetic woman.

Dearest Pickle my beloved let's think about the boat and the dark blue, almost purple of the Gulf Stream, making eddies at the edge of the current and flying fish going up in coves and us on the flying bridge steering in shorts and no tops and at night anchored behind the barrier reef down at Paraiso with the sea pounding on the lovely sand and breaking on the horse-shoe of the reef and we anchored fine and *burn* inside with no motion only the tide pull and we lie with our legs touching and drink a tall cocoanut water, lime and gin and see the lovely blue miniature mountains over our right shoulders and I say "Pickle, do you like very much?" (Maybe you will know better mts. and that is OK. But these lovely) and you say whatever you say and then there is that night and the next day is another and in the morning we can sleep as late as ever and have breakfast and afterwards dive over board and swim ashore and walk on the far beach of the atoll with no suits while Gregorio polices up the boat and we have many things to do my dearest Pickle . . .

When Mary Welsh arrived at Finca Vigía after World War Two, things changed abruptly. She took over the house completely. While Ernest was on the fighting fronts of Europe, a hurricane struck Cuba on October 19, 1944, leveling the area, knocking down royal palms, damaging the tennis court. There was extensive restoration to be done and Mary, barely settled in, got to work at once helping and supervising.

Mary Welsh is remembered affectionately by the townpeople

for her charm, her efforts to learn Spanish, and the energy she bestowed on her rose gardens. "She'd come from there," says Pichilo, the former gardener, "covered with sweat." "And full of mud," adds Herrera Sotolongo. In the end, she would be the one remembered as the true mistress of Finca Vigía.

Mary took good care of the house and of Ernest Hemingway, too. Later when they quarreled, she showed more understanding than he did; friends claim that he was harsher than Mary during their time of discord.

Finca Vigía, described in official language as "a country place" or "Farmhouse," became the writer's permanent "headquarters" after Mary Welsh's arrival; a fine and sunny property with a distant view of the Gulf Stream and the lights of Havana. Here Ernest Miller Hemingway, the well-fed Nordic intellectual marked by a tragic destiny, would stay among the lush tropical vegetation flourishing on a hilltop southeast of Havana, weathering endless rainstorms, hurricanes and droughts, in the midst of his many Cuban friends and neighbors.

Nevertheless, some have seen a negative symbol in Finca Vigía: a towering estate over the humble houses of San Francisco de Paula. But the people of that little town think differently. To them, Hemingway will always bring pleasant memories.


[2]


In spite of its proximity to Havana, San Francisco de Paula has grown slowly since it was founded toward the end of the eighteenth century. In the *Historic Record of Guanabacoa*, by G. Castellanos, one reads that in 1774, "Augustín Francisco de Arocha, a native of Canary Islands, favors the construction of a chapel at San Francisco de Paula."

At that time there existed a few cattle ranches whose owners were in constant litigation. Somehow they got together and agreed to build the chapel as a center around which the village would grow, as was customary in Spanish townships. Today, two centuries later, on one of the hills adjacent to Finca Vigía, the old chapel still stands.

In the *Geographic, Statistical and Historical Dictionary of the Is-*

*land of Cuba*, by Jacobo de la Pezuela, published in 1886, the following appears:

> San Francisco de Paula (village of) - It is situated at 4-½ leagues west of Santa María del Rosario, on uneven and high terrain on the north side of the Bacalao Hill near the source of the Luyano River. It is a cheerful-looking place, formed by 26 houses with 141 inhabitants of all ages, sexes and colors. There is a chapel built in 1795 with contributions collected by Don Francisco Arocha, who, in support of the church, donated 3 farms. Statistics for 1846 listed it with 7 houses and 53 inhabitants and for 1841 with 57. By the road which it borders, the village is ¾ of a league from Santa María del Rosario to which jurisdiction it belongs, and 2-½ from Havana.

Much later, the Spaniards built a small fort on the grounds where Hemingway's house stands today. It consisted of a wooden structure which was used as a watchtower with a heliographic communication systems; hence, the name given to the place. One finds such vigías throughout Cuba.

A Frenchman named Joseph D'Orn Duchamp, with a real estate business in Havana, had owned Finca Vigía since the nineteen twenties. He is remembered to this day by the townspeople of San Francisco de Paula as "Mister Don," following the curious Cuban custom of believing that all wealthy foreigners must be Americans.

Finca Vigía cost 18,500 Cuban pesos (at par with the American dollar). In Carlos Baker's biography of Hemingway the price is mistakenly given as 12,500 pesos. Baker says Finca Vigía was Hemingway's gift to Martha Gellhorn and himself, with Otto Bruce, their aide-de-camp, conducting the negotiations. The money came from the royalties paid for the film version of *For Whom the Bell Tolls*. (Gregorio Fuentes remembers that he was with Hemingway on board the *Pilar*, moored to one of the docks of Havana bay, when the writer received the check from Paramount. Gregorio says the amount was one hundred thousand dollars, and Hemingway waved the check over his head as if it were a banner and exclaimed: "Our old age is secure!")

When Hemingway bought Finca Vigía from Monsieur D'Orn on December 28, 1940, he had acquired 43,345 square meters of Cuban territory, or about 21 acres. As soon as Hemingway acquired Finca Vigía, "Mister Don" took away his great guard dogs which for years had denied the boys of San Francisco de Paula access to the farm. Luis Villarreal, Rene's twin brother, now in his mid-fifties and a neighbor of La Vigía since birth, remembers it well.

"The war between us and Mister Don's dogs had ended forever," reminisces Villarreal. The cause of war had been the beautiful and succulent mangoes of the farm, which, following an old Cuban custom, the boys would try to steal during the season. Many of these boys, grown to manhood today, remember how grateful they were for the change in ownership of Finca Vigía.

There are still people in San Francisco de Paula who claim to remember the first time Hemingway came driving up to the farm in a big black Cadillac (other people claim it was a black Lincoln). All the boys gathered at the entrance gates of the Vigía to see what Mister Don's successor looked like. They saw a ruddy hulk of a man, strangely dressed in khaki shorts mated with a soiled and sweaty guayabera, the white, pleated overshirt typical of the tropics.

[3]

The Vigía is situated above the sea on one of the high points in that region. The highest point, less than a kilometer from there, is known by two names, Loma del Yoyo and Loma del Bacalao. In this lofty region San Francisco de Paula, although rural, seems like a district of Havana.

At the beginning of the century some villas like the Vigía were built when it appeared that the area might become a fine residential section of the city. The rest are small, a few made of wood with tin roofs. Most have traditional red tile roofs. But now there are only half a dozen sizeable houses besides the Vigía. Among them are the big, expensive old house of the Steinharts and the one called the Little Castle.

"The major additions to the farm during Hemingway's time were the tower and the little guest house near the pool," says

Luis Villarreal. "The tennis court was always there and so was the garage, a remodeled old stable. On one side of the farm when Hemingway acquired the land was the Vigía dairy, owned by Julian Rodriguez, who sold his milk in long bottles marked La Vigía—Grade A. A common entrance served both the dairy and Hemingway's house until Hemingway bought the entire property." Villareal remembers that the land from the entrance road down to the woods in back of the farm was planted with cattle foddering. Beyond the wooded region there were a few houses. Not far away was the "gallera," a pit for cockfights owned by Gerardo Dueñas, a local potentate.

When Hemingway bought the dairy, almost the whole hill belonged to him—the top and much of the surrounding land, except for the side to the northeast with Frank Steinhart's house on it. Ernest at the top, Steinhart on one side, and the small houses bordering the Vigía on the other side were separated by a low and thick enclosure called "pigs' fence."

Finca Vigía is on the outskirts of San Francisco de Paula. At times its fence borders the town, its houses and buildings, but then it trails off into open country. There are two roads that border the farm, forming a V whose summit is at the farm's gate. To the left, beyond Steinhart's house, there is open country and the cattle farms that belonged to Representative Dueñas.

In the Alley of the Vigía, Hemingway had five neighbors: in the first house, Diego del Otero, a tinsmith; Carlos Medina in the second house, a Communist and streetcar mechanic; in the third, José Gutiérrez, who owned a plot when Hemingway arrived but took years to get enough money to build his house; David Fernandez in the fourth house, a laborer in the brewery (Hemingway got him his job); and in the fifth house, Manuel Antonio Angulo, office worker in a court house. Beyond this area were some small apartment buildings also owned by Gerardo Dueñas; and to the east there were some more small apartment buildings, again owned by Gerardo Dueñas; a little farther to the east there were empty lots and a semi-clandestine cockpit well known to the locals.

In the nearby houses across the street, Hemingway's neighbors were a weaver, a cigar maker, a night watchman, a tractor driver, a mechanic, a widow and a pensioner. Twenty-five years after Hemingway's death, these people or their heirs are still living and working in the same places.

San Francisco de Paula is a small town with steep, crooked streets following the contours of the land. Only the main road 50 meters from the Finca Vigia gate, for 50 years Cuba's Central Highway, is fully paved. The town's own streets start out well enough, but then suddenly turn into dirt.

There were times when Hemingway, after a few drinks with his merry neighbors, would get lost wandering through these twisting alleys. Victor's, Ignacio's and Anibal's were some of the names of the local shops where one could buy cheap rum and excellent Cuban beer, which then cost ten cents a bottle.

The sources of work for the local folk were the brewery in Cotorro, a nearby town; a textile factory called Facute; and a metal plant, the Antillana Steel Plant. The brewery made Hatuey Beer, which Hemingway mentioned in his books more than once, much to the joy of its owners, who, taking advantage of the publicity surrounding the award of the Nobel Prize to Hemingway—the first and only time the glorious prize, medal, diploma and money landed in Cuba—organized a tribute to the writer. The Havana newspapers dated Tuesday, August 14, 1956, described the event:

> At noon yesterday there took place in the gardens of the Modelo Beer Factory in Cotorro, a tribute to Ernest Hemingway, the great American writer, author of *The Old Man and the Sea*, who has long lived among us. The affectionate tribute was offered by several Cuban cultural institutions.

The lunch offered by the sponsors was served in the afternoon. Hemingway, dressed in a white guayabera, looked, in the words of one of the guests, "weary and prematurely aged." He was nearly stifled by an overenthusiastic crowd of photographers, newspaper people and would-be writers, all Cuban. Hemingway, "maybe for the first time in his life, looked really frightened." The tribute was held outdoors in an immense garden, with plenty of free Hatuey beer and Bacardi daiquiris. The lunch consisted of roast pork, fried bananas and rice, served cold.

Later, surrounded by his buddies, a group of fisherman from

Cojímar who arrived at the last minute, Hemingway said, "For a man supposed to be lonely, I have plenty of friends."

There was a huge sign which said: "Hatuey beer salutes ERNESTO HEMINGWAY." When the local fishermen arrived, the master of ceremonies said: "Here are the humble fishermen of Cojímar, *great* friends of the *great* writer and friends of Hatuey and Bacardi, who take great pleasure in their presence here. Welcome, fishermen of Cojímar!"

The ceremonies started with the Cuban national anthem and when someone asked why they didn't play the American anthem as well, he was told in all seriousness that Hemingway had become a Cuban citizen.

Later, typical native trios interpreted a new chachacha bravely titled "Viva Hemingway," and a guaracha without a title, whose egalitarian lyrics consisted only of "Hemingway! Campoamor! Pessino!"

Fernando Campoamor, the organizer of the tribute, was a newspaperman and a drinking companion of Finca Vigía's owner. Even as recently as 1980, he could still be found lolling in Hemingway's haunts in Havana, especially the Floridita bar. Pessino was the manager of the Hatuey brewery.

One of the musical numbers received with great emotion was a song interpreted by Amelita Frade, played to the tune of *La Guantamera:*

> *He got the Nobel Prize*
> *because he is a writing tiger.*
> *He makes us see*
> *the moments he has lived.*
> *The panthers of Zambeze*
> *trembled before him.*
> *His book seems to say*
> *that the old man was Hemingway*
> *but the sea was of Hatuey.*
> *He deserves the prize he won.*
> *He likes the strong winds*
> *on the decks of El Pilar.*
> *And at night he talks*
> *to the jungle and the river.*
> *He loves this land of ours,*

*and loves our ocean.*
*He likes to shake the hand*
*of our humble people*
*and enjoys the daiquiri,*
*healthful, delicious and Cuban!*

Finally, Hemingway was led to the platform, where he said: "The man who cannot speak a language well should not speak it at all, not even at home." He then proceeded to deliver a speech "in perfect Spanish, though with a strong American accent," according to one of the columnists present. Hemingway repeated his old maxim that the writer should write and not speak, and announced his decision to give the medal from the Nobel Prize to "Nuestra Señora de la Caridad del Cobre," the virgin who is the patron saint of Cuba. Campoamor then thanked him with these words:

"Hemingway, Cuba loves you like a mother."

The next day the *Diario de la Marina* referred to Hemingway in a column written by an overzealous Father José Rubinos: "Hemingway has now embarked with all of us on the boat of the Virgin of Charity. . . . The great novelist is on the way to the Great Illumination. . . . I like to imagine that from now on his novels will have the perspective of the infinite nature of the Christian soul."

In a souvenir of the tribute—printed on brown paper—appears the mention of Hatuey beer in *The Old Man and the Sea* and *To Have and Have Not*, with the additional note:

SOUVENIR
Luncheon held in the gardens of the Modelo Beer Factory in Cotorro, Havana, Monday, the 13th of August, 1956. Copy of a page from *To Have and Have Not* published by Charles Scribner's Sons, of New York, USA, where the great novelist mentions our Hatuey beer.

On the reverse side of the brochure appears the same text, but with reference to *The Old Man and the Sea*.

[4]

Great trucks loaded with lime continue to travel the main East-West highway, the Carretera Central. Nearby are several active quarries that supply construction material to Havana. Since lime is extracted by means of dynamite, each explosion is felt intimately at the Vigía. The house shakes, a white column of smoke can be seen rising in the near distance, and one feels close to a battlefield.

In the street that leads to the farm, long considered an extension of the Alley of the Vigía, there is still the drugstore that Hemingway, chronically resentful of medicine, always avoided looking at.

Out in the Central Highway on the way to Havana, there is a cafe called El Brillante, which has a great sparkling diamond painted on the wall. The landscape was described by Hemingway in *Islands in the Stream*, as Thomas Hudson drives through on his way to the American Embassy and his favorite bar, the Floridita.

[5]

Of all Hemingway's neighbors, Frank Steinhart, Jr., was the most affluent, and the most annoyed by the writer's mischief. Under cover of night, Hemingway feuded merrily with Steinhart for many years. Steinhart lived on a handsome income, derived from the fortune of his notorious, allegedly corrupt father. His father had once owned the Havana Railway, the company that operated the street cars of Havana.

A scandal surfaced when it was discovered that large sums of money, which were to have been used for emergency public works, found their way into the pockets of President Gomez of Cuba and his German and American advisors, and into those of Steinhart, Sr.

This scandalous chapter of Steinhart family history happened years before Hemingway came to Cuba and had no bearing on the "commando tactics" used on his neighbor. According to Herrera Sotolongo, the physician, they were merely childish pranks on Hemingway's part. The writer enjoyed the "undeclared war" on Steinhart and there were great battles at the "frontier," the boundary between the two farms.

Herrera Sotolongo remembers how they made use of firecrackers and stink bombs whenever Steinhart gave one of his grand parties. Hemingway would drag Herrera and his brother, Roberto, into the fray, in addition to any other friends who happened to be around.

The best time for the operation was at midnight, when Hemingway would lead his men under the cover of dark, through the trees, to the enemy fence. He demanded strict silence from his followers and one could see how excited and happy he was as he approached the site for the action. They were armed with hollowed bamboo stalks which were used as bazookas to shoot fireworks.

After the "attack" Hemingway was always the last one "to cover our retreat," as he put it, but, according to Herrera Sotolongo, it was really to see the cups and saucers of the dinner guests jump on the table when the fireworks exploded, and to see how the grand ladies daintily excused themselves and left when the air wafted the aroma of the stink bombs their way.

The action got really wild when Steinhart unleashed his dogs. Once when Hemingway and friends interrupted still another soirée with fire from the makeshift bazookas, Steinhart got so furious that he retaliated by shooting his gun four or five times in the general direction of Hemingway's house. But in Herrera Sotolongo's words: "Luckily, we were all lying on the ground in the darkness. He couldn't see us and no one was hurt."

Mary Welsh disapproved of these foolish games. Thanks to her, Hemingway and Steinhart agreed on a truce and early in the fifties the war between them ended. By then the underground struggle against Batista was spreading and all types of explosions were considered subversive. When Mary speaks of the Steinharts in her book *How It Was*, they are described as charming and distinguished neighbors. She neglects any mention of the curious nocturnal battles in which her husband was captain of the guerrillas.

Steinhart's house is a reminder of the architecture favored by millionaires of the twenties. Compared to it, the Vigía seems

The library at Finca Vigía. The lion is a trophy from Hemingway's first safari in Africa, 1934. (Enrique de la Uz)

The library at Finca Vigía. The leopard was hunted by Hemingway in Kimana Swamp, 1953. The round stool was purchased by Ernest and Mary in Cairo in 1954. (Enrique de la Uz)

The living room at Finca Vigía, kept as Hemingway left it. (Enrique de la Uz)

Hemingway's favorite easy chair. On the right is the table-bar he designed to have drinks at hand while he read, usually in the afternoon. (Enrique de la Uz)

Hemingway often dropped the mail on his bed. To this day, some of the last newspapers and magazines mailed to Finca Vigía after his death are kept there. (Enrique de la Uz)

On the bookcase is Hemingway's Mannlicher carbine, which Mary Welsh Hemingway offered as a gift to Fidel Castro in August 1961, shortly after the writer's death. Above it is a buffalo head from Hemingway's 1934 safari. (Enrique de la Uz)

Tower of Finca Vigía, built in 1947. First story, the baths; second story, the cats' lodgings; third story, the arms room; top floor, the military library and working retreat. (Enrique de la Uz)

Finca Vigía: the path to the swimming pool, as viewed from the house. (Enrique de la Uz)

A happy Hemingway on the porch of Finca Vigía, circa 1941.

Martha Gellhorn, photographed in London by Lee Miller. Hemingway kept this photo at Finca Vigía. (*Vogue*)

Hemingway and Martha Gellhorn on the beach at Waikiki, Hawaii, 1941. (UPI)

Hemingway and Martha Gellhorn beside the swimming pool at Finca
Vigía, circa 1941.

Marital dispute with Martha Gellhorn aboard the *Tin Kid*, the *Pilar*'s
auxiliary.

Shortly after their honeymoon, Ernest Hemingway and his fourth wife, Mary Welsh Hemingway, hold pets in jai-alai *cestas* at Finca Vigía, March 1945. (UPI)

demure, modest, rustic—barely good enough for a prosperous farmer. The Steinhart mansion, with its grandiose and eclectic architectural style, was an expression of native *art nouveau* appropriate for a tycoon residing in Havana. After the victory of the Cuban Revolution, it was converted into a basic intermediate school, its student body comprising most of the adolescents of San Francisco.

The school was named Fernando Chenard Piña, in honor of a revolutionary hero. Piña was a photographer by profession who died in the attack on Moncada, July 26, 1953. The wall that encloses the old Steinhart estate is of stone and much higher than that of the Vigía. The swimming pool is empty, but the road is full of children every school day.

There is a sign at the gate of the old Steinhart residence saying, in the words of the revolutionary Chenard Piña: "If I die and this is saved, dress in red, for it will mean that our country is saved."

[6]

The fireworks action was not limited to the boundary between the farms of the street railway magnate and the writer. Often at Christmas, Ernest Hemingway could be seen surrounded by about 20 boys, roaming the streets of San Francisco de Paula and setting off rockets. He always kept a supply in his house for his private war with Steinhart.

"The firecrackers were sold either singly or in strips, and Hemingway, running around with us, carried his strips in his pockets and also in a bandolier," recalls Gilberto Enriquez, one of the boys who belonged to Hemingway's gang. "The firecrackers could have been lit with matches, but traditionally we used cigarettes, which gave us the sense we were part of a demolition team. Since Hemingway didn't smoke, we vied with each other to carry the Partagas or Lucky Strikes.

"We worked like commandos. For example, we would approach the barbershop stealthily and toss in a bunch of firecrackers. These made a noise like a machine gun and the people in the shop would fling themselves to the floor. Then someone would say: 'Oh, that was nothing, just the kids with their fire-crackers.'

"Sometimes they saw that Hemingway was responsible and they would get mad: 'Damn it, that American is too old for this kind of thing!' But that was all. In the first place, Hemingway was very big and strong and you had to think twice before tangling with him. And in the second place, he was well liked and people forgave him for his childishness. Of course, he didn't want to be seen. He used to run away with the boys as fast as he could, but you can imagine what this must have looked like; that big man among fifteen or twenty kids running uphill or downhill through the streets of San Francisco de Paula. People would say, 'Why, it's Hemingway!' and when they heard the explosions: 'Hemingway and his fireworks!'

"Hemingway, excited, would laugh and send one of the boys to the barbershop or whatever to find out what had happened, and when the boy returned he would question him as if it had really been a guerrilla operation. 'So they got down on the floor, eh?' he would ask. And the scout would tell his tale. When something pleased him, he would turn to the rest of the group as if asking for our approval."

For the boys, the greatest fun was the skyrocket battles. Hemingway placed the "troops" in two different trenches, dug into any of the slopes in the land of the farm; he would captain one faction while he sent some of his friends, usually guests in his house, to lead the other one. The boys were armed with wooden launchers.

"We would take aim, and then the rocket war would start," recalls Gilberto, one of the "survivors." "Anyone could lose his head there. You had to be fast."

Once Herrera Sotolongo was not "armed" and they caught him inside the house with their "bazookas." The doctor had to run at top speed because they were actually shooting at his feet point blank. They wanted to see him dance.

# "*Las Estrellas de Gigi*"

In summer, Hemingway ran around the farm shirtless and in shorts. At times he carried a .22-caliber pistol in his belt. He would tell the boys from San Francisco de Paula: "Take all the mangoes you want home with you, but do not throw stones at the trees." His desire not to have the trees mistreated was an obsession. He particularly prohibited the throwing of stones at fruit on his property. Naturally, this was difficult to enforce, for to a Cuban boy, the best way to get mangoes is by throwing stones at the branch.

Someone once asked Hemingway: "Look, don't you want these kids to be good baseball players? It's good practice for them!"

Hemingway mulled this over and then said he would see that they learned pitching with gloves and a ball, not stones and mangoes. He said he would pay for their equipment. And he did. He ordered baseball uniforms and bought them bats, balls and gloves. Then for the first time the boys of San Francisco de Paula had their very own baseball club. They called themselves "*Las Estrellas de Gigi*" (Gigi's Stars) in honor of Hemingway's youngest son, Gregory.

Many times during Hemingway's stay on the farm, the team of "*Las Estrellas de Gigi*" had to travel to play other teams. Hemingway loved to load his pickup truck with boys and their equipment, and play the part of their manager.

After he organized "*Las Estrellas de Gigi*," he realized that it was absolutely necessary to form another baseball team, so they'd have someone to play against. Once more he dug deep into his pockets to equip nine new players—the competition—and then there were two baseball teams on his payroll.

Something of the feeling Hemingway had for these boys can be appreciated in a passage from *Islands in the Stream*, where the author describes the sense of joy and love Roger experiences as he walks to the beach surrounded by Thomas Hudson's sons.

Yet there were times when Hemingway "went about his own business" and rode down from the farm in the pickup and the boys saw him go by, silent and alone. They remember other times when Hemingway was driven to town and sat in the back seat, drink in hand, or with a thermos in which two or three ice cubes floated in a sea of rum. Then, because they weren't with him, they felt something they couldn't define, something between nostalgia and jealousy.

[8]

The boys were allowed to come to the farm barefoot and bare-chested, and often Hemingway boxed with them, which he enjoyed very much. He taught them how to dodge blows. He let them hit him and never hit back. One saw, that big, smiling, good-natured man, so strong and healthy, perspiring, encouraging his opponents to jab him hard, telling them he could stand any-thing. The boys of the neighborhood gathered around him, yelling, cheering each other on, as Hemingway, enjoying every blow, played the sparring partner.

One afternoon Felix Sosa, a small boy growing into ado-lescence, was boxing with Patrick, Hemingway's second son. He was observed hitting Patrick below the belt several times. Hemingway stopped the action, separated them and told young Sosa: "That's not the way to box. I'm going to teach you how it's done."

When Hemingway started to put on his gloves, Felix Sosa tossed his to one side and ran away, out of the farm. A few days later Hemingway sent for Felix to make peace, so that he would not feel hurt. "The truth is," says Gilberto Enriquez, "that Hemingway didn't have a mean bone in his body."

"We became attached to Papa," said Luis Villarreal, "through a strange circumstances. One day, we, the children of the neigh-borhood, were playing in the street, when Rodolfo, a younger brother of mine, fell off a wagon loaded with yuccas. The wheels ran over him. He was badly crushed and seemed to be in agony." We didn't know what to do. He was lying in the street, scream-ing. The news reached Hemingway in his home on the hill that

Rodolfo had been run over by a wagon. Hemingway came down, picked him up and took him in his car to the private clinic. He told the doctors: 'Save this child's life! I don't care how much it costs, I'll pay for everything.' Unfortunately, all efforts were useless, and my brother died. I don't know why Hemingway did what he did, but what I do know is that he was a compassionate man."

After Rodolfo died, Hemingway decided to take René, one of the brothers, into his house and train him as a secretary or butler. From that day on René became increasingly important to the writer, until he became second in command at the Vigía and the man who took charge of the place in Hemingway's absence. He is an indispensable character in any account of Hemingway's life in Cuba.

In *Islands in the Stream*, Mario is the name Hemingway gave to the character based on René Villarreal. There's a scene in the book in which the dead child is mentioned. Thomas Hudson and his chauffeur are on the way to Havana, and since there is no gatekeeper the usual problem arises: Who will get out of the car to close the gate behind them? "A Negro boy was coming up the street and he called to him to close the gate and the boy grinned and nodded his head.

" 'He is a younger brother of Mario.'

" 'I know,' Thomas Hudson said."

After Hemingway's death in 1961, René was put in charge of the house. He managed the place with great care and understanding. Once when a Cuban writer had a talk with him, René pulled out from his shirt pocket a letter that looked as if it had been folded and unfolded hundreds of times. He must have known the contents by heart, yet he had tears in his eyes as he read it solemnly.

"It was the last letter written by Hemingway."

No doubt he meant that it was the last letter written to *him* by Hemingway. In it Hemingway told him of his illness, how he'd lost a great deal of weight and that "Old Papa is no longer what he used to be." He also said that he was not fooling himself about the future.

In his will Hemingway asked Mary Welsh to give René Villarreal a splendid gift, Hemingway's Winchester carbine. Thus, it is not to be found among the objects at the museum.

René Villarreal may be seen and heard in the Cuban film "Memories of Underdevelopment." At one point, the off-screen voice of the main character accuses him of having been "a slave" to Hemingway. This part of the film is based on the essay, "The Last Summer," by Edmundo Desnoes, co-author of the film.

"I was the only person who could go into his room while he was writing," René Villarreal explained with pride, while he accompanied us through the house, now a museum. Many years ago, the famous American writer found this poor black child in the streets of San Francisco de Paula and took him into his home. He took care of him and molded his personality to his own, and to the needs of the house. When Hemingway wrote, he allowed René to enter his room because he moved as quietly as an African panther. When Hemingway went away, it was René who was left in charge of the farm. "All of us ate at the same table together," added René, to prove that Hemingway treated him as part of the family.

In the film this is said while the camera explores the estate, the rooms of the house, and shows close-ups of Hemingway's hunting trophies.

"The man did not seem to understand that the film was a work of fiction," says Tomas Gutiérrez Alea, the director. "When the film was shown in the theaters, René got a gun and went looking for Edmundo and me. He wanted to kill us."

René Villarreal emigrated to the United States in the seventies, with the help of Mary Welsh. He became a master goldsmith in the jewelry trade, working in a New Jersey shop. His family still lives in Cuba. Another brother, Oscar Villarreal, is a prominent trade union leader.

Luis Villarreal was interviewed at the farm one afternoon in November, 1977. It was the first time in many years that he had visited the old place, although he lives only a few blocks away. It was late in the afternoon. When we passed by the old stables, later converted into a garage, Luis said: "He had a Plymouth and a Chrysler, and a Buick pickup truck." Night fell, and the house, 20 years after Hemingway's death, loomed up from the darkness, with the majestic silhouette of the great ceiba tree lending an imposing presence. A pair of street lights gave a yellow glow, attracting clouds of insects.

Luis Villarreal remembered the many times Papa went away on his travels.

"Sometimes he stayed away for a year and my brother René was left in charge of the house. When Papa returned, everything was in order and I came to welcome him back along with many of his neighbors in San Francisco. I no longer like to come here. It saddens me—a part of my life was spent here, close to a man whom we loved and who loved us so much. And now it is gone."

## Circo Miguelito

[9]

Many people in San Francisco like to tell anecdotes in which the narrator always appears close to "Mister Güey." One of them, Kid Mario, tells the tale of a pair of old lions, three or four clowns and a tent made of well-patched cloth: the Circus Miguelito.

Kid Mario, an old prizefighter, was once Hemingway's masseur. He relates that this battered circus came to San Francisco for a couple of days, and Hemingway, as was his custom, went to see the animals in their cages and to "talk to them." There he casually boasted in front of curious onlookers that he could get into the cage with them.

Maybe he never really said it, maybe it was a figment of the onlookers' imagination. In any case, the news quickly spread that Hemingway was going to tame the lions. He could do it because of his African experience.

The owner of the circus took it seriously. He announced it to one and all. That night all of San Francisco filled the seats awaiting "Jemingüey's" performance. He actually arrived in his African hunter's outfit, with chair and whip in hand, and spent two hours working with the animals.

"The next morning," says Kid Mario, "I was giving Mr. Güey his massage, when he sent for the owner of the Miguelito.

The man arrived in short order and Mr. Güey asked his man-servant to bring his guest a drink. Then he said: 'Do you know why I performed in your show last night? I did it because I do not like to cheat the public and because you announced that I was going to tame the lions.'

" 'It was a good act,' the circus owner said.

" 'Don't worry about my fee,' Hemingway said. 'I have gotten in touch with my lawyers in New York, and they will collect it for me. My price is ten thousand dollars per performance.' "

At that point Kid Mario had to stop the massage he was giving Hemingway in order to help revive the circus owner and pick up the pieces of broken glass when his drink hit the floor. When the man regained consciousness, he assured Hemingway that he had never in his life seen ten thousand dollars, not even a thousand. Hemingway sternly admonished him and then told him that he would commute his sentence. "Let us hope you never again use my name without proper authority," the writer warned the circus owner.

[10]

Hemingway's pal and partner in the business of cockfights was "Pichilo," which is what they still call the gardener, José Herrero, in San Francisco de Paula.

Many claim that they knew Hemingway, but Pichilo can prove it. There is a photo taken of him in the small cockpit he built at the Vigía, with Hemingway standing by his side, watching him closely. Behind Hemingway, a youthful René can be seen.

Pichilo loved fighting cocks more than anything else. He confesses: "I was a gambler. A real gambler."

He was lucky in the business of breeding gamecocks in partnership with Hemingway. They started in 1942 with "a special cock, a Spanish jerezano," a beautiful specimen of fighting cock famous for its stamina, and acquired at a rather steep price. But the favorite of the Hemingway-Herrero partnership was a white-tailed "malatobo," which won a memorable encounter in Guanabacoa, after a bloody fight.

"Badly hurt, but he won," boasts Pichilo. Hemingway's immediate profit was $800, a considerable sum in those days.

"He sent us there to gamble. I always gambled and made good bets."

They owned some 20 fighting cocks. When the birds were ready to fight, when they became "pollones," they were made to wear little cloth boots to prevent hurting each other with their naturally sharp spurs.

"Naturally, in this 'sport' as in any other you can lose," reasons Pichilo. "Hemingway was a good loser, that's the honest truth."

" 'Bet anything you like,' he'd tell me, because he respected my advice. Sometimes we lost, but he never complained. He had faith in me. Of course, I shared the losses as well as the winnings from our bets. When it came to money, neither of us was shy."

The Cuban cockfighting gamblers are the loudest in the world. Hemingway shared the world of these bizarre characters as an equal, and enjoyed with them the wild spectacle of two birds trying to rip each other's eyes out.

Hemingway told the other gamecock breeders: "What I like is to watch the fights." And so he'd give a sum of money to Pichilo, and let him place the bets. The betting was the thing for the *aficionado*, the real thrill, before cockfights were outlawed in Cuba. It was quite a sight—those men in the cockpits, perspiring heavily in their guayaberas, work pants and straw hats, wearing solid gold jewelry, cigars in hand, yelling their bets: so many *monedas* on a favorite bird. A *moneda* was five dollars, a term left over from the old Spanish days. There in the midst of the throng, Hemingway watched the fights, enjoying the excitement.

In the decade starting in 1950, an attempt was made to lure American tourists to the cockfights. Promoters even built a cockpit in the nightclub cabaret, Sans Souci. But all attempts failed. The American public couldn't accept the cruel nature of the sport.

After the fights, Hemingway usually invited his cronies to a bar where great quantities of beer and rum were consumed while they enjoyed much loud talk. More than once his drinking companions heard Hemingway's advice: "Drink all you want, but don't be a drunken shit. I drink and get drunk every day, but I never bother anyone."

Pichilo tells us that Hemingway could spend a long time just quietly watching him prepare the spurs of the cock that was to fight. The fighting spurs were made of mother-of-pearl or of steel. The natural spurs were cut, leaving only a small stump to which the artificial combat spurs were attached. The details connected with the cockfights fascinated Hemingway, and he would spend hours watching and learning, as he did with the fishermen, observing their great preparations, or the Masai warriors in Africa, learning how to hunt with spears.

The "Vietnamese" was the nickname given to Rafael Romero, one of the few fighters in the Rebel army who, as late as 1975, still wore the olive-green campaign uniform and a Colt .45 revolver with a golden handle of the kind that was once popular in Cuba and almost always captured from Batista's men.

One day in 1959 Lieutenant Romero was in a cockpit in San Francisco de Paula, smoking his cigar, as usual, when the betting began. He shouted his bet of 50 *monedas* on a black-legged cock that looked unusually scrappy. Hemingway accepted the bet and Pichilo approved it. The fight went on while the other gamblers screamed and yelled.

Hemingway's choice won and the "Vietnamese" had to play him 250 dollars. The black-legged fighting cock lay dead on the ground, and as the gamblers filed out, Hemingway's voice was heard, loud and clear, "Bad luck, Lieutenant!" and the "Vietnamese," shrugging his shoulders, agreed, "Yes, bad luck."

The "Vietnamese" did not see Hemingway often after that. It was his last bet.

"That day in December of 1959, I decided my days as a cockfight gambler were over. I got so pissed off at Hemingway's mention of my bad luck that I got into my car and went straight to the disbursement office of the Rebel Army Air Force, where I was stationed. I went to see the cashier, who had been an old officer in the Batista army. I told him: 'I lost a fighting cock and 250 dollars on a bet with Hemingway.'

" 'I don't know Hemingway and I don't follow the cockfights,' said the cashier.

" 'That money was to pay the rent on the house and for the family Christmas party,' I told him.

" 'Gambling is no good. Saps the moral fiber,' he lectured.

"At that moment I was blind with anger at myself, and without realizing it, I placed my .45 on the ledge of the cashier's window. I wasn't even holding it, but it worked like magic, for the next thing he said was: 'Well, what we could do for you is give you a personal loan.' He did so right away and the following week I went to see Hemingway and told him: 'My bad luck is over, for I will never again bet on fighting cocks. Now all I have to do is pay that damn debt, and I'll have nothing to do with the game ever again.'

"Hemingway said that the best thing we could do was go have a drink."

Manuel Hernandez is now in his late sixties. He worked as a gamecock breeder for the Dueñas family, and remembers that when he ran into the writer in a café in San Francisco, Hemingway would always ask: "No fights today?"

"What I like is to watch the fight," Hemingway would invariably explain. "What I like is to *see* it."

A dry, taciturn type, Manuel says he clearly remembers one of Hemingway's difficulties with the sports protocol: "When the fight started, Hemingway would yell at his favorite cock: 'Get him!' But that is not what one does at a cockfight. What one does is propose bets. It's done this way: I bet *so many monedas on that cock!* You may yell and swear as much as you like, but no one ever says 'Get him!' Never."

[11]

Hemingway's presence was a welcome one in San Francisco de Paula for weightier reasons. He made generous contributions for the improvement of the town, including the two thousand dollars he gave for the construction of the aqueduct.

Collections were made with frequency in San Francisco de Paula for water pumping equipment, or for some festival, or someone's funeral. During the Christmas holidays there were additional collections of money. Hemingway was always generous and good-natured, and for this he was frequently praised in the local press. He made it a practice to send beautiful floral wreaths to the family of anyone who died in San Francisco.

There was also soliciting of funds for personal reasons, common in Cuba before the revolution. If someone was sick in the family, the thing to do was to go to a wealthy person's house and ask for money. In Hemingway's case these visits were frequent. Luis Villarreal remembers how they were handled. Hemingway would turn to Luis's brother, René, and ask him: "Do you know this person?" If René said yes, Hemingway would ask another question; all this in front of the person asking for the money.

"He says someone in his family is very sick and that he needs help. Is that true? Do you know if someone is really sick in his family?" The answers were usually in the affirmative, and then Hemingway would take some money out of his pocket, according to the merits of the case, and make a contribution.

However, if René's answer was in the negative, and Hemingway realized that it was a scheme to take advantage of his good nature, he would explode.

"If the person was telling the truth," says Luis, "Hemingway would quickly give him fifteen or twenty dollars, but if the person was trying to cheat him, he would become furious and swear like the devil. On one occasion, a character well known in San Francisco went to see him and told him he was collecting money to outfit a local baseball team. Hemingway knew he was lying, and you should have heard him scream: 'I shit on your fucking mother, you dirty cheat!' "


[12]


Hemingway employed Kid Mario to keep him in shape. Kid Mario is his professional nickname; his real name is Agustín Sanchez Cruz.

In the thirties and forties he was Cuba's welterweight boxing champion. Later he earned a living as a private masseur, and used to work at the Steinharts' on alternate days. Mary Welsh, who had lower-back problems, heard about him and requested his services. That was how he started working at the Vigía, going there every other day to make five dollars. Each one of his sessions lasted two or three hours. Ernest began to take notice of Mario when he heard him say that he had sparred with Gene Tunney. Ultimately, he became Ernest Hemingway's official masseur.

When Kid Mario started at Finca Vigía, the sculptor Boada was doing a bust of Hemingway, the clay model for the bronze bust that can be seen today in the Floridita bar.

"He certainly took his time doing it," comments Kid Mario. "I massaged Mr. Güey while the man worked on his bust. Well, each one makes a living the best way he can."

In August 1961, Mary came to Havana to gather Ernest's belongings, and saw Fidel Castro. During their interview, she told the Cuban leader, "The one thing I'd appreciate is your sending Mario to me in the United States once in a while. He's the best in his specialty, even though he's a militiaman now." According to Mario, Fidel replied that it was *much better* that he was a militiaman now.

In July of 1977, Mary brought Mario a present: matching denim Levi pants and jacket. She didn't see Mario, but sent it to him through mutual friends.

According to Kid Mario, Hemingway was a gentle and gracious client, very democratic. They traded blows with Everlast 16-ounce gloves, but the Vigía lacked much in the way of gym equipment. They threw a 12-pound ball around to strengthen Ernest's arms and chest, and, at EH's request, did some calisthenics.

Hemingway weighed 200 pounds and had developed a belly, which Mario attributed to drinking.

"Once he passed his fiftieth birthday he developed a paunch, but this did not stop him from doing his exercises; he could still bend over and touch his toes. He was really in good condition. And he had great posture."

In July of 1960, Hemingway said goodbye to the Kid with these words: "When one hits sixty one should hurry whatever one is doing so as not to leave it half done. But I am already past sixty. There's nothing to hurry for."

Kid Mario is still a robust and enthusiastic character. Twenty years after Hemingway's farewell, he goes on earning a living as a private masseur. Interviewed one recent summer, Kid Mario said that on a certain occasion while he rubbed oil on Hemingway's neck and shoulders, the writer confided the great secret of his life to him. Any biography of Hemingway must include this revelation, he intimated.

Realizing that it could be an authentic secret, the interviewer made no comment and continued questioning him on other subjects. He told Mario he wanted to hear the story of Hemingway's performance as a lion tamer in the Miguelito Circus. Kid Mario told that story and then remarked casually that he remembered perfectly well the day that Ernest Hemingway revealed the intimate secret to him.

The interviewer closed his notebook and thanked his host for his hospitality. As they were saying goodbye at the street door, Kid Mario remarked: "He was tormented by that secret."

During the course of the next several weeks, the interviewer received many calls at different times of the day from Kid Mario, in which he expressed interest in the "comrade writer's" health and in how the work was going. He informed him repeatedly that only he knew the "deep secret" of Hemingway's life.

[13]

Gilberto Enriquez had been one of the many children of the town who was Gigi Hemingway's pal. He had belonged to Gigi's gang, and had taken active part in the fireworks battles held on the farm. But in the mid-1950's he was past adolescence and one could see under his jacket the outline of a .45-caliber pistol. Everybody in San Francisco de Paula knew by then that one didn't fool around with Gilberto Enriquez.

Hemingway, being so perceptive, must have noticed the change in this boy as he became a surly young man of few words.

Gilberto headed a clandestine cell of the Socialist Youth. He joined the revolution as part of the guerrilla columns led by the legendary Camilo Cienfuegos. When the Cuban Revolution triumphed, Gilberto was given the key to San Francisco de Paula in a public ceremony and was praised as one of the district's underground fighters.

One day in the winter of 1959, Gilberto was at the El Hoyo, a small and out-of-the-way local bar. Since officers in uniform were not allowed to drink alcoholic beverages in public, Gilberto was at the back of the room, almost hidden from view. When he went to settle his bill, he was told that Hemingway had already paid it. Hemingway was there and approached him saying, "How are you, Lieutenant?"

"I would like you to have a drink on me," answered Gilberto.

"With pleasure," Hemingway said.

And they proceeded to talk about a common enemy.

That "enemy" was not one of the peaceful customers of the barbershop they both patronized, or one of the many cockfight aficionados, or any of the hard drinkers who spent their money at the café called El Brillante and whom Hemingway and his gang of boys had tormented in the old days with their firecracker tricks. No, the enemy was a tall, sharp-featured man, with a big head and round shoulders. A man named Maldonado.

In the mid-fifties, Hemingway's renewed enthusiasm for bullfights had taken him away to Spain; when he returned to his "home town" things had taken a turn for the worse. San Francisco de Paula was in grave danger. Maldonado was always driving around in a Willys jeep wearing the khaki uniform of the Rural Guard, with a wide-brimmed, chin-strapped hat and dark glasses. He was promoted from sergeant to lieutenant for his "outstand-ing" performance in repressing striking laborers. Moreover, he had killed "four or five boys," among them one named Guido Pérez, who had taken part in the rocket fights at the farm and had been taught boxing at Hemingway's house.

During the armed struggle against Batista, Lieutenant Mal-donado was the military chief of the nearby post at Santa María del Rosario. He commanded the patrol that kept a watch on the farm, which was under suspicion of keeping arms. One night, someone in the patrol killed one of Hemingway's dogs, bashing it with the butt of his rifle. Mary Welsh Hemingway and Hem-ingway's biographer, Carlos Baker, say that the victim was Ma-chakos. Others—A.E. Hotchner and José Luis Herrera Sotolongo among them—say that it was Black Dog, Hemingway's faithful retainer. Without identifying his source, Carlos Baker claims that the leader of the patrol was executed: ". . . the Batista sergeant who had shot the dog Machakos in August had been hanged in November 'with the usual mutilation' by some of the boys from Cotorro."

Baker's information is incorrect. None of Batista's officers executed in Cuba during the time of the insurrection was mutilated. And, not only was Maldonado not mutilated, but he was never hanged. In 1980, twenty-one years after the revolution, he was still very much alive.

Early in 1959, everybody in San Francisco de Paula thought that the end had finally come for this bloody henchman, the last of the local officers under arrest. During a public trial, the defendant wept constantly, until his aide, a man of sallow complexion, rose from his chair and said, "Hey pal, stop crying like a damn whore. You did the killing, and so did I."

An old Batista man nicknamed Caballo Loco (Crazy Horse), also present at the trial, fainted when he heard this. He had been a captain, chief of the Rural Guard at Cotorro, and Maldonado's direct superior. Although Caballo Loco wasn't directly responsible for any crime, he was "terrified at the trial."

Maldonado was sentenced to 30 years in prison. That he was not executed provoked angry local protest, including public demonstrations demanding a new trial and the carrying out of the death penalty, as had been done with other Batista murderers in the rest of the country. But at that precise moment, the order came to halt all executions of enemy officers guilty of murder.

"He's a man who needs killing," Gilberto told Hemingway while they had a drink that winter afternoon at El Hoyo.

"A bad man, a hyena, don't you think, Lieutenant?" said Hemingway.

"What distresses me most isn't the fact that he's alive," Gilberto said, "but thinking of those he killed—my comrades who are dead by his hand."

Hemingway listened to Gilberto in silence. The conversation had to touch inevitably on this subject. "He's going to die of old age, damn it. That's what is going to happen. For the good of the town the best thing would be to see him dead and buried."

The air of complicity between Gilberto and Hemingway had previously been established by events which occurred one night three years before, early in 1957.

Gilberto Enriquez had succeeded in arming a small troop of underground fighters. "Little by little I had armed 18 men," he says. On one occasion they planned to hang an "informer"— a traitor—and execute one of the soldiers who had participated in a repressive action against the revolutionaries who had attacked the military barracks of Goicuría, in Matanzas. Due to a lack of coordination, the plans went awry. But, somehow, the news reached the Vigía and there was an answer. René Villarreal spoke to Gilberto about some arms Hemingway had that he wanted delivered to the rebels. "Papa has some arms there—he wants you to have them." They agreed to meet that night outside the farm, in Steinhart Alley. Gilberto, accompanied by José Antonio Rabaza and Alfredo Sumi, arrived at the meeting place in an old Ford.

René Villarreal had just arrived to meet them when someone shone a light in their faces. The man with the flashlight was Panchito, a guard at the Steinhart farm. He was wearing a yellow uniform, boots, and he had a .38-caliber long-barrelled gun in his holster. Panchito, wielding his flashlight, said: "What are you doing here?" And then, in a paternal tone, he advised them to leave: "You know things are pretty bad, boys." It was a very frustrating moment in a disappointing operation.

The next day Gilberto was wounded in an encounter with the police, but he recovered and continued his revolutionary activities as a guerrilla in the mountains.


[14]


One day in 1939, Pichilo had finished a part-time job at the Vigía when the new tenant, a brawny young American named Ernest Hemingway, sent for him. Hemingway asked him if he could paint. Pichilo said he could. Then Hemingway told him, "I have watched you work, and I think you are a responsible person. I'd like you to work for me."

As Pichilo remembers, when Hemingway bought the Vigía

the place was not in the best of condition. Much of it, particularly the floors, needed major repairs.

Martha was in love with the Finca; she found the necessary people to fix it. Pichilo says she was an enterprising woman, and that he would like to know what happened to her and why she never came back. He was told that Mrs. Gellhorn is very much alive and that she appeared on a television program on BBC-1 in London on November 6, 1975, to discuss the authenticity of a famous photograph by Robert Capa—the snapshot of a militiaman as he falls mortally wounded in Somosierra. Pichilo was very happy to hear this: "On television? How nice!"

When Pichilo started to work at the Vigía, he earned 70 dollars every 15 days. He was given permission to let his cattle graze on Hemingway property, which meant a savings for him. Later, his earnings increased through the business of fighting cocks. He assured me that Hemingway always gave fair pay for work done for him.

As gardener, Pichilo's job was one he took pride in, since the flowers for the house and almost all the vegetables consumed at the farm came from its own gardens. Some notes signed by Mary Welsh, found among the papers left at the Finca, show how much Hemingway and Welsh cared for their gardens. Other notes are in Hemingway's own distinctive hand. In a funny one he advises the gardener, in Spanish, "not to bother the master of the house with gardening problems because those problems should be taken up with the Señora Mary, who is the proper person to handle them. He has enough problems with his writing."

Pedro, the gardener who worked for the previous owner, Mr. D'Orn, came to a strange ending in which Hemingway found himself directly involved. Apparently this was what caused that illustrious pair, Hemingway and Gellhorn, to drink water from a well with a corpse in it.

The most widespread version claims that Hemingway had either just acquired the farm or was still renting it, when he asked to see old Pedro and asked him if he was the gardener. "Yes, sir," Pedro answered. "Well, you are the gardener and I am the new owner. I'm only going to tell you one thing—I don't want you to prune the plants. I don't want you to cut anything, not even the grass. From now on your job will be to cut nothing, and I particularly don't want the children throwing stones at the trees."

Pedro swallowed hard and exclaimed: "But I'm not the police! I'm not going to watch the boys so that they won't throw stones at the fruit trees!"

"I won't ask you to do that," answered Hemingway. "You are the gardener, and your job will be not to cut, not to prune."

"But sir," said Pedro, "part of the work of a gardener is to prune."

"Yes," answered Hemingway, "But in *my garden* the gardener does *not* prune." Pedro immediately asked for his pay to date, for he was leaving.

Many contend that this was not the exact conversation, but it seems to agree with Hemingway's opposition to pruning his plants. His theory was that plants should be allowed to grow "as they wish, without restraint." The truth seems to be that later on, with Ernest's permission, the farm's gardeners did indeed prune some plants, and mowed the lawn as well.

Pedro took his salary and went in search of work, but he could not find another job. At the end of two weeks, Pedro came back and told Hemingway that he was right, that he was the owner, and if he didn't want him to prune his plants, then he wouldn't prune them, and that would be that. Hemingway listened to him and then told him respectfully that he was very sorry but that he had already hired another gardener and couldn't give him his job back.

Pedro, disconsolate at having lost his job at the farm, threw himself into one of the wells of the Vigía. Several days passed before the body was discovered. (Suspicion was finally aroused by the large number of buzzards circling above the well.)

The anecdote has different versions. No matter what the story, there really was a gardener named Pedro who jumped into one of the wells on Hemingway's farm, and, it seems, several days did pass before his corpse was discovered. These are the facts.

Pichilo says that the story of the "dead-man's water," as he called it, happened in 1941, and that Pedro, despondent because of his advanced years, "went crazy and threw himself into the well." Pichilo explains that the well in question was surrounded by a plot of bamboo and that in those days it supplied water *"only* to the swimming pool." About three days after his talk with Hemingway, the rumor spread that Pedro was lost, that he couldn't be found anywhere in town. Someone said that he had seen Pedro around the well, and when they got near it they saw the buzzards.

"The swimming pool, which has a capacity of ninety thousand gallons, was always treated with disinfectants," says Pichilo. "But the truth is that Mr. Hemingway never understood what happened and used to ask me: 'Pichilo, explain this to me: Why did this man come to kill himself at my farm?' I couldn't explain it to him. Neither could I remind him that Pedro did not own a farm and therefore, for his grim purpose, he had to use someone else's. But then, it wasn't Mr. Hemingway's fault that old Pedro didn't have his own farm."

[15]

The ceiba tree at the entrance to the house is the pride of the Vigía. It has become the symbol of the place. "There was a gentleman here, one of those scientists, who examined the tree, its branches, its roots, its knots, as if it were an old man, and said, 'At least 90 years old.' But everybody here knows that the ceiba is at least 150 years old," said the gardener of the Hemingway Museum, Gabino Enriquez, nicknamed "El Negro," although he is white.

The ceiba is mentioned in *Islands in the Stream*, when Thomas Hudson goes out to wait for his car, and sees the leaves and broken branches on the ground. The ceiba, the sacred tree of Cuba, is still there, more than 100 years old, with its branches bare most of the year. The tree, it is said, caused Mary Welsh a trying marital problem and provoked Hemingway into running after a gardener with a double-barrelled gun, a scene worthy of an old silent movie comedy.

According to reports from people in San Francisco, one of the roots of the ceiba tree was creating a problem for the inhabitants of the house, since it was lifting the floor. The roots of the ceiba are unusually strong and constantly spread in their search for water. One grew so long that it crossed under the house, lifting the tiles off the floors. Hemingway gave strict orders that nothing be done to the root, in accordance with his belief that plants and trees should grow without restraint.

Hemingway theorized that in this case the roots would recede when they found no water under the house, and then the tiles would fall back into place. A little cement here and there, and no harm done. But the lady of the house (some say Mary Welsh, while Pichilo swears it was Martha) didn't agree with her husband and hired an outside gardener.

She didn't call on Pichilo or any of those they knew, because she knew she couldn't count on them to go against Hemingway's orders. She waited until the master went to Havana one day and then she (in this story it's Mary Welsh) called in the gardener, who had been previously informed that there was "a spoiled, bad-tempered husband who did not want a particularly bothersome root to be cut." The gardener therefore lost no time in getting down to the job.

He lifted the floor tiles in the "Venetian Room," loosened the soil around the root, took out his instruments and after a little work with a machete and a couple of blows with an ax, the root was in his hands. The mutilation of the ceiba was completed.

And there was Ernest Hemingway, standing in the doorway watching his wife and the gardener, who, absorbed in the work at hand, were oblivious of his presence. Had he returned home purely by intuition, the intuition of "the old lion on permanent alert"?

When the gardener and Mary felt his presence and raised their heads, they heard his "Aha!" and saw before them a furious Hemingway brandishing one of his double-barrelled 12-gauge Remingtons. It is said that Mary stayed in the room, but the gardener jumped out the window and ran for his life, the root still in his hand. He didn't drop it until he was half way through the garden, looking for a way out. Hemingway, almost at his heels, was firing shots in the air.

According to Pichilo, the lady of the story was Martha Gellhorn. And it wasn't quite so violent. Maybe the incident happened twice, and there were two roots involved and Pichilo re-

members only the first one. The story featuring Mary had a
religious ending, a funny twist to it, considering the way she
was punished.

For a certain period of time she had to kneel in front of the
ceiba and ask forgiveness in a special prayer. This took place
every morning and lasted quite a while, with Hemingway
watching to see that she carried out her penance. It's very difficult
to imagine Martha Gellhorn, the proud aristocrat, meekly accepting such a sentence. Martha would never have knelt before
a tree.

There is proof of the incident with the ceiba. Even today
one can see in the "Venetian Room" a large piece of ceiba root
placed like a trophy over the door.


[16]

Pichilo has been working as foundryman in the Antillana Steel
Plant since 1962, one year after Hemingway died. His life has
undergone a transformation. He gave up cockfighting. He's still
a robust fellow as he sits in a rocker in front of his house, cigar
in hand, shirtless and wearing a plastic hard hat. Born and bred
in San Francisco de Paula, he is widely known there.

Among his valued belongings are 50 photos of Hemingway,
almost all taken on the safari of 1953-54. He hasn't been as fortunate with his other property. Pichilo explains in all seriousness
that of the four cows Hemingway left him, Josca, Amarilla, Ne-
griblanca and Pisicorre, only one was still alive in 1978. The cow
was 25 years old and had lost all her teeth. Pichilo sold it to the
government for $120, and she went to the slaughterhouse.

Pichilo says that the cows of the farm were all Holstein;
good dairy stock, they gave good milk. "Pity that Hemingway
didn't drink milk," he says.

Proof of the fine work done by Pichilo and the other gardeners at the Vigía can be seen in the 100 famous mango trees
that still bear delicious fruit. These trees are a great attraction
for the children of San Francisco de Paula.

The mangoes are of the best: Chinese, High, Filipino, native, yellow and the succulent mango-peach. There are tamarinds. (Mary Welsh remembers the first time Hemingway showed her a tamarind at the Vigía and asked her: "Isn't it a romantic name?") There is mamey from Santo Domingo, and laichi, the Chinese honeyberry that Pichilo planted and that began to produce around 1970.

"In the vegetable gardens we had everything: string beans, tomatoes, green peppers, lettuce, broccoli, chard, corn, parsley, pumpkin, yucca, carrots, radishes, beets, cabbage, plantains, eggplant, onions. We had to grow a great variety of vegetables because the Hemingways loved salads and Chinese food. Chinese food takes a lot of vegetables. My work originally was tending the flowers," says Pichilo, "but, as we say here, if you can grow flowers you can grow vegetables."

Also of superior quality are the almond trees in the swimming pool area. "The tenderest, biggest almonds," says Pichilo.

The produce that would not be used immediately was given to friends and to the farm help, or else kept in the freezer, together with the mangoes and the pulp of the tamarind.

Mary's great love was her flower garden, particularly the rose bushes she had planted down the hill from the house.

"We planted ixoras, a hardy flower, and roses, the favorites of the house, which grew in profusion." Pichilo adds: "The rose bushes had to be helped with a lot of chemical and vegetable fertilizer. Growing those roses was expensive. But we had roses, which was what the señora, Miss Mary, wanted."

When Mary Hemingway returned to Cuba in 1977, she could see for herself that most of the plants she had started were still alive. She also saw the flamboyán trees, the royal palms, the plantains and the 18 varieties of mangoes among the hundreds of healthy shrubs and trees that Hemingway mentioned with such pride in one of his articles. And the ceiba was still intact, with its enduring roots, defying time.

"The soil isn't good," declares Pichilo. "It's very sandy and full of gravel. Planting a tree wasn't an easy task. We had to dig deep, and then spend a lot of money on fertilizer and truckloads of topsoil. The rains washed the topsoil downhill.

"The worst feature of the farm is its lack of water. You have to drill deep to find it; it's like drilling for oil. We had to dig a well 98 feet deep, and an artesian well, 380 feet. There are no streams on the farm."

For this reason, a system was installed with canals that caught the rain water and deposited it in the beautiful blue-tile cistern in front of the house. Pichilo explains that the cistern water was not used for human consumption.

"The lack of drinking water was solved by digging wells and using a pump that brought the water into two tanks installed in back of the house. Those tanks guaranteed the supply of good water from the springs outside the boundaries of the farm."

The planting was done as soon as the rainy season ended in November, and that way they had flowers and vegetables from Christmas until June or July.

Mary's rose bushes, so highly praised by Hemingway in one of his articles about Cuba, were once old and neglected. Some of the plants were 15 or 20 years old when Mary started to work in the garden in 1945. She did a complete pruning and feeding of the old plants, and in the course of several years bought new plants, among them fine roses from the United States. But she realized that without constant and exceptional care, the plants from the States could live only approximately two years in the heat and humidity, and so she gave up the American roses. Since 1950, the roses grown in the Vigía, still there today, were native to Cuba.

For the plantings and care of the soil it was necessary to take into consideration the climate of the island, although the alkaline soil of the farm—very dry, sandy and thin—is unlike the soil in the rest of the country.

Cuba is situated in the 23rd parallel, a little to the south of the Tropic of Cancer. The temperatures are stable and seldom vary beyond 20 to 26 degrees centigrade. The seasons differ more in change of humidity than in change of temperature. In summer there are very heavy rains, but winter is relatively dry. The average annual rainfall is 40.32 inches.

It is a tribute to the loving care they have received that all the beautiful flowers, climbing vines, rose bushes, trees and shrubs planted during Hemingway's years can still be seen flourishing at Finca Vigía.

In the end, it was Hemingway who walked from the farm to Pichilo's house two blocks away on a hot day in July of 1960. "José," he said, "they say that he who says goodbye often, never leaves. We have said goodbye many times. But this time I'm worried. I don't think there's much time left because I feel very sick. The Cuban doctors can't find out what's wrong with me."

José had a strange intuition when Hemingway suddenly told him that his father had killed himself and then said: "José, animals and human beings should not die in bed, they shouldn't be allowed to suffer or make others suffer."


[17]


"It was a lifetime of very close association, because the friendships made in war are very deep. Of course, we disagreed many times, and even clashed violently sometimes, but we always managed to patch up our differences and our friendship remained strong. Ernest was a rather difficult person who had many problems with his closest friends, perhaps because of his very deep affection for them." ("Oh, shit," says Willie in the last line of *Islands in the Stream*, berating Thomas Hudson for his apparent lack of emotion: "You never understand anybody who loves you.")

The man talking is Dr. José Luis Herrera Sotolongo, native of Spain, and a veteran of the Spanish Civil War, one of the chiefs of the Medical Corps of the 12th International Brigade under General Lucasz. A Franco court condemned him to death, but he survived to live in exile in Cuba, where he befriended Fidel Castro, at that time a university student. Later on Herrera Sotolongo took part in the rebellion against Batista. He had met Hemingway during the years of the Spanish Civil War and they renewed their friendship when they both lived in Cuba.

Herrera Sotolongo, spurning current myths, gives us a very human, intimate image of Ernest Hemingway. He had every reason to know the writer well: He was his personal physician for more than 20 years, he knew his every ailment, his psychology, how he functioned. Herrera Sotolongo was one of Hemingway's bosom friends, not just one of the many individuals who attached themselves to his entourage.

Through Herrera Sotolongo, we can envisage the quiet evenings at Finca Vigía any time from 1945 to 1960, when none of his famous guests interfered with domestic tranquility. We see lights in the house and on the grounds. Inside, after dinner, Hemingway reads a book and sips some of the wine left over from dinner, while Mary plays canasta with Herrera. Ernest will not be up very long; he usually goes to bed at eleven. Of course, he doesn't go to his own room but in the opposite direction, to Mary's. He will leave an empty bottle of wine by his easy chair. He has done the same at dinner; another empty bottle of wine under his chair. These are his small habits.

If it is Wednesday (it was customary for Herrera Sotolongo to come to Finca Vigía every Wednesday), or one of the weekends that Herrera Sotolongo spends there, the doctor plays cards with Mary or talks with her until it is late, but Ernest retires without ceremony, merely saying goodnight in Spanish and going on his way. Herrera is definitely treated as one of the family. A little later he returns to his home in Havana. All the lights in the house go out.

However, if Hemingway is alone, he will make the rounds of Finca Vigía before retiring. He takes his .22-caliber pistol and a heavy stick to use as a cane, and starts his tour. Black Dog follows closely behind, sniffing everything. The farm laborers have gone to their homes in the town down the hill. Mary is probably visiting relatives in the United States. Hemingway makes his nightly patrol. All quiet at the front, and so to bed. Herrera Sotolongo says: "Although it may be hard to believe, that man was up there alone very often."

"In the beginning he kept his boat, the *Pilar*, anchored at Cojímar. There, he got to know the fishermen and this began to form the personality he acquired in Cuba. But he was not yet a famous man in this country.

"Later on, beginning in the early fifties, he took part in the fishing competitions. A prize was even established in his name. He became a member of the Hunter's Club of Cerro as well. In short, he created for himself a nucleus of friendships which in time helped form his intimate social circle.

"After he received the Nobel Prize, he became a very important man in Cuba. He was decorated with the National Order of Carlos Manuel de Céspedes in 1959, which pleased him greatly, since he considered it as a homage of the Cuban people. But he usually refused the many other official honors that were tendered to him. Another decoration he accepted with pleasure was the Order of St. Christopher, given to him on November 17, 1955, in the Old Sports Palace of Havana. This decoration, which had virtually fallen into oblivion in the many ups and downs of Cuban politics, was usually given to drivers who over a long period of time—25 or 50 years—had driven in the city without any accidents. Hemingway said, with some amusement, that it made him very happy to receive a decoration meant for chauffeurs. Certainly, it was one of the things that helped to strengthen his reputation in Cuba and create the legends about him."

Juan David, the most popular Cuban caricaturist of the century, met Hemingway in the Sports Palace when the writer was there to receive the medal of St. Christopher of Havana. It was a crazy encounter. At the doorway of the building Hemingway had grabbed another famous local caricaturist by the throat. It seems that Conrado Massaguer had drawn a caricature of the writer which offended him. Hemingway held Massaguer by the neck with his left hand and was about to hit him in the face with the right, yelling, "God damn it!" when Juan David, a husky six-foot-one, managed to extricate Massaguer from Hemingway's grip.

"And who are you?" Hemingway asked, startled.

"David, the caricaturist," Juan David replied.

Hemingway took a boxer's stance and David also put up his fists. Thus, they continued their dialogue.

"Are you going to do another caricature of me?" Hemingway asked, jabbing in the air.

"No, I only came to pay my respects," David answered, still on guard.

[18]

"During the Second World War," Herrera Sotolongo tells us, "Hemingway served first in Cuba, before going to Europe. He was in charge of a series of actions in coordination with American submarine hunters. He acted as a key liaison agent between the U.S. Naval Forces and the American government. In those days Ernest developed many new friendships. Later he went to Europe and took part in the Normandy landings, distinguishing himself in combat instead of as a war correspondent, which was his official title. He even became a guerrilla. He joined a group of French maquis that went ahead of the American army. When he returned to Havana he was decorated by the United States with the Bronze Star [at the American Embassy on June 16, 1947].

"Those were the things that contributed to the making of the image of the great man. Only a person of great rank could be so honored. One day Ernest pinned his three medals on his lapel and said that was the way he would appear on the currency bills honoring him. It was a joke, of course. He was neither vain nor proud, and he didn't care for that kind of thing.

"I remember that on this occasion the Cuban press criticized Hemingway's 'untidiness.' They said he had come to the American Embassy wearing a soiled guayabera. But that was not so. I drove the car that day. He was a burly man and perspired very much. In the parking lot of the embassy he changed his guayabera for a clean one he had brought, but to no avail. He sweated it again. Thus the comments made by the journalists."

[19]

During the forties and fifties, many celebrities stayed at the farm. There were Hollywood stars like Ava Gardner or Gary Cooper, or a famous bullfighter, perhaps Ordoñez, or some exotic creature, like a certain young Italian countess named Adriana Ivancich. Some of these personalities stayed overnight and some spent long periods of time with Hemingway.

But finally the day of departure would come, and the guests would pack their bags and be driven either in the Chrysler convertible or the pickup, depending on the amount of baggage, to the Rancho Boyeros Airport. Then Hemingway and his friends would get together again on their usual days, and things would return to normal.

Dr. Herrera Sotolongo would again see his friend Hemingway as a quiet and solitary man, at least during a long period of the writer's life in Cuba.

There were private showings of films at Finca Vigía. Among the spectators were the frequent visitors to the house: Dr. Herrera Sotolongo and his brother, Roberto; "Sinsky," an old friend; the priest Don Andrés, and others. They made themselves comfortable in the big chairs of the living room and enjoyed the images cast on the screen by a 16-mm projector.

Hemingway rented the movies from various distributors. Frequently they were boxing documentaries. One particularly interested him: the world championship fight between Rocky Graziano and Tony Zale, which took place in New York on September 27, 1946 (one of their three bouts from 1946 to 1949). "Muy buena pelea [A very good fight]," commented Hemingway every time he screened it.

On one occasion he managed to get from the American Embassy the complete *Victory at Sea* series. This shows the operations of the American navy during World War II. An excellent series of twenty films, each one an hour and a half long, it was put together with action footage taken under fire by American combat cameramen.

Hemingway ran them over and over again and invariably told the projectionist to stop the film at certain frames.

On one of the small barren islands of the Pacific, the marines have just won a victory and Japanese resistance is almost nil. There is one blockhouse which offers no resistance.

The Japanese are forced to come out of their concrete prison. Outside, an American marine sergeant holding a flame thrower calmly waits for the Japanese soldiers. One by one as they come out he executes them, burning them alive. Their bodies swell as they burn. The film was shot from behind the sergeant. Every so often he turns around and smiles at the camera.

"I doubt this scene will appear in all the prints of *Victory at Sea*," Hemingway said.

"Boys," asked Father Andrés once, "why do you keep stopping the film at that wretched scene?"

"Because we have sworn to kill that guy whenever we find him," explained Doctor Herrera Sotolongo, "and Ernest wants us to remember his face well."

And now, under cover of night, the familiar silhouettes of Lieutenant Maldonado and his companions can be seen again approaching the farm in their customary jeep. The social evenings at Hemingway's house are causing certain complications, for they have aroused the suspicions of an unlawful government established by a coup d'état. The weekly meetings of friends at the Vigía continue.

"The cruellest thing they did to Ernest was to kill Black Dog. The Rural Guards from Santa Maria del Rosario did it with the butts of their guns, at Lieutenant Maldonado's command. Now Hemingway's favorite is buried with the other pets."

Of course, the meetings that Lieutenant Maldonado found suspicious had nothing to do with a conspiracy.

"The lieutenant appeared suddenly one evening when we were there. Although it was certainly no political meeting, we always commented on *the situation*. The revolution was the topic of the day everywhere. But most of the time we simply ran the films and chatted.

"One Wednesday, the Rural Guards thought something unusual was going on because they saw so many cars going in and out of the place. They thought, surely there's a conspiracy at the Vigía. No such thing was going on. Of course, we did listen to the broadcasts from the Sierra Maestra, but everybody did that. Besides, that only started in 1957. Before that, they didn't have that kind of clandestine broadcast.

"When Maldonado tried to enter the farm that night, Ernesto stopped him. He went down the pathway from the house to the gate, and faced Maldonado and a half-dozen of his Rural Guards. Hemingway told them that they were on American property and that the only conspiracy going on there involved a bottle of whiskey. He was bold and brave. The Rural Guards decided to withdraw."

[20]

According to Herrera Sotolongo, Hemingway was not really a prodigious drinker. "He drank a lot, but for those of us accustomed to the life of the heavy drinker in countries where drinking is taken very seriously, he didn't drink *that* much." The doctor also assured us that when Hemingway had one too many, "he couldn't write at all."

The most serious disagreement between Hemingway and his doctor was caused by his drinking. It happened during the time when Hemingway fell in love with Adriana Ivancich, the young Italian countess he had met during a hunt in Taglimento, Italy, in 1948. Hemingway wrote to her and invited her to visit him in Cuba.

"He started to drink heavily then, and as a result was having difficulty with his writing," says Herrera Sotolongo, who told Hemingway: "If you keep on drinking this way you won't even be able to write your name." That was the time when Ernest was always drunk. "It was his bad time, when we had our falling out," continues Herrera. "One day I told him, 'Look, kid, you have turned into a drunkard and I hate that. If you don't change, we'll have to stop being friends. I've tried to help you the best way I know, but I have failed, so perhaps it is better that we each go our own way!' "

Then there were the familiar marital problems between Ernest and Mary, which gradually increased in intensity and to which Herrera Sotolongo was witness: "It got so bad once that I had to intervene and he and I came to blows. I left the farm around four in the morning, after I decided that the worst was over and they were no longer in danger, for they had threatened each other with guns. I had to take away their guns and put them in my car. As a matter of fact, I removed all of their arms and took them to my house. This was a risky thing to do in those days, because Batista's police were searching for arms constantly."

When I got home I immediately wrote a scathing letter to Ernest, and brother Roberto took it to him next day. As soon as he got the letter he phoned me and begged me to go see him. When I got to the farm, he said he was terribly sorry to have behaved so badly and to have offended me. He swore he would try to make amends and that he wanted my help. That's how a final break between us was averted and the incident was settled."

The doctor's letter has apparently been lost. After Hemingway's death, all the letters Herrera Sotolongo had written to his friend were found in the writer's files, except that one. When Mary Welsh went to Cuba in July of 1961, a few days after her husband's funeral, she returned to Herrera Sotolongo all the things in the house that belonged to him. Among these she included a file which Hemingway himself had organized, containing all of Sotolongo's letters. Mary told him that it was best for him to keep them.

[21]

Hemingway once tried to explain his inclination to alcohol. In a postscript to a letter written in his own hand to his friend the Soviet literary critic Ivan Kashkeen, dated August 1935, he makes a lively defense of the benefits of drinking, calling it the only relief from the "mechanical oppression" of modern life.

Thomas Hudson, in *Islands in the Stream*, also fights "mechanical oppression" from the back seat of his car: he drinks while he looks at the squalor of the Havana of the forties. In real life, to begin the day, Hemingway would drink two highballs or Tom Collinses in the swimming pool, or have whiskey and soda, or plain whiskey on the rocks. Later he would have wine with his lunch.

He napped until four or five, and then read while waiting for dinner; he usually did not drink again until he sat down at the table. He liked to read again between dinner and bedtime, and we know that this was accompanied by a little wine.

On an average day at the Vigía, three or four friends could help Ernest consume three or four bottles of whiskey. It never seemed to be too much for him.

Sometimes he varied his drinks. He liked to change. Whiskey, gin, campari, Tom Collins, tequila. He also drank different wines: Tavel, his favorite French rosé, then Chianti in the straw bottle, four or five liters with dinner. He liked to serve the wine himself. He held the bottle by the neck while he poured. This was awkward but he justified it by saying: "The bottles, by the neck. Women by the waist."

He called drinking the cure for "mechanical oppression." But Dr. Herrera Sotolongo didn't worry about semantics that

Carlos Gutiérrez and Pauline Pfeiffer Hemingway with a small *costero* on board the *Pilar*, 1934.

*Pilar*, a museum piece in the garden of Finca Vigía. (Celso Rodríguez)

Ernest and Mary on the flying bridge of *Pilar*, along the Cuban coast, circa late 1940's. (Roberto Herrara Sotolongo)

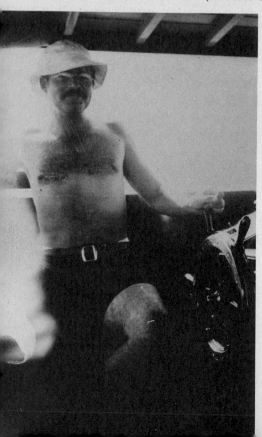

Captain Hemingway on the pilot bridge of *Pilar*, circa 1936.

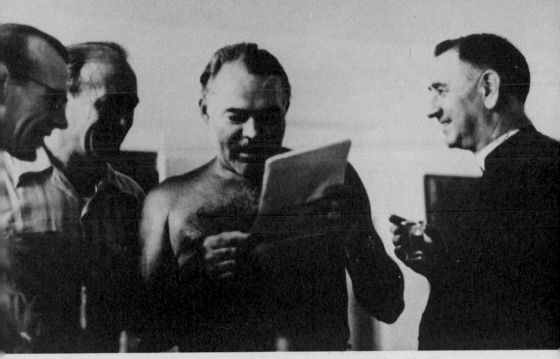

From left to right: Dr. José Luis Herrara Sotolongo, Juan Duñabeitía, Hemingway and the priest Don Andrés Untzaín, Finca Vigía, circa 1947.

José Herrero (Pichilo) in the cockpit built by him at Finca Vigía. Beside Hemingway is René Villarreal.

Drawing the dragnet to catch bait on the Cuban coast, circa 1955.

With the first generation of his special breed of cats, 1946.

*La Granja*, by Joan Miró, the kudu of *The Green Hills of Africa* and Boise, the cat of *Islands in the Stream*.

Hemingway and Mary Welsh are informed that the writer has been awarded the Nobel Prize in Literature, Finca Vigía, October 28, 1954. (UPI)

Mary Welsh and Pauline Pfeiffer, Finca Vigía, 1947. The dedications are to "Sinsky" (Juan Duñabeitía), a member of Hemingway's World War II antisubmarine crew.

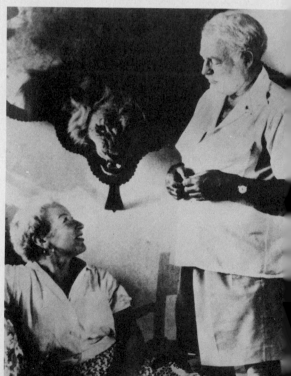

Hemingway and Mary Welsh, Finca Vigía, circa 1960.

afternoon on November 17, 1955. He remembers it as the day Hemingway received the Order of St. Christopher in Havana. They had agreed to meet at the Floridita bar after the decoration ceremony. Sotolongo found Hemingway there and saw that his friend's face and eyes had turned yellow. The Doctor told him: "Tell Juan [the chauffeur] to take you home right away. Go to bed and wait for me."

The next day Hemingway was posing for the sculptor Boada on the top floor of the Vigía tower when Sotolongo arrived. After examining him, Sotolongo called in a specialist, Doctor Infiesta. The diagnosis was immediate: hepatitis. As part of the treatment, Dr. Sotolongo restricted the amount of alcohol Hemingway could drink to a maximum of two ounces a day.

Hemingway referred to this period as being under "the new dry law." His jaundiced condition was one problem Hemingway couldn't solve with alcohol. Usually, a liter of any alcoholic beverage helped him to face storms, wars and moments of loneliness. But not hepatitis. He had to stay dry and in bed.

"Ernest had a tendency to hypertension, but we had it under control. However, it took some time to normalize his liver ailment. Even in those days there were some doctors who did not blame certain conditions of the liver, like hepatitis, on liquor. I shared that point of view. We thought that a good diet and rest could prevent cirrhosis or fibrosis. That's the regimen I prescribed. And sure enough, an attack of viral hepatitis—the second one he suffered—did not become cirrhosis."

In those days, according to Herrera Sotolongo, Hemingway became interested in the medical literature on the subject of diseases of the liver. In his library one finds *El hígado y sus enfermedades*, Alfa Publishing, Buenos Aires, 1949, the Argentine edition of the book by H.P. Himsworth, *The Liver and Its Diseases*, in which Hemingway underlined many passages. An interesting detail is that all the underlined passages refer to diseases of the liver common in the tropics. In this 326-page book, Hemingway marked around 20 passages, which gives us an idea of what worried him at that time.

Although his doctor-friend shared his belief that alcohol was not the cause of his illness, Hemingway was hunting for additional medical confirmation of the theory.

He finally found the scientific evidence he was looking for and underlined a whole paragraph:

> If alcohol by itself can contribute to the development of this lesion by a direct toxic action on the hepatic cells, this is something that has yet to be established. However, even if it had been, such contribution would seem to be unjustified, and the apparent connection between hepatic fibrosis and alcoholism, can more easily be explained as the result of malnutrition than as a consequence of alcohol.

Hemingway's attack of infectious hepatitis, although it took years to be cured completely, never appeared again with such intensity. Herrera Sotolongo had moments of genuine satisfaction during the course of Hemingway's illness. He did not permit his patient to drink more than two ounces of whiskey daily; one in the morning and one in the afternoon. And, not only was the doctor able to get Ernest to obey him, but his patient drank even less than the permitted amount. When Herrera visited the Vigía for his patient's daily check-up, Hemingway would sometimes show him the small, heavy shot glass filled with an ounce of whiskey, saying, "Look, this morning's measure, and I haven't even tasted it."

It was in these days, during his convalescence, that Hemingway enjoyed a rare indulgence. He would settle himself for hours in front of the TV set to watch the outcome of Cuba's championship baseball games. He was a fan of the "Havana" club, a professional team whose red uniforms bore the figure of a lion. His impassioned TV viewing and his heated arguments in defense of the "Havana" made Sotolongo at times fear for Ernest's health. There was a certain American pitcher, Wilmer Mizel (whom the Cubans called "Vinagre" Maicel) who was his special favorite and who broke a record that year, much to Hemingway's delight.

[22]

Hemingway was five feet eleven inches tall, but perhaps because of his beefiness, almost everybody thought of him as a "huge man, over six feet tall."

Gregorio Fuentes explains it easily: "He had broad shoulders and awfully big feet." And he loved to walk barefoot or in moccasins without socks. "Those heavy feet weren't made for shoes," says Herrera Sotolongo. "His old moccasins looked like boats," the doctor adds. He never wore undershorts, which in a Hispanic country is something of a sacrilege, a very bold act.

He cared nothing about clothes, often wearing the same light gray duck pants and a blue gingham shirt day after day.

He was always combing his hair. This is one of the Hemingway quirks that everybody remembers. He kept a small nylon comb in his pocket and was constantly combing his hair and smoothing it with his hands. He is also remembered as leaving the tennis court wearing a visor cap and resting his racquet on his shoulder, like a carbine. Too much sun was bad for him. His face and hands became covered with an innocuous rash that he insisted on calling a "benign cancer."

"Ernesto was well taken care of," says Sotolongo with pride. "He was in good shape. He suffered from hypertension, true, but he had it under control. His blood pressure was rarely above 160. There was always his eyesight problem; he was myopic and had astigmatism. But I prescribed Vitamin A and it did him a lot of good. He used to take off his glasses to shoot and he never missed a pigeon.

"There was a time when he tired easily, and I prescribed a tonic put out by CIBA. This had excellent results. We gave it to him together with reserpine, because of his hypertension. To tell the truth, he was just a bit of a coward when it came to sickness. According to his theory, sickness was truly something to fear. A serious ailment could suddenly appear in an inaccessible place in the body, impossible to control.

"The opposite was true when it came to wounds and other injuries. He used to boast that he had at least two hundred scars on his body and he could tell the story of each one of them."

When he left Cuba in 1960 he seemed in good health. Sotolongo received a letter Hemingway wrote from Spain soon after, saying, "I'm O.K." Doctor Madinaveitia, his physician in Madrid, had given him a check-up.

"Suddenly he became ill," says Sotolongo, "and left for the United States, where he entered the Mayo Brothers clinic. From that moment on I lost contact. Mary didn't give me an explanation when she came to Cuba in August 1961, after Ernesto died. They made him get down to 150 pounds. They destroyed him with those damned electric shocks at the Mayo Clinic."

The possible alternative of suicide had become an obsession with Hemingway. On more than one occasion at Finca Vigía he said he would one day kill himself. He even rehearsed the way he would do it.

"Look, this is how I'm going to do it," he would explain to friends, according to Sotolongo.

"He would then sit in his chair, barefoot, and place the butt of his Mannlicher .256 on the fiber rug of the living room between his legs. Then, leaning forward, he would rest the mouth of the gun barrel against the roof of his mouth. He would press the trigger with his big toe and we would hear the click of the gun. He would then raise his head and smile.

" 'This is the technique of harakiri with a gun,' he'd say. 'The palate is the softest part of the head.' "

"Papa wasn't a great one for jokes," says Gregorio Fuentes. He couldn't be counted on to join his Cuban friends and tell dirty jokes and stories about amorous adventures. But at least one occasional visitor to Finca Vigía, Angel Martínez, remembers him a different way. He says that he visited the writer early one morning in the fifties.

"I was with a bunch of friends. We had some guitars and bottles. We were feeling pretty good and decided to drop in on Hemingway."

The author of "The Killers" and "The Snows of Kilimanjaro" received them at the swimming pool.

"Gentlemen," he said, "please remove your shoes and dip your feet reverently in the water of this pool, where Ava Gardner swam naked this morning."

Herrera Sotolongo asserts that "Hemingway was proud of his manhood even at a late age." In other words, the doctor suggests, Ernest was still pleased with his amorous ability:

"He was strong, and at times weighed more than 200 pounds. He exercised and boxed. He was a good boxer and a hard hitter. Once he even sparred with the heavyweight contender Carpentier."

There was always a tendency in the public mind to identify Hemingway with his alter egos, and attribute to him the adventures and ailments of the characters in his books. For example, there is the problem of impotence faced by the protagonist in *The Sun Also Rises*, which is of a very special kind, since it prevents the sexual act but not desire, according to Hemingway's treatment of it in the novel. However, Hemingway never had that problem, according to Herrera Sotolongo.

Hemingway was the patient and friend for many years of Dr. Frank Stermayer, who didn't share that opinion. When news of the writer's suicide reached Havana, Dr. Stermayer complained bitterly because Hemingway had been allowed access to firearms, "when they know he was deeply depressed and mentally unbalanced."

Ever since the forties, Dr. Stermayer had been voicing repeated warnings on this subject. Contrary to Dr. Sotolongo's opinion, Stermayer thought the electric shocks administered to Hemingway were necessary and inevitable, because psychopharmacology had not yet reached its present level of efficiency. But he was sad and angry that Hemingway's guns were left within easy reach. Stermayer died in the mid-seventies, and on his deathbed he talked about Hemingway, his friend who had been dead for 15 years.

Frank Stermayer never said a word about it, but it was known that he had submitted Hemingway to a Rorschach test and had drawn his conclusions.

Stermayer's widow was interviewed in 1976, and was asked somewhat callously if Hemingway had been impotent. She said that the answer to that question was her husband's professional secret.

Another distinguished Cuban scientist, Gustavo Torroella,

knew through several professional exchanges he had with Stermayer that Hemingway suffered periods of impotence, "a chronic condition that came and went."

[23]

Hemingway never talked about literature. Sometimes he would say, "The work is going well." Often he would inform his friends, "Today I wrote so many words." On other occasions he declared, "I'm writing badly." Then it would be months before he touched a pencil or his typewriter. Those were the times when he complained of being bored and drank excessively. His often-quoted "Inspiration should find me working" was apparently only a beautiful phrase.

His working day at the Vigía could cover six hours, from dawn until shortly before noon, typing standing up at his Royal portable typewriter. When he finished, he placed a copper paperweight on the sheets of paper he had written and jumped into the pool, played tennis, or got dressed and rode over to Cojímar, where he kept his boat, the *Pilar*. But if he decided to stay at the farm, he would spend a long time in the pool, or at poolside, swimming or reading *The New York Times*, or starting on the first drinks of the day—the pair of Tom Collinses, the gin and tonic, or the whiskey and soda—until René Villarreal came down the gravel path to announce that lunch was ready.

With the arrival of Ava Gardner, or Spencer Tracy with Katharine Hepburn, or Jean-Paul Sartre (whom Hemingway didn't particularly admire), or General Buck Lanham, or the bullfighter Ordoñez, or boxing champion Rocky Marciano, Hemingway shortened his working day. They were days of little literary output but much fun, devoted to social activities and entertaining his guests.

[24]

Hemingway was a generous and civilized host. Seated at the head of the dining table at Finca Vigía, there was nothing to remind one of the rough characters of his fiction. When he had special guests to entertain, he would choose the china and silver himself. He had a set of table linen with the symbol of the farm embroidered on every piece. The symbol consisted of three hills, an arrowhead and three lines denoting the double bars of the rank of captain. It was also engraved on the glassware, the silverware and china.

Papa would sing for his guests in Spanish or Basque, but, as many of his guests remember, unfortunately off key. The music lessons that his mother, Mrs. Grace Hall Hemingway, made him take hadn't helped much.

Hemingway presided over the dinner conversation with grace and humor, and he took care of every little detail, although Mary Welsh, like Martha Gellhorn before her, was a charming and efficient hostess.

Hemingway was always well groomed when he sat down at the table. In spite of the informality of his attire, his hair was neat and he looked clean and fresh. If it was a simple lunch on a summer afternoon, he would wear a pair of shorts and a cotton shirt. But for his gala dinners he would wear a plaid jacket, white shirt and tie, and he insisted that the efficient René Villarreal wait at the table in a white *filipina*—a waiter's white cotton jacket—and gloves.

Mary, as hostess, had at least one romantic whim that annoyed Ernest. She loved to dine by the light of candles enclosed in glass shades. Staring at his plate in near darkness, Hemingway complained because they couldn't see what they were eating.

"One of these days we're going to eat a *cockroach!*" he'd wail.

Another one of her husband's complaints was the frequency with which spaghetti was served at the house, albeit with fresh, delicious sauces. Hemingway ate the pasta just the same, as well as the thick soups that Mary sometimes took five or six days to make.

The pantry at the Hemingways was always well stocked. In the cellar they had four or five freezers which held a great variety of food at 30 degrees below zero, among them all kinds of shellfish and turtle meat. Beef was kept in packages and turtle meat in waxed paper.

Everything was wrapped and dated. "Today we are eating

marlin eight months old," Hemingway told Father Andrés one day. Hemingway would cut and wrap the turtle steaks himself, saving the legs and tails for soups. Meats were always taken out of the freezers according to their dates, the earliest ones first.

"You never ate anything fresh there," says Herrera Soto-longo, although without a doubt the greater part of the vegetables consumed came from the Finca's garden, which was Pichilo's responsibility. He remembers that Mary would insist: "Mr. Hemingway likes his vegetables very fresh."

The Hemingways ate a lot of turtle soup, but all frozen. They had a curious custom: They would take it out of the freezer, whip it in a blender like a daiquiri, and serve turtle soup frappé. Only rarely would they thaw it and serve it hot.

Hemingway appreciated Mary Welsh's culinary expertise. There were memorable gazpachos, carefully blended, and a variety of delicately sauced dishes prepared with codfish, which won the favor of more than one dinner guest.

There were a few differences between the eating habits of the two Americans and the Cubans, such as the size of the servings. At the farm there are still notes kept by the servants in which they were asked to cut up the fruit and serve it in smaller pieces. One note in Hemingway's handwriting requests that his avocado be served in smaller chunks, to be eaten as a fruit. This was sacrilege for the Cuban help, who never got used to considering avocado a fruit. The Hemingways never ate it in a salad.

There were two kitchens at Finca Vigía: a modern electric one, and a huge, typically native kitchen with an old, coal-burning stove. This ancient Cuban kitchen was built at the same time as the house. This is where Ramón, the Chinese cook, preferred to work. Ernest greatly enjoyed the creations of Ramón, who started working for him when Martha Gellhorn was mistress of the house.

Ramón combined rare virtues with great faults. The kitchen was his exclusive domain, and he would not allow anyone to enter it or interfere with him.

Ramón loved to prepare elaborate desserts every day, mostly pastry, all excellent. He was unusually patient when unexpected guests turned up.

"Look, Chino, there will be six for dinner," Hemingway would say.

And Ramón would answer calmly: "Chino has no problem."

But Chino, as Hemingway called him, did have a problem: He was an alcoholic. It was foolish to allow the half-full bottles left from dinner to go back to the kitchen, because Chino drank everything in sight—Tavel rosé, Gordon's gin, good red wine, whatever. "Towards the end of the forties, five or six years after leaving Finca Vigía, he died from an alcoholic binge," Pichilo says.

Herrera Sotolongo remembers him as an extremely nervous man who once ran out of the kitchen, eyes popping and knife in hand, looking for Juan, the driver, who had just played a practical joke on him. Unfortunately, it was rather frequent for Ramón to run around with a knife in his hand every time something went wrong. He couldn't take any sort of annoyance or mishap.

Sotolongo says that trouble could pop up any time. Hemingway would be sitting at the head of the table, Martha at the other end and guests at both sides. Suddenly Ramón would burst out of the kitchen yelling that he "could really kill someone."

The slightest thing would set him off. Then one day, when Ramón ran out of the kitchen brandishing his knife, "it was Ernest who screamed the Cuban blasphemy. 'I shit on your whoring mother!' and banged on the table with such force that cups and glasses tumbled all over, while he looked Ramón straight in the eye. After that, there was no longer a problem. There was no longer a Ramón either, for he quit that very moment."


[25]


In the Hemingway home, as in other Cuban homes, there was a special ritual for its cleaning and care. The procedure was complicated because of the idiosyncrasies of the Finca Vigía's owners. There were precise instructions for the care of nearly everything on the premises.

The trophies—the animal heads and their fur—had to be cleaned with hog-bristle brushes, never nylon. Never washed.

Horns were dusted. While any wax-based polish would do for the furniture, for the horns the polish had to be free of oil. Twice a year all the skins, furs and horns were fastidiously cleaned.

Hemingway bought the vegetable fiber rug on the living room floor in the Philippines in 1941. It was carefully maintained by mending and restoring it with fiber from the Pandamus plant. There were two such rugs on the farm. René Villarreal knew how to process and cut the Pandamus leaves to prepare the strips that were braided into the worn spots in the rug. The rug was in poor condition in 1961, but it was repaired when the farm became a museum.

Many of the frames of the paintings were infested with "comejen," a kind of termite common in the tropics. To get rid of them, the pictures were taken off the walls, placed face down on a suitable surface with the canvas protected by layers of paper, and then sprayed.

The Hemingways personally dusted and sprayed all the books twice a year. When Hemingway was working in his room, nothing was allowed to disturb him. No one could clean near him, and so some of his books must have become dusty and moth-ridden.

All the furniture in the house—the mahogany tables in the living room, the dining room and Mary's room, as well as the pieces in the library—was covered with a clear, liquid-plastic coating which was normally applied every two years. This prevented their surfaces from becoming stained. This coating had decayed by 1960 and the furniture showed a cracked surface. Another coating had to be applied.

The floors, especially the living room floor, were uneven. This was caused by the roots of nearby trees, climbing plants or particularly by the roots of the troublesome ceiba. To level the floors, it was necessary to lift the floor planks and dig around the root (often it was cut if the absence of the master of the house allowed it); the empty space would be filled with soil and the planks replaced.

The planks were almost 60 years old in 1961. It was of great importance not to damage them when removing them, since they were very difficult to replace. In a corner of the Venetian Room one can still see a portion of the root that was carefully removed from beneath the dining room floor, so as not to damage the irreplaceable planks.

When Mary Welsh gave the house to the Revolutionary Government, she apologized for its neglected condition. She left the following explanation in writing: "We stayed in Spain too long in 1959 and the state of poor Ernest's health made me forget everything in this past year." She added this curious note:

The little house on one side of the residence was for guests, and there, at different times, stayed a great variety of persons, including Jean-Paul Sartre from Paris, Charles Ritz also from Paris; Gianfranco Ivancich, the poet and artist from Venice; Alan Moorehead, the author from London; Fernanda Pivano, the philosopher; Ettore Sottsass, the artist from Milan; Alfred Vanderbilt, the sportsman from the United States; Denis Zaphiro, leader of the hunting expeditions and a great hunter from Kenya; Ernest's sons and their wives and several beautiful girls from different places.

In the main house, the guest house and the garage, there are fire extinguishers that were refilled for the last time in June of 1960. This work was done voluntarily by the old, hard-working firemen of the Monserrate Street station, near the Morro Castle grocery store. Although they never charged a cent, Hemingway always rewarded them for this task. In time, they became part of Hemingway's "establishment" in Cuba.

Sonia Tsar replaced Ramón, the unpredictable Chinese cook. After this there were no more difficulties in the kitchen, although there are no reports on the quality of the pastry. Today nobody knows Sonia's whereabouts. Of Serbian descent, she was the sister of Ana Tsar, the laundress at the farm and the last of the servants to work for Hemingway.

When Mary visited Cuba in 1977 she saw Ana, who had suffered a stroke. Ana probably didn't even recognize Mary. Her family had dressed her up to look her best, and sent her to the farm to say hello to Mary, "Mr. Güey's" widow. Ana had a fixed smile on her face all the time she was there, and looked around blankly at the Cuban government functionaries and their long black limousines.

This same Ana once witnessed the execution of Bigotes

(Moustache), one of the house pets, a cat turned killer who had temporarily converted the quiet gardens of Finca Vigía into a wild jungle. Bigotes joined a gang of stray cats to form a crime syndicate that "liquidated" several of the Hemingway feline family. Bigotes was already dead in the corridor, and Hemingway was kneeling in front of the animal, holding his gun, sobbing, when Ana appeared and asked him: "Why do you cry for a cat, when you have killed so many lions?"

"Because there, it's war, here, it's peace," Hemingway answered.

Mary Welsh mentions some other former members of the staff at the farm in *How It Was*. The best known is René Villarreal, who appears in every biography of Hemingway as the faithful servant. Hemingway's driver, Juan Pastor López, shows up in *Islands in the Stream* as the literary character "Juan." The author describes Juan with considerable resentment. Thomas Hudson even thinks of him as "a son of a bitch" as Juan drives him from the farm to the American Embassy and forgets to coast and save gas.

In *How It Was*, Mary Welsh offers a different image of him: René once found a purse belonging to Adriana Ivancich in a corner of the garage. It contained $27,000, enough money to solve all the problems in the lives of several Renés. Nobody would have ever known, but René returned it.

Arnoldo was one of the plumbers mentioned by Mary Welsh, but today nobody knows where he is. Another plumber was little Anchía. Ernest once played a practical joke on him, pushing him into the swimming pool on a winter day. There was also Roberto Herrera Sotolongo, another important person at the farm, brother of Dr. José Luis. Roberto managed the farm from the beginning of the forties. He was also one of the participants in the hunting of German submarines on board the *Pilar* during World War II. After Hemingway's death, thanks to the study program of the Revolutionary Government, he received his medical doctor's degree when he was almost 50. He died of a heart-attack in 1970.

A long-time resident of San Francisco de Paula reveals still another domestic facet of Ernest Hemingway: a man preoccupied with building an impregnable sanctuary for himself. In 1979,

Francisco Castro was 76 years old and had lived in San Francisco for 39 years. Pancho, a cabinetmaker, tells us, "I came to live here because of Ernest Hemingway. When Hemingway lived at the Hotel Ambos Mundos he used to see me working there. When he moved over here, he needed a carpenter and cabinet maker. He went to get me at Ambos Mundos where I was installing some windows, and invited me to have a beer with him. We went to the Casa Recalt across the street from the hotel, and he told me: 'Drink your beer and come work for me. All you have to do is tell me how much you want me to pay you.' We came to an agreement right away. He was a fair man and a good guy. I was with him until 1952. By that time I had made a life for myself in this town, where I moved when I started to work for him, and here I stayed."

Pancho built most of the furniture in the house: the magazine stand in a corner of the living room that appeared in many photos of the room taken in the fifties; a round white table placed in the middle of the room; and all the rest of the furniture in that room; the table-bar on the left of Hemingway's easy chair, and all the furniture in the dining room, library and Mary's room. Today all of these pieces are considered valuable and of museum quality.

"Miss Mary usually designed them, although I always added something of my own," Pancho said. "The furniture had to be comfortable and functional and the wood of the very best—mahogany and 'majagua' (a tree similar to the linden)—the precious woods of Cuba. On one occasion, Hemingway asked me to do some work on his boat, the *Pilar*. I had to refuse. I'm no shipwright."

Pancho started to work at Finca Vigía when Martha Gellhorn was there. She was completely different from Mary Welsh, and never bothered to design furniture. She kept him busy on other carpentry work.

Towards the end of the forties, Pancho helped in the most notable new construction, the three-storied tower built on the highest point at the Vigía.

Long after Pancho Castro left Finca Vigía, Hemingway remembered him and used to send him part of the catch from his fishing trips.

These were the people who worked for the writer in his

Havana refuge at Finca Vigía. Hemingway did not forget them. They are present in his last will and testament.

August 23, 1961

Following instructions in a letter addressed to me accompanying his testament, made and certified in 1956, I have given to Gregorio Fuentes, of Pasuela Street 209, Cojímar, Ernest's yacht, the *Pilar*, making known to Gregorio the instructions that he is to dispose of the yacht as he sees fit. Ernest obtained his captain and navigator license for the *Pilar* on April 26, 1934. The *Pilar* and Gregorio helped him a great deal. Not only did Gregorio work on the boat, but he took part in the mission of hunting German submarines during the Second World War, was his companion on the fishing trips and helped in the study of the Gulf Stream in the Cuban seas.

[Signed] Mary Hemingway

Following instructions as described above, I have given in Ernest's name to René Villarreal, of San Francisco de Paula, who was a personal servant to Ernest as well as in charge of the house for 17 years, a Winchester .22 calibre, Model 62A 255364, which Ernest had given him as a personal gift in 1956, but which was kept among our firearms in order to be included in the annual granting of licenses.

[Signed] Mary Hemingway

Following same instructions, I have given in Ernest's name to José Herrera [Pichilo], of San Francisco de Paula, the cows of Finca Vigía. He has been the gardener and has taken care of the swimming pool for 17 years, and has my permission to keep his fighting cocks, whose property Ernest at one time shared, on the grounds of the farm.

[Signed] Mary Hemingway

Pedro Buscarón, who has worked in the house and taken care of the animals for eight years, has my permission to bring his horse to graze on the fields of the farm.

[Signed] Mary Hemingway

Following instructions in Ernest's letter, quoted previously, I am making the necessary arrangements to give gifts of money to several employees, by means of checks drawn on my account at Agencia 4/10/06, Amistad 420, branch of National Bank of Cuba.

[Signed] Mary Hemingway

[26]

In 1957, there were 57 cats at Finca Vigía: 43 large ones and 14 small ones. They lived on the first floor of the tower. Hemingway believed he had succeeded in creating an original race of cats, a cross between native Cuban cats and the Angora. He established the tradition of giving them names that included the letter "s," convinced that these animals liked the sound of that consonant, particularly when it was elongated in pronouncing the names Boise, Missouri, Spendy, etc.

The oldest of the cats was the black and white Ambrosy, who survived Hemingway by eight years, living until 1969 to be 16 years of age. The Cuban help at the farm called him by his Spanish name, Ambrosio, and remembered him for his neurotic spells and frequent excursions into the Vigía pantry.

The most famous of the cats was Boise, who appears in *Islands in the Stream*. In the book, Boise, then a kitten, is given to the protagonist by the owner of La Terraza, a bar-restaurant in Cojímar. But in reality, it was Gregorio Fuentes who gave the cat to Hemingway.

Boise became old and spoiled, jumping on the table at meal times; Ernest permitted it. The priest, Don Andrés, remembers seeing Ernest at the head of the table, giving the cat food and wine. In the background hung Miró's *La Macia*.

The cat Bigotes has his own legend as well. Bigotes and a blond, aggressive stray became close allies. One night, in an out-of-the-way corner of the farm, they killed Mary's favorite cat. "They did it!" cried Hemingway, when René Villarreal came the next day with the news that they had found the cat's body.

Hemingway finished his lunch without a word. Then he went to his room and took out his Winchester .22. In the corridor he found Bigotes rubbing his paws. "He seems unconcerned and remote," Hemingway said, "but I have to do it. He's had a taste of it and from now on he'll be a killer. The first crime is only the beginning for an assassin." From the doorway, he took aim at the cat's head and pulled the trigger.

There were two other rebels who formed their own crime

syndicate: Fatso and Shopsky. Eventually they too had to be put away.

In the summer of 1960, a different kind of feline tragedy occurred. One of Mary's cats fell in love with a black feline who lived outside the farm. The cat made frequent trips in search of her friend and one morning got careless while crossing the Central Highway. Mortally wounded by a car, she crawled to the door of the house. Hemingway heard the cat's anguished cries and told René Villarreal to get his Winchester. René got the gun, cocked it, and asked: "Do I shoot, Papa?" In answer, Hemingway grabbed the gun from him and through clenched teeth said in Spanish: "*Dame aca, cono que a los mios los mato yo*. [Give it to me, damn it, I kill my own]."


[27]


The upkeep of the Vigía averaged four thousand dollars a month. This included property taxes, the salaries of nine employees (the number varied according to the nature of the work done), food and beverages, fertilizer and soil for the gardens, and the swimming pool with its water-purifying system. Herrera Sotolongo and Juan Duñabeitía ("Sinsky") frequently helped with the bookkeeping and in confirming the figures. Also included in this amount was the monthly account from the Floridita bar, where Hemingway signed for his drinks. When he got his bill at the end of the month, he made out a check after only a casual glance at the total.

The Cuban expenses were high. Besides the Vigía and the Floridita, there were other places where Hemingway was a habitué and where his signature had authority. He wasn't the type of man to carry much money on him. His signature was accepted at the Terrace in Cojímar, at the Basque Center, at the Zaragozana Restaurant, and, we are told, at the Bodeguita del Medio as well.

Among the papers at the farm there are bills from these and other places and many onionskin carbon copies from Casa Recalt, where Hemingway bought all his liquor for the Vigía. There are other bills from the grocery store called Morro Castle. Mountains of invoiced deliveries from Florida and New York are almost all addressed to Mary Hemingway.

Once a year during his 20 years in Cuba, around December, Hemingway devoted considerable time to the American income tax collectors. Although he lived in Cuba, he continued to be a citizen of his native country. He reserved special feelings of rancor for the functionaries of the Internal Revenue Service and their labors. In a letter written in 1935 to Ivan Kashkeen he says, referring to the state: "Until now all it has meant to me is the burden of arbitrary taxation."

In some of Hemingway's biographies we are told that towards the end of his life, as a result of his paranoia, he waged an unrelenting war with the income tax collectors. He saw these agents everywhere. But certain facts gave some validity to Hemingway's persecution delusions. According to Roberto Sotolongo, each year he helped Hemingway fix his accounts to reduce his income tax.

[28]

Hemingway was a bit of a fanatic on the subject of papers, particularly letters. He couldn't relinquish them. He was a pack rat who kept any and all printed material, including newspapers and magazines. In the house today there are two cupboards full of old American magazines, in spite of the great number that Mary burned in 1961.

In Hemingway's files there are hundreds of clippings of the reviews which appeared in the United States after his first book was published, sometimes dozens of the same review published in different newspapers. The few intimates with access to the house might see the same letters lying on his bed for years. Dr. Herrera Sotolongo, an amateur philatelist, had Hemingway's permission to tear out the stamps, but not to move the letters from their special place on the bed. "He hardly ever slept on that bed; he shared the one in Mary's room," Sotolongo said.

There had to be some method to the madness. Although

the correspondence covered the whole bed, it was obviously placed there according to a system which only Hemingway understood.

The mail at La Vigía became so heavy that it was necessary to hire a secretary. The perfect person for the job was Roberto Herrera Sotolongo. Roberto organized Hemingway's files and correspondence. Years after the writer's death, in the last few weeks of his own life, Roberto's great worry was what had become of the papers at Finca Vigía. Many documents and letters are missing.

Unfortunately, from the time the news of Hemingway's suicide reached Cuba until Mary Welsh officially delivered the property to the Cuban government in August 1961, Finca Vigía was open territory. Friends and employees had free and easy access to the house and papers for almost six months. Mary Welsh never volunteered information about the papers she took away. The Revolutionary Government gave her authorization to transfer documents and possessions to the United States.

She had access to a metal filing cabinet, a wooden trunk and several boxes filled with photos, as well as a dozen sheets from an old manuscript.

Even when Hemingway was alive, several things were missing, some only temporarily. The Nobel Prize medal was lost on one occasion and the Herrera Sotolongo brothers, particularly José Luis, insisted that Hemingway do something about it. He would answer, "No, let it be—it really doesn't matter." But at their continued insistence, Hemingway finally took the necessary steps to get his medal back. Today it is in the Chapel of Miracles in the Basilica of Our Lady of Charity of Cobre, near Santiago de Cuba. The writer placed the medal in the hands of the newspaperman Fernando G. Campoamor during the tribute given him by Hatuey Beer.

Some time later, it reached the Archbishop of Santiago de Cuba, Monsignor Enrique Pérez Serantes, who sent it to the sanctuary. In the Basilica there is a photo taken by *Life* magazine showing Campoamor, Hemingway and the medal in its case when the writer donated this award.

The medal is now where Hemingway wanted it to be. "There have been false interpretations of this gesture of Ernesto's," Herrera Sotolongo tells us. "He gave it to the Cuban people. Hemingway no doubt thought that inasmuch as the government of Cuba in those days consisted of a bunch of thieves, the only safe place for the medal was the Sanctuary of Our Lady of Charity."

Hemingway may have been remembering certain events that had taken place in the country, particularly the robbery of the fabulous diamond in the dome of the National Capitol. It had disappeared, but reappeared a short time later in a bureau drawer of the president of the Republic!

[29]

"Hemingway was not religious," says Herrera Sotolongo, adding a curious, little-known fact: "However, he was under the protection of the Jesuits. I don't know why—it seemed to be something of a family tradition. The fact is that he was under their protection. He could count on their help at any given moment, hide in one of their monasteries, or make use of them. Hemingway regularly received publications of the Order by mail from the United States.

"Of course, the fact that he was not religious doesn't mean that he was not superstitious. He always carried his 'lucky stone' in his pocket. That's what he called it. 'Do you have yours?' he used to ask me. In all truth, it was just an ordinary smooth stone. In Cuba they called them 'chinas pelonas.' Some people say they have magnetic properties. I carried one in my pocket just to please him."

Hemingway's favorite number was 13, which he considered a sign of good luck, although in Cuba it means the opposite. The license plates of all his automobiles had a 13 in them. He got these easily, because nobody wanted the number. But his superstitions went beyond a fascination with the number 13 and having his friends carry lucky stones in their pockets. On one occasion he wanted to wear earrings.

"You must pierce my ears," he told Herrera. "I must have it done before the baby is born in Africa!"

The purpose of his wanting to wear hoop earrings was in-

volved with the imminent birth of a child Hemingway was supposed to have fathered with a Wakamba girl called Debba.

Mary begged Herrera Sotolongo not to do it, and one day
Hemingway got angry at the doctor for his continued refusal.

"I won't do it," Herrera Sotolongo finally admitted.

Ernest probably "married" the girl during his second African
safari in 1953. According to Wakamba wedding rites, the father
must wear gold hoops in his ears during his wife's pregnancy,
to guarantee the safe birth of the baby.

In April 1947, Hemingway's middle son, Patrick, unexpectedly suffered a prolonged nervous breakdown, shortly after
an automobile accident. Herrera Sotolongo defined it as a
"predemential" state, which may have been caused by the strain
of the college entrance exams for which he was preparing, or by
a crisis of conscience which was brought on when he started
doubting his mother's Catholic beliefs, a faith which they had
shared until then.

Hemingway set up a sort of convalescent's camp at the farm
with those friends he thought could be of help in the situation:
particularly the doctor Herrera Sotolongo, Sinsky and Father
Andrés. The priest, a constant visitor at Hemingway's house,
was a special case. Don Andrés was a Spanish exile, and Herrera
Sotolongo says: "We had opportunities to confirm without a
doubt the very correct position of that man: Don Andrés was a
liberal, a cleric, who considered himself anticlerical."

Patrick thought differently. He accepted all of his father's
friends except the priest. When Patrick saw him he had hysterical
attacks, saying that Don Andrés was the devil on earth. Don
Andrés was obliged to leave the room.

Once they had succeeded in calming Patrick and getting him
to sleep, the four friends would retire to the living room with
the liquor bottles necessary for their "ethylic" conference: Hemingway, looking worried, the doctor, the priest, and Sinsky the
bartender, the official mixologist who prepared the "chemical
compounds," which consisted mainly of gin.

"I think we may have to call an exorcist," Ernest would say
with a sidelong glance at Don Andrés.

[30]

Most of the time Hemingway spoke in Spanish, since the help at the farm knew no second language. He also spoke Spanish with Gregorio and with his friends at the Floridita bar. Unless he met one of his countrymen, all he heard around him was the high-pitched Havana patois. At times, he exchanged a few words in English with Mary.

Naturally he made a few mistakes, but there is little question that he spoke fluent Spanish. He referred to José Martí, the Cuban hero of the nineteenth century, as "General Martí," which is unusual in Cuba. It is true that Martí was named Major General by a revolutionary officers' council in 1895, but in Cuba he is revered as The Maestro. Hemingway liked to acknowledge Martí's military rank; in addition, he claimed total familiarity with Martí's literary work.

"I have read General Martí's texts. I know them well," he said.

However, on taking inventory of the books at Finca Vigía, we discovered not a single copy of the thirty tomes of Martí's writings. "General Hemingway," however, would repeat by memory part of a military dispatch that for some reason or other gave him pleasure: "Our troops continue to advance without losing an inch of terrain." He would pronounce it slowly, with an ironic smile on his lips, while engaging in one sport or another when he was, naturally, losing.

In *For Whom the Bell Tolls* there is a paraphrase of that extraordinary dispatch: "Our glorious troops continue to advance without losing a hand span of terrain," Karkov declares in his picturesque Spanish.

Another Spanish phrase of military origin that Hemingway liked to use was *estamos copados*—we're surrounded. The verb "to be" didn't interest him; what he liked was the sound of *copados*.

Another Spanish expression he liked was *la pepa*, a Cuban slang expression he used when referring to "death." (Pepa is a nickname for Josefa, a girl's name.) Hemingway referred irreverently to the demise of President Franklin Roosevelt: "*A Franklin Delano lo cogio la pepa* [La pepa got Franklin Delano]."

There was a song taught to him by Don Andrés that Hemingway liked to sing:

I don't like your neighborhood
And I don't like you
And I don't like
Your whoring mother
*(No me gusta tu barrio*
*Ni me gusta tu*
*Ni me gusta*
*Tu puta madre)*

[31]

In the eyes of Hemingway, Finca Vigía took on the look of a weatherbeaten boat when a tropical storm swept over her.

In September 1950, a hurricane hit Havana when Hemingway was at the farm. The notes found among his papers show that he experienced many extremes of weather on the island and learned that the best and only way to go through a gale is with a bottle of rum in one hand and an ear glued to a battery radio, after having prudently nailed the doors and windows shut. There are witnesses to the manner in which Hemingway faced these natural phenomena.

Dr. Sotolongo lost track of the number of storms he went through with him on the hill, but he remembers that Hemingway's behavior was always the same: "Those things excited Ernesto. Whenever he heard a hurricane was imminent, his face would light up. If I happened to be there, he insisted I stay so that together we could 'organize our defense.' Of course, when the worst was over and an estimate was being made of the damage outside, inside the house there was another kind of damage.

"That Ernesto—he was quite a character. With a house full of good things to eat, he insisted on fasting during the storm— no food, just liquor. At times he insisted we take off our clothes. Of course, we'd only strip down to shorts or Bermudas. We took off our clothes in case we had to dash out to take care of something the wind or heavy rain knocked down. Anyway, Hemingway, bottle in hand, directed the anticyclone operation from the living room of his home, together with two or three close friends. He looked like the captain of a boat in the middle of a storm."

He not only looked like a captain, but the humorous notes he kept on the storms were exactly like the log of a warship captain; he refers to the "enemy" and his "capacity for destruction," as well as using other military terms.

An incident of meteorological interest for Hemingway happened early in the fifties when José Carlos Millás, director of the National Observatory of Cuba, played the leading role in a catastrophic comedy of errors. He announced with great urgency that a hurricane of tremendous force would hit the island about 60 miles east of Havana.

All the people of Havana hastened to nail their windows and doors shut. Sewer drains were cleared of all obstructions, and shop windows were reinforced, while the city of Matanzas, 60 miles east of Havana, remained completely unconcerned. Sure enough, the hurricane hit and devastated the city of Matanzas, while Havana was left untouched.

The public protest was overwhelming. Millás lost no time in appearing on television to explain what happened. Cuba's chief weatherman asserted that he was not responsible for the people's ignorance of their own geography—the city of Matanzas is 60 miles east of Havana:

"It's not my fault that the observatory is located in Havana, nor that the reference point for this institution is, as you well know, the capital."

This was one of those rare nights when Hemingway watched the television screen closely for more than half an hour. Millás was often the butt of jokes, for being wrong so frequently in his weather forecasts. Hemingway mocked him without pity. Now he listened to Millás's explanation with considerable amusement.

Only a few months later, Hemingway witnessed another strange incident on television.

It was the golden era for flying saucers. Ciudad Deportiva (Sport City) was being built in front of the most pretentious fountain in the city, which the people of Havana called El Bidet de Paulina. Paulina de Grau, "First Lady of the Republic," was the wife of ex-President Grau San Martín's brother. One fine morning, an interplanetary object appeared on its premises.

Round, silver and mysterious, the spaceship raised its chilling periscope, but otherwise gave no signs of life.

The city mobilized the police force, the Chiefs of Staff, an armored force of the National Army, and the Fire Department. The island seemed to enjoy the good fortune—or misfortune— of being chosen for the first public visit from extraterrestrial beings.

In the presence of an event of this magnitude, Hemingway, the old newspaperman, decided to stay put in front of his Admiral television set at Finca Vigía. Armed with a quart of Gordon's gin and lemons from the garden, he fixed his unbelieving eyes on the screen.

Around four in the afternoon, after a day of breathless expectation, a hatchway opened, and to the amazement of the television viewers, a very beautiful and famous model appeared holding a bottle of Cristal Beer in her hand. By that time all local residents had fled from the site and the chief of police, Brigadier Rafael Salas Cañizares, with gun in hand, had taken cover behind his Mercury. Moments later through the same hatchway emerged the 43 members of a popular band, playing a catchy tune entitled "Even the Martians Love Cristal."

This was too much for Hemingway. He finished the whole bottle of Gordon's by himself, without ice, water or lemon. The help at the farm who had been watching saw him get up unsteadily, go to his own room—not Miss Mary's—and fall asleep on top of his mountain of mail, covering his face with a section of the Sunday edition of *The New York Times*.


[32]


Cuba still held a few more incidents in store to shock and amuse Hemingway.

In a passage in *Islands in the Stream*, Thomas Hudson, the protagonist, leaves his house and is driven to Havana. On the highway he recalls a terrible crime which took place in 1939, the year before Hemingway bought the Vigía. A policeman cut up the body of his mistress into six pieces. He then wrapped each piece in brown paper and left these macabre packages strewn along the road. Actually there weren't that many packages, but it is true that the murderer was a policeman and that the victim's head was found in Batabano.

In the book, Hudson calls attention to the curious way in which the Cubans decided the remains belonged to an American tourist. She couldn't have been Cuban, the police claimed, for she wouldn't have had such small breasts. Hudson claims that "He had to give up doing any road work in the country outside Finca, because anybody seen running or even hurrying, was in danger of being pursued by the populace, crying, 'There he goes! That's him! That's the man who chopped her up!' "

When Hemingway wrote that part of *Islands* at the beginning of the fifties, the murderer René Hidaldo, ex-medical student and policeman, was still imprisoned at Isla de Pinos.

Hemingway never knew the end of the story. René Hidalgo was released at the beginning of the seventies, after serving a long sentence. He was an old man by then, working in the passenger terminal of Santiago de las Vegas, some 30 kilometers from the capital. The other workers considered him an oddity. Hidalgo never showed the least interest in knowing that he had been mentioned in one of Hemingway's books. By then he'd had enough of "fame" and press coverage.

[33]

"Señor Ernesto was very generous," says Sergio Anchía González, a class-A plumber now over 70 years old. In his desire to honor Hemingway's image, the old Cuban laborer speaks of Ernest as a man of noble heart, always concerned about the fate of the poor.

Anchía remembers that Hemingway would tell Manolo Asper, owner of the hotel Ambos Mundos: "Manolo, please, I don't want any of my poor to go without the medicine they need."

He also remembers that when he finished a plumbing job at the farm, Hemingway told him: "Anchía, you don't charge enough for your work; here are a few extra dollars, go buy yourself a few drinks." According to Anchía, Hemingway liked to go pigeon shooting and send him the catch, to be distributed among the poor of Tejadillo Street, where the plumber lived.

Anchía tells the following story with great admiration:

"One winter day, he called me to La Vigía. He told me there was a leak in the swimming pool, because he could see the bubbles. It was quite cold, one of those gray days that we see in winter in this country. I leaned over the edge of the pool and asked, 'Where is the leak?' I was concentrating on trying to see beneath the surface of the water, when Hemingway kicked me from behind and threw me head first into the pool. I fell in like a brick, in my overalls, with my tool case.

"Señor Ernesto was laughing like mad, very pleased at how well his practical joke had turned out. Imagine! He had sent his driver, Juan, for me just for the pleasure of throwing me into the pool! And then he jumped in himself, fully clothed. He was very democratic. When he got out of the pool he sent for two drinks and two pairs of pajamas. Since his clothes were much too big for me, he looked at me and laughed a lot. However, the little joke cost him 100 dollars, between my tools and clothes."

Perhaps Anchía remembers this incident with affection and gratitude because Hemingway rewarded the plumber with a letter of recommendation to Howard Soler, Vice President of the Cuban Telephone Company. Thanks to this gesture, little Anchía had a job that offered security and economic stability for the rest of his life.

Anchía's Hemingway is quite different from the man who held a famous dialogue with Scott·Fitzgerald:

—The rich are different from us, Fitzgerald said.

—Yes, they have more money, Hemingway answered.

[34]

CARTELES
July 11, 1954

ERNEST HEMINGWAY
IS BACK WITH US
Text: Lisandro Otero

Late in the afternoon an Italian ship entered the narrow channel of the Bay of Havana, and moments later was at the pier. There were six or seven small boats around the liner waiting for a doctor to order the yellow Department of Health flag taken down, and allow access on board. Up above on the captain's bridge a broad-shouldered man with a gray beard was waving enthusiastically and screaming answers to questions asked him from the boats.

Hemingway was returning to his Cuban home, "the place I love best next to my native land."

When at last the port authorities allowed access on board, more than fifty persons, reporters, photographers and friends rushed up the gangplank. Hemingway waited for them in the ship's dining room. There he chatted with everyone, joking, laughing and downing a few drinks. Finally he went ashore. At the pier there was another human wave. He made his way slowly among them and reached Customs, where he again faced a battery of photographers and general public. Hemingway laughed, pleased at the warm reception.

His luggage consisted of more than forty pieces: wooden boxes holding mounted animal heads, huge trunks, steel boxes filled with firearms, and large canvas bags with his fishing equipment. Everything was loaded on a truck quickly, without the usual customs formality. Minutes later the truck was on its way to Finca Vigía, followed by the novelist's station wagon.

Ernest Hemingway is back with us.

Hemingway felt very much at home on the island of Cuba, which always welcomed him so warmly. There was even more celebrating and many parties on that stormy day, October 28, 1954, when a batallion of Cubans invaded Finca Vigía. At around eleven in the morning, all the radio stations interrupted their regular programs to announce that "one of Cuba's favorite sons" had won a distinguished international competition and had been honored with the gold medal, diploma, and $36,000 in cash, which represented the Nobel Prize. Hemingway addressed the group gathered at the farm. His joy made him adopt a frivolous and light tone, but, like Thomas Hudson at the Floridita, it didn't stop him from saying some pointed things:

"Ladies and gentlemen:

"As you well know, there are many Cubans. But, as in ancient Gaul, they can be divided into three parts: those who starve, those who subsist, and those who eat too much. After this magnificent (and bourgeois) repast, we indubitably belong in the third category, at least for the moment."

Afterwards, in the same bantering tone, he referred to his apolitical stand and his Cuban friends. He claimed that Antonio Maceo, the Cuban hero, was superior to Field Marshal Montgomery (the hero of El Alamein in World War II who was victorious over the Desert Fox, Field Marshal Rommel). He hoped for an early demise of the Dominican dictator Trujillo. Finally, he announced his decision to give the Nobel Prize gold medal to Our Lady of Charity of Cobre. Hemingway ended his speech wryly, explaining that the $36,000 hadn't been delivered yet, and so couldn't be stolen.

# Hemingway on Board

## [35]

The Cuban archipelago lies between two seas: the Atlantic and the Caribbean. It has more than 7,000 kilometers of coastline, and an insular shelf of nearly 70,000 square kilometers, including 1,600 islands and islets, more than 165 lagoons, 290 rivers and 100 dams. The average wind velocity is from nine to 19 kilometers per hour, and tide variations are less than one meter between high and low marks. Its marine flora and fauna possess favorable attributes to make Cuban waters ideal for big-game fishing.

The stars of this sport are the spear* species, like the marlin or sailfish. The waters off the island abound in this type of fish at certain times of the year. Their migratory habits carry them with the currents, according to their biological and other requirements.

On the north coast of the eastern part of the island, in the waters adjacent to Punta Lucrecia, spearfish like the sailfish are numerous during the months of October and November. In the deep water across from Playa Girón on the south coast, white

*Known in the United States as billfish; includes all species of marlin, swordfish and sailfish.

marlin appear around February. But information about these zones and their possibilities for sport fishing is still meager. It is well known that there is a traditional run of marlin in the waters of the north coast, from Punta Gobernadora at the extreme west to the Cruz del Padre Key at the northeast of the Hicacos peninsula. It begins towards the end of April and sometimes lasts until the first cold winds of winter.

In 1932, Hemingway came from his old home in the Florida Keys to explore these coasts. A bootlegger from Key West provided the boat and put the first spools of Catalonian fishing tackle in his hands. Joe Russell, nicknamed Josie Grunts, proprietor of Sloppy Joe's, was Hemingway's teacher in the art of navigation and bootlegging, and a faithful companion who enjoyed having his picture taken with his favorite pupil.

Not content with having him as a customer at his now legendary bar on Duval Street in Key West, where Prohibition was totally ignored, Joe convinced the writer of the magnificence of big-game fishing in Cuban waters. He put his boat, *Anita*, at Hemingway's disposal for only $10 a day, because Ernest was a good friend, and introduced him to Carlos Gutiérrez, an enigmatic fisherman from Havana. Hence April 1932 is the date for the start of Hemingway's trips to Cuba.

On a literary level, this relationship contributed to contemporary literature three important novels, a story of a political nature, and a dozen articles about sports. On a personal level, Hemingway became a Cuban resident and a well-known character in the life of the country.

At Finca Vigía there is testimony of this friendship. There are several out-of-focus photos of Hemingway and Josie Russell at the docks of Havana. These were taken during Hemingway's first trips to Cuba. Josie looks pleased with himself; he is smiling. He is holding a drink in every picture. No wonder it was said at the time that Russell drank a high percentage of the liquor originally destined for contraband and clandestine sales at Sloppy Joe's.

Ten years later, the teacher seemed to have turned pupil. Then it was Hemingway who took along with him and cosseted the pirate of old. Josie had become a venerable grandfather who came on board the *Pilar* at the beginning of the forties. He sat around drinking lemonade with a "little bit of rum," or a glass of lukewarm tea that Gregorio prepared for him.

Hemingway would ask him occasionally, "Are you comfortable, Mr. Russell?" And Josie would respond only with a sad smile. He was a faithful and true friend to Ernest, his "godchild," to the very end.

[36]

In the novel *To Have and Have Not*, while his boat, the *Anita*, swayed gently alongside the pier at the end of two rustic ropes, Harry Morgan, the protagonist, would go ashore and head directly for the "Café de la Perla de San Francisco."

*To Have and Have Not*, a tough and fast-moving novel with the most confused of all Hemingway characters, begins with a shooting in front of this ancient café in Old Havana.

Hemingway had been witness to just such a massacre on August 7, 1933, while he was waiting in Havana for the ship that would take him to Europe and from there to Africa.

Hemingway chose the dawn of a day in Havana, a thirsty beggar and the first sounds of the sleepy square and the bars of the dock to compose the opening paragraph of his first novel about Cuba—how it was with the bums sleeping against the buildings, with the empty square and the fountain and the Pearl of San Francisco Café.

Antonio Rodriguez, the owner of the Pearl of San Francisco, died in 1951, at 86 years of age. He was called Kaiser Guillermo. The only books he ever read were the account books of his business. He wore what he called an Austrian moustache, which made him look like the bellicose German monarch. Rodriguez took pride in the quiet hostelry which his business talent had provided for the people of Havana. He owned a small café where he sold cold drinks, oranges, pineapples, and a 25-cent blue plate; in the same building he also owned a small hotel with 17 rooms. He served breakfast, lunch and dinner to his guests.

Another thing he took pride in was the bar in his café. The counter was made of very fine material, even better than marble, and the bar boasted a ten-door refrigerator unit. The business was valued at $30,000, a substantial amount in 1930, but in later years it lost money and went bankrupt. It was torn down in 1953.

Kaiser Guillermo never knew that Hemingway had been a frequent customer at his establishment, and least of all that his café had appeared in one of his novels. Because of his indifference to literature, he lost a good chance of capitalizing on this. (The owner of La Terraza restaurant in Cojímar certainly took advantage of Hemingway's patronage.)

The original locale of *To Have and Have Not*, in Havana's harbor, seems to have stubbornly resisted the passage of time. Only a few new coats of paint and some bold new picture windows dare to challenge the authenticity of the façades of the old buildings.

In truth, many things have changed since Harry Morgan drank his beer at the Donovan Bar, but the greatest difference of all is the absence of Yankee sailors and adventurers of the Hemingway-hero stripe. In their place one sees on the docks Soviet, Greek, Italian, Polish, Mexican and Panamanian types, which give a more cosmopolitan character to the landscape.

Besides the Pearl of San Francisco Café, there was a Chinese restaurant where Morgan had lunch for the modest sum of 40 cents. After lunch, he enjoyed a quick beer at the Donovan bar and a few more with Frankie at the Cunard bar.

Finally, Morgan's wife, Marie, recalled that the first time she had her hair bleached, it was at a beauty parlor on the Prado.

It is not possible today to find the exact location of the beauty parlor or the Chinese restaurant, because the novel never gave the addresses. Hemingway's favorite Chinese restaurant in Havana was The Pacific, which was near a popular and cheap market place.

Harry Morgan bought gifts for his wife in stores that always had the same sign, in English: "Alligator Goods—Souvenirs." The Prado of Havana, a Caribbean version of the one in Madrid, is still intact, with its great park and the old Hotel Sevilla. Today it is full of beauty parlors and pizza places.

The Cunard bar, three doors away from the Pearl of San Francisco Café, is now an automobile repair shop. Angel Martínez, the former owner of La Bodeguita del Medio, and César

Novoa Esperanza, a well-known character in Havana, recall that across the street from the Cunard there was a shop called the Great Generoso. It specialized in making excellent coffee. The beans were roasted in full view of the public.

Novoa Esperanza is of the opinion that the Donovan bar was "a dive—a lowdown place, where one stopped only for '*el del estribo*,' " which in Havana means the last drink, "one for the road." The building where Donovan's was housed has since been demolished. "A lot of dirty business went on there, whores always on the make," says Novoa. "Definitely not my kind of place."

In *To Have and Have Not* there is a passage that although based on historical facts, does not sound convincing. It is obvious in this case that Hemingway wrote without thorough knowledge of his subject. In the novel Harry Morgan decides to make some fast money by taking groups of Chinese from Cuba to the United States illegally. He agrees with a certain Mr. Sing to take 12 illegal immigrants to the United States in his boat. During the night, Morgan kills Mr. Sing and throws his body into the sea. He then turns around and goes back to the Cuban coast. On reaching a beach near Bacuranao, he tells his passengers that they have reached Florida. The Chinese are aware they have been cheated, but Morgan points a gun at them and orders them to go ashore.

Hemingway must have heard stories about this type of smuggling from the first mate of the *Pilar*, Carlos Gutiérrez. But the old Cuban fishermen and historians are quite sure that it wasn't so easy to fool the Chinese. The professional smugglers charged between 200 and 300 dollars per head, but they had to carry out the deal.

Since the Chinese were the most discriminated against in the labor force those days, they had formed powerful secret organizations to protect themselves. And they had another powerful weapon: until they set foot in the United States, they never paid the full amount of the deal.

Those who tried to fool the Chinese ran the risk of being victims of their vengeance. The number of Chinese who ended up as food for sharks or died of hunger on the keys of the north coast of Cuba had to be very small compared to the great number who succeeded in landing and settling in the United States. Of

The Café de la Perla de San Francisco in the seaport area of Havana, the setting for the opening of *To Have and Have Not*. This photo was taken at the time of the story, in the early 1930's.

Hemingway (striped shirt) stands beside record 468-pound marlin he caught off Cuban coast, 1933. (UPI)

Joe Russell (arrow) drinks a toast with Hemingway aboard the *Anita*, Harry Morgan's boat of *To Have and Have Not*, at old pier San Francisco, which is now renamed pier Sierra Maestra No. 2.

Hemingway catches a *costero* of about 500 pounds. With Carlos Gutiérrez, in Havana, 1933.

Ernest poses with Gregorio Fuentes, who has caught a huge *peto* of 82 pounds.

Fishing for black marlin (Pacific *costero*) for the movie of *The Old Man and the Sea*, near Cabo Blanco, Peru, 1956.

Fidel Castro wins the individual championship at the Hemingway Fishing Tournament, Barlovento's pier, Havana, May 15, 1960. It was the only time the two men met.

the ten thousand Chinese smuggled from Cuba to the U.S. coast, only about one thousand failed to get there, and of these, about one hundred perished in the waters of the Gulf.

There is one detail, though, which tends to justify Hemingway's tale. Strictly speaking, the smuggled Chinese did not always reach a safe port. There is a buoy called Rebeca facing the Florida Keys. In Harry Morgan's time, around the thirties, some people called it Chinaman's Buoy. According to recollections of old-time hands in that area, the buoy owed its name to the fact that on one occasion on that very spot, a smuggler dumped overboard the "passengers" he was taking from Cuba to the United States.

[37]

On the morning of July 3, 1961, the *Key West Citizen* paid grateful tribute to Hemingway. Its front page displayed in large letters the nostalgic and powerful headline: PAPA PASSES.

Hemingway, as we have noted, first became acquainted with Havana when his ship stopped there en route to Key West, that place of aristocratic and at the same time almost revolutionary character.

Hemingway used to call Key West "the Saint Tropez of the poor." The island was only nine square miles and had a population of 11,600, made up of natives called "conchs," blacks imported from the Bahamas, and Cubans. Eddy Saunders and Joe Russell, two important characters in the Hemingway novels of those days, also lived there.

In the twenties, Key West was more Cuban than American, and the conchs were looked upon as the lower stratum of society. Practically everything was in Cuban hands. But with the Great Depression, the tobacco industry, which had employed 2,000 workers, disappeared. The naval base was abandoned, the steamship lines closed, and the cargo boats transferred to New Orleans. City Hall declared bankruptcy on July 2, 1934. This was part of the desolate panorama that Hemingway portrayed in *To Have and Have Not*.

The Hemingways lived in a house on Whitehead Street,

number 907 (today it is a Hemingway Museum), built in 1851 by a naval magnate, Asa Tift. Gustav Pfeiffer, an uncle of Pauline's, bought it for them in 1931 for $12,500.

The couple lived in Key West for nine years, traveling sporadically to Wyoming and Sun Valley, France, Spain, Cuba and Bimini. Hemingway finished *A Farewell to Arms* and *Death in the Afternoon* there, began the first parts of *To Have and Have Not*, and according to some biographers started *For Whom the Bell Tolls* and also wrote "The Snows of Kilimanjaro." On a visit to Key West in 1955 with A.E. Hotchner, they went to the old house, and Hemingway pointed to the cabana by the swimming pool, saying, "That's where I wrote 'The Snows of Kilimanjaro.' "

The overseas highway, finished in March 1938, connected the keys with Florida proper, acting like a blood transfusion. According to Chamber of Commerce figures, more than 450,000 tourists visit the city each year. Of Hemingway's old friends in Key West, only two were still alive at the end of the seventies: Charles Thompson, called "Old Karl" in *The Green Hills of Africa*, who accompanied the writer on his first safari, and Otto Bruce, "Tubby," Hemingway's old valet.

Stan Smith, the owner of Sloppy Joe's since 1962, also remembers Papa. The presence of Hemingway and Russell so many years ago is still excellent publicity, which Smith uses in the promotions that contribute to the prosperity of his business.

In 1928 Hemingway was to meet someone else who was to play an important role in his life, this time not a pirate or a smuggler.

Once, in very rough weather, the *Anita* was forced to seek refuge in Dry Tortugas. Another boat waited out the storm in the same improvised haven. The captain of that boat, a fisherman named Gregorio Fuentes, calmly observed the maneuvers of the *Anita*. He wore a red and black checked shirt reminiscent of the signal flags used by the harbor pilots. He invited Hemingway and his friends to his boat and served them one of Ernest's favorite combinations, wine and raw onions.

Six years later Fuentes had become "the pillar of the *Pilar*," as Hemingway would remark on occasion, delighting in the play of words. Fuentes first appears in "The Great Blue River," an article which is reprinted in *By-Line*, a book of selected Hemingway articles and dispatches. Hemingway credits him with having the cleanest ship that he had ever seen, and adds that Gregorio would rather keep a ship clean than fish, but that he would rather fish than eat. He mentions that Fuentes subsequently saved the *Pilar* in three hurricanes, including the October 1944 hurricane when winds reached 180 mph.

The man described by Hemingway is today a peaceful patriarch, still active as a fisherman. He lives in Cojímar in the same house he bought with the salary Hemingway paid him ($250 a month).

Sitting on a chair in his living room, barefoot, wearing a baseball cap, his drink in front of him on a glass table, Gregorio looks as strong as an oak. His wife Dolores prepares the huge American-style breakfast Hemingway taught him to eat: Quaker oatmeal, great quantities of bread and butter, an omelette, cheese, and coffee with milk. A half-hour spent with him in front of his house is enough to make one aware of his special standing with the people of Cojímar. Everybody greets him. He is one of the best-loved characters of this small fishing city, respected both as Hemingway's old skipper and for his skills and experience as a fisherman.

"As to that Dry Tortugas thing," recalls Gregorio, "Papa wasn't 'Papa' then. He was young, athletic and very likeable. He was around 26 or 27 years old, and always smiling and willing, very talkative, dark-haired and *honest*. There they were, trapped by the storm. They wanted to communicate with Key West and I took them to the lighthouse.

"I loaded my hold for ballast so my sailboat could make it there. He was impressed by this. When we got there, I asked the lighthouse keepers to let my friend use the telephone that was connected to Key West by means of submarine cable. Hemingway didn't know such a thing existed, and was amazed. He still had a lot to learn. Another thing he didn't know was that the lighthouse keepers were my good friends, and that whenever I went by I brought them bottles of cognac."

None of the other fishermen at Dry Tortugas dared to take Hemingway to the lighthouse, three miles out at sea, in a storm. It took Gregorio to do it.

Gregorio carried fresh fish from Cuba to the United States in his decrepit sailboat named *Joaquin Cisto*.

Many years later, Gregorio captained the *Atlanta*, a boat on a scientific expedition for the University of Massachusetts, studying the flora and fauna of the Cuban insular shelf. Julio Hidalgo, an old friend of Hemingway's, harbor pilot for Havana, had recommended Gregorio. Hemingway met him again in a café in Casablanca, across the bay. Ten years had gone by, but they recognized each other immediately. Gregorio accepted the offer to work as skipper of the *Pilar*.

As for the 1944 storm mentioned by Hemingway, Gregorio says that the operation was quite easy. Gregorio cast anchor in a very shallow, swampy area in the bay of Havana, and tied the boat "to every pole in sight, also to any swamp growth, tree trunk or rock. When I was through, it looked like a yacht caught in a spiderweb."

Once secured in this way, his boat gave shelter to about six other fishermen whose small boats had been damaged. Gregorio asked these men to come aboard.

"Then the storm struck. The heavy winds and the angry waters hit us hard, and the boats strained at the ropes, which began to creak, as did the boards of the *Pilar*."

Meanwhile, Gregorio Fuentes, apparently unconcerned, drank Scotch while preparing a succulent *arroz con pollo* (rice with chicken) for all. "It did let up in the afternoon," he continues, "and the fishermen helped me pull the boat out of the swamp. I helped them, and they helped me."

Gregorio says his fate was to be a sailor. When he was four years old, his father took him to see "the big shots of the seaport," in Lanzarote, Spain ("before the generals," he adds, touching an imaginary insignia on his shoulder). There he was asked: "Come here, child. Tell us, how do you want to serve the king? On water or land?" "I choose the sea," he answered. "And that's how it all started," he says.

Gregorio is possibly the only fisherman in the world who owns authentic Robert Capa and Karsh photos. Karsh's famous portrait of Hemingway hangs in his living room.

He married Dolores Pérez in 1922, and they have four

daughters. Gregorio and Dolores have been together over 60 years and he likes to tease her.

"The things I've had to endure in my life with Dolores!" he wails. And she kids him right back: "Too bad he'd never leave me." The old captain of the *Pilar* says: "It was a pleasure to work for Papa. I was the skipper and I also cooked and served the drinks. In those days some good skippers could earn more than I was making. But I enjoyed being with him, and he was a real friend."

The *Pilar* was well stocked. There were always some fresh meat and other quality provisions, and a lot of good canned goods, American soups, beans, hot tamales. Hemingway gave full command of the bar to "Gregorine," as he called Gregorio. As they sailed past the Morro of Havana, Hemingway would invariably say: "Captain Gregorine, please take charge of the Ethylic Department." Gregorio recalls the kinds of liquor and drinks he served:

| | |
|---|---|
| Gin and tonic: | Two fingers of gin, tonic water to fill the glass and a bit of lemon. Never with sugar. |
| Whiskey and soda: | Dewar's White Label, Haig and Haig, or Johnny Walker. |
| Wine: | In decanters. Italian. Sometimes Chilean or Spanish. |
| Daiquiris: | Without sugar. |
| Bacardi: | With ice and lemon. |

Gregorio advises that a drink should be held in the hand no longer than half an hour. Once the sun makes it lukewarm, it should be discarded.

"Papa didn't drink from bottles that had previously been opened. He opened a new bottle every day. Gordon's Gin was his favorite, but there were many brands of liquor on board. He had a lot of guests to please and he wanted each one to drink what he or she preferred."

Gregorio had his own special prescription, which he considered very effective to prevent or cure a cold:

"Take a clean glass and put two tablespoons of honey in it,

add the juice of two lemons, a mint leaf, two ice cubes and rum to taste. Nothing like it," he says.

[38]

One of Gregorio's most cherished anecdotes took place in 1954. Hemingway brought as his guest to the *Pilar* a gentleman named Charles Ritz, the owner of the Hotel Ritz in Paris. Hemingway told his friend, "My chef is better than the one at your hotel." He called Gregorio and asked him: "Gregorine, how are we going to welcome this gentleman?"

In answer, Gregorio told them that he would prepare, during the next three days, "three dishes this gentleman has never tasted in his whole life." Charles Ritz asked: "What kind of dishes are those?" The skipper of the *Pilar* answered: "I call them 'Eat and don't ask.' "

When Monsieur Ritz tasted Gregorio's version of a spaghetti dish, he said that he had never tasted such delicious spaghetti before.

"Everything has its way," Gregorio said.

"What does that mean?" Ritz asked.

"It means that everything good has its own secret way— how it should be done, and how it should not be done."

But finally, all these years later, Gregorio is making an exception. For the first time, he reveals three culinary secrets:

"I take the whole roll of spaghetti and break it in half before putting it in boiling water. First I cook the chicken in a casserole with a special broth. This broth is made with beef and pork bones. When the chicken is done, I strain the broth and take the crumb-like stuff left in the strainer and add it to the chicken. I add a little salt and grind it.

"Then I take some ham from Galicia and some chorizo [Spanish sausage] and grind that as well. I mix this with the ground chicken and the broth, add a little paprika and let everything cook slowly over a low flame. I take the spaghetti out of the water and serve it separately with a pinch of sugar. I put the sauce in another dish, and bring it to the table. When I cooked it for them that time, the more they ate, the more they wanted.

" 'It's a Cuban dish,' " I told Señor Ritz. And he told Papa: 'If you and I weren't such good friends, I would take this man back with me to the Ritz.'

"When they came back the next day I told them: 'Well, now comes the next chapter.' Papa again insisted that his chef was better than the one at the Ritz. (At night he called me at Cojímar to say we had to win the bet. He said it was a moral issue.)

"Next day I took a very fresh swordfish, cut off two slices, marinated them and let them stand. In the meantime, I served them a few drinks and they talked a blue streak. The *Pilar* was anchored at Bacuranao. Later I melted half a pound of butter, and started to fry the swordfish slices over low heat. I squeezed a lemon over them and turned the slices so that they would be evenly browned. I waited until they were seated at the table and brought in the two plates with the dish straight out of the pan.

" 'How did you make this?' asked Senor Ritz.

" 'Easy,' I answered. 'With just a little bit of salt.'

"The other sauce I made was much simpler. I had bought two or three *dorados* at Megano Beach. I filleted the fish, as they were winter fish and nice and fleshy. I made a damned good sauce. Green sauce with peppers, lots of parsley, black pepper, raisins and capers. Everything goes into the frying pan with very finely chopped asparagus.

" 'And how do you make this?' Ritz asked. So I told him.

"Of course, there were many other dishes I prepared for Papa that he enjoyed a lot, particularly octopus in wine sauce, and also fricassee of octopus, and the baby octopus we caught right there from the boat went straight into the pan. What he loved best was crab cooked in lemon. How Papa loved that! And the lobster enchilada. But he preferred the crab dishes the way I prepared them."

[39]

"Four of us went to Puerto Escondido," Gregorio Fuentes tells us. "Adriana Ivancich, her mother, her brother, and I. I was very much attracted to the little Italian countess. I even loved the way she spoke Spanish, but I never had anything to do with her, for she was Papa's guest. Some time later I had to tie her down in order to save her from falling in the water from the lifeboat. It was in rough weather, in the middle of a gale, and I didn't want to lose any of my passengers."

The adventure started one afternoon when Hemingway called Gregorio and asked him to go in the *Tin Kid* (that was the name of Miss Mary's boat, the *Pilar's* auxiliary) to Santa Cruz del Norte to pick up some guests.

"While Papa waited for us on board the *Pilar* at Puerto Escondido, I had my hands full with the small boat, the guests and the first strong gusts of the storm. The captain of Santa Cruz port had warned me: 'Be careful. Bad weather ahead.' I had answered: 'I will be as careful as need be.'

"We had been delayed having some drinks in Santa Cruz. We were just a couple of kilometers out at sea when I realized the bad weather was upon us, and night had fallen. I told my three passengers, 'I will have to tie you down so you won't fall into the water. A big wave may hit us and sweep you all out to sea, and who'd dare explain that to Papa?'

"I started with the mother of the young Italian lady. I put a rope around her, gave her a pat on the shoulder, and told her not to worry. 'Thank you. Thank you, sir,' she said. I gave the brother an end piece of old, greasy rope and told him: 'Do it yourself, brother, and do not move around too much, or we'll sink.' He was calm and smiling, and I'm sure he didn't understand our predicament.

"I found a piece of new rope and asked the little countess to allow me to tie her down securely. I took my time putting the rope around her. 'I think we're going to sink,' she said. But I assured her, 'Nothing to worry about. Look how well we're doing.'

"I had to leave the guests and take the steering wheel, for things were beginning to get really bad. I could see at a distance the Bengal lights Papa was shooting from the *Pilar*. I knew he would feel better if I answered him, but I couldn't let go of the steering wheel. The storm was very bad now.

"Finally, very slowly, we approached the *Pilar*, but the wind was so loud that Papa couldn't hear our motor. I could see him in the half light, standing on the bridge, trying to locate us. The rain had been heavy at times and our clothes were soaking wet.

"As we neared the boat we got both heavy rain and wind. I threw a rope hard against the side of the yacht and Papa heard the sound from up on deck. 'Ah, good. Gregorine has arrived!' he said. I untied the guests and he helped them aboard. He immediately opened a bottle of champagne in welcome. And right away he handed me another bottle. 'Open it, it's for you, Gregorine,' he said. 'You deserve the honor.'

"He saw that I hesitated to get into the party spirit, so he took me aside and asked: 'What do you want to do?' 'I'm thinking of the boat,' I told him. He knew what I meant by that, so he left me alone and went to attend to his guests. Meanwhile, I moved the *Pilar* to a safer position and secured it with two ropes to two buoys and two on land, and got ready to weather the storm.

"Everybody went to bed early except me, of course, and Papa, who came to where I was on the bridge, alone with my bottle.

" 'How do you think we're doing?' he asked.

"Holding up the bottle, I answered: 'Here I am with my compass, waiting for this little hurricane to get tired. But don't worry. Go to sleep, Papa.'

" 'No,' he said. 'I'm going to stay here with you all night.'

" 'There won't be any problems,' I said.

" 'Ah, well, then so much the better,' Papa answered."

Dawn found them sitting on that bridge against which the sea and the wind had dashed all night. It was a slow, gray, wet dawn.

[40]

Alone in the night, facing Havana, waiting for the snap of the outriggers, with half a bottle consumed by each, Gregorio and Papa talked of death and friendship. Following is the dialogue Gregorio relates as he reminisces in Cojímar:

Hemingway:    Do you know what a friend is, old man?

Gregorio:     You and I are friends.

Hemingway:    A friend is more than a father or a brother. A friendship means a past shared. You and I have been together twenty-seven years on board the *Pilar*. Where did we come from? It doesn't matter. One day we met, you with your life story and I with mine. Two friends are two stories that join as one.

Gregorio:     A friend is a chain.

Hemingway:    We have a good boat, Gregorine. A gasoline-powered boat such as they don't make any more. Yet we've never had a fire on board. We have faced many a storm on this boat, and caught great fish on it in the Gulf Stream. With it we also gave chase to the German seawolves.

Gregorio:     I have an idea. Let's wait and see who dies first. If it is you, I will take charge of the boat. I will take it to Finca Vigía and make a glass house for it. But I'll prepare everything the way I always have: there I'll set your fishing rod, a glass of rum ready for you, a book opened on the table, and your writing paper and your pen. And there'll be a statue of you.

Hemingway:    Fine. I like the idea. Yes, a very good idea.

And Papa died first. He left Gregorio the *Pilar*, valued at half a million dollars. But no bank in the world could pay its sentimental value. "There's not enough money in the world for that," says Gregorio.

As was to be expected, however, the upkeep of the *Pilar* turned out to be too much for a humble fisherman. Gregorio decided to donate it to the Revolutionary Government. When Fidel Castro heard of this decision, he ordered that a gift of a small fishing boat be given to Gregorio so that he could go on fishing for his own pleasure. He was given the *Hill-Noe*, a 20-foot launch with a 25-hp Soviet motor.

Gregorio kept the two outriggers and the kerosene stove of the *Pilar*. For some time he also kept the wooden sign that was used on the boat during the Second World War, when the *Pilar* masqueraded as a ship engaged in scientific research.

One afternoon Fidel Castro himself paid Gregorio a visit to

thank him for the gift of the *Pilar*. He assured Gregorio that the boat would continue to belong to him and that he could reclaim it any time he wished.

Today when Gregorio goes out fishing he uses the *Hill-Noe*, in which he installed the outriggers and the stove of the *Pilar*. He has a special authorization to buy provisions and fishing equipment on account at a fishing cooperative. He can fish any time, under the conditions he establishes for himself. He is a member of the Cooperative de Pesca de Cojímar (Fishing Cooperative of Cojímar), where he is considered an important man who enjoys some well-deserved privileges.

Gregorio saw Mary Welsh again 17 years after Papa's death, when Mary visited Havana in 1977. It was a cordial but brief meeting. Mary went to Gregorio's house and after a warm embrace told him, "You haven't changed at all." Gregorio smiled and answered with his traditional courtesy. "Here we are at your service."

They hadn't seen each other since a few weeks after Hemingway's death in 1961, the night the skipper of the *Pilar* went to Finca Vigía to hear Mary read the part of the will concerning Hemingway's Cuban employees.

"We lost him," Mary had said then. "What are we going to do?"

On that occasion Mary had suggested that Gregorio sink the *Pilar*.

"It mustn't fall into strange hands," she said. She also offered the alternative of taking the boat back to Key West with her.

Gregorio merely gave her a long and sad look.

[41]

Inevitably, Gregorio's memories reach his last conversation with Hemingway:

"He came to my house around 10:30 one morning during that summer of 1960. He was dressed as usual, in Bermuda shorts, white shirt without an undershirt, and slippers. I remember him clearly as he stood at the door. That was the last time I saw him. We had a few drinks, a small highball and a

Tom Collins. He fixed his own, and I mixed mine. He took mineral water and an ice cube, but no sugar. He never sweetened his drinks.

" 'Look, old man, I'm all right,' he told me. 'I just had a check-up and my blood pressure is normal. I weigh 190 pounds. That's a good weight for me. I need a rest from the book I'm writing, and that's why I'm going to Spain.'

"So you see, he was in good health. 'Take care of yourself and get a check-up,' he advised. 'Well, I'll be seeing you,' he said, as he had so many times before. He always said goodbye that way.

"I learned of his death from the newspapers.

"It didn't surprise me. What surprised me was the nature of his illness. I wouldn't have wanted to go on living either, if I was going to be a burden. What for, if he really had leukemia of the blood? 'My weight is down to 140 pounds,' he wrote me. I wonder how he looked then. He wrote that he was convalescing in Sun Valley after leaving the Mayo Brothers Clinic. Yet his letter didn't sound pessimistic. He was merely reporting the state of his health.

"Now I regret that I didn't take the necessary steps to go see him."


[42]


All the people who worked for Hemingway speak highly of him, but Gregorio goes further. "Papa was my man," he says, which is something very difficult for a Cuban macho to admit.

But it wasn't all love and sweetness between the two weather-beaten sailors.

Of their quarrels, perhaps the best is the story of the day when Hemingway and Gregorio almost parted for good. Gregorio was having a heated argument with the skipper of a boat moored next to the *Pilar*. Hemingway intervened in such an aggressive and crazy way that Gregorio considered it "a lack of respect" towards him. He was deeply offended and told Hemingway to figure out what he was owed, because he was quitting.

Hemingway left in a fury but was back before long, finally intending to right the wrong. As a matter of fact, he came back three or four times. Each time he had a few drinks with Gregorio, whose hurt feelings gradually subsided, until he finally agreed to stay on the job, "So that Papa wouldn't leave Cuba and burn down the farm and the yacht and all the other things he said he was going to do." Gregorio remembers it as a bad but fleeting moment: "Once in a while old Hemingway was strange.

"We were moored at the pier of the Club International de La Habana. Next to us there was a boat with some very rich people aboard. They told Papa that I had given away all our catch of the day to the local fishermen. It is true that I had given away some fish, but that was our custom. Both Papa and I wanted it that way—he, because of his generous nature, and I because it was a nice gesture and those people were our friends.

"The rich people from the boat saw me giving out the fish. They went to Papa with the story. I was arguing with their skipper when Papa came on board. It was obvious that he had been drinking too much. He was loud and offensive, and screamed at me: 'You gave away fish!'

" 'Yes,' I answered. 'You know I have never done anything against your wishes or interests. If this is the way you feel now, the problem is easily solved. Give me the salary due me and I quit right now.'

"That made Papa very angry; he left saying that I could go away if that was what I wanted. It was around 11 in the morning and he came back at one p.m. or thereabouts.

" 'Let's have a drink,' he said.

" 'Let's,' I answered.

"I had been waiting on the *Pilar* for him to bring me the accounting of my salary. We went down to the bar of the Club Internacional and had a few drinks.

" 'You insist on your decision?' he asked.

" 'I insist,' I answered.

" 'Well,' he said, 'you know, you're the one responsible . . .' And he left.

"He came back at three p.m. More drinks and similar questions. Again he left, and came back at 5:30. More drinks at the bar, without a word between us this time. Then more drinks at the *Pilar*.

" 'You are definitely leaving?' he asked.

" 'Look, Papa, I have to leave. What you did hurt me too much.'

" 'Don't say that. Don't talk about it,' he said.

"We fixed two more drinks. Then he said, 'Listen to what I'm going to say. First, I ask you to forgive me. If you don't forgive me but insist on quitting, I'll burn down the farm and leave Cuba forever!"

At this point in the story Gregorio says that two tears as large as peas ran down Papa's cheeks. The moment had come for patching up the quarrel and having two more drinks.

"We always agree, sooner or later," Thomas Hudson (Hemingway) tells Antonio (Gregorio) in *Islands in the Stream*, the most autobiographical of his novels.

[43]

After Finca Vigía and the hospitable bar, Floridita, the natural ambience for Hemingway in Cuba was the *Pilar*. If the author of *Islands in the Stream* compared his boat with his colonial house in San Francisco de Paula, there is no doubt that he felt more at home in the yacht than in any other place.

He bought it around the middle of 1934, when, on his return from Europe, he received a very pleasant surprise from the bank: three thousand dollars for his African chronicles published in *Esquire* magazine, which served as a down payment on the purchase of the yacht. He contributed to its design and commissioned the Wheeler Shipyard Company of New York to build it. When finished, it was sent by rail to Miami. Hemingway broke a bottle of champagne against its hull the day it was launched. It was registered in Key West and in the port of Havana as well.

The *Pilar* is solidly constructed. Today its appearance has an old-fashioned flavor, but in its time it was an extraordinary boat. It was narrow, but with a broad stern.

In its interior, through the center entrance beyond the

bridge, there are three compartments. The first one has two double berths (the interior ones with drawers), two closets and a little cabinet. The second one contains the kitchen and bath. The third has another double berth and two open shelves called "The Ethylic Department" in the Hemingway "code," because that is where the liquor was stored.

The instrument panel has been preserved intact. Behind the steering wheel are four dials and the following inscription: NORSEMAN POWERED. The dials are for the tachometer, the oil level, the motor temperature and the ammeter. To the left of the helm is the lights panel, with buttons placed from top to bottom:

> anchor light
> running lights
> bilge pump
> wiper
> search light

Behind, on the counter, are the throttle and gearshift levers, and a bronze plaque placed there by the manufacturer:

> HULL 576
> Wheeler Shipyard
> Boat Manufacturers
> 1934
> Brooklyn, New York

Two other dials are on a column in the cabin: a barometer and a chronometer.

The *Pilar* had a cruising range of 500 miles with seven persons on board. Its tanks had a capacity of 300 gallons of gasoline and 150 of potable water. It had a small domestic refrigerator. In her cockpit it could carry 100 more gallons in drums. It was possible to stock another 100 gallons of water in demijohns and 2400 pounds of ice. It was built to sail in rough weather and its owner considered it a great ship in spite of its being powered by gas engines. Hemingway's great pride was that there had never been a fire on board.

It was powered by Universal and Chrysler Mariner engines

in its early days, and later it got new ones by the same manufacturers. The Universal engines had 45 hp and the Chryslers 90. The *Pilar* could reach a speed of 8 knots. She cost around $350 to $400 a month to operate, and was moored at Jaimanitas and Casablanca. At times she was at anchor in Cojímar, the Club Internacional and Tarará beach. The *Pilar* could be identified at a great distance by the enormous outriggers that Hemingway installed on board.

Gregorio Fuentes says: "I kept it shining bright, like gold. It was made of American black oak and I cleaned it every day."

The *Pilar* is intact today, but that doesn't mean she hasn't suffered hardships. Around the middle of the fifties, Gregorio took the boat to the shipyard for general repairs. The yacht had to be caulked and the timber of the keel had to be replaced. It was difficult for Hemingway to get black oak in the United States. He couldn't get enough of it and agreed that some pieces be rebuilt with Cuban mahogany.

This was a good time to adjust the Universal and Chrysler engines. Ricardo, a mechanic for the pilots of Havana harbor, again had a chance to work on the *Pilar*. He was the same mechanic hired by Gregorio to keep the boat in good condition during the Second World War.

The carpenters who worked in the banks of the Almendares river proved to be real craftsmen, and Ricardo demonstrated that he was "the best engine adjuster in the Caribbean and the world," according to his own sincere declaration, carried away by his enthusiasm at repairing one of the world's most famous yachts. Gregorio directed the whole operation.

"When everything was ready Papa came on board, and when he saw his boat shining like new, just like the boat of his youth, he cried, 'Oh, what a pleasure this is, how happy I feel!' And he had tears in his eyes."

But the *Pilar* cannot stay out of water for long. If that magnificent hull doesn't have water pressure, the frame timber tends to open and will soon lose its masts. At first Gregorio kept it at Cojímar, from the time of Hemingway's death until he gave it to the government. From Cojímar it was taken to the Vigía, to be exhibited as the most important item of the new museum. It was her first overland trip. There she remained several years until moved to the shipyard at Casablanca, and then to another shipyard in Cárdenas, 100 kilometers northeast of Havana. The yacht again underwent general repairs before it was returned to Finca Vigía in 1973, more than ten years after Hemingway's death.

It was transported by highway from Cárdenas to the Vigía, as a wide-load. It was necessary to stop the traffic on stretches of the road, because the width of the boat extended beyond the sides of the military vehicle on which it rested, covering two-thirds of the narrow Central Highway.

The return of the boat was cause for great celebration in San Francisco de Paula. It stayed there day and night until 1975, mounted on wooden blocks, much to Gregorio Fuentes' objections.

In 1975 an American company planned to film a documentary about Hemingway's life in Cuba, and again the yacht was taken to Casablanca by land for major repairs. Suddenly, however, the American company decided to cancel the film, and the major repairs were reduced to a superficial once-over, and the boat was returned to Finca Vigía.

Gregorio paid a brief visit to the shipyard before the *Pilar* was sent back to the farm, and seeing someone else directing the operation upset him so much that he was depressed for weeks.

The yacht remained there, losing its looks, in need of paint, sailing on a sea of green ferns between mango trees, until 1979, when it was sent to Casablanca once more—this time for what promised to be the "definitive restoration." But on this occasion Gregorio refused to know what was being done to *his* boat.

Much later, the hazardous route followed by the *Pilar*, without captain or master, or the warmth of blue Caribbean waters, was no longer taken alone. In the famous Chullima shipyards on the city's waterfront, an exact replica of Hemingway's yacht was built. The work is of such precision and high quality that not even Gregorio Fuentes can tell which is the original.

Previously, only one other replica of a boat had been built in Cuba, one more important to the Cubans and of more historical value to them, and therefore in their eyes completely justified.

It is the yacht *Granma*, which on a rough voyage from Tuxpan, Mexico, to Playa Coloradas in Cuba, brought the hope of freedom to the island with Fidel Castro and his men.

Neither Gregorio nor anybody else can explain the reason for the new replica. The captain of the *Pilar* will often wistfully ask his friends in Cojímar, "Why a double for my boat—why?"

[44]

One of Hemingway's favorite restaurants, La Terraza in Cojímar, is described in *The Old Man and the Sea*. Thomas Hudson in *Islands in the Stream* says that it occupies a big old house on the beach, and that "it is very pleasant there." La Terraza hasn't changed much since Hemingway's time, when its owner used the author's presence there to promote his establishment.

A "Terraza" of sorts appears in the movie version of *The Old Man and the Sea*. The original is of masonry, and the one in the film is a thatched hut, or "bohio." The previous owner was slow to make changes, and the only difference in the place then and now is that the walls are covered with about fifty photos of Hemingway, most of them stills from films. Although one might expect to find authentic photos of Hemingway in Cojímar, most of the shots depict the capture of a gigantic marlin in Cabo Blanco, Peru.

In *Islands in the Stream*, Hemingway recalls "the bar at Cojímar, that was built out on the rocks overlooking the harbor," and he describes his first visit there on a Christmas morning. In 1970, Fidel Castro, on a tour of the area, asked about La Terraza. He was told that it was now a roadhouse where great quantities of beer were sloshed down in paper cups. Castro gave orders that he wanted La Terraza restored "at least" to the condition it was in when Hemingway patronized it, and "with the same menu." Today the best crab and shrimp "enchilados" in all Cuba are prepared at La Terraza. It's still a good place to meet Gregorio Fuentes and drink Cuban beer or rum in a tall glass while enjoying the company of seafaring men.

There are a few new apartment houses along the waterfront

of Cojímar. The base for sport fishing is now called "Ernest Hemingway." The fishermen have organized and formed a cooperative. There is a new shipyard called El Cachón. The fishing boats have 25-hp engines of Soviet origin, not very stylish, but efficient.

The big tree on one side of La Terraza, under whose shade Hemingway chatted with the fishermen, is gone. And many of the fishermen are missing. They too have died. But one thing survives: every night the members of the cooperative head for the Gulf Stream. It's not a fleet of yachts, but a fleet of small fishing boats carrying the rugged old fishermen of Cojímar out to sea.

Gregorio endures, still drinking rum smacking of the brine. Alert and shrewd, this bright-eyed mariner still enthralls friends and journalists who visit him in his home. Still roaming "Hemingway's mile" and eating and drinking well at La Terraza.

At times he confuses dates and characters, and even forgets how the stories about Hemingway end. But this is of no importance. One can always check the facts and straighten loose ends. But only Gregorio can give us such a fresh vision of the life he shared with Hemingway. This is the man who tells us that it was he who thought of the title *To Have and Have Not* and furnished the material for *The Old Man and the Sea*. He may tell the same story, but the details often vary from day to day.

The one thing that never varies is his opinion of Carlos Gutiérrez which, of course, can be attributed to professional jealousy. Neither is this important. Fishermen love to add a few inches to their catch, but then, there it is jumping and snapping, defying the tape measure of researchers.

[45]

Sometimes Hemingway would weigh anchor and hide out for a few weeks at Cayo Paraíso (Paradise Key), called Mégano de Casigua in the naval charts. It lies approximately five miles off La Mulata Bay, in Pinar del Río province. The writer would go there with his wife and Gregorio, his Royal portable, a few reams of writing paper and half a dozen number-two pencils. He found a good place to work among the barrier reefs of Cayo Paraíso, a private place, one the press never knew about.

Those excursions to the key became more frequent towards the end of the forties and in the fifties. It gave Hemingway much pleasure to join Gregorio in overseeing the supplies of food and drink for those trips. He would make ambitious plans about what he was going to do and what he was going to write on the island, keeping the same disciplined regimen that he followed at Finca Vigía.

Later, around eleven, he would jump into the water, or run naked on the shore with Mary. He never made clear what Gregorio was supposed to do in the meantime, who no doubt stayed on board the *Pilar*, keeping it in shape while the couple enjoyed the freedom of the deserted key. After one of Gregorio's famous lunches, they would enjoy a siesta in the swaying boat in one of the coves of the shore, and in the afternoon Ernest had another session with the Royal portable under a palm tree, out of the sun.

If they felt up to it, they would sail out to the Gulf Stream in search of fish to catch for the evening's or next day's dinner. This was necessary because the ice boxes aboard the *Pilar* had limited capacity. Refrigeration was always a problem and many times a "military operation" was organized in Havana, headed by Dr. Herrera Sotolongo and involving Don Andrés, the priest, and good friend Sinsky.

On Sundays, after filling the trunk of Herrera's car with ice from the Mariel factory, they would drive along the road bordering the mountains until they reached the port of the Mulata, where they had previously agreed to meet Ernest.

The yacht would be waiting with Gregorio, Mary and Ernest, all deeply tanned. Bearded and smiling under cover aft, Ernest would wave his greeting and the hours of drinking and fooling around would begin. After noon, the friends would say goodbye and Ernest and his small crew would return to the key. In the late afternoon, the *Pilar* could be seen from the shore sailing against the sun with its two long outriggers waving in the sea breeze—a wide, dark boat with its prow pointing towards Mégano de Casigua (Cayo Paraíso).

[46]

Marlin search for food in both blue and green waters. "One looks for the blue water," say the veteran fishermen, "because that's where the Stream is." And Gregorio looked for them often at the *hilero*, the visible borderline between the two waters.

When one cuts open the stomach of a marlin, one finds shrimp, flying fish, squid and other small species that inhabit the borderline. "That's why one must look for marlin there. That's what Papa and I used to do as soon as we passed the Morro."

The fishermen usually have their own landmarks to guide them. "We were guided by an old house we could see on the coastline, near Cojímar. We called it the Pink House or the House of the Priest. On a level with that point was the exact location of the Hondón de Cojímar, a marine abyss, excellent for fishing. Now our old landmark is called 'The Antenna,' because those who look for that spot steer themselves by the tall radio tower that stands where we once saw the House of the Priest."

"Hemingway's mile," which is somewhat longer than the orthodox mile, was measured from the shooting range in La Cabaña fortress at the mouth of Havana Bay to the House of the Priest. That area still abounds with marlin. When the current is strong it brings in many fish.

Fishermen mistakenly believe that marlin run from east to west because that's the way they see them. But scientists have determined that the marlin run in precisely the opposite direction. What happens is that they leave their "run" to find food near the *hilero*. Although they go west to the borderline to feed, their migratory course is from west to east.

Hemingway wrote on this subject in several articles: "The Great Blue River," "Marlin off the Morro," "Out in the Stream: A Cuban Letter," and others, all written between the thirties and fifties.

Hemingway learned how to fight and catch marlin, thanks to instruction from Carlos Gutiérrez during the thirties. But it was Gregorio Fuentes who taught him how to distinguish with professional accuracy between the habits of different species of marlin.

The blue marlin arrive from April to May, but September is the month of the real big ones, the ones Hemingway called "the heavyweights." It was one of these that inspired the story of *The Old Man and the Sea*. The fishermen of Cojímar tell the story of a huge blue marlin like Santiago's fish which fought for 15 hours before being hoisted aboard. The blue marlin is one of the largest sea creatures, and incredibly fast moving.

The crew of the *Pilar* fished in these waters for the largest and heaviest of the marlin, but they also looked for one of the most beautiful and fast-moving of all the fish that inhabit the deep, open seas: the *dorado*. Hemingway claimed that this fish changed colors according to its sensations. To him, the different colors meant hunger, anger, sexual excitement and fear.

The sound of the alarm in the outriggers could also announce the hooking of another species, the white marlin; its back is deep blue, with bright silver lower sides and belly. His sword is fine and sharp, his eyes very large. He's very fast and puts up a stiff fight when hooked.

At other times it was the sailfish, also found in deep waters. When caught and brought on board, rows of light blue spots appear on its sides. Like other marlin, it hits the bait with its rough, hard bill before swallowing it.

Hemingway used to watch closely as Gregorio baited the hooks. He watched with the same concentration he devoted to the Masai warriors when they prepared to throw their spears. Gregorio, very skilled in the preparation of bait, would choose *balaos* and needlefish, the best bait when fishing for marlin. Gregorio used the entire *balao*, but cut up the needlefish in slices, or cut pieces from the flanks. "Papa," he would say, "this has to be done with much care. It can't be done quickly. The bait has to slide through the water and stay fresh and appetizing."

The *balao*, a silver fish, is hooked *por derecho*, in the language of the Cuban men of the sea, meaning that the shank of the hook inside the bait fish is tied to it to help withstand the pressure of the water when trolling. The bend and the barb emerge on the side or the belly of the fish, near the tail, to facilitate hooking the marlin when it attacks the bait.

The needlefish is cut in slices according to the size of the hook. The pieces are attached to the shank of the hook with a fine line and the lower part is left free to dangle and simulate a fish's tail as the bait slides through the water.

When there were no *balaos* or needlefish available, Gregorio looked for other small bait fish. When, however, the *Pilar* went out to fish for the big blue marlin in September, they used big bait, like whole bonitos, mackerel, bonefish, *dorados* and similar species. None of the baiting procedures interfered with the usual private consumption of whiskey and Tom Collinses which continued uninterrupted on board.

In his battles with marlin, Hemingway always wanted to be fair. He tried to make it an even fight between man and fish, and may the better one win. He always remembered that it was not the man who had the hook in his mouth.

His contribution to ichthyology, as an aficionado, should not be underestimated. Charles Cadwalader, director of the Museum of the Natural Sciences Academy of Philadelphia, chose to accompany him in August 1934 on a sea voyage of scientific explorations.

Henry W. Fowler, ichthyologist, obtained sufficient information from Hemingway, just as Cadwalader did, to revise the classification of marlin found throughout the entire North Atlantic.

Hemingway was a master sport fisherman, combining great skill and knowledge. "He was a bull," say the old fishermen of Cojímar. In the defense of his dignity as a man of the sea, he had a row with Alfred Knapp in Bimini in 1935. The American millionaire cast doubts on the number and size of the fish Hemingway claimed to have caught and on the many seafaring adventures he described in his articles. This happened on one of the piers of Bimini.

Knapp, an ugly drunk, gradually raised the tone of his insults. "Slob, son of a bitch," was the last thing the writer endured in silence. Suddenly Papa punched Knapp in the jaw, and followed up with a few swift blows that ended the incident for the moment. This encounter surfaced in a song popular in Bimini. Both, song and boxing match, appear in *Islands in the Stream*.

The truth is that the owner of the *Pilar* reeled in the biggest sailfish ever caught up to that time in the Atlantic. It weighed 119 pounds. In the same Bimini area, after a half-hour battle, he boated a 786-pound shark. In the summer of 1935 he won all the competitions, beating such skilled and famous fishermen as Lerner, Farrington and Shevlin.

# Return to Paradise

[47]

In 1975, many years after Hemingway's death, Gregorio Fuentes took a sentimental journey to Cayo Paraíso in his boat the *Hill Noe*. On board were his coxswain, Santiago el Soltero (the Bachelor), the photographer Enrique de la Uz, and the writer of this history.

Gregorio led his boat with utmost care; he went very slowly, since he knew he was going over coral reef capable of opening a big hole even in the hull of a transatlantic ship. The key, the only refuge for miles around, is no longer a paradise. It is in ruins. The holiday cabins and huts of the fishermen have suffered the same fate over the years; they are completely destroyed. The key is sinking—the palms and the coconut groves of the coast are sinking with the land. However, the pines that Hemingway planted have not only resisted the surge of the sea, but have increased in number, their seed carried by wind the length and breadth of the islet. Today, lost in the Gulf Stream, these pines can't be much different from those towering above Robert Jordan where he lay, belly down, in the opening and closing passages of *For Whom the Bell Tolls*.

Hemingway's excursions to the key started in 1935, but he didn't plant the pine trees until the time of the Second World War, when he armed the *Pilar* and began to hunt German submarines. He needed a point of reference, a visible sign, so that he could locate the key quickly at a distance.

"You may not believe it, but I'm very moved," says Gregorio Fuentes as we anchor the *Hill Noe* in a cove of the key. "I remember Papa playing on the beach so clearly."

A pelican flies over the beach grapevines, the *hicacos*, the palm trees and the mangroves. There are three abandoned huts sometimes used by the fishermen in summer. In one of these there is a wooden icebox which they still use to keep the fish.

Gregorio tells stories of Africa, about the elders who armed themselves with "old guns and silver daggers." He talks about his "Daddy." He invents a new geography, mentions a legendary Dakar and conjures lions in the coasts of Africa.

Gregorio is wearing the same olive-green campaign jacket with the letters "US NAVY" printed on it that Hemingway gave him when he joined the anti-submarine operations. He sips cheap rum and describes the night land breeze, the "terral." "Wherever you see a falling star, that's the direction the wind will come from."

This is the last night the skipper of the *Pilar* will spend in Key Paradise, or what's left of it. The next morning he will leave without looking back—not once.


[48]


With his Royal typewriter, Hemingway joined two good friends, Joe Russell and Charles Thompson, into one character: Harry Morgan, the tough smuggler of *To Have and Have Not*. The influence of the owner of Sloppy Joe's is felt more in the novel.

The many trips Hemingway made with Russell from Key West to Havana, and his own experiences as observer of the revolutionary struggle against the Cuban dictator, Gerardo Machado, provided material for the first two parts of the novel, which was first published as separate stories: "One Trip Across," in *Cosmopolitan*, in the April 1934 issue, and "The Tradesman's Return," published in *Esquire*, February 1936. The protagonist of these two stories appears without the surname Morgan. The Hemingway hero was known only as Harry to the readers of *Cosmopolitan* and *Esquire*.

Harry's fate, with or without a surname, deadly wounded in the Gulf Stream, is quite different from that of the man who was the primary inspiration for the character. But that is easily explained: Joe Russell was a real man and Morgan a typical

Hemingway hero. Gregorio Fuentes has said, in a critical tone, that the Morgan of the novel "is a bit soft." He means that Morgan is a man who shows concern about his fellow man: a feeling of human solidarity not often present in the heart of the authentic smuggler.

In real life Russell died in relative wealth, having grown old peacefully with the help of much whiskey and memories of a life of intense emotions. Harry Morgan's namesake, Henry Morgan, the pirate of the seventeenth century, the adventurer who represented the emerging British middle class, did not possess the virtue of solidarity as shown by the harassed character who bears his name in *To Have and Have Not*.

William Faulkner read the novel and agreed to write the film script. He did this in collaboration with Jules Furthman. It failed completely, a real disaster. It was too rough, too grim and brutal. How could a Hollywood hero fit into this tragic seascape of harsh social conflict?

Gregorio Fuentes knew Joe Russell: "He was a little old man, very thin; he couldn't have weighed more than 120 pounds. Towards the end of his life he didn't drink much. He used to say that Ernest was a very smart boy and that's why he liked him. A boy with a great future."

Fuentes tells us that, during Prohibition, Hemingway went to see Russell and told him: "I'm broke, lend me your boat." Russell and Hemingway made a deal, and the writer went to Havana and managed to get around 600 or 700 cases of cognac from Recalt's, 24 bottles to the case. The cognac cost them 40 cents a bottle, and sold in the United States at $3.50 each.

According to Fuentes, Hemingway smuggled the "goods" from Playa de Jaimanitas. He and Russell agreed on the day and place to meet in jurisdictional waters. They had a prearranged system of signals, using red, white and blue lights. According to Fuentes, that was how Hemingway made enough money to go to Europe and Africa.

The contraband was carried aboard the *Anita*, Joe Russell's boat on which Hemingway made his first crossing to Cuba. It turned out to be very seaworthy, made to sail in all kinds of weather. It was about ten feet shorter than the *Pilar* and is the boat described in *To Have and Have Not*.

[49]

When Hemingway was awarded the medal of San Cristobal in Havana in 1956, in the old Sports Palace, he brought with him some written words which he planned to say during the presentation. The speech reveals his sense of irony, his knowledge of Cuban sports, the great respect he had for the fishermen of Cojímar and above all for Gregorio Fuentes.

As it turned out, Hemingway couldn't read his notes and had to leave with the folded sheet in the pocket of his guayabera, because there were a thousand more drivers so honored for "never having had an accident," and all with the same right to "say a few words." That was the writer's democratic comment. This was the speech, unheard, unpublished and unedited:

> Distinguished politicians, officers, ladies, gentleman and friends:
> My Spanish is very bad, because I learned it in places like Madrid, Pamplona, Andalucía, Regla, and the docks of Caballería, where it is spoken with a different accent in each place.
> Thank you for the medal and all the flattery. But I accept it in the name of all the marlin fishermen of the north coast of Cuba, from Puerto Escondido to Bahía Honda. I dedicate my book, *The Old Man and the Sea*, whatever it may be worth, to my old comrade in arms, Gregorio Fuentes, my oldest fishing companion, Carlos Gutiérrez, and all my old friends who fished for marlin with me in Cojímar: Anselmo, Figurín, El Sordo and the late Marcos Puig, and all others alive or dead. Cojímar is my second country, and so I cannot forget a toast to Jorge Martínez, who, when he was the Naval Delegate, was the best friend of all the fishermen of Cojímar.
> I also want to toast the Cuban team that just won the international competition in Nova Scotia, and also all the fishermen who fish for marlin with rod and reel and do it fairly.
> End of speech.
>
> E. Hemingway

The fishermen he mentions in his speech all contributed in one way or another to his apprenticeship in big game fishing and to his knowledge of commercial fishing, which is evident in *The Old Man and the Sea*.

The brave and good fishermen were many. As has been said many times, the best fishermen in all Cuba come from Cojímar. They are fishermen *of the deep*, who take great risks; as did Negro Arsenio, or El Sordo, or Anselmo (who served as a partial model for the Santiago of the story), and the authentic Santiagos, Santiago Puig and Santiago el Soltero, and the rest of the great fishermen of that town: Bello, Cachimba, Cheo López, Ova Carnero, Tato and Quintín. All of them used to sit down to "chew the rag" with Papa in the shade of a leafy big tree on one side of La Terraza.

They really enjoyed the filming of *The Old Man and the Sea* in their town. They were paid very well to appear as extras in the movie and to look for the big fish to be featured in the film. The people of Cojímar thought of it as a fiesta, a pleasant interruption of their everyday routine to join in the search for the enormous fish, a search which finally ended far away in Cabo Blanco, Peru, which meant that only Hemingway and Gregorio went there.

There is a plaza in Cojímar, near the coast, where a bust of Hemingway has been erected. This is how it happened: the fishermen of Cojímar came together spontaneously a few days after "the American's" death. These men, with their hard faces, their hands scarred by a lifetime of handling fishlines, their skin toughened by the salt from the sea, held a meeting in which they decided that "a statue of the old man" should be made and placed in a park in their town.

The meeting was very quiet at first, and nobody took a drink, thinking that was the best way to show respect for Hemingway. But later on they changed their minds, and each one took a "big swig" in memory of their dead comrade.

They found a sculptor who told them, "There is no bronze for what you have ordered. The country is suffering an economic blockade, and the bronze is scarce."

"We have it," the fishermen replied. "The bronze of the propellers in our boats." And true to their word, they furnished the metal.

The sculptor was touched and refused to charge them for his work. It was enough that they had contributed the bronze.

The statue turned out "real nice," the fishermen said, and it will be in place a long, long time. It is made of enduring material that can resist the perils of the sea and years.

Plaza Hemingway, the first in the world with that name, was inaugurated a year after the writer's death, July 2, 1962. For many years, the plaza had been one of the familiar spots of Cojímar, although nobody remembers exactly when or why it was built. It faces one of the docks where the *Pilar* was moored.

Hemingway often walked in the little plaza without a name. He would be seen there in his Bermudas and long-billed visor cap, after one more battle at sea, quiet but happy, looking for his Chrysler.

## [50]

The current of the Gulf Stream moves in a great circle. It emerges at the southeast of San Antonio Cape and borders the north coast of Cuba. It passes in front of Key West, Miami and Cape Hatteras and then heads in an east-northeasterly direction toward the Canary Islands. It then returns across the North Atlantic and moves again toward the Antilles, where it continues to Yucatan and then starts on the same course all over again.

Across from Havana, it flows in an easterly direction, and east-northeasterly off Varadero beach. In front of Havana it is approximately 60 miles wide, with velocities of between 1.2 and 2.4 knots. The current picks up speed as the marine floor deepens; its water is of a more intense blue than the water around it. As it moves, it drags along masses of sea grass and sargasso which float lazily on its surface.

Manuel Sáenz is 70 years old and has never read a single page that Hemingway wrote about the fishermen of Cojímar. But he knows by memory what happens in those books. He fished with Papa and Gregorio and was a close friend of Carlos Gutiérrez. He practiced the arts described by Hemingway in the fishing areas that served as background for his characters.

Sáenz remembers the garbage scows of Havana, which Hemingway described in *Green Hills of Africa*. They carried all the waste of the city, which in the afternoon was dumped into the Gulf Stream. Groups of fishermen followed the scows, because they knew many species of fish would feed on the garbage.

Sáenz preferred the sharks, which were worth 90 cents a fin. "We fished for them with harpoons, but when the marlin began to run we forgot all about the sharks." He remembers the time Hemingway and Carlos Gutiérrez had a falling out. He says that on a certain occasion during the filming of the capture of a marlin, when it came time to gaff the fish, the moment corresponding to the "moment of truth" in a bullfight, Gutiérrez lost his nerve, messed things up and the shooting was all wasted. He then went to work for Julio Hidalgo, "The Frenchman," who was a harbor pilot.

Carlos had eight children, four girls and four boys. They called him Grandpa. "But Carlos was not as skillful as Gregorio." Long afterwards he went blind and died in the house he had bought in Cojímar. "He was a man of little character," contends Sáenz, and to work for Papa, "you had to have a good deal of character."

Sáenz accepts that Carlos Gutiérrez may have been the model for the protagonist of *The Old Man and the Sea*. "It could have been him, because some very strange things happen to fishermen," he said.

Gregorio Fuentes understandably shows a lack of enthusiasm on the subject of Gutiérrez. As we have already said, it's a matter of professional jealousy. The fact is that Carlos Gutiérrez was as much a friend of Hemingway's as Gregorio. Of course, it is true that the writer's relationship with Gutiérrez was not one between equals, since he sometimes bullied his employee Gutiérrez. It is also true that Hemingway, as they say in Havana slang, *"le tenía cogida la baja"* (knew his weak points).

This was not at all the nature of his relationship with Gregorio, a proud and dignified man who reacted violently to any attempt to bully him. In Carlos there was a certain weakness of character which stimulated the most negative traits of Hemingway's personality. At times Carlos would be remiss, let go of the line and lose a prize catch. He was wise in the ways of the current of the Gulf Stream, but he had his problems.

At the end, Sáenz shows good fellowship among fishermen

when judging Carlos. "It is true," he says sadly, "that we, the poor fishermen, usually lost the big fish because we had only small tackle."

The Hemingway competition was inaugurated in 1950. The team of the Miramar Yacht Club won on that occasion. The Havana Biltmore won the following year. Bob Hopp, an American, won in 1955. It was held continuously until 1958; no competition was held in 1959. Fidel Castro won as the person with "the largest individual accumulation" in 1960. That was the afternoon he and Hemingway met.

Sunday, May 15, 1960, was the last day of the event. Fidel entered the competition on the yacht *Cristal*, property of Julito Blanco Herrera, owner of the La Tropical Brewery. There were some 15 people on board that yacht: three Cuban photographers (Cala, Alberto Korda and Osvaldo Salas), bodyguards and others. According to Cala, the competition was sponsored by Hy Peskin, one of the most prestigious photographers in the United States, whose color photographs have appeared on the cover of *Life*. Also on board the yacht were Baudilio Castellanos ("Bilito") and Jesús Montané. One of the first to arrive was Ernesto "Che" Guevara, with *Le Rouge et le Noir* in his hand and a Contax camera around his neck.

Cala says that Che Guevara greeted him and that he (Cala) praised the camera. "Well, it is more revolutionary than I," answered Guevara. He explained that with it he had earned a living and made money to buy bullets in Mexico.

Fidel came on board around eight o'clock in the morning, and they took off. The fishing lasted until four in the afternoon. Che tried his luck a couple of times with lines, but he evidently preferred to read that day. He took off his campaign shirt and Peskin started to take pictures of him, but Cala scolded the American, telling him that "Che shirtless would make too exotic a photo."

Che Guevara then went below deck and sought the quiet of a cabin. On return to port at four, he had already finished the book and told Cala that he was very much impressed with Stendhal. Nobody mentioned Hemingway, who was nearby on board the *Pilar*. Not feeling well, Che Guevara did not stay to watch the award ceremonies. His asthma was bothering him and he left. He never met Hemingway.

A couple of days before, on May 13, 1960, Fidel Castro had appeared on a TV program to answer questions from newspapermen. One of them, referring to his participation in the Hemingway competition, asked if he planned to continue fishing.

"Oh, *caramba*, of course," was his answer. "Tomorrow I will be one hour short [on his fishing] because I have official obligations, but I have two more days, and tomorrow I'll fish five hours, because for the contest it should be six hours daily, and the day after tomorrow, Sunday, I will fish the six hours, and then, I don't know whether you have read the newspapers, but they have asked me who put the marlin there for me. [Laughter] The truth is that I am in second place and I'll keep on going; I already have enough fish for two months. When I'm through, I'll have enough fish for half a year.

"The competition was organized by INIT [National Institute of Tourism]. The tournaments are very good, very well organized and many foreign fishermen have come to the international competition. I don't presume to be a great fisherman, but I was invited and I was told that Hemingway would take part as well, I believe tomorrow, and as you know, he has always defended Cuba and the Revolution. He is a writer whose presence here is of great satisfaction for us.

"This is the International Marlin Competition, with the 'Hemingway Award,' and I went not because I think I'm a great fisherman or anything of the sort, but because I was invited and I wanted to contribute to its success, and at least encourage the comrades that work for tourism and this competition, that have done so much propaganda, put in so much effort, on such good programs . . . but with the unfavorable campaign against them in the United States, it is difficult to bring tourists. They are the most patient, optimistic and hard-working people, and that's why I'm taking part in it.

"So far I've been lucky, because the marlin have come on their own. Now, everybody can be sure that if I win it will be a clean victory and if I lose, a clean loss."

Lawyer Baudilio Castellanos and Jesús Montané organized the competition. They were in charge of INIT. They recall that

Hemingway had been baffled by the unusual activity surrounding the competition of that year, 1960, no doubt the most publicized of all those held until then. But he appeared willing to help, and collaborated graciously.

Hemingway's biographers usually state that the writer found little pleasure in meeting Fidel Castro. In her book *How It Was*, Mary Welsh says that despite the force of Fidel's personality, she was quite unmoved that day. However, photographs taken on the occasion show a smiling Mary and Ernest Hemingway in the presence of the Cuban leader.

[51]

CUBA INTERNATIONAL
October 1978
IN THE WATERS OF THE HEMINGWAY
Seventeen years after the disappearance of the author of *The Old Man and the Sea*, Cuba remembers Ernest Hemingway in the celebration of the annual Tournament that carries his name.

by Urbano Fernández

For the first time since 1960, the notable event has recovered its international character and in the blue waters off the coast of Havana can be seen the seven teams of the nations that have registered in the first "Ernest Hemingway" International Tourist Fishing Tournament.

*Why the Name*

Some of the old fishermen of the town still call the stretch of water off the coast between Cojímar and the new residential district of East Havana "Hemingway's mile." Marlin is traditionally abundant there.

Fishing for marlin—the most exciting and colorful of all sports fishing—was always known in Cuba. The famous Gulf Stream which crosses in front of the coast of Havana is thronged with marlin on their annual migration.

Started by Hemingway in 1950, the International Marlin Tournament was held yearly until 1961, when it was suspended.

That was the year which culminated in the disaster of the Bay of Pigs.

However, two years after Hemingway's death, in spite of the difficulties faced in obtaining fishing tackle and replacements of motors for the boats, the first marlin tournament in memory of Hemingway was modestly celebrated. It was the first time workers participated in this type of event, which previously had been reserved for the native bourgeoisie.

Since then, various representatives of the country's provinces, ministries and central organizations, national trade unions and the Armed Forces meet each year on the coast of Havana, seeking victory in the tournament.

Each year there are competitions which culminate in the provincial finals, from which the participating teams for the Hemingway are selected. Thousands of aficionados of marlin fishing throughout Cuba compete for the chance to take part in the finals, completely free of charge in a costly sport ordinarily reserved in other latitudes for the wealthy.

GRANMA
23rd of May, 1980
## TRADITIONAL "ERNEST HEMINGWAY" MARLIN TOURNAMENT OPENING TODAY

Today, at nine in the morning, is the opening day of the traditional "Ernest Hemingway" International Marlin Tournament, at the Marina Barlovento northeast of the capital. The classic cannon shot will serve as the signal for the boats to set off to sea in search of the prized game. This kind of fishing is not easy, as it demands great skill to boat these specimens.

Thirty years ago, Ernest Hemingway himself organized the first competition. Since the Revolution this sport and the tournament have attracted more participants each year, since the workers of all the trade unions are able to take part in it. Later, the competition was held between provinces, and a few years ago it became international. The competition is rod and reel exclusively, by the method of trolling. The maximum strength allowed on line is 50-pound test line. Fish caught with lines of less than 30-pound test will receive extra points. Further, only one-hook baitings will be allowed. Double and triple hooks are not allowed.

[52]

In *My Brother Ernest Hemingway*, Leicester Hemingway tells an apocryphal tale of a night in the thirties when, on a spree in Jaimanitas with his older brother Ernest and some friends, they succeeded in getting some twenty naïve and humble fishermen very drunk. For fun, and with the fishermen's help, they set fire to some huts and cabins in the town. They were wooden and thatched structures, and the fire spread rapidly. According to Leicester, the revellers enjoyed themselves thoroughly.

But the tale doesn't hold up. Esteban Arias and Fidelino Pérez, who should know, deny that such a thing happened. Both men were 75 years old in 1977, the oldest residents of Jaimanitas, and they don't remember any such fire. They never heard of the incident Leicester Hemingway refers to. Fidelino Pérez, in fact, gets very angry: "How the hell could they burn our houses?" he asks, and deliberately uses other more expressive words. "What did he think we were to permit such a thing?" Esteban's answer is more controlled and sober: "There was never such a fire in this area."

During the thirties, the beach of Jaimanitas near Havana was one of Hemingway's favorite places. Later he was to change his course and head in the opposite direction, towards the beaches and ports to the east.

Jaimanitas is vividly remembered by Philip Rawling in *The Fifth Column* and is also the background for the only Cuban short story Hemingway wrote, "Nobody Ever Dies." Jaimanitas is a small fishermen's village. Although it has a beach and a river that provides boat shelter, it cannot compare with Cojímar.

Hemingway had good friends in Jaimanitas: the Masons, husband and wife, companions of his first fishing expeditions in Cuba. George Grant Mason was Pan American's representative in Cuba at the time when the great clippers used to touch down in the water at the port of Havana. The Mason mansion still stands in an out-of-the-way, exclusive area of Jaimanitas. In 1977 it was the residence of a Canadian diplomat.

The Mason place seems to be the stage for the action Hemingway describes in his story, the tale of a young Cuban who, after seeing combat in the Spanish Civil War, is assassinated hours after returning to his own country, by order of Cuba's reactionary government. Before he succumbs, he manages to convince his sweetheart that nobody dies in vain if he gives his life for a just cause.

Many Cuban elements supply the atmosphere for the story, from the voices of children playing outside the house to the toothpaste and gasoline commercials on the radio.

Hemingway was in Cuba during April and May of 1936, when several revolutionary actions received sensational coverage on the front pages of the newspapers. He based "Nobody Ever Dies" on these events.


[53]


LA GACETA
September/October 1979

HEMINGWAY and NEGATION
OF NEGATION
by Mary Cruz

Had he lived twenty more years, he would have been eighty years old on the 21st of July, 1979. But on the first day of another July (in 1961) he voluntarily introduced into his life—already irrevocably lost to all creative activity due to bad health—that which Engels called the "essential element" of all existence: death, the dialectic negation of life.

After very careful study of his work, I dare to divide it into two different stages, separated by his connection to the Gulf Stream of Mexico and his assimilation of lessons which, particularly in Cuba, added depth to his intellectual viewpoint. By this I do not mean to imply that from then on Cuba and the Gulf Stream formed the only framework for the action in his narratives . . .

He bought a yacht to be able to enjoy his favorite sport: fishing. He also went to hunt in Africa, another sport in which he could not only experience physical exertion but which also gave him time to analyze the motivation for all his actions. Fishing, to some, is a boring sport, but fishing provides plenty of time to think.

Hunting is a perfectly useless occupation: but during the safari of 1934, Hemingway intended to see whether it was possible to write about real events in the form of fiction and achieve the effect of a novel. Moreover, in the expertise of a sport that had meant work for the men of another age (and which still does for some) he wanted to study the relation of man and his occupation under simplified circumstances . . .

With unerring instinct, the people of Cuba always appreciated the worth of this American writer who, under cover of a careless attitude, observed with deep interest and affection the things of Cuba. Much to the displeasure of those who didn't know how or refused to interpret his writings correctly and thus judge the man by them, there is the bust of Hemingway donated by the fishermen of Cojímar, and there is the museum in San Francisco de Paula, with a constant stream of visitors. Hemingway has not died . . . on the 80th year after his birth . . . and twenty after his death.

[54]

A hurricane hits the straits of Florida, sinks the Spanish ship *Valbanera*, and provides literary material for Hemingway.

The passenger ship of the Pinillos, Izquierdo & Co. line had left Santiago de Cuba in the easternmost province of the island. It had arrived there from Spain, and after one stop it was enroute to the bay of Havana.

On the night of September 8, 1919, the blow suddenly hit the ship a few miles off the coast of Havana. It was unable to reach port. The storm swept it to the Florida Keys, where it sank in waters six fathoms deep.

Hemingway used this disaster as the basis for "After the Storm," a story in which Eddy Saunders tells in the first person his memories of the looting that went on, his diving among the ruins of the ship, how the corpses floated inside the cabins and how the Greek divers got in ahead of him and carried away most of the booty.

Another hurricane provided a lasting traumatic experience for Hemingway. Slow and devastating, it crossed southern Florida and left numerous victims behind, among them hundreds of veterans of the First World War who had been working for the federal government in the construction of the Overseas Highway. These were the former soldiers who were pictured as fun-loving and likeable types in *To Have and Have Not*. The catastrophe killed more than a thousand people in the Florida Keys on September 2, 1935, particularly in Upper and Lower Matecumbe Keys.

Hemingway helped in the rescue operations aboard his *Pilar*. He found only the dead. Weeks later, old infantry boots were seen scattered along the beaches. Birds of prey hovered over the keys and the stench of decomposing bodies was everywhere.

It was like a field after a lost battle. In his indignant attack published in *New Masses*, Hemingway accused the authorities of neglect, indifference and finally responsibility for the death of the men he considered his comrades in arms.


[55]


In his essay "The Last Summer," the Cuban critic Edmundo Desnoes saw a connection between Hemingway's stay in Cuba and his avowed devotion to Spain. According to Desnoes, Hemingway established residence in the former Spanish colony, Cuba, because the same language is spoken there and many aspects of the Spanish culture are preserved; it is an ideal place for an American who loves Spain.

Hemingway's early Cuban years turned out to be very useful. He learned how clandestine organizations operate. His visits to Cuba to fish for marlin, and as an intelligent observer during the thirties, provided him with material on the anti-Machado activities.

A summary of what he thinks he has learned in Cuba appears in the words of the character P.O.M. in *Green Hills of Africa*, who describes the revolution as having been "Beautiful. Then lousy." He speaks of crouching behind tables in saloons while men in cars raced through the streets shooting up the town, and like any good Hemingway character was proud of not having spilled his drink. The shooting became so common that children asked their mothers if they could go out on the streets to watch it.

In spite of the superficial view of the revolutionary process reflected in P.O.M.'s words, what is interesting is that during the time he was writing *Green Hills of Africa*, Hemingway acknowledged the revolutions that were breaking out in Turkey, Spain and the Balkan countries. But he considered them events from which the artist should remain aloof. His Spanish experience was to make him change his mind and understand once and for all that a revolution never happens without a reason.

[56]

Sometimes while working he permitted himself the luxury of going fishing in his yacht. He would return late from the high seas. His impressions as he neared the coast are recalled in one of Robert Jordan's monologues: " . . . the smell of the land breeze as one approached Cuba in the middle of the night."

The first work written by Hemingway at the Vigía was *For Whom the Bell Tolls*. What remains of those 18 months of effort are some sheets on which he wrote a few draft pages of his novel in his large, round schoolboy script. These fragments serve to reveal his working method, and how the artist slowly forms his book. They represent the 500 words he wrote every day, equivalent to a sheet and a half on a typewriter, double spaced.

This is one of the fragments of his rough draft:

41-43
. . . no treason and if all worked together for it.
"No," he said. "Rien a faire. Rien faut accepter. Comme toujours."
The hammering roar of the planes was getting deafening now. Golz watched them with his hard proud eyes.
"Nous ferons notre petit possible," Golz said into the receiver and hung up. But Kotz did not hear him. All he heard was roar of the planes.

The name Kotz, of Russian origin, was replaced in the final version by Duval, a French character, member of the International Brigades, an officer under General Golz. Duval receives the message to cancel the offensive action from Robert Jordan, because the enemy knows of their plans and has taken precautions. But Duval hesitates and cannot decide to take on such responsibility.

The only thing he does is telephone Golz, who is at the airbase watching the planes take off on a mission that is doomed to fail. It is well known that Golz is based on the real Russian-Polish general Karol Swierczewski, who was in charge of the offensive at Segovia. His name during the war was Walter.

What follows is the first draft of Pilar's long narrative (Chapter X in the novel) of the massacre in her village. The parts crossed out in the original appear here between brackets and the added parts or words are italicized.

> . . . and across the square the trees shining in the moonlight and the darkness of their shadows and *the* benches bright too in the moonlight and the scattered bottles shining and beyond the edge of the cliff where they had all been thrown and there was no sound but the splashing of the water in the fountain and I sat there and I thought we have begun badly. The window was open and [three houses] up the square from the Fonda I could hear a woman crying. I [looked] *went* out *on* the balcony standing there on my bare feet on the iron and the moon shone in the faces of all the buildings of the square and the crying was coming from the balcony of the house of Don Guillermo. It was his wife and she was on the balcony kneeling and crying. Then I went back inside the room and I sat there and I did not wish to think for that was the worst day of my life until one other day.

The following text is part of a monologue by Robert Jordan on the last night of his life. The moment in the story is indicated by Hemingway in the heading of the passage. However, in no part of the book is there a passage that corresponds exactly to this fragment in the draft, although his ideas and thoughts are scattered in the thoughts expressed by Jordan in Chapter XXXI.

Jan. 24

(Rewrite in conversation on the last night)

He was awake in the night now thinking and he thought, now that this has come to me it is a great complication. Before there was only the work. Now there is the work and this girl *that I love*. I must not think about that now nor ever worry about it, but my life is changed now. I must take good care of her. Now when I was thinking of going off to Gaylords I left her there at the Hotel where she knows no one and where there could be a shelling and she with no papers even.

I could have come back and found the police had picked her up. No, first I must get her good papers. Karkov can help me with that and I will send Petra out to buy what she needs. Petra will take good care of her. She could live with Petra perhaps while I am away. No, that's not practical but I do not want her at Gaylords with those people.

Maybe we can get an apartment. Certainly we can. I will find out all about that. Somewhere by the Park along there near where the book fair is and now in the spring we can walk in the Park with the horse chestnut trees coming into bloom. I can show her all of Madrid that's left, he thought.

Karkov's girl will help me to dress her even though she will be jealous. But she will do it. I've quite a lot of pesetas still and *more coming and* Karkov's girl has quite good clothes. I never notice what women wear except whether it looks good or not. But we can get her a suit and some good sweaters. A suit has to be made though there are fine sweaters still at Samarands on the Gran Via. She'll look lovely. In what? He thought, in whatever we buy for her. I don't know what it will be, whatever she wants. She'll need shoes too. She'll have to have underwear, stockings. Don't worry about it. She ran get all that with Petra while you're up at Gaylords. We can go to the coiffeur's together. They can cut her hair once the same way mine is so it will be neat and then it can grow out.

I wonder how long it takes for a girl's hair to grow out? She has beautiful, beautiful hair. Hers will be like sun burned corn silk. I'd like to see her wear it down to her shoulders. I wonder how long that would take? She's lovely enough looking now. I guess I couldn't stand it if she were any more beautiful. But she will be. All the time.

*The best thing is to get married too because you never know and you're going to take her to Missula too. That will be funny but it will be good too. She can throw away that razor blade once you are across the frontier.* And you must get her nightgowns and pajamas and a dressing gown and bedroom slippers and a good comb and brush and a suitcase.

Stop it, he said to himself. Just stop it, will you? You and your beautiful young wife, you and all your domestic problems. You loving someone and letting yourself really go so that you know now what that can be, in love and what Maria means to you. You and your Maria. *Well, you had a nice time didn't you. It was mighty nice in Madrid, wasn't it?* Yes. You and your Maria and the other little item you've forgotten.

You're wonderful, he told himself. You really are. What was your big problem? How long it would take her hair to grow out to glamour girl length? That was it, wasn't it? That was what was on your mind. That was all you had to worry about.

You're pretty good, he told himself. You really are, and if that is all you have to worry about I think you had better go to sleep. Your beautiful young wife is asleep already. Because pretty soon it is going to be morning and in the morning see if you can remember what your problems were last night.

Another draft preserved at Finca Vigía:

Epilogue
It was night [on the road] when Golz rode (back) in a staff car [down from the pass] on the road down from the pass to El Escorial.

Around July 14, 1940, Ernest debated whether to add an epilogue to the novel, in which General Golz and Karkov would pass judgment on the failure of the offensive of Segovia and comment on Jordan's death.

Another chapter in this final section would be the return of Andrés to the camp abandoned by Pablo's guerrillas, a kind of anticlimax. Following Max Perkins' advice, however, Ernest didn't go ahead with this plan; he left the novel at the moment in which Robert Jordan, lying face down with his heart pressed against the grass-covered earth, waits for Lieutenant Berrendo, who is framed in the sights of his gun.

The first-draft material of *For Whom the Bell Tolls* which is preserved at Finca Vigía is scant and disorganized. (Hemingway gave the final draft to Gustav Pfeiffer.) It is written by hand on ordinary paper. The writing seems to have been done slowly and tends to slant toward the right-hand margin.

[57]

There are only two families in the world, the Haves and Have-Nots.

—A woman of the people in *Don Quixote*

When Hemingway decided to join the Spanish Republican cause, he did so decisively. His main objective was that the war must be won. It was a clear break: he was no longer the Hemingway of the twenties, solitary and disillusioned, who wrote "Soldier's Home" or *A Farewell to Arms;* Hemingway was leaving behind his earlier views about the function of art and the artist as expressed in *Green Hills of Africa* and *Death in the Afternoon.*

He was also abandoning the life of ease enjoyed during his marriage to the wealthy Pauline Pfeiffer, including the big house in Key West and his role of The Consummate Writer. He told his brother Leicester that before his Spanish experience he had never worried "about the meaning of life, as long as he was able to create and produce."

If on one occasion John Dos Passos had been the object of Hemingway criticism because of his leftist views, the Spanish Civil War was to change that situation radically: Hemingway was to occupy the role abandoned by Dos Passos.

The execution of a professor from Valencia, José Robles, accused of passing information to the Franco rebels, served as the reason Dos Passos gave for deserting the Spanish loyalist cause. Hemingway was angered that "Dos" was so concerned over the life of one man that he put aside the genuine interest of the Spanish people.

At last, Hemingway had something like an ideology and a flag to defend. Although the idea was not clear and was colored by individualistic sentiments, the flag represented a cause: Spanish Republicanism.

Hemingway was to change his way of thinking during the course of the war; he was to have his doubts and contradictions; but always, even during the most difficult moments, he held firm to his position and to his new political consciousness. Robert Jordan, the protagonist of *For Whom the Bell Tolls* and the most faithful exponent of Hemingway's ideological strategy, says: "If we win here, we will win everywhere."

In the autumn of 1937, Ernest Miller Hemingway, war correspondent, accredited by the North American Newspaper Alliance, was stationed in the eastern sector of Madrid with his NANA credentials, American passport, Magnum .357 gun (not declared at customs), explorer's knife, a pocket full of onions and flask full of cognac.

He was so proud of his magnificent knife that he showed it to everybody; it was of Solingen steel, with a mother-of-pearl handle. It opened up like the legs of a spider and held a pair of scissors, a corkscrew, a can opener and three types of blades. Many illustrious personages slaked their thirst from the canteen hanging from his belt: people like Joris Ivens, Ilya Ehrenburg, André Malraux and Robert Capa.

Ernest carried the raw onions in a pocket of his suede jacket. His way of assuaging hunger was to take a long drink of cognac and a bite of raw onion. He usually carried other personal items in the pockets of his jacket: his passport, credentials, money, a notebook, a fountain pen and a couple of number-two pencils.

Of these things, the only one still at Finca Vigía is his passport, a dramatic document by means of which one can follow not only his route through Spain but also the ups and downs of the Spanish Republic. The passport is covered in red cloth and frayed at the edges. The many French and Spanish customs stamps on it reveal Hemingway's comings and goings.

One of the characteristics of the passport is that as one turns the pages, the quality of the visa stamps deteriorates. If the early ones were elaborate, some showing flying flags, coats of arms of the country, or some proud inscription of the Republic, the later authorizations are hurriedly written in pencil, and lack the official aura.

The Republican fighters soon learned to recognize Hemingway by his height, bulk and the way he dressed. He used to visit the different units wearing his suede jacket, great hunting boots, a Basque beret on his head and his metal-framed glasses. A lucky man who walked calmly through many bombings, he rarely neglected to share his flask with the combatants.

He was brave, a man of experience in war. He was familiar with the whizzing of projectiles made by Krupp. He knew when to protect himself by jumping head first into a trench. Years before, he had been wounded by fragments from an Austrian shell. Together with his canteen, two medals for valor and a pair of pants stained with blood, his souvenirs from the war of 1914 included a few hundred shrapnel fragments, some of which were left in his legs by the doctors. Another souvenir was an artificial kneecap, which he wore when he arrived in Madrid.

The famous war correspondent who was paid $500 per cable and $1,000 per article was now pursuing a new objective that was superior to the hunts in Africa, trout fishing and bird shooting in Michigan, big-game fishing in the Gulf Stream, or his passion for the bulls. He was now part of an optimistic, cultured, brave group that included Ehrenburg, Malraux, the legendary Hungarian photographer Robert Capa; the Germans Gustav Regler, Hans Khale, Werner Heilbrun and Ludwig Renn; the Soviets Roman Karmen and Misha Koltzov; the generals Petrov, Walter and Lucasz; Cuban writers like Carpentier, Guillén, Marinello; other Latin Americans, like the Chilean Neruda; the Spaniards Alberti and María Teresa León; and Hemingway's countrymen, Langston Hughes and Paul Robeson.

The war strengthened old friendships and brought him new ones, friends who would later visit him in Finca Vigía in the long period following the war. He helped them as much as he possibly could. He gave Werner's widow the publication rights to the film *The Spanish Earth*. He was part of the effort to get Gustav Regler out of a French concentration camp after the war. Regler's novel based on the Spanish Civil War, *The Great Crusade*, was published with a prologue by Hemingway.

It is probable that at times Hemingway's stay in embattled Spain had the appearance of an adventure. He had enlisted people like the bullfighter Sidney Franklin and the poet Evan Shipman in his activities, along with his old Spanish friends, but the background of dissipation and fun in *The Sun Also Rises* had turned into one of destruction and death.

His first trip to Spain during the war started on February 27, 1937, when he sailed to France on the *Paris*. From Toulouse he flew to Barcelona and from there to the east coast to Valencia and Alicante, where the Loyalists were happy over the victory in Brihuega. He visited the battlefield where the unburied bodies of Italian soldiers had been shattered by the artillery and the rocks.

This was the period in which he collaborated in the production of the film *The Spanish Earth* with the Dutch communist filmmaker Joris Ivens and the cameraman John Ferno. Previously he had participated with a young Spanish writer named Prudencio de Pereda in the preparation of the documentary *Spain in Flames*.

Ernest was a member of the organization called Contemporary Historians, which originally included John Dos Passos, Lillian Hellman and Archibald MacLeish. Its objective was to promote the cause of the Spanish people and collect money for the Republic. In 1937, MacLeish asked Hellman to work with Ivens and Hemingway in the making of a documentary about the war. He wanted the benefit of her experience as a playwright in the writing of the script. But an attack of pneumonia prevented Hellman from leaving Paris, and she couldn't work on the film.

Towards the end of the sixties, she saw *The Spanish Earth* again and said that she still liked it. She thought that Ernest and Joris did an excellent job. "Hemingway was much better qualified than I to make the film," she said.

The making of *The Spanish Earth* and his work as a correspondent took Hemingway to the front, where he saw how the fighting really was in that war. He always returned to Madrid, turning his room at the Hotel Florida into a sanctuary for himself and his friends. There he got together with his "gang," worked and had fun.

Arthur H. Landis, in his *The Abraham Lincoln Brigade*, describes the service at the Florida this way: "The flatware at the Hotel Florida—headquarters for Hemingway, Herbert Matthews and Martha Gellhorn—was still polished with great care. The linen was magnificent, but the menu, although served with real elegance, was invariably the same: a slice of bread, chick peas cooked in olive oil and onions, and sometimes lentils or beans.

"That's all there was. Dessert, if any, consisted of a solitary orange. Liquor was no longer served at the marble-top tables of the outdoor cafés, nor in the cabarets, but we know that somehow, mysteriously, Hemingway was able to get the generous supply he served his guests."

Hemingway paid a low rent for his room, because it was in the direct line of fire of the Fascists' batteries in the Sierra Garabitas. He enjoyed showing his guests the still warm and unexploded projectiles he picked up near there.

His comrades, Ivens and the photographer John Ferno, didn't take a back seat when it came to taking risks. Ernest wrote MacLeish claiming that they would probably lose their good friends. Besides being a cinematographer, Ivens served every day as "an officer in the regular infantry."

The biggest risks and dangers they faced came while they were filming the tank and infantry attack in Moratas de Tajuña, and during the bombing of Madrid. Together they withstood a number of machine-gun attacks and escaped from collapsing buildings. They also had their diversions, hunting for bars in the midst of war, looking for one of Hemingway's "clean and well-lighted places." In the middle of all this commotion, Hemingway was busy writing the script for *The Spanish Earth*.

Recalling that spring in 1940, Ernest said: "That period of struggle, when we thought the Republic would win, was the happiest of our lives."

*The Spanish Earth* was shown to the Roosevelt family at the White House on July 8, 1937, thanks to the good graces of Martha Gellhorn, who knew the president and Eleanor. The first public showing took place in August of the same year in New York. The film provoked one of the many fights Hemingway had with intellectuals throughout his life. Orson Welles and Hemingway sat side by side during a private screening of the film. Welles was to have narrated the film, but for some reason he never did. At the end of the screening, Welles turned to Hemingway and told him that the film was "shit." Hemingway reacted with quick anger and the two men came to blows.

Hemingway had returned to the United States in May of 1937. On June 4th, he delivered the first formal speech of his life at the second Congress of American Writers, which took place at Carnegie Hall in New York. He told about his experiences in Spain and spoke of "the mission of the writer in our time."

Sitting beside him on the dais were Donald Ogden Stewart, president of the League of American Writers; Earl Browder, secretary of the Communist Party of the United States; and Joris Ivens. Archibald MacLeish was the master of ceremonies.

Hemingway's seven-minute speech received an ovation from the 3,500 spectators in the house and the throngs outside its doors. This was a high point in his political evolution: not only did he conquer his shyness about public speaking, but he expressed the belief that writers should take an active part in the defense of freedom and democracy.

In the midst of this turmoil—his trips to and from the fronts of Spain and back to the United States—Hemingway was involved in writing *To Have and Have Not*. From New York he went to Key West, and from there to Bimini, where he proofread the galleys. He considered the book in many ways "the most important work he had ever written," according to his brother Leicester. He had already finished the novel at the time of his first wartime trip to Spain, and the text was much longer than the one finally published. But when Hemingway returned from Spain an ardent defender of the Republic, he tore up part of the manuscript and changed the ending. Then he wrote Harry Morgan's final words, which became a kind of Hemingway manifesto: "One man alone ain't got . . . No matter how, a man alone ain't got no bloody fucking chance."

The book reached the marketplace in 1937. American critics seemed baffled by this new work. They said that Hemingway had destroyed his style in an attempt to enter the field of social significance. They also said that the title was a parody of Shakespeare's most famous monologue, although Cervantes, hundreds of years before Hemingway, had already expressed the simple economic equation.

During this time of his life Hemingway wasn't worrying about the small world of the writer's community. But he did exchange some blows with critic Max Eastman, as repayment of an old literary debt.

In his new role as political agitator, Hemingway, accompanied by Ivens, went to Hollywood and took part in the campaign to collect funds for the Spanish Republic. This campaign was carried out under the auspices of Fredric and Florence March. Ivens traveled with the reels of *The Spanish Earth* under his arm and Hemingway with the 15 pages of his second speech.

Lillian Hellman remembers those collections made in the United States. Once at the home of the Marches, $13,000 was raised to buy ambulances. The actor Errol Flynn disappeared at the very moment the collection started, saying that he was going to the bathroom. Nobody saw him again that night. According to Arthur H. Landis, Flynn had gone to Spain as a Republican sympathizer on "a kind of tour for tourists," and had been hit by a stray bullet. The tour had included a visit to the front, which could be dangerous. The news item about this appeared in *The New York Times* in May 1937.

Hemingway tried to convince his rich friends to finance shipments of bandages and other first-aid material to the Spanish Republic, but many of them refused, saying that would be tantamount to collaborating with the communists.

As president of the Commission for Ambulances of the American Association "Friends of Spanish Democracy," Ernest raised enough money in 1937 to buy ambulances and medical equipment for Spain. He contributed a considerable part of the funds himself. He was able to pay for 12 fully equipped ambulances, but they were blocked in the port of New York by order of the American Neutrality Act, which prohibited the shipment of any kind of merchandise to Spain.

[58]

Hemingway limited his activities in Spain to the 12th Brigade, his favorite international brigade. This is acknowledged by almost all the authors of books about the writer, including Carlos Baker.

Hemingway visited other units, and naturally spent some

time in the posts occupied by Americans in the "Abraham Lincoln" Brigade. He spent most of his time with the people under Paul Lucasz, which was the *nom de guerre* for Maté Zalka, a novelist and one of Stalin's envoys to the Spanish Civil War. Baker states in his book *Ernest Hemingway: A Life Story* that the 12th Brigade "most engaged his affections, chiefly for the people and their *esprit de corps.*"

That group included the physician José Luis Herrera Sotolongo, who years later was to become Hemingway's close friend and doctor in Cuba. Sotolongo recalls his first meeting with Hemingway and the writer's first contact with the 12th Brigade:

"It happened this way: after operations at the front in Madrid in 1937, we gathered in an area west of Madrid with the purpose of recouping, because we had many losses. Since November 26 we had been in a series of battles, including the Casa de Campo, the Pardo, Las Rozas and Villanueva del Pardillo. The 12th International Brigade carried the brunt of this combat.

"In the last few days of December we successfully carried out an offensive in Brihuega. We left the troops of the fourth corps there and returned to Madrid. But in the last combats we saw in Madrid and Las Rozas, we again suffered many losses.

"The brigade was left in deplorable condition; there were great losses of personnel and equipment. We got reinforcements in a town called Moratas de Tajuña, east of Madrid. We had one of our batallions there; the other one was in Perales. In other words, we dispersed, because a brigade should avoid concentration in one place when it stops to rest.

"One afternoon during our stay there, the Chief Health Officer of the brigade, the German Werner Heilbrun, came to me and said: 'You are the best-dressed officer here. Go to Madrid and pick up an American journalist who wants to visit for a few days to write a story about us. My wife Matilde will be waiting at the Hotel Florida in Madrid.'

"Sure enough, when I got there, Werner's wife was waiting for me with a young American woman who turned out to be Martha Gellhorn, the journalist who later married Hemingway. We got in the car and drove to our lodgings in the hospital of the 12th Brigade. That hospital was a kind of hotel for tourists.

"At that time Ernest was in love with Martha. He had gone

to the southern front of Madrid in the Getafa zone. When he returned to the Florida Hotel and didn't find her, he asked where she had gone. He was told that she was with the 12th Brigade. He joined us the next day.

"Martha stayed there a few days and Hemingway was her constant companion. He seemed to like the brigade very much, and from then on made it his meeting place. Most of the time he lived with us, where he went off to do his work as a reporter. He was our guest for a very long time.

"His first visit to us was at the beginning of 1937, when we were stationed in Moratas de Tajuña. After that he was with us the whole time the Jarama offensive lasted, almost a month. Then he was away for a while on other fronts, and we carried on the Guadalajara operation against the Italians. When Hemingway realized it was a big offensive he tried to reach us. We were dismantling the hospital in a palace, but when he arrived we had already left. He took some pictures of the palace, which can be seen today at the Finca Vigía.

"He joined us when we went to Moraleja to rest. All we did there was relax. We even played football. After that he went away again. We went back to Aragón for the attack on Huesca, and that was when General Lucasz was killed. When we returned to Madrid we established contact with Hemingway again, who came back to live with us. After that we were separated again, almost permanently, because the 12th Brigade had become a division and we were sent to the front.

"Our paths crossed again during the offensive and the taking of Teruel. Hemingway always appeared during the most important operations, and we were together again for a few days. After that he was assigned to other fronts and we lost contact. I didn't see him again until I came to Cuba."

Herrera laughs, recalling *"las cosas de Ernesto."* There was an officer from a Slavic country named Makakos. Hemingway used this name often to form a variant of his favorite blasphemy: "Makako en Dios!" It sounded like the terrible *"Me cago en Dios!"* (I shit on God). In the front line, people would joke about anything, to ease the tension for a brief time. Makakos was one of the officers of the Dombrowski Brigade who was lost in action at Puente de Arganda.

Herrera tells another anecdote, one in which Ernesto was the butt of the joke. It happened during the 12th Brigade's rest period after the Battle of Guadalajara. The Heads of Staff and some of the officers were relaxing at La Moraleja, in the palace of the Duchess widow of Aldama in the outskirts of Madrid. The place had acquired a grim reputation, because many Fascists had been executed there. But, afterwards, official receptions were held there, partly because its silverware and furniture were in good condition. The offensive of Guadalajara over, some officers had been promoted, among them Herrera Sotolongo, who was made a captain.

"One night there was a big reception at the palace, and Paul Robeson, the singer, made an appearance. Ernest drank too much and fell asleep during the festivities. Someone thought of a good joke to play on him: He was carried to the field infirmary and tied to a stretcher. Everyone put on white gowns and masks.

"When Ernest awoke and found himself in bondage, he started screaming with all the voice he could muster. 'I thought I was in the hands of the Fascists and that they were preparing to torture me,' he later said. He screamed, *Me cago en Dios!'* and, 'Sons of bitches, kill me!' In perfect Spanish, of course."

On one occasion they "executed" a record: Ravel's "Bolero." It was one of the records in the Duchess of Aldama's collection, one of the few they liked, but they had played it so often that they decided to condemn it to death before they left.

They threw stones at it to see who could score a bull's eye in the spindle hole. Nobody did, although it was conceded that Hemingway came the closest to the center. But Hemingway played it down, saying he had had a lot of practice shooting pigeons.

Someone suggested that the record's sentence should be commuted, because it survived the execution. Everyone agreed, and Ravel's "Bolero" returned to the Duchess's collection.

# Hemingway in Moscow

[59]

At Finca Vigía, besides the red passport he used during the war, there are 200 postcard-size photographs taken during the filming of *The Spanish Earth*. There is also a collection of photos taken by Robert Capa. Others are of Lucasz, his staff, and Hemingway with Ludwig Renn, all faces and people who have disappeared. On a certain occasion Herrera Sotolongo was looking at these photos when he stopped at one that shows a very short individual standing next to Hemingway. Herrera said, "This was Aliosha, aide to Lucasz."

Forty years after that picture was taken, December 15, 1976, on a day when the temperature was 23 below zero, a small but sturdy and energetic man of 71 years opened the door of his Moscow apartment to me, thanks to an appointment arranged by a third party, a friend named Yuri Greding. The man was Alexis Eisner.

Two things contributed to a pleasant interview with Eisner: the letter and greeting he received from his old comrade Herrera Sotolongo, and the picture I showed him in which he appears with Hemingway, a copy of the one kept at Finca Vigía.

"Of Hemingway's books I had read only *The Sun Also Rises*," said Eisner. "I realized that he was a man of genius, but only literary genius. When Mikhail Koltzov of the 12th Brigade, or maybe it was Herrera Sotolongo, I don't remember exactly who, took Hemingway to meet the high command of the 12th Brigade early in January or February 1937, I was an aide to Lucasz.

"Lucasz went wild with excitement when Hemingway was introduced, for he had read *A Farewell to Arms*. Hemingway consequently held a special place as a visitor within the brigade. But to me he was only one of the comrades.

"He looked like an older sportsman. He had a round face and small eyes. He wore glasses. Although he was dressed in good American clothes, he never looked neat. It was the 'thing' there at the time to get your raincoats good and dirty. All his clothes seemed old and soiled. He always carried a flask full of whiskey in his breast pocket. He drank a lot, but I liked him for it.

"The High Command of our brigade was very hospitable. They fed everyone who came to visit, and even gave Hemingway gas for his car. Lucasz spoke Hungarian, Russian and German. Hemingway spoke English, French, Italian and Spanish. I translated French into Russian. Lucasz was annoyed because he had read only *A Farewell to Arms.*"

Alexis was amazed that "Hemingway was not like other writers." He never talked about literature or art and was uncomfortable when they talked to him about literature.

"That big guy would blush when someone told him he had read his books. He'd get angry, because he thought that was not a proper subject to bring up at the front. This was a strange reaction, because in his heart he knew that his was a serious profession."

When Alexis got to know him better, he realized that Hemingway knew what war was about and behaved among them as just one more soldier.

Alexis claims that Hemingway never had official permission to go to the front. But his collaboration with Ivens and Ferno on *The Spanish Earth* allowed him to go to the trenches. He carried their cameras and gave them a helping hand whenever necessary. He could go anywhere they went. "He never wrote about that," Alexis says.

"He felt good in the company of our High Command. I can understand his friendship with Regler and Heilbrun, and his interest in Lucasz: he was intrigued by the writer who is also a man of action.

"But Lucasz never became a good writer—life did not permit it. He wrote in Hungarian, a language he was forgetting. He translated what he wrote into bad Russian.

"Hemingway found Lucasz an interesting person, and everyone in the High Command loved Hemingway except Randolfo Pacciardi, who was an Italian captain and a patriotic Republican. Pacciardi never forgave Hemingway for what he wrote about Caporetto.

"After the Christmas of 1936-37, we organized a banquet

to celebrate the first victory of the Republican army. We had occupied three villages on the Franco side: Almadrones, Alcora, and Mirabuena. The hero of that encounter was Pacciardi, who captured the house of the commander of Franco's battalion, along with his wife and horse. The wife was a young woman, and Pacciardi, being a gentleman, decided to take her to Madrid in his car. But on the way a howitzer crashed into the car and only Pacciardi survived.

"Hemingway went to the banquet with Martha Gellhorn. When Pacciardi saw Martha he told Albino Marbin, another Italian fighter, 'Sit next to the American and hold his attention.' Pacciardi was very handsome. He courted Martha and she wanted to leave. Ernest insisted that they stay.

"Pacciardi then offered to take Martha home in his car. He drove her all the way to Madrid, some 50 kilometers. He returned two hours later. Hemingway was still drunk. Pacciardi confessed to me later: 'I got nowhere with her.' Of course, in *Across the River and into the Trees*, Hemingway poked some fun at Pacciardi. He hadn't forgotten Martha's 'Caporetto.' And maybe he suspected that the Italian had actually 'gotten somewhere' with Martha the night of the banquet."

Alexis now asks himself: "Did all women leave him like they did Pushkin? Who knows!"

"The last time Hemingway and I saw each other," says Alexis, "we had already buried Lucasz. I was on a ten-day vacation, walking on a street in Valencia. Hemingway was coming in the opposite direction. We embraced—Spaniards don't kiss.

" 'Lucasz' death was a great loss,' he said. Then he described Lucasz as a hero, and said something I have never forgotten: 'Death is badly organized in war.'

" 'How are things with you?' I asked. 'What are you doing?'

" 'I'm going back to America, and I don't know if I'll come back to Spain,' Hemingway answered.

"But he did come back. It is very sad when two soldiers say goodbye," says Alexis Eisner. "He had his hands in his pockets and kept tapping his foot.

" 'Come see us,' he said. 'I'm married to a millionairess. I have a home in Florida.'

"Then he took his checkbook out of his pocket. It was from

the French Bank of Paris. He wrote the date and signed the check, but he didn't fill in the amount, leaving that up to me. On the back of the check he put his Florida address. Then he put the checkbook back in his pocket.

"We embraced again and he said, '*Adios, amigo. Buena suerte.*' It was very sad."

It was Eisner's last meeting with the writer, and it would have been better if they hadn't met. Hemingway had given him the blank check in case Alexis should need money; it meant that they knew they were on the side that lost the war. Hemingway also invited him to go to New York or Key West (luckily Beria's police didn't know about this). Alexis returned to the Soviet Union in January of 1940 a few months after the start of World War II. In April, his home was searched and they found the blank check signed by Hemingway: *a blank check signed by an alien*.

Sentenced to 25 years in Siberia, Alexis was released in 1956. When he returned to Moscow, he was older but not elderly. He found a lovely young woman with the Spanish name Ines, 26 years younger than he. They were married, and at age 57 he had a son, Dimitri. Later he started to write. A book of his Spanish war memoirs was published in Moscow in 1968.

The deaths of Lucasz and Werner Heilbrun in the offensive of Huesca in 1937 closed a chapter of Hemingway's activities in Spain. Lucasz died on a road near Aragón on June 11, 1937. The road had been camouflaged to cover the military movements, but the Fascists released their bombs at intervals and by sheer chance hit the car in which Lucasz was riding, a 1936 Ford.

Lucasz was buried in Valencia three days after his death. Herrera Sotolongo signed the death certificate and embalmed the body. The funeral was held in Valencia. A telegram of condolence from Joseph Stalin was the high note of pomp at the funeral, and proof of the esteem in which he was held.

The road on which Lucasz died was "cursed." Only a few days before, Werner Heilbrun's driver had met the same fate under similar circumstances, attacked by an airplane. Ernest was spellbound when Alexis told him the curious story. A heavy caliber bullet from a German plane cut the driver's throat and almost severed his head; death was instantaneous. Perhaps it was only a reflex action, but somehow the driver was able to reduce speed, throw in the clutch and stop the car.

The Spanish Civil War provided Hemingway with a prolonged and intense relationship with Soviet military personnel and journalists, and European communists. He was a friend of Líster, Lucasz, Swierczewski and especially the enigmatic Mikhail Koltsov.

Hemingway described Karkov (Koltsov) in *For Whom the Bell Tolls* as the third most important man sent to Spain by Stalin. Hemingway gives him such importance in the book that one of the last thoughts of Robert Jordan, his protagonist and alter ego, is dedicated to Karkov. Jordan would have liked him to see the way he was facing death. He frankly admits that Karkov had been his teacher.

In all the great political moments of *For Whom the Bell Tolls*, there is the presence of Mikhail Koltsov and the influence he had on Hemingway. He appears every time Robert Jordan faces a moment of doubt or when his conscience must make some moral judgment. Despite his falterings and misgivings, Jordan's conclusions are always positive. That is part of the education he received from that hard but capable professional.

The theme of loss of innocence comes up again in *For Whom the Bell Tolls*, just as in the series of Hemingway's Nick Adams stories, only now the subject is an adult and the lessons he learns are political. At times these lessons are difficult to accept, like the episode in which Karkov convinces Robert Jordan of the need, when occasion arises, of sacrificing his own wounded compatriots to prevent their falling into the hands of the enemy, who would use them to justify greater intervention on the part of the Fascist powers. In the end, Jordan has to kill one of his comrades.

The education and the transmission of the experience became a cardinal point in the novel, but it is natural that this was the objective of a writer who was also a moralist. Hemingway's novel gives a clear picture of the results of such an apprenticeship.

At Finca Vigía after the war, Koltsov was an ever-present ghost. He was often mentioned in conversations with Herrera Sotolongo and veterans of the war who visited Hemingway. When Herbert Matthews, *The New York Times* correspondent, went to Cuba to interview Fidel Castro, then leader of the rebels at Sierra Maestra, he spent a few nights with Ernest at Finca Vigía. They had dinner together, and Matthews told Hemingway what he had seen on his return. These two great journalists of the century recalled their old friend Koltzov, and drank a toast to him.


[60]


Alexis Eisner draws a sketch of the positions the 12th Brigade occupied on the outskirts of Madrid. The precision of his memory is admirable. He takes obvious pleasure in writing the Spanish words, almost all correctly spelled, adapting the Cyrillic alphabet to the Latin.

He draws Madrid first. On the outskirts, Ciudad Universitaria; beyond it the School of Medicine Hospital; and then the bridge called Puente de los Franceses. On the other side, opposite Madrid, he places Fuencarral. Between Madrid and Ciudad Universitaria he puts Durruti's Command Post, and a little farther back, the Lucasz staff headquarters, although he says the latter was later moved to another place.

He tries to locate the place where the photo in which he appears with Hemingway was taken, and says: "That was in Fuentes del Carril or in Fuencarral, a place near the road to Guadalajara. Across there is the Palacio de Don Luis; farther on, the road leads in the opposite direction to Brihuega, and then to Zaragoza, and then to France."

On one occasion in Cuba, Hemingway tried to define the meaning of friendship for the skipper of his boat, Gregorio, and he used as simile a chain of interwoven events: "Two friends are like two joined histories." This applies to Alexis Eisner, far away in Moscow, still alive and feeling the warmth of a friendship born in a few days at a combat front in Spain, a land to which neither of them belonged.

"Like Hemingway, I made many friends there: Heilbrun, Lucasz, Herrera . . . "As to the blank check Hemingway gave him: "Although I needed the money, I never used the check. I brought it with me to Moscow, and Beria's police used it as proof that I was receiving money from a capitalist."

One July day in Moscow, 1961, Ivan Kashkeen, the Soviet critic, called Alexis Eisner to tell him: "The radio has announced that Hemingway is dead. Seems it's a suicide." Eisner answered: "What terrible news! If it is suicide, it will not be disclosed here." But he was wrong. At least two Soviet writers wrote about the American's suicide: Leonid Leonov, probably the most widely read and admired foreign correspondent in the Soviet Union, in *Pravda*, July 4, and Genrik Brovik, on the same day in the *Literaturnaia Gazieta*.

Upon my return to Havana, I brought back a note Eisner had signed, which greatly pleased Herrera Sotolongo.

Dear Herrera:
    When I first talked to Fuentes, I couldn't remember who you were, but now I remember perfectly. I am glad to know that everything is well with you. I am also glad to know that you and Hemingway became good friends and for this I envy you.
    Forty years have gone by since the time we were friends and comrades, but that is not over and will never be. I embrace you with all my heart, and I wish you much health and happiness.
    Salud!

Old Aliosha,
11th of December 1976, Moscow

# Hemingway in Combat

## [61]

In *The Spanish Civil War*, Hugh Thomas says that Hemingway actively participated on the Republican side, "going beyond his duties as a mere correspondent" and training young Spaniards in the use of guns. Furthermore, according to Herrera Sotolongo, Hemingway took part in armed combat in Spain. He saw action with English Vickers tripod machine guns as well as with Maxims and Soviet guns. "He liked to get in the trenches and fight. He did so in Guadalajara and Jarama. He took great satisfaction in that kind of contribution to the war effort." He acted like a combatant; his old comrades remember it well.

"Not only that," says Herrera Sotolongo, "but he even thought of himself as a tactician, and sometimes even a strategist. He discussed the operations and got involved in matters that were the concern of the officers."

Such interest is evident in his dispatches distributed by NANA and in the article about "the ill-named battle of Guadalajara," in which he states: "I have been studying the battle for four days, going over the places in which it took place with the officers who led it. I can clearly confirm that Brihuega will occupy a place in military history among the most decisive battles of the world." The article appeared in June 1937. Hugh Thomas refers to it in his book.

There is evidence that Hemingway was not bothered by the carnage he witnessed. He had no trouble training the young members of the militia, or in knocking off some Fascist heads with his own machine-gun fire. When a group of Fascist suspects was gunned down point blank towards the end of the war, Hemingway didn't hesitate in joining in, as monstrous as this may appear. Later he would make fun of this action of the Civil War.

The shooting, which illustrates Hemingway's moral complicity, took place in a garbage dump near Tielmes. Today most people admit it is a dirty page of the Spanish Civil War, but we must take into account the circumstances in which it occurred. Bitter political hatreds were unleashed, at a time the Republic was in grave danger, when the Loyalists had suffered such atrocities that only the Nazis would surpass. The story involves the execution of an undetermined number of prisoners from the Cárcel Modelo de Madrid (Model Prison of Madrid), composed of upper-class young men *suspected of being Fascists*, who were arrested at random in the streets of Madrid.

Franco's troops were approaching the city. Commander Carlos Contrera, an Italian whose real name is Vittorio Vivaldi, directed the operation. Of him it was said: "With Carlos Contrera in command, the militia has no fear."

In a letter to Joris Ivens, Hemingway makes light-hearted reference to the dump in which Vivaldi carried out the regrettable action. He also used to parody the name of a Cuban town, San José de las Lajas, calling it San José de las *Latas* (San José of the

Tin Cans), a bit of gallows humor referring to the site of the execution.

Hemingway told friends that he knifed several German soldiers to death during World War II. As far as his friends could tell, he never gave a thought as to whether these soldiers were the sons of poor German families. No war is won with such considerations, although cruelty should never be glorified. Besides, Hemingway's thesis was that, above any other considerations, the Spanish War *had* to be won. Anything else said about it was a lie. His humanitarianism was linked to the cause he was defending, the cause of the Spanish people.

It is impossible to break away from the sentiments that inspired "Old Man at the Bridge"—the story of a poor refugee facing Fascist barbarism—to embrace a boundless humanitarianism in which dead Italian Fascist soldiers would be as deserving of sympathy as the poor refugee.

In this light one must consider the killing of the Spanish Fascists in *For Whom the Bell Tolls*. It is not an attack on the Republic. It is merely a picture of what all-out war was like, the prelude to a greater struggle in which the fate of the world would be decided.

The attitude of Hemingway the novelist was not the same as that of Hemingway the militant. His partisanship remained in his articles and in his own personal contribution to the fight. He made it quite clear that in *For Whom the Bell Tolls* he exercised his freedom as a writer to express his own ideas about what he had experienced and observed. Hemingway didn't soften the blows when he turned to fiction.

As a result of his experiences after the end of the hostilities, in *For Whom the Bell Tolls* Hemingway attacked some high officers of the Spanish War, in particular the *habitués* of Gaylord's. Of these, Marty and Líster carry the heaviest burden of his criticisms. André Marty is his principal target. Hemingway, although writing a novel, uses Marty's real name and mentions real charges. There are many contradictory opinions recorded about the Frenchman. Ilya Ehrenburg, for example, described him as an authoritarian individual who "suspected everybody in the world of being a traitor."

This old member of the Comintern, secretary of the French Communist Party and founder and highest political chief of the International Brigades, acted with extreme military rigidity and "had people shot for any minor offense." Even within the left he was called "the Butcher of Albacete" because of his objectionable behavior.

Hemingway's acid characterization of Marty provoked some unfavorable reactions, but the writer was determined to present the Spanish tragedy with total freedom and honesty. To write without holding back anything was the only way to do it. During the war and to its end, he was the loyal trustworthy soldier. As an artist, he felt loyalty only to his truth.

Hemingway's reflections on the war do not justify the opinion expressed by Stephen Spender when he wrote in *The God That Failed*. "All the good books about the war—the ones by Malraux, Hemingway, Koestler and Orwell—describe the Spanish tragedy from the liberal point of view and they attack the Communists."

These are not the sentiments expressed by Hemingway in his novel. Robert Jordan, although he has no clearly-defined political views, may be considered a person with leftist ideas who considers it his duty to fight for the Republic. He accepts communist discipline and places himself under it for the duration of the war because it was the best and sanest for the prosecution of the struggle "*here in Spain.*"

[62]

Hemingway's correspondence about the Spanish Civil War would be incomplete without the following letter, until recently little known in the West (although published in the USSR), dated Key West, March 23, 1939. Hemingway wrote it to Ivan Kashkeen (in *For Whom the Bell Tolls* Jordan's friend, Kashkin, is clearly an homage paid to the real life Kashkeen):

 . . . We know war is bad. Yet sometimes it is necessary to fight. But still war is bad and any man who says it is not is a liar. But it is very complicated and difficult to write about truly. . . . It is just that now I understand the whole thing better. The only thing about a war, once it has started, is to win it—and that is what we did not do. The hell with war for a while, I want to write.

That piece you translated about the American dead was very hard for me to write because I had to find something I could honestly say about the dead. There is not much to say about the dead except that they are dead. I would like to be able to write understandingly about both deserters and heroes, cowards and brave men, traitors and men who are not capable of being traitors. We learned a lot about all such people.

Well it is all over but the people like these [who] did nothing about defending the Spanish Republic now feel a great need to attack us who tried to do something in order to make us look foolish and justify themselves in their selfishness and cowardice. And we having fought as well as possible, and without selfishness, and lost they now say how stupid it was ever to have fought at all.

In Spain it was very funny because the Spaniards where they did not know you always thought we were Russians. When Teruel was taken I had been with the attacking troops all day and went into the town the first night with a company of dynamiters.

When the civilians came out of their houses they asked me what they should do and I told them to stay in the houses and not go into the street that night under any circumstances and explained to them what good people we reds were and it was very funny. They all thought I was a Russian and when I told them I was a North American they didn't believe a word of it.

During the retreat it was the same. The Catalans all moving steadily away from the war at all times, but always very pleased to see us, the Russians, moving through the traffic in the wrong direction—that is toward the front.

Another Soviet personality to receive a letter from Hemingway was Konstantin Simonov, author of such important novels about the Second World War as *Days and Nights* and *Nobody Is Born a Soldier*.

When the letter was published (in *Soviet Literature*, and included by Carlos Baker in *Ernest Hemingway; Selected Letters 1917–1961*), Simonov said: "It was . . . in the spring and summer of 1946. . . . Ilya Ehrenburg and I were invited by Hemingway to visit him in Cuba. . . . To our great regret, we couldn't go. When told this, Hemingway wrote me a long letter while I was still in New York." Here is the letter:

Dear Simonov:

. . . your book came last night. I am reading it today and will write you to Moscow when I finish it. . . .

I should have read it when it was first translated but I was just back from the war and I could not read anything about it. No matter how good. Am sure you know what I mean. After the first war I was in I could not write about it for almost nine years. After the Spanish war I had to write immediately because I knew the next war was coming so fast and I felt there was no time.

After this war I had my head very badly smashed up (three times) and bad headaches. But finally I have gotten writing again all right but my novel, after 800 mss. pages is still a long way from the war. But if I live O.K. it will get there. Hope it can be very good.

All through this war I wanted to be with the army of the U.S.S.R. and see that wonderful fight but I did not feel justified to try to be a war correspondent there since A - I did not speak Russian and B - because I thought I could be more useful in trying to destroy the Krauts (what we call the Germans) in other work. I was at sea for about two years in a difficult job. Then went to England and flew with R.A.F. as a correspondent before the Normandy invasion, and then spent the rest of the time with the 4th infantry Division.

The time with the R.A.F. was wonderful but useless. With the 4th Infantry Division and with the 22nd regiment of Infantry I tried to be useful through knowing French and the country and being able to work ahead with the Maquis. This was a good life and you would have enjoyed it.

I remember how after we had come into Paris ahead of the army, and the Army had caught up with us, André Malraux came to see me and asked me how many men I had commanded. I told him never more than 200 at the most and usually between 14 and 60. He was very happy and relieved because he had commanded 2,000 men, he said. So there was no question of literary prestige involved.

That summer from Normandy into Germany was the happiest I ever had in spite of it being war. Later in Germany, in

Oldest photo of Hemingway in the Finca Vigía archives. It is a postcard and was shot in Pamplona in the early 1920's. On the left is Harold Loeb, who served as the model for Robert Cohn in *The Sun Also Rises;* on Hemingway's left is Guy Hickock, Paris correspondent for the *Brooklyn Daily Eagle.*

In March 1928 Hemingway had "the most peculiar of all accidents," when the glass roof of his apartment's bathroom fell on his head. This photo was taken when the wound was still recent.

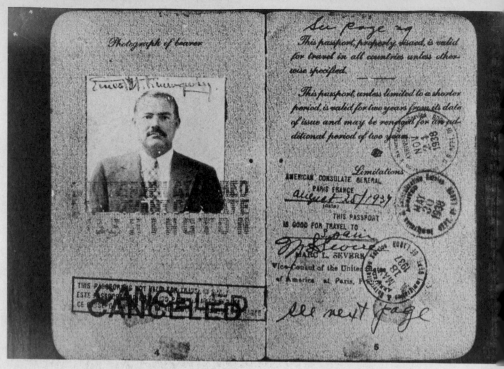

A document of extraordinary value. Hemingway's passport during the Spanish Civil War, as it is kept today at Finca Vigía.

Mijail Koltsov, the Soviet journalist on whom Hemingway based the character of Karkov in *For Whom the Bell Tolls*.

Dr. José Luis Herrara Sotolongo, Medical Commander of the Spanish Republican Army, around 1937.

First encounter with Herbert Matthews in a war zone, Madrid, 1937.

With Joris Ivens, Dutch filmmaker and director of *The Spanish Earth*, Jarama, 1937.

Hemingway with Alexis Eisner, then lieutenant and later aide to General Lucasz, in *Fuentes de Alcarría*, March 1937.

(7th page of 466 to 475)

was what was on your mind. That was all you had to worry about. you're pretty good, toed himself you really are. and if that is all you have to worry about S think you had better go to sleep. your beautiful young wife is asleep already. Because pretty soon it is going be morning and in the morning see you can remember what your problems were last night.

A page from the handwritten manuscript of *For Whom the Bell Tolls:* part of the monologue of Robert Jordan during the last hours of his life.

the Schnee Eifel, Hurtgen Forest and the Rundstedt offensive it was very bitter fighting also quite cold. Earlier there was much bad fighting but re-taking France and especially Paris made me feel the best I had ever felt. Ever since I had been a boy I had been in retreats, holding attacks, retreats, victories with no reserves to follow them up, etc., and I had never known how winning can make you feel.

Now, since the fall of 1945, I have been writing so hard, and all the time, that the weeks and the months go by so quickly we will all be dead if we do not know it.

I hope you had a good trip in America and Canada. I wish I would have spoken Russian and gone around with you because there are really many wonderful people to meet and fine things to do. But few of those people speak Russian. I would like you to have known our Colonel of the 22nd Infantry (now General Lanham) who is my best friend and the commanders of the 1st, 2nd and 3rd battalions (those that are alive) and many Company and Platoon commanders and many wonderful American soldiers.

The 4th Infantry division from D day on Utah Beach until VE Day had 21,205 casualties out of a strength of 14,037. My oldest boy was attached to the 3rd Infantry Division which had 33,547 out of their 14,037. But they were in Sicily and Italy before landing in Southern France. He dropped in ahead as a parachutist and was later wounded very badly and captured in the fall in the Vosges. He is a good kid, a Captain, and you would like him. He told the Krauts (he is very blond) he was the son of a ski instructor in Austria and had gone to America after his father had been killed in an avalanche. When the Krauts finally found out who he was they sent him to a Hostage camp. But he was liberated at the end.

It is a damned shame you could not have come down here. Are your poems or the journal translated into English? I would like to read them very much. I know what you are talking about. As you say you know what I am talking about. After all the world has gotten far enough along so that writers should be able to understand one another. There is so much *govno* (probably misspelled) that goes on and yet people are so good, and intelligent and well intentioned and would understand each other well if we could have understanding of each other instead of the repeat performance of a Churchill; doing now what he did in 1918-1919 to preserve something that now can only be preserved by war.

Excuse me if I talk politics. I know that I am always supposed to be a fool when I do. But I know that nothing stands between the friendship of our countries. . . .

There is a boy (now probably old man) in the U.S.S.R. named Kashkeen. Red headed (probably greyheaded). He is the best critic and translator I ever had. If still around please give him my best regards. Was *For Whom the Bell Tolls* ever translated? I read a review by [Ilya] Ehrenburg but never heard. It would be easy to publish with small changes of, elimination of, certain names. Wish you could read it. It isn't about the war as we knew it the last few years. But about small hill war; it is all right and there is one place where we kill the fascists you would like.

Good luck and have a good trip,

Your friend,

Ernest Hemingway

In May 1937 at Gaylord's in Madrid, Ilya Ehrenburg met Hemingway. The two men chatted. Ehrenburg described the writer as "tall, taciturn, a whiskey drinker." The American confided to the Soviet writer: "I don't understand much about politics, but I do know about Fascism. The people here are fighting for a just cause."

Expanding on his beliefs, he said: "I read somewhere that my heroes are neurotic. They forget that life in this world is dirty. And, generally, they call a man neurotic when things are difficult for him. The bull becomes neurotic in the ring, though he may be sane in the meadow. That's what we're talking about."

Ehrenburg believed that this relationship with Hemingway in Madrid was of great help to him. Ehrenburg, whose style was usually mordant and lean, wrote this paragraph in his memoirs, thirty years after the Spanish Civil War:

And now I, thinking back over my own life, see that two writers whom I had the good fortune of knowing, not only helped me to get free of sentimentality, long discourses and narrow perspectives, but they simply taught me to breathe, write and to endure: Babel and Hemingway. At my age, a man can confess it.

Milton Wolf, who was a 22-year-old platoon commander in the Lincoln Brigade machine-gun company when he met Ernest, draws a sketch of Hemingway as a loyal and attractive figure, in an article that appeared in *American Dialogue* in 1964: "I had the vague impression at the time that Hemingway's rooms at the Florida were headquarters for Phil Detro, battalion commander, and Freddie Keller, commissar." But at the end of 1940, Wolf had called Hemingway a "rooter."

Hemingway's answer to that was not long in coming. He was sarcastic and furious, declaring that they were not friends any more. According to Carlos Baker, a few weeks later Hemingway was sorry he had been so hard on Wolf. Seven months later he sent Wolf $425 to help him buy a farm.

Roman Karmen, a Soviet writer and filmmaker, has vivid memories of Hemingway during the Spanish Civil war:

> In those days, in the front lines along the road to Valencia, many times I would meet a man who went awkwardly among the trenches. He was successful in getting to the most advanced positions, and there he sat and talked to the combatants of the International Brigades. He was the well-known writer, Ernest Hemingway. He was collaborating with the cinematographer, Joris Ivens, in the filming of a documentary about the struggle of the Spanish people. . . .
>
> Hemingway usually wore a light raincoat all muddied from the trenches, a sweater, a loose jacket, thick-soled shoes, a black Basque beret, and round metal-framed glasses. I gave Aliosha Eisner, the Lucasz aide, a Leica, and he took our picture with Ivens.
>
> Hemingway lived at the Hotel Florida. Koltzov and I had previously stayed there. I spent a few evenings with Hemingway. Usually his room was bursting with people; most of them in the uniform of the International Brigades. There were always two or three guns leaning against the wall. The host usually received us with a cordial "hello," and with a nod of the head indicated the table where he had put the bottles, canned food, oranges with stems and leaves still on them. Talk went on in English, Spanish, and some French and German. The window was covered with thick drapes; a bluish gray fog from the tobaccco smoke filled the room.
>
> I remember that on one of those nights I saw a beautiful young woman reclining on the bed. She wore a military uniform, and her soft golden hair was spread all over the pillow. She spoke

in German, with a few Spanish words sprinkled through her conversation. She was drinking straight whiskey. Someone said she was German and a doctor, the medical officer of one of the International Brigades. Our host sat beside her on the bed and they talked a long time.

Karmen regrets that he didn't keep notes of some of Hemingway's words, perhaps a joke or an angry retort: "Why is it that I can't remember who the other guests were? Why wasn't I aware then that my contact with that man of simple conversation, the cordial host in that room of the Florida, would one day become a priceless memory?"

One of the last letters that Hemingway received in Finca Vigía was the one Roman Karmen wrote 20 years after the end of the Spanish Civil War:

Moscow, July 10, 1959

Roman Karmen
Bolshaira Polianka 34 KV 35
Moscow USSR

Dear Hemingway,

I have been wanting to write to you for a long time. The last time we heard from each other was during the war. How happy I was to get your letter at that time! It was forwarded to me to the front and amidst the roar of the guns I read and re-read your warm lines with profound emotion. A letter from Hemingway from distant Cuba! It was like a miracle. . . .

I do not know whether you ever received my reply. Later, I heard about your landing in Normandy, about the motor accident, and that you had been wounded. In a photo printed in *Life* I first saw you with a beard. I think the photo was by Capa, our mutual friend from Spain.

The memories of our meetings on Spanish soil are very precious to me! Do you remember the Jarama? You and I had our photos taken with Joris Ivens at the command post of Lucasz' 12th Brigade. I am sending it to you, perhaps you have not got a copy? Yes, many hard and grim years have passed over our graying heads since then, but Spain, dear Spain, and the dear Spaniards have remained a bright and warm memory in my heart.

I recall our last meeting. Your hotel room (I think you moved from the "Florida" to the "Gran-Via"?) almost hidden in clouds of tobacco smoke. A lot of men wearing the uniform of the International Brigades, their boots smeared with yellow mud. Somebody lying on the bed. Bottles, a lot of bottles on the table. The Madrid nights were sad and grim in those years. We spoke Spanish and English, and understood each other perfectly. Do you remember, I promised you excellent trout fishing in Armenia and salmon fishing on the Kola Peninsula? You promised to come to the USSR.

After leaving Spain in the autumn of 1937 I have roamed far and wide with my camera. I spent two hard winters in the Arctic. The year of 1938-39 I spent in China, tramping on foot over the mountains to reach the 8th Army and Mao Tse Tung's cave in the mountains of Northern Shenhsi.

Four years passed on the roads of the war against Hitler, from the first day to the storming of Berlin. Then ten months of filming the Nuremberg trial. My film was called "The Court of the Peoples." It was not a picture of the trial but of the crimes of fascism, of vengeance.

In the jungles of Vietnam I filmed the Vietnamese people's struggle for freedom. That was the fourth (I hope and believe the last!) war in my life. I have made many pictures about my country, of Soviet people and their work, and films about India and Burma. I have brought up two sons and cultivated an orchard. Such in short is my report for the past twenty years.

I would like to show you my latest film. It is a cinema-poem about the courage of people drilling oil in off-shore wells from a steel island in the Caspian Sea. You would like those people. I spent six months with them there, on their steel island, amidst storms and hurricanes.

The film, called "Conquerors of the Sea," was released recently and received most flattering press notices.

Your 60th birthday was celebrated with much warmth and good feeling in our country. I wish you many, many happy returns with all may heart. I am enclosing some press clippings, which might not reach you otherwise. I would like you to feel the great and sincere love which millions of readers in our country cherish for Hemingway. Your stirring *Old Man and the Sea* has been read by a countless number of people, young and old, students, workers, collective farmers, who love and admire the author of *Fiesta* [*The Sun Also Rises*], *Farewell to Arms*, *The Fifth Column*. You probably do not even suspect how people love Ernest Hemingway in the USSR. But why, do tell me why, have you never visited our country? After all, Carl Sandburg flew here with Nixon, in spite of his venerable age! There was a rumour that you were also to come with Nixon, and I was already anticipating the pleasure of our meeting!

Have you made your home for good on Cuba? I can understand why you have done so, I understand your love for the Cubans. In reportages from Cuba, printed in our magazines, I can never tear my eyes away from the photographs of the Cubans. What a noble people! Their sad eyes shine with almost fanatical honesty, purity and courage. Apparently, you have grown to love them dearly. Just as we loved the Spaniards?

I often have the feeling that I must set off for Cuba to make a film about that country and its people. The images of the people with the delicate oval faces, with long hair falling onto their shoulders, images of courage and sincerity, give me no peace. I sometimes think that I would put titanic, nuclear energy into the creation of such a film.

I want this letter to reach you. I want to receive your reply from afar. I want to believe that we shall meet again sooner or later. My wife, Nina, and my sons, Roman and Alexander, send you their warmest greetings.

I embrace you warmly, dear Hemingway,

Sincerely yours,

R. Karmen

Roman Karmen's attempt to reestablish contact with his friend of the Spanish War failed. Hemingway never responded.

The Hemingway who got that letter was 60 years old, and beginning to behave erratically. Depression, loss of memory and feelings of persecution complex were wearing him down. His correspondence piled up on his bed unanswered, and his excursions aboard the *Pilar* became less frequent.

Karmen got his wish and the Soviets sent him to Cuba, late in 1960. He shot 35,000 feet of film, but the timing was wrong and he could not locate his old friend at Finca Vigía. Hemingway had just left on his last trip to Spain, where he intended to do research for his work in progress about bullfighting. It was a fruitless and nostalgic trip, which he spent roaming through all the places he had known in his youth.

Karmen was to live 20 more years. He spent much of that time writing his memoirs and reviewing the material he had filmed during his long career. In 1977, on the occasion of his seventieth birthday, Karmen rented one of the biggest theaters in Moscow for one night. It was a kind of rally and many Soviet veterans of the Spanish Civil War attended. In December of that year I told Karmen that I had read one of his letters, preserved at the Hemingway Museum in Havana. He seemed surprised: "From me to Hemingway? How is that possible? That letter was written such a long time ago."

When Karmen made his second trip to Cuba in 1962, Hemingway had already died. Many Cubans saw Karmen filming during the height of the October Crisis.

He wore the olive-green uniform of the Cuban Revolutionary Army and was escorted by two uniformed Soviet aides, who carried his cameras and sound equipment. He was often seen going towards the ramp at the San Antonio de los Baños airbase, which had been built by the Americans during the Second World War. Ironically, it would have been one of the principal targets of their bombs in the October Crisis if a peaceful solution had not been found.

Karmen's hair had turned white and his skin ruddy. He moved around with great ease among the combat troops. He did not visit Finca Vigía. At that time, although it had been announced officially, the place, a year after Hemingway's death, had not yet been converted into a museum. He would have found a group of adolescents at Finca Vigía, armed to the teeth, belonging to a troop called the Young Rebels.

Roman Karmen's last reference to Hemingway was to honor him by including him in a posthumous work, along with Paul Robeson and other great personalities who went to Spain to defend the cause of democracy. That is the way Hemingway appears in the early scenes of the film, *The Unknown War*.

Some time later, *La Gaceta de Cuba* ran an article on the death of Karmen in the spring of 1978, using the Hemingway title "Nobody Ever Dies," and this subheading: ". . . on the 28th of May . . . in Moscow, the bell tolled for the last of the great reporters."

In a chapter of *They Shall Not Pass*, Karmen told about "one of those amazing coincidences that happen to people" during the course of the Second World War:

> . . . something happened that to this day seems incredible to me. It was at the beginning of 1943. On my way from one front to another. I stopped two days in Moscow. I was staying at the Studios, but I went alone to my Polianka apartment, a cold and solitary place, to take some of my things. No sooner had I set foot in it when the telephone rang. I picked up the receiver. The call was from the Soviet Foreign Cultural Relations Society. "We have a letter for you. Judging from the envelope and the stamps it is a letter from Cuba. Where do you want it delivered?" Without a notion about what kind of letter it could be, I told them I would go pick it up myself.
>
> The letter covered only a small page. I carried it in the top pocket of my campaign jacket for a long time. I reread it many, many times. Much was lost in the war, but a bitter loss to me was discovering two years later that I had lost that letter from the faraway friend who was so dear to me. He had written approximately the following, for I remember it almost word for word:
>
> "Dear Karmen: I wonder where you are and whether you will get this letter. Knowing you, I am convinced you are in the very midst of battle, in the furious fight that your country is waging against Fascism. I, on the other hand, am writing from distant Cuba, away from the struggles. But don't think I am seeking refuge in the present calm. . . . I am sure that we will meet again, perhaps in the battlefields of Europe when they open up the second front. Cordial greetings! Salud! Yours, Hemingway."
>
> Later we learned of Hemingway's heroic fight against the Nazi submarines that prowled near the northern coast of Cuba, attacking allied transports. He was referring to this between the lines of his letter.
>
> That is how our paths parted. When I went to Cuba, it turned out that Hemingway had just left for Spain. Before that, Anastas Mikoyan, who visited Hemingway at his villa near Havana, told me that when the master of the house showed him his library, he took from a bookcase and showed him my book, *A Year in China*, which I had dedicated to him. I sent him the book just before the war.

[63]

Hemingway's *For Whom the Bell Tolls* was not well-received in certain sectors, especially by the leaders of the Communist Party in Spain. Hemingway was far from pleased with these criticisms, although he tried hard to contain his displeasure within the confines of his intimate social circle.

Sam Putnam, in the Communist Party's *Daily Worker,* bitterly criticized the novel.

Hemingway was understandably annoyed when the review appeared in this paper, since years before Putnam had criticized *A Farewell to Arms,* but from a fascist point of view. Curiously enough, in those days Putnam had been a fascist sympathizer and had actually accused Hemingway of writing a "socialist" novel.

There was another article, written by the Argentinian García Tuñón, entitled "Hemingway the Traitor," which was reprinted by the Cuban Communist newspaper *Noticias de Hoy* in its Sunday supplement, under the direction of Angel Custodio, a Spanish Republican playwright.

Upon receiving an evasive answer regarding this attack on Hemingway from Custodio, José Luis Herrera Sotolongo went to see Juan Marinello, then president of the Cuban Communist Party, to straighten things out. Herrera Sotolongo made it clear to Marinello that Hemingway always had a positive attitude about the communists and had given considerable economic aid to the cause. To prove his claims he showed Marinello certain documents.

Herrera Sotolongo managed to convince Marinello, who said: "Well, this campaign against the book must end, but we reserve the right to criticize the motion picture." When Herrera Sotolongo repeated Marinello's reservation to Hemingway, the writer said: "Tell Juan that if he wants me to write that review, I'll be more destructive than anybody else." By then everyone knew Hemingway's opinion of Hollywood.

It is not generally known that his novel was published in the Soviet Union in a special pocket-size paperback edition for the Red Army. Maxim Litvinov, the Soviet Ambassador to the

United States, sent Hemingway two copies of the book and three or four of *Pravda* from Washington. On the front page, a review by Ilya Ehrenburg gave high praise to the novel. The article ended by saying that the Soviet fighters were inspired by Robert Jordan.

In the cover letter he sent with the books and papers, Litvinov explained to Hemingway that the money for his rights as an author had been deposited in rubles in the Soviet Union. These were the documents Herrera showed Marinello.

The greater part of the political criticism—there was literary criticism as well—came from the left or from former combatants in the Spanish Civil War. For example, difficulties arose with Milton Wolf, a brave man, the last commander of the Lincoln Brigade who once swam across the Ebro River with what was left of his battalion, reorganized his command and turned back to fight the enemy. Wolf was outraged by the contents of the novel, and said as much to Hemingway in a letter. Besides immediately breaking off their friendship, Hemingway answered: "Okay. Did it ever occur to you that there were around 595,000 . . . troops in the Spanish army, besides the 15th Brigade, and that the entire action of my book took place and was over before you personally had ever been in the front lines . . .?" He didn't just leave the problem there, but went on to ask what Wolf would have liked him to have done to aid the cause of the Spanish Republic that he did not do.

In Arthur H. Landis's book about the Lincoln Brigade, Hemingway is described and quoted many times, always in terms of praise. Landis claims that Hemingway's bottle of Scotch was thought to have some special magic; it never seemed to diminish, either in quality or quantity, and no member of the American brigade who came to visit him was ever denied the pleasure of his company, cigars, or a long drink from his bottomless bottle.

Landis adds that although the American volunteers were friendly with all the correspondents, only Herbert Matthews, Hemingway and Vincent Sheen (from the Paris edition of the *New York Herald Tribune*) were considered their own; the soldiers and the other reporters were worlds apart.

Today, so many years after its publication, it seems that the controversy regarding *For Whom the Bell Tolls* was excessive, particularly considering that the novel does not depart from Hemingway's artistic standards, applied to the heroic tale of one of his typical characters—an alter ego—in one of his typical situations.

In his other novels these elements had won sympathy and approval. It was rather the historic and geographic aspects of the Spanish Civil War that proved controversial; that and the fact that so many intellectuals from so many countries participated in the conflict. If ever there was an instance in which the Civil War caused a radical change in Hemingway's writing, it was in *To Have and Have Not*, which he finished during the interval between his trips to Spain. It is a crucial turning point, a book that represents a real break with all he had written before.

Hemingway's opinion of Líster as expressed in *For Whom the Bell Tolls* is cutting and sarcastic. He refers to him as a simple stonemason from Galicia who now commanded a division, and also casts some aspersions on his intelligence as a commander.

Líster's opinion of Hemingway is of some interest: "When I read *For Whom the Bell Tolls*, several years after the end of the war, I was furious, but not greatly surprised. I have not the slightest doubt about Hemingway's identification with our cause during his lifetime and up to the day he died.

"How can we explain, then, his writing that book, which is a coarse caricature of our war and the heroic struggle of our people and the Volunteers for Freedom? I believe he wrote it because at that moment he was incapable of writing anything else. In spite of his talent he was not able to understand it in all its depth. Hemingway, like many others, looked only at the external, the anecdotal, the superficials of our struggle, without really going into it deeply.

"When I read his book and saw the things he said about me, I wasn't surprised at all: that was his way of getting even, for I knew, and he had told me so many times, that he would never forgive me for not letting him see everything he wanted to see . . . because if it is true that the book as a whole is an insult to the struggle of the Spanish people, it is also treason to the opinions that Hemingway himself had expressed of that struggle, not only during the war but after the war as well, in much of his work, in different media. Among these is the excellent film he made with the cinematographer Joris Ivens in 1937, and that is why, in spite of that book, I always hold for Hemingway the affection born during the war in Spain, and that, until his death, I know he had for me."

The Spanish Communist Party condemned *For Whom the Bell Tolls* when it first came out. It even went as far as to ask the Soviet Union not to publish the book there. But the book was not anti-communist or anti-Soviet and its possible defects clearly did not prevent the appearance of a special edition for the Soviet Army.

Herrera Sotolongo has his own opinion. He totally defends Ernest: "I have seen famous writers take notes for a book and then come out with something that was a disaster. I knew a German writer, Gustav Regler, a political commissar who fought actively in the Spanish war. He kept a diary and every night he would take home several sheets of paper covered with very small writing describing the events of the day. But when his book was finally published, it was a disaster. It had no literary value whatever, in spite of the fact that Ernesto had written a preface for him. Yes, they were good friends.

"Ernesto's attitude towards the Spanish Republic was always sincere and helpful. Although there has been a lot of controversy on this point, I know he was convinced that the Spanish people were in the right.

"An effort has been made to denigrate him for what he wrote in *For Whom the Bell Tolls*. I am sure that those who have attacked the book have not interpreted it correctly. The book is both easy and difficult to understand. I discussed it with Ernesto, we talked about it profoundly at times, and we reached the conclusion that the book has been misunderstood by many of its readers.

"Some see it as a story of an adventure, others as a book about a war, and still others as an attack on various aspects of Spanish politics. They are all wrong. The book expresses a very authentic feeling, which is the great impact the Spanish war had on Ernesto. As a novelist, he may have fictionalized the record at times, but he truly poured into it his innermost feelings about the Spanish people."

Herrera Sotolongo says that Ernest's commitment could be expressed in the true meaning of the English term "fellow traveller," which when translated into Spanish becomes "*un companero de viaje*"—a travelling companion.

That opinion was not shared by the leaders and intellectuals of the Lincoln Brigade: Wolf, Bessie (author of an extraordinary book about the Spanish war, *Men in Battle*), Keller and Goff, all of whom attacked Hemingway in the pages of *New Masses* and the *Daily Worker*.

The publication of *For Whom the Bell Tolls* caused a break-up between Hemingway and his old comrades of the Lincoln Brigade. The organization VALB (Veterans of the Abraham Lincoln brigade) also came out against Hemingway, ignoring the novelist's excellent record of support for the Spanish cause. VALB's resolution to condemn Hemingway was unanimous and led to his exclusion from the anthology *The Heart of Spain*, sponsored by VALB. But a group of veterans visited Hemingway in New York to declare their support.

A decade later, during the chilly days of the McCarthy era, the old romantic friendships ended and turned into something grim and distasteful. However, contrary to many who had upheld more advanced ideological positions and later recanted, Hemingway remained loyal to Spain up to his death.

In the Venetian room at Finca Vigía, usually reserved for guests, there is a document titled and accredited in this manner:

Subversive Activities Control Board—Docket No. 108-53
Herbert Brownell Jr., Attorney General of the United States, Petitioner
Veterans of the Abraham Lincoln Brigade
Respondent
May 18, 1955

Between pages 167 and 168, marked by Hemingway, it states that Alvah Bessie published, in 1939, an article in the publication of the American Communist party, *New Masses*, attacking Hemingway for his characterization of André Marty in *For Whom the Bell Tolls*.

[64]

Fidel Castro has his own opinions about the writings of the master of Finca Vigía and in particular about *For Whom the Bell Tolls*. Almost twenty years after he came down from the Sierra Maestra, where he led the guerrillas who defeated a professional army, Castro held this dialogue with two of Hemingway's countrymen, Kirby Jones and Frank Mankiewicz:

J & M:　Do you read a lot?

Castro:　Everything I can.

J & M:　What kind of books do you read?

Castro:　Political literature concerning the Party, as well as economics and history, for which, unfortunately, I don't have at my disposal all the time I would wish. Sometimes I read classic novels. . . .

J & M:　Which authors?

Castro:　I must say . . . practically all the classical authors. Really, I read a great many books. About economics, energy, monetary crises and developments in general. Today a great quantity of books is being published, more than one can read. Recently, the president of Mexico and a Mexican publisher presented me with a complete library, and I wish I had time to read the interesting books that make up that collection. Of the American writers, Hemingway is one of my favorites. He was a friend of ours.

J & M:　Did you know him personally?

Castro:　Yes, I met him after the triumph of the Revolution, during the ceremony of the awarding of the Hemingway Prize in a fishing competition. But I knew his work long before the Revolution. For instance, I read *For Whom the Bell Tolls* when I was a student. It was all about a group of guerrillas and I found it very interesting, because Hemingway told about a rear guard that fought against a conventional army. I can tell you now that that Hemingway novel was one of the books that helped me plan the tactics with which to fight Batista's army.

There were other books in which we studied our own War of Independence, especially the story of Máximo Gómez. One of the subjects I have always liked is the history of Cuba of that epoch: the writings of the men who were making history then. I have read practically everything written by the men who fought in our war for independence: Máximo Gómez, Antonio Maceo and other patriots. All of them presented and discussed the problem to which a solution had to be found: how to carry out successfully a revolution against a modern army. There were many writers, including those who wrote during the commune of Paris, who came to the conclusion that is was impossible to fight against a modern army. Some-one, I think it was Mussolini, once said that the revolution could be waged with or without the army, but never against it. We were in the same situation here, fighting a modern army that had absolute control of arms. The methods the men of that other time used to solve their problem helped us con-siderably to find a way to do it. Those elements were in Hemingway's book *For Whom the Bell Tolls*.

J & M:  Very interesting. Did he ever know you thought that?

Castro:  Never told him. He used to travel a lot and died soon after the Revolution. He lived in a house near Havana, which we have converted into the Hemingway Museum. Of course, you must know that he is one of the most admired writers in the world. He is much admired in the Soviet Union and other Socialist countries. Of the many people who come here, whether they are part of delegations, sailors or tourists, the first thing they want to do is visit Hemingway's house. Everything in that house has been kept intact: the rooms, his library, the high table at which he used to write standing up for hours every morning. . . . Everything has been perfectly preserved.

J & M:  Any manuscripts preserved there?

Castro:  I don't know if there are any manuscripts there, but I do know that many of his personal effects are.


[65]


Part of the correspondence preserved at Finca Vigía refers to Hemingway's Spanish War experience. Many are letters received after *For Whom the Bell Tolls* was published. One letter from Joris Ivens written in New York antedates these.

Ivens had been trying to communicate with Hemingway.

The following pages will show the marked difference between the language and spirit of the letters written about the Spanish Civil War and those that arrived at Finca Vigía in the fifties.

Like Karmen, Ivens went to Cuba after the revolution. Throughout long and difficult years he had been an active pro-Cuba militant. But his political views became paradoxical in the seventies. At that time he contracted to make a documentary series for the government of China under Mao Tse Tung.

The maestro, already an octogenarian, returned to Spain in 1977 for the first time since the war. It was then that *The Spanish Earth*— 40 years after it was produced—had its public premiere in that country at the film festival in Benalmadena, Andalusia.

Ivens was the object of many well-deserved tributes, and a delegation from the Cuban film industry was instructed by their government not to mention the China episode.

He was then terminating his relationship with Peking, which never stained the image of the true Ivens in Cuba. The important thing for the Cubans was that Joris Ivens was what he had always been for them: a committed artist and an international militant.

In his travels to Cuba at the beginning of the Revolution, he refused to visit Finca Vigía. It's easy to understand why neither he nor Karmen would wish to go to their old friend's house when he was no longer there. He spent his time more profitably than going on sentimental journeys. Ivens was the first instructor of the Cinematographic Department of the Cuban Revolutionary Armed Forces.

Testimony to the friendship that existed between Ivens and Hemingway must include the following letter, now in the Hemingway Museum:

Feb. 27, 1940

New York

Dear Hem,

Good to get your letter. I got proposal from Educational Film Institute of N.Y. University (financed by Sloan foundation) to do a picture for them about the frontier of the U.S.A. I asked full artistic freedom. They're considering that now. I proposed as follows: 1 reel (10 minutes) frontier moving from east to west composed of the best shots of old Hollywood pictures f.i.: the landscapes of *Covered Wagon*, *Stagecoach*, etc., maps, cartoons, a good score and commentary. Then 4 or 5 sequences each a reel of what is considered now to be the frontier: 1) World market 2) in science, busting of an atom 3) consumers market. A complicated theme. Nobody knows anything and I have to stay at economical frontiers—for treatment of social frontiers, no Sloan money. Friends here advise me to make this film a $40,000 project, pretty good for a documentary if I am completely free in direction and editing . . .

Gustav [Regler] saw Jay [Allen] and told him what you wrote me. Jay showed me letter from Gustav in which G. writes: "*La visa pour Chile est déjà accordé.*" So I think that as soon as Sweeney gets to Paris G. Will get out of France. Sweeney, on your demand, has done a lot for G. now with guaranty—but Von Hemingstein even now does not fit in Sweeney's staff, as far as alien can see.

Want to play against trio in the partidos. That is like the wall of the pelota. I think 198 pounds is a good weight for a net man. Miss those partidos anyway. Fat is growing again, not yet in brain.

I think some mistakes are made in dealing with good friends like Jay in relation to the work they do for our cause. On one side they help us with their personal connections and friendships—on the other side we keep them too long in our public work, which will harm them and us in the near future. Many of us here think like you do: War is very near and anybody saying something against France or England is suspect and a red.

Fine that book is going ahead—like to read what the fascists did to us, because what we did to them is still vivid in my mind. That row of good people from bullring to the river.

Are you coming to N.Y. soon, saw something in paper about alien committee. I am still looking for a good backroom—and a large office for [word illegible] President with the smile of the winner.

Do not mind your troubles too much. The gas station against big oil is always right. Marty is fine. Got letter from her. Will answer her tomorrow.

I do not think that the S.U. [Soviet Union] wants anything from Sweden, as long as England does not spoil the relations. President is playing that game. We will see.

My work: The Rural Electrification Picture is still resting. P. [Pare] Lorentz who has to write the commentary has been away for 2 weeks. Like to show you the material when you are in N.Y.

If I do the Frontier picture, work with Hawks is impossible.
But next work I hope will be with you. See how war goes. We
do not know much more than you.

Best regards from Helen, also from Johnny [Ferno],
[Robert] Capa—See you soon.

(signed) Joris

The letter mentions Gustav Regler, the political commissar
of the 12th International Brigade, led by Lucasz. Regler, a militant communist, was a courageous soldier in Spain, but he felt
the collapse of the Republic a bitter personal blow. Disillusioned
with the tragic climax of the war, he left the Party. He lived in
Mexico a long time and wrote *The Great Crusade*, published in
1940 with a prologue by Hemingway.

Regler had miraculously escaped alive, although wounded,
from an air attack on June 16, 1937, while he rode in a car with
Lucasz during the preparations for the offensive of Huesca. This
was the attack that killed Lucasz. Joris Ivens and Hemingway
later helped Regler get out of France and helped support him in
exile. That's what Ivens refers to in the letter.

There are also some references to Jay Allen, whom Hemingway met in 1931 in Madrid, where Allen worked as correspondent for the *Chicago Tribune*. During the war, Allen and
Hemingway were in close contact. There is also mention of
Charles Sweeney, a friend of Hemingway's since the twenties
in Paris, of whom Mary Welsh, commenting on his photo found
in Finca Vigía, said, "He was one of the few heroes admired by
EH." Sweeney had been in the Foreign Legion, but this military
man was not good company for the Gustav Regler of that time,
according to Joris Ivens.

There is a reference to Basque "pelota," a game in which it
is possible for two to play against three. The two that play against
the three must be extremely skilled and strong players.

A sentence in the letter is written in the secret code between
Ivens and Hemingway. According to Herrera Sotolongo, the
reference is to the punitive action under orders of Commandant
Carlos. Ivens says that he would like to know "what the fascist
did to us, because what we did to them is still vivid in my mind.
That row of good people from bullring to the river." This phrase

is recalled in one of Robert Jordan's monologues in *For Whom the Bell Tolls*, when he was just heard Pilar's tale of the killing of the Fascists in a small town in the mountains.

The cable Ivens sent Hemingway about four months after the letter recounts his further frustrations in the United States and the reorientation he is trying to give his situation. By that time, Hemingway had finished his novel and had returned corrected galley proofs to Scribner's. One of the first readers would be Joris Ivens.

CDA29 UD NEWYORK 55 17
NLT ERNEST HEMINGWAY
  HOTEL AMBOS MUNDOS HAVANA-

HEAR YOU FINISHED BOOK FINE ARE YOU COMING TO NEW-
YORK WANT TO TALK OF POSSIBILITY MAKING FILM TOGETHER
IN SOUTHAMERICA WHAT ARE YOUR PLANS MR SLOAN DIS-
CONTINUED MY FILM ABOUT NEW FRONTIERS SO I AM FREE
HOPE TO HEAR SOON BEST REGARDS ALSO MARTY +
  JORIS 46 WASHINGTON SQUARE

[66]

Hemingway had just received the first printed copies of *For Whom the Bell Tolls*, and Pauline Pfeiffer, his second wife, was concluding proceedings for their divorce when she sent him an encouraging and enthusiastic cable from San Francisco, on September 17, 1940. She addressed it to "Ernest Hemingway, Sun Valley Lodge, Sun Valley, Ida." Referring to the book, she says that it is *so* carefully done, *so* sound, *so* intelligent, *so* engrossing, *so* moving that she thinks it impossible that it could have been done better: "All my admiration and appreciation of the super-human effort involved. Salud, Maestro."

In a letter dated September 20, 1940, Maxwell Perkins, Er- nest's editor at Scribner's, told the novelist that he considered it a miracle that he had written *that* book in only 15 months, and that he had done it magnificently.

Hemingway himself thought he had taken too long over it. Perkins assured him that even if he had taken five years to write the book, nobody would have thought it too long, because nobody else could have written it. "Now I am looking out for books for you, since you at last have leisure," says Perkins. "I did send you one about a judge which makes good and easy reading, and tells some interesting things about criminals."

In another letter dated October 15, 1940, Perkins tells Hemingway about a favorable review of the book by critic J. Donald Adams which appeared in the newspaper the editor considered the most important and influential, *The New York Times*.

Of another review in the *Herald Tribune* Perkins says: "In spite of its simple beginning, it is quite good . . . particularly from the sales point of view." He adds that he will take the reviews to Maurice Speiser, Hemingway's lawyer and literary agent, in order to make photocopies of them with a view to using excerpts in the publicity for the film. He also expresses a wish to have Gary Cooper act in the picture, because of his looks and other qualities.

A third review was published in *Time* magazine. Perkins writes that he regrets only that it was written in *Time*'s biting style, but that he considers it very good, and quotes the last line: "The bell in this book tolls for all humanity."

The letter goes on to other personal news and gives Ernest the addresses of Scott Fitzgerald in Hollywood and John Bishop in Massachusetts. Then Perkins says that the publication of the book is an event of great importance and general interest.

"Even people outside editorial and literary circles are interested," he writes, "for the word of mouth is that this is really a great book. You must come to New York so you'll see the bookstore windows when it goes on sale."

John O'Hara, author of *Appointment in Samarra* and *Butterfield 8*, was such a great admirer of Hemingway that in 1950, after the publication of *Across the River and Into the Trees*, he compared Ernest to Shakespeare. In a wire dated October 16, 1940, excited over the new Hemingway book he had just received and read, he says: "IT IS A CLASSIC. YOUR THIRD. I AM PROUD TO BE YOUR FRIEND. O'Hara."

Jay Allen, correspondent for the *Chicago Tribune* and considered "the best-informed journalist in Spain," met Hemingway in Madrid in 1931. Six years later he helped Ernest get settled in the Spanish capital at the beginning of the war.

In spite of his great knowledge of Spain, Allen somehow never wrote a book about that country. His articles about the war, however, are considered extraordinary; for example, the one about the bloody action in Badajos, published in the *Chicago Tribune* on August 30, 1936.

Allen interviewed General Franco during the first few days of the war and reported Franco's determination to kill half the people in Spain, if necessary. He also interviewed Felangist founder Antonio Primo de Rivera a few days before he died.

Shortly after *For Whom the Bell Tolls* was published, Allen sent a cable of congratulations to Hemingway:

2171 NT XC-TDBSV EASTHAMPTON NY OCT 21
ERNEST HEMINGWAY
    SUN VALLEY IDA-
ITS A BLOODY MIRACLE. ITS WHAT YOU SAID IT WOULD BE
AND MORE; YOU COULDN'T HAVE KNOWN. THE TRUTH WAS
WITH US BUT WHAT WITH THE FASCIST LIES AND THE LIES
OF THE PHONIES, THE RACKETEERS AND THE FRIENDS IT WAS
PRETTY DAMNED NEAR DEAD. ALL ALONE—AND HOW ALONE
I CAN IMAGINE—YOU WON A KIND OF VICTORY FOR THE GOOD
GUYS WHO DIDNT COME OUT. IN A WAY, ERNEST, ITS THE
FIRST VICTORY. YOU WON IT WITH A TRUE BOOK. WITH ME
IT CUT INTO WOUNDS I HAD ABOUT FORGOTTEN AND
CLEANED THEM. I FEEL BETTER AND ALL TODAY FOR THE
FIRST TIME IN OVER A YEAR I HAVE BEEN REMEMBERING
THINGS WITHOUT DUCKING. ITS WONDERFUL TO SEE THE OB-
SCENITY CRITICS TONGUETIED FOR ONCE, AND WITH SIMPLE
AWE I MEAN IT. SAILING WEDNESDAY OR FLYING WEEKEND
FOR LISBON MOROCCO MARSEILLES WHERE ANXIOUS SEE
ABOUT OLD FRIENDS. ANY MESSAGES? PACCIARDI AND SCORES
OTHERS THERE AS YOU KNOW. AIR MAIL ME ANY SUGGES-
TIONS. THANKS FOR THE LIFT ON THE EVE-
                    JAY

Archibald MacLeish, the poet, was another friend whose praise for the book was high. He cabled Hemingway from Washington in October of 1940 as follows: "THE WORD GREAT

HAD NO MEANING IN OUR LANGUAGE UNTIL YOUR BOOK. YOU
HAVE GIVEN IT BACK ITS MEANING. I AM PROUD OF HAVING
SHARED ANY SMALL PART OF YOUR SKY." He dedicated a poem
to James Joyce and Hemingway entitled "Years of the Dog."

According to Leicester Hemingway, Ernest and Archie
MacLeish went fishing near Key West in the summer of 1936,
and during the day they had an argument because they had not
caught a single fish. Tempers grew heated. On board the *Pilar*,
they decided to continue the discussion on land and headed for
a key.

MacLeish got off first and Ernest sailed away and left him
there. It was one of the islets between Boca Grande and Snipe
Keys. Ernest, "The lad with the supple look like a sleepy panther," returned to his home in Key West, where he stayed until
Pauline, "horrified," made him go back for MacLeish.

One can understand that this incident damaged the friendship between the poet and the writer for the time being; the
breach was eventually healed.

At Finca Vigía there is a copy of the February 1939 issue
of *Esquire* containing "Night Before Battle," a literary reminis-
cence of the Spanish Civil War. One can see several corrections
Hemingway made in pencil on his own published material, revealing the same critical sense and perfectionist zeal with which
he attacked the printed texts of Fitzgerald and Algren. He substituted and crossed out words that seemed all right, but which
he would not have overlooked if he had had another chance at
the copy. He made the corrections in the copy of *Esquire* that he
kept on his bookshelves. Later he told Scribner's he decided not
to republish any of the four stories written in the Florida Hotel
in Madrid, including "Night Before Battle."

A collection of 40 extraordinary photographs taken by Robert Capa during the course of the war and two hundred shots
by John Ferno and Joris Ivens taken during the filming of *The
Spanish Earth* heighten the nostalgia and close the dossier of the
Hemingway of that spring, when he believed that the Republic
would win the war: "That time—the happiest of our lives."

[67]

In *How It Was*, Mary Welsh Hemingway says that in 1950 Hemingway got a letter from the Soviet writer Ilya Ehrenburg. Writing in the name of the World Peace Council, Ehrenburg urged Hemingway to take part in the international movement against atomic armaments.

Mary says that her husband was irked. He started to frame an answer to the letter in which he told Ehrenburg that "for his information" he was not only against atomic arms but anything exceeding the strength of .22-caliber sporting guns. He went on to list all the things he opposed and ended with the statement that if his country were attacked, he would fight against any aggressor, including the USSR.

According to Mary, Ernest started the letter in May of 1950 but never finished it or sent it. So, all we know about it is what Mary tells us. This letter has not been found in Finca Vigía.

The Hemingway image of the Cold War period as presented by the bibliography consulted is always tinged with anticommunism. Hotchner in *Papa Hemingway* and Leicester Hemingway in his biography contribute to this: the writer as soldier blue ready to go to war against the Red Menace. Today, political exhumation of Hemingway is not an easy task. Several Hemingways are conjured up: Hotchner's and Leicester's and the writer himself who, in his 1954 article, *The Christmas Gift*, mocks Senator Joseph McCarthy and his hysterical anticommunist campaigns.

There is an interesting typewritten document at Finca Vigía with the heading "Finca Vigía, San Francisco de Paula, Cuba" and dated 8/11/50. It is a kind of declaration of principles. Hemingway's text starts with a reference to an unidentified book: "Since that introduction was written we have won a war and lost a peace and are now fighting an undeclared war while preparing to fight a war on a world-wide scale."

The "introduction" he refers to is probably the one he wrote for *Treasury for the Free World*, the book edited by Ben Raeburn. Hemingway wrote and signed it in San Francisco de Paula, Cuba, in September 1945. Both documents are similar in style and tone. In Raeburn's book Hemingway wrote:

We have fought this war and won it. Now let us not be sancti-
monious; nor hypocritical: nor vengeful nor stupid. Let us make
our enemies incapable of ever making war again, let us re-educate
them, and let us learn to live in peace and justice with all countries
and all peoples in this world. To do this we must educate and
re-educate. But first we must educate ourselves.

In the paper at Finca Vigía, after saying that his country
has won a war and lost the peace, and that it is now waging an
undeclared war, Hemingway states that: "People of the mentality
of those who were going to Beat Japan in Sixty Days are now
prepared to fight all Asia." (Evidently a reference to the Korean
conflict and even a premonition of what was to happen in Vietnam.)

Hemingway also states that anyone critical of this insanity
is considered a potential traitor. "Any two war-mongers together,
neither of whom will fight when the chips are down again, constitute a nucleus of super-patriotism. Three war-mongers are no
doubt regarded as having the same value as a well-trained, and
blooded, Infantry Division."

He concludes bitterly that:

The people who fight will fight again. The people who talk will
talk again. The ten percenters will know how foolish they were
to be content with ten (very few were) and they will do better
out of this new one until the inevitable end of such folly comes.

War is the biggest and finest business ever invented for those
on the island. It was brought to its perfection in this last war and
it is still the health of the state.

We could possibly afford to give every inhabitant of all the
countries some people envisage fighting one deep-freeze unit; a
television set and a collected edition of the Works of Ralph Waldo
Emerson for the cost of fighting them and conquering them. Not
to mention occupying, re-educating and feeding them. We could
probably put two cars in each of their garages and build the garages. We might be able to put even two chickens in their every
pot and we ourselves be left without a pot to eat in.

But no, Gentlemen. To horse again; and the Ghengis Khans
of the super ten per-centism to lead us from the rear.

And he adds, ironically, that surely that is not what a real American should feel about "our great, new, contemplated Preventive War," the one that Pentagon spokesmen had recently explained so clearly. However, the writer made this final declaration; here, as throughout the typewritten document, the words are well-spaced:

> . . . that is the way the writer of this Introduction feels and he loves his country and will fight for it.

Hemingway signed with pencil, the way an artist would sign a drawing. These pages disprove a conservative and politically narrow-minded Hemingway; here he strikes at warmongers and jingoists, declaring that war is business for profiteers and folly for the rest of mankind.

In the preface to *Men at War*, Hemingway presents the theme of what one feels in war. Here, he questions why war is made at all. The writer is now politically maturer, in spite of the bitter undercurrent one feels in his "manifesto."

Ehrenburg never read Hemingway's angry letter mentioned by Mary Welsh, nor did he receive any other answer from him, yet, two decades after Hemingway's death, he reminisced about his friend: "It was not an accident that Hemingway stayed in Madrid; nor was it an accident that he, as a correspondent in the Second World War, visited the French guerillas and not the high officers of the United States army, or that he hailed the victorious Castro guerillas. Throughout his life he was consistent with the line he had set for himself."

[68]

GRANMA
August 2, 1977
JOURNALIST HERBERT L. MATTHEWS DIES
New York, August 1 (PL)
Herbert L. Matthews, *New York Times* correspondent for 45 years, died at the age of seventy-seven in an Australian city. Matthews, who retired in 1977 . . . interviewed the Cuban revolutionary leader Fidel Castro in Sierra Maestra, in 1957.

GRANMA
May 2, 1978
ROMAN KARMEN, CELEBRATED SOVIET FILM
MAKER DIES
MOSCOW (TASS) The Central Committee of the CPSU, the
Presidium of the Supreme Soviet and the Council of Ministers of
USSR announce with deep sorrow the death on the 28th of April,
1978, at 71 years of age, of Roman Karmen, outstanding person-
ality of Soviet culture, Hero of Socialist Labor, artist of the people
of the USSR, and honored with the Lenin and National awards.
He was a graduate of the Moscow Institute of Cinematography.
He acquired fame as a cinematographic reporter during the years
of the revolutionary war in Spain (1936–1939). Several documentaries were based on the material he filmed in Spain.

GRANMA
May 3, 1978
ROMAN KARMEN—FAREWELL TO A BROTHER
By Raul Rivero
Spring has come suddenly to Moscow. These days, so long awaited by Muscovites, the trees have turned a deep green and the
parks overflow with flowers. Roman Karmen, the legendary Soviet
cinematographer, the exemplary international revolutionary, will
not see it. . . .

[69]

A key figure throws light on how contemporary Cubans view
Hemingway's true relations with the communists and the Spanish
Republicans.

Roman Nicolau, born in Havana in 1905, was a trade union
leader and member of the Cuban Communist Party since 1926.
In 1930 he already belonged to its Central Committee. Jailed for
organizing opposition against the dictatorship of Gerardo Machado, upon his release he travelled to the Soviet Union where
he studied in the Frunze military academy.

Returning to Cuba, he helped organize the peasants of Ori-
ente province during their revolt in the thirties. When the Civil
War broke out in Spain, he was responsible for recruiting Cuban

volunteers for the International Brigades and providing their supplies.

Nicolau managed to send sugar, tobacco and coffee shipments to the Republican Government, sponsored a school for 300 war orphans in the Spanish town of Sitges, and, when war came to an end, launched a campaign to rescue the Cuban survivors in French concentration camps.

His contribution to the Spanish conflict was only one of the many activities of that man of unprepossessing appearance—short, gaunt, informally dressed and unarmed—who would, several years later, sit in an easy chair lecturing Hemingway and Martha Gellhorn about the necessity of winning the war against Finland.

During the Civil War he met Hemingway at the Majestic Hotel in Barcelona. They were introduced by Nicolas Guillén. That night Hemingway was with Paul Robeson, the black American singer. Although both in their own way were serving the same cause, Hemingway and Nicolau did not become friends in Spain. After the war, again accompanied by Nicolas Guillén, he visited Hemingway in Finca Vigía. Nicolau had gathered a group of intellectuals who were providing economic aid for the revolutionary movement and he wanted to request the writer's cooperation. Nicolau found Hemingway willing to help and he paid him frequent visits. Now he tells us:

"How did we work out the interviews? I simply called him on the phone and said: 'Hemingway, I must see you.' He knew right away what I wanted to see him about, and we'd make an appointment, usually the same day.

"I never asked Hemingway for much money. But he was very generous and used to give me more than I requested. He gave us a total of twenty thousand dollars. It gave him pleasure that we were doing *something* against the government.

"We had to buy the paper for our newspaper *Hoy* in Canada. We had a publishing house, the *Editorial Páginas*, which was run for political purposes, not profit. Hemingway gave three or four thousand dollars for the publishing house on one occasion, and said to me: 'Nicolau, I pay you more for your lectures than I get for one of my books.'

"However, Hemingway himself asked for these 'lectures,' as he called them. He used to call me whenever he wanted to discuss certain political problems. For example, he couldn't understand the reason for the Russo-Finnish war, and I went to his house and explained that it was a preventive war, that it involved the defense of Leningrad.

"The one who really didn't understand about the war was his wife, Martha; he sent for me so that she would hear the explanation. He was already convinced of the necessity of that war, but didn't know how to convince her. He would have preferred that there be no war, but, anyway, he had that problem with his wife and wanted me to help him out.

"I don't know if we convinced her in the end, but, at least, there were no more arguments on that issue. Hemingway, however, understood the point of view of the Party and the USSR in this matter. I was left with a good impression in my contacts with him. He hated the anarchists.

"I never mixed our political discussions with my collection visits. When he called me, it was always to talk about politics. Then he'd say: 'Nicolau, I'd like to you to come over for a drink.' When I visited him on money matters the dialogue was different: 'How much do you want?' he would ask, and I would answer, 'Whatever you can spare.' He would sit there figuring his bank account, and at the end he would make his contribution. He would usually give a few hundred dollars, but sometimes it was more. When the CP was legalized, I went to see him and told him that I wouldn't bother him anymore, but that if he would allow a suggestion, I thought his help should go to the exiled Spanish Republicans in Cuba, who needed it badly. He thanked me for the suggestion."

Now Nicolau comes to a crucial assessment:

"He may not have been a communist," he says, "but he was a humanist and so he cooperated with us."

Nicolau remembers that he used to call Hemingway "compañero" (companion, friend), but that Hemingway called him "camarada" (comrade). Nicolau figures that Hemingway got used to that form of address during the Spanish War.

He assures us that, of all the foreigners, Hemingway contributed the most money to the Communist Party in Cuba. He states that he always forgave Ernest's political errors, adding that he felt very uncomfortable when he read Líster's attacks on the writer.

"Líster is a Eurocommunist and disavows the past. This doesn't mean that I approve or disapprove of Eurocommunism. That's another matter. What is important is that we all change. What does today's Eurocommunist Líster think of Hemingway? It would be interesting to know his opinion."

Nicolas Guillén tells us that he took Nicolau to the Majestic, and when they saw Hemingway with Paul Robeson, Nicolau asked Guillén to introduce him to the writer. This done, they sat with him and had a few drinks together.

Later he would take Nicolau to the Vigía "for the assignment in which Monguito [Nicolau] had to collect money for the Party."

[70]

Hemingway loved Spain. The Spain he saw under fire and ravaged by the war would cross his mind many times in later years. He felt a close, deep commitment to that country, a commitment he always acknowledged.

When Luis Delage, a member of the Political Bureau of the Spanish Communist Party, found exile in Cuba, the Party decided that he should return to Spain to organize its clandestine work. Delage was exhausted and run-down and was sent to Guanabo Beach near Havana to recover before going back. Hemingway paid all his expenses at the beach, and for his trip back to Spain, through Emiliano Loza, the intermediary between Ernest and the Spanish Communist Party.

Herrera Sotolongo frequently received money from Hemingway for the Party. "The sum," he says, "was never lower than five hundred dollars and he gave it as a natural thing to do."

"Besides," says Herrera Sotolongo, "he sponsored the Party's Committee in the district of Guanabaco when the Cuban Communist Party became legal on the island. He paid their rent, lighting, and telephone." This fact can be confirmed by the volunteer aid bonds kept in the fifties at Finca Vigía.

# *Patente de Corso* (Orders of Marque)

[71]

The photograph is yellowing. In it one can see the *Pilar* with a sign on its prow which serves to camouflage its true purpose. It says simply: *American Museum of Natural History*. There is also an official-looking document which reads:

OFFICE OF NAVAL ATTACHE AND ATTACHE FOR AIR
AMERICAN EMBASSY
HAVANA, CUBA

18 May 1943.

To Whom It May Concern:

While engaged in specimen fishing for the American Museum of Natural History, Sr. Ernest Hemingway, on his motor boat PILAR is making some experiments with radio apparatus which experiments are known to this *Agregado Naval*, and are known to be *arreglado*, and not subversive in any way.
[signed]
Hayne D. Boyden
Colonel, U.S. Marine Corps
Agredado Naval de los Estados Unidos, Embajada Americana.

This document and photo are all that remain at Finca Vigía of one of the most romantic and naïve of all the undertakings organized by Hemingway in his lifetime.

Gregorio Fuentes, captain of the *Pilar*, still has the sign with the inscription, *American Museum of Natural History*, and an olive-green jacket with the insignia of the U.S. Navy. There was some talk about the existence of a map of Cuba marked by Hemingway, but it was never found. Missing as well is the "Orders of Marque" document given to Hemingway by the naval authorities of the United States.

In 1944, when Hemingway was in London, on the first stage of his adventure as war correspondent and captain of guerrillas in the Second World War, he saw his brother Leicester and confided how he had intended to save himself and his crew if they were ever taken prisoners by the enemy while on their antisubmarine assignment.

"We had *orders of marque* drawn up, as in the old days. I have the document at home. It stated that the ship was manned by a crew of different nationalities, but was acting in the interest of the United States and on an authorized basis. In this way we hoped to acquire some legal standing and avoid being executed if luck wasn't with us."

The document dated May 18, 1943, was a kind of informal authorization extended to Hemingway by the American naval attaché. It has the words "arreglado" (arranged) and "Agregado Naval" (Naval Attaché) underlined. These Spanish words seem addressed to the Cuban authorities.

The question arises: Why on earth would a naval attaché state "to whom it may concern" that Sr. Ernest Hemingway was carrying on *certain* experiments with radio equipment? This blunt approach seems to prove the thesis that American Intelligence in those days was in its infancy. It is also worthy of note, given Hemingway's penchant for professionalism in all things, that an unmistakable flavor of improvisation pervaded the whole operation.

For those who took part in the antisubmarine activities on the Cuban coast, the name Ernest Hemingway suggests an adventurer who hobnobbed with the high officers of the American navy and to whom the supply section delivered extra rations of liquor for use aboard his boat.

"A playboy who hunted submarines off the Cuban coast as a whim," declares Captain Mario Ramírez Delgado, a man now nearing sixty, strong, bitter, nostalgic, one of the most authoritative voices on the World War II submarine hunt in the Caribbean. He was the only captain to sink a German submarine in Cuban waters: The U-176, hit May 15, 1943, position: latitude 23 degrees, 21' north; longitude 80 degrees, 18' west, approximately seven and a half miles to the southwest of the lighthouse of Bahía de Cadiz Key.

There was plenty of opportunity for Ramírez to run across

Hemingway and his boat the *Pilar*, for they shared the same zone of operations. His opinion of Hemingway is biased: that of the professional regarding the efforts of an amateur.

Lured by the reports of the presence of German submarines, Hemingway sailed for the first time into the waters of the archipelago north of Camagüey. After the war, U.S. Intelligence found out the identity of his wartime enemy: Captain Reiner Dierkin, chief officer of the U-176, the same submarine later hit and sunk by Captain Ramírez, who caught up with it ahead of Hemingway.

Dierkin came through the pass of Crooked Islands early in May of 1943. East of the city port of Nuevitas, he sank a small tanker and the freighter *Nikerliner*, and it was then that American Intelligence alerted Hemingway.

At the time Hemingway was on patrol near Port Purgatorio, not far from Key Paraíso on the north coast of Pinar de Río, in extreme western Cuba.

Hemingway had been involved in the mission since the spring of 1942. It was deemed sufficiently important to be labeled "Top Secret" by the American naval command. Hemingway called it "Friendless" in honor of one of the Finca Vigía cats. He took to sea and for more than two years went after anything that moved around the Cuban coast between Pinar del Rio and Camagüey.

According to his plans, it would be profitable to locate a German submarine, capture it, take the crew as prisoners and if possible seize their secret codes. The success of such an action would make possible a vast operation against the German fleet known to be in waters of the North Atlantic. Some considered it a crazy plan, but Captain Daniel V. Gallery, commander of Task Group 21-12, studied a similar project and actually put it in practice in African waters. In May of 1944, shortly before the Normandy invasion, Gallery succeeded in capturing a "live" German submarine. So the plan was not really that farfetched.

In the Atlantic, German submarines worked in what became known as "wolf packs," while in the Caribbean they operated individually.

The U-boats hung around Cuba until the end of the war. At first they met little opposition. They were like dolphins on the high seas. Maybe one fine day an officer of the Nazi navy on sentry duty picked up in the cross lines of his periscope the disconcerting presence of an armed luxury yacht. We'll never know if they considered this discovery a threat, but the truth is that they did not fall for the bait. And Hemingway never forgave what he considered their condescension. He was fighting his own war. But he tried to do it at a time when the defense of the Gulf Stream was still sadly inadequate, and he had very little in the way of weaponry.

How in the world could anyone successfully attack with hand grenades and bursts of machine-gun fire a submarine armed with 88-millimeter cannon and two or three others in the 20-millimeter class? And the German IX models even boasted a 105-millimeter cannon!

Although he did not score any victory, Hemingway was able to put together a fairly efficient military unit with official backing, an operative combat organization of which he was the captain and in which he had enlisted men who shared his own life style. Moreover, he was participating in an adventure in which terms like "confidential," "paramilitary" and "intelligence missions" were used, whose official nature served to mask adolescent yearnings for heroic actions for which Hemingway succeeded in enlisting not only the folkloric characters who were his companions on his pleasure rounds in Havana, but two intelligence officers and one American ambassador as well.

[72]

"Key Paraíso was our training base," recalls Gregorio Fuentes. "Our marksmanship practice consisted of shooting at some old fuel drums on which we had painted faces we named *Hitlers*. We also simulated boarding ships and throwing grenades. We liked that key and always went back there. But one day we got a radio message instructing us to go to a certain point to pick up orders."

It was an important message. Hemingway sent Winston Guest, his second in command, and Gregorio to Bahía Honda, where they were to receive their secret orders.

"The weather was very bad," says Gregorio, "but Papa told

us that, dead or alive, we had to come back with the orders. We got to Bahía Honda around eight or nine that night, after a very rough crossing. We got a sealed envelope from our American contact, had a bite to eat and slept a while, before returning to the yacht. Soon after, we weighed anchor and headed for Camagüey, and we didn't leave that area for the next three or four months."

Those orders had taken Hemingway to an area of Cuba foreign to him: the keys north of Camagüey. Previously, the *Pilar* had sailed only from Mégano de Casigua Key to Varadero and Key West. What Hemingway saw and experienced in Camagüey, although colored by his imagination and with the addition of fictitious events, would later serve as the background for *Islands in the Stream.*

But not all of his experiences in the keys north of Camagüey went into his fiction. Some incidents remained only memories for Hemingway and his crew.

They may have been unprepared to fight German submarines, but from that adventure emerged new friendships. The men became deeply suntanned as they spent their leisure hours hunting iguanas and trying to capture some of the wild horses of Key Romano. Hemingway consumed great quantities of his favorite dish: raw crabs with lemon. He would buy crabs by the bucket from the local fishermen.

It is easy to understand how Hemingway was able to enlist nine men in his adventure, since it seemed to be such an attractive project, offering some possibility for real action and much for having a good time. As the captain, Hemingway was zealous in his duties, however, and he made his selection among men he considered to be in tune with the operation. That is why he picked a sprinkling of strong jai-alai players, that violent sport of which he had been a fan ever since his first trip to Spain. They would guarantee the muscle necessary to throw their grenades down the hatchway of the submarines when they surfaced.

This kind of operation, similar to that of the guerrillas, suited Hemingway perfectly. He wouldn't have to adhere to the army's iron discipline. Guerrilla warfare was itself rebellious, and liberal in the sense that he could wear what he pleased and use any type of weapon in a style of combat in which conventions gave way to personal ability and devotion to a cause.

Behind his preference for this type of action was his hatred for the army, as expressed in *A Farewell to Arms*, his high praise of Pablo's guerrillas in *For Whom the Bell Tolls*, and his own irreverent and undisciplined behavior in the Second World War, when he wandered through the front lines, cut off from the army, with the French guerrillas and the weapons he chose.

[73]

There are some legends that still endure about Hemingway's mission. One is about a submarine sighted by his crew which the airforce sank, thanks to their timely information; but the truth is that the Q-boat *Pilar* failed to record a single victory during the two years of its contribution to the war effort.

Previously, Hemingway had organized a group whose purpose was to infiltrate organizations in Havana which were supposed to be pro-Nazi.

According to Carlos Baker, there were three thousand Falangists in Havana at that time. In those days most of them belonged to Spanish societies which were openly in favor of Hilter. The newspaper *Diario de la Marina* supported the Axis; the German submarines roamed the region's waters with impunity.

Ellis Briggs and Bob Joyce from the American Embassy listened to Hemingway's plan for his group. Hemingway confided to Joyce that he had taken part in organizing a private intelligence agency in Madrid in 1937, and that he thought a similar organization was needed in Cuba.

The project was submitted to Spruille Braden, the new ambassador. Hemingway asked only for "minor supplies" and a little money. He offered to finance the rest of the operation, and put his home, Finca Vigía, at the disposal of the project. After discussing the plan with the Cuban premier, Braden approved it.

Baker says Hemingway's motives for the project were personal: patriotism, of course, but also the pleasure of carrying out secret plans and his desire to lead any operation, particularly if it involved firearms and taking risks. He recruited his people mostly from the Basque Club of Havana, with its anti-Fascist membership. Father Andrés, an old friend who was familiar with machine guns from the war in Spain, helped in the selection.

Hemingway tried to recruit his friend, Dr. Herrera Sotolongo. He even chose a code name for him in advance. But the Spaniard proved stubborn: "I won't be a policeman," he said. Hemingway and Winston Guest explained again in detail the purpose of the mission while relaxing by the pool at Finca Vigía, but Herrera was unconvinced: "God damn it, I'm a soldier, not a policeman! I never liked the police or spies!"

Hemingway explained that everything would be secret and that it was an important mission. "Oh, Ernesto, don't bullshit me!" was Herrera's only response. Herrera Sotolongo says that Hemingway had given himself number 08 in his secret code. Agent 08.

In the end, the Crook Factory, as this operation was called, turned into the other type of naval adventure. Hemingway tired of spying from his hilltop and getting little important information for his pains.

Gustavo Durán, former art critic and commander of the 69th Division of the Spanish Republican Army, was called from the United States at the request of his old friend, Hemingway, to take over the Crook Factory. In Cuba, Durán became American Ambassador Braden's right-hand man. He was put in charge of intelligence matters at the embassy.

Durán was called Alexander the Great as a joke by Hemingway and the people who frequented the Vigía. It seems that on a certain occasion, Hemingway invited some Franco diplomats who were passing through Cuba to a luncheon at his home. Durán and Herrera Sotolongo were invited as well. Herrera Sotolongo doesn't remember the reason why Hemingway invited them, although he was aware that it had something to do with the Crook Factory.

After a while, their conversation turned to military matters, and there was much talk about battles and their mutual contribution to the war, all apparently without anybody getting offended and with a high degree of diplomacy. Suddenly Durán broke into the conversation to declare, most emphatically, that Alexander the Great was his only master. Thereafter Hemingway called him Alexander the Great.

[74]

Born in 1894, Spruille Braden had considerable expertise and much experience in Latin American affairs. He started his career as a mining engineer and advisor to Chile on the electrification of railroads. Then he went to New York, where he was tremendously successful in business ventures.

At the age of 42 he began to represent the United States in various international assemblies. He always remained intensely interested in South America and had many investments in that region. (He married a Chilean woman.) Between 1939 and 1942 he was ambassador to Colombia.

Braden was considered a diplomat of advanced social thinking as compared to his other colleagues. Many Cubans considered him the best ambassador the United States had ever sent to Havana. However, almost all his activity there necessarily had to be military: the first instructions he received from Secretary of State Cordell Hull were that the War Department wanted "to establish, with the least possible delay, a unit of heavy bombers and operational training in Cuba," under command of United States officers, for the purpose of training Americans and British RAF personnel. This was rapidly agreed to, and San Antonio, near Havana, and San Julián in Pinar del Río, became training centers for the Allies.

Braden received instructions in July to get approval to buy land in San Julián in order to build a landing field with a seven-thousand-foot runway and to station five hundred men there under operational and administrative control of the United States. The Cubans agreed. No doubt their willingness to cooperate was conditioned by their many losses at sea from German submarines. Several Cuban freighters had been sunk in August of 1942.

During the McCarthy period in the United States, Braden and Durán were accused of being communists.

"The real leftist is Hemingway," Durán declared before a Senate Committee. "I met Braden in Hemingway's house."

He had no qualms in declaring that Hemingway was a communist, and Braden gave similar testimony. The writer was not in Cuba during the committee's session, but Herrera Sotolongo kept the newspapers that carried the story, and Hemingway was livid when he read them on his return. He swore that Durán and Braden would pay dearly for what they had done.

However, when Braden flew back to Havana, he asked to see Hemingway immediately. He claimed that he answered the questions the way he did before the Senate Committee in order to save his career. Hemingway told Herrera, "That's how he justified the lies in his testimony. However, he said he was sorry and expressed all kinds of apologies and seemed to be sincere."

Durán, on the other hand, stayed in the United States and was never heard from again on the island. Herrera Sotolongo says of Durán: "He was an art critic in Spain and during the war he joined the militia and saw some action. His fighting unit, the Duran Column, achieved some fame by carrying out successful missions in Guadarrama. But later he became Braden's 'gray eminence,' as chief of Intelligence and Information.

"On the other hand," says Herrera, "I don't remember Hemingway ever being against anything progressive. After the Civil War in Spain ended, Durán was the only Spanish exile admitted into the United States. They refused to let me enter the country because I had been in the Brigades. Later they refused to let me join the U.S. Army when I wanted to fight in Europe. Not even Hemingway's recommendation helped, and he did everything he could to assist me when I wanted to enlist."

José Regidor was one of the agents who worked with Hemingway in the secret operation called the Crook Factory. Regidor had been a corporal in the Spanish Legion in Africa before the Civil War, around the twenties. He won a decoration called "Laureada," but nobody ever knew exactly what he'd done to win it. Hemingway used to joke about it, saying: "He may be a laureate, but he's a coward. Most heroes are heroes by mistake."

Regidor had joined the expedition for the submarine hunt

on the *Pilar*, but lasted only one trip. He quit when he realized it was a serious undertaking and that it involved taking risks.

Félix Ermúa, the jai-alai player nicknamed *El Canguro* (The Kangaroo), was another participant in the operation. He was the kind of man Martha Gellhorn liked: tall, strong and handsome. According to his boasting, it seems there had been a romantic interlude between them. Later he went to Mexico and claimed he was going to marry Martha.

One day in 1943, about 40 friends gathered at the Club de Cazadores del Cerro, the hunting club, at a dinner honoring Hemingway on his birthday. One of Hemingway's so-called friends, a certain Thorwald Sánchez, a cattleman from Camagüey, started to tell some atrocious jokes about the supposed infidelities of Hemingway's wife.

Herrera Sotolongo was told by Cucu Kholy, one of the guests, to get Sánchez out of there quickly before his slander reached Hemingway's ears. "We are going to have big trouble here if Ernesto gets wind of it." Herrera managed to get Thorwald to his car and they took off at reckless speed, Sánchez at the wheel. They were on the wrong side of the narrow road and had to swerve sharply more than once to avoid an oncoming vehicle.

"When we got to the Floridita, Sánchez urinated all over the place," says Herrera Sotolongo. "I was disgusted and told the bartender, 'I'm leaving. I can't stand drunks.'

"No sooner had I left than he got into a fight, and was beaten by other customers and the help. Next day Ernesto phoned, because when he saw us leaving the club without knowing what Thorwald had said, he had whispered to me, 'Stay with him.' I told him I'd left Sánchez at the bar because I didn't enjoy going around with drunks, but I never told him the dirty gossip Sánchez had been spreading about him and Martha."

Another character in the undercover group was Adonis Rodríguez. A Spanish aviator, he had sought refuge in the Dominican Republic during the start of the dictatorship there, when Rafael Leónidas Trujillo was still willing to receive Spanish exiles.

Trujillo had not yet won his unenviable reputation as an assassin. Years later he resumed his relations with his counterpart, Francisco Franco, and decided to persecute and liquidate Spanish

Republican exiles. In the good times, Rodríguez even got to be one of the leaders of Trujillo's air force. He made frequent trips to Havana. He was charming and very articulate. He later became assistant director of the American Life Insurance Company in Havana.

The story of the Crook Factory operations had an epilogue which was conveniently hidden until very recently. Although Hemingway had been in close contact with the American authorities, from that time on the FBI engaged in surveillance of his activities. The FBI tried to hinder Crook Factory operations, for they wanted to wrest that information network from Hemingway.

J. Edgar Hoover, the FBI director, accused Hemingway of being a "communist." American researcher Jeffrey Meyers discovered the Hemingway dossier, which the FBI jealously concealed in its files. Hemingway, like Thomas Hudson, hunted fascists in one of the islands of the Stream, but, on the other side of the Old Bahamas Channel, he was the hunted one. It would have been excellent material for the novelist, but he was never aware it existed.

EL DIA
Mexico, March 13, 1983
EDGAR HOOVER CALLED HIM A "COMMUNIST"
WASHINGTON (EFE), March 12. The writer Ernest Hemingway was in charge of an "amateur spy network."

*The Washington Post*, based on the revelations made by a professor at the University of Massachusetts, said today that Hemingway's network operated in Cuba during World War II.

"The FBI agents . . . accused Hemingway of meddling in their affairs."

Edgar Hoover accused Hemingway of being a "communist." The FBI feared him because "he was already a famous writer, of international prestige, and could harm the FBI."

Hemingway committed suicide in 1961, and his *dossier* in the FBI was kept up to 1974, including numerous references, even private ones, according to his biographer, which "the FBI gathered with its own point of view as to what could be negative or damaging."

[75]

The *Pilar's* becoming part of American Intelligence caused the boat to be completely refitted.

Gregorio Fuentes received orders from the Cuban Navy to take the boat to the Casablanca shipyards for major repairs. There it was overhauled and its old gas engines renovated. Under Gregorio's supervision, carpenters built some glass holders, which were really to be used to store hand grenades out of sight. Fuentes said later, "The .50-caliber machine guns proved too heavy for the boat, but the refitting was very convenient. After the war they repaired it again. We were allowed to keep all the weapons, including antitank guns, several bazookas and Papa's S&W magnum."

Gregorio stored the arms below deck, in the cabins and in secret coves and cabinets not visible from the outside. The sign installed on the *Pilar* after its renovation work read *American Museum of Natural History*. It was meant to confuse the enemy and give the impression that the *Pilar* was a peaceful vessel on a scientific investigation.

Their scientific classification amused the crew of the *Pilar* and was the subject of many jokes. They classified everything on board—even their hats—as "scientific." The hats, wide-brimmed native *sombreros*, were used as a protection from the sun, since there was very little cover on the *Pilar's* decks. The business of the "scientific sombreros" was later used by Hemingway in *Islands in the Steam*.

Years after through the magic of fiction, Hemingway accomplished what had never happened in real life. If his Nazi submarine hunt never amounted to much, in *Islands in the Stream* he succeeded in engaging the German boats in combat, using all his war potential on an equal basis. If in real life the hull of the *Pilar* could not withstand the installation of two .50-caliber antiaircraft guns (instead there were magnetic mines, dynamite charges and antitank guns), in the book it easily accommodated two—one foreship and one astern.

The Friendless operation continued for approximately one

year. When Hemingway took off for the war in Europe, Gregorio was left in charge of the crew.

[76]

July 9, 1943
12 noon.

Dear Papa,
I shall be brief, as I know you want the conclusion first.

1. You are to return home.
2. Saxon is *not* coming to Confites.
3. Gadget was supposed to arrive July 5 or July 6 and has not arrived as yet (July 9). When gadget arrives it will be installed in Habana.
4. The Colonel himself mislaid (or lost) the Permiso, so Bob says. By now you will have received a wire from Habana office from Col saying "Permiso granted. Proceed according to Plan. Permiso will be at Cayo Frances waiting for you." Translated it means go home and pick up copy of permiso at Cayo Frances.
5. As instructed and decided between us, I have emphasized the fact that we wish to do a 100% job and would stay two weeks more if necessary to do what Bob and Col considered a first class job. I read your first (1) underlined sentence to both Bob and Col and emphasized our willingness to do whatever they desired.
   Answer: (1) Come home now.
   　　　　(2) No gadget and not sure when it will be in Habana.
6. Bob said "Come home but don't beat your brains out doing it."
7. Bob discussed Col's letter dated July 5 with Col and read it. It means "If gadget does not arrive today or tomorrow (July 5 or 6), come home." Bob again discussed the letter of the 5th yesterday (July 8) with the Col and wondered:
   (1) Why the letter of the 5th did not go out on the Margarita on the 7th to Confites (Courier brought it in Wed. P.M. and Margarita left Wed. A.M.)
   (2) Why they had not heard from you on the 8th that you were returning "according to plan."

8. I have been more than 100% conscientious and leaned over backwards to make sure we were carrying out the wishes of *both*.
9. Please keep this so, if there is any discussion about the rightness or wrongness of our move, you can take up these points one by one with the Powers that Be.

[signed] Wolf

I have discussed the mislaying of the Premiso with Don, Col and Miller. I am sure Miller forwarded *all* the mail Don gave him. I know Miller is very thorough so I am inclined to believe *he* did not mislay it. Don did not show him the contents of the envelope to be forwarded.

W.G.

This is the language of *Islands in the Stream*, its tone, its jargon, like a secret code between Wolf and Ernest.

In the next letter, the style is maintained. The characters now know each other better; the subject is similar but mixed with personal references, mention of military operations and enigmas we cannot decipher. The following names appear: Gregorio, Pache, Bumby, Marta. As in the previous letter, there are other unidentified names, probably American contact officers or Cuban operators whom they met in different ports: Miller, Bob, Roy Hawkins. Little Winston refers to the auxiliary boat of the *Pilar*, called *Tin Kid*.

(Letter written on Floridita letterhead)
Aug. 24, 43

Dear Papa -

Spent morning on boat and made the complete list—or rather complete inventory—We did not list some old tinned goods that were under my bed.

I left the map in front of car above the pedals.

Will get Polaris this PM

Left 5 large (6 lb) tins of tinned vegetables in car for Marta to use at the Finca. Gregorio quite rightly points out that boat cannot use 5 or 6 lb tins of vegetables without considerable wastage.

Can we buy what we need now through Don Saxon's *commissary*? It will save us 75%.

Re Pache and cradle for Nino—Gregorio has it written down and will see him about it tomorrow AM at 9. For the holder of the fire extinguisher Gregorio will get a carpenter.

There is nothing else except that I hope you bring my "Smoking" suit in the evening about 7. I have the other white suit for you. The dry cleaners promised it back for this morning at 10. I haven't been home but if it is not there I will call you and we can work it out with Bumby's pants and my two coats.

The current has not been running worth a damn. 7 marlin caught in the whole season. Yesterday they caught a big blue so maybe the current is starting again.

I gave Gregorio $100 to pay for work on Little Winston and other expense.

I am wiring Roy Hawkins today to find out what day we can expect the new engine—also baker attachment.

Gregorio will call Juan and go with him to have old cocina mended. The new cocina is too small but ok as spare.

If it is ok with you I won't meet you here. I am very tired and would like to rest at home—F5723 and be in good shape for tonight.

If there is anything I can do please call me there.

Your pal
Wolfie
[Winston Guest]

Winston Guest, the executive officer on board the *Pilar*, won Hemingway's affection and enthusiasm. Gregorio states that he was "Winston Churchill's nephew" and that he was "*muy preparado*," meaning well-educated and highly cultured.

"Wolfie" had won fame in England as a virtuoso polo player and also as a lady killer. The sportsman and the writer met in 1933. When Hemingway arrived in Kenya, he heard that a certain Winston Guest already counted two giant elephant tusks among his trophies. Years later Ernest succeeded in enlisting him in his antisubmarine adventure.

Lillian Ross described the emotional meeting between Guest and Hemingway in a New York store. Guest is one of the principal people who inspired Ernest's nostalgia, as expressed in his war poem "To Mary in London," written in 1944.

Mary Welsh, in her introduction to the two love poems by Ernest published in *The Atlantic Monthly* in 1965, says that her husband "shared with Winston Guest the financing of that undertaking [the antisubmarine fight]. . . . " She also says that they once sighted a Model 740 submarine and got within a mile of it.

The submarine took a northeast course and the crew of the *Pilar* later heard that it had headed for the Mississippi River, where it had put several men ashore near New Orleans. The *Pilar's* radio picked up the presence of two other submarines, which perhaps were destroyed by other forces, but "Ernest never realized his dream of entering into combat with them."

The one-time warrior, Winston Guest, ended his days as an obscure tycoon, owner of an airline. William Green's *The Observer's Aircraft Directory* stated in 1961 that "Guest Aerovías de México, S.A. is the smallest of the three Mexican international airlines," and that it carried the name of its founder, Winston Guest.

Herrera Sotolongo has no idea whether Guest was actually Churchill's nephew or any relation to him, but, on the other hand, "I was positive that he was a British agent—not as tall as I, very blond, always well groomed and very pedantic."

Juan Duñabeitía, Sinsky, and Sinbad the Sailor were one and the same person. He was a captain in the Cuban merchant marine and had worked for the García Line, which later merged with the Ward Line. That company possessed the few Cuban merchant ships in existence.

When its owners took them to the United States in 1959 at the start of the Cuban Revolution, Sinbad refused to go with them and stayed in Cuba. However, he didn't take a job and decided to return to Spain where, with the last of his money, he opened a maritime supplies store in Bilbao.

From Spain he wrote several letters to Herrera Sotolongo. One day he stopped writing and Herrera later heard that he had died. The doctor still holds all the documents that Sinbad gave him to keep for him. "Really, I don't know to whom I should send them. I'll probably burn them."

In the CIA Bay of Pigs operation in April, 1961, the following ships were used in the invasion of Cuba: the *Caribe*, the *Río Escondido* and the *Atlántico*. Strangely enough, these were the very ships on which Sinbad had been captain. The *Río Escondido* had once belonged to one of the Somozas of Nicaragua. It was a small ship of approximately two thousand tons. (Ernest was amazed at the luxury of the captain's cabin, which was completely out of proportion to the rest of the vessel.) The *Atlántico*, Sinsky's favorite boat, was the last ship in the CIA convoy the day the mercenary Brigade 2506 landed on Cuban soil. Another friend of Hemingway's, a certain Captain Zenón, was the skipper of the *Atlántico* that morning.

Zenón was at his command post and was going at half speed as his boat neared the Bay of Pigs when he became aware of the bombing. He saw the planes diving and the landing boats sinking in the bay and the thick black smoke rising where the boats sank. Then he saw an unbelievable sight: the *Río Escondido*, whose cargo was war material, including airplane fuel tanks, exploding like an atomic bomb.

He decided he had seen enough and refused to enter the Bay of Pigs. He gave orders to get out of there at full speed.

That was a bloody, interminable day for many Cubans. It was also the day in which the engines of the *Atlántico* proved they could reach a rate of speed considered far beyond their range. They went like crazy. The ship left the war zone and gained open sea, went around Cuba by the Cape of San Antonio and reached Miami with its military cargo intact: a hundred mercenaries who never saw combat and who hailed the captain as a hero, while the telegraph operator on board received a coded message from the commander of the Brigade which said: "The fish is needed at home." In other words, the *Atlántico* was ordered to return to the Bay of Pigs.

Zenón never sailed again.

He had a reputation of being tight with his money. Hemingway used to tease him about it. "I'm broke, Captain," Ernest would say. "Couldn't we arrange a loan until I win another Nobel Prize?"

[77]

In *Islands in the Stream*, Antonio tells Thomas Hudson that somebody has burned the shacks of the turtle hunters of Camagüey and there are bodies in the ashes. Hudson asks how many there are, and he is told that there are nine.

There were changes, sometimes new people, but although it could have been unplanned, the help at the Finca Vigía always numbered *nine*. When Lillian Ross visited Finca Vigía for *The New Yorker* magazine, she noted that the place was *nine* miles from Havana. She said that at the Finca there were: "his wife, a domestic staff of *nine*, fifty-two cats, sixteen dogs, a couple of hundred pigeons, and three cows."

In *Islands in the Stream*, when Hemingway compares the two houses to boats, he says that when it goes to sea, the crew of Thomas Hudson's boat numbers *nine* men. Nine bodies are found by his crew after the massacre on the key, and, of course, there are *nine* survivors of the German submarine. Those *nine* bodies are a warning of destiny, an omen which Hemingway needed in this novel of exorcism and magic, to balance the strength of his forces against the enemy force.

In the fight against the Germans they must be neither superior nor inferior. The crew under Hudson's command may have some advantage in weapons, but the Germans have in their favor time and the serenity born of the belief they had a perfect war machine.

During Hemingway's meeting with his brother Leicester in London a few days before D-Day, he mentioned the nine men of his crew and the purpose for which he had obtained the "order of marque" as in the old days.

But the original crew of the *Pilar* in the days of the Friendless operation is not reproduced with complete authenticity in the pages of the novel. The characters and anecdotes appear in combination. There are also some omissions. Only the number remains unchanged.

*Friendless:*　　　　　　　　　　　*Islands in the Stream:*
Ernest Miller Hemingway　　　　Thomas Hudson

*Friendless:*

Winston Guest (Wolfie), second in command, executive officer, millionaire, athlete, owner of an airline company.

John Saxon, telegraph operator, assigned by the American Embassy. "Not very tall," according to Gregorio, "nor very blond. But very nice." Good drinker. His transmitter didn't break as often as it does in the book. He knew his set well, and could take it apart and put it together in seconds. Very brisk in action

Gregorio Fuentes

Francisco Ibarlucia, alias Paxtchi or Pachi, jai alai player, supplier of the Fronton cafeteria. Hemingway's coach in the sport. Died in Mexico in the fifties.

Juan Duñabeitía, alias Sinsky, or Sinbad the Sailor.

Dine, Basque, strong, could easily lift the many 100-lb. containers of fuel needed for the trip. Gregorio remembers him as a "young man who suffered a lot in the Spanish war."

*Without counterpart in the book:*
Fernando Mesa, exiled Catalonian, a waiter in Barcelona, "physically weak, dark, weighing about 120 pounds."

*Islands in the Stream:*

Henry Wood

Willie, but only a "slight resemblance," according to Baker. "No one aboard was one-eyed," states Gregorio. But the Willie of the novel is one-eyed. "Neither was he hateful," adds Gregorio, although most of the characters in the book become "difficult," at one time or another.

Antonio, simultaneously cook and pilot. Hudson disapproves of the jokes the others make about Antonio's double role.

Ara, a "faithful image," according to Baker.

Juan in the novel. It's possible Hemingway gave him some of the characteristics of Dine, another member of the crew who does not appear in the book.

With Colonel Buck Lanham on the Siegfried Line, September 1944.

The map Hemingway is holding can still be seen at Finca Vigía.

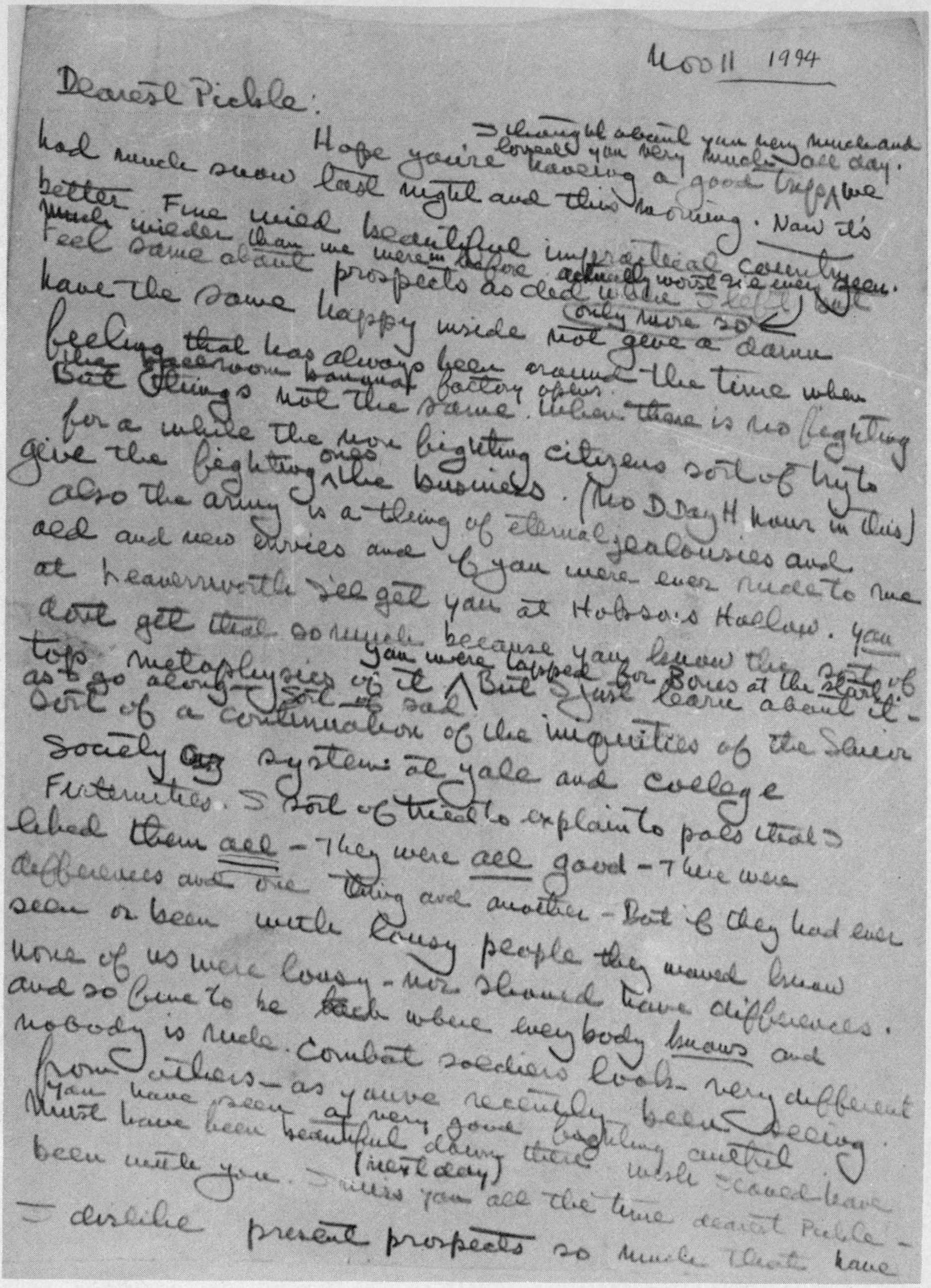

Nov 11 1944

Dearest Pickle:

Hope you're having a good time all day. I thought about you very much and loved you very much all day. Now it's fine wild beautiful impractical country...



Letter from Hemingway to "Pickle" (Mary Welsh), sent from the 4th Infantry Division advancing on Germany, November 11, 1944.

"The famous novelist Ernest Hemingway, correspondent in the battlefields of France for some time, has just arrived in Havana on the Clipper of the Pan American World Airways. The novelist will stay with us for some time."—*Diario de la Marina*, La Habana, March 25, 1945. (PAA photo)

73—HEMINGWAY—Across the River—12-15-24 Jan.

Then there was one other thing, I remember. We had put an awful lot of white phosphorous on the town before we got in for good, or whatever you would call it. That was the first time I ever saw a German dog eating a roasted German kraut. Later on I saw a cat working on him too. It was a hungry cat, quite nice looking, basically.

How many could you tell like that? Plenty, and what good would they do? You could tell a thousand and they would not prevent war. People would say we are not fighting the krauts and besides the cat did not eat me nor my brother Gordon, because he was in the Pacific. Maybe land crabs ate Gordon. Or maybe he just deliquesced.

In Hurtgen they just froze up hard; and it was so cold they froze up with ruddy faces. Very strange. They all were gray and yellow like wax-works, in the summer. But once the winter really came they had ruddy faces.

Real soldiers never tell any one what their own dead looked like, he told the portrait. And I'm through with this whole subject.

Would you join me in a glass of Valpolicella? What time do you think I should wake your opposite number? We have to get to that jewelry place. And I look forward to making jokes and to talking of the most cheerful things.

What's cheerful, portrait? You ought to know. You're smarter than I am, although you haven't been around as much.

All right, canvas girl, the Colonel told her, not saying it aloud, we'll drop the whole thing and in eleven minutes I will wake the live girl up, and we will go out on the town, and be cheerful and leave you here to be wrapped.

I didn't mean to be rude. I was just joking roughly. I don't wish to be rude ever because I will be living with you from now on. I hope, he added, and drank a glass of the wine.

Chapter—Set Style

9 IT was a sharp, cold bright day, and they stood outside

A novel in trouble? Hemingway's corrections and additions on the galley proofs of *Across the River and into the Trees.*

*Friendless:*
Lucas, Cuban, "unknown origin," according to Baker. "He helped us a lot," according to Gregorio. A pilot in the port of Caibarien, he served as guide in the keys of Camagüey.

*Islands in the Stream:*

*Without counterpart in real life:*
Peter, the hateful radio operator, evidently not a true portrait of the real radio operator, John Saxon.

Gil

George

# "The Old Man in His Bearing"

[78]

The third part of *Islands in the Stream* tells of the hunt for the survivors of a German submarine, who, it is assumed, must be heading for the Cuban coast.

At the start of the tale, Thomas Hudson and Antonio, on the flying bridge of the *Pilar*, are scanning the beach, they suppose, of Guinchos, or Jumentos. They can't find any evidence of the *tortugueros*, the turtle hunters who ordinarily live there.

It is a bad sign. They land on the key to replenish their water supply and look for traces of the Germans. What they find are the bodies of the *tortugueros*. They have been massacred. Two turtle boats are missing.

When they finally discover the corpse of a German, Thomas Hudson concludes that the German survivors must be on their way to the Cuban mainland. Unless they can capture them before they slip through the keys and reach the Central Highway, they will probably escape, for once in Havana the Germans could be smuggled into a Spanish ship bound for Europe.

The exact location of the key where the massacre took place is not made clear in the book, probably in order to fulfill the demands of the narrative. Just as Conrad changed the course of a river in the Congo to exploit it for the terrible fate of one of his characters, Hemingway altered the position of the home of the *tortugueros* and of the channel scene of the final encounter between the Nazis and their pursuers. It was not the first time Hemingway added a touch of fiction to alter a real locale.

In his story "The Big Two-Hearted River," the scorched earth is Hemingway's invention; there had never been a fire in that area. Although Hemingway described it in almost photographic detail, he did it for the sake of the story. It was not a faithful picture of the place.

The Camagüey archipelago is a series of keys, islets of irregular shape, that look like pockmarks on the face of a map. On the north the keys end in silvery beaches, and to the south in muddy swamps. The charcoal makers used to build their pyramid-shaped ovens right in the center of the territory, and at night, to the unwary sailor, a key might resemble an erupting volcano.

In *Islands in the Stream*, Thomas Hudson and his antisubmarine crew searched for the invisible enemy in this very area. "We will come back some day after the war," says Hudson. And almost forty years after Hemingway's wartime mission, Gregorio Fuentes, in the company of a photographer and a journalist, went over the region with *Islands in the Stream* as their naval chart.

Only the rustic constructions of some lookout posts of the Frontier Guard and a few fishermen's camps intrude upon the landscape that in the old days met the eyes of the *Pilar*'s crew. Yet for those who knew it then, the archipelago is greatly changed. "It has become," says Gregorio, "empty, boring."

Gregorio went back as a guest of honor. He didn't have to steer the ship or worry about kitchen duties. He wore his best tropical suit and a fine Panama hat, in the style of the forties. He thought it advisable to bring his dentures in case there was some formal occasion, but there was none. He brought an enormous suitcase, heavy with the things his wife Dolores packed with infinite patience: shoes, socks, handkerchiefs and shirts, as if he were making a trip overseas.

"Be good and write," she told her husband when they said goodbye at the door of their home in Cojímar. In contrast, the photographer's and the journalist's belongings, including cameras, film, tobacco and rum, fitted neatly into one plastic bag each.

The boat is a small vessel of the Frontier Guard, an old luxury yacht converted into a combat unit to hunt down counter-revolutionary infiltrations. In the early days of the revolution, they were the only boats that could compete with the powerful CIA speed boats. They were equipped with .50-caliber machine guns, painted gray and sent into combat. This information didn't surprise Gregorio Fuentes. He understood it perfectly, for a similar transformation had happened to the *Pilar* during another war.

To reach Key Romano, the key that figured prominently in *Islands in the Stream*, it was necessary to cross the mouth of Punta Practicos to reach the lighthouse of Maternillos, on Key Sabinal. Nearing Romano, a place where in the last century very good horse meat was sold to Havana merchants, we went slowly through the Old Bahamas Channel.

"Go on tiptoe, this is a dangerous spot," was Gregorio's advice to the helmsman, a young man wearing an olive-green uniform. The prow of the old luxury yacht took a northeastern course. It seemed days, not just a few hours, since we had left behind the city port of Nuevitas.

"I hadn't noticed all that industry before," Gregorio said when he saw the city, on our way to the bay. "My memory is failing," he added. But Gregorio couldn't remember things that did not exist in his time. The industrial buildings were of recent construction.

Navigation is complicated in the inner zone of the keys, where the charts indicate shallows of barely two feet of water. If there is an accident, you have to do the best you can with no hope of getting any help, because hardly anybody lives there now. After the revolution the keys were abandoned. The old inhabitants went to try their luck on the mainland, where living conditions were getting better every day. Only in Cayo Romano does one find some inhabitants in the houses of the settlement called Versailles. There are three families living there. On the point of the key there is a wooden house with a zinc roof. Alcides Fals Roque and his family live there.

The vessel anchors about one hundred meters from the beach, at a place called Punta de Mangle. "The Falses must be at home," says the helmsman. "They have sunk their nets." He examines the landscape through his Carl Zeiss binoculars. "There are lots of fish on that point," he adds, without taking the binoculars from his eyes.

Although Fuentes and his two companions are on a war vessel, there is no war. It's as if they were going to dig up some treasure, or find some forgotten thing in those keys, something perhaps irretrievably lost that nobody else came to look for. Hemingway's novel is their only secret chart, their only reference. And they are almost there.

They will soon be in a world lost for forty years, lost with old Papa. Gregorio is present, but he is like one more character in the novel, absorbed in his thoughts and poised on the edge of fantasy and reality. "Gregorio, don't you feel well?" "I'm all right, kid, just dozing." Maybe he meant to say, "Just dreaming."

Alcides Fals Roque has lived in Cayo Romano for more than half a century, in the same wooden house that has grown according to his needs. He kept adding rooms as the children were born, and when they grew up and married, he added more. For the last fifteen years Alcides has amused himself by papering the walls of his home with full-color magazine covers. The first covers to decorate the living room were photographs of Fidel Castro and Ernesto Guevara.

His house is the only one that can be seen from the Old Bahamas Channel, even at a distance of one nautical mile. "That house is like a beacon," says Gregorio solemnly, looking at the horizon as a flock of gulls flies overhead on its way back to land.

[79]

It ain't a place a man wants to go back to; the place don't even need to be there no more. What aches a man to go back to is what he remembers.

WILLIAM FAULKNER

Gregorio is better preserved than Alcides. He looks strong. His skin has toughened and wrinkled, but his body is still muscular. "That's because I have spent seventy years at sea," he says. But Gregorio's sea is not exactly the sea Alcides has known. Gregorio went to sea aboard the *Pilar*, handsomely paid by Papa. Alcides is twenty years younger than Gregorio. "But I'm worn out, my poor back is bent," he says.

Gregorio is well dressed. But now he wears a baseball cap instead of his impeccable Panama hat. Alcides wears an army cap whose visor is lined in red. Gregorio's voice is clear and steady, almost boyish; Alcides speaks in hoarse, broken tones, as if he had something stuck in his throat. But they understand each other; they are fishermen.

We are introduced to Alcides' family and the women retire to the kitchen to make us some coffee or to gather some coconuts and prepare a cool drink for us. Only his wife, Zoila, remains in the room, ironing some much-mended and patched pants.

"We used to sail around here many years ago in a dark boat with two long extensions on the side," says Gregorio. Alcides half closes his eyes, as if looking for an image in his personal file of memories. Gregorio adds: "A dark boat with two wings."

"Ah, but that boat was used for other things besides fishing," says Alcides. "I remember it well . . . a dark boat with Americans on board."

"Oh, God," exclaims his wife. "I remember it, too. I was a little girl then. . . . " She recalls that her mother used to do the laundry for the crew when the *Pilar* came to Versailles.

"How long ago was that?" asks Alcides, with a trace of nostalgia.

"A long time," answers Gregorio. The women come with freshly brewed coffee. Gregorio puts his cup on the table.

"Don't you want it?" asks Zoila.

"I just like to let it cool a bit," answers Gregorio.

Gregorio and his companions went into Key Confites. A heavy squall obscured the sun and the afternoon suddenly grew very dark. By nighttime a strong wind from the west whipped the north coast and pushed the squall to another zone.

Gregorio was on deck. Thirty-five years ago there had been a naval station here, the one mentioned in *Islands in the Stream*, and it was here the *Pilar* picked up such supplies as pigs, turkeys and chickens. A boat called *La Enviada* brought ice regularly.

"Papa used to strut ashore, vigorous as all hell, as if he owned the place," says Gregorio. But by 1977, all that was left of the old Confites was the trace of old gardens, all gone to weed.

The beach where Hemingway and his men used to land has receded and the rocks are naked. Gregorio seems annoyed, as if someone were responsible for the key's yielding land to the sea. "There were so many plants here before—now it is bare. So many beautiful palms, and now not even one left. The key has grown old." But there are seven pine trees left on the key. No more, no less. They were planted by Hemingway in 1943. "I'll be damned!" exclaims Gregorio when he sees them. "If only the old man knew that his pines are still here!"

When Gregorio returns to the boat, he adds: "A merchant ship ran aground near Confites once and it became one of the landmarks for the crew of the *Pilar* as we approached the coast." The ship he refers to is the *Colabi*. The only thing left from the wreck is a metal sheet, difficult to identify, abandoned on that lonely beach.

That night Gregorio was a happy man. He was given an AK-U7 gun and allowed to fire it. He was entrusted with the wheel of the old yacht, now guarding the coasts. He was a proud captain. He became talkative and confident, in full command of the situation. He drank rum and seemed to be thoroughly enjoying himself.

Lieutenant Humberto Pascual, chief officer of the boat, told him: "Old man, you are a barometer, a real sailor who has spent his life observing the weather. You could steer this ship with your eyes closed. You're very cautious, but that's good. You'll live a long time."

"Like Papa's pine trees?" Gregorio asked, and then, with a laugh: "Yes, that's it, like Papa's pine trees."

Gregorio knew the novel *Islands in the Stream* only by hearsay. We had to read him the parts where he was mentioned, explaining that the character Antonio was meant to be Gregorio. That night he was not amused by a joke in the book about his double role as skipper and cook.

In the novel, Willie, a character slightly based on John Saxon, makes fun of Antonio because of that double occupation. Willie thinks it improper that on a warship, or any boat of distinction, the captain should also be the cook. At that moment Hudson tells him sternly: "Antonio knows more about the handling of small boats than the rest of us together, including you."

Everybody on board the boat that night had a feeling of well-being as we sailed near the coast of Camagüey. It isn't every day that one can take a literary character into the real-life scene of his fictional story.

Next day Gregorio Fuentes landed once more at the Paredon Grande, site of the lighthouse painted in black and yellow squares. In the book Antonio goes there in search of information. Now Gregorio says: "This is exactly the same as it was then. Maybe that little house back there is new."

The lighthouse serves a busy navigation zone in the Old Bahamas Channel. In the time of Hemingway's adventures it had a powerful beam that could be seen for 35 miles. Now its light is more powerful and reaches an extra 15 miles. The lighthouse is 120 years old.

"The one at Maternillos has a bronze handrail that shines like gold," recalls Gregorio. "Papa loved the well water we drank here in Paredon Grande, but he also liked going to Maternillos. I remember that we went aground between Media Luna and Guillermo."

"Yes," answered Lieutenant Pascual, who is very knowledgeable on this area. "It is very possible that you were grounded there."

It is true that they were grounded at that point. The experience was used in *Islands in the Stream*, in a passage that mixes frustration and relief. Hemingway describes Media Luna as a cheerful key, where he was happy. In the book, Thomas Hudson uses the key as a point of reference to guide his boat towards the Pasa de Contrabando, a narrow channel known only to the fishermen, deep enough to carry his boat. Hudson was searching through his binoculars for the keel of a half-sunk ship, one of the many wrecks found in the area, when his boat ran aground. The place where that ship foundered was marked on his map.

When we got to the place, Gregorio Fuentes, the photographer and I couldn't find the wreck, even with the Carl Zeiss binoculars. It seemed to be the first inaccuracy of the novel. Gregorio and I went in a rowboat to look over the area, Gregorio at the oars. We rowed away from the boat, made a half-turn—as the book indicates—but no luck. Gregorio couldn't remember the exact place.

"I told you—my memory is failing," he said.

The oars hit some iron, and I jumped into the water. It wasn't deep. The sand was white and very fine. Then I saw a steel beam, a boiler, pieces of a boat resting just beneath the surface. At first sight they seemed rusty and useless. Thirty years is a long time, even for an old hull.

"As I told you—if Papa says so in his book, you can bet on it that it's true," Gregorio said.


[80]


Gregorio told some tales about his trips around that area. One of them had to do with a fisherman they had found adrift, half dead, on the Gulf Stream. Gregorio sighted the fisherman's boat and brought the *Pilar* near it, the rest of the crew on alert.

Hemingway asked his captain: "What can that be, Gregorine? What could have happened?"

Gregorio answered that they had to get to him first, and then find out what had happened. They found the man with a foot mangled by a spearfish, "a marlin," they thought.

Hemingway immediately offered a bottle of whiskey, for the man was in unbearable pain. He had been drifting under a hot sun for hours, with a seriously injured foot and no medical attention.

The nearest landfall was Nuevitas, some hundred miles away. The fisherman's turtle boat didn't have a chance to make it there. Neither would the *Pilar*, because of its weight and crew.

Hemingway turned to Gregorio and asked: "What do you think we can do?"

"I'll try to make it in ten hours, through the inshore keys," Gregorio answered.

"Get going, Gregorine," Hemingway said.

Gregorio boarded the *Pilar*'s auxiliary, a small motor boat, and got the wounded man. Hemingway gave him three bottles of whiskey. The man drank the first one without even stopping for breath, and got groggy. "He needs that," said Hemingway approvingly. "It's the only thing he can do." They were all heavy drinkers, but they admired the way the man grabbed the bottle and gulped it down. He was half asleep now.

Gregorio starts off for the keys. Now he recalls that day: the glassy-eyed, wounded man and the bottle of whiskey. The man moans, almost asleep, and the leg is swelling rapidly.

Gregorio offers him more whiskey. He no longer gulps it down but takes big sips, and Gregorio, who needs some fuel as well, joins him. There's not a drop left and they have thrown the bottles overboard when they sight the pier at Nuevitas. An American army ambulance is waiting. The *Pilar* had sent a message ten hours before, and now help is at hand.

They carry the man to the ambulance. Gregorio will stay behind to take care of his boat. The fisherman has just enough time to shake his hand in gratitude.

Gregorio hadn't been back to Nuevitas since that day. Now the conversation turns to the fate of the old fisherman of that time, during the war. An officer of our Frontier Guard boat suggests we visit one of them.

Miguel Montenegro Roque is 80 years old. During the Second World War he sailed the area where the German submarines roamed, but can offer little information about those days, because he is senile and cannot put his thoughts together.

From the interior of his house, another fisherman emerges to attend to the unexpected visitors. He is a short, solidly built man. Lame, he walks dragging his feet. He asks us to excuse him; he wasn't expecting anybody.

The officer of the boat tells him that we were passing by and decided to drop in. He explains that Gregorio is an old fisherman and sailor who was in the area during the war and now has come back with a photographer and a writer who are doing a "documentary" about that time.

José Roque, 63 years old, is called Felo. He sits down with some difficulty because of his handicap. "Oh, this arthritis in my knee," he moans. He is a native of Nuevitas who fished in the old days, but fishing is no longer the same, because the "*quelonios*"—tortoise shell turtles—are no longer plentiful.

"That's true," agrees Gregorio. "Fishing has declined a lot."

"The problem is that the line now in use is a marvel," says Felo Roque. "It's a '*capron*' line from Spain. Any fish that touches it is a fish done for."

"There's too much fishing," Gregorio says. As always, when he talks, he seems younger than the other fishermen.

"That's because there are many fishing grounds. Before, there were only two, three or four. They were Punta de Piedra de Sabinal, Punta de Ganado, Aguada del Inglés, Cayo Romano, El Mangle, and another one in La Guajaba."

Those were the fishing grounds where the *Pilar* sailed during its antisubmarine adventure. On board the *Pilar* they were drinking rum and offering themselves as bait to lure and catch the Germans. Meanwhile, the humble fishermen of North Camagüey went about earning a living at their ordinary occupation.

"Too much fishing makes the fish disappear," Felo Roque says. "Now they even catch the turtle eggs."

Roque remembers that he did a lot of fishing during World War II: "We sold the tortoise shell for forty cents a pound. Very cheap. Nothing was worth anything."

We ask him to tell us the characteristics of the turtle boats that sailed the area in times of war. In his novel, Hemingway describes the skiff used by the shipwrecked Germans as a turtle boat.

"Well, the turtle boat was a small sailboat, not a motorboat. The *Canario*, belonging to Alcides Fals, was one of those boats. The turtle boat is an open boat. More comfortable that way to work on all sides. As you work, you go either by sail or rowing. We catch them in the nets. We sink the nets inshore up to very near the reefs: 12 or 15 hundred feet of net, and we used to bring a small glass box with us, which we dropped into the water so we could see.

"One tried to catch the turtles live. The smallest ones are 40 or 50 pounds. But some caught are between 200 and 400 pounds.

There are differences between the green turtle and the logger-head. The loggerhead has a dark shell and is very fine. The green turtle is speckled, but very fine, too. The hawk bill is very nervous, and its colors are brighter.

"My boat was 18 feet long and six feet wide. Only one mast and one *botalón* sail. I tied it to the mast when I worked. No anchor, of course. And an open boat without cover, under the sun.

"We lived on the fishing grounds. We had nothing to cook on board. The net is cast for nine days. We used Spanish twine and later very bad cotton cord. We lived in a tent. We had a wood stove in the key. We ate rice, fish and turtle meat, and drank coffee. And a little rum to tone the body."

It's a good time for Gregorio to uncork a bottle. He opens it skillfully with a knife, and we start to drink.

"Did you also fish in this zone?" Roque asks.

"Fishing, really fishing, no. I was on a mission."

"What kind of mission was that?"

"A scientific mission," Gregorio explains. "We were on a boat doing scientific research."

"You probably ran into each other around here," I said.

"I used to come in a dark boat—the *Pilar*."

"A dark boat," Roque says, looking steadily at Gregorio. "A dark, strong boat. A wide boat with two long sticks on its sides that looked like two lobster feelers. A boat full of Americans, with a skipper from the Canary Islands. A strong guy who was a millionaire. And another one, with a beard, whom they called the Americano."

"That was my boat," Gregorio says. "And I was the Canarian."

"Oh, damn," says Felo Roque. "Oh, balls! This fucking life. So it was you! One day you appeared on the horizon, and another fine day, months later, you disappeared."

"We left forty years ago, a whole lifetime. And you remember."

"I used to go on board your boat every day," Roque says. Don't you remember that boy, kind of short and stocky, on the ugly side, but strong, to whom you used to give the catch of the day? That was me."

"That was you. . . . " Gregorio says. And he admits frankly, "I truly couldn't remember your face."

"That was me," says Roque. "There was a guy, a friend of mine, Vincente the Andalusian. If only he were here now! He used to say that he would be in debt to all of your forever, because one of you saved his life. He was taken by boat all along the inner passages of the keys until they landed in Nuevitas, where they took care of his injured foot."

"I was the one," says Gregorio. "I took that man to Nuevitas. Where is Vincente the Andalusian?"

"Oh, damn! Balls!" exclaims Felo Roque. "Let me shake your hand, by God."

The two rise and shake hands.

"Let's have some rum."

"If only Vincente could have seen you."

"Doesn't he sail any more?"

"He's been with God some years now—he was already an old man when you saved his life. He's been dead around twenty years."

"What happened to him that day?"

"A stingray gored his foot, like a nail. I was alone taking up line when I saw him lying there, eyes bloodshot and popping out of the sockets. He was foaming at the mouth from great pain. He managed to tell me that a *lebisa*, a ray, had pierced his foot with a lash of its tail. I told him to hang on and wait for the American boat, a very good yacht. I told him you were well-supplied, with a canteen foreship. And that I knew you. 'Go find them, damn it,' he said. But I didn't see you on the way I took. It was he who ran into you."

Gregorio is amused by the reference to the canteen, and tells him that although it was not exactly a canteen-bar, the kitchen, it's true, was very well supplied.

The Andalusian recovered from the foot injury. He was very grateful to Gregorio.

"Every afternoon I went on board your boat. You gave me the fish."

"You didn't drink much," Gregorio says.

"That's right, not much. I used to tell Montenegro about

the boat and how well you treated me. But I never saw arms on board."

"That's because we worked well," Gregorio answers with pride.

"I remember the wine you offered me," Roque says. "The leather wine bags hung everywhere on the boat. I remember that boat—how could I ever forget!"

[81]

It was a little bar on the roof of the Hotel Ambos Mundos. There Ernest Hemingway would often sit, a drink in front of him, watching night fall slowly over the Havana of 1934. He would also stand in front of the window on the fifth floor, where he could see Old Havana, the Plaza of the Cathedral and the roofs of the city. Behind the roofs, all on one level, he could see part of the port. This is the fragmented landscape he described in his *Esquire* article, "Marlin Off the Morro."

Today, opposite that roof and window there is a building which hides the view he loved from sight. And the new building has mortally wounded the colonial architecture.

Marcelino Piñeiro was the waiter assigned to Hemingway's room in the Ambos Mundos. After the writer's death, Piñeiro kept Hemingway's thick, moth-eaten set of *Don Quixote* in Room 525, where it had always been. He would frequently make the old mahogany bed and dust the empty work table.

Downstairs, at the entrance on Obispo Street, there is a plaque with the information that during the decade of the thirties, the author of *The Old Man and the Sea* lived there.

In 1934, the Cuban writer Fernando G. Campoamor met Hemingway. The Cuban, an intimate of the famous, had already corresponded with Faulkner and Dos Passos.

One day at Ambos Mundos he went over to Hemingway and embraced him. From then on the two men were companions during the sunsets at the little bar. Their friendship lasted more than twenty years.

Campoamor recalls that one of Hemingway's great friends

in those days was the boxer Kid Tunero. The author of *A Farewell to Arms* was impressed by the gentlemanly manner of the Cuban prizefighter.

"The guy is decent and elegant," Hemingway would comment softly. "He never hits in excess. With his opponents, he is the master, but never abusive."

In a photo of Kid Tunero which Campoamor kept, and which can be seen in the living room at Finca Vigía, the fighter is smelling a flower.

[82]

In Old Havana, next to the Plaza of the Cathedral, Cubans have a very special place to drink their rum. Three generations of artists have passed through its doors. It's an uncomfortable, hot place, but in the turbulent Havana of the fifties it managed to steal customers from the luxurious Tropicana.

The place is called La Bodeguita del Medio. Its founder, Angel Martínez, arrived in Havana in the late thirties. One of his customers was Ernest Hemingway, who started to go to the Bodeguita during the forties, accompanied by Paco Garay, a Cuban customs inspector married to an American girl, who exported parakeets to the United States.

According to hearsay, around that time Hemingway coined the phrase that appears on the sign which still graces the bar of the establishment: "My daiquiri at the Floridita. My mojito at the Bodeguita."

Angel Martínez says that he told Hemingway the story of the origin of the mojito, the drink that immortalized the Bodeguita. It is a cocktail made with rum, sugar, ice, water and mint. Martínez claims that Francis Drake invented the drink, which is why it was initially called the Drake.

Campoamor, however, has another story. He says that Hemingway never set foot in La Bodeguita, and that the sign is only a publicity stunt he invented to help his friend, Martínez, when he owned the place. Visiting Havana in 1978, Margaux Hemingway, the writer's granddaughter, said that the names of Martínez and Bodeguita were legendary in her family. After the revolution, Martínez turned over the business to the government and he is now manager of the place he once owned.

Martínez sticks to his story. He also remembers that "Hemingway feared the company of solitude," and says that we, the Cubans, should keep his memory close to us, although if truth be told, he was "kind of hard to take."

Martínez uses a popular Cuban expression to describe the American writer: *"Era un saco de madarrias."* In other words, a difficult guy.

[83]

The Havanese, who during the thirties walked frequently along the busy thoroughfare called Obispo Street, sooner or later would run into a certain extraordinary character at any point in the nine blocks between the Hotel Ambos Mundos and the Floridita.

This character was a thirty-year-old American, heavy set and absent-minded, who strolled in the direction of the bar with a resigned air of someone doing his duty. He would be wearing moccasins and a cotton shirt. But what caught the attention of passersby and provoked more than one mocking comment were the faded khaki shorts he insisted on wearing.

In the distance he covered between the Ambos Mundos and the Floridita, Hemingway gave international fame to a myth: the daiquiri. Cubans had other means of combating the tropical heat, but the writer preferred Mr. Constante's frozen cocktail.

The landscape of the old part of the city, the writer's walks and the existence of the Floridita remained unchanged for a decade.

Then the installation of a powerful air-conditioner in the neighboring bar called the Pan American seemed to mark a new era: the beginning of the end of the Floridita.

The Pan American opened between 1948 and '49, though its regular customers can't remember the precise date. It was the first bar in Cuba to have a cooling system. Antonio Meilán, one of the oldest barmen at the Floridita, remembers that it wasn't long before his customers left him for the refrigerated Pan American.

"Everybody said that the drinks we prepared here were delicious, but the heat was unbearable. We had great four-bladed fans rotating on the ceiling, but the draft they created mussed the ladies' hairdos."

The moment came when, in 1948 or '49, Mr. Constante, the owner of the Floridita, had to break tradition and deeply rooted custom centuries old. For a long time he had insisted on keeping the Floridita as it had always been, with its eleven doors wide open.

Cuban bars and grocery stores, called "bodegas," always had long, dark wooden counters flush with the sidewalk and open to the street. This was the classic native bar, with a space behind the counter where the barmen worked. The shelves behind them held hundreds of bottles of liquor.

Each day the Floridita was opened and closed by means of great metal shutters that were rolled up or down. When they were rolled up the whole place was open, which gave one the impression of being out in the street and under cover at the same time. Originally it was a Spanish custom, but is now widespread in Cuba.

It became the custom to have a "bodega" at every corner, and most of these stores had a bar as well. Sometimes it was just a bar, like the Floridita. One drank standing up, resting a foot on the rail, even though most bars provided high wooden stools for the customers.

When Constante begrudgingly consented to install an air-conditioning system in his bar, he did it on one condition. He told the technicians: "All right, install the damn thing, but leave my place open." They had to explain to him the technical impossibility of such a request. Constante argued and extolled some of his strange theories about "keeping something cold." Not in vain had he been the creator of the frozen daiquiri, to this day considered the most refreshing and appropriate drink for Cuba or any other country with a hot climate.

"The important thing about ice," he said, "is to present it with a challenge. It is on this island where it acquires its own personality."

Antonio Meilán, the veteran bartender, recalls the exact day he began to work at the Floridita. It was October 30, 1939, and by then Hemingway was already its most important customer. He doesn't remember clearly whether Hemingway was there that day or in Spain, but he does recall that the two most important people at the Floridita were Constante and Hemingway.

"Hemingway didn't seem to care about the installation of air-conditioning at the Pan American Bar. He remained loyal to the Floridita."

He may have been influenced by the fact that the installation of air-conditioning required putting up cement walls to enclose the place. It was well known that Hemingway loved open spaces and liked the possibilities offered by all those open doors.

On the occasions when he had to settle problems with his fists at the bar, the absence of walls gave him more freedom of action and the opportunity to throw his opponent into the street.

After the air-conditioning system was installed at the Floridita, Hemingway did have one or two encounters; but it was never the same again, because he had to go outside to fight and by the time he reached the street he was no longer angry.


[84]


Lisandro Otero, the writer, recalls that when he was a young newspaperman he recognized the famous novelist one afternoon at the Floridita, as Hemingway sat reading and writing with great concentration. Otero went over and introduced himself. For an answer he got a fast jab, which he managed to dodge and which suggested that he should find a place to sit at a considerable distance.

Hemingway tried to explain his action by saying that "a writer must never be interrupted," especially when he is concentrating.

There are several variations on the "interruption" theme; for example, "When a man is drinking, nobody has the right to interrupt him."

In the case of the young writer Lisandro Otero, the experience left him with a slight feeling of frustration. Hemingway had been the idol of his student days, and to suddenly see him in the bar only a few feet away, alone and writing, was "like meeting God."

Otero explains: "I wanted to tell him that I was a student and that I admired everything he wrote. In those days I thought it was fine to admire *everything*."

Otero wasn't alone that day, and his companion was no weakling but an athlete who exclaimed: "What the hell is the matter with that old drunk?" But Otero showed great patience, and he and his friend ate their dinner in another room of the Floridita. Then they were told that Hemingway had paid their bill.

When they were leaving, the "old man" signalled to them and greeted them, and then attempted to explain his behavior.

"The thing is that people are always interrupting, particularly when one is concentrating." Then he told Otero: "Do you know where I live in San Francisco? Well, stop by some afternoon."

The following Sunday, Otero showed up at the gate of the Finca Vigía. He told the gatekeeper that he was the student Hemingway had met recently at the Floridita.

"Naturally," says Otero, "I wasn't about to tell him I was the guy he had tried to punch."

He doesn't remember how the information was relayed from the gate to the house, 300 meters away—whether it was by telephone or intercom. He doesn't remember anyone being sent over with the message. All he remembers is that Hemingway gave orders for him to proceed to the house.

Hemingway greeted him at the door. There was a party, or some similar affair, going on at the Vigía. The living room was packed with people, "almost all of them American," and there was a Spanish trio singing Flamenco songs.

After a polite exchange of courtesies, Hemingway told Otero to feel right at home and enjoy himself. He then asked to be excused, because he had to attend to other guests.

René Villarreal, wearing his *filipina*, was going around carrying a tray of drinks. He offered Otero a whiskey on the rocks. After half an hour, Otero decided he felt out of place, and, without taking leave of the host, left Finca Vigía.

Almost twenty years later, Otero, now considered one of Cuba's most prestigious revolutionary writers, wrote an essay on Hemingway in which he praised the American's literary and political values and told the anecdote of their meeting at the Floridita.

Hemingway remains one of his literary idols and he regards Lady Brett, in *The Sun Also Rises*, as one of the great female characters in all literature.

Juan David, the caricaturist, tells a similar story about Hemingway's character: his apologetic sincerity for his "bad behavior." Hemingway was drinking in a café in Old Havana, near the Floridita. David was there with some friends. Hemingway and a lady were at a table nearby. The lady was Mary Welsh. The place, called El Templete, still exists, although today it offers a different menu. David remembers the exact date, because it marked Germany's surrender in Europe—May 7, 1945.

A wandering artist appeared on the scene. He started to sketch Hemingway's portrait without Ernest being aware of it. He finished it in a matter of minutes and approached the writer's table in the hope of making a little money. Usually he'd get a peso or two from his subject. He interrupted the conversation between Hemingway and Mary to say: "Please help a Cuban artist."

Hemingway looked at the sketch in amazement—a few wavering pencil lines, with erasures, on an ordinary piece of paper—and then slammed his fist on the table, crushed the paper between his hands and threw it on the floor, saying: "My boy can do better!"

The man, seeing the sad end of his labor, answered: "But your son has enough money to pay for his studies. If I had money, I would be a better artist. The little I know I've learned on my own." And he left El Templete.

Hemingway asked the bystanders if they knew the man. Their answers were too vague for Hemingway, who guiltily went out looking for the man. But he couldn't find him. Later, Hemingway left a twenty-dollar bill with the manager of El Templete to give to the poor artist when he came around again, with the message that he was truly sorry.

David thinks that Hemingway's reaction was simply irritation at being interrupted. Also, he just didn't like any drawings of himself.

David drew half a dozen caricatures of Hemingway which were published throughout the years in the most important publications in Cuba. "We met often," he says, "but he never said a word, never made a single comment about them."

[85]

The liquor store known as "El Florida" was originally called "La Piña de Plata"—The Silver Pineapple. The name change occurred almost a century later. The shop was opened in 1820 in a city shaped like a cogwheel, due to the many right-angled indentations in the wall that surrounded it, in the style of such European towns as Avila in Spain, Nancy in France and Turin in Italy.

The population (85,000 inhabitants) overflowed the perimeter of the walled city, and a marginal village grew outside its limits. Through the gates in the stone wall of the city there was a constant flow of people coming and going, in carts, carriages or on foot.

The population within the wall depended for its existence on the land and cattle brought from the ranches and farms outside the wall. Among entrances and exits no gate was more important than the one at Monserrate, connecting with O'Reilly and Obispo Streets.

Pedestrians gathered in great numbers at the gates, and according to reports: "At the corner of Obispo and Monserrate one heard all about what was going on and who was going by, if one went to or near the *bodega* called 'La Piña de Plata,' a strategically located tavern, where the traveler fell into a pleasure trap as he stopped to down some wine or stronger spirits."

Citizens of every description drank together at its rustic tables and counters. It was a typical colonial combination store and tavern called *bodegón*, where well-dressed gentlemen drank their gin, rum or vermouth, while the ladies, under their silk parasols, waited in their carriages for their drinks of honey water, sherbets or fruit juices.

Although La Piña de Plata opened in 1820, the "Era of Ice"

had its start ten years earlier, when in 1810, the first shipment of block ice arrived in Havana from Boston.

Since the introduction of this novelty, drinking fruit juices, either iced or frozen into sherbets, quickly became a habit in the stifling Cuban heat. The serving of all kinds of tropical fruit in the form of cold drinks, shakes, ices, sherbets or ice creams, "opened a gap in the wall of prejudice that had surrounded women," and which until that time had kept them out of all bars.

Naturally, there had to be some changes made in the architecture of places like La Piña de Plata and in the image of the rough *bodegones*. But from then on in La Piña de Plata and other similar establishments, "native ladies" would sit and freely enjoy their cold drinks or confections behind discreet shutters or screens which allowed the light from the street to filter in.

It was during the period of the first American military intervention (1898-1902) that the name La Piña de Plata was changed to "El Florida," more pleasing to the taste of the new masters of the Cuban economy and political life. Other customs were introduced as well. Cocktails became very popular. The newly christened bar became known to its customers as "El Floridita." In many of Hemingway's books it appears with the feminine article, "La Floridita."

Constantino Ribailagua, a *cantinero*—later to be called barman—started working at the Floridita in 1914. He was a Spaniard from Catalonia, and the customers renamed him Constante. In time, thanks to his considerable savings, he became owner of the Floridita. He must have arrived in Cuba before 1902, when the country became independent, for it was then that a law was passed which said that all foreigners who applied for citizenship would be considered native-born citizens.

Today the building remains basically unchanged. Alterations were made over the old structure. In this way the style of the Floridita was created: a kind of "Cuban neoclassic," with columns and a wooden frame, a solid structure with great mirrors behind the bar.

Here in this ambience in the forties, invariably at noon, the leading personalities of Cuban society, merchants and politicians, gathered daily. It became their favorite place to meet and discuss business.

Constante soon became known as the master of his trade. Certainly, Hemingway considered him number one. He used to say of him: "His work is a ceremony of order and cleanliness." Constante invented an estimated 150 drinks, with an accent on rum, sugar and Cuban fruits.

His masterpiece was the daiquiri. According to Fernando G. Campoamor, who is "the historian of Cuban rum," the daiquiri owes its prominent place in the manuals of the trade to Constante. Hemingway had only words of praise for that notable drink and the clean mahogany bar which he used as background for one of the longer passages in his literary works.

In a review of the world's most famous bars which appeared in the December 1953 issue of *Esquire*, the Cuban Floridita was compared to the Raffles Bar in Singapore, the Hotel Shelbourne in Dublin, the 21 Club in New York, the Ritz bar in London, the Ritz in Paris, and the bar of the Hotel Palace in San Francisco.

In the thirties, during one of his strolls along Obispo Street or on the street parallel to it, O'Reilly (another one of the streets he loved), Hemingway dropped in and soon became a regular at the Floridita. Before long, he made a cozy corner for himself at one end of the bar, acting as a sort of host to all comers, personalities of the most diverse hues and professions, both Cuban and foreign.

Until the end of the fifties, the Floridita was the meeting place for most of the celebrities living in or passing through Havana. From the mid-sixties on, that honor fell to the Bodeguita del Medio. There is no doubt that Hemingway's bulky presence contributed to the prestige of the Floridita.

Not long after Hemingway received the Nobel Prize, his friends decorated his favorite corner with a bust of the writer. For years after the Floridita became the property of the state, the waiters and management of the place didn't allow anyone to occupy the one seat under the bust that had always been reserved for Hemingway.

Fernando G. Campoamor says that "it is very sad to go to the Floridita," and he seldom goes there now. He comments in a mocking tone that on the fact that it is forbidden to occupy the seat that had belonged to Papa. He confides that he told the new management of the Floridita that it was time to forget about the legend and put the corner back in use.

"It is not that they had put up a rope or chain, the way they do in museums—it's just that they didn't let anyone sit there."

It was in that first corner to the left, according to Campoamor, where Papa invented the Daiquiri Special, also known as the Papa Double or Hemingway Special, or the name that is seldom used but which Hemingway much preferred, the "Wild Daiquiri."

The difference was suger. The daiquiri and everything Hemingway drank was absolutely sugarless. Some people said that Ernest never had anything sweet because he was diabetic. But his doctor, Herrera Sotolongo, assures us that this was not the case.

In *Islands in the Stream*, Thomas Hudson comments while he shaves: "I don't use sugar, nor smoke tobacco, but by God I get my pleasure out of what they distill in this country."

He was referring to the good Cuban 90-proof pure sugar cane alcohol, which he not only drank when refined into native rums but liberally doused over his face after shaving. It is still as cheap in Cuba as rubbing alcohol.

The classic daiquiri is a mixture of rum, lemon and sugar over crushed ice, with a dash of maraschino.

Hemingway simply asked Constante to give him a daiquiri without sugar. Later, doubtless to save time and energy, he started to order doubles. And the Wild Daiquiri came into being, the "daiquiri a la Papa."

Hemingway's war against sugar in his drinks is described at some length in *Islands in the Stream*. During his many conversations with Honest Lil, the waiters, the Worst Mayor, and Ignacio Natera Revello, every time he orders a drink (invariably a daiquiri), Thomas Hudson adds the stipulation *without sugar*.

At the end of this passage, when his beautiful ex-wife appears, she asks him how many drinks he's had and Hudson tells her he's had about a dozen.

Another time the bartender, Serafin, asks him if he is going to break his own record, and he replies that he is just drinking with calmness.

But no mention is made of what the record was. A dozen daiquiris seemed to have been his average at one sitting, an amount equal to approximately a 26⅔-ounce bottle.

Antonio Meilán, a barman recognized in Havana as an authority on the daiquiri, says that Hemingway could drink more than a dozen daiquiris in one afternoon. If he had neglected to bring his thermos bottle, he would carry one of his Specials home in a large chilled glass filled with lots of ice and wrapped in a napkin. Hemingway had every right to call this drink "one for the road."

There are other legends about the true origin of the daiquiri, but if it wasn't really created at Constante's Floridita, it acquired both its fame and notoriety there. It was mixed with finesse and precision, exactly timed in the blender and served in a frosted glass.

Constante never claimed he had fathered the daiquiri. He merely said that Floridita was the place where the daiquiri had been cradled, not born.

Constante, born Constantino Ribailagua y Vert, died on December 2, 1952. Hemingway went to his funeral and said: "The master of saloonkeepers is dead. The Floridita was his creation. He was a very clean man. Bartending to him was an art."

At Constante's death, his widow took over the business. In honor of the great saloonkeeper, she planned a memorial approved by Hemingway and some of his friends. She placed a portrait of Constante on the first column to the right, as one enters, and ordered a laurel wreath of gold to serve as a border for the picture.

Mario Arellano, a decorator who at the time was doing over the Floridita, had a wreath made of a yellow metal at a cost of $500. When the widow saw the bill she asked why it was so little. The decorator explained, and the widow insisted that it be made of real gold. Hemingway approved the motion, saying, "Constante deserves a gold crown."

The new wreath cost five thousand dollars, but it still wasn't real gold. The decorator had merely given the metal a golden bath, and pocketed the balance of the money. Until he left Havana for the last time, Hemingway remained a faithful customer. He honored Constante in *Islands in the Stream*.

The Floridita has survived. Thirty years later the waiters

are just as busy, and today you can still see Antonio Meilán there, wearing the sumptuous white and purple uniform of the bartenders and waiters. But in the bar's latest remodeling in 1975, Constante's picture and the wreath were eliminated. The place isn't the same without Constante and Hemingway.

Mary Hemingway refused to visit the Floridita during her return visit to Cuba in 1977. She said that there were no longer any prostitutes or *maricones* (fags) there and she was no longer interested. Some members of the Cuban escort resented her comment, but, in a way, one can understand her attitude. She didn't want to revisit a place which, for her, would have a museum-like quality.

Today the Floridita still offers some of the best cuisine in Havana. You can find choice lobsters and seafood, and the bar is still first-class. Fernando G. Campoamor says that "there's still the Hemingway aura in the place."

There are twenty-one bar stools; on the other side of the room are the ten tables; separated from the bar by a wall is the restaurant. The decoration is English and the glassware Baccarat. In 1954, when the bust of Hemingway was unveiled, a bronze plaque was placed over the first seat to the left, where the writer always sat. It reads:

> To our friend Ernest Hemingway
> Nobel Prize in Literature
> Floridita

"I don't deserve so much," Hemingway told the waiters at the unveiling. "It's too great an honor."


[86]


In *Islands in the Stream*, Hemingway's devotion to the Floridita had been immortalized with his customary accuracy.

The description of Serafín García Lago is a faithful one. It is true that Lago was bothered by the presence of people like Honest Lil at the bar. Another character in the book is Pedrico, whose model in real life was Manuel Lopéz Laza, known as Pedrito. Ignacio Natera Revello's prototype was Alvaro González Gordon, younger son of the old Marquis of Torre Soto, head of the family González de Jerez de la Frontera, owners of the company that produces González Byass wines.

One of Hemingway's Cuban friends, Mario Menocal—"Mayito"—identified Natera Revello for Carlos Baker, but neglected to say that the portrayal of the Worst Politician was patterned after his own brother, Raul García Menocal, mayor of Havana in the forties.

Another character, present when Thomas Hudson and the Worst Mayor visit the lavatory, is Emmanuel Seale, native of Barbados, remembered at the the Floridita as a very neat individual who earned his living as a men's room attendant. Seale tried to hide the fact that he was a Rosicrucian, but Hemingway knew his secret, and the character in *Islands* appears reading a manual of that organization.

Hemingway gave his character some of the characteristics of Juan Eleuterio García, known as "Juanito, the Jehovah's Witness," a man who seemed to possess a great faith in mystical theology.

Hemingway was amused by Juanito's condition and the burden placed on him by his job as *"guardiajurado"*—the term Cubans used for policemen on private duty. Since Juanito's duty was to keep order, he frequently had to break his faith's vow about love for his fellow man, and club a few heads when customers became insolent or refused to pay their bills.

[87]

There were seven or eight whores who frequented the Floridita, but Leopoldina la Honesta—who appears in *Islands in the Stream* as Honest Lil—was the most notorious.

At the bar or one of the tables, indispensable to the atmosphere of the place, were Hemingway's friends and those who sought him out: Spencer Tracy, Errol Flynn, Marlene Dietrich, Ava Gardner, Barbara Stanwyck and Robert Taylor; and the Latin Americans whose relationship with Hemingway was rather sketchy: Hugo del Carril, Libertad Lamarque, Pedro Armendariz and Arturo de Córdoba, the latter having played an important part as one of the guerrillas in Paramount's movie of *For Whom the Bell Tolls.*

Wearing Basque espadrilles or moccasins, Bermuda shorts and a light cotton shirt, Hemingway reigned over the Floridita.

Unlike Cubans, who customarily go to bars to socialize, Hemingway didn't talk much. When he did speak it was in a deep, well modulated voice. The bartenders remember him as a very strong man: "He was like an oak, he knocked down whomever he hit." Hemingway said that was his way of *advising* those who got noisy and made trouble. In this way he was a great help to Juanito, the Jehovah's Witness.

Hemingway would arrive early at the Floridita, or, if not, later in the morning, around eleven, drink a couple of daiquiris, leave at noon, return at five in the afternoon and drink a dozen more.

He began to cut his normal schedule short somewhere between the winter of 1959 and the summer of 1960. He had lost a lot of weight.

"He started to fail suddenly," says the barman, Antonio Meilán. "He became ill. He said he was going to Spain or the United States for an operation, but he killed himself instead."

In the summer of 1960, Havana was a city at war. The well-being Thomas Hudson enjoyed in *Islands* during the Second World War, when he drank at the Floridita, was the result of a special time in the country, when a state of curious tranquillity resulted in very little change in the flow of supplies, despite hostilities.

But the situation changed radically in 1960, when the revolutionary government faced its first major problems with the administration in Washington and the start of the longest-lasting economic blockade of the century.

Meilán recalls that customers would ask him to obtain a Hemingway autograph, because that was the only way they could get it. Many times Hemingway would bring him a number of choice marlin filets to take home. The bartender also remembers that Errol Flynn as *"muy pala paga,"* which means not trustworthy at paying his debts, although he always had open credit there. Hemingway said many times that the money pocket in Captain Blood's pants had been stitched closed.

Hemingway was extremely generous, says Meilán. Before he left on a trip, he always paid his outstanding bill at the Floridita and an additional 20 percent as a tip for the staff. He said he did this because "in case something happens, I want them to remember and miss me."

"A Situation Report," next to his last journalistic piece, rebuts the expatriate charge made against him by some fellow Americans because he didn't live in his native country but made his residence in Cuba.

In the days when McCarthyism was in full swing, Hemingway answered his critics by saying that whenever he wanted to see his compatriots, all he had to do was get into his car and drive to the Floridita bar.

[88]

Honest Lil (Liliana la Honesta) is the most important character among the many habitués of the Floridita who throng *Islands in the Stream*. Her model in real life, Leopoldina Rodriguez, called Honest Leopoldina, was very similar in appearance and hypersensitivity to ugly actions and obscene words.

Hemingway describes her as she sits in the corner opposite the one where he usually held court. That was the gathering place for the five or six prostitutes who frequented the Floridita.

Some remember her as a "very elegant, refined, well educated" mulatto, who started going to the Floridita "when the walls of the place were marble." Fernando G. Campoamor and Antonio Meilán remember Leopoldina and say that they never knew what she did in "her private life," all they knew was that she was at the bar practically all the time.

Leopoldina was a poor woman, "a prostitute through need." Ernest would take her to the Finca, help her and give her many gifts, all for "sentimental reasons."

Some say that she was forced into that kind of life in order to pay for her son's unbringing and medical studies, but this may be a myth. No son appeared at the cemetery when she was buried towards the end of the fifties. A solitary man who accompanied her remains to the cemetery paid for her funeral.

He was gray haired and bearded, an American wearing a short-sleeved guayabera, large moccasins and a pair of very wide and baggy pants.

[89]

The area around the Floridita has changed very little. O'Reilly is still a narrow street in which pedestrians may get bumped if they're not swift enough to dodge the traffic. Obispo Street, which was the most important thoroughfare linked to Hemingway's years in Cuba, looks much the same. It begins—or ends— at the Floridita, and nine blocks later crosses in front of Ambos Mundos.

Two blocks farther on is the building once occupied by the American embassy, which had the same fate as the old house of the Steinharts: it was converted into a secondary school named "Forjadores del Futuro"—Makers of the Future—which houses what sounds like the noisiest body of students in the world.

The Zaragozana, one of the great Cuban restaurants during the forties and one of Hemingway's favorites, survived until the beginning of the sixties. Today it is in ruins. Many of the places fashionable during Hemingway's time have vanished. But the characteristic smells of these streets, as described in *Islands in the Stream*, still survive. In the book, Hudson did not like to walk those streets at night, because then the windows of the warehouses were closed and there was no smell of roasting coffee.

[90]

William Faulkner believed at one time that Hemingway had found God. It was in 1952, when *The Old Man and the Sea* was published. All those who had inveighed against Hemingway and had taken him to account for the failure of *Across the River and into the Trees*, a sentimental and romantic novel in the eyes of many critics, now had to bow down before a new example of the old master's skill.

In this brief novel, barely over 100 pages, Hemingway told the simple story of an old fisherman's battle with a great fish. Faulkner confessed that he was very moved by these pages. So were many other American and European writers. Vladimir Nabokov, who on another occasion (comparing Hemingway with Conrad) had said that Hemingway was "a writer for children," conceded that "the description of the iridescent fish and the rhythmic flow of the famous tale is superb."

Considered Hemingway's great Cuban novel, *The Old Man and the Sea* is now a classic. This, in spite of some sentimental passages (like the one in which Santiago prays for the baseball player, Joe DiMaggio). Hemingway said at the informal celebration of the Nobel Prize award at Finca Vigía:

> This is one prize that belongs to Cuba, because my work was conceived and created in Cuba, with my people of Cojímar, where I'm a citizen. Throughout all the translations, this, my adopted country is present, and here I have my books and my home.

The immense and bottomless sea of the book in not necessarily Cuban. With the exception of a few strokes of local color, the novel could just as well have taken place in Java or the Mediterranean. Any fisherman in the world would feel at home in Santiago's small boat, and would act in the same brave manner. There are minor exceptions; when Santiago believes he is lost, he studies the horizon and decides that he can still find his bearings by the island's coastline. But he immediately turns back to his faith in the sea, and reaffirms his belief that no one need get lost if he knows it well.

According to Carlos Baker, the first rough copy of the book was finished in April, 1951. The original completed manuscript reached Scribner's March 10, 1952. It appeared in *Life* magazine on September 1, 1952, and the book was published by Scribner's on the 8th of the same month.

This novel has an interesting background. The basic story appeared in an anecdote included in an article, "On the Blue Water," published sixteen years earlier in *Esquire*'s April, 1936, issue. But the text written by Hemingway was to be part of a major work. Hemingway intended to write an extensive trilogy on "the earth, the sea, and the air," a vast Proustian ambition he discussed with Malcolm Cowley.

Within that plan, *The Old Man and the Sea* was to be the coda of the section about the sea. Apparently the other parts, representing the earth and the air, connected with his World War II experiences, remained only as good intentions, or, as Baker says, "in the walls of the imagination."

According to Baker, Leland Hayward, who eventually produced the film, was the person who convinced Ernest to publish *The Old Man and the Sea* independently. At first Ernest didn't agree. Hayward insisted, arguing that when Hemingway finished the sea section of his projected work he could add this one, but that the story had a special value independent of the rest.

When he received the Nobel Prize, Hemingway said that he could have written a 500-page story about Cojímar and its inhabitants, but he preferred to concentrate on the tale of Santiago and create an authentic old man and fish. He was possibly referring to other material he had put aside in order to achieve a more highly distilled narrative.

Two climactic scenes of both *Islands in the Stream* and *The Old Man and the Sea* center on the action of catching a great fish. It hardly seems possible for Hemingway to have used a similar action without establishing different moral implications between the two.

There are nuances to be taken into consideration. In *Islands in the Stream*, there is the boy, trying to attain manhood through killing a noble beast. In *The Old Man and the Sea*, Santiago is a symbol of tenacity itself, of the need to prove at any moment that long-attained manhood, exemplified in the struggle between man and fish. Identical dialogue makes brothers of the two characters. Joined to the fish by the line, each one, the young and the old, exclaims: "Oh God, how I love you!"

Although he never read *Islands in the Stream*, William Faulkner, from his own point of view, referred to that identity:

Early in life he learned a method by which he could do his work, he has followed this method, he has handled it well. If he continues to write, then he will do his best work. His last book, I believe, *The Old Man and the Sea*, is his best, because he has found something he had not found before, and that is—God. Until that moment, his characters moved in a vacuum, they had no past, but suddenly in *The Old Man and the Sea* he found God. There is the great fish— God made the great fish that had to be caught, God made the old man that has to catch the great fish, God made the sharks that have to eat the fish, and God made them all and loves them all, and if his work goes on from there, it will be even better, which is something not all writers expect to do. Many dry up tragically when young and then become unhappy. That happened to Fitzgerald, it happened to Sherwood Anderson. They crumbled.

Hemingway kept a number of clippings about *The Old Man and the Sea* at Finca Vigía. In the most notable, Faulkner returns to his theme:

SHENANDOAH MAGAZINE
Fall 1952
William Faulkner
Time may show it to be the best single piece of any of us. I mean his and my contemporaries. This time he discovered God, a Creator. Until now, his men and women had made themselves, shaped themselves out of their own clay; their victories and defeats were at the hands of each other, just to prove to themselves or one another how tough they could be.

A touching refutation of Faulkner's God-centered view was written by Ernest's old friend Kashkeen:

VAPROSY LITERATURA
1964
Ivan Kashkeen
Santiago is written from the inside. Many have seen in this novelette Christian symbolism. But Hemingway is always in evidence in the frame of a simple, real character—let us leave other interpretations to the conscience of those who suggest them.

[91]

A man alone in a small boat drifting in the Gulf Stream is hard to find. Even when the Coast Guard boats and airplanes joined in the search, they couldn't find him.

His fishing companions in Cojímar must have considered him lost. But a child, Manolin, the apprentice fisherman, waited for him with his eyes fixed on the horizon. He had faith in the old man. He believed that solitary man could face tides and all the elements of the Stream and survive, and so he waited, even though the old man's cabin on the beach was empty.

The old man kept up his lonely struggle in the Stream. No help could come from the airplanes. It is impossible at that height; the mass of water of the sea appears like a sheet of solid and immovable metal.

He hadn't caught a fish in 84 days, and Manolin's parents no longer gave the boy permission to accompany him. They said that the old man *had bad luck*. Then he sailed away from the coast. After a whole day's navigation he found his marlin and he knew immediately that it was a big one.

The character of old Santiago is patterned on another individual, a man Hemingway met in the days of Prohibition, when he began his adventures on the Gulf Stream.

Carlos Gutiérrez appears in most of the pictures taken of Hemingway as a young man, wearing shorts, posing with his first marlins. Hemingway mentions him in "On the Blue Water," and was very fond of him.

Gutiérrez was the first skipper of the *Pilar* and as good a friend of Ernest as Gregorio, the second skipper. Gregorio likes to believe that his own version of the old fisherman's tale is superior to Gutiérrez's: he says that towards the end of the forties, in the latitude of the port of Cabanas, he and Ernest saw a fisherman being dragged through the waves with unusual force, as if his boat had a motor.

It was a rickety old boat. They thought they should offer their help, and got near it. A man and a boy were in the boat. The man was straining against the board of the seat, gripping the line, which was taut, and then they realized that it was the force behind the line that was pulling the boat, which was cutting the water like a knife. To keep up with it, the *Pilar* had to go full speed.

The man was shirtless, thin but strong, and screamed at them in greeting:

"Get out of here, you sons of bitches! Leave me alone!"

Hemingway ordered Gregorio to keep the *Pilar* at a distance of half a mile, while they observed the fight between man and fish. Hemingway understood how the fisherman felt; he respected the man's decision and solitary effort.

The struggle lasted half a day. Finally Hemingway told Gregorio to take the auxiliary boat with some provisions for the fisherman.

Again the man yelled: "Son of a bitch! Get away!"

But Gregorio quickly reached aft of the small boat and threw in a package containing a few snacks, beer, a bottle of rum and beef sandwiches.

"It was around here," says Gregorio, pointing to a spot in the water. We are in the latitude of Cabanas, on board the *Hill Noe,* his own small boat.

"He was a fisherman from this port, who came from Mallorca. He is dead now."

One wonders how Gregorio can point to the exact place in the Gulf Stream where, so many years ago, he and Hemingway witnessed that magnificent battle.

Maybe his story is true, and the writer took some of it for his book. Or maybe it's a tale remembered and colored by Gregorio. The truth is that such a story of a great struggle is not unusual among the fishermen of the north coast of Cuba.

*To Have and Have Not* represents an early chapter of the Hemingway epic on the Gulf Stream. It bears more than one similarity to *Islands in the Stream:* three stories, originally independent ones, joined in one narrative; a gallery of memorable characters whom the narrator discards gradually without returning them to the story; and a similar locale, on board a vessel where the protagonists fall victim to machine-gun fire.

Men and locales of this geographic area are present again in Hemingway's writing when he returns from the Second World

War. But now the artist is more skillful and mature, more controlled. A rough, nervous personality like that of Morgan in *To Have and Have Not* no longer seems to have a place in the work of the postwar Hemingway.

There is no doubt that Hemingway was aging, and that the anxieties of previous years were giving way to the memories of a man whose days perhaps were numbered. The conflicts that demanded immediate solutions, the just or unjust wars, social and political struggles, the procession of refugees in the Balkans, army veterans abandoned to their fate in a Florida Key—all of those lost urgency for him. His inner drives narrowed to cope with the eternal questions of man: life and death, love and hatred.

The Hemingway heroes—the deserter, Frederick Henry; the outlaw, Harry Morgan; and the combatant, Robert Jordan—became philosophical old men and characters who turn back to the past: Colonel Richard Cantwell; the artist Thomas Hudson; and the fisherman Santiago.

The war is over and Hemingway, the withdrawn, hard man, aspires to write a Proustian book, a transcendental and extensive memoir. He confides to his friends that he intends to tell all he knows about the earth, the sea and the air; about his young days in Paris, his impressions of a six-day bicycle race, and his experience in a low-altitude bombing as part of the crew of a Mitchell.

He directs his efforts toward this goal, but a succession of unexpected incidents spoils his plans: illnesses (his own and his children's); traffic and airplane accidents; family problems. The Proustian memoir is never realized and the Hemingway legacy is fragmented.

His production at Finca Vigía included: *A Moveable Feast* (a return to the locale of *The Sun Also Rises*); *Across the River and into the Trees* (return to the scene of *A Farewell to Arms*); "The Dangerous Summer" (returning again to *The Sun Also Rises*, and the theme of *Death in the Afternoon*); and the articles about Africa for *Look* (a final return to the background of *Green Hills of Africa* and the stories of Harry Street and Francis Macomber).

The result of his major effort, only half done, was *Islands in the Stream* and Santiago's tale, both of which he apparently intended to include in his larger work. In any case, the vital stages of man (and Hemingway) are registered in these unique books:

First, childhood, represented by Hudson's children in *Islands in the Stream* and Manolin, the boy fisherman who accompanies Santiago in *The Old Man and the Sea.*

Then Rogers, representing Thomas Hudson's lost youth, and Hudson himself as the experienced, mature man despairing when he recalls his past life. Last of all is the depiction of old age in Santiago, whose basic philosophy has been shaped by the blows life has dealt him.

The chronological ladder and the separation of elements in temporal planes correspond to the application of the cubist literary techniques that Hemingway learned from Gertrude Stein when he was beginning to write.

He made good use of these techniques in the last period of his creativity. Not only do separate characters converge in one identity, but there is a scene in *The Old Man and the Sea* in which Santiago addresses the different parts of his body and talks to his hand, his head and his nerves.

[92]

When Hemingway has Santiago say that it would be better not to bother the great fish at sunset because that is a bad time for all fish, an ichthyologist might well be amazed at this information.

But the fact is, thanks to his power of observation, experience as a fisherman and extensive reading, Hemingway knew what he was writing about.

The truth is that fish swim toward the light or away from it, depending on the kind of fish. The swordfish, for example, is caught at night, and the blue marlin proabably descends to the depths at night, since it is caught in the daytime.

What Santiago feared was that his fish would go deep and break his line. There may have been some error or poetic license in the statement that the fish wouldn't surface until the following day. Blue marlin always give battle and surface to see what is going on.

With Gary Cooper at the Floridita on Obispo Street, New Year's Eve, 1951.

With Errol Flynn at the Floridita, 1960.

Hemingway and Spencer Tracy during the filming of *The Old Man and the Sea*.

While filming *The Old Man and the Sea* at La Terraza in Cojímar. Seated is "old" Ramirez, one of the veteran fishermen of the village. (Henry Wallace)

"THE OLD MAN AND THE SEA"    3/26/56
                                    83...

320. (Cont.) *p.138*

OLD MAN
We must get a good killing lance and always have it on board. You can make the blade from a spring-leaf from an old Ford. It should be sharp and tempered so it will not break. My knife broke.                    *heavy*

THE BOY
How many days of wind will we have?

OLD MAN
Maybe three.

THE BOY
I will have everything in order. You get your hands well, old man.

The Old Man looks down at his hands.

OLD MAN
~~They will be all right in a few days.~~

*Old Man*   *See page 138 of book —*
*" I know how to care for them.*
*In the night I spat something strange*
*and felt something in my chest*
*was broken"*
*" get that well too.*
*Boy — (and what follows)*

*(you lose your story here*
*and there is no previous reference in the*
*script to the damage to his chest*
*EH*

Hemingway's yacht anchors in Cojímar. The belvedere near the dike is the site of Hemingway's bust, installed the year following his death. (Raul Corrales)

Gregorio Fuentes poses in front of the bust of Ernest Hemingway in Cojímar, the first sculpture in the world dedicated to the writer after his death. The bust was cast from melted bronze pieces from the local fishermen's boats, collected by them in tribute to their friend.

Santiago of *The Old Man and the Sea* was partially based on this man, the late Anselmo Hernández.

October 1947. Gregorio Fuentes (the Antonio of *Islands in the Stream*) lands on Cayo Confites, thirty-five years after the closing of the little base that served as supply port for the *Pilar* during Hemingway's anti-submarine adventure of World War II.

Gregorio Fuentes returns to Cayo Paraíso (Mégano de Casigua) in the winter of 1974. The *Pilar* made countless trips to this key.

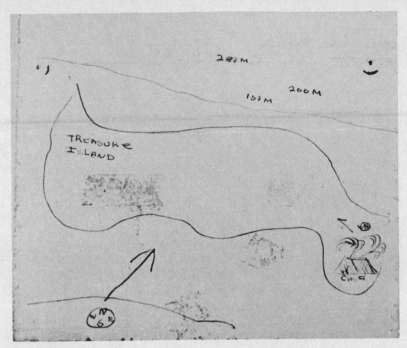

Drawing by Hemingway, probably of Caya Paraíso. It was renamed "Treasure Island" on this occasion.

On July 3, 1961, the day after Hemingway's suicide in Idaho, bartender Eugenio Rob Iedo cleans the novelist's favorite spot at the Floridita bar in Havana. The bust of Hemingway on the wall was placed there by his friends after he won the Nobel Prize. (UPI)

As for fish lines, three were thrown in the days before the use of the boulter, a long fishing line with hooks attached along its length. The depth to which these were lowered depended on the moon. The short one was used if there was a new moon, and the long one if the moon was full.

Santiago had his own method. He went out alone in a boat meant for two, and the depth of his lines varied somewhat, although he used three classic fish lines for marlin.

In *The Old Man and the Sea* the preparation of bait is described in detail. The professionalism of Cuban fishermen in this task is admirable.

Marlin can be caught with the boulter. Its meat is highly prized and has great commercial value. Santiago knows he has hooked one by the kind of strike he feels in his line. Marlin hits the bait with its spear two or three times and then starts to eat it. Not so the shark. The shark bites and pulls the line. When fishing is done with outriggers, the clothespin which clips the line vibrates with each hit by the marlin and then snaps it loose when the fish takes the bait.

In spawning season, marlin usually travel in pairs and even threesomes: a female and two males. They can then be caught easily, because wherever one goes, the other will follow. The problem is to keep the fish with its mouth facing the fisherman.

Santiago's marlin was not in that position. The fishhook caught in its mouth was not well placed.

The fact that Santiago, upon entering the area called "the great well" in the book and which the fishermen of Cojímar call "*el hondón*," is fishing in an easterly direction with the current, opposite to ordinary practice, appears to be literary license. This is as strange as stating that the fish would take 24 hours to surface.

[93]

Fred Zinneman, the director, sent Hemingway the script for *The Old Man and the Sea*, and the notations made on its pages by the writer constitute a most revealing document showing Hemingway's deep knowledge of fishing and his manner of getting close to the Cuban characters he immortalized in his book.

Hemingway made notations in his round handwriting with the traditional number two pencil. In the changes he indicated, one sees his concern with details more technical than literary.

Hemingway's involvement with the movies was character-ized by seriousness. *The Spanish Earth* was a statement of restraint. His observations on the script of *The Old Man and the Sea* at-tempted to eliminate typical Hollywood absurdities.

In September, 1956, in one of the last articles he wrote for *Look*, he confessed: "The motion picture script is finished, and I will never do this kind of work again."

The first entry in the script corresponds to scene 25. The narrator says: "It made the boy sad to see the old man come in each day with his skiff empty, and he always went down to help him carry the harpoon or the sail."

Hemingway crossed out "harpoon" and put "heavy coiled line" in its place, adding "mast and" so that the weight would be shared when carrying the items: ". . . and he always went down to help him carry the heavy coiled line or the mast and sail."

The rest of the scenes with notations by Hemingway follow this logic of narrative objectivity. In scene 45 he added the word "either" to the narrator's voice-over: "There was no cast net and the boy remembered when they had sold it. But they went through this fiction every day. There was no pot of yellow rice and fish either and the boy knew this too."

In scene 50, in a description for the benefit of the script writer and director, Hemingway put a question mark where he doesn't understand the inclusion of the words "in Spanish." It concerns the description of a baseball game: "The catcher is jab-bering away in Spanish (?), signals for the pitch . . ."

Scene 54 presents a direct concern. Martin, owner of the restaurant La Terraza, serves some draft beer, takes a drink, and moves slowly towards the boy. Hemingway wrote: "No draft beer in such a place." Which is true. In Cuba, beer was always served in bottles.

Immediately following this, Hemingway modifies a de-scription. The text reads: "Martin thinks of himself as a wit, and enjoys ribbing the boy." Hemingway crossed out "ribbing" and substituted "teasing."

In the dialogue Martin says: "Well, you can have some black beans and rice for that." Hemingway crossed out "some." Martin starts to fill the metal container with the food, which he spoons from two enormous casseroles. Hemingway added: "Martin also adds two servings of fried bananas and some stew."

Then Martin says: "All right," and the boy takes out the money to pay and hands it to him, saying "Here." Hemingway crossed out "here," and adds a joke for the boy to say:

Martin: All right. Do you want an egg too?

The Boy: No, keep the egg and cackle when you lay it.

One must remember Hemingway's comment that most Spanish jokes are off-color. In most Latin American countries, the word egg has a double meaning: the second is the vulgar expression for testicle.

Scene 58:
The Boy: The great Dick Sisler's father was never poor and he played in the big leagues when he was sixteen.
Santiago answers:
Old Man: When I was sixteen I was before the mast on a square rigged ship that ran to Africa and I have seen the lions on the beaches in the evening.

Hemingway added some text for the narrator and inserted it between the lines spoken by the boy and Santiago:

Narrator: The boy was not accurate here.

In Scene 72, Manolin asks Santiago: "Why is it no one ever takes food in the boats? Why is it they only take water?" To which the old man responds, with the help of Hemingway's addition:

Old Man: Because it is not certain you will always have money to buy food and this way, as you are not used to having it, you will never miss it. *Also, if you had just eaten and hooked a big fish, you would be in trouble.*

In scene 76, in the following passage: "He thinks better of it and drinks the bitter liquid himself," he crossed out "bitter" and substituted "unpleasant." A few lines later this is repeated. In the script: "The boy accepts the cup reluctantly and drinks as much of the bitter liquid as he can." Hemingway again crossed out bitter and inserted "unpleasant," writing on the margin: "Note: It is not bitter, only very oily and distasteful."

In Scene 99 the narrator says: "There was no part of the hook that a great fish could feel that was not sweet-smelling and good-tasting." Hemingway answered: "He must hook on the sardines first." In other words, first, the bait. Hemingway is appealing here to the sequence of acts which produce sensory emotions, which, according to his literary method, will be transmuted into art.

In scene 123 the script says: "The bait being towed behind the old man's boat. The fish are circling and driving it." Hemingway put parentheses and a question mark around the first phrase and noted the following: "They are not driving this bait but the shoal of bait fish the size of minnows."

Hemingway was criticized by some because of a few technical inaccuracies that appear in *The Old Man and the Sea;* it's possible that as a result he felt compelled to clear the script of any ambiguous passages from the book. And so he pointed out that tuna did not attack Santiago's bait, but that it was the shoal that had attracted these fish of prey.

In Scene 131 the script writer says: "He is getting sleepy." Ernest scolds in a marginal note: "Why is he getting sleepy so early? It's silly. EH."

In Scene 133 the script states that the fish line is over Santiago's shoulders, and Hemingway again remonstrates: "Not yet! Not until the fish is hooked."

In Scene 135, Hemingway scolds again. The scene shows the moment in which Santiago is about to take the fish, the point of the hook about to pierce its heart. Santiago is kneeling, but Hemingway notes: "This is all done on foot."

In Scene 147, when Santiago recalls the baseball teams, he says in script: "I wonder how the baseball game(s) in the big leagues came out today." Hemingway added the letter "s" to the word "game" and comments: "Games plural. They follow many clubs."

Nine scenes later, Hemingway's note makes clear for the

benefit of the script writer the fact that marlin have many little sacks along the backbone, not just one. "It is plural," he noted, "there are many sacks."

In Scene 147: ". . . and he saw a flight of wild ducks etching themselves against the sky over the water." Hemingway added: "then blurring, then etching again," a precision worthy of his alter ego, painter Thomas Hudson, the protagonist of *Islands in the Stream.*

In Scene 203: He added the verb "do." "but it is good that we do not have to kill the sun or the moon or the stars."

In Scene 320: Hemingway added the adjective "heavy" to "wind," without which the sentence wouldn't make sense: "How many days of heavy wind will we have?"

Almost immediately he offered his most extensive commentary and his most severe scolding of the script writer. First he crossed out Santiago's speech: "They will be all right in a few days," and tells the script writer to reread page 138 of *The Old Man and the Sea.* Not happy with this, he quotes the passage in question: "I know how to care for them. In the night I spat something strange and felt something in my chest was broken."

Hemingway advised the script writer to go on reading and warns: "You lose your story here and there is no previous reference in the script to the damage to his chest."

In his last two notes on Scene 320, he crossed out the second sentence in Santiago's dialogue: "Bring any of the papers of the time that I was gone. *I want to read about the baseball.*" In the scene following, when the boy Manolin cries as he leaves Santiago's cabin, Hemingway insisted in his notes that the script stress the fact that the old man suffers from chest discomfort.

[94]

Miguel Angel Quevedo owned *Bohemia,* the Cuban magazine that had the greatest circulation in the country. He was gay, and was proud that no woman had ever entered his property, a farm where he gave great weekly fiestas attended by the most outstanding impresarios and politicians of the nation. The victory of the revolution in 1959 was a tragedy for him, and he left the country in 1960.

He continued to publish his magazine in different Latin American cities, although with a change of name: *Bohemia Libre (Free Bohemia)*. He committed suicide in Caracas in 1970. But in 1955 he was the czar of the Cuban press and resented the fact that *Life* magazine had beaten him with the publication of *The Old Man and the Sea*.

He pulled some strings, put pressure on the American Embassy and succeeded in obtaining publishing rights for the complete Spanish translation of the book.

The caricaturist David says that Quevedo called him one afternoon and told him: "You, who know everybody, go see Hemingway and tell him that I want to publish his story."

"Well, I don't know Hemingway very well," David answered.

"It doesn't matter. Go and tell him I want to publish that book."

Located at the Floridita, Hemingway quickly accepted the offer of five thousand pesos, on two conditions: that the translator be Lino Novás Calvo and the five thousand pesos be invested in the purchase of television sets which he would donate to the patients of the El Rincón Sanitarium.

It isn't clear what finally happened to the money. A dozen documents found at Finca Vigía show evidence of some irregularities. In those letters, the management of *Bohemia* assures Hemingway that the sets will be acquired without delay, or that they are about to be installed at the sanitarium. There is a letter from Lino Novás Calvo explaining to Hemingway that he had nothing to do with the irregularities of the management and that he is concerned about Hemingway's long silence and not answering his phone calls.

The story ends with the installation of the television sets, and years later, in the sixties, Lino Novás Calvo becoming one of the counterrevolutionary Cuban writers residing in Miami as chief editor of *Bohemia Libre*. Quevedo's farm, where at one time women were not allowed, was ironically turned into the first camp for young revolutionary women, where they got militia training as members of the batallion named "Lidia Doce."


[95]


Carlos Baker tells of seven readers who wrote Hemingway in 1953 to point out that "The old man could not have seen Rigel in that part of the world at that time of year," as the book states. Hemingway's comment was: "They were so good to write."

Dr. Herrera Sotolongo insists that "the cancer of the skin" attributed to Santiago, the fisherman, as one of his characteristics, does not exist scientifically speaking. Sotolongo says that he discussed this with Hemingway, but that the writer insisted on leaving it in the book as his invention, not to be stubborn, but as an act of artistic freedom. Santiago's condition could have been a "cloasma," an unpleasant scaly condition of the skin which can be caused by over-exposure to the sun, but it was certainly not cancer, "a benign cancer of the skin," as claimed in the story.

Not surprisingly, Hemingway himself had this skin condition. It dated from his long exposure to the sun during his adventures on board the *Pilar* and his wartime mission hunting submarines. Because of his low tolerance to the sun, his skin burned easily. He had scales on his nose and forehead. As protection he used an electric shaver, never a razor blade. Sometimes in those days he would go a month without shaving to avoid irritating his already damaged skin.


[96]


The news of the conspiracy appeared on the front page. Hemingway kept the page, marked the item in red and underlined the paragraph in which he was mentioned so prominently.

## DIARIO DE LA MARINA
October 17, 1947

SANTO DOMINGO WILL ACCUSE CUBA, VENEZUELA AND GUA-
TEMALA BEFORE THE INTERNATIONAL TRIBUNAL.

Among the accused functionaries is the ex-minister, Alemán,
who is charged with contributing $350,000 to the cause and of
handing over to the revolutionary army trucks belonging to the
Government.

NEW YORK, October 16 (By Amador Marín of the I.N.S.)

A three pound "dossier" accusing high functionaries of the governments of Cuba, Venezuela and Guatemala, of having participated in the recent failed attempted invasion of the Dominican
Republic, will be brought before the International Justice Tribunal
by the government of President Rafael Leónidas Trujillo, it was
announced today by the office of the Dominican Republic in New
York.

The preliminary text of the report will be submitted to the
highest International Justice Tribunal together with an enormous
quantity of documents to prove that the "great quantities of arms
were bought for the attempted invasion by the governments of
Cuba and Venezuela with funds contributed by the Soviet delegation in the capital of Guatemala."

The documents try to prove that the President of Venezuela,
Rómulo Betancourt, helped to finance the invasion forces against
Santo Domingo. However, the report adds, according to data obtained in Venezuela, President Betancourt withdrew his support
after "he was convinced that his money was being wasted fool-
ishly." It further states that after Betancourt's withdrawal from
invasion plans, most of the support for the revolutionaries came
from functionaries of the governments of Cuba and Guatemala.
Adding fuel to the report of the plans for the revolution, is the
statement in said document, that a group made up of two dozen
veterans of the American and Canadian air forces had the mission
of bombing military installations in Ciudad Trujillo and other
strategic points in the Dominican Republic.

*These men, according to the Dominican report, were given lodging
in the home near Havana, Cuba, of the American novelist, Ernest Hemingway, who on several occasions acted as spokesman for the revolutionaries.
The American aviators implicated in the plot returned recently to Miami,
Florida, declaring that although they had been well fed and provided with*

*drink in Hemingway's home, they had not been paid the sums they had*
*been promised for their part in the adventure.*

Some of them received only around a hundred dollars, of
the six or eight thousand promised to each one. The report states
that there is proof that the bombs found aboard the planes belonged to a shipment sold by the American War Surplus Administration to the government of Venezuela.

It points as well to "a consistent apathy on the part of the
Cuban government about documentary proof brought to it on
revolutionary activities," and it adds that even after an agent of
the Dominican government was informed by the revolutionary
spokesman, Ernest Hemingway, that the invasion army "had
grown to seven thousand men," and that their training was being
carried out publicly in several places in Cuba, the government of
President Grau San Martín denied rumors that such a movement
existed.

In the information center of the Dominican Republic in New
York it was also said that news of the current arrest of invasion
forces and confiscation of their arms by the Cuban Army was
considered by the Dominican press proof of the existence of the
conspiracy about which the press of the United States and other
American countries had expressed doubts.

The report points out that some American newspapers considered the news of the existence of an invasion force a fabrication
of President Trujillo to benefit his own political goals.


This time Hemingway was forced to flee. He had to run
because the press had implicated him in an international plot of
great political proportions. It was a conspiracy, orchestrated by
the opportunist government of Ramón Grau San Martín. Its
strategic purpose was to get rid of some "particularly rebellious"
university students, among them young Fidel Castro. A number
of them ended up in Key Confites, waiting for arms and for the
boat that was to take them to Santo Domingo to fight against
Trujillo's dictatorship.

It was apparently only one of several conspiracies in which
Hemingway became involved with what seemed to be a sporting
spirit; a repetition or echo of the memories of his participation
in the Spanish conflict.

"Hemingway gave some money for the Confites thing,"

confirms Herrera Sotolongo. "But we heard he was going to be arrested, and so I went to the Aerovías Q offices on Prado Street and got him a ticket for Miami. The plane was to leave at three. We got to the airport just a few minutes before the plane's departure. He was already in the States when they went to search the farm."

Lieutenant Correa, heading a squad, appeared at Finca Vigía that afternoon. When Mary ordered them out of the house, Correa pointed his gun at her. Mary saved her life by telling him that she was pregnant and that she held the rank of captain in the American army. She couldn't stop Correa from taking away all of Hemingway's firearms, but these were returned next day, thanks to Herrera Sotolongo's intervention.

Correa had fought in Spain, but had then joined the corrupt politicians who had ravaged Havana during the forties. He became a "career army man," and was assassinated during the armed struggle against Batista. He had become a bodyguard and confidant of a hated official of the Batista dictatorship.

A week after Correa's appearance at Finca Vigía, Hemingway returned to Havana, took his arsenal on board the *Pilar* and jettisoned it in the bay around the bend from the town of Casablanca. Herrera Sotolongo disapproved of this action, particularly since the weapons included his favorite Luger.

Hemingway was well informed about many of the conspiracies active in Havana between the thirties and the end of the forties.

In his 1949 article, "The Great Blue River," he describes what it feels like to leave the port of Havana on board the *Pilar*, passing the fortress of Cabaña where most of his friends had been political prisoners.

In 1951 in another article, "The Shot," he tells of two political fugitives who succeed in getting five hundred dollars (actually two hundred) from him in order to leave the country, because they have been unjustly accused of being in the second of two cars which had killed two and wounded five in what is known as "the old one-two": A lead car fires on a house known to contain enemies, and when the men in the house rush out to fire at the speeding car, a second car comes by and wipes them out.

One of the men claimed to be a friend of a friend of Hem-

ingway's who was shot dead in the street with thirty-five cents
in his pocket while he held a government position.

He was referring to Manolo Castro, a gangster gunned down
on February 22, 1948. President Grau San Martín had named
him to the post of Director of Sports, in spite of his implication
in a number of crimes, such as the murder of a student, Hugo
Dupotey, at Bar Criollo. Although he was over 30 years old,
Castro was registered at the Engineering School of the University.
He was supposed to teach in the Department of Design and at
the same time was considered a member of the Revolutionary
Legion. He was closely connected with Masferrer, another known
gangster of that era.

[97]

Julio Suárez was born twice. First, in a natural and human way.
His mother had him christened with the sonorous name of Indamiro, and from his father he inherited the equally euphonious
surname of Restano. His second and definitive birth took place
at Sierra Maestra, in the days of the struggle against Fulgencio
Batista's dictatorship.

As a member of the underground, Indamiro Restano was
sent to La Plata, where the command post of Fidel Castro's guerrillas was located. When they were introduced, the leader of the
revolution made him repeat his strange combination of names—
strange indeed to an ear used to the plain sound of Pedro, García,
Juan and González. In a sudden burst of native humor, the guerrilla leader advised Restano to give up such a fancy name and
suggested something simpler, for instance—Julio Suárez.

At the end of the war of liberation, the underground fighter
called Restano entered Havana wearing a faded uniform and a
thick beard, and with a new name and title: Captain Julio Suárez.

He had begun his friendship with Ernest Hemingway long
before the war.

In 1942, the writer, driving a convertible, went to the offices
of the Communist Party in Havana to ask for an address.

Julio Suárez was there and recalls their first meeting: "He
was a young guy then. He had a slight foreign accent and pro-

nounced his words very slowly. We struck up a conversation. I said I had my opinion about 'The Killers.'

" 'Well, then, if you have opinions, get in.'

"He opened the door of the car, I got in and he took me to the farm. There a servant served toast, butter, tea and whiskey. Hemingway poured himself whiskey on the rocks, a *whole glass*. Then he lay down on the sofa.

" 'I have money in all the banks in the world, but I have the most money in the USSR, where they publish and read my books,' he said.

"I was dying to recruit him into the communist movement. I wanted the rest of the world to be communist.

"I particularly remember some small details about him. For instance, I was impressed by the fact that he had very long fingernails. He said he never cut them. I don't remember whether all his fingernails were long, but I do remember his thumbs. The nails curved beyond the flesh of the thumbs and were highly polished.

"On one occasion he had a big rip in his shorts and you could see his behind. That day we discussed the Democratic and Republican parties. 'Well,' I told him, 'in your country one is as bad as the other.'

"The day he was to receive the Bronze Medal, he told me: 'Excuse me, Restanito, but today I am going to be decorated.' He looked elegant that day. 'I'm getting the medal because of my wartime articles.' I was also impressed by the number of shirts he had hanging from a clothes rack. All of them were white and ironed.

" 'I don't know why I have so many shirts,' he said. 'In Cuba it's so hot that one should wear very light clothing. Or none.'

"I was very young and eager, but he never contradicted me. I imagine because he didn't want to discourage me. He used to listen a lot.

"We talked a lot about the Second Front. He sidestepped the issue. The Yankees kept postponing opening up the Second Front and he would tell me that it was no easy thing, that it took time.

" 'Yes,' I would argue, 'but you can build a destroyer a day.' "

" 'That's because it is paid on the basis of piece wages,' he'd answer. 'Stalin would win the war with such payment of labor.' "

"We often discussed the complex political coalition of the Allies. I admired the Red Army, and so did he."

[98]

Samuel Feijóo says he used to go to Cojímar from Casablanca in a little train. There he would rent a boat for one peso, and for that money he could use the rowboat all afternoon. One day he went alone up the Cojímar River to almost unknown places, "where there are some beautiful bare cliffs and resonant echoes."

He had his watercolors and a canvas with him. On a small island of white sand, he would stop and take advantage of the complete isolation to do his painting.

Samuel Feijóo, one of our most restless and versatile artists, perhaps the best of all and the most daring, likes still waters, solitude, rocks, translucent fish in the water, sunsets and landscapes. It was only logical that Hemingway and Samuel Feijóo would meet one day in one of those out-of-the-way places. And they did meet, around 1941.

Feijóo says that on a certain afternoon he saw a boat approaching and in it a muscular, ruddy man who looked foreign. He was alone in his boat with a few bottles. The man rowed past him but immediately turned around and asked, in a loud voice in English: "May I come over?"

Feijóo says that he was annoyed, for he didn't like interruptions when he was painting, but he said yes, that the man could come over.

The American sat by his side and said that the watercolor was very good.

"You know about painting?" Feijóo asked.

"Yes, I know a great deal about painting," the man replied. "I have been to Paris and I know enough about art. This is a good watercolor. And this is a great place to paint it."

They ended up discussing many things, but the main issue

was the solitude both men felt. In truth, they had met on that little island because each in his own way had been looking for seclusion.

"I turned around because I saw your watercolor. It's a diamond. A diamond!" the man repeated.

Feijóo says: "My watercolors were very good. They *are* very good. I have kept them all. In New York Chagall once wanted to trade one of mine for one of his, but I told him nothing doing. What a fool I was! Today I would have been able to sell it for forty thousand dollars, and I would have money to buy all the material I need."

He says of Hemingway: "We talked about solitude. I explained that I went there to paint in search of solitude. He told me that he did the same, that he needed solitude because he was bored with the world around him, and that people made him mad. He said that he was misunderstood, that he had no friends and that those around him were there because he was a famous writer. They were really the friends of his fame."

Feijóo didn't ask him who he was. Up to that time he had read only one Hemingway book, *A Farewell to Arms*, in English.

Then Hemingway started to sniffle.

Feijóo told him that at least he had company in his boat: the bottles of whiskey.

"No," answered Hemingway. "That is not company. I don't even get drunk. They only offer me a mild escape from the world around me."

Hemingway started to cry a little louder. Feijóo patted his head as if he were his son, and told him: "Damn it, kid, don't cry like that. Don't let it get you down."

"Definitely, our problem is that we are two failures unto death."

"Oh, how he loved that phrase!" recalls Feijóo.

"*Failures unto death*!" Hemingway repeated in his tremendous voice. He was crying copiously now.

"Such a big, strong, vigorous man and yet he cried with great abandon. I patted his head again and told him not to cry. Later on he started to sing in a beautiful voice which echoed among the cliffs. He even taught me a song:

*Don't sit under the apple tree*
*With anyone else but me . . .*

and he cried again and clung to me and hugged me.

"Finally, after three or four hours of emotional release, he took me back to Cojímar. He tied my boat to his and pulled it. He wanted to be the only one to row. I told him that I wanted to row, too. He said he needed the exercise and I told him I needed exercise as well. And so we returned to Cojímar with both of us at the oars, he on one side of the boat, and I on the other.

"Then when we docked, everybody came to greet him: prostitutes, pimps, smugglers. 'Heming, Heming!' they called to him. It was then that I realized he was Hemingway. He was much in need of affection and those people gave it to him in their way. I told him: 'These people are like dirty water. They're here for the tips you give them.'

" 'I don't care about the color of the water. I need to quench my thirst!' Hemingway answered."

He invited Feijóo to eat something with him at La Terraza. Hemingway ordered lobster thermidor.

"I need affection. I don't care where it comes from," he confessed.

They discussed *A Farewell to Arms*, a book Feijóo was fond of.

"I told him I liked Gary Cooper's interpretation in the movie."

Feijóo says that Hemingway asked what he thought of the book.

"It is the work of an artist," Feijóo answered.

"But it took guts to write it. Many writers have genius but no guts. They waste their genius because they lack the courage to do anything with it."

On another occasion he said: "I'm looking for solidarity. That's why I came to Cuba."

"But life here is terrible!"

"Yes, but it's worse in my country. Here at least people smile at you. That's the truth."

Feijóo says: "Afterwards, we saw each other a few times. But I didn't like the type of people around him."

# Sailing into the Wind

[99]

The opinion of Nicolas Guillén, Cuba's National Poet, about the Bronze God of American Literature is at best mixed. He starts by saying that Hemingway spoke Spanish badly, with a heavy accent.

"I told him: 'You should talk more to P&P.'

" 'Who's P&P?' he asked.

" 'Prostitutes and Peasants,' I answered.

"I remember something he did one of the few times I went fishing with him on his boat. There were five of us on board: Hemingway; his wife; the skipper; a snobbish lady who was introduced to me as a very prominent American woman; and I.

"Hemingway sat down with a drink in his hand. When we passed El Morro and were out on the open sea, we heard a loud, explosive sound over the hum of the motors. Its origin was unmistakable.

" 'Ernest!' Mary cried in protest.

"In answer, Hemingway raised his leg and let loose another barrage.

" 'Oh, God!' Mary exclaimed.

"Hemingway's face was expressionless. I didn't know what to do in such a situation. But the boat continued sailing into the wind, full speed ahead."

The Cuban also remembers during the Spanish Civil War: "His hotel was close to the telephone company, and so it was bombed regularly. His position then was very progressive."

An evaluation: "He didn't really know Cubans. I know this from experience. He translated the first part of my *West Indies Ltd.*—only the first part, where certain expressions taken out of context could be considered pejorative, against the people. It is only further into the work that the poem grows in stature and acquires its true feeling and dimension.

"In Spain we saw each other, of course, because of our connection with Ramón 'Monguito' Nicolau's mission, and we also met when we went to the Alianza de Intelectuales de Madrid (Alliance of Intellectuals of Madrid). We had our picture taken there with Langston Hughes and Mikhail Koltzov. The four of us with our arms around each other. Or maybe it was only Hemingway's long arms around the rest of us."

[100]

Alejo Carpentier plays the leading role in one of the tales which merits investigation in relation to Hemingway's stay in Cuba. It has to do with some of the most important luminaries of contemporary literature, or at least those who at one time strolled along the left bank of the Seine. And it involves four, five or six cartons that were once filled with Hemingway's correspondence and that are alleged to have been consumed in a fire that burned for several hours at Finca Vigía.

Lisandro Otero was the first one to mention it. I started my research in July or August 1973 and Otero asked me: "What have you found at the Finca? Documents?"

The early search produced a number of interesting letters, though not many, and almost all of them were about family matters, intimate subjects. It was good material from any point of view, but there had always been the hope of finding letters from Gertrude Stein, Scott Fitzgerald and Sherwood Anderson, at the very least. There were none.

Otero said it would be impossible to find any, because they had all been burned in the famous fire Mary Welsh built a scant few weeks after her husband's suicide in July 1961, when she returned to Cuba to pick up his belongings.

According to the story, Mary had a servant bring her a can of gasoline. She cleared a space in the ground and started to throw the letters there.

Alejo Carpentier was allegedly witness to the operation. Other

Cuban writers knew of the incident from Carpentier. He told the same thing to two Cuban poets, Pablo Armando Fernández and Roberto Branly. Both mentioned it when I started my research. They bemoaned Mary's authority to destroy that correspondence.

" 'I have seen the burning of the most fabulous letters,' " Pablo Armando Fernández said, imitating Carpentier's French accent and expressive gestures. " 'Letters from Scott Fitzgerald, Gertrude Stein and Joyce.' "

Carpentier claimed that Mary told him she was acting according to Ernest's wishes as stated in his will: his personal correspondence was to be burned.

It happened this way: Mary came from the States a few weeks after Hemingway's burial to collect her husband's unpublished manuscripts, which were in a safe deposit box at the National Bank of Cuba. Among these were the original of *Islands in the Stream* and in all probability parts of *A Moveable Feast*, some unpublished Nick Adams stories and the rough draft of *The Garden of Eden*. She also wanted to take back some pictures, books and correspondence. Fidel Castro visited her at the farm and they agreed to establish the museum that is now in existence.

Then one afternoon, Mary Welsh called Carpentier to tell him she was going to proceed with the burning of the letters, and she needed his company. Vividly described, the scene had a certain beauty: Hemingway's widow crouched before the fire at Finca Vigía, amidst the exuberant foliage of the garden, accompanied by Carpentier, to whom she handed each letter for one last look before throwing it slowly into the fire to be turned into ashes.

This is what Pablo Armando Fernández recalls Carpentier telling him.

But when I interviewed Carpentier to confirm the information about the incident, his answer consisted of stupefied amazement and absolute denial.

"Burning of letters?" he asked. "I never participated in any such ceremony!"

"Well," I answered, "several people have given me the information. For instance, Branly and Pablo Armando."

"No, no," he said, "they must be mistaken. I don't remember anything of the kind."

"Well, they said you had read incredible letters from James Joyce and Scott Fitzgerald."

"No, my friend, you may be sure that the reader was not I."

There are many ways in which such legends grow in Cuba, and it's possible that Carpentier's visit to Finca Vigía could have provoked the controversy.

I met with Carpentier early in an afternoon in January 1975, in room 240 of the Hotel Nacional in Havana. In a certain way, the antiseptic condition of the room (really the foyer to the suite) provided the wrong atmosphere. Carpentier looked like an Indian god. He was seated but rose to greet me. The interview had been arranged through a mutual friend, who had convinced Carpentier of the necessity of providing information I needed.

Carpentier offered me a drink and said that although he would try to help, he didn't think he would prove of much use. Evidently the subject I was interested in went against his grain.

Whenever he had the chance, Carpentier changed the subject, and then his conversation flowed smoothly. Nevertheless, the discussion of Hemingway went well when Carpentier reminisced, at the same time, his own experiences of the twenties.

"I knew Hemingway in Paris, in the twenties. In those days there was no control in the money exchange and the franc had free conversion. I could get 4500 francs for 75 dollars, a good sum then. I think this is one of the reasons so many American artists went there. The truth is that when exchange control came into being, they all ran away.

"I always thought: well, the culture that this *lost generation* is absorbing has a lot to do with the money exchange. They were all there: Sherwood Anderson, Gertrude Stein, Scott Fitzgerald and the famous hard man, Hemingway.

"I'll tell you this about Hemingway: I have fond memories of *The Sun Also Rises* and of his descriptions of Montparnasse. If at times his descriptions of Havana were unsuccessful, or not pleasing, his descriptions of Montparnasse were vivid and beautiful.

"I also remember the world of the French Basques described in the same novel. *The Sun Also Rises* is a great book.

"The last time I saw Hemingway," Carpentier said, "was

at the Floridita. He was all alone. I had never seen anyone look so sad. He was drinking a Colonial. He drank it all down and didn't even greet me. I had to get out of there.

"During the war I met him at the Club del Cerro. In those days Robert Desnos was suspected of being a Nazi collaborator. When I met Hemingway he told me, 'I would put my hand in the fire for Robert Desnos.' And he raised his hand and held it over an imaginary fire. Desnos, as it turned out, had not worked with the Nazis."

Carpentier recalls the thirties in Cuba: "Evan Shipman went fishing with Hemingway around 1933, and they saw Machado's police boat throwing some bodies into the waters of the Gulf Stream. Evan later told me the story in Paris."

Carpentier used this anecdote in his novel, *La consagracion de la primavera—The Consecration of Spring.*

Later, Carpentier compared Hemingway with one of the greatest Cuban journalists of all time, who died in the Spanish War:

"Pablo de la Torriente Brau, one of the best young writers of my country. His style has many similarities with the 'brutal style' of your friend Hemingway, although I doubt that Pablo had any literary models. He was the least 'literary' of writers."

Further on in *La consagracion de la primavera*, when the protagonist returns to Cuba, he sees Ernest Hemingway at the Floridita, "elbows on the bar, sitting with his back to the entrance, his woodsman's torso bent over, gesticulating in the heat of a discussion about jai-alai technique with a picturesque friend of his, a charming Basque priest who was a combination of worldly wiles and holiness. 'Go say hello,' Vera asked me, eager to meet him: 'Remind him of Gertrude Stein's place. Mention Adrienne Monnier. Tell him we were in Benicassim with Evan Shipman.' 'He's busy with something else,' I said, glad that the writer wasn't looking our way. I had no desire to bring back such shadowy silhouettes: The Café des Deux Magots, the Rue de L'Odeon, Sylvia Beach's bookstore, Shakespeare & Co.—and Joyce crossing the street with the blind man's groping gait behind incredibly thick glasses . . . All that was in the past . . . they seemed to be part of another existence. . . . "

One day toward the end of 1959, Hemingway landed in

Havana and his friend Fernando C. Campoamor met him at the airport.

"Oh, Ernest, Carpentier tells me he wants to convey his greetings. He is thinking of visiting you at the Finca," Campoamor said.

"Georges Carpentier?" Ernest joked, "the boxing champion?"

# The Champion

## [101]

If you had only one choice, which one of all the American writers of your time, now dead, would you bring back to life?

Nelson Algren, author of *The Man With the Golden Arm*, did not hesitate: "For me, it would have to be Hemingway, Hemingway all the way." (Nelson Algren, *Notes from a Sea Diary: Hemingway All the Way*, New York, 1965.)

The choice could have been dictated by literary taste, by experience or admiration, but not out of gratitude, since Algren knew nothing about the marginal notations Hemingway made on the pages of *The Man With the Golden Arm* during a careful reading in 1949.

Hemingway received the book at Finca Vigía. It has an admiring dedication: "For Ernest Hemingway, the man with the golden typewriter."

The record shows that he started reading the novel in the Finca Vigía and finished it in a room at the Ritz Hotel in Paris.

There is an unusual note about the copy of *The Man With the Golden Arm* that Hemingway read. A poem written for Miss Mary at the Ritz, dated November 1949, was scribbled hurriedly on a blank page inside the cover of the book. Under the same date this note appears: "Read and Finish."

Hemingway wrote brief opinions and corrections on the narrow margins of the book, which show his concern with style, spelling and vocabulary. The notes either praise or criticize, but always from the position of the old professor who sees a bright student err or triumph on the everlasting battlefield of words and ideas.

Hemingway gives a resounding "bad" to a literary image Algren uses on page 296: "like a clock with a broken heart," but is excited about a sentence in which snow is described as falling "with a slow movement, suspended," and writes "beautiful" after and then "wonderful" over another phrase: "the slow snow trailing the evening trolleys."

Page 300 he qualifies as "wonderful" without exception. On the left-hand margin of page 302 he turns critical again, indicating to Algren in this imaginary dialogue that he "goes bad." On the following page, he indicates that all goes well with a brief "OK."

Hemingway thinks Algren is a poet. On page 324 he notes: "Is a poet—goes into straight poetry."

The author of "The Killers" invented or reinvented a word to qualify a passage of Algren's book: "OK-issimo," followed by "you're winning now."

On page 321 he interrupts his reading, and writes on a blank space, "No more notations, too late. Chips all down."

When he returns to the book he is more severe. He crosses out page 337 with a diagonal line, noting "Horrible," and addresses the author: "You ought to finish better." And then he adds, "But, see page 343." That's the last page of the novel. There one finds a note that is full of praise, of a more intimate character, and in the best Hemingway style:

OK Kid, you beat Dostoevski. I'll never fight you in Chicago. Ever. But I will knock your brains out in the other towns I know and you don't know. But: you are going to be a champion. But: and these are hard buts, you, repeat, you, hope to knock a champion out to win (unless he is Max Baer) OK. EH.

It wasn't exactly a lack of discipline on Hemingway's part that was responsible for the resounding critical failure of *Across the River and into the Trees*. The same severity he applied to his notes on Algren's book is present in the corrections the author made on the galley proofs of the book which is generally considered to be his worst.

Hemingway often answered this criticism with irony and unusual courage: "The best novel I ever wrote," he told *Time* magazine on September 11, 1950. Hemingway was very protective of *Across the River and into the Trees*, and he fought for it zealously.

"It's amusing to feel I have to defend my title again at age 50. I won it at 20 (*A Farewell to Arms*), I defended it at 30 (*To Have and Have Not*) and again at 40 (*For Whom the Bell Tolls*) and I have no objection to defending it at 50." The title of the *Time* article was: "The Champion Against the Ropes."

Raymond Chandler tried to justify Hemingway: "He is trying to sum up in one character, not very different from himself, the attitude of a man who is finished and knows it and is bitter and furious about it. Apparently he had been very ill and didn't know whether he would recover, and he poured on paper, hurriedly, how it made him feel as he faced the things in life he appreciated the most."

But the champion did not limit his defense of the book to outside the ring. Its galleys, revised and enriched by Hemingway at Finca Vigía, are testimony to his method and training. He once said that he welcomed any opportunity to revise his texts. These galleys, full of circles, arrows, additions and deletions, are a good example of his striving for perfection.

Galley No. 6 has one of the more illuminating additions to the orginial. Colonel Cantwell returns to the scene of his youth, when he fought in Fossalta, and Hemingway adds some important lines: "Where fertility, money, blood and iron is, there is the fatherland. We need coal, though. We ought to get some coal."

There is a note on the back of page 10 in which Hemingway observes, "This is wonderful and moving but in the last sentence I lose my way." Hemingway is referring to the description of a landscape. And then he does further editing: "I read it this way: 'Where the children play in the mornings and in the evenings; maybe they would still, etc. The punctuation I have suggested gives me its full meaning." And then he adds for his own benefit: "You lose your way too easy, kid. You lost it in Fossalta, Fornaci (Fornace) and Monastier (Monastir). But if that is the punctuation you want, OK. Probably better. *But* I don't leave a comma out always to be slovenly."

*Across the River and into the Trees*, delivered to the editors in October 1949, could be viewed as a study of how a 50-year-old man faces death after having lived as intensely as Hemingway himself.

Everyone who has read the novel knows that towards the book's end, Colonel Cantwell discusses with his driver, Jackson, the last moments in the life of General Thomas "Stonewall" Jackson, and repeats the words the general is reported to have said before he died: " . . . let us pass over the river and rest under the shade of the trees . . . " This was not just simple recall. It was the artistic use of information Hemingway had gathered from a book he had read, *I Rode with Stonewall*, by Henry Kyd Douglas.

On page 228 of that book, found at Finca Vigía, the six lines that suggested Cantwell's comments and the book's title are framed in blue ink. On the left side margin, written crosswise on the page, one can see in Hemingway's handwriting, in the same blue ink, the words *Across the river and into the trees*.

[102]

William Faulkner told literary critic Harvey Breit: "The five best contemporary novelists are Wolfe, Erskine Caldwell, Dos Passos, Hemingway and me." And referring to a previous statement of his: "I put Wolfe in first place, and myself second, and Hemingway in last place. I said that we were all failures. I selected the authors according to their efforts in their splendid failure to reach the impossible. I think Wolfe attempted to reach the greatest of impossibilities when he tried to reduce to literature the whole human experience. I placed Hemingway last because he always stayed within the limits of what he knew. He did it admirably, but he never tried to reach the impossible."

Faulkner's words angered Hemingway. He felt Faulkner had called him a coward because he had stayed "within the limits of what he knew."

A critic suggested that the clearly autobiographical aspect of *Islands in the Stream* and the exaltation of the courage and integrity of Thomas Hudson could have been a reaction to Faulkner's opinion. In one of the papers found at Finca Vigía, Hemingway writes:

. . .on his death-bed if possible, that I think he is a chicken-shit man who had great talent as a writer and for lack of application, rummy-hood, Hollywood and the usual faults of the professional southerner turned out to be a morning glory. But never did he fault to turn up in N.Y. for the launching of a new book, nor to kiss the ass of those who gave him prizes. Tell him I touted him all over Europe for years as the greatest writer in the U.S. because I was sorry for him in his rummy-hood and hoped he could get where he could make a living without whoreing in Hollywood. Tell him he is a whore and a sad cunt with a mellifluous voice and all the un-expended corn-directed talent of the Southern coward.

The original of this fragment is written on the letterhead Finca Vigía, San Francisco de Paula, Cuba. Only the sheet number 2 exists. There is no title. It is evident that he is referring to Faulkner: southern, drunk, the greatest American writer, Hollywood, etc.

William Faulkner's statement had deeply upset Hemingway, since, pride and principle were involved. Despite this, he kept an autographed picture of the author of *Sanctuary*, and in the *Paris Review* interview with George Plimpton he said that Faulkner was the writer he would have liked to edit.

Hemingway's pride was hurt. He had his friend Colonel Charles T. Lanham write Faulkner a letter listing all Hemingway's wartime and personal acts of courage.

"I was only earning my $250 fee," replied the Master of Yoknapatawpha County to the hard man of Finca Vigía, "and I said some things off the record, not for publication. I hope you accept my sincere apologies."

[103]

TIME
February 5, 1979
MILESTONES
DIED. Elizabeth Hadley Mowrer, 87, the first of Hemingway's four wives; in Lakeland, Fla.

Mowrer (née Richardson) and Hemingway were married in 1921. Five years later, he divorced her to marry Fashion Writer Pauline Pfeiffer. Remorseful, the novelist dedicated *The Sun Also Rises* to "Hadley," assigned her its royalties, and wrote fondly of her and their one child "Bumby" in his memoirs, *A Moveable Feast*. In 1933 Hadley married Paul Scott Mowrer, a Pulitzer-Prize-winning foreign correspondent and later editor of the *Chicago Daily News*.

[104]

"I believe completely in the historical necessity of the Cuban Revolution."

—EH to General Charles T. Lanham, 12 January 1960

The financial connection of Ernest Hemingway with the "26 de julio" clandestine movement led by Fidel Castro was discreet. It was limited to the purchase of a small statue of José Martí made by the Cuban sculptor Fidalgo, which was sold to enlarge the funds of the Fidelista organization.

His solidarity with the anti-Batista fighters was rather an emotional one. Throughout the insurrection Hemingway kept well informed about the course of the war, but his position, except in a few instances, was what could be called distant. Herrera Sotolongo recalls that at Finca Vigía they listened to the station Radio Rebelde, which transmitted directly from Sierra Maestra.

Recently, a red and black bracelet, symbol of the rebels, was found in one of the drawers at Hemingway's Cuban home. That was the extent of the writer's partisan part in the fight against Fulgencio Batista.

When Herbert Matthews went to Sierra Maestra to interview Fidel Castro in 1957, he naturally stopped at Finca Vigía. Hemingway and the old *New York Times* expert in Latin American affairs had been in Spain together. The owner of the Vigía had once called Matthews as "brave as a badger."

After his interview with Castro, the newspaperman spent a night at Hemingway's. Herrera Sotolongo was there.

"Despite Batista's claim that Castro is dead, Fidel is alive and fighting in the Sierra," Matthews told his friends. He confirmed this with photographs a few days later in *The New York Times*.

Two years later, Hemingway was intensely active on behalf of the Cubans. Because of the circus atmosphere of the trials and executions of war criminals of the Batista dictatorship, the revolution became the target of the American press. Twenty-four days after the triumph of the Cuban Revolution, Ernest Hemingway became a militant again.

Interviewed by telephone for a local radio station in Ketchum, Idaho, Hemingway stated that Castro's government was bound to succeed if it remained free of foreign intervention. He described Batista's people as assassins and torturers and declared that the revolution was good for the people; that the trials were fair and open to the public, and that Cuba, his home for many years, finally had "a decent moment in history."

According to newspaperman Luis Gómez Wangüemert, when the false news of Fidel Castro's death in the Sierra Maestra campaign was circulated and appeared in a UPI cable, Hemingway declared, "That is a lie! They say it in order to discredit the Movement. Fidel cannot die! Fidel has to make the Revolution."

Four years later, arriving in the United States from revolutionary Havana, he was accosted by a group of reporters who had been waiting for him. They mouthed disparaging things about the Cubans and their Revolution.

Hemingway let them talk a while before interrupting their chorus. "Are you through, gentlemen? I think everything is fine there. We, the people of honor, believe in the Cuban Revolution."

He had one year left to live. That meeting with the newspapermen as he stepped down from the airplane was the veteran's own farewell to arms.

"The story of Hemingway's last days in Cuba is interesting," says Herrera Sotolongo, "because it defines his ties to the Revolution, which frequently have not been properly judged. He was sincerely in favor of the Revolution. He liked Fidel personally. "They had not been friends, but Fidel admired him. I remember that around 1949, Fidel was very interested in going to

Hemingway's house to meet him. Fidel wanted to talk to him. The visit was never realized, although we talked about it often. Fidel would say: 'Listen, I feel like going there with you. I want to meet him. I'm interested in talking to him.'

"Several times I told Ernest: 'I'm going to bring someone here, a friend who wants to meet you.' But because of Fidel's activities, his involvement in politics at the University, we could never get together.

"They finally met years later at the fishing competition, during the ceremony of the Hemingway Award. It's curious— from the beginning one of the most important voices raised in the world in defense of the Cuban Revolution was Hemingway's. This is not well known, because when the Revolution triumphed he was in the United States.

"He went to Sun Valley for the ski season. He was getting ready to return to Cuba, but in those days there was a campaign being waged in the States against the Cuban Revolution. Fidel's first visit to the United States followed, and the campaign intensified, particularly in the press, which was very vocal against the trials and executions carried out in Cuba.

"Hemingway raised his voice against this campaign, a scarcely known fact because his statements were little reported. He wrote an article for a local paper which was published on its front page. In it he stated that the 'blood bath' propaganda was false, and that he had knowledge of the Cuban revolutionary process and could assure everyone that the number of executions carried out in Cuba did not correspond to the number of known criminals.

"Then, not satisfied with only the printed word, he made a record of it and had it broadcast on a local station. When the item reached the news syndicates, however, they ignored it. Not one important newspaper in the United States carried Hemingway's comments.

"A few days later Hemingway came to Cuba and brought the article with him. It is in Fidel's possession, for we sent it to him. In one of his first appearances on television, Fidel had the article with him and commented on it. Hemingway was always on the side of the Cuban Revolution. He would have died in Cuba if circumstances hadn't hastened his death."

Gregorio Fuentes tells us that from the beginning of the insurrection Hemingway approved the use of the *Pilar* to hide arms for the revolutionary movement.

"He saw what I was doing, but never interfered. He let me be. After the triumph of the revolution, when he came aboard and saw me wearing the militia uniform he embraced me and said: 'I love you more each day!' And he cried. We had our own secret conversations. Absolutely secret. They will go with me to the grave. We had our own way of talking or *not* talking. But we understood each other. That's the only way to be a revolutionary. Tight-lipped. I took part in the revolution with the boys at Cojímar who were in the '26th of July' movement. But I never asked Hemingway his opinion on the subject. And he didn't ask me. On the contrary, we both knew that each was doing his own thing, and that neither would harm the *other*."

### [105]

Rodolfo Walsh, a newspaperman from Argentina who at the time was a correspondent for *Prensa Latina*, was the man who wrote the cable about Hemingway's arrival in revolutionary Cuba.

This happened early in November 1959. The cabled report was printed in its entirety in several Havana papers. *Bohemia*, the magazine with the largest circulation in Cuba, published it without giving credit to the agency.

*Prensa Latina* was notified from New York that Hemingway had left for Cuba. Walsh waited at the airport from midnight on; nobody else from the press was there. With Walsh was a photographer named "Mickey," who was also interested in welcoming Hemingway.

The writer stepped down from the plane and greeted them cordially.

"Well, what news do you have? What do you hear about Camilo?" he asked Walsh. Camilo was the guerrilla hero who had recently disappeared on a flight from Camagüey to Havana.

"No news," Walsh answered.

"Listen, the northern hasn't reached here yet," Hemingway said, referring to the weather.

He was wearing a sports jacket, knit tie and mustard colored pants and was "loaded with small valises, tickets and strings," Walsh says. Antonio Ordóñez, the bullfighter, looking "very elegant," was with him.

"What do they say about Cuba in the States?" Walsh asked.

"Nothing," answered Hemingway. "The only thing New Yorkers talk about these days is a TV program, 'The $64,000 Question.' But Miss Mary is the one who keeps me informed about what's happening in Cuba. I am well informed."

REVOLUCION
November 5, 1959
ERNEST HEMINGWAY
again in Cuba
ARRIVES
—One more Cuban
—Not a Yankee
—With Fidel

HAVANA, November 4 (PL)—"I am happy to be here again, because I consider myself one more Cuban," said the American writer Ernest Hemingway as he arrived tonight in Havana from New York. "I don't believe any of the information about Cuba being published in the foreign press. My sympathies are with the Cuban government and all our difficulties," he said, with emphasis on the word "our." And he added: "I don't want to be considered a Yankee."

Hemingway was accompanied by the Spanish bullfighter Antonio Ordóñez and wife. At the airport he was greeted by his relatives and by a large group of admirers from the town of San Francisco de Paula where he lives, and reporters from *Prensa Latina* who were successful in getting an exclusive interview.

Asked if he still held the favorable opinions about the Cuban Revolution that he had expressed earlier in the year, he reaffirmed them fully.

"In New York, where I stopped on my way back from Europe, the only thing they talk about is the scandal of a program of questions and answers and about Van Doren's part in it."

Upon leaving customs, the neighbors of San Francisco de Paula give him a Cuban flag in gratitude for the favorable comments that Hemingway had made about Cuba in other countries.

In May 1959 (according to *Granma* in a recent tribute), the writer, answering the continuous attacks of the American press against Cuban revolutionary justice, wrote in an article: "I knew one of the men who were executed. If he had been executed a hundred times, it would not have been enough punishment for the terrible crimes he committed."

Hemingway referred to the situation existing in Cuba before January 1959: "I knew three men who were qualified teachers, but who couldn't find work because they didn't have the hundreds of pesos necessary to buy a teaching job." He concluded by saying: "I have complete faith in the Castro Revolution because it has the support of the Cuban people. I believe in his cause."

Euclides Vázquez Candela, then assistant editor of the newspaper *Revolución*, tells of his own experience with Hemingway. In April of 1959, on the eve of a possible trip by Fidel Castro to the U.S.A., Luis Herrera Sotolongo went to see Candela with a message from Hemingway. The writer wanted to express privately his opinion about the Castro visit and to make certain recommendations which would reach the ears of the Supreme Leader of the Revolution so that he would know "how to face American public opinion."

Candela allowed Herrera Sotolongo to lead him to Hemingway's home. On the way there, Dr. Herrera made a further comment: "Ernest must be very interested in communicating with you. Lately he has been seeing very few people, particularly at night."

For more than two hours, Mary Welsh and Hemingway briefed Vázquez Candela about the subjects which "the monopolists of the Yankee press would harp upon": the executions; the laws that were being announced to modify the economic structure of the country—above all, the Agrarian Reform; international policy; and the determination of the Revolutionary Government to stop depending on the dictates of the American State Department.

In the days when Guillermo Cabrera Infante was the movie critic for *Carteles*, he used to say between beers in the local shops: "Some day I will be like Hemingway." At other times he would assure his friends that he would be like Faulkner or Fitzgerald.

In fact, he ended up being the editor of the literary supplement of the publication *Revolución*, eager to play a leading role in Cuba's new revolutionary cultural policy.

It was while engaged in these activities that he met the famous writer. When Hemingway saw Cabrera Infante briefly in a restaurant in Madrid, he conveyed his "best regards to Castro."

In 1967, Cabrera Infante turned against the Revolution. He went to live in London in a flat decorated with Cuban flags and Persian cats. His work on Hemingway presents personal testimony of the great writer's loyalty to the Cuban Revolution. It's one of the rich possibilities life offers: a soon-to-be traitor vouching for another man's loyalty:

". . . the people of the town gave him a flag when he arrived. Hemingway kissed it. The photographers missed the gesture and asked him to repeat it for the cameras. Hemingway became furious: 'Gentlemen, that kiss was sincere,' he exclaimed. This gesture marked Hemingway's return to Cuba, the country he knew best, which he had described in 1935 as 'a beautiful ulcer in another part' . . .

"At that time Hemingway had also said in his advice to a young painter: 'Cuba is a place to leave rather than return to.' And he explained why: 'Because a young painter cannot earn a living here.' Now he was returning. 'Why is it a place to return to? Because every artist owes the place he knows best two things: He either destroys it or perpetuates it.'

"Hemingway had returned to Cuba more than once to perpetuate it. Was he returning now to perpetuate the Revolution? He had said several times that he wanted to write a book about the Cuban Revolution. Had he lived, perhaps he would have.

"In any case, Cuba was still his home. I remember seeing him in October in Madrid, where I stopped on my way to the Soviet Union. He was dining with friends in a restaurant near the Gran Via. 'How is Cuba doing?' he asked me, and immediately added: 'Everything is fine. I didn't have to ask.' He seemed about to go back to his dinner when he said: 'Give my best regards to Castro. We have faith in him.' He accompanied this with a gesture I couldn't understand. Did he mean Spain, his friends, or only the two of us?"

[106]

Scarcely a month after Hemingway's funeral, at the end of August 1961, a ceremony was held on the open porch of Finca Vigía.

Mary Welsh held a 30-page folio of very fine paper with the Finca Vigía letterhead printed in red, and with a signature at the bottom of each page. Fidel Castro was present in the role of official representative of the Cuban people. Also present were Gregorio Fuentes and the Herrera Sotolongo brothers, José Luis and Roberto.

A brief social exchange preceded the reading of the document. Mary Welsh handed the folio to Castro, but he refused it with a shake of his head, saying: "No, *señora*. You do it."

The thick document was written alternately in English and Spanish. It was a testament which included the transfer "for the welfare of the Cuban people" of Finca Vigía and the personal belongings of the writer. It suggested that a meeting place for young artists and a center for botanical studies be established there. The library, with more than nine thousand literary and technical volumes that would be left in the house, could be used for this purpose.

The document also included much useful advice on the maintenance of Finca Vigía, and a detailed description of the objects therein.

In accordance with the document, the ownership of the *Pilar* was formally handed over to Gregorio Fuentes. Hemingway also left to various friends in San Francisco de Paula a Winchester .22 carbine, a 1950 Buick and a 1953 Plymouth. The National Bank of Cuba would take charge of issuing the checks on Hemingway's account to pay the last salaries of his employees, including a bonus for each.

At the same time, Mary Welsh asked the Cuban authorities to find work for the former help at Cervecería Modelo Nacionalizada (Nationalized Model Brewery), a short distance from San Francisco de Paula. The document authorized Pedro Buscarón, who had worked at the farm for eight years, to continue to graze his horse there. To José "Pichilo" Herrera, head gardener at Finca

Vigía for 17 years, Hemingway left the cattle of the farm and the right to continue breeding his fighting cocks there.

Mary Welsh would take the most important works of art in the house back with her to the United States. She would also take possession of a number of prized unpublished manuscripts on deposit at the National Bank of Cuba, including the text of *Islands in the Stream*. The final clause stated that she would also keep for her own use the little house at the left of the main house, which would not be part of the museum and which she could use as lodgings in the event of her return to Cuba.

Several days later, the putative story goes, Mary Welsh proceeded to burn all the Hemingway correspondence in a fire she built, some claim, in the patio of the house. It is alleged that, if the story is true, she was following the writer's very precise instructions.

"Fidel phoned Finca Vigía in order to arrange a convenient time to visit Mary. I was invited to go there," recalls Herrera Sotolongo. "But I didn't make the arrangements, as Mary says in her book."

Fidel arrived at dusk. The three 1960 Oldsmobiles, dark purple, the means of transportation for him and his entourage, parked under the trees in front of the garage. Nine men in olive-green campaign uniforms, drivers and bodyguards, remained quietly standing around the cars. Fidel went into the house alone. He shook hands with Mary and Herrera Sotolongo, and was quickly introduced to the rest of the reception committee at Finca Vigía.

"This is your home," Mary said. "Please sit down."

Fidel was about to sit in Hemingway's easy chair, with the beret on his head and a big cigar in his hand, when Mary said: "That was Papa's chair."

Fidel didn't actually sit. He straightened up quickly.

Mary, smiling, exclaimed: "Oh no, you misunderstand! Sit there, please."

A light meal prepared by Mary was served.

"Anything you want to take, you take," Fidel said.

"The paintings, our painting collection," Mary answered.

Later on she chose a bureau she had in her room and the Hemingway manuscripts kept in a safety box at the bank. She was also interested in taking the bed linen, the tablecloths, the china and silverware.

Together they made plans for the museum. There was a valuable collection of antique editions of Hammond's *American Atlas* and another one of the works of Mark Twain. They agreed these should be put to use. There was talk of turning the garage into a reading room. (It is now used as an art gallery.)

Fidel stayed at Finca Vigía for two hours. He was particularly interested in the hunting trophies. He listened to the story of the greater kudu mounted in the dining room, and carefully examined almost all of the firearms. Mary said she would give him as a present the Mannlicher Schoenauer .256, "Papa's favorite." Fidel thanked her but said he would prefer to leave it in the house as part of the Hemingway Museum.

It was the same thing with the phonograph records: Castro and Mary agreed they should serve some useful purpose.

"There was always music playing there," says Herrera Sotolongo, referring to the Capehart so prized by Hemingway.

At the very moment that the official transfer of the house was going on, Glenway Wescott wrote in *The New York Times* that the destruction of unpublished works by Ernest Hemingway should be prevented; he thought Mary entirely capable of such a thing on her trip to the Cuban capital.

Mary explained in *How It Was* that it was only hundreds of old magazines kept by Hemingway that were destroyed in the fire she built below the Finca Vigía's tennis court. Among them, she says, were extensive collections of the bullfight magazine *El Ruedo* and *The Economist*. She adds that their close friends Roberto Herrera Sotolongo, Valerie, Mayito Menocal, Elicio Argüelles and René Villarreal wheelbarrowed loads of periodicals in the bonfire operation.

In the same book, Mary states that she took advantage of the opportunity provided by the Cuban leader to withdraw close to half a million dollars in jewels and various valuable objects left in her trust by a disaffected Cuban. These valuables were smuggled out of the country in her handbag.

Finca Vigía remained closed for more than a year. The Steinharts, Hemingway's neighbors, left the country about the time of the writer's death and an antiaircraft unit was provisionally installed in their home to defend, from the heights, a section of the city.

The fine crystal in the homes of Steinhart and Hemingway and other residences in San Francisco de Paula was saved, because no suspicious plane flew over the zone. The sixteen 100-millimeter Soviet cannons installed in the patio of Villa Steinhart remained silent.

At the same time, a batallion made up of orphan boys and former beggars was quartered at Finca Vigía while they received military instruction. They were not allowed in the house, but their camp was put up in the grounds. Somehow, before they were transferred, they found a way to open the door to the cellar of the main house and "liberate" a vast quantity of Hemingway's stock of liquor.

Luc Chessex, a Swiss photographer who arrived in Cuba late in 1961, decided to begin his photographic essay on Cuba with a few shots of the recently deceased writer's home. He was greeted at Finca Vigía by a very cheerful and lively bunch of boys:

"I arrived there the afternoon of December 30, 1961, and they took me out of there on January 4, 1962, practically unconscious, because of the great quantity of liquor I had drunk."

Together with Chessex, the boys were removed from the premises. The first visit by Fidel Castro to the Hemingway Museum was made almost a year later. The Cuban leader appeared with a captain of one of the American ships which brought food and medicine as part of the compensation from the Kennedy Administration for the return of the captured members of Brigade 2506, which in April 1961 landed and were promptly defeated at the Bay of Pigs.

[107]

GRANMA
July 11, 1977
HEMINGWAY WIDOW IN CUBA

At present in our country, at the invitation of the Commander-in-Chief Fidel Castro, President of the Council of State and

Council of Ministers, is Mary W. Hemingway, widow of the American writer, Ernest Hemingway, who lived for many years in Cuba and who wrote here the novel, *The Old Man and the Sea*, inspired by the life of a Cuban fisherman.

With Mrs. Hemingway came a group of motion picture people who propose to make a film based on the book she wrote about her life with the novelist. The group includes Jay Weston, producer; Sidney Pollack, director; and Waldo Salt, script writer.

Since their arrival in Cuba, Mary Hemingway and the film group have visited the Hemingway Museum, the town of San Francisco de Paula and Cojímar. . . . In the next few days they will visit other possible locations for the film and other places of interest.

Mrs. Hemingway's last visit to our country was in 1961, when she came to Cuba to donate to the Revolutionary Government the farm she and her husband owned in Havana, today the site of the museum that bears the name of the famous writer.

[108]

BOHEMIA
September 30, 1977
HEMINGWAY ALWAYS SIDED WITH
THE REVOLUTION
says Mary Hemingway, his widow, in an interview for *Bohemia*
by Luis Baez

Speaking in Spanish, which she hasn't used in 17 years and for which reason she had to resort to English to recall events and express some opinions, Mary Hemingway talked to this reporter a few minutes about some subjects related to Ernest.

"I wrote a book," she explains, "about my life. But it's only natural that it should have a lot of Ernest in it. I wrote it because so many lies have been written about Ernest, and I wanted to set the record straight. Thousands of lies. Thousands of lies have been written.

"When Fidel entered Havana, we were completely for him. One must remember—I'm old enough to remember—the regimes under which Cuba had suffered. The governments always stealing. All of them the same: Grau San Martín, Prío or Batista. We lived through all those times, so no one can come to us with stories.

As a matter of fact, Batista invited Ernest to lunch with him several times, but Ernest always found some excuse to refuse.

"He was positive," she stresses the point, "that with Fidel there would be changes that would benefit the people. He had put great hopes on Fidel, from the time he was still fighting in the mountains. That is why he was so happy when they finally met—and it was the only time—at the fishing contest.

"He was always on the side of the Revolution. Always on the side of Fidel. Anything else that has been said has been part of the thousand lies and innuendoes that have been written about Ernest."


[109]


She had returned to Cuba after 16 years. On a hot day in July 1977, she went up the pathway of Finca Vigía, perhaps for the last time.

She had her picture taken outside the house. A battery of Metro-Goldwyn-Mayer cameramen accompanied her under the supervision of Sidney Pollack, who was preparing to make a film version of *How It Was*. She visited her old dressmaker, Josefa, in San Francisco de Paula and presented her with a huge plastic bag containing one thousand aspirin tablets. Josefa, who suffered from arthritis, said she was moved by the present. Mary was pleased.

She went to Cojímar and saw Gregorio Fuentes. Then she returned to her old house, now the Hemingway Museum, and asked to be allowed to take some of the books from the library. She had brought a list of the books she was interested in taking from Finca Vigía, more than 173 of them from 45 authors, among them the ones Hemingway had mentioned as his favorites in his interviews with Lillian Ross and George Plimpton.

Fidel Castro received her at the Palace of the Revolution. He explained to her that a recent law passed by the National Assembly made it impossible to take any works considered national patrimony out of the country, Hemingway's possessions included. He regretted not being able to please her, but to make up for it he offered to help in any way he could in the filming of *How It Was*.

On her return to the United States, Mary Welsh expressed enthusiasm about her trip to Cuba. She had found all the things that had belonged to her and Ernest in perfect condition.

Mary had asked for a bottle of Gordon's gin, but none could be found in any bar in Havana. Just as with the prostitutes of the old Floridita, this aromatic liquor seemed to have disappeared. The much sought-after bottle of Gordon's gin finally appeared at the table during Mary's last dinner in Cuba. This was on the eve of her departure at the restaurant Atlantica at Playa Santa Maria del Mar, not far from Finca Vigía.

Margaux Hemingway, granddaughter of the writer, was at Finca Vigía a few months later. Her visit was quite different. Margaux went through every room of the house, its gardens, its paths. She stopped in front of one of the lounging chairs around the pool, one in which her grandfather had had his picture taken with her. She asked the photographer who accompanied her to wait outside. And they say that Margaux, that aloof and lovely girl, sat there and quietly cried.

LUNES DE REVOLUCION
August 14, 1961

### REQUIEM FOR AN AMERICAN
by Carl Marzani

His death, like his life, was strange. One of the greatest writers of this generation, a superb stylist whose impact in the world of letters can be compared only to that of James Joyce, he was, deep in his soul, a stranger in a world he had not created, a world that, represented by his native land, he had basically rejected. As a result, he made a cult of Individualism. . . .

I write with sorrow about the subject, because a family's privacy should not be violated and Mrs. Hemingway has said that her husband's death was accidental and the authorities and the press have supported that statement. But in our confused and fragmented society, where we are in such great need of intellectual beacons, Hemingway's death is so significant that it supersedes considerations of grief and delicacy of a private nature. He was a vibrant writer of great impact on the older generation, and a permanent influence on the younger ones. He lived according to his own philosophy and the circumstances of his death have an importance that cannot be denied. I believe that Hemingway himself, a man of such unquestioned honesty, would wish that the truth be known.

The facts, as printed in the press, leave almost no other conclusion but that of self-destruction. It is not only that it is questionable that a man accustomed to the use of firearms practically all his life, would try to clean a loaded gun. The press reported that no firearm cleaning material was found in the place where the "accident" occurred and that death was instantaneous. The almost bare police report, as well as the death certificate, says: "Bullet wound in the head produced by the deceased." The sheriff said that the wound was through the mouth, upward, and that both barrels of the gun had fired. Any knowledgeable person, and Hemingway was an expert in death-dealing methods, knows that certain and instantaneous death is produced by a shot through the roof of the mouth. The mechanics of the operation, including the simultaneous pulling of both triggers, practically excludes the possibility of an accident.

What motivated that last decision? Hemingway was ill and perhaps he feared the slow decline of his physical and mental faculties. However, in spite of private reasons, I cannot believe that his motives were totally separate from the contemporary social climate, the tensions and desperation that sounded in his ears like trumpeters of a humanity on the edge of a holocaust. I don't believe, for example, that the invasion of Cuba did not have an effect on Hemingway. He lived a long time in Cuba and loved that country. Many of the bearded leaders were his friends. Commenting on his death, the newspaper *Revolución* said that, "he was one of us." Hemingway loved loyalty and truth and it couldn't have been easy for him to remain quiet the last few months.

The American press, which has never respected a celebrity's privacy, has been dry and reserved in its comments on Hemingway's death. . . .

The depression that engulfed Ernest Hemingway had a fatal ending far away from Cuba. It seems that Hemingway, like many wild animals, went to die in the place of his birth.

His last steps were taken in an effort to find a set of keys: the keys that had been deliberately hidden from him. He found them, opened the closet and readied the gun. The hunter, according to his brother Leicester, used a silver double-barreled

12-gauge Richardson; Carlos Baker refers to a double-barreled Boss shotgun of the same caliber.

Whichever the firearm, some family friends later cut it up. The pieces were buried in secret places to prevent their falling into the hands of souvenir collectors.

The Cuban stations were among the first to broadcast the news that Sunday morning, July 2, 1961. A just and sincere epitaph was added to the information by the Cuban media: "A friend of Cuba has died."

There were two places affected in a special way by the sad news: Cojímar and San Francisco de Paula. The next day, Monday, as is the custom in Cuba, there was only one morning paper published—*Revolución*. That paper featured the story in a sober and deeply felt manner.

Ernest Hemingway was buried on July 6, 1961, in a cemetery near the mountains of Sawtooth, Idaho. There were about fifty people at the ceremony, almost all of them residents of Sun Valley. Hemingway's three sons and Mary requested the services of Reverend Robert L. Waldmann, of Our Lady of Snows Church at Sun Valley, for the reading of a special passage from Ecclesiastes:

"Oh, Lord, grant to thy servant Ernest Hemingway the remission of his sins," said the Reverend at the start of his prayer. "Eternal rest grant unto him, oh Lord . . ." But when he opened the Bible, he read only the first line of Hemingway's favorite verse: "One generation passeth away and another generation cometh, but the earth standeth forever." Either in confusion or reticence, the minister omitted the phrase that had been the motto of the Lost Generation: "The sun also rises."

[110]

In a desk drawer at Finca Vigía there is photographic testimony to the care Hemingway, the artist, bohemian and carefree, took to project a public image which would serve him as protective armor.

In his first safari in 1933–34, he seemed to delight in the role of the omnipotent white hunter.

Edmund Wilson took advantage of what he saw as an opportunity to compare Hemingway with a Hollywood actor. Later he would comment on Hemingway's book about Africa: "Almost the only thing we get to know about the animals is that Hemingway wants to kill them. As for the natives, although he includes a sharp description of a tribe of wonderfully agile runners, the main impression we get is that they are a simple and inferior people and that all of them admire Hemingway enormously."

In the fifties, when Hemingway went back for his second and last safari, *Look* magazine was paying for the adventure and Ernest had to deliver a report. He carefully checked the proofs of the pictures taken by Earl Theisen and rejected those he thought inadequate, where the shots were unflattering or unsuitable.

Long strips of these proofs are kept at Finca Vigía. He had written in pen a resounding *NO* on a photo that showed him smiling sarcastically at a dead lion. But he approved of those that showed him wearing the expression of the experienced, hardened hunter.

In a way, he was very proud of those pictures; he often showed them to his friends and told them how he had learned to spear-hunt with the Masai warriors and how he had faced "a tank with horns"—a rhinoceros—and resisted its frontal attack at a distance of a few yards.

There are some two thousand other pictures at the Vigía, among them the ones taken with Taylor Williams in Pahsimeroi Valley in the forties; Ernest's collection of war photos by Robert Capa; one in which he appears with boxing champion Tom Heeney in Bimini: those with members of the USAF at Finca Vigía; and those inscribed to him by Ordoñez, Dominguín, Marlene Dietrich and Rocky Marciano, among others.

Looking at these pictures one gains an idea of his great passions: fishing, docks, beaches, coastal birds, ports and shores. We see Hemingway with Mary at the tower on the farm; unknown visitors; caught marlin; Hemingway posing with an elephant at the Ringling Brothers Circus; Hemingway in Africa and at the Floridita; Robert Capa originals of Spain; photos of the Sino-Japanese war with Hemingway's notations; and, of course, the *Pilar*.

Among all the pictures and papers left at Finca Vigía, there is not a single photo of Hadley Richardson, Ernest's first wife.


[111]


In the spring of 1960, Hemingway stood for the last time at the converted bookcase he used as a worktable. Part of the time he worked on the long piece "The Dangerous Summer" (commissioned by *Life*), and on the final revision of *A Moveable Feast*. But when the time to leave arrived, he cleared the desk of the many sheets of rough drafts and quantities of blunt pencils. He put his Royal Arrow typewriter on top of a volume of *Who's Who in America* and placed two new, sharpened pencils on top of the worktable as well as a dozen sheets of carbon paper, the chunk of copper ore he used as a paperweight, his glasses, a writing board he used when he wrote dialogue and a book about the conquest of the west.

The metal-framed glasses prescribed for his myopia were made by the optical firm Lastra of Havana. In the volume of the 1954-1955 edition of *Who's Who*, a corner of page 1191 has been folded to mark the place where it says that Hemingway received his education in public schools and that he married Mary Welsh on April 11, 1946. It also mentions wartime activities and decorations received. It says that he belonged to the following clubs: Meyer, Philadelphia, Gun and Vedado Tennis.

The two pencils he placed on the worktable are Mirado 174 #3. The writing board was a present from his firstborn, who had it inscribed: "To Ernest from Jack." On the shiny surface of the board Hemingway wrote in ink the sums of the number of words written by him during one of his creative journeys. But he wasn't good at figures. There is an obvious error in the addition of the first column:

|     |     |
| ---: | ---: |
| 156 | 61 |
| 161 | 220 |
| 208 | 187 |
| 515 | 468 |

The chunk of copper ore weighs 570 grams. The carbon sheets have been used and from them one can make out the text of letters written by Hemingway; apparently he kept copies. The other book on the table, with uncut pages, is *A Pictorial History of the West*.

He finished his last work session at Finca Vigía, writing about the rivalry between Dominguín and Ordoñez, and revising his Paris memoirs. Then he closed shop.

Now, on the flat surface of the worktable, what's gone forever are the piles of paper, the books, pamphlets and newspapers he kept around him as he worked. He was in the habit of spreading sheets of paper as if they were bedsheets, perhaps to hide or protect the manuscript he was working on. The photos taken of him at work in the fifties show a man surrounded by so much paper that there is hardly any room for his typewriter.

He worked standing up, in Bermuda shorts, shirtless, almost always barefoot, his feet resting on a lesser kudu rug, or else wearing moccasins, but without socks, and with a bottle of Vichy water handy.

Knee-high, on the middle of the bookcase, he kept a magazine and four books: a German translation of his stories, the novel *Guadalquivir* by Joseph Poyre, *John Colter* by Burton Harris, *The People of the Sierra* by J.A. Pitt and the first issue published in 1953 of the magazine *Nucleus*.

At his back was his bed, which he used as the first stop for the correspondence coming into Finca Vigía and where the newspapers and magazines received after his death still lie.

The bottle of Vichy was at his left as he worked. A bottle sits there now, empty. The first object one sees at the left on entering the room is a huge aviation manual which Hemingway put on the floor to keep the door open.

The collectors of personal data on the writer will surely be interested in the contents of the table-bar he kept by his chair in the living room. There were six bottles of El Copey sparkling mineral water, bottled in Havana; a bottle of White Horse scotch; a bottle of Gordon's gin; six bottles of Schweppes Indian tonic; a bottle of Bacardi rum; a bottle of Old Forester; a bottle of Cinzano vermouth; and an empty champagne bottle without a label.

Hemingway reads the notice announcing that he has won the Nobel Prize for Literature, 1954. (UPI)

Hemingway pours a vodka toast to peace at Finca Vigía for Soviet first deputy premier Anastas Mikoyan (right) and Vladimir Bazikin, Soviet ambassador to Mexico, 1960. (UPI)

In his doorway at Finca Vigía, after being awarded the Nobel Prize, 1954. (Hans Malberg)

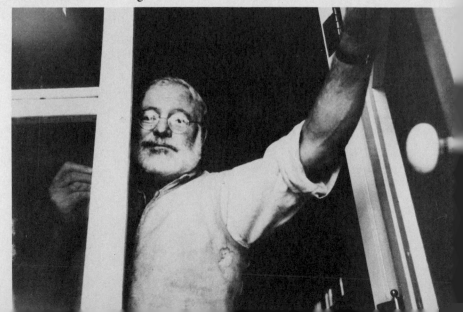

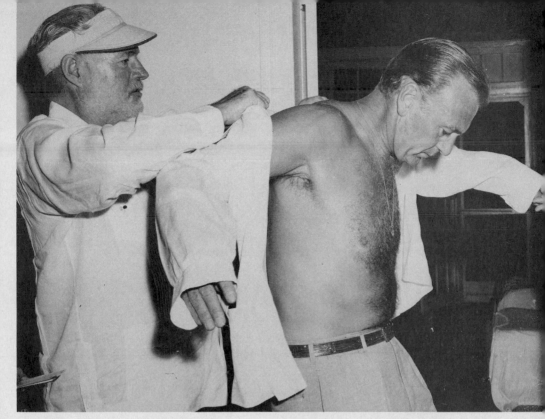

Hemingway helps his friend Gary Cooper into a guayabera after Cooper's arrival in Cuba as the novelist's guest, 1956. (OPI)

Marlene Dietrich wrote on this photo to Hemingway: "Oh, Ers I love you!" (John Engstead)

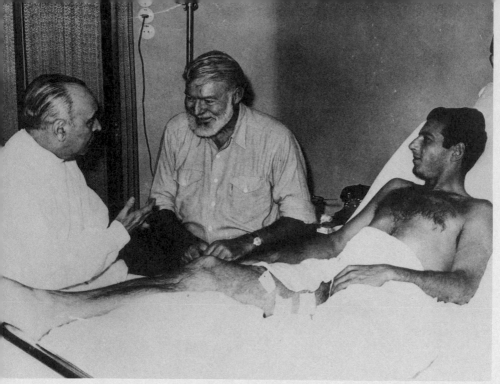

Hemingway visits matador Antonio Ordoñez in a Madrid hospital after Ordoñez was wounded during a bullfight, 1959. At left is Dr. Manuel. (UPI)

Matador Antonio Ordoñez salutes Hemingway at a bullfight in Spain, 1959. (UPI).

The museum collection also contains nine thousand books, and five hundred phonograph records that Hemingway kept in a bookcase behind his chair. In classical music his favorite was Beethoven, while in popular music he preferred Benny Goodman.

The inventory at Finca Vigía discloses the presence of 1,197 objects or 3,000 to 4,000 pieces, depending on who's counting. A bureau at Finca Vigía can be one piece or it can be many if it is counted by each drawer and its contents. The task is difficult, and it has fallen on the shoulders of two or three young men in white coats, the technicians in the house, who from 8 A.M. to 5 P.M. spend their time counting, recording and cataloging objects.

Hemingway's library has a copy of the 1951 edition of *Tender Is the Night* by Scott Fitzgerald. Turning the pages slowly, one notices that they are unmarked until we get to page 243, which contains Hemingway's only observation. Where the text reads "forward and clapped," he places two question marks and writes the correct word, "slapped," in place of the one that slipped past the editors and proofreaders.

Few books in the library have notations, but frequently the corner of a sheet of paper peeps out from between two books and we find a handwritten phrase on it. This was probably the case with a note scribbled on the back of an ordinary envelope: "Any woman would rather dig her grave with her mouth than earn her living with her hands."

The number two copy of the first edition of *A Bibliography of the Works of Ernest Hemingway* by Louis Henry Cohn, published by Random House, New York, in 1931, bears notes by Hemingway. The sharpest comment is on page 88. Cohn refers to "The Killers" and quotes a paragraph from one of the writer's letters in which he says:

> "There really is, to me anyway, very great glamor in life—and places and all sorts of things and I would like sometime to get it into the stuff. People aren't all as bad as some writers find them or as hollowed out and exhausted emotionally as some of The Sun generation. I've known some very wonderful people who even though they were going directly toward the grave (which is what makes any story a tragedy if carried out until the end) managed to put up a very fine performance en route."

Hemingway marks the page and writes: "What shit—Lousy violation of confidence." He makes a similar comment on page 115, when Cohn informs the reader that Hemingway took the title for *The Sun Also Rises* from Ecclesiastes, *The Torrents of Spring* from a book of the same name by Turgenev, and the title of *A Farewell to Arms* from a paragraph by George Peale. Hemingway disposes of the paragraph by commenting: "Some shit."

Hemingway inked in numbers on a copy of Emily Bronte's *Wuthering Heights*, published in London in 1935. The numbers appear in three columns on the cover, inside the cover, on the first few pages, and even over the title of the English classic. At the time, Hemingway was obviously worrying about his health. The first column of figures indicates the time of day, the second his temperature in centigrade and the third his pulse.

| | | |
|---|---|---|
| 0745 | 35.9 | 60 |
| 1200 | 37 | 66 |
| 1600 | 36.7 | 66 |
| 1800 | 36.6 | 54 |

He kept this strangely self-conscious record from November 25 to December 6 of an unspecified year, with brief explanations of the movements which might have influenced the slight changes in readings. "Up to dinner," or "Up to telephone."

There is a notation of an entirely different kind on the last page of the copy of *Wuthering Heights*. It concerns the first draft of Hemingway's Parisian memoir, which here is titled "The Lean and Lovely Years." Much later its title would be changed to *A Moveable Feast*. Hemingway started this book at Finca Vigía between the fall of 1957 and the spring of 1958. He had begun a first sketch in 1956 on the early years of his friendship with Scott Fitzgerald.

The writer reminisces about his adventures with "the lost generation":

THE LEAN AND LOVELY YEARS
The Three Mountains
Connection
The Lyons Trip

Scott date was agreed on and I confirmed it by telephone.

The tale of the journey to Lyons is one of the best parts of *A Moveable Feast*. Hemingway and F. Scott Fitzgerald had agreed that they would travel together on the train. But when the moment of departure arrived, Scott, an absent-minded young man, was missing. He had forgotten. As a result, Hemingway found himself speeding southward alone on the train, with very little money.

Another interesting item found in the library at Finca Vigía is the original manuscript of the famous story "In Another Country," in which the other well-known tale, "Now I Lay Me," appears as the second part, although without a title. Nick Adams, alter ego of Hemingway's youth, is the protagonist. The material later appeared as two separate stories in *Men Without Women*.

"In Another Country" was published for the first time in the March 1927 issue of *Scribner's Magazine* and "Now I Lay Me" premiered with three other stories in *Men Without Women*. Nick Adams is also the hero of one of the first novels conceived by Hemingway, although he never got very far with it. The original manuscript found at Finca Vigía combining the two stories may have been a fragment of that projected book.

There was, curiously, an intramural correspondence at Finca Vigía between Ernest and Mary. They sent each other postcards and Christmas greetings. Hemingway would also take copies of famous works of art, particularly the French Impressionists, and in his unmistakable handwriting dedicate them to Mary in extravagant French, signing the names of the artists. Gauguin and Van Gogh were two of his victims. These benevolent forgeries provided Mary with a collection of personal messages from the greatest masters of the century.

There are humorous Christmas, Thanksgiving and St. Valentine Day cards. On a card with the picture of a duck with plastic eyes Hemingway writes:

Monsieur le Conde de
Hemingwé
Chateau La Vigía
SF de P

Another card, showing a Christmas tree, but without a message or date, is misspelled in Hemingway's own handwriting:

Heddy Lamar

A sincere and tender message to Mary is written on plain cardboard:

To my dearest and blessed Kitten
who makes sense of this Christmas
and all the other 364 days of the
year

A card with a Paris subject is more enigmatic:

To *mi* Kitten with love

and it is signed:

Christopher Columbus

Under that name Hemingway drew two claws.

Another postcard: A different duck with the same plastic eyes. On it Hemingway wrote an address with politically suspicious overtones; the writer was inviting McCarthy's inquisitional interest.

Tovarich Hemingstein
Hotel Better World
Havana, Cuba
USSR

[112]

Of several curious Cuban tributes to the writer, none was more bizarre than the naming of an electric ceramic insulator after him. It was manufactured in the ceramics workshop called Gilberto León Alfonso. The workers themselves selected the name Hemingway as appropriate because "of its great resistance and the high voltage the insulator is capable of taking."

Another fine tribute was naming a dam after him, one recently built near Finca Vigía: the Hemingway Dam. In this case the workers in the hydraulic project did not bother to invent a reason for the choice of name, nor did they volunteer to make any comparisons between the life and work of the writer and the curtain of concrete holding back the waters.

Some of the places that were important in Hemingway's Cuban geography have vanished. One of these is the Club de Cazadores del Cerro (Hunter's Club of Cerro), where he and his youngest son, Gigi, used to compete at pigeon shooting. The place is an empty lot today. The Club Internacional de Pesca on Havana's waterfront has seen some changes.

The ex-International Fishing Club was used as a unit attached to the High Command of the Cuban Navy, and as a berth for Soviet submarines. Recently there has been talk of turning it back into a tourist attraction. The remote possibility exists that some fine day the *Pilar* may cast anchor there again. The Morro Castle, the grocery store at Zulueta 259 which he favored, is still there. But La Zaragozana, the restaurant frequented by Hemingway during the war, is no longer in existence.

Another restaurant, The Basque Center, was once located at Malecon and Prado streets, a memorable intersection in the Havana of those days. It is mentioned in *Islands in the Stream*. Juanito, the chef, made enough money to open a new Basque Center at Third Street in the Vedado section of the city, and it is quite famous today.

Some of the secondary characters in the story of Hemingway's life in Cuba were still alive in 1980: Ramón Jordán, Hemingway's drinking companion at El Brillante, a bar in San Francisco de Paula; the waiters at the Floridita, Armando Blanco, Luis Blanco and Guillermo Ramos; and Antonio Sánchez "Cotan," the guitarist of a trio that performed at the Floridita and to whom Hemingway gave some horns of animals he had killed. Ana Tsar (The Yugoslav) went insane around 1976. Marcelino Piñeiro, the waiter at Ambos Mundos, died in 1977.

Ana Tsar was the last of Hemingway's employees to leave Finca Vigía. When the estate became a museum, she was kept on to care for the cats and their descendants that survived the writer. Later on she widened her scope and took care of all the strays that appeared at the farm. She was very punctual. Every day at noon she walked up the path to the farm, carrying two steaming pots filled with a mixture whose pungent aroma was described as "penetrating and demoralizing" in a complaint signed by hundreds of local people.

Ana and her cats created a problem. The hour in which the sun reaches its zenith was renamed "the lethal hour," because it was impossible to remain in the vicinity and inadvisable to admit tourists or foreign delegations to Finca Vigía at that time.

Finally, the management of the museum decided "to retire our colleague, Ana Tsar" and to get rid of the 60 remaining cats, which by that time bore "no resemblance to the authentic feline race Hemingway had created."

The locales in Cojímar described in *The Old Man and the Sea* still exist: "La Tiburonera," the factory which used shark tails as raw material; La Terraza, where Santiago ate and drank, as did Thomas Hudson in *Islands in the Stream*; the Bodega de Perico; and, of course, the beach where Santiago's boat landed. On one side of the beach the Ernest Hemingway Fishing Club has long since been established.

The locales and some details of *Islands in the Stream* have changed considerably. But there actually was a bar for "crazy guys" near Havana and those unfortunate creatures indeed wore uniforms made of óld sugar sacks, exactly as described in the novel.

The shacks where the beggars lived went up around 1933, the last year of Machado's dictatorship. They made Thomas Hudson say that he "drinks to forget such misery." There were four of these slums fairly close together: "Isla de Pinos," "Llega-y-Pon," "La Cueva del humo" and "Las Yaguas." They lasted until the day the Revolution triumphed.

Hemingway's collection of paintings is said to have been valued at several million dollars when Mary Welsh took it from Cuba. It included "The Farm" by Joan Miró; Andre Masson's "Dice Game," "Composition" and "Landscape"; Paul Klee's "Monument in Arbeit"; and Juan Gris's "The Bullfighter" and "Guitar Player."

"Guitar Player" was one of Ernest's favorite paintings. It hung over his bed. In *Islands in the Stream* Thomas Hudson says, in Spanish, that "Guitar Player" is *nostalgia hecha hombre* (nostalgia in human form). The text also says that "across the room, above the bookcase, was Paul Klee's 'Monument in Arbeit.' " And adds: "Above the other bookcase was one of Masson's forests."

The trees of the farm described in *Islands*—the flamboyant, mango, avocado, the ceiba in the garden—are all there. The avocado tree, whose produce Ernest appreciated as much as the Cubans, is still producing.

In *Islands in the Stream* Hemingway describes the quarter of Jesús María, the expulsion of the French prostitutes in the thirties, the smoke from the tall chimneys of the Havana Electric Company, the part of the bay where the clippers landed, and the Castle of Atarés where Colonel Crittenden was shot.

The long list of plaques, busts, memorials, institutions, and even the line of ceramic electric insulators named after him guarantee the memory of Ernest Hemingway for years to come among the Cuban people. José Martí, Cuba's national hero, is the only man of letters who surpasses Hemingway in the number of tributes—and the extravagant love and devotion—he receives on the island.


[113]


The Hemingway who lived in Cuba has been compared with Gauguin. His vivid descriptions and acute interpretations of the island are a homage and an act of love. One Cuban literary critic showed real understanding when he asserted that the detailed physical descriptions of Cuba in Hemingway's work are on a par with the best he wrote about the woods of the American midwest, the rugged Spanish sierras or the snow-covered peaks of Austria and Germany. The critic adds: "This legacy will not gather dust locked in the Hemingway Museum, but to the whole world will represent a permanent tribute to Cuba."

Of the eight novels Hemingway wrote, three have Cuba as their main background: *To Have and Have Not*, *The Old Man and the Sea* and *Islands in the Stream*. Two novels have Spanish settings: *The Sun Also Rises* and *For Whom the Bell Tolls*; two have Italian backgrounds: *A Farewell to Arms* and *Across the River and into the*

*Trees*; and only one, *The Torrents of Spring*, takes place in the United States.

Parts of *The Sun Also Rises* are set in France, mostly in Paris, and some scenes in *A Farewell to Arms* have a Swiss background. There are geographic variations in *Islands in the Stream* as well, for part of it takes place in Bimini; and in *To Have and Have Not* there are chapters with a Key West background.

Hemingway's output from *For Whom the Bell Tolls* on had to do with Cuba in one way or another, because such work was either started or written entirely on the island. He had only praise for the two places in Havana where he found it easy to write well: Hotel Ambos Mundos and Finca Vigía.

Much of what Hemingway wrote in the thirties was done at Ambos Mundos, particularly his articles about fishing. When he returned to journalism after a lapse of ten years, he wrote "Marlin Off the Morro" in October of 1933. The first paragraph, a genial description of Old Havana as seen from the window of his hotel room, reflects the writer's excellent frame of mind.

Hemingway was to take advantage of the favorable writing conditions offered by that fifth floor corner room at Ambos Mundos: the view, the cool air coming in through the windows, the good service. He wrote several articles and stories there and started *For Whom the Bell Tolls*, although there are differences of opinion about the latter. McLendon, for example, says he started it in Key West, while other authors claim it was in Paris, on his way to Spain. Be that as it may, it was at Ambos Mundos, and then Finca Vigía, where *For Whom the Bell Tolls* took shape and where most of it was written. ·

After buying Finca Vigía, Hemingway finished the prologue to *Men at War* and on his return from the war in Europe started writing his final books. He began the rough draft of "The Sea Book," which eventually became part of *Islands in the Stream*. He finished *Across the River and into the Trees* as well as *The Old Man and the Sea*. He started and wrote most of his book of memoirs, *A Moveable Feast*, and started the novel he left unfinished, set on the French Riviera in the 1920's, *The Garden of Eden*.

Then, with great effort and the help of many friends, he finished and delivered to *Life* the long chronicle of "The Dan-

gerous Summer." This, and a few newspaper articles, some pro-
logues and two small fables, besides some notes, constitute his
entire Cuban output, most of which was written at Finca Vigía.

It is a trivial thing to give importance to the place where an
artist does his work, but Hemingway himself insisted on taking
up the subject: The Ambos Mundos in Havana and the farm are
referred to several times as splendid places to work.

The fact is that he lived 33 years in his own country, the
time divided into three stages, of which the most important one
lasted twelve years.

The first was from his birth in Oak Park, Illinois, until 1918,
when he went to Kansas City to work as an apprentice reporter.
The second, the years in Key West, took place between 1928
and 1939. The third consisted of the last two years of his life,
spent in hospitals and short stays in Ketchum, Idaho.

He lived for long periods of time in Europe: Spain, Italy,
Germany and France. Sporadically, Paris held him for a total of
four years, in the early days of his writing career. He traveled
in Africa, Asia, Canada, Mexico and Peru. But Cuba was the
country to which he invariably returned.

Havana was the place where he wrote and from which he
mailed his manuscripts to New York. Although painters had no
fine photographers to reproduce their work there, as a writer he
could rely on efficient typists to make clean copies of his manuscripts.

He would get up at dawn and start to work. He always said
that sunrise at the farm was the ideal time for his occupation.
He sounded like the exemplary dedicated professional: getting
up at daybreak, drinking a cup of coffee, sharpening a few pencils
and then giving complete devotion to his work.

But there are conflicting opinions on this. The old servants,
laborers and gardeners at Finca Vigía remember that he often
slept late; sometimes he stayed in bed all morning, and occasionally he would start work at nine, which is not exactly daybreak.

Though he may not always have been an early riser, there
was iron discipline when it came to keeping the boys quiet when
they played on the grounds near the house in the morning. No

sooner did they raise their voices than either René Villarreal or Mary Welsh would appear to scold them, reminding the youngsters that Mr. Hemingway was writing.

Ernest Hemingway spent one third of his life in Cuba, 22 years of continuous residence at Finca Vigía. With a distant view of the Gulf Stream and of the towns near the city, Finca Vigía, a house built on a hill at the beginning of the century, caused jealousy in the hearts of friends and critics of the writer. Why didn't he live in the United States instead of in a Cuban village surrounded by modest houses and cabins owned and occupied by carpenters, gardeners and factory workers? He was breaking the tradition of Mark Twain and William Faulkner by escaping a few hundred miles to the south.

His living in Cuba was and still is a cause of serious concern for some. Elizabeth Hardwick, reviewing Carlos Baker's biography, *Ernest Hemingway—A Life Story*, asked in 1969: "What was there in life in the United States from which Hemingway had to get away?" A reasonable question. The problem to her was not that he lived in Cuba, but that he did not live in the United States.

Actually, he never stopped being an American writer. He never even stopped being essentially *an American*. It was evident in his appearance and mode of dress: a big man with a ruddy complexion, wearing a light plaid jacket, or, nonchalantly, Bermuda shorts and sandals in a city where even today its inhabitants insist on wearing heavy trousers, shirts and street shoes in the classic Spanish tradition.

Hemingway, answering his critics, gave many reasons, some bantering, for making his residence in Cuba. Among them: the wide variety of mangoes growing in his orchard; the boys he coached and with whom he played baseball, who even ran for him; the cockfights; and the world of tiny insects and miniscule tropical animals that lived on the edge of his swimming pool.

These reasons were offered in innocent amusement, which unfortunately became a double-edged sword as the Cubans entered the fray and accused him of looking at the country with the eyes of a tourist. "Tourist vision," they called it, something greatly resented in a country that bled as it prepared for a revolution.

Where, they wondered, was the political view and interpretation of a writer of his magnitude? Zero politics, but a lot of talk of mangoes, small lizards in the pool, daiquiris and cockfights!

But of course those were not the reasons why Hemingway lived in Cuba. He had real reasons and they were numerous. He had made many references to them, in great detail and with affectionate enthusiasm.

The negative reaction of American foreign policy to a political event of global importance—the Cuban Revolution—gave free license to those who wanted to settle accounts with the island, and inevitably caused several Cuban critics to join in the controversy.

And thus it began. It started soon after Hemingway was buried; a squadron of American biographers fired the first shots. Carlos Baker, an otherwise well-informed writer, hurried into the trap. His chapter on the last phase of Hemingway's life in Cuba is contradictory. It seems, as one reads those pages, that Cuba is merely an exotic place and an accident in the life of the writer.

Leicester Hemingway, a writer with questionable intentions, and A.E. Hotchner, a journalist, did not hesitate to present Hemingway as a reactionary, selfish old man who worried about saving his collection of paintings and was forced by circumstances created by the revolution to close his house in San Francisco de Paula. Even Mary Welsh at times has portrayed an unknown and petty Hemingway.

The specter of an international conflict and the strained relations between Cuba and the United States—at times on the verge of war—have contributed to the remaking of a story. But the resentment Hemingway's long residence in Cuba aroused antedated the revolution, and it may be that subsequent political developments have strengthened an anti-Cuban sentiment in some individuals which should be judged in part as a reaction to the question without an answer: Why did Hemingway choose to live outside his country?

Friends and biographers of Hemingway should not forget that he was a voluntary exile. His restlessness started in the trenches in Fossalta, where the doctors removed 277 grenade fragments from his right leg; it continued in garrets on the left bank of the Seine; and later in Spanish inns and hotels. In Paris, when he decided to be a writer, he lived in two different places.

His first address was the fourth floor of 74 Rue du Cardinal, in the Latin Quarter, and then he moved to 113 Rue de Notre Dame des Champs.

It is touching to see among the papers he left at Finca Vigía the clippings of the first reviews of *In Our Time* sent from the United States to the expatriate's French address.

On his return from Europe he went to live in Key West, at the mansion on Whitehead Street. Later came the 22 years at Finca Vigía, and finally the house in Big Wood River where, old and worn, he decided to end his life.

Hemingway was obviously sincere when he said that he enjoyed his trees, his breeding of cats and dogs and the beautiful, sunny city nearby. He was equally sincere when he said that The Great Blue River—his name for the Gulf Stream—with the most abundant fishing he had ever seen was one of the main reasons for living in Cuba. And there was another factor: the cost of living. Besides being beautiful, Cuba was cheap, and Hemingway lived like a lord.

Today that sounds bad in a country which had to struggle hard to survive, where stores, bars and restaurants were poorly supplied or closed for years.

Even the Gulf Stream where Hemingway once fished for marlin became a zone of military operations. Yachts appropriated from millionaires were equipped with artillery and transformed into pursuit units. Their powerful engines and speed helped them serve as "pirate fighters" in the first detachments of Cuba's coastal defense.

Hemingway's yacht, although in good condition and a veteran of other wars, was spared this fate simply because it was owned by the famous writer. His house and farm were saved for the same reason. Finca Vigía would have been perfect for a day nursery, a school or a military establishment. Its location

high on a hill with a wide, unobstructed view is superb for antiaircraft defense.

But, above any other personal considerations, there are
Hemingway's three novels, the collection of articles and the story
that he wrote about Cuba. His relations with the island went
back 40 years: first when he fished for sport in Cuba's waters,
then as a guest in the Ambos Mundos, and finally as owner of
his own home.

Hemingway had deep roots among Cubans. He wrote about
Cuba and described the landscape and the people.

In a writer of his stature, who has been called the creator
of "the only intrinsic style of the century," this is most significant.
It means more than his taste for mangoes and cockfights. More
than living cheap amidst beautiful scenery, which, at times, reminded him of Spain. Cuba won him completely. There he settled, lived, worked, made friends, enjoyed life and transformed
his surroundings into art. What more could a writer demand
from his abode? He lived on the island because no where else
did he get that feeling so fully.

[114]

Hemingway killed a beautiful kudu bull in the Masai region, east
of Kondoa in Tanganyika territory, and described it with reverence and awe in *The Green Hills of Africa*. Fifty years later the
trophy head can be seen with its twisted brown horns and great
solid neck. It occupies the silence of an almost bare wall at Finca
Vigía.

Hemingway described the hunt and how much he had desired this trophy and how he didn't recognize in the heavy gray
bulk the most beautiful kudu he would ever possess. The gun
he used is well preserved: the old and greased Mannlicher carbine,
with its pull set at a thousand grams of pressure. It is a precision
instrument for professionals and was Hemingway's favorite gun.
It will never be used again.

And where it always stood, beside the sharpened pencils
and the chunk of copper mineral, is the portable typewriter with

the black frame, the only machine which gave Hemingway the feeling that he was really writing. American collectors have offered as much as fifty thousand dollars for it.

There are his books on the same bookshelves, placed the way he liked, without any order either by author or genre. There are the photographs of family and friends, small souvenirs, the ammunition of different calibers and the insignias, his own and the ones he had captured in the Second World War. His beautiful hunting boots are in their place and the last correspondence received at the farm remains unopened on the bed.

But no longer are there the works of art by Paul Klee, Juan Gris and Miró that Hemingway acquired in the Paris of the twenties, under the guidance of Gertrude Stein. Although they added value to Finca Vigía, they never affected the practical and informal feeling of the house. The paintings and ceramics, however valuable, merely shared the premises with the shells of .50-caliber bullets, gardening books, boxing gloves and 50 or so fighting cocks.

And outside, visible from the cement hallway which leads to the tower, is the view that Hemingway described. From there one can see the nearby hills and the towns near the city. If you look north over the refinery in the harbor, you can see the definite line of purplish blue which is the current of the Gulf Stream.

# Soldier's Home

[115]

As Hemingway would say, every story has an ending.

The man with the moustache, steel helmet, paratrooper vest, cluster of grenades at his chest, three canteens at his waist and a carbine in his hands was one of the most popular characters on the Siegfried Line in the winter of 1944. He could be found in the smoking ruins of a farm less than 500 yards from the German batteries, where he had installed an advance command post known officially as "Task Force Hemingway."

Germany was almost at the point of surrender. Hemingway

was rendering outstanding service not only as a daring war correspondent but as a courageous captain. Perhaps for the last time, he was giving free rein to his adventuresome personality. The officers and soldiers of the 4th Infantry Division must remember the "old fighting lion" and "General" Papa's canteens filled with wine, gin or cognac.

And yet, something came to an end there.

"When he came back from the war, his hair had turned gray," recalls Gregorio Fuentes.

He returned to the past aboard a silver plane, an aluminum Pan American twin engine that made the crossing between Miami and Havana. He landed in Cuba on March 24, 1945, at Rancho Boyeros airport. He wore a gabardine uniform, campaign boots and a scar on his forehead. He still looked good.

"The uniform was as becoming to him as it would have been on a West Point officer," said Herrera Sotolongo.

But the smile he gave the photographer who met him was suspect, and he kept his hand in a tight fist as he stepped down from the small DC-3.

The man had aged in the war, the man who, according to his own prediction, would never die.

He lasted sixteen more years.

[116]

So we beat on, boats against the current, borne back ceaselessly into the past.

—F. Scott Fitzgerald, *The Great Gatsby*

The hurricanes, the squalls, the bad times are over and tranquility returns to Finca Vigía. Once again there are film screenings and family chats in the living room, or games for the canasta championship after dinner.

Discreetly, Hemingway retires to his easy chair with a book and a glass of wine left over from dinner. He leaves the championship games to Mary, Herrera Sotolongo and one of the "boys": Sinsky or Father Andrés.

But what is going on inside that house besides friendly chats, innocent games and the running of the film taken so far away which shows the sadistic marine against whom the writer has sworn such extravagant vengeance? Nothing. Not much more is to happen in the house. According to the select few who entered there, the appearance of constant festivities at the top of the hill, "at the American's house," was only part of the legend.

Except that Hemingway has had a full day: he has been writing the love story of Renata and Colonel Cantwell, or the tales of desperate Thomas Hudson, or about Santiago, the old man of Cojímar. The morning journey has been intense: moving like a boxer, resting one foot and then the other, bathed in perspiration as he covered with words the sheet clipped to a board. This is Hemingway at work, in search of that clean, precise English prose.

Perhaps his three sons are visiting him, or maybe only two of them. Hemingway writes the story of a man named Thomas Hudson, who is plunged into the most painful loneliness in the world as he reads the telegram announcing the death of his two younger sons in an automobile accident on a French road.

"We'll play our cards to come out the best we can," Thomas Hudson says in the book. Hemingway, with his own life and work, is doing the best he can.

He once put Robert Jordan on a hill in Spain, lying quietly after blowing up a bridge, with Lieutenant Berrendo approaching as Jordan has him centered in the sight of his automatic rifle. Now he has an old fisherman named Santiago in a small boat surrounded by sharks, fighting to save his big fish and knowing that it is possible to be destroyed but not defeated.

Or he is dealing with Colonel Cantwell, stricken with heart failure and in love with a young woman, but trying to attain something, searching for something beyond the river, beyond the trees. In a way, this was Ernest Hemingway's search, too.

Maybe Adriana Ivancich is a guest at Finca Vigía and he is trying to flatter her, seeking a name for the girl's alter ego in the book. (He settled on Renata.) Perhaps he's heard from an old friend, or one of them is present and he feels the need to write about male companionship, so he tells the story of a group of apparently rough, determined guys who decide to take a stand and face the cunning crew of a German submarine.

Hemingway's heroes are forever in combat, forever making confrontations and taking risks. ("Whoever seeks danger will perish," is a warning in *Don Quixote*.)

In *Across the River and into the Trees*, a romantic novel that never did ring true, Richard Cantwell, a colonel in the American army, old and suffering from a heart condition, tries out different formulas to keep sacred in perpetuity the places where Dante, Giotto, Titian and Piero della Francesca created their masterpieces. Conversing with his friends, Hemingway also expounds on the thesis that the places inhabited by Dante should be preserved forever.

What to do, then, with that corner of a room in a Cuban house where the lonely writer created some of the most indestructable characters of our age?

Mary Welsh said that the place was nothing without Ernest. We can also understand Herrera Sotolongo's desire not to return to his second home, although occasionally he goes to see "how things are there." And there is the nostalgia shared by all those who used to visit Ernest there: Gregorio Fuentes, Kid Mario, Luis Villarreal, Pichilo, Pancho Castro, Gilberto Enríquez. The clock has stopped at Finca Vigía. The place is "frozen in time."

Gertrude Stein, who taught Hemingway some key lessons in matters of art, was never there, nor was Scott Fitzgerald, another friend of the Paris years. Would Gertrude Stein have admitted that Finca Vigía was in fact "a good place to live"? If Hemingway was not the one who found it, he at least had the good sense never to leave it. And one wonders what Fitzgerald, that shy man with squinting eyes and a half-smile, would have done in a Cuban forest of gigantic ferns, flamboyant trees and tamarinds?

Scott died on October 21, 1940, just a few weeks before Hemingway received title to the property. He never heard of Finca Vigía, though it might have been good for him to come.

Hemingway, however, was rather cruel in his description of his old friend in *A Moveable Feast*. He told of a visit to the Fitzgeralds' apartment in the Rue de Tilsit, where Scott showed him an enormous ledger in which he had listed all the stories he had published, year after year, with the sum he had been paid for each:

"He showed it to us with a special pride, as if he were 'the curator of a museum.' "

There is not a similar book of accounts among the objects and documents found at Finca Vigía, but between the folders in the files there are some papers in Hemingway's handwriting on which he kept an exact record of the selling price of his books.

Hemingway left instructions to have all his personal papers destroyed, although he yearned for the inaccessible future.

He always fought for complete control of every detail of his existence. But inexorably, the time came when all pretense of control disappeared.

No one can be a stoic all the time, or keep struggling forever. Nor is it necessary. Rest is part of the program, death and destruction as well. Maybe Finca Vigía should have disappeared with its last master. But it stands today, a solid white house resting on strong Spanish foundations, a lasting reminder of Hemingway's life in Cuba.

François Mauriac once declared that he was not afraid of being forgotten when he died, but rather of not being forgotten enough. Ernest Hemingway worried about something else. And the strong man in the end became weak and erratic, losing his last battle to a 12-gauge silver-barrelled gun.

# Appendix I: The Finca Vigía Papers

Among the personal papers that Ernest Hemingway left behind when he departed Finca Vigía for the last time, shortly before his death, were a number of letters, many of which display his affection for his friends and, particularly, for Mary Welsh Hemingway, his fourth and final wife.

The 16 long love letters Hemingway wrote to Mary from Europe during World War II are full of longing and a lover's passionate declarations. They are also a writer's diary of his life as a correspondent on the fighting fronts. One of them is prophetic, the letter of a romantic seer who successfully predicts a future in which he will be strolling the beaches of a deserted key off the coast of Cuba, hand in hand with his beloved.

These letters, published now for the first time, were written between early November and Christmas of 1944. They form a discovery which could rightfully be called: "Hemingway's Lost Love Letters to Mary." This wartime correspondence and the peacetime notes EH mailed to a young Italian countess, Adriana Ivancich, bring us closer to an appreciation of the man's character and his genuine fondness for women. This is an understanding that has escaped some observers.

Mary Welsh Hemingway and Hemingway's relatives have said that he did not want his letters published. But they finally made them public, believing in the words of Carlos Baker, his biographer, that "they deserve the wider audience that his books have always commanded."

The first Hemingway letters to be published in his lifetime appeared in an essay by Edmund Wilson, "Emergence of Ernest Hemingway," and put the writer in a bad light. Perhaps Hemingway's refusal to have other personal papers published arose from that experience. Early in 1981, Charles Scribner's Sons published an extensive selection of the Hemingway letters with the consent of Mary Welsh and with Carlos Baker as editor. This literary event, turning against the writer's explicit wishes, dispelled my own scruples in the matter.

Some words by André Gide also contributed to my decision to publish the papers Hemingway left at Finca Vigía:

> No doubt there are literary men always so delicate and of such easy modesty, that they prefer not to see any more than the busts of great men and rebel against the publication of intimate papers, of private letters: it seems that they object mainly to the flattering pleasure that mediocre spirits may derive on discovering that their heroes are subject to the same imperfections. They talk then of indiscretion, and in a romantic vein they even write about violation of the grave, or at least, unhealthy curiosity and say: Let the man be! Only his work matters! Evidently. But to me, the admirable thing, the inexhaustible source of learning is what he has written *in spite of* himself.

—Gide, *Dostoiewski*

The earliest paper found at Finca Vigía is a letter written by Gregory Clark to Ernest Hemingway dated March 12, 1924. Clark, a journalist, and his wife Helen were friends of Hemingway's youth. They met in the offices of the *Toronto Star*. It was Clark who back in 1920 took Ernest to see J. H. Crostone, who would almost immediately give him a job on the paper.

Hemingway resigned from the *Star* in 1924 because, among other reasons, he couldn't get along with the irascible City Editor, Harry Hindmarsh. He left Toronto on January 12th of that year with Hadley and their son John. The Mary Lowrey mentioned in the letter was a member of the editorial staff of the *Star* and the only person from the newspaper to see the Hemingways off on that cold afternoon in January.

Both fascinating and heartbreaking is a paper dated June 1953. That was a particularly bad time for the Hemingways. Papa was romantically interested in the young and beautiful Adriana Ivancich and this must have been difficult for Mary to accept. Hemingway wrote a long, pathetic note to Mary about their difficulties, particularly sad in view of his high hopes for an ideal marriage, as expressed in the "Dear Pickle" letters of 1944.

There are long letters from his dear friend Marlene Dietrich, and from the young Italian beauty who embodied his last romantic dream.

Then there are the letters he received and wrote at Finca Vigía. These include letters to relatives, friends, business associates and ex-wives. Obviously, he maintained good and even affectionate relations with his former spouses.

And last, but certainly not least, are the typewritten fragments, perhaps for some work in preparation. One could have been for a wartime article. Another is a bitter tirade against women.

Here then, the Finca Vigía papers. We present them unedited, as we found them, including the eccentric spelling, grammar and punctuation that Hemingway affected in his private correspondence.

NOTE: In view of Hemingway's fondness for nicknames, the following may help the reader to more readily identify the person referred to:

*Wives:*

| | |
|---|---|
| Pickle | Mary Welsh |
| Marty, Mook | Martha Gellhorn |

*Sons:*

| | |
|---|---|
| Bum, Bumby | John |
| Mousie | Patrick |
| Gigi, Gig | Gregory |

*Sisters:*

| | |
|---|---|
| Beefy | Carol |
| Sunny | Madeleine |
| Marce | Marceline |
| Ura | Ursula |

*Women friends:*

| | |
|---|---|
| Kraut | Marlene Dietrich |
| Daughter | Adriana Ivancich |

*Men friends:*

| | |
|---|---|
| Buck | Gen Charles T. Lanham |
| Wolfie | Winston Guest |

# Contents

36. Letter from Martha Gellhorn, May 28, 1945.
37. Letter to Martha Gellhorn, undated.
38. Notes for a story.
39. Letter to General Charles T. Lanham, June 9, 1945.
40. Letter to "Raymond," September 18, 1945.
41. Letter to sister Carol, 1945.
42. Letter from Sidney Franklin, June 5, 1950.
43. Letter from Ingrid Bergman, December 12, 1950.
44. Letter from Ingrid Bergman, January 28, 1952.
45. Letter from Malcolm Cowley, August 3, 1952.
46. Letter to Bernard Kalb, August 17, 1952.
47. Letter from Michael Lerner, August 20, 1952.
48. Cable from Marlene Dietrich, August 28, 1952.
49. Letter from William Randolph Hearst, Jr., September 10, 1952.
50. Note to Mary Welsh, June 1, 1953.
51. Letter to Gregory Hemingway, August 7, 1954.
52. Letter from Adriana Ivancich, October 6, ?.
53. Letter from Adriana Ivancich, October 20, 1954.
54. Part of letter to Adriana Ivancich, undated.
55. Undated cable to sister Ura.
56. Letter from Marlene Dietrich, August 25, 1955.
57. Letter from Leonard Lyons, April 18, 1956.
58. Telegram from Ellen Shipman, June 25, 1957.
59. Letter to Minister of the Interior, undated.
60. Notations and fragments.
61. Fragment.

[1]

Letter to Hemingway from Gregory Clark, a friend from the staff of the *Toronto Star*.

March 12, 1924

Dear Hemmy,
    Seven weeks today, the first of May.
    That day, I go with Messer Mossop, mgr. of Allcook Laight and Westwood, tackle makers to his majesty, to his preserve on the pine river seventy miles nor, nor-west of Toronto, two days later I celebrate the opening of the season proper by going to Dunc Campbell's preserve

near Milton with Wm. Milne, and then on May 17, in company with wife, father, brother, Milne and wife, I go to Agwa Bay, 103 miles north of the Soo on Algoma central ry. to fish in three rivers that empty into that water, the Sand, Agwa and one other river that nobody has yet had time to name, so busy have they been catching Lake Superior trout.

Following your unspoken but inferred suggestion, I got me a fine split cane fly rod, nine feet long, five ounces, stiffish backbone for laying either wet or dry fly. I have been down to Sunnyside beach at unfrequented hours and practised with it, using level line, and you'd be surprised the length I can lay out . . . Surprised.

I deeply regret that Messer Mossop has not yet completed my long ordered hatch of flies, so I can't send you the promised selection yet. But he says they will go duty free marked "gifts."

We got Hadley's letter. How happy you three will be. I can now that Hadley has given us the setting, see why we have had no letter from Hemmy. I can see Hemmy loafing furiously about Paris, seeing everything, reassuring himself, taking a drink here and there, calling on friends, coming home late, making sure Paris is just where it was and nothing further from his mind than that he would write a letter.

You old bum.

I have sent for the Chicago Trib review of you and I intend putting it on the office board in the local room.

Nothing has changed. Nothing. Mary Lowrey if abstracted over her coming marriage, oddly concerned with painting and plumbing and furniture. Can get no arguments in the Womens Room. Hindsmarsh still thumps about, unconquered by sciatica, a grizly lurking about a cattle range. Cranston is still concerned with the "number" I have in hand for coming week, never the kind or quality. No kick in anybody. Lately I have been coming down at six am and by this device I get a slight kick out of myself.

I wonder if someday I mightn't get into mischief out of sheer ennui.

I have completed scene Eight of my MacKenzie playlet. Curtain rises on darkness, in which you can see long, perpendicular cracks in a barn wall. Large double barn door opens backstage and wind blows both halves open. Scene, a wide, snow landscape under moonlight, another barn in distance. Farmer enters, silhouette only, and speaks Mackenzie's name. Mackenzie rises from hiding in straw pile on floor. Also silhouette against the white snow background outside. Other furtive figures appear, come and stand within barn. One woman stands out in snow, slightly lighted herself, only looking in occasionally, but watching off to east. They tell Mackenzie a party of horsemen went up the next side road. They have a horse saddled for him. They have a sack of provisions. Mackenzie silhouette, makes his final speech on the things he lived for in pitiful halting speech to five farmers in which he slips into the parliamentary manner, as though addressing the assembly of Upper Canada. Woman makes a sudden gesture and says something inaudible. In midst of speech, they all hasten out of barn, out of sight. You are left looking at snow landscape out barn doors for a moment of silence. Then curtain.

By silhouette, I return the thing to legend, as I took it in scene one out of legend.

Needless to say, I like it.

But will it ever get done? . . .???

Hey?

Hadley's letter was gorgeous. Artful woman, she knew how we would be interested in the domestic details, and the hourly progress of John Hadley Nicamor. Now Helen is terrified at the prospect of answering such a long, generous letter: (she hasnt written her brother in Paris for thirteen years!) But I have agreed to collaborate with her.

Hadley we love. And what a wonderful girl she is considering the husband she has got! He is wonderful for a lover, I dont doubt; but as a husband . . . Ah, well: history records the lives of the wives of genius; they always had a time of it.

The big slob.

With all our love,

Greg

[2]

The following sketch or vignette was no doubt written in the twenties. It has the return address he used to write on the upper left side of all his literary output of that time.

Ernest Hemingway
Guaranty Trust Co. of N.Y.
1, rue des Italiens
Paris O France

Benchley: The Image and The Man

The story up until now—The story stars about two expatriates named Frances E. Butcher. They are both in the publishing business but it has been a long hard winter in the publishing business and they are thinking of growing full beards and becoming six day bicycle riders. Only one thing keeps them from this. They cannot count and they have never been on a bicycle. But they are not dismayed by this and soon they have gone in for raising rabbits. We see them engaged in this for some time. Then, knowing raising rabbits can be carried only so far they take to lowering rabbits. This pays better but the police step in. Just as the old place is being sold Benchley comes along. He is only a step behind Lincoln. Lincoln speeds up but Benchley knows what makes the old mare go and slipping a five dollar confederate bill under the saddle he is soon an easy winner. Lincoln dismounts and they follow one another down Fifth Avenue. This is before the day of the cable cars and Benchley cannot understand it. He appeals to passersby but no one will buy the gasoline he offers as it is before the day of the motor car. Benchley has a pack filled with copies of the Old and New Testament which he is willing to sell but no one makes an offer. A passerby steps up and informs Benchley politely that it is still B.C. Benchley thanks him but is plainly puzzled. Just then the Misses Frances E. Butcher pass. Driven on by poverty they have taken to raising and lowering rabbits in the streets. Benchley is horrified and resolves that if he ever has a chance to strike a blow at the shameful traffic he will do it. This is the point we have now reached in the story.

### Benchley and the Young Lincoln

Some one clapped Benchley on the shoulder. A strange place, Benchley thought, but he looked up.

"Benchley," a tall man in a battered cocked-hat said. He put out his hand.

"The rail splitter," Benchley greeted.

"How did you know I wasn't Washington in this hat?" Lincoln asked quickly.

"Ha ha," Benchley said. "Fancy not recognizing the old rail splitter."

They fell into step together along the Avenue.

"Split many?" Benchley asked.

"Not many. And you, Robert, how are things going with you?"

"A little dull," Benchley said.

"Like me to tell you a story? A new Lincoln story?"

"No," said Benchley.

"Like me to tell you about how I wrote the Gettysburg address? Some woman writer wrote a pretty nice piece about that."

"I read it," Benchley said. "Nice piece."

"Like to hear what I did to Stephen Douglas out in Illinois?"

"Let's have a drink," Benchley suggested. They entered a saloon. (This is important. Everybody drinks in Biography now. As a matter of fact everybody drinks almost everywhere now. The whole thing is pretty reprehensible)

"Seen Washington?" Lincoln asked.

"No," replied Benchley. "Seen Connally?"

"No," replied Lincoln. "Seen Stonewall Jackson?"

"No," Benchley answered. "Seen Stewart?"

"No," Lincoln said. "But I've seen Andrew Johnston."

"That's all right," Benchley said. "I've just seen Charlie Mac-Arthur."

"What's MacArthur doing now?"

"I don't know," Benchley answered. "What's Johnson doing?"

"Oh, let's stop it," Lincoln said. "Like me to tell you about freeing the slaves?"

"Sure," said Benchley. "What about the slaves, Lincoln?"

"I freed 'em," Lincoln answered.

"How do you think it will work out?"

"It's a little early to tell yet. What have you been doing yourself, Robert?"

"Writing."

"Get any of it published?"

"Faster than I can write it."

"Make you feel pretty good?"

"How do you mean?"

"Like this," Lincoln took a deep breath and flexed his arm. "On top of everything."

"I keep pretty busy," Benchley answered.

"They call me the Emancipator now," Lincoln said.

"Nice name," Benchley said. "Sounds better than rail splitter.

"I don't know," Lincoln said. "I was fond of the old name."

"Well," said Benchley, "I've got to get along. Come around and look me up some time, Emancipator."

"Rail splitter to you, Robert," Lincoln said and put his arm kindly on the young man's shoulder.

Benchley walked out into the street. It had been strange seeing Lincoln again. Odd how tall Lincoln was.

[3]

Letter from Leicester Hemingway.

Tuesday, March 19th, 1940
Off the dock at Cozumel Island,
Quintana Roo, Mexico.

Dear Stein:

You were dead right about all young Cubans, and it took just 24 hours to find out. The great Rafael Cortez Y Horseshit, descendent of the conquistadores, modern conquerer of the seas and far places, is a seasick kid who is in the way, can't cook while the vessel is moving nor steer in a seaway.

We had a hell of a good crossing, and further test of the boat and crew and Tony and I functioned perfectly and are getting along at a great rate.

First day ran down to Bahia Honda before the wind gave out, got a good departure from Gubernadora light at five in the afternoon and streamed the log. Made seventy miles due west during the night, and by noon of the next day we were fifteen miles west of the Cape, with a heavy swell, light following breeze, and every prospect of another good night. It was good, we made another forty miles out of it, breeze picked up in the morning but died at noon. The high white haze of a norther was filling that whole half of the sky and at noon of Thursday I ran the motor a couple of hours, spoke a Cuban coming off the banks who swore he was 50 miles NE of Contoy light, and who was pushing with his own motor to get across the channel before the norther hit.

It came as a healthy line squall at three in the afternoon, and scared the crew green. The day before he swore there was quite a sea on one of the lovliest days I've ever seen, and vomited copiously. But when this norther came and we reduced sail and were still driving along like hell in a rapidly rising sea, he swiped my bunk aft, pulled a blanket over his face, and was of no use for 24 hours. Eighteen of 'em were as fighting as I ever want to see. We had to run down those fifty miles to pick up the Cape Catouche light, then bear off to the east to clear Contoy with a long reef off to the north of it, and then hold her out to the eastward the rest of the night to be well clear of the reefs north of Mujeres that the 2 knot current sets on. At daylight we jibed her over, just the foresail [?] stay up, and both in great danger of blowing clean out of their boltropes. The boat was a perfect lady. Filled the cockpit repeatedly with the tops of seas but they were really big, and it was excusable. Tony and I spelled each other every couple of hours, and changed clothes and rubbed down every time we climbed down into the cabin. At ten in the morning we made in a few hundred yards under the southern tip of Mujeres, and heaved the hook. It was still blowing about 40 miles an hour and the ace crew wouldn't believe we'd made land.

We spoke a smack before dark Thursday, running down on it like a stationary object, and they were reduced to staysail alone and wollowing badly. Looked damn lonely and they were glad to see a boat smaller than themselves out in it because it was a bitch out on that bank, shoal water yet plenty of wind. After we got into Mujeres the smacks kept coming in, all within a few hours and with storm trysails and jibs alone. This was the only lee for a hundred miles. We ate like hell and felt good and slept and moved up into the settlement the next morning and formally entered under protest. Very nice customs, nicked us five bucks only, and we got to see the sort of town that lays at the northwestern tip of the island. Extra pretty place, with lots of turtling, and friendly citizens, and we lay in until Monday, yesterday, first day of sun since Thursday morning. Then got our papers and shoved down here to see this greatly-talked-of spot, and get to see the people. Wish to hell we could get a good young Mexican crew, but great paper-changing business needed, and no American Consular rep., here.

Tony says we might keep the bumbling beef for his neusance value, because we can apparently forever put in places on account the crew is sick. He is truely a sleazy twerp though, and to think of paying him a salary for his presence, is preposterous.

Got sick yesterday afternoon coming down here on a 40 mile run in the gentlest of easterly breezes, no sea, sunshine and absolutely no motion to the boat. He has no explenation for his, and simply claims he was never like this before. He moves his bowels properly, eats like hell, sleeps tremendously, cowers spectacularly and wants to know when we will fetch the land, even when it is in plain sight. Neither of us has been the slightest bit sick and we have done every bit of the work except seven meals he has cooked in harbor, and two he prepared off the Cuban coast that first day.

He damn near broached the boat in the following sea when we were forcing him to handle the tiller for ten minutes while putting on a reefed main off Cape Contoy that Thursday midnight.

The hell with him. I'm for signing him off in Belize. He's too good for our egoes.

This is a pretty place, and Mujeres was a lulu.

Getting some nice pix, though the clouds made stuff bad for a while.

Everything on the boat functioning well except the motor which absolutely refuses to work. Got drowned out in the breeze and no juce passes the distributor, no matter how I clean, wipe and adjust it.

This island is hot, in many ways.

I'll write you from Belize as fast as we get there. Ought to be about three days, bucking this two to three knot current. No counter current, at least where we can get in, and coming down here, we were held in the grip of it for six hours last night within fifty yards of the island, exactly balanced between the strength of the wind, as it fell off, and the healthy stream, which we were making about 3 miles in. Some feeling.

My best to Marta and Gregorio and Manolo at the hotel. I can't thank you enough for the hundreds and the unbuyable help there in town. You deserve the best the godam world can give.

Tony is full of words of appreciation too.

Keep writin' it down, Stein.

Les

[4]

Letter to Anthony Jenkinson. Anthony served with Leicester in World War II in Central America and the Panama Canal after introduction from Hemingway in Havana.

Finca Vigía, May 1, 1940

Dear Tony:

Damned glad to hear from you from Puerto Cabezas and know everything going well. I'd written to Blue Fields and forwarded one letter. Sent to Poste Restante. But they should have it in General Delivery. That's all the mail you've had since Belize.

Bad luck about the cracked cylinder. Blocked off, though, it still should do what you need it to do.

No news here. Been blowing like hell from the North-East ever since the boat got over. If it drops tomorrow may run down, trolling, as far as the Gobernadora or maybe Cayo Jutias to give Mr. Josie a little trip. Marlin haven't come yet in any numbers.

Lost a partido finally but then won again and stand 22 out of 24. On Chapter 37 in the book For Whom the Bell Tolls, Marty, Martha

Gellhorn, is toward the end in a long, very long story. She wrote a very good short one.

This machine needs to go to the vet. Will have Otto take it in while we are on the water.

Have the phonograph fixed finally there is no shock. It was a couple of bad condensors that opened and let the current permeate the whole damned machine.

No word from Joris. His friends and ours are splitting up the Spanish refugee committees in order to attack France. If Hitler moves into Sweden I think they will have to make another complete turn.

Play still does business but will have to close when Tone goes to Hollywood in June. Four or five more weeks of the golden or gilded eggs. They say they will re-open in the fall.

Have been feeling on the seedy side for quite a while. Stale and working too long. Max Perkins was crazy about the book. Said it was best I'd written. I wish the hell he had to finish it insead of me. But I'll finish it.

Awfully glad your refrigerator is refrigging (that sounds an odious business—refrigging). Johnny Ferno and his girl were down here. He has a good forehand drive. The radio must give you all the news. Give the Baron my best. Of the two you write the better letters so tell him not to bother. Big may Day here. Haven't gone out maying yet myself. May may a little later.

Good luck Tony. Thanks for writing. Best to you both.

> Ernest
> Marty sends Love

[5]

There are several pages of Hemingway's ship's log for 1940-1941 at Finca Vigía. Most of the material would be of interest only to fishermen and sailors, but the entry for June 10 is of more than passing interest. Here are three selections.

May second—out at 11:30 glass 29.92 Breeze going around from S to W.—then N.W.—freshened from 1 pm on—Travelled westward and at 2:55 had strike from a sailfish about a mile west of Banes. West of Madrid at 3:50 a good sailfish pulled down the port outrigger—he fought well—jumped 10 or 12 times and then headed out northwest—gaffed him at 4:20. (No 1) [Hemingway kept a running account of marlin caught.]

About 3 miles further west toward Cabañas caught a good *balao*[?] at 4:50 wind was freshening plenty—fairly rough when we ran into Cabañas at 6 pm—Two strikes off harbour going in—anchored to west of port—but many mosquitoes came out so we headed out of the harbour and anchored outside the buouy—Marty rowed out in the skiff and then swam while Gregorio cooked dinner—no mosquitoes until daylight—light rain at midnight—

May 7—out at 2:45 glass 30.08—same current—fresh ENE Brisa—sea rough but not the huge seas there would be with this amount of brisa if the current were running—water clear and deep blue—plenty of small flying fish—at 3:10 off Cabañas fortress brought in a barracuda—at 3:20 caught a big good female dolphin at 3:35 off the cement factory Gregorio sighted a pair of marlin travelling westward—turned boat sharply and headed them off in heavy seas—one came to port outrigger one to starboard—EH hooked the port fish—it started jumping and the other larger fish took the starboard bait—jumped and threw hook before [?] could [?] him—followed boat for a long time while EH fighting other fish—EH fish pulled hard in heavy seas—on 18 thread line— jumped 15 times then fought heavy and steady to N.W. Brought him alongside and gaffed him at 4 pm (No 3) 6 feet 9"—afterwards we caught one small dolphin and had a valeos (?) strike trolling up past Baeuraneo and back—much flying fish and many birds—fish should be in soon.

wrote 870 words June 10
out at 3 pm—glass 29.97 current not as strong as other days— water paler blue—breeze fresh ENE. Pat aboard—we trolled to westward as most fish been hooked off Punta Brava between Nacional Hotel and Almendares River/
    Today Italy declared war—24 years since last time—still same vile jackal politics/
(B) 54 lb.


[6]


Letter from Hemingway's mother.

Grace Hall Hemingway
Studio-551 Keystone Avenue
River Forest, Illinois

Hemingway with Adriana Ivancich, the model for Renata in *Across the River and into the Trees*, Cortina d'Ampezzo, 1950.

His favorite drink in the 1950's—the *ginebrazo*.

In his doorway—last years at Finca Vigía.

Four recipients of the Airman-of-the-Month award for good behavior visiting Hemingway at Finca Vigía, 1954.

Hemingway oversees the fishing scenes for the movie of *The Old Man and the Sea*.

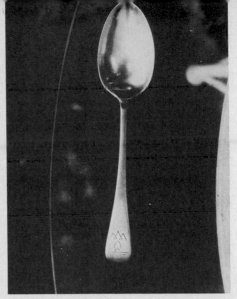

The symbol of Finca Vigía used on the cattle brand and tableware. At the top are the three *monts* of Paris—Montparnasse, Montmartre and St. Geneviève—as well as the three hills of Finca Vigía. The arrowhead is that of the Ojibwa tribe of northern Michigan and Minnesota, where Hemingway spent much of his childhood and early youth. The two bars (represented by three lines) indicate the rank of captain, which was held by both Ernest and Mary during World War II, as well as by John, eldest son of the writer, who was a captain of paratroopers. (Celso Rodriguez)

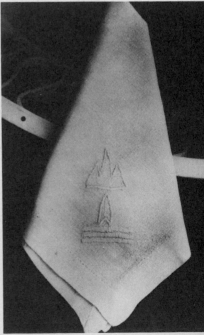

His typewriter, in its usual place. (Enrique de la Uz)

July 17th 1940. At Home.

Dear Ernest—I received the deed this week—Cannot tell how long it will be before I receive the money as this long delay, during which the buyers returned north may cause them to change their minds about purchasing.

Everything in the world is so unsettled at present. Only God gives security.

I'm so sorry to have done something to displease you.

You have always seemed the one person who had abundance of money. I have always feared to send you any, because you would only be insulted. You destroyed the $4.00 I sent you for expenses incidental to making this deed.

However, if I may send you $100.00 when, or if the money comes in the next 2 or 3 months, I shall be *glad* to do so—I like nothing better than giving to my children when they need, and you are no exception. You are the one who was able and willing to make it possible for me to live comfortably and be able to help my children when they needed help—and they have frequently. I hope you will have a happy birthday, 41 is still young.

I shall send you a typewritten copy of the Chronicle (9000 words) which I have written of the past 5 generations covering 200 years. I'm having copies made now. Don't lose it. Your boys & grandchildren will prize it.

Lovingly Your Mother
Grace H.H.

[7]

"Heritage" by Grace Hall Hemingway.

Also found at Finca Vigía was a twenty-eight page type-written manuscript by Hemingway's mother, Mrs. Grace Hall Hemingway, tracing the history of her side of the family.

The genealogy, entitled "Heritage," contains some interesting surprises. According to Grace, Ernest Hemingway's maternal grandfather, Ernest Hall, knew Charles Dickens and "steadied" the famous novelist when Dickens drunkenly strolled the streets of London.

Grace also writes that her mother, Caroline Hancock, "was

a daughter of Captain Alexander Hancock . . . (a grandnephew of John Hancock of Revolutionary fame.)"

She repeatedly praises the members of her family for their renunciation of worldly pursuits in favor of a selfless dedication to God and humanity.

Grace sent the manuscript to Ernest with a handwritten note dated July 25, 1940, which reads:

My Dear Son Ernest:
This is the Chronicle which I wrote last summer of our heritage. It covers 200 years and five generations.

My sources are: a published memoir of Wm. Edward Miller (your great great grandfather), which told much of his father Dr. Edward Miller . . . of Oxford. My grandmother's word of mouth concerning her father and mother, husband and children. My father's word of mouth concerning his parents, sisters and brothers. My mother's word of mouth concerning her forebears, and my own word concerning my husband.

I trust you will take care of this for your children. There are no more copies. While I have no gift for writing I have at last set down some interesting data that otherwise would have been lost to posterity.

Hoping it will seem worthwhile to you. Lovingly your mother.
Grace Hall Hemingway

This was to have been your birthday gift

*Selected excerpts from "Heritage"*
(Grammar and punctuation are unedited)

§ Regarding William Edward Miller, Ernest Hemingway's maternal great-great grandfather:

(Pages 4-5)

Upon his marriage William Miller established his residence in Sheffield. He became very popular as a musician, since he possessed the Cremona violin which seems to have been the idol of his soul. He was accounted the second, if not the first violinist in England. His life revolved around the fashionable world. He was successfully teaching his beloved Art when one evening drawn by the music which he heard in passing, he strayed into Norfold Chapel. His appearance . . . for he was very handsome and majestic in bearing . . . created a sensation. His dress was surely fantastic for a Methodist Chapel. He was powdered and ruffled as a beau of fashion. But there he listened to the impassioned preaching of the great John Wesley. In a flash his whole life was changed . . . he experienced conversion.

He went up to the altar-rail and fell on his knees, dedicating his life unreservedly to the preaching of the Gospel. When he had made this decision, he felt that his beloved violin stood in the way. It was the thing he loved best in the whole world. He decided never to touch it again. It remains in the British Museum to this day.

(Page 7)

Prosperity and all the temporal blessings have followed the descendants of William Miller in a remarkable manner.

§ Regarding Ernest Hemingway's maternal great-grandmother, Mary Dunhill Miller Hall:

(Page 9)

She was a woman of great strength of character, dominating her husband, also her children during their early lives; but they all inherited her strong will. She was devoted to the Methodist Church, never missing prayer-meeting, a deeply spiritual service, which came at nine o'clock on Sunday and lasted until church time. Frequently she led this meeting.

She was a widow all the years of my remembrance, strong and able, absolutely without fear. I have seen her duck under a train at the railroad tracks, if it did not move on fast enough when she wished to cross. She was always dashing in front of, or between vehicles on the city streets. She seemed to lead a charmed life.

§Regarding the immigration to America:

(Pages 10-11)

After the death of their youngest child, Florence, Charles Hall and his wife Mary, followed their married daughter Marianne to America. They left behind them Ernest twelve and Gillum ten, and took with them their son Miller, nineteen, and their small daughter Alice. Marianne who had gone before, had married William Ludley Mandall, a trained musician and organist, who later had a pipe-organ built into his house in Chicago. This journey for the family was a matter of six weeks in a sailing vessel.

§ Regarding Ernest Hemingway's maternal grandfather, Ernest Hall, after whom he was named:

(Page 11)

Ernest who had insisted on refusing a clerkship, took an apprenticeship with a carpenter across London town. He walked the three miles each night and morning, taking never-to-be-forgotten joy in frequent encounters with Charles Dickens. Ernest was already a devoted reader of the novels of Charles Dickens, and when the latter would come reeling along, sadly in his cups, Ernest gladly steadied him. . . . Both Ernest and Gillum, who was training at Westminster Abbey [he possessed an "extraordinary soprano voice"], were in charge of their brother Charles Jr., a capable guardian. After three years the parents, who had established themselves on a small farm in Dyersville, Iowa, a place settled by an English community, sent for their remaining sons to come to them. The ocean voyage for the boys and trip by rail as far as Dubuque, and from thence to Dyersville by horse and wagon, consumed two months. But it was highlighted by thrilling tales of the glorious future in Iowa. Upon their arrival, it seemed heaven to these London boys.

(Pages 18-19)

One morning my father said to his family: "I want you to sit down and listen. I have something to tell you that is important. I have had a very wonderful experience. It happened to me once before, but I was so upset and frightened by it at that time, that I could not speak of it to anyone. But now that it has come again, I feel compelled to tell you."

"Don't imagine that I was dreaming. It was the middle of the day and I was sitting there quietly in the store, amid the noise of business, trying to solve a problem, when suddenly without warning, I had the most wonderful experience! The atmosphere was bathed in radiant color! Wonderful sounds! Exquisite joy! Such amazing happiness!" . . . As he hesitated for lack of words, I exclaimed: "Well, what did you see, Daddy? What did you hear?"

"That's just it," he said, with a gesture of despair. "There are no words, no language to express it." And then, after a pause, in which he struggled for lucidity . . . "The only way I can make you understand is with a parable."

"Suppose an angle-worm came up out of the ground, and for a few minutes, was able to experience and appreciate all the joys that we human beings know . . . great orchestras and symphonies; the note of birds. Able to appreciate gorgeous sunsets and white sails on turquoise waters. Able to understand poetry and great literature; the beauties of Nature and the joys of human love and companionship. Then suppose the angle-worm went back into the earth and tried to tell the other angle-worms about it. No words! No background of experience! I am the angle-worm," said my eloquent father. . . .

As nearly as I can explain it, he saw the world and everything in it from God's standpoint, not man's.

(Page 20)

He had no fear of death, being confident of immortality. Of old, they said of men like my father: "He walked and talked with God." Many times I have burst into his room, as daughters do, and found him kneeling at a little table, looking up, smiling, with his eyes wide open, talking to God. The picture remains. . . .

(Page 22)

When my children, Ernest Hemingway and his sister, were little tots, their grandfather, Ernest Hall, used to give them scraps of bacon from his breakfast. He called them his "scrap-dogs." Many times, at intervals, he has said to me when we were keeping him company at breakfast: "Grace, this is a remarkable boy. If nothing happens to him, he is going to stir the world."

§ Regarding Ernest Hemingway's father, Dr. Clarence E. Hemingway:

(Pages 27-28)

A year after my mother's death, Dr. Clarence Edmonds Hemingway and I were married. Dr. Hemingway had just finished his course at Rush Medical College and begun his work as a general practitioner in Oak Park, Ill. He had served three years as assistant to Dr. Nicholas Senn, the great surgeon, and in his Senior year had permanently furthered the great science of surgery by inventing and perfecting a laminectomy forceps, for spinal cord and rib resection operations. . . .

My father loved my husband so deeply and my husband so loved him. It was the joy of my life. They never either of them entered upon any project or investment, without consulting the other. Doctor said often: "How rich I am to have two real fathers!"

Dr. Hemingway was one of those generous, high-minded souls, who loved people; longed to help them at any cost to himself. He often wished that he never had to send a bill. If people thanked him, he was happier than if they paid him; and if they did both, he came home as radiant as a school boy with a prize. . . .

We were blessed with six children:

*Marcelline* . . .musician, sculptress, playwright, having four suc-
            cessful one-act plays to her credit

*Ernest* . . .the novelist and short-story writer

*Ursula* . . .sculptress

*Madelaine* . . .musician, harpist and pianist

*Carol* . . .writer

*Leicester* . . .magazine editor

[8]

Letter from Leonard Lyons, columnist for the *New York Post*.

Oct. 29, 1940.

Dear Ernest:-

Your book arrived, and I immediately read 150 pages, and sat up all the night doing that (by all the night, of course, I mean all the morning. Because I finished the column at 6 A.M., and started reading then). It's as wonderful as I expected it to be, and I'll finish it tonight— or rather, to-morning.

That was a helluva mix-up in Havana, and we're sorry we missed you. We had hit a hurricane off Hatteras, which delayed us six hours. We waited at the pier for some word from you—and then along came Maurice Habif, who owns The French Doll, and he took us around hunting for you. We went to El Jardin for chicken and rice, after a quick trip around the city before the sun went down. Then to some 5 and 10¢ dancehall, the cemetery, at least 50 sightseeing spots, then San Souci and La Playa, winding up at 5 A.M., at Jiggs—but no Hemingway. We got your note 36 hours later, in Panama. That fishing trip would have been wonderful, even though my guts can't take it. But it would have been wonderful.

Dottie and Alan sent us a postcard from Sun Valley, and set us wondering when you'd come back. It will be safe after Tuesday, when the Stork will be clear of the politicians ready to slug you at the mention of Roosevelt. By the way, that reminds me—Sylvia and I went to the Garden last night to see the President. On the platform, in charge of the works, was a husky guy whose face seemed familiar to me. It puzzled me all night, especially when I saw him running around, escorting Gov. Lehman and the other dignitaries who preceded the President. Then it came to me—he was the guy you slugged at the Stork—Chapman. And I thought he'd surely be a Willkie man. Maybe that short hook knocked some sense into him.

Anyway, what I started to write you was that the book thrilled me, and Sylvia is looking forward eagerly to reading it forthwith . . . that we both are looking forward also to seeing you in N.Y. shortly— and if not shortly, then at least to hear from you.

With best regards,
*Len*
Leonard Lyons

[9]

## Letter from Pauline Pfeiffer, November 1940.

Dear Ernest,

The children arrived in superb shape. They look wonderful and are full of animal spirits and a great pleasure. Gigi has gone back to school and Patrick is being tutored by guess who, Canby. I never dreamed he would do it when I mentioned it to him—in fact I had already made arrangements with Evan. But he (Canby) is in so much better shape this year, drinking much less and is all there, that I am very pleased to have him take Patrick. He needed an interest and he is throwing himself into the job. I really felt under the circumstances that I should give him the job as it may be the means of rehabilitating him, and Esther is *so* pleased. I wrote Evan and sent him two weeks salary and explained the situation to him and he was understanding and charming about it as Evan always is. So everything is hokay.

The pheasants were beyond compare. I never tasted anything so perfect, texture, taste, quality, age, weight and occupation all perfect. Thanks for the memory—don't think that means much, just an old song, I believe, of the Hit Parade. But they were lovely.

Had a letter from Uncle Gus saying you had written him Patrick was a phenomenal rifle shot and had suggested that if he had any Christmas problems he might give Patrick a gun. He asked me if I thought it would be all right to give Patrick a rifle. It seems its a shotgun Patrick wants. I haven't written him yet, but it seems to me one of those ninty dollar Winchesters Patrick pointed out to me, more than a hundred dollars cut to measure is rather a large present to suggest, and rather a big present for a boy of twelve. What do you think? You used to have quite a lot of fun at that age for a lot less money. If you *should* decide that you think he should have this don't you think it would be better if you and Uncle Gus gave it to him? I know either of you can afford to give it to him alone, but I think the effect on Patrick would be better, and then we wouldn't be asking such a big present for a little boy from his uncle even though he is rich. I note from Patrick's letter than you are to be in New York, so I am writing to Uncle Gus to take the gun business up with you when you get there. Just wanted to tell you how I felt. You probably feel the same.

Didn't get around to charging any books to you after all so don't pay any strange bills. But thanks all the same. And thanks a lot for the warthog. I love him so. Otto is packing the books with careful lists and leaving them open for your once over. Quite a lot of books.

Yes Bumby did write, I am glad to report, a very nice letter, and then on election day he sent me a charming little note by his roommate which was very cute and a thoughtful thing to do. The roommate was a very manly slightly on the slight side fellow with top coat collar turned up like an old newspaper man. Said Jack was a fine fellow.

Let me know when you will be down as soon as you know. Good luck,

Pauline

Next Morning—
Just heard that you and Mart are married. Best wishes and much happiness.

Pauline

[10]

Letter to Ingrid Bergman.

Sun Valley, Idaho
November 15, 1941

Dear Miss Bergman,

I was very glad to hear from you about the Paramount matter, although the news in your letter was not cheerful. I think that there is still a chance of your playing "Maria" though as there are various deals, or attempts at deals, going on about the picture.

Sam Goldwyn first refused to let Cooper, who is here now, play for Paramount, but now it looks as though he might. Paramount has great difficulty in making the picture if they cannot get Cooper, and there is a great effort being made for David Selznick to take the whole thing over from Paramount for Cooper, Howard Hawks as director, and you as "Maria". All of this is confidential and I write it to you so you will know that we have not given up hope of having you play the girl. There is no one that I would rather see do it, and I have consistently refused all suggestions that I endorse other people for the role.

Mrs. Hemingway sends you her best regards, and we both hope that we may meet again sometime when there is not all the hurry of going away to China on the same day.

All best wishes.

Yours always,


[11]


Letter from Patrick Hemingway to his father, March 8, 1942.


Dear Papa and Marty,

I am putting the date of easter vacation in P.S. because I am writing this letter on Sunday and tomorrow I find out.

I cleaned out my workroom and I am going to have a cement floor put in so it will stay clean.

There haven't been birds around, I guess it's the wrong season.

I am trying to learn all the insignea on the navy (I know all the commissioned officers, but I'm having tough time with the enlisted men.)

Ada has a bad cough, but otherwise we are all well. How is every body over there?

Mr. Henry gave us a very nice tool chest, he is gone now.

How are the cats?

I am doing ok in school did not have any lessons over the weekend, because the head of the sisters in this district was down here. (We always have none to celebrate.)

I was going out fishing today for jacks, but it was too rough for a rowboat.

Love,

Patrick

[drawing of boat with
person rowing]
Me in rowboat. Kiss.

P.S. Vacation begins on
Wednesday in Holy Week
and ends next Tuesday

[12]

Letter from John Hemingway.

1942

Dear Papa,
    This is to let you know that we got a reservation alright for the 26th. I will be coming over with the kids if my passport comes through alright. Mouse is here now and we have had a great time so far. Gigi has a little cold and a sore throat which have kept him out of school for the last couple of days but he'll be ok very soon.

Much love,

Bum

[13]

Letter from Pauline Pfeiffer.

Oct. 7, 1942

Dear Ernest,
    Thanks for your cable, which relieved my mind considerably. Mr. Guest had written Patrick that Gigi was sick and they thought he might have had infantile paralysis, but at the end of three days HE COULD MOVE HIS LEGS ALRIGHT, and that he was fine now. I thought it was probably a scare until I read in the paper there were 54 cases of

polio in Cuba and that they were closing the schools. Then I did begin to worry. Please write me the details. And do keep him quiet if the Guest report is in essence true, because the doctors up here tell me that sometimes the spine is affected later if the patient over does. I know how careful you are in taking care of the children, but please tell me what did happen.

Also, will you please cable as soon as Gigi's reservation is sure, as I must give Ada notice to leave Syracuse and get to Miami to meet him.

New York and Washington are both places not to be in now, I think. Everyone keyed up and I never know what sacred cow I am slaughtering. I shall be glad to get back home, where I shall go sometime before the fifteenth of November. Tell Gigi I would like to hear from him. The address is 144 E. 61st. I hope you are well and happy—tho I must say the personal life seems to be a thing of the past for the moment.

Yours,

Pauline

[14]

Letter from Christopher LaFarge.

Dec. 5, 1942

234 EAST SIXTY-SECOND STREET

Dear Earnest:

I was just about to write you when I got a letter from Ross saying you had called me a bastard for not writing. Well bastard yourself, you old writer you. My correspondence has gone to hell in a bucket anyway, I'm so far behind now that I'll never catch up, and I guess I won't even try. The damn doctors got their hands on poor Louisa last August and said frightening words to her (in such a fatherly way, too) and then they proceeded to cut her up into assorted little pieces, and then they sewed up the pieces again and got her reassembled in a pretty fair order. Boy, did that raise hell with the LaF works! I was suddenly a commuter between N.Y. and R.I., a governess, tutor, father, husband, writer, farmer, housekeeper, questionnaire-filler-upper, drunkard (not yet chronic), and the man who took care of the sugar ration cards. All very enrvating. I spelled that word wrong but it looks about the way I felt.

I wanted like hell to try to get out to Sun Valley this autumn, but, Christ, it just was out of the question. I wanted badly to see you and Marty again and to do a spot of the old Idaho butchery, and find out how your movie was going. I got into an awful rut sitting in the middle of the huckleberry bushes and the poison ivy in R.I. and I needed someone like you to kick me the hell out of it. However, I'm sort of pulling out now, slowly. I tried to get back into the Army, but hell, they wouldn't have me. At least they said, "Not now, but ah! you're so patriotic to offer your services and maybe some day when we've used up all the others, we'll take you up on it." So now I just write. Or try to. As best I can. Very difficult. I won't write propaganda as such, and that's about all they seem to want. I make speeches telling people that they have to find out what the hell the whole thing is about and how bloody important the word is, and then I go home and figure how damn important it is for me to be fighting instead of talking and so feel miserable. If you're not weeping by now, I guess I'd better stop trying to make you to weep. Why do writers have to be such god damned egotists?

In re shooting, which we weren't talking about, I wish to God I could come down to Cubia, and take you up on the simple but beautiful thought of 150 Doves per diem. But what in hell would I use for money, pal? I'm not the sort of man who can go anywhere on his face and I've never liked trying to travel on my arse. Which is the only possible alternative as I see it. If my COUNTRY would only send me to Cuba to write beauty about that spot, that would be O.K. But I can't think how to rig that one. Unless I get Ross to send me for the New Yorker. What a hope!

Shooting this autumn was good in spots. There were the hell of a lot of ducks, which was very soothing. But they have the woodcock season now frozen in November, and so there are no birds of that succulent variety left by the time its legal to shoot same. Quail are on the increase, on account a lot of R.I. is now being farmed which hasn't seen a plow since the boys left for the great frontier country of the Susquehanna Valley. So war does do some good things. The partridges were none too plentiful, so I didn't pursue them with any ardor. I had a very fine time shooting crows with that owl I shot and had stuffed in Idaho. It worked every time. It's an amazing spectacle to see the crows, several hundred of the black bastards, wheel around and around that owl. I got as much fun watching that happen as I did in the shooting.

I've read most of your Men at War. The introduction is damn stimulating. I read it first to myself and then aloud to Louisa. You spoke plenty true, pardner. It's a very warming thing to find someone else you like and respect and are fond of saying in public the things about writing that you've been trying to practise for a long time. The only thing that matters in the whole world is the truth, but by God, that's easily and often forgotten. As to the matter of the book, double O.K. I found quite a few I didn't know, notably the Joinville St. Louis. which is wonderful. Am I crazy, or are you wrong when you say there was nothing on the last War fitten for to print? Isn't Nason O.K.? I never got to France but fought the glorious battle of Camp Grant ILL, a great and sanguinary and confused engagement, so I'm no judge. But his Chevrons always seemed to me a good picture of a certain sort of battle, without any slop or attempt to mitigate or pretty it up. Maybe I'm wrong. Anyway, it's unimportant, and the book is valuable as the devil. My, The Red Badge of Courage rereads wonderfully well! It's the damndest mixture of colloquialisms and poetic prose and occasional highfalutin sentences I know. And the mixture works. It oughtn't to, but it does.

Write me a line, pal, when you get a chance between doves, or make that far too atractive wife of yours do so. Attractive with two t's, I mean. And I've put my telephone on this, in case you've lost it and you'll both be the children of Shaitan if you come to N.Y. and don't let me know. I missed M. Gellhorn by one night, and could easily have been here that night, damn all. I have vast stocks of liquor, and even a bed or two.

My love to you both,

Kipfer

P.S. I had a fine, illiterate Scotch letter from Jean Ramsay. She has had peritonitis (no disease for a virgin [?], either, if any). Says John the Earl of is well & busy & gets to shoot when the Government gives him the gas to do it with.— What is Honest John Hemingway doing?

K.

[15]

Letter from Alexander Woollcott.

THE WHITE HOUSE
WASHINGTON

12-18-42

Dear Hemingway—

I hope that by this time—I shall know nothing until I get back to New York three days hence—you will have wired Max Perkins your consent to our use of "Fifty Grand" in that reader which differs from others available chiefly in that, thanks to thin paper, it will be portable— 600 pages that will go in one pocket.

I thought you might be interested to know that I was hovering undecided over the Caporetto retreat, "Wine of Wyoming," "Big Two-Hearted River", "The Killers" and "Fifty Grand" when along came Willa Cather as one of my consultants and plumped for "Fifty Grand" so I let that settle it.

Tell Martha that I find the White House lonely without her.

A. Woollcott

[16]

Letter from Evan Shipman.

May 2, 1943

Dear Ernest;

Thanks for the money. It helped me out in a difficult and unpleasant piece of business last week connected with Garey. I was trying to get her transferred to another hospital in the hope that closer attention might help her case. As things turned out, nothing came of this for the time being, but at least I know exactly what the situation is now, together with what I can and cannot expect. The truth is that I can expect God damned little.

As usual I had been waiting for an answer to my last letter to you to write you, but we're both such wretched correspondents that it is foolish to depend on replies. Much better to just go ahead and write when the spirit moves us. I'd wanted to tell you how pleased I was at your mention of me in the preface to the anthology. Also how much I'd enjoyed the book. Thank you particularly for introducing me to Marbot. I was able to pick up the five volumes in french, and every page interested me. Aside from the extraordinarily cool picture he gives, Marbot must have been a very unusual man. While it is hard for me to reconcile his qualities, I am completely convinced, and also fascinated. This is one of the books in which I have no reference at all to any known (understood) character. And I dont think that it is just because I have known few soldiers. I've read enough writing by soldiers. For instance, how different Marbot is from that Marine what's his name who translated him.

I have been in the Army a year today. Its been a good year, and, all in all, I've been happy, and I've learned a lot. Not enough, but a lot. I'm lucky enough to still have an opportunity to learn, although I will be leaving here the middle of next month as a cadre non-com teaching a new outfit the ropes and then going over with them. This Armored Force business demands a lot of skills of the kind I was always slow at. I've had to sweat, and there have been many days when I have been pretty discouraged, but the little I have actually mastered has been a real satisfaction to me. In the beginning, I worked as a radio operator, and that was like pulling teeth, and I was always pretty humiliated about where I stood in my class and how long it took me to catch on to code. Finally however I got the hang of it—graduated a 16/16 man—and made a T/4 rating last January. I was as proud as I could be. But I realized that radio was really not my game, so I quit it for combat intelligence the day after I got my rating. That meant being broke, and even if the demotion was "without prejudice", it still hurt to lose those stripes. And it looked like a long road in front of me to start learning a new trade from the ground up. This time it was more plesant than I'd expected. I made sergeant about a month ago, and on the 15th of the month I get my five stripes as a Tech. That will be plenty to live up to, but there is no job that I know of that I would rather have.

I told you briefly about going to New York to try to arrange about Garey. Of course my distress at Garey's condition is bound to color my feeling about a furlough, but I still am sure that we here at camp have little to envy the people outside. For most, I am sure it is a sad, uncertain time. We here in camp are spared a great deal that is dismal, together with much confusion of mind. I think you are wise to have avoided New York lately.

While I was in town I saw Marty, about to leave for California. Not in a good way at all. He and Sana have broken up in spite of the baby. I was glad to see him of course, but I worry about him. He does not even have the things to depend on that he used to. He should be in the Army, but of course the Army wont take him with his leg.

Mary is in California. She quit the horse business and went to work for Consolidated Aircraft. Her first promotion was as head of women personel at the San Diego plant, and now she is head of that department throughout the country. She has sold the farm in Virginia, and I would'nt be surprised if this changed her whole life. When she was first thinking of taking a job out there, I advised her strongly against it. It just shows you how wrong you can be about someone else, not to mention yourself. Consolidated has a plant in Nashville, so I manage to see her every once in a while. The work agrees with her, and I have'nt seen her so well in years.

Andre had a show a while back. I saw him one evening in town. Glad to see him, and the same old Andre, but he is tied up with an awful bunch. How he can stick that defrocked priest Breton is beyond me, and the bunch of rich women that pay the bills for that Trotskyite crew.

Have read very little these days except manuals. I find thinking about books I have read and enjoyed almost takes the place of reading. Do you know Silone's Bread and Wine? That's one that is a real satisfaction to think about.

Your Marty wrote me a nice letter last month, and this of course is for her as well as you. I was glad to get the news of John Sanakas. I know that we will see him again. And I never will forget the time I spent with him in Madrid, nor how kind he was to me. I am sorry Patrick is having a hard time. It is hard to imagine anyone giving Patrick a hard time The visits to you all ought to help make it up to him.

And Bumby an MP! He's probably a husky young devil now, and I'll bet it wont take him long to learn how to keep order on Saturday night. Give him my best when you write to him. And Ernest this time do think and let me hear from you once in a while. Your letters are very welcome, and you'll see that I'll answer promptly. I think of you very often. Some day I hope I'll see Havana again. It is one of the things worth looking forward to.

My best to you both always,

Evan

Sgt. Evan Shipman
Hdg. Co. 28th Armored Regt.
A.P.O. 444
Camp Campbell, Ky.

Note on reverse side of last page of letter from Evan Shipman dated May 2, 1943:

Ernest; Somehow this letter has hung around my cluttered desk all week! I've been out on the range so much lately that the desk has quite escaped my attention.

I've been working on a map problem about a dozen miles out from the post—surveying about a square mile. This is nice country—something like France south west of Paris and something like Tarazona near Albacete where I trained in Spain. Its hardwood country, with oak and beech and black walnut, and this spring there has been first the red bud and then the dogwood.

Out on the back roads I see the units training all day—the platoons of the new men marching. It came to me the difference—this is an army that does not sing.

You may remember a poem I wrote a couple of years ago—July 1937—I think I showed it to you. I have added a new verse to it that I am enclosing. Perhaps you will like it

Goodbye again, and write me.

Evan

## *JULY 1937.*

In Memory of Harry Hines, Jim Lane, Harry McSorley.

### I.

We shout our song tonight against the night—
Our feet mark time upon the waiting road—
The great wheel turns in space and space is bright—
We shout—trucks groan beneath the load
Of guns, in gear climb the straight white road
Out of our sight, toward morning, toward light.

We shout our song, hoarse chorus, and our song
Has pulled one star slanting across the sky.
Our hobnails grind the stones—the stones belong
To us now, and with our gun butts we try
Beating our refrain on the road, while high
Above the ash streak splits the sky.

The morning, when it comes, will trail thin mist
Across the parched grass and the dusty leaves.
The sun will rise blood red. The wheat is grist
For the ox now. Fields are stubble. The sheaves
Are on the earth floor. Let the ox persist,
Tread kernel from chaff, While we exist,

We shout, we'll sing. The star slides to the West.
Our stamping feet grind fire out of the stones.
The column clatters quiet, and the rest
Of the song, as the column stretches, groans
In creaking leather and the collected tread
Of tired feet resuming the road ahead.

## II.

Nobody has asked you anything
Nobody knows you
Nobody sees you
Nobody can hear you now
You are alone
They have all gone away.
There is no need to call
No need to whisper
You are talking to yourself
You are listening to yourself
You are looking at yourself.
What are you waiting for?
What are you looking for?
What are you listening for?
Everything will be explained
Everything will be clear
And there is only one way,
Only one sun in the sky,
Focus of all the days and all the hours.
The sun does not belong to you.

## III.

It is not the dead we honor;
Rather we honor the brave.
All of the dead were not brave;
All that these gained, a grave,
And for tomb the emblem of honor
Perhaps, perhaps the wish,
The frantic wish, the desire for honor
For emblem to weather the wind and the sun,

Even with nothing done
And the glamor of giving gone;
Only the gift
Worn, ragged, and seasoned
By that hard straight rain and the lift
Of that wind. They had reasoned,
But the colors of reason ran in the rain.
So, faded and tattered, this emblem for pain
Still follows the wind, and the wish
Is there in the wind, as the white hills are there,
Sharing the hard earth with the hard honor, ready to share.

IV.

Clay is the motto of chance.
There against purple and tan
Spirals of dust in the wind
Gathered by the gust in a dance,
The red dust shakes like a fan.
Crumbling clay takes to flight
Winding the spiral of light.
Come, swell, as a child's voice bids you rise—
Wreathe as smoke over fire
Above this pyre
While shrill a child cries
Beckoning the horizon with her hand.
Some of us loved this land;
We told this child,
Her fingers in the dust, to sing.
Dust was a scarf, wild,
Skirting her dancing. We watched her fling
Red pebbles down steep walls. Today
Dry winds have turned the echo,
To us mourners bring
Up canyon walls the ass's bray.

EVAN SHIPMAN

[17]

The original of this affectionate letter was found at Finca Vigía.
It was never mailed:

To Allen R. May
Rural Route No.1,
Port Credit,
Ontario, Canada

August 31, 1943

Dear Allen:

Marty and I were so happy to hear from you and I only wish you
would have sent me the letter that you said you wrote last spring. For
Christ's sake, all we can do is to help each other out in these things
when they come up and you know that Marty and I are your pals (for
lack of a better word in war time) and please always write me about
everything.

You must be terrific on the radio as the Voice of Labor, something
like I was back in 1921 when I was seeing Europe for the STAR through
Canadian eyes.

Last night after we read your letter Marty and I were talking it
over and she said that there were always periods in everyone's life when
they were absolutely stalled and she figured that you had just come
through one of those. But now you have shaken loose and you have to
write. You can call it the strange necessity or any other name they put
to it but it is what all of us bastards have to do in order to feel good
in the evenings when we are with our wives and listen to the radio. So
always remember you have to bite on the old nail and that biting on
the old nail never feels good nor makes anybody very happy when they
are doing it unless they have rubber teeth or something. But in the end
that is what we were thrown in here for and that is what we have to
do and if we do not do it we end up as bad fathers and everything else.

Our news is not so easy to convey and is rather complicated. I
have been away a good part of the time and expect to be away, with
luck, even more. Marty is shoving off the first of this month for New
York and then to Europe, or whatever parts of Europe available, for
Collier's. She is lovelier than ever and we love each other very much
but I cannot go with her to the sector of the war that they send her to
any more. Once, when we had only one war at a time, it was easy and

we could have a nice GHQ in the Hotel Florida. But now there is such expansion that husbands and wives cannot make the same shows any more together without somebody being unfaithful to something. Unfaithful is not used as a sexual word.

Your daughter sounds lovely and if she looks like Ingrid you have something that I wish we had very much. I wish you would send me a picture of both of them and one to show how time is treating you, and that you would give our love to your wife and know, always, how fond we both are of you.

P.S. If Rohrbach, your pal, should turn up in these waters, we will treat him accordingly.

[18]

The Spanish writer Prudencio de Pereda and Hemingway were friends since the thirties. Pereda collaborated with Hemingway on two documentaries about the Spanish Civil War: *Spain in Flames* and *The Spanish Earth*.

To:
Private Prudencio de Pereda
Headquarters Company, Second Battalion
480 A.I.R., 20th A.D.
Campnell, Kentucky.

Dear Prudencio:
I finally got both of your letters at the same time and am very sorry I didn't have them sooner. Am enclosing the letter you asked for and hope it will be some use to you.

You must have had marvelous basic training with the Armored Forces and I envy it very much. Agree with you about everything that was wrong with the film although I haven't seen it. Have heard from enough friends who have to know your account of it is accurate. They would not let me have anything to do with it and would not let me send anyone out to tell them how it should be. Sam Woods was set from the start on making it into a "Great Love Story" and nothing else and naturally he lost what it was all about. Dudley Nichols, in spite of his great reputation, I think writes terrible scripts. You may remember the awful one he did for Joris on that China picture and how

Joris had to call in poor old Papa to rewrite it as it was absolutely hopeless and simply a rotten imitation of THE SPANISH EARTH.

You ought to be damn good at making documentaries and I only wish we were all starting out together again to do one now. The Signal Corps will have a wonderful chance to make some when we invade on a big scale. I hate to think of not having had a chance to use that wonderful background in Sicily. But I suppose someone has and done it well.

Do you have any news of Joris or of Johnny? Will close this letter now, Prudencio, so as to get it off to you in a hurry.

Martha sends you her very best. She is just off for England. I hope to be getting away from here again shortly.

Best to you always and un abrazo de tu amigo.

Accompaniment.

TO WHOM IT MAY CONCERN:
Prudencio de Pereda worked with me in 1937 in the making of the documentary film "THE SPANISH EARTH". He is an excellent writer and skilled, loyal and untiring craftsman in this field. If I were working on documentary films at this time I know of no one I would rather have working with me than Prudencio de Pereda.

> Yours very truly,
> Ernest Hemingway

September 6, 1943


[19]

Letter from Howard Hawks.

October 11, 1943

Mr. Ernest Hemingway
Finca Vigia
San Francisco de Paula
Cuba

Dear Ernest:

It was nice to talk with you on the telephone.

I bought "To Have and Have Not" from Howard Hughes paying him a stinking big price. It was a good business deal for me, but next time let's fix it so you get the dough. We are about half way through with the scenario and should be finished by the end of the month.

We'll probably come down to Havana about the fifteenth of November and make some waterfront scenes, harbor scenes and maybe some of the fishing stuff. Slim is crazy to come and wants to live in sin with you while I work. Will let you know more about the possibilities. Transportation seems to be the great difficulty nowdays.

Ernest, do you know any politico down there that would be a help if we come down to make scenes or some boat man who knows his way around the keys and Havana. Any dope you can give me on this will be appreciated.

Slim, David and I had a good dove shoot the other day down in Imperial Valley, and the freeze box has been full of doves, and every time we eat them, we think of the Hemingsteins.

I have been having a lot of fun teaching gunnery to the 4th Air Force. You'd get a great kick out of how quickly the kids learn.

Let me know if you're going to be around Havana at the time I mentioned, and as soon as our plans are a little more coordinated, I'll let you know.

> Best regards,
> *Howard*
> Howard Hawks

P. S. By the way, Humphrey Bogart is going to do Harry Morgan and he ought to be a good one.

> H. H.


## HEMINGWAY'S LOST LOVE LETTERS TO MARY


### [20]

Letter to Mary Welsh.

> Wednesday
> Nov. 8, 1944

Dearest Pickle:

Not long after you left Sergt. Kurt Show of the irregulars came in with Jean and Marcel from Div and a letter from Stevie. So have transport and will be off. Certain amount of repair necessary on transport and we will be off daylight day after tomorrow. Jimmy Cannon also in.

Moretti has come in with gen for me on Bumby and am meeting him in bar in few minutes. Dave Bruce called up to have me dine with him tonight. I will go see Shaef this aft. and get my orders. Am not takeing Richard. Am leaveing Marcel.

Don't care nothing for the prospects. But suppose will brighten up as get closer. It has always worked that way. Am not very bright right now and Know I always soften up away from battle or is it bottle and get wonderful ideas about wanting to live, write, have a double bed and have our good fine life that we have ahead of us. Stevie writes this is the real works and we are to have the honor.

Teague must look forward to it. I hope we drew good replacements.

Mary my dearest beloved I love you so and there is nothing much I can add. Except that I love you more all the time. I'm just empty, sick, lonely for you all the time as though half of me were gone, more than half.

Dearest beloved let's be patient and brave and good through all the things people and the world will try to do to us. I regret exposeing our common property this way, i.e. assault - But it is the last time and I do not think it would be all we want it to be if I did not go now and let down Buck and Co. just because I do not want to go. I can make them a little happier in the fucking great sorrow we all share - which is war.

I respect truly, as I told you after seeing Beadle, the fine intelligence and the fascination of haveing participated in the direction of such a huge, unbelievable, world changeing thing. To be trusted, to understand and to really know about it and above all about the air as you do.

All I can ever do to compensate you for leaving it is to try to make something, with your help, that will be good enough to justify your sacrifice.

I understand *so well* you going off to the front now - *not* for kudos - not for category - But (maybe I'm just egotistical and wrong) to learn something of my end. Just as I was proud to learn about your end. I do not mention you doing me a great favour about Bumby. I know you know about that.

I write in this stupid, moral, probably trashy way because one of the loveliest adventures we have had is the one of trying to learn to understand each other and each others things and values, not just loveing, and quarrelling. You know the sort of thing "I love you you're a slut. But ah God how I love you" school of loveing. But instead trying to have an understanding as solid as cement, sand and water can make into concrete reinforced with the good iron bars of our love.

Dearest Pickle I want *so* to make a good life with you. I won't always be solemn like this. I will be as gay as gay can be. But inside I want to serve you well and true the way some very dull people want to serve their country and even sadder people want to serve their god - But sometimes are very happy at it. You're a very small god with a face that breaks my heart every time I see it and the lovely body with the jolly big behind but Pickle I love you - and together we make us - and us is much better than either of us separately.

(Could now go into that. But no time)

Pickle I will try to make you a good husband and to work so you'll be proud of us - and because the work is US have to do it alone. *But I could not do it alone.*

Poem was made on the Schnee Eifel and in bed. I had to write it. But we made it. We and all the guys.

Well Pickle I have to go.

Don't trust Phil - he is a crook - or rather, a weak and twisted fake soldier.

He had said to the *MP* him a Col.

Just before Eddy and the Col. came in on after him on that Sunday "Why couldn't he have a girl if E. Hemingway had a girl?"

And the only way he knew or thought he knew I had a girl was that I had excused myself to him night before by saying I had to leave to go talk to a lovely girl. The poor swine confessed this to me last night comeing drunk and staying till 2 a.m. I was very cold. It was bloody awful. You know the guy had had drinks in my home. Had fished on my boat.

I just asked him to look around the room and see if there wasn't something he could denounce. Made him cry. For which he will probably do something much worse.

I really hate shits, Pickle. Mistake is being nice to shits ever. But I don't trust my shit detector, I guess. There's where *you* can help. *Anybody* can tell Butch is a shit. But they come in such varied plumage.

So long Dearest Pickle. I love you with all my heart.

Only.

Enclosed your check we bet in *large amounts for big Dough* for the fun of it. Between us. But in our family (me and you) we settle for 10% of bet. Sometimes 1% of bet. This is house rule. You owe me 5 quid - Please use it to buy bedroom slippers from me as haven't time to get them. I love you.

EH

Big Sporting House Rule.

[21]

Letter to Mary Welsh.

Nov. 11, 1944

Dearest Pickle:

I thought about you very much and loved you very much all day.

Hope you're haveing a good trip. We had much snow last night and this morning. Now it's better. Fine wild beautiful impractical country much wilder than we were in before actually worst I've ever seen. Feel same about prospects as did where I left, only more so, but have the same happy inside not give a damn feeling that has always been around the time when the ballroom banana factory opens. But things not the same when there is no fighting for a while the non fighting citizens sort of try to give the fighting ones the business. (No D Day H hour in this) also the army is a thing of eternal jealousies and old and new envies and if you were ever rude to me at heavenworth I'll get you at Hobson's Hallow. *You* don't get these so much because you know the sort of top metaphysics of it. You were tapped for Bones at the start. But I just learn about it as I go along - sort of sad, sort of a continuation of the iniquities of the Senior Society system at Yale and college Fraternities. I sort of tried to explain to pals that I liked them *all* - They were all good - There were differences and one thing and another - But if they had ever seen or been with lousy - nor should have differences. And so fine to be where everybody *knows* and nobody is rude. Combat soldiers look - very different from other - as you've recently been seeing. You have seen *a* very good fighting outfit. Must have been beautiful down there wish I could have been with you. (next day) I miss you all the time dearest Pickle - dislike present prospects so much that have had to throw you away a little earlier than usual. I mean throw away as in Poem - (not *really* throw away - nor cease to trust, love and have all hope in-) yest was very close to the old whore people's ignorance - avoided by caginess - what a braggy sounding thing - actually - you would have appreciated it.

Been snowing, snowing, snowing, raining, raining, raining - lousy weather - Hope you had better where you were. Snow makes mine problem a problem - yest a jeep with the windshield so muddy and snowy practically unseeing came within 20 feet of running into a mine field on a road been told was OK enroute to a town told was OK but which outurned was held by Krauts. Sort of thing could produce unfortunate results.

Going up now see Buck my pal. He's been feeling lousy - grippe and sore throat and things generally not so good.

*Later*

Pickle what a lousy miserable letter - Buck and I ate together in the trailer (3 hrs) and talked together about a lot of things - technical things and problems that came up with winter etc. and I told him about you and our hopes and our good prospects and how happy I was with you (read am with you)

We have all been kidding very rough and gay and all my winter clothing has been promised in case - Blazzard gets the yak nest and or I get his next liquor ration - you give Buck the boat if you don't want it -

Christ I hate waiting around. Each morning like all ready to pitch in ball game - nothing.

You cant walk Pickle because the snow, slush and mud is over your boots and on the roads the trucks ride you off - If you walk any where else you might but something or trip on something - I eat three meals a day which is good for me but will make me fat as pig - or people play cards somebody gets snappy or petty fights start - (Not me) - My favorite thing of going and looking over all terrain and learning it and understanding it is out because with the rain and snow and mud you cant see anything and in the woods you cant see anything anyway.

(Will write some more tonight)

Later - (Night of 13th)

Before dinner I read (San Ten) out loud to the guys - have read it twice now and find finer stuff all the time - also read Marechal de Saxe again - Hard to read anything that hasn't teeth in it - understand why you cant read most of the time - Because you're always waiting for something to start - with you it's like that all the time - you always have something starting by 10 a.m. every day.

I'm cheerful as hell and clown all the time for the guys so don't think I'm walking gloom house - But this ready to move every day and then not move is *not* my racket. (nor my dish) very difficult for me to decide to do anything I guess but certainly like to go when have prepared to - If I were sentenced to be shot at 6 a.m. on a certain day and they did *not* shoot *me* I would sue them - It's all right to write this because

I won't send this until something is moveing. I just write to you a little each day to take away some of the loneliness - in action you can write a lot - but waiting around you can't write anything.

Will add some more tomorrow if no ball game. Good night Dearest Pickle. Please love me very much. I look forward very much to hot bath (joint)

We live here all together in a sort of joint dining, living, work, map and bath room - no privacy - not like the old farm house.

### Next day - 14th Nov.

Just too gentil to spit on the floor - But so swell that we all bathe in the kitchen sink - I sleep in my rof sleeping bag on a bed by the window - another guy next on cot - two others in connecting undoored room, which is also dining room and contains stove. We stopped in Epernay and Jean bought 37 bottles of excellent Brit - same as Ritz - 1.20 per bottle - I have an old stone pipe with a sort of flash cone on the head and a toilet seat that use as a . . . base plate and can fire a champagne cork through this and have hit a cigarette out of the cooks hand - Hit Pelkey behind the ear - calling both shots before hand - This is known as Dr. Hemingsteins' Secret weapon - we yet shelled plenty - Every night - Today went up with Buck again - Didn't talk any shop at all - Just the Marshal de Saxe, jokes, writing, future, etc.

### - Next day Nov. 15 -

Had the what do you call it shelled out of us last night - not really bad but would impress a visiting fireman fairly semi-rugged day today - Germans have about 19 Battns of artillery around here - Stevie and I walked down and back through it to put it in its proper perspective - House rocking quite a lot - up in the lines snow and foggy - woods pretty dropped up - went all over everything trying to get things good and clear in my head and then stayed and ate with Buck and we bull shitted and he told stories of when-a-boy certainly made me feel like a cissy - Feel very ashamed how I never fucked my teacher in High School - But was too shy.

Pickle if I wasn't such a security minded dull . . . could write you damned interesting letters. So simply picture your man riding in jeep (Boom) trudging through snow (Boom) mud up to knees (Boom) in forest (Boom) trees falldown *(Boom)* in renewed house outgazing over Kraut-land (Boom Boom) in partly kraut villages (Boom Boom Tot Tot Tot Tot) in bed (Boom Boom double Boom) talkeing ½ hour before expect to get up for the ballroom bananas each morning saying to self "I will think of absolutely nothing and lie here quietly, neither asking nor hopeing just straight not thinking and rest my fucking heart." And instead think of my Pickle, comeing into the Bar, comeing into the room, sitting at the table, awake and talking, asleep, awake, on the days they have hot water - walking by the river, in bed, repeat in bed, in bed, on the boat: especially on the boat and in the double bed, takeing a drink and arguing, explaining to me when I'm stupid, loyal to me when I'm attacked, makeing magic together. Oh Pickle I love you so much. So terribly much. Waiting around not good for me. But make fairly good jokes and when they shell say very much and people inclined to be serious say, "Sir, are these c - s - ers attempting to intimidate us?" cheap stuff like that all same Teague says, about himself "who ever saw a dead mule?"

Pickle I'm going to stop now. I love you as you will know. I hope you're well and please write. I won't send this till later will write you a quick one now.

I love you my darling,
Only.

From
E. Hemingway, War Correspondent
9o PRO Hq 4th Infantry Division
APO 4 US Army

[22]

Letter to Mary Welsh.

9o PRO Hq 4th Infantry Division
APO 4 US Army
From E. Hemingway, War Corresp.
Nov. 15, 1944

Dearest Pickle:
Have written you a long letter, written some of which each day which will send you soons get to work. Meantime short note to tell you I love you as stated. (More than ever stated) In very tough racket cant possibly be back before 7 to ten days due conditions. Week to 10 days.

Tubby fine, Buck fine, pals fine. Prospects same envisaged.
My morale good.
Havent heard from you yet. Just send you this so you know about times of back getting. My dearest beloved I love you more all the time.

In earlier letter it tell how much and how and why - altho I do not write very well under censorship. Never been in tougher racket than now and unrosiest.

Please have fine time, see and know and go out with everybody but know I am as faithful to you in head, heart and what shall we say, balls, I guess as though you had sent me on a patrol through a thickly wooded country, with considerable snow, many trip wires, ruines, one thing and another - (you didn't send me. I waned wather be with you. Just went to finish up and help in bad time.) But have fine time because no D Day. *But look after us.*

Did you get the letter from Willie?

Hope it wan't too lously solemn and ungay - I am gay 90% may be more of time and make pretty good jokes whiles been *bad*.

Pickle: a sextette or octette of ghouls, Belden etc. even Carson, will come in for 20 minutes and go up to a Regt and receive the dramatic untrue handout which blossoms in their hands like one of those dried Chinese sticks that turns into a dragon in water (remember) but *we live here* - and am now *so* fearless that I struck on ice even to myself - that we must go to the guignol and be comfortable scared together. Much Boom-Boom here now. I love you my dearest darling beloved.

Please write if you have time. But if you haven't I know about it and is OK.

Dearest Pickle pretty soon on boat. Xmas in Havana (or Bermuda).

Your

*Only*

Nov. 16 a.m.
Feel fine and cheerful.
Love you very much.
Papa


[23]


Letter to Mr. Henry La Corsitt for Mary Welsh.

Pickle:
For your files copy of
letter to be sent in case
of my death. Ernest Hemingway

November 16, 1944

Mr. Henry La Corsitt
Editor Colliers

Dear Henry:
    You never asked me to name a beneficiary for the insurance Colliers took out for me. I hereby name Mary Welsh of *Life* and *Time Inc.*, 4 Place de la Concorde as sole beneficiary of this insurance revoking by this letter any previous beneficiaries that may have been named.
    My wife Martha Gellhorn Hemingway entered into a mutual property agreement before leaving New York and she has been fully provided for.
    In addition to the money Colliers has advanced me I have spent $3950.00 of my own money on Expenses for Colliers. Will you please send $1500 of this to my wife Martha G. Hemingway since she advanced it to me and deposit the balance in my account in the Guaranty Trust Co. of N.Y., Fifth Avenue Branch, N.Y.C.
    Yours very truly,

                                 Ernest Hemingway

Enclosed is copy of letter to be mailed from here in case of decease.

Ernest Hemingway, War Correspondent
9o PRO Hq 4th Infantry Division
APO 4 US Army


[24]


Letter to Mary Welsh.

                    Nov. 16, 1944
                    E. Hemingway, War Correspondent
                    PRO Hq 4th Infantry Division
                    APO 4 US Army

My Dearest:
    Today we had fine weather - First since I've been here and we kicked-off beautifully, were going rain or shine - Snow or shit - and instead had air and all - I would have given anything for you to have seen it - I woke early and wrote a letter in case of (the Insurance is 50,000 they say. Seemed simpler than to be saddled with place not

knowing what shape it is in) to Colliers and a PS and enclosure to you on last night's letter and then had no problems and felt as happy as going to follow hounds across good country on a fine sharp autumn day.

We had quite a morning (can you marry a man who writes "we had quite a morning") but I'll write it well for you sometime. Anyway slapped the old wh—RC on the ass a couple of times. Then, after, the open country show went into the woods with Buck. Everything fine. Tomorrow we will have a tougher time but we will be OK and anyway once fight starts it is fine. Today we could have killed 6 krauts (I mean Jean and Red could) - They got away across a field and into a ravine right under our noses - But so much Brass around they could not intervene - Krauts galloping - Strong, sound, husky Krauts - getting away to fight another day - Red saying, "Papa, please Papa!" and Jean saying, "Mr. H. don't you think we might Sir?" They broke out of a house when the armour passed. We had them marked down perfectly. It was a funny morning - The O.P. shelled much, much, you would have loved the sight of the battle, everything as clear as in an old time battle painting place found reconnoctering the other day. Best place to see a battle I've ever been. The krauts galloped clean across the whole front. That was the smallest incident but I guess the only one can mention.

Buck very confident. Things going exactly as he expected - Fighting where expected to fight - easy where thought easy - Bad where figured would be some -


Nov. 18 -


Darling had to skip two days - No good to write about - worsen the poem place - Possible *never* was worse. No. Forest was never too good - The Krauts are beaten and we only have to destroy this crust - But it is like facing the pitching of an old Pitcher who knows everything and has 4 fine innings in his arm - or an old boxer who can go 4 of 10 rounds - or even six - But in this, while the old worthless is going well, everyone is greeting the old whore more or less *everybody*. Sort of impossible to conceive. I heard Red Moeller on the radio yest. morning (Combat Diary) and the difference between his reading the communique and our strange life was almost obscene. I understand about and like Red but I'm so glad you went to the front (not to be contemptuous as Sam, and hate some guys for instance) but just to have perspective and see and balance and know our end. Hell I must try and just understand and never be prejudiced. But Pickle this war is like almost nothing now - I'm right back where was in 1918 - Have almost cut out drinking on acct. need head very sharp and mean. Also would like to be fine for you. Also would like many krauts to be done away with.

In the nights *where* we sleep shakes solidly all night long - ripping cracks in the walls - when Sam awake I think of you and love you and think of us and the boat and how lovely it will be to be married - not to be yoked - to be privileged - and to be proud - when Sam asleep I can dream about *anything* I want. This is sort of miraculous. For instance the day before the jump off - knowing there was some - I thought now I have seven hours - So I dreamed about you - really - not make up or pretend dreams - nor day dreams - just magic lovely dream about you - then I dreamed about Boise my principal cat and then Littlest Kitty and then I woke up and just thought happy and good about you and how lucky I was to have run into you. Almost every night I dream about the White Tower very strange. I think because I saw you there first. Dearest Pickle my beloved let's think about the boat and the dark blue, almost purple of the Gulf Stream, makeing eddies at the edge of the current and the flying fish going up in coves and us on the flying bridge steering in shorts and no tops and at night anchored behind the barrier reef down at Paraíso with the sea pounding on the lovely sand and breaking on the horse-shoe of the reef and we anchored fine and *burn* inside with no motion only the tide pull and we lie with our legs touching and drink a tall coconut water, lime and gin and see the lovely blue miniature mountains over our right shoulders and I say "Pickle do you like very much?" (Maybe you will know better mts. and that is OK. But these lovely) and you say whatever you say and then there is that night and the next day is another day and in the morning we can sleep as late as late as ever and have breakfast and afterwards dive over board and swim ashore and walk on the far beach of the atoll with no suits while Gregorio polices up the boat and we have many things to do my dearest Pickle. We can have a lovely life on the ranch too. Good things to read and good music and keep healthy and work hard and well and always love each other.

Nov. 19 -

Pickle this is the evening of the next day but it seems so much longer it's stupid. Today big fight in woods; ditto yest, day before same - if you could see would appreciate - Krauts tough, smart, very professionally intelligent and deadly. We will kill and destroy some - But meantime Bod.

Today Red and Jean were bloody lions.

Woods, much, all knocked down and all over every way. Mines,

mines, booby trapped, booby traps, booby trapped - all fine breaks through woods tabed for mortar and M.g. fire. Smart Krauts infiltrating. Bod times.

So let's leave it Pickle and think about how, when you come in from the plane from Miami, I will be out at Rancho Boyeros airport and you'll come through customs and we'll drive through lovely country to the place and then we'll be where we'll start our fine life. You'll be scared - But unless everything on earth is completely blown down - it will be very lovely, Pickle - and if everything is blown down then we'll just have a fine house, like an intact C.P. to write and work in amid desolation - and better off than most everybody - and anyway our job is write and not simply live in perfect conditions - and we have a boat and some part of the coast the hurricane didn't hit and we'll hit that part -

Will write again tomorrow -

Nov. 20 -

Darling I got the letter about Bum - Very fine job. Nothing to do. Then no worry. All comes under heading "Too Bad" now. Bad luck for our Bum though. But been bad luck for everybody. But you were wonderful and beyond praise to go so quickly and do everything so dearly and beautiful and well. Will tell you - not write about it - Head all clear about that now. You're my hero - glad was good trip - Also got your letter of the 14th about telling Wert about going home - That is wonderful - Really wonderful - Will write you separate letter on it - Pickle we've had *another* day - Am not punchy tonight but am sort of tired. Put it in with Buck all day - We had problems - Pickle this fight has Belleau Wood etc. completely chickenshitted - I woke, thinking about yest. and what today would bring - and woke happy as always, but then started to think about how wanted our life together and had a real deffaillance (like when you had one on us once) so did 50 belly exercises and had ⅛th of bottle of Scotch left so drank that in 4 drinks with water and no left at all and then piled out into the rain and the rain washed it all away and when I found Buck I was feeling fine and he said "Ernie do you *know* what those chickenshits are trying to do?" and I said No. And he told me and we were off to the ball game. Pickle wish I could write you about it. This is one of bitterest and worst fights in history. That's why I write you in such a stupid constipated way. The artillery and mortar fire is most intense I've known since I was a kid on P cave in 1918 (only this is woods) and when there is a big fire fight it rolls like a storm.

Buck says, "I like counter-attacks. Let the chickenshits counter-attack - We'll kill them all right. We're hurting. But we'll make those chickenshits wish they never were born."

I suppose right now the most useful thing a man could do, beside the most pleasurable, is killing krauts. Very parochial view point. But I have seen you angry and I know you are a fighter and you understand. I promise you I do nothing show-off, nor stoopy (stupid) and as far as I know how I take care of our interests.

And soon we will have smashed them and I will drag down. Tubby told Hank Gorell that I would never be able to drag down etc. But no one knows me but you my dearest beloved. It's like all of your friends who never know you really write but *you* know and I know and I want to write better than I ever could and be a credit to you and take care of my children and love you and be straight partners with you and try to make you happy and be a good husband and father and writer and to never be away from you ever in my life if we can work it.

What you said about how careful we should be when *we are not attacked* to not be critical and contemptuous of each others things and picky is maybe the most important thing of all. Pickle we are both smart and essentially very just and let us be *so* careful to never be prejudiced and to always be understanding. It is just a grown-up adjustment to make - I'm sometimes *unbelievably* stupid. But if you put up with that and *know* I am never stubborn I don't see why we cant work and anything.

I'm saving you all my cigarettes - Think that is OK because offer them to everybody if they are short - if anyone *is* short you won't have any.

Am tired tonight Pickle. Excuse lousy letter - will write more tomorrow - Maybe in the morning - all I know good and sound is that I love you and the good news about (from Rather) Wert is best I've ever had. I'm so proud of your trip and of you I can't write it Mary - I am so happy about things being settled and OK I cant write about it either. Just believe it. Let's start our life soon and good and fight it as bravely and skillfully as Buck fights - But we can be kind and not be ruthless - only thing we'll be ruthless about is the people that waste our time and our life - you teach me how to be *polite and* ruthless over the telephone - and I'll learn - and Pickle one time you asked me what we could drink in Bermuda when woke up and I'd forgotten that have 7 cases of Pre-War Gordon gin - last in World - I don't think it is so good for night drinking - But anyway you have it for anything else (I can make lovely Martinis) and have Noelly Prat too. I think we'll be so happy and tired and fine feeling we wont have to drink in the night

- But for wake-up drinking when there isn't any Perrier-Jouet - Scotch is good - I can always hear Wolfie moveing around on the boat "What's the matter Wolfie?" "Just haveing a drink, Papa."

Do you like Scotch and good Soda without ice? Very good. Also Whisky and lime and soda to make Whisky sour.

But Pickle in the morning the breakfast of the 2 eggs any style, *good* fried ham, or Canadian bacon, or good crisp bacon and tall tomato juice, or grapefruit or orange juice and papayas and mangoes and each breakfast good and lovely on each tray - one ring for mine and 2 for yours - or 3 for both - and sleep as long as you want - and sometimes me with work all best before you ever wake up - and then fun all day with work whipped before-hand - and otherwise when Im working you can do any damned thing you want (the mornings *are lovely*) and all time in world to read an loaf at pool - and let everything in you thats been tired come back slow and strong and good (me too) - and you may not be bored at all - just maybe happy the way we always were when you didn't have work - and there's fine music on the capeheart - and anything you want we'll buy in N.Y. at the Liberty Music Shop. Anyway I'll make the best attack for you I can ever make - (am a judge of them now - I swear thát) I'll write the best, and be a good loveing husband - and I know what you bring me and will try to show you how I *value* it and it will be such fine fun Pickle - and now we start it - isn't it fine -

Theres a little matter of putting it all on the line tomorrow - But tomorrow looks sort of good in comparison to yest and today - and then a few more days - Then I'll come into Hotel - Not tanned like in the rat race - Everybody is sort of grey dirty colour - about the colour of singed chicken - no sun, rained out, youre a good man now. To your (. . .) and I'm hungry all the time and eat like a bastard, ate 5 steaks yest from cow killed by artillery, saw her killed, marked the co-ordinates and sent John out to butcher out the tenderloin. Between us and Krauts. They killed them while they were butchering. Red cooked a couple of steaks and brought them to me when I was asleep. Then yesterday we ate her up. But do 50-60 belly exercises every morning and a certain amount of up-hill and down-hill. John and Red fought all day again today. Nothing spectacular like yest just good, sound, useful - over country they learned yest.

I just set around up forward learning how to read a map and keeping track of the horrid intentions of the kraut as they manifest themselves in hostile form. Part of ones education. Pickle will write some more tomorrow - Seem to have written that once tonight - Good night dearest love. Been too tired *to stop* writing - sorry so dull - Love you - Hold you close and *tight* and always.

Your only true love ever
Papa


[25]

Letter to Mary Welsh.

Nov. 21 1944
E. Hemingway, War Correspondent
APO 4 US Army

Dearest:

So what to write tonight? We're on the 6th day of the fight and it has been the father and mother of all fights today with a driving thin rain and the trees comeing down as a hurricane. Mary other things comeing down too. Hank Gorell who went up to the bad part today for a couple of hours is writing it for all clients of U.P. (He hasn't ducked it. Was flying in Piper Cub day before and plenty shot on 1st day) and I cover him with us. He has a wife and kid and makes 150 a week and it is wicked to have to go around this any more than necessary if anybody can cover you. I see his copy gets off and bring him and find hot hot stories. Am tired of it and will be glad not to have to do it - But its only a few days more.

If you liked the hair breadth escape instead of flowers could fill every vase with them. But I've never cared for them either and you *must* have had to read enough of them in your husbands copy. I thought of Noel today and hated him before I thought which was cheap. I just hated him simple for takeing your money and (. . . .) so many suits and not makeing love to you. Here the hair-breadth or 2 yard or foot and ½ breadth escape is as unremarkable as the sardine in Portugal, or the worthless gin in our fine home Bar in the Ritz.

There is *nothing* to drink - neither before nor after todays show.

Everyday in the woods is like Custer's last stand if that distinguished leader had fought his way out of it and slain the red men. Yest one fine outfit jumped off simultaneously with the Kraut - the kraut counter-attacking, attacking, attacking, attacking - moving like the Lemmings in a migration into death - The guys wait until they are at 20 yards - and you can walk knee deep in them - Some places they come on now cockeyed as japs. I guess I start to sound as sensational as Noel.

Please forgive that chickenshit remark - But very sensational fight - Nobody here to make it historical but me and Gorell - He writes it so cheaply it's sort of sickening - I cant write you in detail or truly about it - And I promise you I will never be chickenshit nor D Day H hour about it - But it is a fight such as has been fought very few times *ever ever* in the world - and the people so damned *unbelievably* wonderful no one could ever believe it - I've seen the flower of the Union and the flower of the confederacy fight so that Pickle it would break your heart - So lovely, and happy and immortal - without this one I would never have known about Americans - You're a technician Pickle and so am I - and I could impress you with figures and details - But in a battle that is not permitted - So please believe that I am not just enthusiastic nor impressed nor sensational -

So - tomorrow is another day and tomorrow we will do tomorrow -

I think things go very well. I love you my dearest beloved. Excuse me if I write so under wraps and badly -

I hold you very close my dearest darling and you are all my love and all my hope and all our fine life and future - I love you always and especially tonight and tomorrow morning and always.

EH
*Only.*

[26]

Letter to Mary Walsh.

Nov. 21 1944
E. Hemingway, War Correspondent
9o Pro Hq 4th Inf. Div.
APO 3 US Army

Dearest Pickle:

Been writing you every day since kick-off except two when couldn't make it. But thought better send you a quick note to tell you how grateful I am for your news of Bumby and for makeing such a fine also damned proud of you! Also how happy about how you came out with West and that we have an actual factual future. Wonderful.

Pickle I write to you in the evening sort of in place of talking to you - always people talking and interrupting and lots going on - so its defficient to mail it getting to be an awful long letter and I just write some every night - about the boat and us and how I love you - and take it easy about what goes on. It's hard not to though. So much to write if could write it.

For actual news - I'm ok. Had been very jolly, etc. Hope I've been some use. I'm just sort of general bitching post for all corners.

This is the toughest fight I've ever known. Belleau Woods chickenshit alongside of it - if can ever write any part of it very fine story. Cant write of The Soul of Man like hearty But man himself is there for to be admired. You can imagine it haveing seen a woods front, a real battle in a woods is something. The fire rolls like the sea. Guess that is all the news Pickle except that I love you.

Red and Jean been fighting very well. I have to head back in a week.

Will send the long letter soon as have chance to read it over - your letter came through in 4 days. Please write when you get this.

All my love to you my dearest always. I love you more and steadier and always.

Only
E. Hemingway, War Correspondent

I sent you two other letters -
a long day to day dull one I wrote
before the kick-off and mailed
4 days after and a short one.


[27]

Letter to Mary Welsh.

Nov. 22
In Germany

From E. Hemingway, War Correspondent
9o PRO Hq 4th Infantry Div.
APO 4 US Army

Dear Pickle:
    Had your letter of Nov. 17 today - which is only five days and wonderful to get. I love to think of my Pickle, smallest gen officer in

the world, striding along through the tables being looked Doggers at by the tall long legged citizens who over-shot their bolts. Hell why wasn't I there to be with you? Good old Willie our Partizan. I can see him and hear him comeing over to see you and hear him, long lipped, telling you the crack and see my Pickles eyes light up. Pickle I miss you very much. For two bad days I couldn't see you in my mind - Knocked out of it visually - Then two days ago you came back completely and fine and now I can see you and be happy about it any time see you wonderfully with the dogger lookers looking.

Another tremendous fight today. We on all objectives through Buck's sagacity, foresight, attention to detail and absolute damned genius as a commander and braver than a badger - or a mongoose I guess - or a wounded leopard (only *not* wounded) but as dangerous as same. I don't know what's brave but Buck is and *so* intelligent and such a lesson to me. I know all his faults now - which is fine for human understanding. We haven't had any liquor for 2 days and you'll be happy to know that am all same without it as with it - Think maybe steadier and better - although have loved it, needed it, and many times has saved ones damned reason, self-respect and what all. Besides great pleasure and I love it. We always called it the Giant Killer and nobody who has not had to deal with the Giant - many many times has any right to speak against the Giant Killer.

Pickle if I could give you details, figures or anything concrete of the sort you and I understand we would have to understand and appreciate.

I cant though this show. But just know it is, today, toughest day of toughest fight ever. - Today it was magnificent. I'm really useful to Buck - only morally I mean or morale-ly rather I'm just his bitching post - and soon will be back I hope. Please love me very much the way I love you and I will be back and we will start our fine life. My dearest, blessed most beautiful and lovely.

Your
*Only*

Nov. 23

Next day:

You know I write you every night just to be near you and to talk to you. Miss that almost as much as anything. Being with you makes a feeling same as knowing both your flanks are OK. Being away is the opposite of that. Pickle first we had the snow then a couple of days of good weather and now its the rain and rain and the rain. The people are soaked wet through in it all day and all night - Just to live in it without the constant shell and mortar and small arms fire would be enough - But they endure it and fight and fight.

Pickle *I'm* tired and I sleep in a dry sleeping bag on a bedstead - and the people fight on and on and to the 8th day - Everybody is the colour drowned people with Mauldin looking beards and the forest, forward, is just the wreckage of where there was a forest. The streams flooded up to your waist running yellow mud and you can walk in the woods knee deep through dead krauts. Nobody will ever know how many krauts we've killed because there's no way to count them and they get a lot of their dead away too. If I tried to tell you you couldn't believe it. But this has been one of the great fights of our history.

You know how I was spooked of it before it started because know how sad it would be - But then about yest. and day before just like a gift - stone cold and with nothing to drink - just as though someone were leaveing you a million dollars. I get the old feeling of immortality back I used to have when I was 19 - right in the middle of a *really* bad shelling - not the cagy assessment of chances - nor the angry, the hell with it feeling - nor the throw everything away feeling - none of those - just the pure old thing we used to operate on - It doesn't make sense - But it's a lovely feeling - So I just split it with Buck all same as though it were a liquor ration - So it was fine because after giving it without haveing it - Doing it without feeling it - Then suddenly I had it again. This is dull as hell in a letter. But would be OK in a novel done objectively *(and about someone else)* and I'm so stupid I have to.learn about other people through myself - Pickle I write you such dull and self centered letters - Buck is braver than any man I know (who is completely sane) and I don't mean this chickenshit was helping either him or me to be brave - I meant to say it helped us to be happy and the bases of happinesss in the midst of prolonged and continued tragedy is a serious subject - am learning so much Pickle - and no you to talk to - you with the fine, clear intelligence to put me right - I love so being with you Pickle and you are as necessary to me as a compass -

Now, all the time, I think about how much fun it is with you and what a good time we have -

I like to think of how hard it is when we are together to break away to have to go to work and how we can spend rainy days happily and how happy I was just being around and reading while you worked and of all the fine places I know to go and fine jolly places to go evenings in towns I know that you will like. I know N.Y. pretty well and how to get around there nights in places you would like I think - the smarty ones 21 - Stork - El Morocco - The Colony (Don't like) and good low saloons with Thurber and Co. and the places the Mob goes - Do you know the rough joints? and boy, Pickle will be wonderful to put an *eater* like you up against the 21 chow - But I want us to be eating up on the roof of the old Pacífico in Havana - which is the best food in strangest surroundings in the world - I told you about it once. (. . . .) I stay hotel - Wolfie has eaten all over the world and is an old 21 and Colony habituée and he thought it was the best - There's no such thing as the best - But it's marvellous anyway -

Fats Waller is dead - But there still are joints where Maxine O'Sullivan sways and there are good places in the big town. To stay up well you have to be able to sleep till anyway 10 a.m. So you just do it (ordinarily I'm out wakeing at 7.45. I get tired but know how to handle that). Put a stop on phone calls - and if I wake early will read the papers and then go back to sleep and then can play up all night all same as when worked on morning papers. - We can go to the Museum of Modern Art and the good shows of pictures and the Metropolitan (4 wonderful to break your heart pictures) and the Museum of Natural History (which you scoff at maybe but is lovely (parts) and walk through the Park always to everywhere and see shows and wander around.

I learned, deliberately, to go to bed by 10:30 or so on acct. of knowing early morning only intact time for straight writing - you can protect it, your head is best then, and you have no alibis.

But instead of just protecting my lousy habits against unreasonable bitches (as have had to fight for in past) with you can say, reasonably, will switch habits in town since we understand and respect and are *not* unreasonable - (Pickle it is so *wonderful* to love someone who is not as unreasonable as a Bitch giraffe from Bryn Mawr in heat backwards, read cold) that it is like emerging from the valley of the shadow of Ball Room Bananas into a country of the kind we were brought up in.

Pickle wrote you another long page but threw it out. (too personal for mail. Very much loveing you)

Don't think this letter has anything cant said.

Good night my dearest love. Tomorrow is another day - and the next one and the next - But I know when I'm comeing back (Soons we OK to leave) and you clear up yours (plans, travel arrangements, office, etc.) and get it all straight so you can move good - and I'm your man for always and if we start out in the world another time (if they have other times which they *may*) all I ask is that we start out earlier together - But I think it is wonderful the way it is - and I love you now and always -

My judgement about our guys and what a fight this is, been confirmed today - very confirmed -

Well good night dearest Pickle - Been up in the ball room banana racket this p.m. again. Tired.

Love you. Wish could write poem to tell you. I love you so my darling lovely beautiful dearest always Pickle -

> Your only -
>
> E. Hemingway, War Correspondent
> (See head *of letter*)

[28]

Letter to Mary Welsh.

> E. Hemingway, War Correspt.
> 9o PRO Hq 4th Infantry Div.
> APO 4 US Army

My dearest Pickle:

I've written you every night but hard to write to who you love about a battle and write letters that you know other people will read. So I just send this note to say I've written three letters — one of them a very very long one that I would write on every night and I'll send them soon. I love you so my dearest beloved and this is just to tell you I'm not not writing - have just not been mailing.

This is the toughest fight I've ever even known about by hearsay let alone been in. But if I start on that I won't be able to mail this one either. So just remember about the poem, double it and redouble it and that's how she goes.

But I don't throw you away - I keep you as all I have or ever hope for -

Have written you a lot about things we'll do and lots of good details about the future. Pickle please love me very much - as much as I love you - because I need you very much.

Big ball room bananas today - Been up all morning with Buck - just going again. Been with him all the time. He's fine. Will be a gen. sure. All I want to be is in bed with you.

Everybody, sort of tired. But we've got sun again today. The sun of Austerlitz only news is I love you my dearest beloved -

Re-read poem. It tell you what I think of you. I've been very lucky - would like it to have a few more days and then come home to you and never be away the rest of our lives.

Your lovely husband.

Only.

[29]

Letter to Mary Welsh.

Nov. 25, 1944
E. Hemingway, War Correspt.
9o PRO Hq. 4th Infantry Div.
APO 4 US Army

My very dearest:

Wrote you a letter this noon and sent it off this aft. back through army I haven't been there since came up.

It's been another of those days. I stayed with Buck and ate with him and just drove home through the forest in the moonlight. Felt pretty low today. Wish you could spend a day with us in a battle. You are so much better reporter than I am and I am so involved and mixed up in it what with knowing the people that one day knocks another out of my head. You could write it straight and fine and I would explain what you don't understand. I am so tired of explaining to journalists who are incapable of understanding. Pickle I miss your lovely clean, sound un-lying competent head as much as I miss your pocket size miracle of a body and your beautiful face that breaks my heart every time I see it.

In the end I will have absorbed and digested the stuff about this show - and if I cant write it accurately as it is Will be able to invent a good battle for a book sometime out of my knowledge - But I wish you were here for historical purposes and to see things so I would see them. I get so involved that I have to force myself to see and notice instead of just consider problems and results. ½ the time I'm too tired to look - To overcome that I ride standing up and with butt against back of jeep seat and make myself look, conscientiously, at everything I'd gotten so I was just going from place to place and only noticing technical things and thinking.

When writer begins to quit noticing he's gone. So am noticeing again, my Pickle, but I wish I could pass all this in front of your lovely, accurate, and fresh eyes. You know what it's like from your hip up in the heels and this is one of toughest battles ever, ever, *ever*.

I'm so damned anxious not to be killed. Pickle on acct. of loveing you that knowing I'm at the end of my tour of duty it makes me hurt where I don't usually. I *can't* throw you away. You see because we made a decision on that. We quit that "I can lose anything and you too." That I did that time before our trouble taught us not to be stupid. I've quit that easy, cheap defence against love. If any bad luck should happen to me please remember, and tell Willie because would like to have him know that I have loved you all the time *repeat* all the time, and have fought this one (inside myself) all the time without throwing you away, nor the children, nor the work I have to do afterwards - as sort of a step toward growing up. But I'm a son of a bitch if it's not the hard way.

Pickle you know how we tell each other the things people say or do that make us proud: that we cannot say to other people. Like the things you tell me the air citizens say of you and then I am proud. This is just a small thing. But up at Bucks all the GI's salute me and the sentries present arms and I explained to them all I was a civilian and did not rate salutes and everyone knows I don't and there are no mis-apprehensions - and everyone continues to salute and the sentries continue to present arms.

It isn't the above which holds me here. My Pick as you would realize if you had a look at our country.

So now what? Did I tell you that for 2 bad days I couldn't see you in my mind? Didn't lose any confidence though - Didn't lose any confidence - (that's a bad sign - when you repeat sentence) and the next morning there you were as clear and lovely as though George were unlocking the door of the Bar to let you in and I see you way across the room before you see me.

Pickle I guess we better figure on me being here a week longer - I have to set a limit - So I better set that and I'll tell Buck - Then I'll stick to it unless he is in some sort of awful jam - and then I'll just make it soonest - He's my only obligation any more in this racket -

If I am jamming up your travel dates you could go ahead and see your people first and get Cuban visa on passport - It isn't a Cuban visa - that is unnecessary for US citizens I think - it is just to have passport validated for Cuba - I'll plan to be in Paris then by Dec. 2 - Maybe before - Frankly don't think can last a week at present rate of exchange - But will put that as maximum -

In N.Y. all I have to do is my business - 1 day Colliers, 1 Day

Scribners, 1 day my lousy lawyer. Am too tired to start boxing - altho if stuck there will go work with George.

Mornings will see Dr. and get check-up. (Try to take care of your property) Is large old truck and better see if it needs oil, gas or a grease job.

If youre there we will have some fun (write a long letter about things we could do)

I wrote the children to get their passports validated and make reservations via Panamerican for Cuba at start of their Xmas vacations. Usually they get 7 to 10 days. Just before Xmas through New Years.

How long does it take to get home once you decide to go? Am sure can get air transport.

Didn't get letter from you yest. nor today. Now am afraid you're not writing because expected me back. There won't be any time to answer this letter. But God I hope I didn't ball things up with original predictions on return 20 no more are comeing - Later very great help beside great pleasure.

Pickle am stopping now. The damned radio is going and people are talking and letter is deteriorating so I'll stop.

I love you now and all the rest of my life.

*Only*.

Later: Buck just called. Had slept 12 minutes and thought it was morning and he wanted to talk to me and the guy wanted to thank me for hanging around today and I said "Fornicate you Col. Sir. I just hang around for fun. Don't get sentimental on me you, willy, wicked, worthless old man and get a real sleep now and we'll open up the ball room banana factory tomorrow."

Please give Bill Walton my love. Tell him I miss him very much and the advice I gave him is straight, OK and my considered and reconsidered advice.

Truly. It's just a personal thing and he will know what I mean.

EH

[30]

Letter to Mary Welsh.

November 26
E. Hemingway, War Correspondent
9o PRO Hq 4th US Infantry Div.
APO 4 US Army

My dearest:

Well, today we had another day and tomorrow is another. Nothing to write any more Pickle. Tonight comeing back in hurry from Buck I dined with Tubby - afterwards the chief gave me two bottles of Brandy which I will take up tomorrow to the mob. Yest. was a day I wrote you once when I had to come back at noon and again last night. Oddly, I feel better about tomorrow and I've just finished reading a 42 page report (or informal observation) by the Division Psychiatrist. Much very interesting. But encouraged me because he knows all about fear and nothing about courage. I think *he even* thinks it is sort of cheap and actually it is bad from his standpoint as it would, if it ever over-ran the country probably put the Psychiatrists out of business. (cheap statement by me)

But we all live up there with our damned sorrow and our blunted pride and the broken shaft of our spear and no son of a bitch on earth will beat us - and the Psychiatrist doesn't know about that. Or I guess he does but he is in a different racket. A good and kind one I guess. He sounds kind. (I've never spoken to a B.T. Carried them. But never spoken with their heels healing.)

Pickle if I come home tired forgive me in advance because it will pass quickly and I will try not to be a bore about it. Nor favours. Just lay a long time in bed and tell you anything that comes in my head. And maybe nice like for Bumby to break the damned choke and then *it's over*.

Didn't get letter again. Maybe will tomorrow. Here I'm in the good example racket. Very boreing!

Pickle this isn't a self pity letter. It's that really I am a writer and I can turn my imagination off like a faucet to function as something else - But I pity people, all people, but above all infantry and now I'm going away. I know I've been inhumane and only considered results (I've loved my friends but I had suspended pity except when I was away, and so I start to notice and noticeing - it is tough - Every day is poem day now.

The Blitz made you tired didn't it? Even though you were always brave and good? I think sometimes I am tired from the boat too. I know before I came over I was very tired. The hell with tired. Let's get in shape and rested and healthy and work good. Us and we the Partners.

I love you my dearest most beautiful most true, most complicated, most simple and most lovely.

Can see you now and it is a lovely sight.

I hold you very close my dearest heart.

Your
Only

[31]

Letter to Mary Welsh.

> November 27, 1944
> E. Hemingway, War Correspondent
> 9o PRD Shaef Press Hq.
> APO 757 US Army

Dearest Pickle:

I was going to send five letters for you that I didn't want kicking around post boxes - in today by Hank Gorell - But thought he might be tight in Paris or forget to deliver them or something - (none of the things I've asked him to do for me at the rear has he ever done - forgot my mail - forgot other things) so think better wait until I can send them surely. They just tell you I love you - But they are what I write at night with only you to talk to. Last night, in the night, I woke up and realized that anybody could take any letter from me to you out of your box and know it was from me to you and what was to stop entire Fleet Street from doing same and I thought I had been stupid and careless for you. Also that maybe why I didn't hear from you last 4 days was that you had *never* gotten my letters. So I had fine idea of sending these in and now have just abandoned it. I plan to leave here Sat. the 2nd and be in Paris that night - Hope so.

We've had it toughest ever - I hear Bill Walton was at 1st army and called and tried to get him but no luck. Then had to get out to Buck's in a hurry - yest was big bananas festival, today easier, not much, tomorrow is another day of those days. I don't give importance to Colliers except try to write good pieces since am a Pro but today I found they had cut all the good first part - the funny part - protection for their phonies I guess and had not used the pictures, nor any of the names, numbers, etc. the censor authorized be re-instated. The poor god damned mentions that guys have instead of immortality. How's that? Just to make you feel good after what we've been doing. (I sent them the appropriate cable).

Dearest Pickle I love you very much and always.

Send this now in haste as have to get back to the ball room banana factory.

(You would like the letters if you ever get them.)

It won't take me long to get set to go Statesward soons get back. Much all my love always to you.

(Am writing this for the Daily Mail, your bank account chiseling ex-mate, if *he* happens to pick it up, and any pricks who read it who shouldn't.

*Only*

[32]

## Letter to Mary Welsh.

Wed. 29th November
From E. Hemingway, War Corresp.
9o PRO Hq 4th Infantry D.
APO 4 US Army

Dearest Pickle:

Am takeing advantage of letter of Willie to send this. Pickle we won't be back on Sat. Hope be back by Monday, or Tuesday, or Wednesday night. I was comeing back on Sat. but couldn't leave Buck. It is wonderful to see Willie and be able to talk about you. I haven't heard from you since the night Willie was with you—his last in Paris— So I sweat out each day but no letter. Last was about night you bought wonderful present and Willie read from Book. Have taken Bill in with the guys and he loves it and is very impressed. He is haveing chance to see wonderful fight from inside and all the guys love him and he is very chic and fine. Am very happy now he is here because if anything happens he can write the story of the fight and feel a little because he is our Bro. that you are here. Nobody understands this fight and nobody will go near it (only us). I fix so Willie sits in sames me in all stuff forward, also sees everything, only am very careful with him without seeming so.

Pickle darling I love you so - I want - hell wont write what I want -

Anyway we are winning our fight - am trying to see and notice all the things I haven't fooled with for when I write - I don't want to compete with the fine kids who have been through this and have the right—and will write wonderfully. The young, the new, the always comeing that we hope will write better and sounder than we can - That we blast the trail for and that will be *good*—to write of it. I will just take my small piece of a tiny part of it and buttress it with the forgotten sometimes punchy knowledge and the new will work the mess so the old magic will work - and then we will have book a day at a time.

Would give anything to have you here now to see and feel better than I can.

We need a photographer here for Willie Mary heart breaking shots Christ wish I could have made a movie of this fight like we did of Spanish Earth. I took Willie up with Buck in the morning and didn't bring him back till after supper.

Hell Pickle don't know any news. We took all our objectionables today and tomorrow is another day. Tomorrow is a real one.

Red lets me read the letters from his girl because I never get letters. He got a wonderful one tonight. He has terrific problems but he is wonderful. Couple of days ago he looked at the Big Picture map in the kitchen and put his finger on Milheim, past Cologne and said "Papa by god ain't that the town we took yesterday?"

Must turn off the light now to go to sleep. I love my very dearest always and for always. Hope you are fine and your news is all good and soon I will be there with you and then we will be starting our fine life. I cabled Colliers asking permission return home for urgentest business reason repair hurricane damage Cuban property - only agreed stay over for them through July anyway -

Did I tell you they cut all the Dorothy M. Dennis part of the Story - also all the stuff about male correspondents etc. Also unuse pics. Also all mention of released units. Was not heartening. I cabled congratulateing them complete sabotage piece. Lets get into our own racket.

> I love you
> Only

My dearest lovely darling.

## [33]

Letter to Mary Welsh.

> Thursday
> November 30 1944

Dearest Pickle:

Don't know if you ever get any of the letters from me nor from Willie Walton and me. Lahst heard was from you written on No. 17 which was one day after the ballroom banana factory went into full production and hardly a sonofabitch is now etc. that remembers that famous day and year. Willie and I had a fine day today. A lovely day in these latitudes is one you can walk away from and (mis-set typer) sentence was intended to read that a lovely day in this parish is one that you can walk away from. Willie is fahscinated by the infantry that obsolete profession that takes over from all others at the dictates of meteorology. Today we laid the ballroom banana on the line definitively. I mean we throwed it over the woodshed. Willie is wonderful guy and I have tried to show it all to him same as would show to you and guys love him same as they would love you. Am always careful.

Expect to leave here and be back Paris Tuesday night Dec. 5 or morning Dec. 6 - Pickle would it be possible if you are leaveing work to have it set so we could have three four five days to see Paris really without you haveing just to work. Would be worth it. There are all the fine things to do we could do if you didn't have to hit the bag every day and I can write my piece NY or anywhere and could even write Paris piece that way if we need dough. Because if you are laying off we have right to see what it was we captured (I've never had time to see because care nothing about see alone and except Sundays just wait for you to show up from work) Think this sound project. You could turn in suit on definite date and we have few days for to see town. I love town very much and would make no other engagements and would like to see Cirque, races, Music Halls, Montparnasse, Montmartre, Pac Montsauris, Montmartre again (slower), le Boxe, the Salon D'Automne, Salon des Refuses, and take several hot baths. Also eat good at any price and walk all over rain or shine.

I have bitched up my needing to be back to fix place as should have gone instantly. Is like fireman arriveing five weeks late. So let's salvage all we can of Paris and can still get to N.Y. plenty time to get down for Xmas.

I wrote the childries, Mouse and Giggy, would be back for Xmas. Tonight we had very funny time with the Division Psychiatrist. He came in to study us all for his future works. Will tell you much funnier to tell. Willie and me going to write play. Div. Psych in as comic villain. Everything getting so screwball now - 4 more to go for us, you and me I mean.

It is wicked not to have a photographer here to get pictures of something like today. I love you always my dearest Pickle. Will see you very soon.

Excuse worthless letter. Since no hear begine everything just runs for the intercepts. (only)

Papa
I love you

Ernest Hemingway
War Correspondent
9o PRO Hq. 4th US Infantry Division
APO 4 USA


[34]


Letter to Mary Welsh.

Christmas Night [1944]

My dearest love:
Your letter was the loveliest and finest thing that ever happened
to me. It was so strange, too, that while you were writing the first part
I was thinking what I phrased so badly to you when I came upstairs
but meant so truly.
Last night after I sent a message to you so you would know I loved
you and that everything was OK. Mrs. M. showed up. (This is just
news) I was good and kind on acct. of Christmas. (Explained to Buck
I was marrying you if you would have me.) But she came and robbed
us of what we should have had together. But the counter-attack broke
down of its own weight. Did not say a mean thing. Nor act one. But
everyone, and me, and she, finally, dumb in the confidence of her
beauty, (like the Germans confident in their armour) knew finally that
my true love was not there: nor was my heart there and it all ended
in politeness and niceness and no one being fooled. But I was heartsick
for us and how it would have been to have you there. Because the
fighting men do not like Miss M. In some circles she is wonderful -
But not there, anymore. But if you had been there it would have been
as though by some miracle all our true loves had been there instead of
we haveing a ration of Bryn Mawr, Bergdorf Goodman and the Lan-
caster.
Pickle, the weather has been clear and sharp and cold, very healthy
after Paris. Like a lower Switzerland good for the chest I think and so
wonderful for your Big and middle sized and small friends! Such wonderful air.
I was quite ill when I hit here. Then had great confidence in the
feel of the air and sun and gambled on staying out (could hardly walk
first day. Was a lot sicker than I knew) and feel better and stronger
every minute. Felt strong and good tonight. Your leather jacket a truly

life saver. We are all fine. The fight was wonderful and almost un-believable. I have gotten it all technichalled out and will give it to Wert tomorrow. 9.30 a.m. (He is here and will bring this to you.) It will all be garbled in that sheet. But I married into Life and Time (though I hope you truly will leave if I am good enough) for you to leave for me. Not because I have a job building the Sphynx or own a ballroom banana factory - But because I hope you will marry me to marry a good man - if he proves he is a good man.

Pickle, as soon as I am working, as out here, I am so un-drunk and so un-stoopy. It was a big destroying thing to be un-working at ones true trade and to be sick too and confined to quarters in that lovely town also not to have had a chance to work at ones trade 4 years etc. (insert self pity ad lib) am sick of it myself.

Marty thought maybe I was marrying you (I don't mean you have to) defensively and I told her you marry me straight and truly and why and how much I loved you you know them so I will not bore you with enumerating. But maybe I can summarize in such a fashion that the succinctness (never wrote that word before) will amuse you. They are: lets see if can summarize in winter.

Head, body, bed, heart, future, face, soul, belief in, trust of, desire to be partners with, T W H, B W H, or if anyone bitches us T H W, B H W. (Mr. Scrooby has risen at this point) desire to live with rest of life, (some of these I didn't mention) nor did I mention our clothes, and wishing to lie with your head where it belongs and listen to the Capeheart, nor about the sea which is ours for the takeing, nor that you are littless kitty my only animal or showed we just say fun-ed love, nor that you replace for me religion, King and country, family, home, state, economics, chastity, the First National Bank of Key West Florida, all bonds, mortgages, liens, or assigns, the flash of a breaking school of mullet with the morning sun on the water, un-read copies of the New Yorker; touch-downs from kick-off, frozen daiquiris, (it could go on for 6 pages).

Dearest lovely Pickle in the yellow bed jacket with the magic lovely mouth and the figure heads of all my ships and the place that knows exactly what it wants to do and has, lying beside you, its partner who wants to do that and no other. I love you very much.

I want to be exactly as you want me to be (within my own-ness as you have your own-ness) (This sounds lousy but you know how I mean it) and I want you to help me to be what you want the same as you would help a horse - and I will race well for you as a horse - but at home will be neither a horse nor a horses ass and instead your good

loveing, sound, but funny husband who or whom I hope you will marry
and have a fine life with.

I love you darling dearest Mary and I will love you all my life.

Yours very truly,
Ernest Hemingway

I love you dearest Pickle.

Day after Xmas a.m.

Just saw Wert and he says no matter whether Willie goes or not
you can come to be there within 30 days of me. We've been haveing
conference.

It seems there is some doubt about whether he Willie goes or not.
But there are ways he can work the replacing. If Willie doesn't go you
can come as soon as you like.

Note: That Christmas, Hemingway was at the 22nd Regiment Command Post at Rodenbourg. Col. Ruggles sent a jeep
to bring Martha Gellhorn from Luxembourg. He thought this
would be a pleasant surprise for Ernest.

[35]

Letter to Mary Welsh.

December 27 8 a.m.

My dearest beloved:

I wanted to write you last night but was too tired. Night before
I couldn't sleep until 6 a.m. and wrote you the other letter then.

This morning am flying over the whole show in a cub to get it
straight in my head yest worked it all out with the maps and accounts
and turned over all material to Wert so he could use any he needed.
Have a fine technical account that I could supplement with inserted
colour in Italics (the way I did in that Schnee Eifel story) and he thought
if Colliers did not want it with the maps it might be good for-Life.
(. . .) to take it over with me if the censor passes it. He wanted me to
work for Life etc. But I would love it if neither of us ever had to write
journalism again. I think we would work it that way and still leave a
happy life. I have not lost any faith and more now that I know all your
views. But if you want it *with* journalism we can do it that way. But

do not worry about me moveing in on you in the same organization. All I want to do is what you want to do.

If it were possible I want to write a book. More than anything almost - not as a work of art - But all same as it is my work that I have for all my life. If you could stick with me through that we could concentrate on whatever you wanted to do most and would respect it.

I don't think it's selfish, maybe to do mine first, any more than we ever had any trouble about who should have first turn at the bathroom. I haven't seen M since her counter-attack altho she is staying here at Wert's hotel.

Pickle I wish the over-cast were clearing a little better maybe it will. Am going out to Bucks afterwards to stay night.

What I would like best if for us to be married and me be the one that works, not to be a big shot or to be privileged, but so you would have plenty of time to be my wife if you liked being it - not wife of E.H. writer - just your husbands wife, partner, fun partner, good and bad tunes partner and mother of our children. But if you don't want that then I'll take what I can get. I really hate journalism - worse than you hate drinks or the Roman Catholic Church maybe even - but I would do it rather than not have you. Though I suppose doing what you hate and what is against nature would probably destroy one sooner or later. It's had me pretty well down as it is.

I truly think you would have a chance to be happy with me working because it is not against nature for you to have a husband and be healthy and economically sound and nothing says you have to stop useing your head, nor going fine places, nor learning and you would have time to learn the things you are interested in really. And when we come to London and Paris you would see and talk to all the people whose minds bring you pleasure.

Here he goes trying to sell something I guess. Excuse me Pickle. It was just that I suddenly remembered telling M. how things had to be over because of how you and I loved each other and we, (you and I) could and would work things out and then I thought maybe you and I'll do whatever you want. But really I want to take us both out of journalism and into a sounder life - the advantage of it being writing is that writing gives us great freedom of movement in between working - If it were a factory I wouldn't have as much to offer you and I don't think it would be fair to take you from your friends - But as it is we can always come back and see them.

Oh well - Have to get dressed now and go to work. I love you very much. Littless I hold you hard and tight and kiss you.

Things look OK here now banning possibilities. Hope to clear up story. See remaining friends and get back end of week or first of next. Don't worry if I don't. Will try and send message.

I love you my darling. Chest and head much better but am still weak. Think Dr. had something in that convalescence idea.

All my love. Excuse dull (frosty) letter. The other is a love letter.

Your loving husband
*Only*.

[36]

## Letter from Martha Gellhorn, May 28, 1945.

Dear Bug; Now that Bumbi's safe, I really consider the war in Europe over. I didn't know of course and went mooching about Munich, Nurnberg and other 7th army territory, trying to find out about him. But there was no finding out anything about prisoners; they moved apparently largely on their own and were reported in when they finally found some of their old people. I met Neil Regan in the street in Paris, after V-E day and he said he'd seen Bumbi, and then I got a note from Charlie Scribner, and then I came back here to London and Mike Burke and Bob Thompson said he'd been through and gone home, looked fine and I hope he's there with you now. Please give him all my love and kiss him for me. So now all is truly well.

I hope the house and grounds are fine and that you are all enjoying yourself very much. I am going home in about two weeks to spend the summer with Mother, and will either go to the Pacific or back here in the fall. Do not want to go to the Pacific as am very tired and Japs sound like mean citizens. When in Nurnberg I saw the patch of your division and spent the night in a billet apartment house that was okay except no water with George Goforth and his men. He was very tired and very glad to be out of it all; a lot more were dead apparently. It was only overnight but they were sweet to me and sent many loving messages to you.

I understand there has been a complete announcement of our separation in the US, including Winchell on the radio (Audrey wrote to ask me if true) so that's all finished with now and you needn't worry about publicity. It sounds as if it had gone off extremely quietly and pleasantly. Would you mind getting some lawyer in Cuba to get busy on the divorce; I think it will only mean a telephone call. I do very much want to get it all tidied up, as I am sure you can understand.

Have you been able to start on your book yet? It will be a fine one and I wish you very much success. Please kiss the Mouse and Gigi and I hope I will not lose them entirely and for always.

Am fine and healthy again, weigh 124 pounds and have a faint sunburn (very faint) and in excellent spirits. Your friends, the sixth floor staff at the Dorchester, send love: they are my family now and this beat-up room is as cosy as if one had built it oneself or been born in it.

Love.
Mook

May 28, London
P.S. Better write me care Charlie Scribner; I don't know where I'll find a room in NY, though will try the Gladstone. If you left any clothes there, I'll have them sent on to you if you want them.

[37]

A long, affectionate letter to Martha Gellhorn, undated, and probably never sent.

Dear Marty,

I guess you didn't see Mousie as he got out of school the 19th. Thought you may have. Bumby is fine. He lost 50 lbs on a one soup a day five times a week and 2 soups twice a week diet. They made one break and were recaptured. Finally they marched them from Nuremberg to Moosberg (200 miles) with the S. S. dealing with those that fell out. Now he has put back 35 lbs (it came on first just as fat) but is takeing good exercise and eating well and building up soundly.

He loves you very much and we talk of you very affectionately. His wounds are through shoulder and fore-arm. Due to infection they had to remove a muscle across the back of the shoulder but he claims this has only helped loosen up his nerve. The wounds are big, from that stepped up automatic carbine at about twenty yards range and the krauts also threw an egg grenade that exploded just alongside his head. We've had a lot of luck with him. He is "entero." Not spooked nor nervous. Has grown up terribly in some ways and not at all in others. He loves you as much or more than ever. So don't ever feel lonely for him because you always have him.

We were terribly worried about Mousie when Dr's reported he had a spot on lung. But it was an error in the plate. He and Giggy are due here tomorrow. Gigi is much better and sounder; as good a joker as ever but can joke against himself now and has gotten rid of much of the fierce competetiveness.

Mousie started to paint last year and is painting really beautifully. I know he would like to send you a good one if you would like it. It reminds you of Van Gogh only it is Mousie and I think it is really good. Wouldn't it be wonderful if he should turn out to be a really fine painter? He is so modest and quiet and good about it but the way it works is that you don't see him and what he is doing is painting. I have two of the best ones framed and they stand out with the other pictures.

This will have to be an awfully long letter to give you all the Gen. So just be patient. It is ten a.m. now and by one o'clock ought to be able to get most of it down: Wish could talk instead. It was lovely talking the last time at the Dorch and such a pleasure not to be enemies.

That's the more or less minimum of Gen on the childies except that Giggy is probably a little shorter and much broader. Mousie is terribly tall, stooped, and very thin. Must build him up and look after posture. They both love you and are proud of you.

When I got home the cotsies looked like something out of Daschau. It was heart-breaking. Have them all o.k. now. Blindie drowned in the hurricane. All other name cats o.k.

Hurricane in its effects on grounds too sad to talk about. But most of the best royals remain and place still more beautiful than any other I've ever seen. Big Ceiba and most flamboyan-tes fine. Anyone who hasn't seen it before would think it was the way it had been planned I guess. We lost all the best mango trees; most of the key royal palms looking off toward the Mts. No use listing all the losses. Were plenty. But place and grounds essentially intact.

What raised the devil was that for eight months after there was a drought. Until four days ago everything dried to a crisis. My replantings withering, earth cracking open, no water in well [something illegible] sucking mud, really right up against it.

So on last Wednesday it starts to rain early in the morning. But just a shower not the real sort of seasonal rain you needed to save the place and the whole Island which was drying up like the dust bowl with cattle dying, chow almost inexistent, etc.

At the point have not brought Thomas Hardy to the coast to write the scenario. It's just our old friend The Hand of God.

As filler for scenario should state I'd told columnists what you asked me to in London. Spoken highly of you. Everybody friendly. Everybody respectful. No scandal. Two people been married and were busting up. About as dignified as could be. Everybody wishing us both good luck. Friends of yours saying like to stay friends with me too. Friends of mine saying how much admired and loved you. Exchange friendly letters between Walter and me. Mother and me understanding each other.

Welsh set to get divorce by appearing in court by 28th when term closes. (suspended for summer) Leaving on plane last Wed with all passage arranged straight through and a five day lee-way to be sure and have everything o.k. (Passage difficult to arrange) I'd been assured could get un-publicitized divorce in one month and waiting until could check with you on representation etc.

So it all looks like something built by Henry J. Kaiser except for the fact that I'm writing on a novel which is never quite that smooth. We start for the air-port at 1235.

So, crawling along in the rain up the hill behind the Club de Cazadores, Lincoln tops hill and starts down the Montilla road, downhill, and starts to skid. It is just as slippery as though it had been soaped. (First rain of eight months on a place where trucks had been hauling clay) I took her out of four skids and went into ditch, finally, between a tree and a stone wall. Mary: cut in forehead and bad one across left cheekbone. Me: chest stove by the steering wheel (buckled steering column with chest) very deep cut in center of forehead where rear-view mirror drove into head, and left knee hurt pretty bod.

Mary is going to be perfectly ok with plastic surgery (That Prince Rodríguez Días really is a good surgeon) but awfully painful and American Hospital full and you know Cuban clinic? All same like where Mr. Josie died.

I have *no* fractures. Cartilage split a little from ribs and pleura bruised. (You probably had same on your jeep spill) Knee has that elephant look but no fracture and think the internal hemmorage is largely blood rather than cynoveal fluid as is absorbing good already and the purple runs all the way up to the crotch.

So that's that. Mary misses what was needed to do. Comes out of the Clinic today but can't smile, laugh nor talk so don't think should travel and can't get there for 28th. C'est la hard luck tu sais. Toi qui la connais bien. (My french still pitiful) But will all come out all right and just have to start the attack all over again.

Now we are past the Drahma let's see what other news have for you. Oh Yes. Cucu, Mrs. Cucu and I packed all your things with sad reverence and they are in all the good suit-cases in moth-balls in the top floor of little house. All your papers, etc. sealed. Leather etc. things that would deteriorate packed in blue hall closet kept locked and regularly aired by Maria Esther. Have taken really responsable good care of your things and all your china things, silver things, ornaments etc. all packed and cared for. Please don't worry about anything.

Nobody knew how bad my head was after 2nd and 3rd concuss until get home. José Luis been looking after it and he has more experience and sense. Seems was lucky didn't have the works. Not to bellyache but honest to godliness it is bad luck to hit it again right now and hit the other place where I'd had trouble.

On the other hand we've lost a lot this last year and a half (you and me) but we got Bumby back, Mousie *hasn't* TB, we've beaten the Krauts and I hope you've got a fine play. (By the way about that I said exactly to Colliers what you told me to and built you up tremendously not that you needed it)

They admitted cutting my stuff and changeing it to improve it; they released those comic fotos they took at Georges (bearded wrestler stuff) they had promised solemnly not to use and only took as a gag and did me great and irreparable damage thereby; and they have never yet paid me $6,000 of my own money I spent for them and gave them an expense outline on. They cabled they only wanted a summary so I gave them a summary (much less than actually spent and told them to wire me when it was deposited) instead got a letter (un-airmailed) from LaCossitt wanting all details. They also forwarded me cable from Mike Burke saying Bumby was o.k. (when was worried blind about him) in a 3 cent envelope. Not even air-mailed. A cable they had opened about your own son being o.k. took seventeen days when every day had no word and the last camps over-run. I have to get my passport back from State Dept. to get dates and write London for expense details and meantime they have been useing my money since last April (a year ago).

All I did for them was hit beaches on D Day when should have been in hospital and have had terrible headaches ever since; fly interception against robot bombs; write them good breakthrough story (The GI and the General) and be First into Paris, and admitted by all correspondents First into Germany. So they don't pay the expense money they have owed you for over a year. It seems the one thing I mustn't do is get angry so I can't write La Cossit. But if you see him just suggest he send me the 6000 he owes me pending whatever amplification he wants in the account I sent him.

Have such a darb of a headache now that maybe better lay off. Dearest Mook if you want to marry anyone or have *any* urgency for the divorce will go downtown tomorrow and start it no matter what repercussions on me or others. You have a right to anything you want. But if there is no hurry and the separation status is adequate will get it the soonest it is tactically most favourable considering the angles that exist and have come up. If it is a question of *telling* people you might tell them we are divorcing in a month or a couple of months or in the fall. Please know I will never stall on it. If can swing right away you can just tell them we are divorceing sooner than we expected.

Don't know how is with you but *terrible* hard for me to write immediately after war. As though all the taste buds were burned off and as though you had heard so much loud music you couldn't hear anything played delicately. But I promise you I will try to get in as good a shape as I can be and write as well as I can to make up (there is no such thing) for all the things we lost.

Down to 202, been down to 194. Never drunk, never rum-drunk (my own opinion of course) Haven't been mean nor cruel nor said mean nor cruel things. Have some other new good qualities but cahnt remember same. Bleive they are Sex--1.

Mary has been awfully good; wonderful on boat; can't get rough enough for her. Will skip eulagies. That was the poem Eulagy in a Country Churchyard. Cahnt spell it.

Will be nice to see Childries. Wish you were seeing them too. But see no reason why if you ever have a place we can't split them with you if you want them. Also if you and Mother ever want to use this place no reason why not. Hope to spend a lot of time in Africa once things are clear and you would love this as a place to go once you didn't feel it like an albatross.

[38]

Notes for a story.

But Gentleman your old friend Hemingstein's popularity waned around Hurtgen. I'd had three days in Paris and been briefed, debriefed, bigotted, bull-shat and befused. So we sat in the trailer (caravan) and the Gen had not one but two guards outside and said, "What do you think of it Ernie?"

I said, "Do you want me to be frank, General?" and the usual; you know.

I said, "It looks like the worst, murderous, fucking balls-up I have even seen on an overlay."

(Too frank)

Gen: "I feel the same way you do. But we must never take counsel from our fears."

Poor Old Papa: "General, Sir. I have no ——ing fears as far as I know except for your 8th, 12th and 22nd rgts and the poor god-damn combat engineers and the medics."

Gen: "Why don't you call me Tubby instead of General?"

Me: "I'll call you General all the time through this one, Sir."

Gen: "Do you really think it's that bad?"

Me: "General, Sir. You couldn't cut it with a shit knife if you'd laid it to the grindstone all day."

Gen: "Would you please send Dick in? (His Chief of Staff who was in love with one of my sisters before he went to the Academy) Are you eating with us?"

Hemingstein: "Only if the General requests it."

Gen: "All right. Get up with Buck then. That's what you've been wanting to do all the time isn't it?"

Hem: "After I'd seen you, General."

Gen: "Tell him to quit coon-dogging and wanting more light. 81 mm."

Hem: "It's for three bursts, General. They heavy comes through the trees and goes into the ground. The grounds all soupy with the rains."

Gen: "It's liable to freeze and harden up."

Hem. "It's liable to snow and mush up worse Sir."

Gen: "Well get up there and come in and see me when you come back. I've got a bottle of bourbon for you."

Hem: "Thank you, Sir."

Gen: "If we are not on a first name basis find your own liquor."

Hemingstein: "Yes sir, General. I have. But yours is better."

Gen: "Get the hell up there. I'll be up when you get back. Tell me how much light 81 he really needs and how much he's trying to steal from the other rgts."

Hemingstein: "Good-bye Gen. I'll send in Dick."

Up at regt.

Buck: "You old son of a bitch. You reprobate. You worthless character. What did you do in Paris?"

"What do you think?"

"What did our Lost Leader say?"

"Nothing."

"When is it for?"

"We have to get some weather for the air Listen

Buck: "How much light 81 do you really need?"

"All I can get and all I can steal and more."

"What would you be satisfied with?"

"Tell him I'm never satisfied. What does he think we're going to do with it? Eat it or sell it?"

"He's got his troubles too."

"Tell me about it."

"I can't. I'm bigotted."

"I always thought I'd see you hanged. But never bigotted."


[39]


Letter to General Charles T. Lanham.

June 9 1945

My Dear General:

The D is capitalized as in Adulation. Just a mannerism I picked up under our lost Leader. The C.S.[1] Just received your pathetic communication of May 29 1945. Contents noted and reply herewith.

Only thing I can do about any of the upfrucks and injustices you mention is to attempt to obtain and read a copy of Hank (B.F.) Gorell's piece. Where the hell did he get battle fatigue? In Spa with me telling him over the wire what gave in Hurtgess Forum as I now refer to it with my battered memory. I'll be a sad son of a bitch. What type of neuropathology do you think that son of an opera tenor could have developed if he had to sweat out that 1800 bomber through that overcast rap with type of infantry you affected who couldn't explode pole charges waiting to make what I have nicknamed The Assault.

Maybe it is a good piece but honest to Christ Buck so many things are simply comic to me now that I may get to be like one of my granfathers (the other was a big G.A.R. man) who fought all through the civil war and never once spoke of it thereafter and never allowed it to be mentioned in his presence. On the other hand he was a man of convictions and never knowingly sat at table with a Democrat.

The biggest boy got in day before yesterday without telegrams or preliminary communication via a taxi-cab with the damndest holes in him you ever saw. The krauts shot him at 20 yards with that stepped up carbine job you sent me sample of they were lying around free up

[1] The initials C.S. refer to Chief of Staff Richard O. Barton. Hemingway's "The GI and the General" was a tribute to Barton, a man he respected and admired. After the war Barton proposed Hemingway for the Bronze Star decoration, for his valuable assistance in the search for and securing of information.

in Tom's disorganized country when we were there one cold day remember before we were souvenir conscious and he is 35 pounds under weight but ok and a lovely soldier. He put in for Pacific and has same but wish had more than 30 days to put him in shape. He had sixty days leave but has spent 30 of same in bed with anything that's warm and hollow and he wants me to tell him what to be after the war (he's been a soldier since he made 18) and has strange gray eyes and hollow cheeks and looks like something out of the Civil War. This sound corny but I honestly don't think he was been anymore spooked than I was (sensibly you know) and where I was always ashamed of my chickenshit kid bro. who is no more like a soldier than a yak is like a race-horse and I had to explain and apologize for same so you wouldn't think was from this stable; this kid is as good as the best of Swede (not the lazy Southern shit of Swede with the faint scum of the athlete on him) I mean the wonderful jolliness and the sound common sense and good info (most valuable of all) of Swede and the other thing that Kemper has. Excuse me General I become maudlin over my children. But this one is good children. He wanted to be flier and they turned him down for some visual defect (maybe my fault) said could be corrected by exercise of eye muscles etc. He applied for immediate induction when was 18 on acct speak French (brought up and educated in same) put in MPs sent to OCS commanded platoon negro mp battn. Soft like North Af. Everybody like. Much spoilage, invitations, Duff Coopers etc. Has lots of fun but felt like shit. Police a Casbah when 19. Hears I'm killed. Has attack of conscience. Applies for paratroop. 28 boogies in platoon apply for paratroop. Jumps in way ahead of seventh landing and organizes resistance kills krauts etc. and takes Montpellier. (this from other not him) Oh well. Take it away. Bumby is good guy and you would like him all same as though he were both of our son. (no syntaxer he) (Mean me)

We have been haveing lovely life and I have been working hard to write novel. Is difficult on acct. five years do opposite of writing novel. Buck, honestly, not romanticism, you don't know (of course you do) how opposite it is from the other thing. China gave it to me first and then the boat. I have no facility you see and I know much more than I can ever write, properly, and I have such an obligation to do it right that you must never think I am stalling when I am trying to get something right.

In 32 days Mary was only lonesome for the Grande Monde once and it was the 3rd day of the business. I can't be the houses of Parliament and Westminster Abbey and Churchill and all those citizens nor take place of same. A fait l'amour cinquante cinq fois dans le mois de Mai quelle Mois. Tres peu for wild man and such peoples but a good fine life for us guys and to wake in the night and find who you love there is all my war aim.

I wrote you about the fishing and all. Now come to serious part of letter. Can you and Pete[2] come down here and we go on boat?

Here is my gen. Children will be here. Are o.k. You will like. We have room. Bumby is here until 14 July. Then probably go to take some courses before pacificing.

If I have guts enough to put off writing it (writing) will be that much better.

You and Pete as welcome as anything in the world.

Mary's divorce should come through end of June. I can get in a month. Not starting proavoid scandal. Will make attack fast and not put self out on limb to be range of nobody. Mary very good about everything. Behaveing exemplary.

Anytime, any day you and Pete come down fine. We have whole small house where can live. We will make fine trips in boat. Swim, (if you want) drink no more than you want, eat good and have a lovely time. Catch as small or as big fish as you want. There is a fine trade wind now and this is a cockeyed wonderful place. Buck if money has anything to do with it I have a thousand bucks that would make me happier than anything in the world if you would use. You and Pete are my best friends and money is something sould take from you if you had and I didn't have.

Practically:

Need passport. Apply State Dept. No difficulty for Cuba. Mrs. Ruth Shipley Passport Division. $10. each.

Transport Air- or train to Miami. Pan-American Miami-Havana. Or William Lyons an American Miami. Say sent by Papa. No difficulty. They will off-load Jesus.

Get permission from W.D. to leave country. That's all there is to it.

Please you and Pete come down and we will have a wonderful time.

[40]

Letter from Hemingway to "Raymond." This appears to be a letter to Raymond Guest about Winston ("Wolfie") Guest. It is

---

[2] Pete is Mrs. Lanham.

a fine example of the sarcastic, bellicose tone Hemingway used to express his anger.

FINCA VIGIA SAN FRANCISCO DE PAULA CUBA

September 18, 1945

Dear Raymond:

Couldn't you grow up a little and lay off Win and stop needling him?

I don't know what your duties are nor give a damn but if you were Dickie Mountbatten himself you would have no right to criticize Win's actions in this show. I have probably spent as much time at wars as you spent at kindergarten, school and the university and have as many wounds as you have apples from or for teacher. So get this straight. If you want to criticize Win criticize me instead and to my face. Needling is out.

I know under what circumstances he wrote you and was unable to sign the letter. I know how he learned your brother was ill early this year and the sound steps he took about it. Your brother was in Canada fishing when he was in N.Y. last and your letter asking him to come up for the 18th arrived today the 18th. He could not come up to N.Y. now unless it were a life and death matter and then it would depend entirely on circumstances whether he could go.

We are not friends, you and I, merely acquaintances, so I ask you on that basis, and no other, to not make a further fool of yourself by criticizing Win's actions in this show and acting as though a war were fought under the Polo Association with annual published rankings. It is not. It is fought to win and only shits care about rank or ranking.

Yours always,
Ernest Hemingway

[41]

Hemingway writes to his youngest sister, Carol, around the time of his divorce from Martha, 1945.

Dear Beefy:

Thanks for the letter and the pictures. Glad you have the kids for company. Have three good kids too altho, unfortunately, Bumby 1st.

Lieut. Parachutist wounded and prisoner (no word yet), Mousie and Gigi in school. Will get them end of June.

It was almost this same time you were down here. Certainly was nice haveing a kid sister. I bungled it badly but only thing to have done would have been shoot John and that wasn't practical in N.Y.

It's just no good Beef. Now, when I think of it, and hadn't for long time, hate that guy just like I hate the Nazis. It's childish, I know, but it is as strong as something in a Faulkner book. Didn't get it out of any Faulkner book though.

Les (the Baron) our kid bro. has turned into a good guy if he is still alive. You know I could never stand to look at him on acct. he looked like our mother. But in London, when I was smashed up, I found if I kept my eyes shut could make friends with him. His marital etc. problems are completely unsolvable so the war is sort of a gift to him. He turned out to be a very brave guy and lots of people liked him very much. When Bumby had his bad luck Les volunteered at once for same unit. He wasn't qualified so he finally got out of his Signal Corps job and into the 4th Inf. Div that I'd been with since July. Had him with me for a while and everybody liked him. He was re-joining Dv. when I left.

Ura is in Hawaia (can't spell it) with her husband. Her daughter is a dancer on skates. In Ice Follies or something. She was always a cute little rat altho deadly spoiled.

Haven't heard from Sunny nor Marce for a long time. Only contact with families been through the Baron. He's really a good guy now; funny, unconceited, over-enthusiastic of course; but a good, civilized guy. War entirely to be deplored; but been very good for the Baron.

Had a lovely letter from our Mother in which she was sure God would look after me no matter how little I deserved it. And WHO was Mary Welsh? Finally got cured of Martha. One writer enough in a family (if not too much) and I need wife who will be in bed at night instead of in some different war. [something crossed out] theater. Need such wife very much, very badly and immediately and hope have same in Mary Welsh. She wants to quit writing and journalism and I am going to try very hard to be good husband to her whenever we can be married. Writing is terribly tough racket Beef and you need somebody to help you instead of compete with you. Marty was a lovely lookeing girl and I taught her to write very well in her own way (she had a lot of talent and writes a hell of a good magazine piece too) also taught her to shoot beautifully. But very selfish and imperious girl and as I say what I wanted was wife in bed at nights not somewhere haveing even higher adventure at so many thousand bucks the adventure. I loved her very much but finally got cured of it flying.

(The letter, unsigned, ends here)

Note: The John mentioned in this letter refers to John Gardner, Carol's husband. Ura, Sunny and Marce are his sisters Ursula, Madeleine and Marceline. Les is his brother Leicester.

[42]

Sidney Franklin, the only really successful American bullfighter, was past his prime at the time of this letter, already too old for that dramatic spectacle Hemingway called "Death in the Afternoon."

> Sidney Franklin,
> Matador de Toros,
> 1538-East 29th St.,
> Brooklyn, 29, N.Y.

June 5, 1950.

Hello Ernest:-

Please accept my congratulations and best wishes for Pat on his forthcoming marriage. May they live happily ever after.

It's quite a jump from that to more prosaic matters. But as you know, I spoke with Charles Scribner Sr. prior to his European trip about the possibility of you selling the title 'Death in the Afternoon' to a movie outfit here that wanted to make a bullfighting epic abroad. Rice, your agent here, informed me when you came through that you weren't interested. So that was that.

Since then I saw Scribner and showed him one hundred twenty five pages I did on my own autobiography. He liked it but others in his outfit didn't think the subject timely enough to warrant a contract. And since another publisher had been on my neck, I told Scribner about it and he said it was okay for me to go ahead with them. He even offered to help me in any way he could to get a good deal.

Now, I know you're busy. And I know you've had more than your share of rough times with your health and have plenty of work. And with one thing and another, after all this time I truly don't know what the score is between us. But recalling the many times you said you'd help me if I ever got around to doing my autobiography, could I impose on you sometime between now and the middle of October to edit the works for me or whatever you believe best in order to turn out something decent?

I've got one hundred twenty five pages done in straight narrative form. I just put down the facts as I recall them with hardly any trimmings. The complete works should run to between four and five hundred typewritten pages. I made an outline of incidents by chapters to follow in proper sequence. There are thirty now but it probably will boil down to twenty five chapters of twenty typewritten pages each. I hope to have the whole thing done by early October so it can be published in the spring.

This past week, with George Bye as my agent, we agreed with the publishers on the general terms of the deal. Sometime this week we'll sign up on the basis of what they've seen. They feel it's fair enough not to require a ghost writer or collaborator. But they did say they'd have to do some heavy editing. As I told you many times, I never wanted to tackle it before because I always had hoped you might do it. But we're not getting any younger and I may as well get what I can out of it before it's not worth anything at all. And maybe this can be the means of straightening out everything between us. And though it may surprise you, this winter I hope to be in action in Venezuela and Peru. I've got to do that to revive interest for the book and make it timely again, aside from the dough for the corridas.

The way things stand right now, after signing up this week, I'll take off by car for California and Mexico and be back here in about a month. Then I'll fly to South America to iron out contract details and return in late July. After that I'll make a quick trip to Spain for uniforms and stuff and be back by October. I set myself a schedule to turn out at least one twenty page chapter per week and believe I can finish the whole thing by late September.

If it's okay with you, I could stop in at Havana to see you on the way back from Mexico early next month. Or I could do it on my way to South America or when I return from there. Any way you say is okay with me. All I hope is that you consent to help me with it.

Hope your health is improved to where you can enjoy life as you did in the old days. Meanwhile, best regards to everyone and please let me know what's what. And above all, take care of yourself.

As ever,
Sidney Franklin

[43]

Letter from Ingrid Bergman.

Rome, Dec. 12, 1950

Dearest Papa and Mary;

.So long ago and so far away . . . But I think of you often and I read about you and am hoping that soon you are coming back to Italy or Paris, as we are going to be there in the beginning of the new year.

Dear Papa, I have several times read nice things you have said about me and I hug your big heart and thank you with mine. (quite a phrase!)

Christmas is coming and for once I am writing in time to send Holiday wishes. Usually they arrive long after. So - Merry Christmas and may the new year arrange itself so that we will find one another in the same spot.

With all good wishes to you two from us,

Ingrid

[44]

Letter from Ingrid Bergman.

Rome, Jan. 28 1952

Dearest Papa and Mary;

Yesterday arrived an envelope from the postoffice with excuses for the delay delivering this letter, but the plane it was on had burned! And inside I found your Christmas card, all burned black I could barely make out your name. I do think the postoffice is very efficient in Italy!

I was so happy to hear from you. Are you living quietly with your cats for a while. When are you coming back to Italy? Before Robertino was born you wrote me wishing I would have twins that you could be the proud Godfather and carry into St Peter's. You didn't come, probably because I didn't have twins. I am trying again now in June. Maybe if I have twins you'll come?!

Roberto joins me in all kinds of good wishes and we hope all is well with you, dear friends!

Fondly,
Ingrid

[45]

Letter from Malcolm Cowley.

Sherman, Conn.,
August 3, 1952.

Dear Ernest:

*The Old Man and the Sea* is pretty marvelous—the old man is marvelous and the sea is too and so is the fish. I'm proud of them all and of you and glad that I'm reviewing the book for the Herald Tribune. As yet I don't know what I'm going to say, because I'm getting a lot of space to write about such a short book, but it will be a pleasant task to fill the space. Maybe among other things I can talk about your prose, which has that quality here as elsewhere of being absolutely fresh, with the words standing out separately on the page, as if nobody before had ever used the simple words of the English language. And to point up what you do in the story I can talk about the present rage for symbols and myths, with the kids saying, go to, I will use symbols, go to, I will create a myth—and all of them forgetting that if a character doesn't live it can't be a symbol and if a book doesn't tell a story it can't be a myth. So you give us a character and a story and the reader is privileged to read into them whatever symbolic or mythical qualities they suggest to him, but meanwhile the character and the story have their own life. There is a curious contrast with *Moby Dick*, where the whale comes to stand for the impersonal power and malignity of nature. Your fish and your fisherman are equally parts of nature—brothers, as the old man says; each of them plays his assigned role as if in a ritual drama. The old man loves and honors the fish and one suspects that the fish loves and honors the old man, and in the end fish and man have collaborated (like bull and matador) to make life on this planet seem more dramatic than it was before their battle started.

Oh, I'll fill the space all right, and try not to be unworthy of the book. I'm reviewing from page proofs and there's one error in them that I hope you caught before the book went to press: the albacore on pp. 43-44 turns into a bonito on p. 64 when the old man eats him. What are you going to do with the other three stories that were in the same group? Bring them out together next year?—or separately?—or wait to use them in some other fashion?

You must have read in the papers that July was the hottest month in New York since the weather bureau started keeping records in 1871. It was tough on me because I'm not a hot-weather animal—I begin to come alive after the first frost. This time I missed the four hottest days by a trip to Martha's Vineyard, which I hadn't seen before. I thought it was wonderful—a hundred square miles of land that actually has topsoil and used to be a prosperous farming area, with trout brooks and bass ponds and too many deer, surrounded with beaches, inlets and lagoons. The little harbors are crowded with draggers and swordfish boats—the latter have a double lookout at the masthead and a long bowsprit ending in a "pulpit" where the harpooner stands to wait for the fish. I'd love to live on the Vineyard for three or four months of each year and go out for swordfish and live on lobster and chowder.

At home this has been the rabbit year. They moved in on us like tribesman from the desert, set up their tents, started raising families, became tame, then impertinent, so that the young ones used to come up and smell my shoes. Then the garden began to come up and they moved into it; also into Muriel's flower garden, where they devoured phlox, platy-codon, canterbury bells, even chrysanthemums, looking first at the price tags so as to be sure they were getting their money's worth. For a long time I couldn't bear to shoot them, but then it got to be a question whether we or the rabbits would survive. One morning I saw two in the garden, lost my temper, went out with a double-barreled shotgun and killed both of them sitting. But there were four rabbits, not two, and the others simply looked at me in amazement, so I went back into the house, loaded the gun again, came out and found them still there, and it was a rabbit massacre. Seems that the foxes have been dying of mange, so that there's no check on the rabbit population. Coons are multiplying too and raiding the cornfields. Strange that this country is raising a new sort of people who aren't used to guns and who, if they catch a coon in a trap, just bury it instead of eating it. O pioneers, who can't eat food unless it comes in packages.

Rob is liking it in the Grand Tetons. Two weeks ago he was shoveling snow so the tourists could follow the high trails. Now he and three other kids have gone for a three weeks' trip far back in the mountains (still at $1.35 per hour) rebuilding pack trails. They carry their food with them. Wonder if I couldn't hire out as cook of the expedition. Hope you're bearing up under the Cuban heat and are able to sleep. Why don't you get in the boat and start north at times like these? I hear there's wonderful fishing off Nova Scotia. Oh, since you inquired about my adventures in nonalcoholism--I stood it for two months, then decided that white wine wouldn't hurt me too much. It wasn't the strain of doing without liquor, it was the strain of being bored to death at parties that made me fall off the wagon. But I still haven't gone back to hard liquor, because the doctor threw a scare into me, and he wasn't a bluenosed doctor either, he was a specialist with such a red nose that I believed everything he said.

As ever,
Malcolm

[46]

Letter from Hemingway to Bernard Kalb, newspaper and TV correspondent.

August 17, 1952

Dear Mr. Kalb:

Your letter came this morning and today is Sunday. Your deadline is Wednesday so this may be worthless to you.

Let's skip the clippings. There will be new ones now. Anyway, for better or for worse you wouldn't want a man to believe his own clippings would you? He would certainly get confused over a period of thirty four years.

Four hundred words are a lot of words on a Sunday morning unless you are delivering the sermon. Maybe we better put this in question and answer form.

Question: How is the writing going?

Answer: About the same as always. Some days better than others. I've worked two and a half years steady now and could use a vacation.

Question: How is the big book?

Answer: Very long. I am in no hurry about it.

Question: When may we expect it?

Answer: As and when it seems best to publish it.

Question: Do you mean your answers to be curt?

Answer: No. Truly. I do not like to talk about any work when I am writing it. Some people do. But, unfortunately, I do not.

Question: How is the fishing?

Answer: It was very good through spring and early summer. It was worthless during the time of the sun spots and is picking up again now with a very heavy current in the Gulf Stream. We've caught twenty five marlin this season and should get quite a few more. The best year I ever had we caught fifty four. The fish that are running now are very big. I work in the early morning and fish when I've finished work.

Those are the questions you asked Mr. Kalb and we are pretty short on the four hundred words. Would it be any use to know that it has been very pleasant and cool here at the farm all summer (we had our heat-wave last year). The other night it was so cool coming in from the Gulf Stream that I had to put on a flannel shirt and last night I put on a sweater steering home. Mary, my wife, is very well. She loves the ocean and has never been sea-sick and she fishes beautifully. She sleeps in the morning while I wake and work early and she handles all the problems, when she wakes, that I neglect because my head is in the writing. She reads what I write most days and I can tell if it moves her if it gives her gooseflesh. She can't simulate gooseflesh. Now I had better knock-off writing this and write something else.

Good Luck.
Yours always,
Ernest Hemingway

[47]

Letter from Michael Lerner.

Michael Lerner
730 Fifth Avenue
New York 19, N.Y.

August 10, 1952.

Dear Ernesto:

I received a galley proof from LIFE Magazine of "THE OLD MAN AND THE SEA." I have just finished reading it, and am so enthusiastic and happy. It is one of the best stories I have ever read, and I am sure it ranks with the tops that you have ever done. There isn't any doubt in my mind that the book will receive great recognition. The character of the old man can well set an example for this generation—or any other generation to come.

I returned from Bimini about ten days ago and am just about caught up with a lot of back work. I am leaving this afternoon for Saratoga Springs and will return to New York September 19th. Ernesto, if you are in New York at that time and don't call me up, I'll really be deeply disappointed. I am very anxious to have you take luncheon with me, and if Mary is with you, we can make a foursome with Helen. Otherwise, you and I can have a bite of lunch at my place at 730 Fifth Avenue, and have a chance for a good oldfashioned talk.

I wrote you thanking you for your fine letter to Arthur Gray and

I do want to express again, for Helen and myself, our appreciation for your friendship in relieving me of the anxiety that some day anything might interfere with the view we have come to love so much. Some day I hope you can see the layout in Bimini. I don't know whether you get the magazine "National Geographic", but in the event you do not, I am sending you the issue of last February which contains an article that will give you some idea of the work of the laboratory.

    With love from Helen to Mary and you, and hoping you are both in the best of health and trying to relax, with every good wish,

Your Pal,<br>Mike

My love to Mary

[48]

Marlene Dietrich cable to Hemingway.

Aug. 28, 1952
New York, N.Y.

Ernest Hemingway
Finca Vigia
San Francisco de Paula

HAVE BEEN ASKED BY TIME TO SPEAK ON AIR PROGRAM CALLED TIME CAPSULE ABOUT BOOK AND YOU RECORDING TO BE BURIED AND DUG OUT AFTER HUNDRED YEARS BOMBS PERMITTING STOP KNOWING MY PLACE FELT THIS OUT OF MY TERRITORY TO GIVE OPINION ON YOUR WRITING STOP THINK QUOTES OF ALL SORTS OF PEOPLE IN CURRENT LIFE IN LOCAL NEWSPAPERS RATHER SILLY AND THAT GAVE ME COURAGE STOP PLEASE TELL ME IF YOU WANT THIS OR WOULD IT BE CHEAP STOP MAYBE YOU TELL ME WHAT TO SAY SHOULD YOU WANT IT STOP THANKS FOR LETTER MY ONLY BLOOD SUPPLY IN MY ANEMIC EXISTENCE STOP WOULD LOVE TO COME BUT MARIA WORKING I HAVE TO TAKE CARE OF CHILDREN STOP MAYBE LATER KISS MARY AND KISS HEMINGSTEIN AND THE OLD MAN AND THE FISH

KRAUT

[49]

Letter from William Randolph Hearst, Jr.

> W. R. Hearst, Jr.
> 959 Eighth Avenue
> New York 19, N.Y.

September 10, 1952

Mr. Ernest Hemingway
c/o Charles Scribner's Sons
597 Fifth Avenue
New York, N.Y.

Dear Ernest:
Thanks a lot for sending me a copy of your book. I had already read it in Life on the West Coast.

It's really great as anyone who ever had a fishing rod in his hands will unquestionably agree.

I am sure that even those who have been foolish enough never to expose themselves to that experience will be moved by the story and the writing.

Let me know if you expect to be in the neighborhood of our concrete jungle, and we'll plan to have a drink and get that additional bit of writing done on the front end of the tome.

Best to Mary.

> Sincerely,
> Bill
> W. R. Hearst, Jr.

[50]

This note, written by Hemingway to Mary during a time of domestic conflict, is particularly sad in view of the writer's great expectations for an ideal marriage, passionately expressed in the "Pickle" letters of 1944:

June 1, 1953

Honey:
I wrote these notes to clarify something in my head. Please return them.

Your exact words this morning were "You want to hog everything. You get angry if anybody even writes anything about the same country you are in. Look at that man who wrote that book about Spain."

Q: Who?

A: That Frenchman.

Malraux explained. Q. Who else?

Answer: Look at the way you got angry about Mr. Dos Passos just because he wrote about Michigan.

Mr. Dos Passos and Native Country explained. Mary had not read the book.

At another time Mary: You never told me you had any offer from Look. You did no such thing. You did not show me any letter from Rice with any offer from Look.

Explanation offered that we had talked about it when the Leland Haywards were down here. And that Mary was tired of hearing me discuss it.

Mary: You didn't tell me anything about Lowe's offer. You just whispered something to me.

Explanation that offer was fully explained to her after the Lowes had left. They left almost immediately after Mary arrived. They had called up and asked when they could come out. We had talked the whole matter over and after I had made our objections. Lowe had made his offer which Mary and I talked over at length that afternoon and evening. They came out the next day and we talked it over together discussing the character of the photographer etc. Lowe sent in his written agreement which Mary read and said was exactly the terms he had proposed except for the photographer to be three weeks rather than two.

Things getting sort of hopeless. Yesterday at lunch was shouted at, scolded and tongue lashed about clothes. Shut up and left the table. Came back and the tirade continued shouted so that servants and deaf Taylor could hear. Made no answer and did not get involved in it and did not bring it up.

The night after fishing the whole First day in the tournament was awakened at one thirty a.m. by scolding and bawling out. No way to stop it. Did not answer except to ask if would please stop as had to be up early to be out the next day. Scolding and tongue lashing continued and left and sat in the chair in the living room until five a.m. when came in with Mary asleep and slept until six when had to get up to organize sandwiches, breakfast, etc.

This scolding and tongue lashing was a continuation of a very violent one given me in the car in front of Taylor and Roland. This scolding tirade was exceptionally violent. A scolding for delaying our getting home early by stopping and talking too long with people at Floridita was probably justified and deserved. The violence of this one in the car and the vituperation in front of other people, however, was exceedingly embarrassing. The picking it up to say it all over again at one thirty a.m. I do not think was justified nor sound.

Got all preparations made and was leaving the house before Mary woke. Waved cheerful good-bye never mentioned the scolding nor the bawling out. Mary very good tempered and pleasant when we came in from the Tournament last Sunday night.

Enough tension during the week with that bloody Roland around and a pile-up of people at Wednesday lunch to make anybody bad tempered. But got Roland set to leave on Friday, which he did, and then tackled all problems that could be handled by phone. Then went to see about postponement of Saturday's tournament (for which everything had to be ready until the moment of postponement) and to the Country Club-Jaimanitas residence of the Holman's.

Don't believe I was bawled out or scolded at all on Friday. Next was the violent outburst at the table Saturday noon May 30th. Took no notice of it and obtained a quiet afternoon and pleasant evening with storm raging outside.

No bawling out in the night. Awake at 5 a.m. checking house. Storm of a tropical disturbance moving North-west into the Gulf of Mexico.

Scolding and bawling out came with the morning mail when I was asked to read a letter from Carl Brandt and made the mistake of saying Brandt was mistaken when he said that neither he nor Mrs. Hemingway knew of any negotiations with Look. These had been initiated by Look four or five months before and Mary and I had many times discussed them their disadvantages etc. what was true and correct was that we had no committments with books when Mary sent Brandt the samples from the diaries. But they had been making offers for several months.

The trouble is that I see no way of avoiding those terrible angry out-bursts. They used to be almost always in private and there were long intervals between. Sometimes months. Very often I deserve to have it done without rages or false accusations. They are no help.

I have tried being as good as I know how, to give no cause for jealousy with other women, and made an earnest effort, since I was thoroughly scolded for it, to get to the house at the exact hour I say will be back for lunch. Not to telephone saying I will be late. But to stop anything that would make me late and get there.

Try to be thoughtful about Mary in every way I know how: especially in seeing she gets her morning sleep. But I cannot hear the telephone unless I am close to it and she *can* hear it. So if it rings early I am defeated on that.

Had always heard women like presents and to be made love to lovingly. But on the day after Mary had a homecoming present and we had made love lovingly and understandingly and, certainly, at some length I had the worst public bawling out I have ever received in my life followed by being waked up at one thirty a.m. to hear it all over again. That night when I was listening to it I thought of saying, "I am a little deaf. Do I understand that you are thanking me for the little yellow convertible?"

The temptation to say this was strong enough so I got out of bed immediately to avoid starting answering. The only thing I have learned is that it is better not to answer at all. Women have no memory of what they have said to you. But if you finally say something bad in answer THAT is what was said during the evening, or how it was: the morning; the noon; or the night.

Right now the question is whether I should accept Mary as a scold and give up another illusion. Or whether I should ride along and learn not to give a damn. I know I can do that but it will mean losing something I value more than anything: our love and companionship.

The strange thing is that Mary will come to me and say what can I tell her to do that will make her a better partner and a better wife. But if I should ask her now to seriously think about this problem, or habit it is now, of scolding she would probably answer, "What? Me a scold? I have the kindest tongue and the best disposition in the world and who are you to say a horrible untrue thing like that." So I might as well let it go.

But maybe we could both have some luck and she would admit she has been scolding very much lately and very violently.

[51]

Letter to his son, Gregory Hemingway.

August 7, 1954

Dear Gig:

It certainly did not sound like a letter from a crazy and I am certainly proud of you.

The procedure now is to instruct them that all manuscripts be sent to Lee Samuels at 155 John Street, N.Y. Give them a receipt and ask

Mouse to do the same. Lee Samuels will receipt for them to Mathew G. Harold.

I have been turning over all my first editions, late manuscripts and original stuff that could be of value to Lee and he has willed it to the New York Public Library where it will be available to students.

He will hold these manuscripts for me in an air-conditioned safe and when any of us, you, Mouse, Bum or me are in trouble I can have one sold, intelligently, to someone who will agree to give it to a University library on his death. Selling them intelligently can bring in plenty of money. Dumping them for sale would mean they would bring nothing at all of their real values.

Maybe it is better to skip all talk about that Committee that took over Uncle Gus when he had lost his memory and his judgement. I gave Uncle Gus the manuscript of For Whom The Bell Tolls after mother and I were divorced. He said he would love to have it because it was a great pleasure to him to possess my manuscripts but that he was always holding it in trust for me and I could have it any day I asked for it to give it to anyone I wished and to dispose of it as I wished. He wrote me this and wrote me the same thing about the other manuscripts.

It looks as though the committee etc. wanted to get away with them for the estate which they administer. But they were spooked. I will tell you when I see you why they were spooked. I have checked all this gen very slowly and carefully and it is all at your disposal in case they ever try to put anything over on you. I had better skip it now and give it to you with the witnesses and if necessary affidavits if you ever need it. Some of it is really spooky. Mayito Menocal's evidence of a member of the Committee who arrived in Havana and represented himself as Uncle Gus and got Mayito to take him out to the house with women companions and a man to open my safe is the most shocking. I only learned about this when Mayito and I learned that Uncle Gus was dead while we were on Safari in Africa. It was so shocking that I did not want to talk about it with Pat or think about it. It made you sick. But I took it slow and by evidence.

The Key West business was even rougher. But not so awful because nobody represented himself as Uncle Gus. You know Mayito is a very serious character. He knew what good friends Uncle Gus and I were so he did everything he could for the man who said he was Uncle Gus and was acting in my behalf.

Let's skip that. All the news from Mouse is good. I wrote you we got him a good cook. Someone who can run his joint efficiently (I hope) He was painting fine. I am buying a painting of his a month and when he has enough for an exposition will see he gets it in N.Y. All the paintings will be his to sell and he can keep what they bring. What he does not sell I would like to have for myself. I haven't seen the paintings yet, nor paid for them, but I will and he says he is going good. Anything he has that gets valuable he can sell and just pay me back the original cost. Think this is a sound fair way of staking a guy and giving him a professional interest in his work. I wanted to teach him about the big animals but we did not have enough time. Now he has old Mumu a fine gunbearer and ivory poacher of the old days and since Mouse speaks Swahili well Mumu can teach him much better than I could.

If you don't mind and it does not bore you will write a fairly long letter and the hell with work. I've digested what you told me about you not feeling ok when you were writing those bad letters. I know, beside accepting what you told me, that it is true on acct. of the penmanship. Now everything is straight. Not chickenshit like forgiveness. Rubbed out. Any time you want to show up: show up I am working hard now and not seeing anybody.

Shatz, Bum is the member of our family that I am worried about. I think he is making a beautiful try there in civil life but it is straight down Domesday road complete with twin cypresses. Except for the fishing. I sent him the cash for his Warner-Hudnut trust and have not cashed it and am still holding it in his name because I do not know when he will be broke next and I can have it still producing for him and keep it as a surprise. I sent him an extra $4,000 but I never hear anything from him unless he needs money. He has had the burnt stick on inheriting monies and he has been a good husband and a very good soldier and an excellent fisherman. But it is a problem to me to stake him with taxes as they are and Mary's father now in a nursing home etc.

This is not a cry towell letter. It is just to give you the gen. In the aircraft nonsense I got smashed really bad. I never had a broken back before, certified anyway, and it can be uncomfortable and shitting standing up, while not a difficult feat, can get to be a bore. I don't know whether I wrote you about it. I went 22 days when I couldn't unlock the sphincter. Then shat a species of white hard nobby rocks about ball size. Then got up to 62 a day. It was really comic. One time when I missed from my berth to the can Miss Mary said, "Don't you know that no gentleman ever shits on the floor?"

"Well, you have just seen one who has," I said wiping up busily.

Now have my bed-room air-conditioned for work. Have done one short story and am six days along on a second. Miss Mary is fine and healthy and very happy. She loved Africa. This is between us and on our old technical basis. You know you could never know where she was going to shoot. I think mayby the 6.5 Manlicher she shot was too long for her and with variations in clothing it could go off as she brought it up. She would make wonderful shots at 350 yards. Kill things dead through the neck at 375 (one beauty lesser kudu) and miss all of a whole lion as big as the biggest lion rug at twenty yeards. Everybody loved her and everybody was with her all the way then she would miss Our Lord sitting in William Faulkner's lap posing as a corporal at 40 yards with the light behind her. But since we were always training Miss Mary she always had to shoot everything for meat so she had a lot of wonderful shooting. What was against her was her height. A lion looking like a lion rug to me who was tracking and flanking in brush and some grass would just be a big lion head to her when it came up Will get her a gun that really fits. I have signed to go there in a year to make a documentary. Lots of chances to have fun and work and back up the photographers. Maybe we could work it out so you and Mouse and me could shoot together.

Gig must send this now. Think it has all the news. Of course it hasn't. There is the Key West stuff which I will write you about. It is a whole separate letter and please be patient if I take my time writing it. Mary is going over to put the Pool House in shape to rent for winter. That is where the dough is. The other people who had the big house move out the 21st of this month but will have it rented immediately. I know it seems that nothing comes in but you know I paid all expenses and some of that was siphoned back to me until your share and Mouses were paid. I enclose the check that Rice sent me endorsed to you to buy something for your wife so that you will know I am not trying to make monies for myself.

The Key West situation is very complicated. From the minute we wanted to, and agreed to, sell it the locals started to knock down the price in order to get it for nothing. they have it rigged so it would not bring $50,000 today. But I know how they work and counter-act all their moves and it is not really an anchor around the neck. I am manoevering to the best of my ability for it to be a valuable property for you, Mouse and me. Uncle Gus bought it for $12,500. I put over $60,000 into it and it would be criminal to let it go for less than it is worth. You are not making money on it but the check I send you is the interest on quite a lot of money. If I can rent it this winter it will make everybody money not much; but cash money.

Gig I am having a sort of rough time getting back to working good. It is necessary to be ruthless about not seeing people that waste my time and at the same time get the exercise I must have to build back basic strength and to use the head well and not tire too much. It took a very bad beating. Knowing you and Mouse will get those Mss. into Lee Samuels hands is like hearing your reserves have come up in the middle of a battle. It means I do not have to worry about having to do hack work and forcing my head faster than it can go and I do not have to worry about being able to help Bum.

First he wrote me he was getting out of the army to open a small sporting goods store in a good fishing country, live modestly etc. The next thing I hear from him the sporting goods business is out and he is working for a security house (it sounds as though on a drawing account but maybe it is salary and a percentage of sales). He needs cash to buy a house (which is ok) but he also needs cash to entertain and live up to his job. Where this cash is to come from I couldn't figure.

This year I have a good chance to win the Nobel prize unless they give it to some great Iceland poet, or, say Synghman Rhee. If I do I will cut Bum in on a piece of that. But transfusions won't keep him going forever if what he is doing is not basically sound. On the other hand you can't ask a loving husband and father to make his living forever by jumping out of an aircraft even if they provide him with free parachutes.

I would be glad to make my own living shooting the incoming rhino or stoning the irascible elephant. But I couldn't guaranty to make my living on the incoming cotsie because he comes faster than the correo and sooner or later you will miss one. The trick, of course, is not let him get incomeing.

Some time I'll tell you some funny stories about the last trip. It was long enough so we learned a lot. I think Mouse will be a good hunter. He's not spooked at all. And he always was a good shot. He is not a great shot like you. But he is a very good shot and the natives love him.

Sometime I'll tell you about the comic trip we made down the Great Ruaha and about how we went to the Chulu Hills where no white woman has ever been including Miss Mary. There were some funny things about crashes too that you would have liked. Also Miss Mary's lion after thirty seven days of intensive and horror striking lion hunting. If anybody ever deserved a really great lion or if a great lion ever really deserved anybody it was Miss Mary and this beast. Gig, after Miss Mary's lion hunting there is nothing. She and her gun-bearer old Charo are so short that no animals have any fear of them. Wild dogs want to eat them up. A wart-hog will trot cheerfully toward them thinking they look like attractive companions. Zebra's merely bare their teeth as they approach.

Better stop this and get it off.

Best love to you and your family.

Papa

Want to study that famous document a little more and then will ship it back. The part where the characters decide what Uncle Gus would really want to do in direct violation of what he has written he wished to do are in the great tradition. Would you let me know when you and Mouse have written to have to Mss. delivered to Lee Samuels? Then I can start to set up the sale of one of them for around before Christmas time and then we can all split it. If I can do it well enough could make you dough enough to fly out and see Mouse for the Holiday's. Or for him and Henny to fly here. We could get Bum and company down too and all have Christmas together. And charge it to The Committee, gentlemen, who tried to steal Mr. Papa's best and closest property and did not know that he had honest sons.

It might be better and more fun for you to go and see Mouse. But you can gen that all out.

Love,
Papa

[52]

Letter from Adriana Ivancich. Year omitted.

October 6—Age of gold

Crazy, good, sweet old lion . . . did you fall on your head . . .? *I did*, when I saw the "millions". . ."My god, I am seeing double", I said to myself, "I am seeing triple . . ." And, instead, it was true. Papa, I was never capable to thank you for all you did for me, and I am afraid I will not be able to begin now . . . And, anyhow, how can you thank properly somebody that sends you millions as if they were peanuts? Papa, dear Papa, you made me became so rich, that I can't even realize how rich I am.

The first five hundred dollars I had to return to you because, as I told you, no bank would accept it - not because they did not believe you had a current account in the N.Y. bank, but because it was not legal for you to send it to me. "We trust Mr. Hemingstein, but the law is the law," they said. But this time I was fed up. Because I thought it rediculous for this money to cross the ocean and then have to cross it again in a matter of days. And so, taking my courage into my hands, I decided to face Mr. Masprone, telling him (listen well) that you had asked me to do some shopping for you and pay some bills and that you had sent me the money to do so. Mr. Masprone was very happy at the idea of doing you a favor and said that he would "take advantage of the occasion to write you a letter." And tomorrow morning he will let me have the money. Until I have that money in my hands I won't realize how rich I am. I think it very strange that such a small bill should have the power to give reality to so many things and so many desires. . . .

Do you know which is the first wish I'll be able realize, thanks to you? In a way it makes me tremendously happy and in another way it makes me sad. Now I tell you and please understand why: Last year Marina Cicogna (daughter of Anna Maria Cicogna, nee Volpi, grand-daughter of Guisepe Volpi, aunt (or almost) of Giovanni, son of the Contessa Lilli, mother of Anne Marie la Cloche, etc. (understand?)) had invited me to go to Tripoli, AFRICA. I thanked her but said I couldn't go, because Tripoli is not Cortina or Paris, because in Paris, if one is a guest of Monique, one can live economically, but staying with Cicogna, Volpi, in Africa one needs a lot of dough if one wants to hire a camel as one would a taxi, or take some side trips, so it's more complicated. So I said "thanks" and didn't go.

This year, I don't know why, since I am no great friend of hers, Marina invited me again. I told her thanks and that I would think about it. One should always leave the door open to luck, don't you think? And luck arrived a week or ten days later, in the form of your check. Now I have accepted the invitation, and I am happy, so happy, and I will see a bit of Africa and I will rent a camel all for myself, and will take a lot of pictures, and will be happy. I will be happy but a little sad, because I will not be seeing Africa with you, through you, as I would have wanted, YOUR Africa, with the lions, good or bad, and your blacks and all the unexplored regions where "the white man has not yet set foot." But I am happy and I will write long letters to you and will tell you all I have seen, if it will not bore you. Papa, think of it! I am going to Africa! How can I ever thank you! Papa, I think I am very happy . . . You know what I will buy for myself? Inasmuch as I am always cold in winter, I will get a cashmere sweater which is soft, warm, and fine and . . . very expensive! (While on the subject of clothes, you remember the cloth you gave me in Nervi? I had it made into a dress, copied from "a classy model", that has had truly, great success. All the women ask me who made it for me (a dressmaker made if for me for 5,000 liras) and all the men tell me "how very elegant" I look. I wouldn't tell you this if it hadn't happened many times because if they tell you only once it could be just a compliment, but when people tell you many times then it could be true. And to think that that happened during the festival when Venice was full of women wearing important clothes and jewels! I, of course, was most proud and would have liked to tell everyone the "real story of the dress made from the cloth given to me in Nervi by a GOOD LION before leaving on a sunny day." One night, at the Lido, they took my picture wearing your dress, with Monique. I wanted to send it to you, but I'm sorry to say I lost it. But one day I'll show you the real thing, the dress with, I hope, me inside it.

Papa, I love you very much—aside from the millions—because everything I have seen with you I remember as if it had happened yesterday. I remember our first hunt together, our meeting at Geitti's, the first time you had lunch with me, dressed all in blue, and you brought a box of caviar—and then you boxed with Gherardo—and Cortina, Villa Aprile, and Venice, again to Cuba, and Venice and Nervi . . . There is much I have forgotten about my life, so many years have passed that I remember only fleetingly, having forgotten dates, situations, those many evenings in night-clubs . . . But, believe me, everything I have done with you, trips, discussions, the book covers, problems—I remember and keep in my heart. I love you a lot, Papa, in my way and in spite of everything and because, as I have told Percotto, you have such charm . . .

Tell me . . . what did I say that made you feel "so much better and very happy, to send the money W.T."? I remember only that I wrote and wrote all one night and then sealed the letter without reading it over in the morning, because I thought that "if I wrote it, it meant that was what I felt, and that was enough." I remember that the letter was long and that I had many ideas in my head and did not know how to express them and was very confused. I remember also that when I sealed the letter I said to myself: "Papa will understand." But what you were to understand, I don't remember. I remember only that I wrote with all my heart, and I hope I wasn't too fresh. Papa, I am happy that you are working and very happy that you are feeling a little better. Please go on. My idea is very selfish, because I intend, gossip permitting, to go on seeing you for many years, even when I am old and ugly. I will find you, show you my best photograph and say "Remember?" and you will have to talk to me. No joke,

Have I told you I will go to Paris? If I go, it will be perhaps this winter, when all the Soapinelli family will be in Sicily, unfortunately, and Jackie will go to Paris to study. Maybe Mamma will go get him (because Jackie doesn't want to be away from the family a long time) Mamma cannot stay away from me a long time either. It's all very simple and complicated at the same time.

Poor Ava, terribly bad publicity without deserving it. It's a sad thing. It makes you hate humanity, an uncomfortable thing, as one has to live in the midst of humanity.

Too bad about the documentary about Africa: it was a good idea and no one else could have done it better. But why did they give such a short time? If you are working, and working well, I understand why you didn't accept.

I never believed for a second that you had become an actor in a movie. Though being an actor, I suppose, is not a dishonorable career. It amuses me to see now and then things in the newspapers about you which I "feel and believe" are not true. I trust you felt the same about me when you read that "Anna Maria and Adriana had killed Vilma Montessi." (Aside from the fact that his would have been worse!)

Papa, believe me, I too "hate to leave you even in a letter" but the letter is getting too long and, after having read a letter in English, I write very badly Italian, and it can't be very funny to read.

Obeying your orders, I don't thank you but I kiss you . . . Is it all right?

Your faithful daugther called, as always,

AI

Note: The Vilma Montessi mentioned here was a prostitute of a certain category who was found murdered on a beach in Venice early in the fifties. The crime developed into a political scandal that kept the Italian press busy a long time. It involved prominent Fascists, high government functionaries, aristocrats, even including Mussolini's son. One of those indicted was Adriana Bisaccia, arrested for giving false testimony.

The money mentioned in this letter could perhaps have been in payment for the book jacket Adriana designed for *The Old Man and the Sea*.

[53]

Letter from Adriana Ivancich, part in English and part in Italian.

October 20, 1954

(In English)

This night I had a dream:

You just arrived, by plain, from Cuba to pay me a visit for a couple of days. Everything was very nice and . . . legal, because Mary was there too, and we were all having lunch at Calle sin Remedio. But you were not eating much, as usual, and were standing near the window, watching the canal.

So I came near you and said: "I really am very happy to see you, Papa."

"So am I, daughter . . ."

"I am very happy with my millions, Papa. You gave me so much money that I nearly don't know what to do with it.

"This is not at all kind of you!" you said.

"But . . . but . . . but it was a joke, Papa! Of course that I . . ." but it was no use to go on speaking, because you hade allready gone away, with a gondola, very angry.

"So I begain to run and run but, as always happens in the dreams, my feat where very heavy and I couldn't run fast and your gondola was allways more far away and I was allways more sad and begain to cry. So I stopped, and I decided to take a "vaporetto," but, of course, I had not I cent in my pocket, as I just was having lunch in my home and you don't usually have money with you when you have lunch at home.

"And your gondola was far far away and the vaporetto went away to . . . and then I don't know what happend next, because I woke up.

"Funny dream, eh? I hope it will never happen in reality.

\* \* \*

(In Italian) The money arrived. Thank you. It is marvelous to go around with full pockets. You told me to change my Rolley for a new model: I regret I have not done so, as I am so terribly fond of it that I'd be very sorry to change it even for a much more beautiful one. I think I am so fond of it because I have always had it, and after all, better something good than new. So, if I may, I will keep it as long as possible.

I was sorry to hear about poor Negrita. I understand her loss must have made you all unhappy? All of you, including Black Dog.

I hope the cyclone did not hit Cuba. I think I read somewhere that it had turned around to, to, to . . . I can't remember where.

I am sending you some photos: tell me what you think of them. And tell me when you will get tired of keeping my photos.

I kiss you hard and thank you again for everything.

Your

A

Have I told you that at this time millions fall on me, like the summer rain on very dry earth? After all that I have gained another million: 1,020,000 of . . . red blood cells! I have made the analysis and the result is:

| Before | | Now | |
|--------|--------|--------|--------|
| Red cells | 3.270.000 | 4.250.000 | |
| Hemoglobin | 67 | 85 | |
| neurofili | 3.432 | 3.974 | |
| monociti | 264 | 128 | (down) |
| eosinofili | 397 | 448 | |

Good, right?

AND YOU, HOW ARE YOU? I recommend you follow my example.

[54]

Part of letter (undated) to Adriana Ivancich.

I tried to sell my share in the Key West property at a big loss to have money so that I could try to solve the problems of your finca (farm). But since they are rich Gigi will not and Patrick cannot answer letters. It is very funny when little boys who know nothing and can make no judgements must be considered as adults and everything must be agreed on by three people with two of them incapable of writing a letter; much less makeing a decision. Patrick is a kind and intelligent and loveing boy. But he cannot stick to a decision about anything. We had a consejo de famiglia and decided to sell the property for $150,000 since no one wanted to live in it. Then Patrick decided he did. Then that he didn't. Then that he didn't for other reasons. Then confusion and Gigi too busy with his inheritance to answer any letter ever. Patrick decided he thought it was better to make money renting the property because he did not need money, he said, and land was better. So I offered to sell him my part for half what it was worth. He wanted to buy it. But did not want me to lose money. So finally he left it last week with no word to me and nothing has been accomplished. This must seem very silly to a European. But then the cuggini were silly too although they thought they were intelligent. Certainly children should become adults legally at some time. But the age is different for everyone.

How are you my beauty? Spring should have come now and soon there will be the season. Here we have wonderful weather: cool every night; a great heavy current in the Gulf Stream; many torneos and concursos; small rains in the afternoon to keep the grass and flowers green and blooming; and everything here but you.

As long as I have no money I accept not seeing you as I would accept being in prison if it was for a short and determined time. But when I have some money (which God hope will be soon) I will see you Adriana.

Won't it be fun? Please hold Europe. Cuba is not lost. It has only changed masters. Will tell you when I see you.

Please give our love to your mother and tell her how often we think of her and with such happiness remembering all the jokes and fun and hardships (Escondido) when we were all a family as well as a partnership.


[55]


Undated cable from Hemingway to his sister Ura (Ursula).

NLT
Mrs. Jasper Jepson
4668 Aukai Avenue
Honolulu 15
Hawaii

Dearest Ura happiest operation successful hope you dont hurt worse than can bear stop am your old brother do you remember named gladly thy cross-eyed bear stop mailed longest letters may twentyfirst june eighth last 1800 words telling how maybe if we settled for happy hunting grounds you and I could be wonderful complete with prospectus stop will write registered but what became of lovingest letters to best beloved sister or best loved anybody stop best jep thanks wire insides are nothing stop without luck we might never have had them and been like other people stop love you the most dearest Ura Ernie

Sender E. Hemingway Hotel Ambos Mundos—Havana.

[56]

Letter from Marlene Dietrich, August 25, 1955.

Dearest Papa,

I was happy to get your letter—I had waited so long for it. Am leaving Saturday for 704 N. Beverly Dr. Beverly-Hills till Sept 30th—then Sahara Hotel, Las Vegas, Nevada, till Nov. 1.

I got the script. I cannot begin to tell you how dissappointed I was. The choice of material is as un-theatrical as can be. The presentation is amateurish. I always knew that we need an *adaptor and a director*, either to work *together* or better *one man who is both*, like Laughton functiones for Paul Gregory's Readings. This new medium which was so successfull when Laughton started it is *not an easy* one. It still is *theatre*. The Readings which Emlyn Williams does of Dickens and the Bible-Readings Laughton does, are different. But if one distributes the dialogue between three or four actors it becomes *more* than *Readings*

The *frame around* your stories is *all important*. It has to have the dignity you require, and the intelligence and showmanship in the presentation you require. I don't know if you have read the final script. I nearly was sick when I read that *I am brought on* with the words: And now, ladies and gentlemen, the star of our show! (MUSIC: La Vie en Rose! Miss D. appears, lights a cigarette, taking her time e.t.c.) Hemingway Reading—and I arrive to the strains of La Vie En Rose! I light a cigarette? What do I do with the cigarette once I reach the microphone and start on the story?

I am just citing this in order to show you that whoever wrote this is *so far away* from what we want that it is almost hopeless to discuss it with him. I know that I can change my introduction easily, the point I am making is that whoever *can write this* kind of crap down in connection with *your* material, someone who has been thinking for months about this presentation, *is in the wrong business*.

All the way down the line the script is impossible. To put the 'Hills are like white elephants' *first!* After the Vie en Rose and the cigarette plus the impact of my stage appearance I am supposed to make the audience believe I am the girl of that story?

The script then goes without connection into the next story, one does even know that it is the next story. The guitar player, who has been introduced: And now, ladies and gentlemen, I want you to meet our Guitar player!, strums the guitar while the reading goes on and plays louder when the story is ended. How amateurish can you get!

The choice of the 'Farewell to Arms'-scene is ridiculous and this shows again that no Theatre-Man had his hand in this presentation. Acting Labor-pains and death while standing (in the simplest of eveningdress) at a microphone on a stage in the company of other actors will get giggles from the audience even if Duse stood there. And to choose that scene as the last one of the *whole evening* is just murder.

*I* could do a better job. But I would not *dare* to do it. Not with *your* stories. When you fool around with the great you have to be up to their standard at least *and* up to the standard which has been set for the medium.

Hotchner, to whom I told all this, claims that 'THEY' wanted it done this way. Who 'THEY' are, I do not know and he wouldn't tell. I told him that he should have refused to put his name to the script if he felt it was wrong. The way it is I can only blame him. I told him that when Gregory and Laughton planned the first Shaw-Reading they worked years on the project. Throwing great material together like that is criminal.

Please understand the one important point: Readings of one person alone, reading all the parts, sitting at a desk *alone* on the stage is *one thing*— having different actors read the parts is *quite another*.

The second-one is the one which requires theatre-sense in choice of material, staging and acting.

The way I see it: we cannot do it this coming spring.

Orson Welles should be made to adapt and direct. Then I can vouch for something worthy of you.

Forgive my being so vehement about this—but my respect and love for you as a writer makes me so in this particular instant.

I kiss you hard

> and love you to death
> Kraut

[57]

Letter from Leonard Lyons.

18th April, 1956

Mr. Ernest Hemingway,
Vinca Virgia,
San Francisco de Paula,
Cuba

Dear Poppa:
Next Thursday and Friday, the 26th and 27th, a good friend of mine will give concerts in Havana. His name is Isaac Stern. He not only is one of the world's foremost violinists, but he also is different from the other musicians in that he has a great deal of warmth and goodness. From Havana he has been invited to fly to Russia for a tour.

He, of course, would be most honored if you and Mary would care to attend either of these concerts. I told him, naturally, that you were busy with the new book, and that I doubted you would find the time. But just in case you would like a little break from the daily routine, this would be a pleasant one. In any event, you would adore each other. He will be at the Presidente Hotel—of course, I did not give him your number.

I read that you may be off to Peru, and another report that you would head for Africa—the first to catch a big fish; the second to find a big son. I hope both quests are successful.

Sylvia plans to leave for a quick trip to the Riviera tomorrow. I wish she could go by way of Havana, to convey to you in person all our affection and good wishes.

Sincerely,
*Leonard*

[58]

Telegram from Ellen Shipman.

NEW YORK JUNIO 25 1957 8-55 PM

LT ERNEST HEMINGWAY
FINCA VIGIA-
    SAN FSC PAULA-

EVAN DIED MONDAY MORNING YOUR CABLE GAVE HIM GREAT HAPPINESS

ELLEN SHIPMAN ANGELL

[59]

Letter from Hemingway to Minister of the Interior.

FINCA VIGIA
SAN FRANCISCO DE PAULA,
CUBA

Minister of the Interior
City

My dear Sir:

I have the honor to address you in order to explain the following:

For many years I have been an aficionado of the hunt and target shooting. I have at home a Colt pistol, 22 calibre, Match Target type, which I keep there as I am not the sort of person that carries firearms.

Inasmuch as the law requires that all firearms be licensed by your Department, and as I do not wish to break the law, I applied for a Class 7 license, which is the one that permits the possession of arms in one's own domicile.

Three days ago I received a communication from the director of the Department of Firearms in which he advises me that it is not possible to grant me said License Class 7 as it applies only to other types of firearms and not to a pistol, even one used only for sport, and that therefore I should apply for a Class 5.

Because in order to obtain a Class 5 License the application must be accompanied by a letter of recommendation from a Military or Police officer, and not knowing personally anyone in either service, I hereby address you, as Minister of the Interior, to ask for your help in obtaining said license by writing a letter of recommendation for me so that I can enclose it with rest of the documents necessary to obtain it.

Hoping for your understanding in the matter of this application and thanking you in advance for any interest you may give it, I am

Very truly yours,

Ernest Hemingway

Note: Original of this letter was written in Spanish.

[60]

Several notations and fragments for stories were found in different drawers at Finca Vigía.

The two handwritten notes are:

Jimmy was one of the most pleasant people that ever lived in that, finally, particularly most depressing quarter of Paris.

It's funny
one thing you notice as you go along is the intense intolerance of the people who call themselves liberal.

A Hemingway typewritten fragment, perhaps part of a wartime article:

It turned out wrong because in the end I always [thought?] of Torney Island as Coney Island and my impression of the Mitchell is if you have to get out get out the same way you came in And Five in a panic when he couldn't get his heels down and did not know the manual drill (newly scraped bottom of the barrel) and the tower saying, "Shut up Five. Shut up Five) That day we lost two kites out of the same box bombing a launching site foe VI near abbebille at 12,000. Or flying in the lovely mosquitos with Pete Wyckham-Barnes. He was my true and legitimate hero. But I was only a guest and spectator and a half assed or worthless occupant of co-pilot or navigator space. But could always find Brighton or Hastings. And it was damned nice to have a hero. There aren't very many around that I would have. I never had one in ground fighting since I can remember.

[61]

This typewritten fragment written by Hemingway could have been part of a letter, or part of a story:

You are right about women being good friends. They are good friends and dreadful enemies; crazy and completely unreasonable every 28 days and off and on whenever it hits them in change of life. But they can be wonderful friends as you say. But it is better to watch yourself on the breaks though. Woman is the only female two legged animal that stands upright and will always hit after the bell. Maybe the female kangaroo does too. I wouldn't know. I think most sterile women were clapped early and just didn't notice it. Most of them don't even know when they have the clap or the old rale and they give it to you with true love and affection. They always have to be jealous of something and if you give them no cause for jealousy except your work they will be jealous of that. But if you convince them that writing brings mink coats, or a mink coat, etc. they will love it for its-self alone. You have to back up your play though. After that they usually keep the mink coat in storage as an asset. They forget everything that is ever given to them but remember for a hundred years any cashable asset they did not get. Finally they get it. You must learn never to speak against their family, naturally, but also never to agree with them if they speak against them. This last is just as bad as the first. I would like to write about a bitch sometime except that real bitches are abnormal. Most lovely women bat over 750 at not being bitches and as long as you can 1 to their 3 you can play in their league for ever and they will even love what you write. Being able to f———is esteemed far above being able to write except with abnormal women. They can always tell whether you can f———or not like bird dogs can tell whether the cover is there. No one of them knows anything about whether you can write (exception for a woman whose name begins with M) Shit.

Read Joe's piece. Very good. Afternoon mail just came with request from Donald Friede that I write an introduction for a collection of your pieces. Am glad to do it if you would like me to. It would be easier to do if I saw the pieces but I can write a piece without seeing them. Let me know when you should have it and give my best to Donald. Please excuse me to him for not writing on the grounds that I am working. Or if you prefer I will write to him.

# Appendix II: Chronology

With particular reference to activities and literary work of Hemingway during his residence in Cuba:

**1899**
Ernest Miller Hemingway, second of six children, born to Clarence Edmund Hemingway and Grace Hall in Oak Park, Chicago, the 21st of July.

**1916**
Hemingway's first published work, a story titled "Judgment of Manitou," published in *The Tabula*, a literary review of Oak Park High School, in February.

**1917**
Graduates from Oak Park High School. The United States enters the First World War. The Army rejects Ernest Hemingway because of poor vision in one eye. In the fall starts to work as reporter for the *Kansas City Star*.

**1918**
Takes part in the First World War as member of an ambulance corps. Wounded by mortar grenade in Fossalta del Piave, Italy, the 8th of July. Convalescence in a Milan hospital and romance with Nurse Agnes H. von Kurowsky, on whom he modeled the character Catherine Barkley in *A Farewell to Arms* and that of Luz in "A Very Short Story."

**1919.**
Returns to the United States in January. Joins editorial staff of the *Star Weekly* in Toronto.

**1921**
Marries Hadley Richardson in Horton's Bay, Michigan, the 3rd of September. They leave for Paris where he works as correspondent for the *Star Weekly* starting the 8th of December.

**1922**

Correspondent in Switzerland, Italy, Germany and Turkey. In December, Hadley loses a suitcase full of Hemingway's original unpublished work in a railroad station in Paris.

**1923**

In the spring, a trip to Spain to see the bullfights. His first book, *Three Stories and Ten Poems*, published in Paris by the Contact Publishing Company, 300 copies, probably in July. Birth of John Hadley Nicanor, his first son, in Toronto, on October 10. Leaves the *Star* in December.

**1924**

Goes to the San Fermín festival in Pamplona. First edition of *in our time*, 170 copies, published by Three Mountain Press in Paris.

**1925**

Goes again to the festival in Pamplona in July. Begins first draft of a novel, *The Lost Generation*, which would later be titled *The Sun Also Rises*. *In Our Time* (this time capitalized) published in New York by Boni and Liveright, 5th of October, 1,355 copies.

**1926**

Charles Scribner's sons of New York becomes his publisher for life. *Torrents of Spring*, 1,250 copies, published May 28, and *The Sun Also Rises*, 5,090 copies, on the 22nd of October.

**1927**

Divorces Hadley on March 10. Marries Pauline Pfeiffer on May 10. Publication of *Men Without Women*, 7,650 copies, on October 14. Begins residence in Key West.

**1928**

Trip to Europe with Pauline. In April returns to Key West on board the *Orita* which makes a stop in Havana. It's his first known visit to that city. Patrick, his second son, is born in Kansas City, the 30th of June. First exploration of the Gulf Stream. He meets Eddy "Bra" Saunders, plunderer of the *Valbanera*, on whom he would pattern the lead of "After the Storm," and Joe Russell, owner of Sloppy Joe's in Key West and owner of the boat the *Anita* as well, and who was to serve as the model for Harry Morgan in *To Have and Have Not*. He meets Gregorio Fuentes when a storm forces him to seek refuge in Dry Tortugas. His father commits suicide the 6th of December in Oak Park.

1929

Residence in Key West. Trips to Spain and France in spring and summer. *A Farewell to Arms* is published the 27th of September, 31,000 copies.

1930

Stay in Spain. Hunting in Wyoming. In November, automobile accident and hospitalization in Billings, Montana. During his convelescence he grows a beard for the first time.

1931

In the summer, to Spain again. First motion picture version of *A Farewell to Arms*. Gregory, his third son, born the 12th of November in Kansas City.

1932

"After the Storm" published in *Cosmopolitan* magazine in May. Joe Russell puts him in contact with Carlos Gutiérrez. Fishing on board the *Anita* around the north coast of Cuba. Use of Hotel Ambos Mundos as base of operations in Havana. *Death in the Afternoon* published the 25th of September, 10,300 copies.

1933

Observes revolutionary events that culminate in the overthrow of Dictator Gerardo Machado in August, in Havana. In the fall, after a lapse of ten years, returns to journalism with the publication in *Esquire* of "Marlin Off the Morro," his first article about Cuba. *Winner Take Nothing* is published in October, 20,300 copies. He makes plans for a book on the mysteries of the Gulf Stream. Goes on an African safari in December.

1934

Evacuated to Nairobi suffering from an amoebic fever in January. Starts over again in the safari and shoots a beautiful specimen of a greater kudu in the Masai region, February 15. Returns to Key West in April. He commissions the construction of the yacht, *Pilar*, from the Wheeler Shipyard. The story "One Trip Across," first part of the book about Harry Morgan, *To Have and Have Not*, published in *Esquire* in the April issue.

## 1935

"Who Murdered the Vets?" an indictment on the death of hundreds of American veterans, victims of a hurricane in the Matecumbe Keys, published in the *New Masses*, 17th of September. *The Green Hills of Africa* published the 25th of October, 10,550 copies.

## 1936

"The Tradesman's Return," a story that later became the second part of the book on Harry Morgan, published in the February issue of *Esquire*. "On the Blue Water," an article including the anecdote that years later would be expanded into *The Old Man and the Sea*, published in April in *Esquire*. The African stories, which Hemingway later would declare his favorites, appear: "The Snows of Kilimanjaro," in the August issue of *Esquire*, and "The Short Happy Life of Francis Macomber," in September in *Cosmopolitan*. His troubles with Carlos Gutiérrez begin.

## 1937

In February goes to Spain as war correspondent for the North American Newspaper Alliance (NANA). Takes part in the filming of "The Spanish Earth." Returns to the United States to collect funds for the purchase of medical equipment for the Republican Government. Makes a speech at the Second Congress of American Writers in Carnegie Hall in New York, the 4th of June, the first political speech of his whole life. Returns to Spain in August. Serves as militia instructor and fights in the Spanish fronts. *To Have and Have Not* published the 15th of October, 10,300 copies.

## 1939

Starts work at the Hotel Ambos Mundos in Havana on the final draft of "The Undiscovered Country," later to be titled *For Whom the Bell Tolls*. "Nobody Ever Dies," the only one of his stories to take place entirely in Cuba, published in *Cosmopolitan* in March. In April, at Martha Gellhorn's insistence, he rents Finca Vigía for a year.

## 1940

*For Whom the Bell Tolls* published the 21st of October, 75,000 copies. Divorce from Pauline final on November 4. Marries Martha Gellhorn on the 21st of November. Buys Finca Vigía the 28th of December.

## 1941

Ralph Ingersoll, editor of *PM*, a New York newspaper, sends him to the Far East to report on the Sino-Japanese War. Hemingway takes

Martha with him on a kind of honeymoon. Returns to Cuba in July. Joe Russell dies.

1942

Creation of the Crook Factory, a secret agency of anti-Nazi operations, with headquarters at Finca Vigía. Guns installed on the *Pilar* and hunt for German submarine starts. *Men at War* published by Crown Publishers in New York, the 22nd of October.

1944

In March, first stay in England. Automobile accident during a London blackout takes place in May. News spreads of Ernest Hemingway's death. From May to December takes part in combat: several air force bombing missions and reconnaisance, the landing in Normandy, liberation of Paris and operations on the Siegfried Line. Accused of disregarding his obligations as war correspondent, he is questioned in October by an investigating officer of the Third Army.

1945

Returns to Cuba via New York. Starts two drafts, one for a book titled *The Sea Book* and the other *The Garden of Eden*. In June, another automobile accident, this time on the Mantilla road near Finca Vigía. Divorces Martha the 21st of December.

1946

Marries Mary Welsh in Havana on the 4th of March.

1947

In April, stops works temporarily on *The Sea Book*, of which he has written 997 pages, because his son Patrick has suffered a nervous breakdown. Maxwell Perkins, his editor, dies on June 17. Takes part in the conspiracy to overthrow Dominican dictator Rafael Leonidas Trujillo; Finca Vigía is raided in October and firearms are seized.

1949

Trip to Northern Italy and his return to the locale of *A Farewell to Arms*. Meets Adriana Ivancich who will be the model for Renata in *Across the River and into the Trees*. Starts to write this novel in Cortina d'Ampezzo. Returns to Cuba in the summer.

1950

*Across the River and into the Trees* published the 7th of September, 75,000 copies. The novel receives the most unfavorable reviews of all of Hemingway's work. Goes back to work on *The Sea Book* in the fall.

1951

Hemingway's mother dies in Memphis, Tennessee, the 28th of June, and Pauline Pfeiffer in Los Angeles, California, the 22nd of October. Puts *The Sea Book* aside again, although he decides to publish part of it: the story of Santiago the fisherman.

1952

Charles Scribner dies the 11th of February. *The Old Man and the Sea* published in *Life* the first of September, and in book form, 51,700 copies, the 8th of September. The novel immediately becomes one of the biggest successes of Hemingway's career.

1953

In May receives the Pulitzer Prize. Goes to Spain for the first time since the Civil War. Goes hunting in East Africa. Suffers two consecutive airplane accidents in Uganda in January. Again the world press announces the death of Ernest Hemingway. Some of his friends rush to write and publish their post-mortems.

1954

Hospitalized in Nairobi in January. In the summer he returns to Cuba via Venice and Spain. He receives the Nobel Prize in October.

1956

Goes to Paris and Spain. In September *Look* publishes "A Situation Report," his last article on Cuba. Helps the revolutionary movement in Cuba.

1959

Ernest Hemingway publicly declares his support of the Cuban Revolution. Visits and recalls old times in Paris, goes to Spain for the bullfights, stops in the United States and returns to Cuba the 4th of September.

1960

Last stay in Cuba, which lasts until the summer of the year. Meets Fidel Castro at the Hemingway Fishing Contest on May 15, 1960. Anastas Mikoyan visits Finca Vigía. Hemingway finishes writing *A Moveable Feast*. Begins to show signs of mental unbalance. Goes to Spain to write *A Dangerous Summer*, a report about the rivalry of the two great bullfighters, Dominguín and Ordóñez. Has much trouble finishing it. Feels ill and returns to Ketchum, Idaho, in October. First admission to Mayo Clinic in November.

1961
Returns to Mayo Clinic in April. Submits to electric shock treatment. Back to Ketchum in June. Commits suicide on Sunday, July 2. Mary Welsh Hemingway goes to Havana in August. Meets with Fidel Castro for the official donation of Finca Vigía and its contents to the Revolutionary Government. Hemingway Museum is established.

1964
Posthumous publication of *A Moveable Feast*, 83,800 copies. May 5.

1970
Mary Welsh and the editors of Scribner's revive *The Sea Book* and decide to publish it under the title *Islands in the Stream* on the 6th of October, 75,000 copies. The backgrounds of the book include the Bimini islands, a deserted and remote archipelago north of Camagüey, Cuba, and the two most important places of the Hemingway legend in Havana: the Floridita bar and Finca Vigía.

# Appendix III: Bibliography, Notes and Sources

*Three Stories and Ten Poems*. Contact Publishing Company, Paris and Dijon, 1923.

*in our time*. Three Mountains Press, Paris, 1924.

*In Our Time*. Boni and Liveright, New York, 1925.

*The Torrents of Spring*. Charles Scribner's Sons, New York, 1926.

*The Sun Also Rises*. Charles Scribner's Sons, New York, 1926.

*Men Without Women*. Charles Scribner's Sons, New York, 1927.

*A Farewell to Arms*. Charles Scribner's Sons, New York, 1929.

*Death in the Afternoon*. Charles Scribner's Sons, New York, 1932.

*Winner Take Nothing.* Charles Scribner's Sons, New York, 1933.

*Green Hills of Africa.* Charles Scribner's Sons, New York, 1935.

*To Have and Have Not.* Charles Scribner's Sons, New York, 1937. The first novel by Hemingway with a Cuban setting. The action takes place in Havana, on the nothern coast of Cuba, on the Gulf Stream, and in Key West. It was made into a film by Howard Hawks, with a screenplay by William Faulkner and starring Humphrey Bogart and Lauren Bacall. The film's exterior scenes were shot in Martinique and the seagoing scenes in a Hollywood tank. The film retained the title of the book, but little else.

*Short Stories of Ernest Hemingway.* Charles Scribner's Sons, New York, 1938.

*Men at War* (ed.). Crown, New York, 1942.

*Across the River and into the Trees.* Charles Scribner's Sons, New York, 1950.

*The Old Man and the Sea.* Charles Scribner's Sons, New York, 1952. Set entirely in Cuba and on the waters north of the Cuban coast. Almost all of the exteriors in the film version were filmed in Cojímar, but because the Cuban waters could not produce a fish of the required size, the final fishing scenes were shot off Cabo Blanco, Peru. The narration required that a pride of lions be seen on the African coast; the lions appear, but not on the coast. Hemingway and Mary appear in one of the final scenes as tourists who discover the skeleton of Santiago's enormous fish on the beach at Cojímar.

*A Moveable Feast.* Charles Scribner's Sons, New York, 1964.

*By-Line Ernest Hemingway.* Charles Scribner's Sons, New York, 1967. Contains all of Hemingway's Cuban pieces for *Esquire.*

*Islands in the Stream.* Charles Scribner's Sons, New York, 1970. A novel in three parts: the first set in Bimini, the second in Havana, and the third in the waters and archipelago north of Camagüey. This was also made into a distorted film version, starring George C. Scott as Thomas Hudson, the memory-plagued painter who hunts German submarines while smuggling Jewish immigrants pursued by Cuban government boats.

"Nobody Ever Dies," is the only short story by Hemingway set in Cuba. Despite the excellence of the title, it does not succeed in capturing the essence of the revolutionary struggle in Cuba before and during the

Second World War. It has been published in Spanish under the title "The Revolutionary Education." It was first published in *Cosmopolitan*, New York, vol. 106, March 1939.

## ARTICLES

"Marlin Off the Moro," *Esquire*, Fall 1933. Hemingway's first article on Cuba. Introduces Carlos Gutiérrez and describes the embarcation of the *Anita* and the passage to Havana. The city is described from his room in the Hotel Ambos Mundos. Relates his first experience fishing for marlin.

"Out in the Stream," *Esquire*, August 1934. Hemingway becomes an experienced fisherman and a lover of Hatuey Beer.

"On Being Shot Again," *Esquire*, June 1935.

"On the Blue Water," *Esquire*, April 1936. Introduces the tale of the old man and the sea.

"There She Breaches," *Esquire*, May 1936. Leaving Havana harbor and skirting machine-gun target practice from the Cabaña fortress; also a humorous description of an uncommon occurrence: an abundance of whales off the coast of Cuba.

"The Great Blue River," *Holiday*, July 1949.

"The Shot," *Ken*, April 1951.

"A Visit with Hemingway" (also known as "A Situation Report"), *Look*, September 4, 1956.

## THE GULF STREAM

Hemingway proposed a book on the mysterious origins of the Gulf Stream to Maxwell Perkins in a letter dated February 10, 1933. The project, along with others, failed to materialize. But the first trials and fishing experiences suggested to Hemingway material for future fiction and articles. Following is a list of pieces which include the events that were retold or referred to in *To Have and Have Not*.

"After the Storm," *Cosmopolitan*, May 1932. A story in the idiom and of an ambience similar to that of the Harry Morgan stories. Based on an experience of Eddy Saunders and the wreck of the Spanish vessel *Valbanera*.

"One Trip Across," *Cosmopolitan*, April 1934. The first part of *To Have and Have Not*.

"Old Newsman Writes. A Letter from Cuba," *Esquire*, December 1934.

"Remembering Shooting-Flying. A Key West Letter," *Esquire*, February 1935.

"The Sights of Whitehead Street. A Key West Letter," *Esquire*, April 1935.

"Who Murdered the Vets? *New Masses*, New York, September 17, 1935. The death of thousands of World War I veterans who were abandoned by federal authorities in the path of a hurricane on the keys of Alto y Bajo Matecumbe is used by Hemingway as the basis for an angry political tract. There is a brief reference to Cuba: One does not encounter the yachts of millionaires in those waters during hurricane weather; that is not the time for fishing. He reveals the idea that no one has a chance "as long as there are rich sons of bitches who decide to make war." The experience is crucial. Following this, *To Have and Have Not* was changed into a strange and nervous novel. This hardening process was to reach its climax in the Spanish Civil War.

"The Tradesman's Return," *Esquire*, February 1936. The second part of *To Have and Have Not*.

## GATTORNO AND ROWE

Hemingway wrote the texts for presentation brochures of the paintings of Antonio Gattorno, a Cuban, and Reginald Rowe, an American resident of Cuba at the time. The one on Gattorno is interesting because of the observations on the hardships of the artistic community of Cuba during the thirties. The brochure was published by Ucar, Garcia y Co. in Havana in 1935 and reproduced in *Esquire* in May 1936. The Rowe piece is a folder containing a paragraph of Hemingway's observations on the light in Cuba and how to render it artistically. Unpublished.

## "IT IS AN ISLAND LARGE, BEAUTIFUL AND UNFORTUNATE . . ."

In Chapter VIII of *Green Hills of Africa* there is an essential paragraph on Cuba. Hemingway describes the eternal and mighty movement of the current of the Gulf along the coasts of the island. Elsewere in the book there is a brief and pessimistic dialogue concerning the revolutionary movement that overthrew the Cuban dictator Gerardo Machado in 1933.

## PHILIP RAWLINGS IN CUBA

The protagonist of Hemingway's only work for the theatre, *The Fifth Column*, recalls Havana at dawn, before the Spanish Civil War. The Sans Souci, dances on the patio "under the royal palms," and breakfasts on the beach at Jaimanitas are part of his evocation. In Cuba, the character explains, he began his revolutionary indoctrination. At another time he mentions the Cuban terrorist organization of the thirties, the ABC.

## HEMINGWAY AND CASTRO

Baez, Luis, "Hemingway Always Favored the Revolution," interview with Mary Hemingway, *Bohemia*, Havana, September, 30, 1977.

Castro, Fidel, Statements, in *Revolutionary Works*, Havana, Saturday, May 14, 1960. Transcribed version of his television appearance the previous night, in which he referred to his participation in the Hemingway Fishing Competition which was to be held at the end of the week.

————, Statements, in *Revolución*, Havana, Saturday, July 9, 1960. A transcription of his television appearance the previous night, in which he said: ". . . why don't we consider those North American citizens who have a house or a parcel of land on the Isle of Pines, *like Hemingway who has his house and lives here*. They are fine North Americans who selected this country for settling down and living and those North Americans will have nothing to worry themselves about, because we well understand the feeling that has drawn them to our country. Who have come here not to exploit our country or to frustrate the longing of our people." Obviously, the Cuban leader pronounced these words at a moment of deteriorating relationships with the United States. Hemingway underscored the words referring to him and kept the newspaper clipping, without date, in one of the bookshelves in the guestroom of Finca Vigía.

————, Speech delivered as President of the Movement of Unaligned Countries before the XXXIV Period of Sessions of the General Assembly of the United Nations, New York, October 12, 1979. He made a paraphrase of the title of a novel by Hemingway in exhorting the governments of the world to work for peace and growth. The last paragraph of the speech: "We say farewell to arms and shall consecrate ourselves in a civilized manner to the most pressing problems of our time. . . . That is, moreover, the essential premise for human survival."

Desnoes, Edmundo, "The Final Summer," *Points of View*, Instituto del Libro, Havana, 1967. This essay, although it presents an unfavorable evaluation of Hemingway, popularized a phrase of Fidel Castro's concerning the novelist: "All the work of Hemingway is a defense of human rights."

Mankiewicz, Frank, and Kirby Jones, *With Fidel. A Portrait of Castro and Cuba*. Playboy Press, Chicago, 1975. Contains statements by Fidel Castro on Hemingway and his friendliness towards Cuba, and an opinion regarding *For Whom the Bell Tolls*.

Matthews, Herbert L., *Fidel Castro*. Simon and Schuster, New York, 1969. His sole reference to Hemingway in this book is stimulating. After mentioning the possible intervention of the CIA in the sabotage that destroyed the ship *La Coubre* in March 1960 in the port of Havana, Matthews added the following note to the foot of the page: "And while one the subject of my March 1960 trip, I find this in the conclusion of my memorandum: 'Ernest Hemingway is still the great hero of the Cuban people. He is staying at his home working as a deliberate gesture to show his sympathy and support for the Castro Revolution. He knows Cuba and the Cuban people as well as any American citizen. I was glad to find that his ideas on Fidel Castro and the Cuban Revolution are the same as mine.' "

Otero, Lisandro, *Hemingway*. Casa de las Américas, Havana, 1963. Popularized another statement, but this time one attributed to the writer: "If I were younger I would climb the Sierra Maestra to join Fidel Castro."

Vasquez-Candela, Euclides, "Hemingway Worried About Cuba and Fidel," *The Cuban Gazette*, Havana, vol. II, no. 13, February 13, 1963.

## THE CUBAN SCENE

Boudet, Rosa Ileana, "Hemingway: Always *La Habana*," *Cuba Internacional*, Havana, December 1969.

Cabrera Infante, Guillermo, "The Old Man and the Mark," *Ciclón*, Havana, September 1956.

Campoamor, Fernando G., "Ernest Hemingway's Cuban Life," *Bohemia*, July 21, 1967.

———, *The Hemingway Circuit* (Havana, 1980). A tourists' guide enumerating and describing some of the spots frequented by Hemingway in Havana.

Carpentier, Alejo, *The Consecration of Spring* (novel). Editorial Letras Cubano del Libro, Havana, 1979. Contains references to Hemingway and his friend Evan Shipman, and a memorable description of Hemingway in the Floridita. There is a comparison between Hemingway and the Cuban writer Pablo de la Torriente Brau.

Cirules, Enrique, *Conversation with the Last North American*, Instituto Cubano del Libro, Havana, 1973. Contains a description of the continuing presence of Hemingway in the archipelago north of Camagüey.

Cruz, Mary, "The Cuban in 'One Trip Across,' " Annuario L/L, Havana, no. 5, 1974.

———, "A Cuban Revolutionary Short Story by Ernest Hemingway," *Casa de las Américas*, Havana, no. 116, September-October 1979.

———, *Cuba and Hemingway on the Great Blue River*, Ediciones Unión, Havana, 1981.

Desnoes, Edmundo, "Hemingway's House," *Cuba*, Havana, April 1965. Contains a collection of excellent photographs by Mario García Joya.

Fuentes, Norberto, "A House to Defend," *Revolution and Culture*, Havana, no. 55, March 1977.

———, "Mas vale ver una vez que escuchar cien" ("Better to see it one time than hear of it a hundred"), interview with Anastas Mikoyan, *Revolution and Culture*, Havana, No. 69, May 1978.

———, "Nobody Ever Dies," *The Cuban Gazette*, Havana, no. 168, June 1978.

Gonzáles Bermejo, Ernesto, "Hemingway's Fishermen," *Cuba*, September 1962.

Hemingway, Margaux, "Playboy and Margaux Go to Cuba," *Playboy*, vol. 25, No. 6, June 1978 (with photographs by David Hume Kennerly, produced by Hollis Wayne).

Manning, Robert, "Hemingway in Cuba," *The Atlantic Monthly*, vol. 216, August, 1965.

Otero, Lisandro, "Ernest Hemingway Among Us Again," *Carteles*, Havana, July 11, 1954.

Paporov, Yuri, *Pilar*, Sovietski Pisátiel, Moscow, 1975. A novel based on the life of Hemingway in Cuba, his fishing expeditions in the Gulf and his participation in anti-submarine warfare. The line between fiction and fact is often blurred.

————, *Hemingway na Kybe* (Hemingway in Cuba), Sovietski Pisátiel, Moscow, 1975.

*Revolution Monday*, literary supplement to *Revolution*, no. 118, August 14, 1961. Edition devoted to Hemingway on the occasion of his death. Contains, among others: Edmundo Desnoes, "The Spaniard in Hemingway," Guillermo Cabrera Infante, "Hemingway, Cuba, and the Revolution," and Lolo Soldevilla, "Two Encounters with Hemingway."

## BOOKS ON HEMINGWAY

Aronowitz, Alfred, and Peter Hamill, *Ernest Hemingway, The Life and Death of a Man*. Lancer Books, Inc., New York, 1961.

Baker, Carlos, *Ernest Hemingway, a Life Story*. Charles Scribner's Sons, New York, 1969.

Buckley, Peter, *Ernest*. The Dial Press, New York, 1978.

Burgess, Anthony, *Ernest Hemingway and His World*. Charles Scribner's Sons, New York, 1978.

Gajdusek, Robert E., *Hemingway's Paris*. Charles Scribner's Sons, New York, 1978.

Hemingway, Gregory, *Papa, a Personal Memoir*. Houghton Mifflin Company, Boston 1976 (with an incisive and irreverent prologue by Norman Mailer).

Hemingway, Leicester, *My Brother Ernest Hemingway*. The World Publishing Company, Cleveland, 1962.

Hemingway, Mary, *How It Was*. Alfred A. Knopf, Inc., New York, 1976.

Hotchner, A.E., *Papa Hemingway*. Random House, Inc., New York, 1966.

Klimo, Vernon (Jake), and Will Ousler, *Hemingway and Jake: an Extraordinary Friendship*. Doubleday, New York, 1972.

McLendon, James, *Papa Hemingway in Key West*. E.A. Seeman Publishing, Inc., Miami, 1972.

Ross, Lillian, *Portrait of Hemingway*. Simon and Schuster, New York, 1961.


CRITICAL AND ANALYTIC

Baker, Carlos, *Hemingway. The Writer as Artist*. Princeton University Press, New Jersey, 1952.

Baker, Sheridan, *Ernest Hemingway. An Introduction and Interpretation*. Holt, Rinehart and Winston, Inc., New York, 1967.

Broer, Lawrence R., *Hemingway's Spanish Tragedy*. The University of Alabama Press, Alabama, 1963.

Cunill, Felipe, Introduction to *The Snows of Kilimanjaro*. Editorial Arte y Literatura, Havana, 1975. Presents the first collection of Hemingway's short stories published in Cuba.

Defalco, Joseph M., *The Hero in Hemingway's Short Stories*. University of Pittsburgh Press, 1963.

Fenton, Charles A., *The Apprenticeship of Ernest Hemingway. The Early Years*. The Viking Press, New York, 1954.

Fuentes, Norberto, Introduction to *For Whom the Bell Tolls*. Editorial Arte y Literatura, Havana, 1980.

Gurko, Leo, *Ernest Hemingway and the Pursuit of Heroism*. Thomas Y. Crowell Company, New York, 1968.

Lewis, Robert W., *Hemingway on Love*. Haskell House Publisher Ltd., Austin, Texas, 1956.

Portuondo, José Antonio, "The Literary Process of Ernest Hemingway," in *Intellectual Heroism*, Tezontle, Mexico, 1955. This is one of the more serious, and in turn destructive, analyses that has fallen on the works of Hemingway. Although written from the Marxist point of view, it is essential to any interpretation, even though the Hemingway hero emerges rather battered from these pages.

Rodríguez Feo, José, "Ernest Hemingway: A Discordant Note," Ediciones Unión, Havana, 1962. This work was published a few months after Hemingway's death but put forward philosophical and political judgments that other critics made only much later.

Stipes Walls, Emily, *Ernest Hemingway and the Arts*. University of Illinois Press, Chicago, 1975.

Suarez, Silvano, *The Leopard's Skeleton*. Havana, 1955. Treatise by the only Cuban who occupied himself in studying extensively the work of Hemingway before the triumph of the Revolution. Lisandro Otero affirms that this essay says sensitive and brilliant things about the writer.

Young, Philip, *Ernest Hemingway*. Holt, Rinehart and Winston, Inc., New York, 1952.

————, *Ernest Hemingway, A Reconsideration*. Pennsylvania State University Press, University Park, Pennsylvania, 1966.

## ANTHOLOGIES

Baker, Carlos (ed.), *Hemingway and His Critics*. Hill and Wang, Inc., New York, 1961. Contains, among others: George Plimpton, "An Interview with Ernest Hemingway," and Ivan Kashkin, "Alive in the Midst of Death: Ernest Hemingway."

McCaffery, John K.M. (ed.), *Ernest Hemingway. The Man and His Work*. The World Publishing Company, Cleveland, 1951. Some of these pieces are essential reading: Gertrude Stein, "Hemingway in Paris," Malcolm Cowley, "A Portrait of Mister Papa," Max Eastman, "Bull in the Afternoon," John Groth, "A Note on Ernest Hemingway," Ivan Kashkin, "A Tragedy of Craftmanship," and Edmund Wilson, "Hemingway: Gauge of Morale."

Weeks, Robert P. (ed.), *Hemingway. A Collection of Critical Essays*. Prentice-Hall, Inc., Englewood Cliffs, New Jersey, 1962.

## OTHER BOOKS

Aldridge, James, *One Last Glimpse* (novel). Little Brown and Company, Boston, 1977. Although this is a work of fiction, it is well informed concerning the complex friendship between Hemingway and Scott Fitzgerald.

Armero, José María, *Spain Was News*. Sedmay Ediciones, Madrid, 1976.

Babel, Isaac, *You Must Know Everything. Stories 1915-1937*, Alianza Editorial, Madrid, 1976. In the Appendix of this Spanish edition he recalls Ilya Ehrenburg's moving discussion at the reunion in honor of Babel celebrated in Moscow on November 11, 1964, in which, among other important information, Ehrenburg revealed the following: "I remember what Hemingway said to me in a hotel in Madrid [during the Spanish Civil War]. Having finished reading Babel for the first time, he said; 'I have never believed that arithmetic was important for the appreciation of literature. I am criticized for writing in an excessively concise manner, but compared with the style of Babel, his is more concise than mine, which is more verbose.' "

Berg, Scott A., *Max Perkins, Editor of Genius.* E.P. Dutton, New York, 1978.

Bessie, Alvah, *Men in Battle.* New York, 1939.

Busch, Harold, *U-Boats at War.* New York, 1955.

Carmona, Darío, *Prohibida la sombra (Ban the Darkness).* Ediciones Unión, Havana, 1965. Contains the report "Graham Greene in Havana," with an account of the writer's visit to Finca Vigía.

Collins, Larry, and Dominique Lapierre, *Is Paris Burning?* Simon and Schuster, New York, 1965.

Cowley, Malcolm, *Exile's Return. A Literary Odyssey of the 1920's.* The Viking press, New York, 1951.

Chandler, Raymond, *Raymond Chandler Speaking.* New York, 1962.

Doenitz, Karl, *Memoirs. Ten Years and Twenty Days.* New York, 1966.

Dos Passos, *The Best Times. An Informal Memoir.* The New American Library, New York, 1966.

Douglas, Henry Kyd, *I Rode With Stonewall*, University of North Carolina Press, Chapel Hill, 1940.

Ehrenburg, Ilya, *Gente, anos, vida; primer libro de memorias (Men, years, life: First Volume of Memoirs).* Joaquín Móritz, Mexico, 1962.

Eisner, Alexis, *La 12a. Brigada Internacional.* Prometeo, Valencia, 1972 (Russian edition: *Dvenadtsiaia internatsionalnaia*, Moscow, 1968).

Garosci, Aldo, *Gli Inteletualli e la Guerra di Spagna.* Einaudi, Turin, 1959.

Gill, Brendan, *Here at the New Yorker.* Random House, New York, 1975.

Gwynne, Frederick L., and Joseph L. Blonter, *Faulkner in the University.* Vintage Books, New York, 1959.

Hellman, Lillian, *An Unfinished Woman*. Little, Brown and Company, Boston, 1969.

Hughes, Langston, *I Wonder as I Wander*. Hill & Wang, New York, 1964.

————. *El inmenso mar*, Editorial Arte y Literatura, Havana, 1978. Contains a prologue by Nicolas Guillén, "Recollections of Langston Hughes." This is the Cuban edition of *The Big Sea. An Autobiography* (Hill & Wang, New York, 1963).

Karmen, Roman, *No pasarán (They Shall Not Pass)*. Editorial Progreso, Moscow, 1976.

Landis, Arthur H., *The Abraham Lincoln Brigade*. The Citadel Press, New York, 1968.

Lister, Enrique, *Nuestra guerra; aportaciones para una historia de la Guerra Nacional Revolucionaria del pueblo español (Our War: Contributions to a History of the National Revolutionary War of the Spanish People)*. Paris, 1966.

Mailer, Norman, *Marilyn. A Biography*. Grosset and Dunlap, Inc., New York, 1973.

Milla, Fernando de la, *En La Habana está el amor* (novel), Havana, 1949. One of the most extravagant literary works of all time, and the first—and perhaps the only—novel to contain advertisements. The characters and the plot are used to publicize certain establishments and to salute the friends of the author. The dedication is in English: "To Ernest Hemingway, for whom the bell of old and new Spain shall always bring a glorious chime of greeting, jubilees and thankfulness. *Fernando*."

Raeburn, Ben (ed.), *Treasury for the Free World*. Arco, New York, 1946. Contains a foreword by Hemingway.

Thomas, Hugh, *Cuba, la lucha por la libertad (Cuba: The Struggle for Liberty)*. Mexico, 1974.

————, *La Guerra Civil español*. Ruedo Iberico, Paris, 1967.

Thompson, Hunter S., *The Great Shark Hunt*. Random House, New York, 1977. Contains the article, "What Lured Hemingway to Ketchum?" published originally in *The National Observer*, in which he states that Hemingway left Cuba because "Castro's instructors" were telling the people that Hemingway "exploited them." Thompson is the creator of "Gonzo journalism."

Tijomirov, Mijail, *El general Lukacs* (novel). Editorial Progreso, Moscow, 1971.

Weintraub, Stanley, *The Last Great Crusade*. New York, 1968.

## OTHER SOURCES

*The Los Angeles Times*, November 10, 1975. *Bohemia*, July 4, 1954; March 6, 1964; February 2, 1979. *Carteles*, July 11, 1954. *Cine Cubano*, Havana, September-November 1963. *Cuadernos para el diálogo*, Madrid, November 5, 1978. *Cuba Internacional*, Havana, March 1980. *Esquire*, New York, October 1970, March 1979. *Historia*, Paris, December 1973. *La Gaceta de Cuba*, March 1967, September-October 1979. *Granma*, Havana, July 11, 1977; September 15, 1977. *Noticias de Hoy*, Havana, July 7, 1961. *Juventud Rebelde*, Havana, July 2, 1966; January 22, 1970. *Life en español*, New York, March 30, 1953; December 1, 1958. *Mar y Pesca*, Havana, February 1980. *The Miami Herald*, March 5, 1977. *El Mundo del Domingo*, Havana, July 5, 1962; August 6, 1962. *Newsweek*, New York, March 14, 1977; May 30, 1977. *The New York Post*, July 3, 1961. *The New York Review of Books*, May 12, 1977. *The New York Times*, August 21, 1974; January 31, 1975; October 5, 1975. *The New York Times Magazine*, October 16, 1977. *Revolución*, November 5, 1959; July 3, 1961. Supplement to *Revolución*, August 31, 1962. *Revolución y Cultura*, Havana, April 1978. *Saturday Review*, New York, February 3, 1979. *Soviet Life*, Moscow, December 1979. *Tass* dispatch from Washington, January 9, 1975. *Time*, New York, December 13, 1954; April 19, 1976; June 26, 1978; February 5, 1979. *Triunfo*, Madrid, July 29, 1978. *Unión*, Havana, April-June 1964.

## INTERVIEWS

The text does not mention the following persons who offered information: Luis Crespo and Gustavo Iglesias, on fishing the northern coast of Cuba; Victor Pérez, on Cuban warships of the Second World War; Rafael M. Miyar, on the anti-submarine campaign; Juan Pérez de la Riva, on Chinese immigration (he disqualified as inaccurate some of the information given by Hemingway in *To Have and Have Not)*; Abelardo Abreu, on coastal geography and smuggling; Monsignor Pietro Sambi, Mariano Tomé, rector of the Seminary of Santiago de Cuba, and Rita Llaneza, of the Social Sisters, on the disposition of the Nobel Medal; Dr. Darío Guitar, on ichthyology and fish in general; Dr. Mirta

Aquirre, on a sentence by Cervantes; and Dr. Manuel Fuentes, on medicine in general.

CONTRIBUTORS

Access to materials was provided by: Manuel Pico, of the Fishing Cooperative of Cojímar; Natalia Bolivar, of the Numismatic Museum of Havana; Jose Manuel Penaranda, of the Frontier Guards of Punta Alegre, Camagüey; Saúl Yelín, of the Cuban Institute of Art and Cinematographic Industries; and Raul Guadarramos, Jorge Selva, and Reynaldo Robaina, of the Customs Office. A special word of gratitude to Gladys Rodríguez, Luis Fuentes, Araceli Feria, Máximo Gómez, and the rest of the staff of the Hemingway Museum.

# Appendix IV: Inventory of Hemingway Museum

LIVING ROOM:  On top of the magazine stand, a photo of Nancy Hayward, friend of the family, holding the dog Negrita. The magazine stand is the one designed by Mary and built by Francisco Castro. To the right of the stand is a marine clock and the original painting by Roberto Domingo for a bullfight poster, bought by Hemingway in 1929 or 1930.

To the right of Miss Mary's room: Photo of Hemingway taken by Karsh of Ottawa. Above the photo, a jai-alai basket. Underneath, two miniature cannons and a Mexican ashtray. Hemingway used to fire the cannons to welcome special guests.

On the wall, to the right of the main door, between the lower shelves at the windows: a jug Mary and Ernest bought in Toledo, Spain; two Russian dolls; a Danish jug, a present from Hemingway to Mary on her birthday, April, 1956; a miniature crystal boot, a gift from Don Pedro Ganaderías, of Madrid, with the branding mark of his cattle ranch engraved on it; another Russian doll and another Danish jug, again a birthday present for Mary.

In the bookshelves: a Cuban jar; ashtray made from bronze pieces from the *U.S.S. Shenandoah* of the U.S. Navy, given to Mary; another ashtray; a box for tobacco, a gift to Hemingway from Jaime Befill in 1952; a Mexican tray bought by Hemingway in Mexico in 1942.

On the opposite wall: two bullfight paintings by Roberto Domingo. On the bookshelves: three Spanish candlesticks formerly in a church at Extremadura, Spain; a bowl from Peru belonging to the Inca civilization of pre-Colombian times, a gift from the Club Marciano, Chiclayo, Peru; a footstool made by Pauline Pfeiffer; a poster of a bullfighting scene by Roberto Domingo.

On the white round table designed by Mary and made by Francisco Castro: Venetian platter from the 19th Century; ashtrays and a plaque showing the *Pilar* and a jumping marlin, a gift to Hemingway from Earl Theisen, *Look* photographer, who accompanied him on the first leg of the African safari of 1953.

On the far corner to the right: A copy of a Goya painting, Christmas present from Hemingway to Mary, one of the few articles in the house that is not original. Underneath: bookshelves, Venetian crystal decorations, a Mexican tray and a Soviet sputnik.

On the far corner to the left: a bullfight painting by Roberto Domingo. Underneath: the record player; Venetian crystal decorative objects bought by Mary in Venice in 1951, broken and repaired. More shelves with classic, Spanish and popular records.

The living room furniture was designed by Mary and T. O. Bruce, of Key West, and built by Francisco Castro and Cecilio Doma, the carpenters from San Francisco de Paula; the fiber rug is the one Hemingway bought in the Philippines in 1941.

Tables: small table in the northeast corner of the room; on it, a green and gold bowl, present from friends in Venice. There were always flowers on the long table behind the sofa; on it are some cards, a lamp bought in Cuba and an ashtray. On the other long table behind the two chairs in the living room: a box for cigars, two Venetian glass ashtrays in the form of conch shells; a corkscrew made from the tusk of a wild boar, and two lamps made from Sheffield silver candlesticks, brought by Mary from England. The table-bar designed by Hemingway and made by Francisco Castro at the farm.

DINING ROOM:     In the cabinet to the right of the glass door, on the top shelf: miniature of a model-T Ford made by Lee Samuels, Hemingway's lawyer; a bucket inscribed by Roy Marsh, the pilot who was flying the Hemingways when the accident occurred near the cataracts at Murchison, Uganda (the inscription includes advice for good conduct); tile, a gift from the bullfighter Antonio Ordoñez with the branding design of his ranch and the one used at Finca Vigía; a large drinking glass, a present from Venetian friends; a pitcher from one of Hemingway's favorite restaurants, "El Callejón," in Madrid; small pitcher from a restaurant in Segovia, Spain; French jars; tile with flower design from Bergamo, Northern Italy (this decoration is typical of that region); large goblets for the table (the first ones Mary bought for her first apartment in Chicago, 1932). There is another cabinet to the left of the glass door. On the top shelf there is a silver platter, a gift from the Cuban Institute of Tourism; a crystal Steuben plate, a wedding present to Mary and Ernest, March 1946; china from Bergamo; glass made of gold and crystal from Murano (Italy, 1770), gift from Venetian friends; a pair of wine glasses with a design of animals and flowers, bought by Hemingway for Mary in Venice, 1951; a group of serving platters, some with designs of pastel flowers and some all white, bought by Mary in Venice in 1954. On top of the sideboard, two hurricane lamps; figurine of a Danish polar bear; a crystal angel; crystal Danish platter; a Danish matchbox and cat. Inside the sideboard: dishes and glassware with the Finca Vigía symbol.

Among the decorations spread around the dining room, there is a Spanish plaque with the figure of Don Quijote, and several dinner plates with a flower design. There are also Italian crystal plates and others, white with a gray border and the branding sign of the Vigía stamped on them.

Table at left of the shelf: books in Russian, gifts from Mikoyan and Khachaturian (two of them were given to Mary by Mikoyan in March, 1960, when he visited Finca Vigía; the books contain reproductions of the painting collections at the Hermitage in Leningrad); there are also stones carved by Siboney Indians and some auriferous mineral.

On the stand to the left, between the living room and the dining room, there are various African wood carvings and a bird carved on an African antelope horn.

The furniture of the dining room was designed by Mary and T.O. Bruce and made by Francisco Castro.

LIBRARY:    Facing the room, golden candlesticks in the shape of heads of angels, placed at the door. They were bought by Mary Welsh in Venice in 1950. There is a piece of wood found drifting in the waters off Paraíso (Megano de Casigua). On the left, a poster of Juan Belmonte, bullfighter friend of Hemingway's, from September, 1927; a plate with a drawing of a bull's head by Picasso, bought in Paris in 1957; it cost around $150 (the most expensive one Mary acquired). On top of the bookcase, a corner shelf with an amplifier, and a roulette wheel bought by Hemingway but never used. On the adjacent wall hangs a tempera by Schrums, depicting an Austrian moutain village where Hemingway and Hadley Richardson, his first wife, spent several winters before and after 1925. Hemingway skied in those mountains and also worked there as a guide for skiers. The person in the lower part of the picture is Hemingway.

The bookcase has four drawers: the top one on the left holds files and Mary's documents about gardening, the swimming pool, the servants, insurance policies, Cuban tax papers and weapons licenses, records of taxes paid on Finca Vigía and also some postcards of old Venice. In the lower drawer on the left, there are drawings of the film *The Old Man and the Sea* and some advertisements from Curaçao. The upper drawer on the right is empty. There is a white chest of drawers with a flower vase on top, a gift from Hemingway to Mary on April, 1958, and over it a painting by the Dutch artist Paul Hyckes. The inscription reads: "La poule et le Fer à Cheval. A Monsieur Ernest Hemingway, avec ma trés grande admiration."

On a bookshelf, a photo of his boat, the *Pilar;* three barometers; a painting of a parrot; two lion skulls; a brass lamp of the *Pilar;* dry coral; a spritsail; modern Italian dishes.

On the opposite wall: a bookcase with four drawers and two vases on top; a porcelain bird and an African figure. There is a filing cabinet with a safety box; on top of this there are pencil sharpeners and a Mexican tray. The drawers contain manuscripts and documents concerning various matters belonging to Hemingway and Mary.

There is an Italian modern bookcase and an old American cranberry vase, of a type very popular in the 19th Century.

A curved table completes the furnishings. It is in front of the door, and on it are a lamp and an atlas. There is also a sofa in the room, a coffee table, a bench, chairs, bamboo tables and a ladder.

This room was at one time used as a guest room. The door behind the white bookcase opened onto Hemingway's study. Due to the progressive accumulation of books, and the necessity of making room for them, Mary turned it into a library in 1949. She also designed and had the furniture built, everything except the rug by the sofa, which is an authentic piece, a Moslem prayer rug from South Mombasa, Africa. Mary bought the round pouf in Cairo in 1954, as well as the camel-skin bench. The large tables are made of *majagua*, a Cuban wood. The drawer pulls and the drawers themselves were designed by Mary, as were the wall lights, and made by Francisco Castro.

HEMINGWAY'S BEDROOM:     Over the table, an old Mexican painting bought by Hemingway in Mexico in 1942.

On the left of the bed, Hemingway's typewriter. It rests on top of the bookcase to the left of the door. He worked with the typewriter placed on top of a table-desk standing on the skin of a lesser kudu that Mary shot in Africa.

In the corner to the left of the door: a black-and-white drawing, a present from an Italian friend in 1951. It is a map of East Africa.

On top of the bookcase, a photo by Charley Sweeney. Mary Welsh said of him: "Colonel Sweeney was Ernest's friend since the twenties. he attended West Point but was expelled. He fought with Pancho Villa at the Mexican border, and in many Latin American revolutions. He was a Colonel in the French Foreign Legion. He became an expert in military tactics and strategy and was promoted to General in the French army. He organized and was the leader of the Eagle Squadron of the British Royal Air Force during the Second World War, made up of American aviators that had gone to England via Canada. One of his last appearances as a military expert was at a conference he organized in 1950 for the Chiefs of Staffs and his colleagues during the war. He made a brilliant analysis of the situation in France at the time with valuable recommendations on how to improve it, recommendations that were not followed. He suffered a cerebral hemorrhage in 1956. He was one of the heroes Ernest Hemingway had admired all his life, being, like himself, the eternal rebel."

In the bookcase: a cane, photos, insignias taken from German prisoners, a corkscrew and a belt.

On the floor, a lion skin and head.

On the wall opposite the window of the study: a buffalo head, a map of Cuba and a jar that holds a frog preserved in formalin.

On the window wall: a painting of Merganser ducks and a photograph of two of Hemingway's sons: Gregory and Patrick. A photo of his eldest son John, his wife, and David Bruce, American ambassador to Great Britain, taken at John's wedding.

A Daumier lithograph, an original; "Short-snorters;" an American bank note signed by other "short-snorters," which meant people who had flown across the Atlantic or Pacific oceans (when Ernest Hemingway flew to China in 1941, crossing the oceans by air was still quite rare); 26 small objects, all presents from friends or unknown persons. Camouflage cloth of green and brown silk, a gift from British friends, 1944.

A shoe holder.

More bookshelves, and on them 13 knives, a belt and canes. The canes were presents from African tribal chiefs: the Wacamba and Masai tribes. The knives are used to skin animals and in ceremonies. They were all gifts from friends who knew of Ernest Hemingway's fondness for knives.

Next to the books there is a photograph of his first granddaughter, Jean Hemingway.

On top of Hemingway's bureau there are some carvings of animals, bought by Ernest and Mary from the same artists in Machakos, East Africa. There is a key from the city of Matanzas given to them when Hemingway and Mary arrived there on the French transatlantic *Île de France* in 1957. Also, a tray in the shape of a fish, full of shells and other objects which Hemingway considered bearers of good luck. A leather bookmark with the following inscription: "I never write letters. Ernest Hemingway." He never used it. There are different types of paper which he used during the last seventeen years. Other objects are: a hand-drawn map which Ernest used when the troops of the Fourth Infantry Division of the U.S. Army were approaching Paris. Foreign coins and bills, wallets, checks made out to Hemingway which he never cashed. Three unopened letters, the last ones to reach Finca Vigía. Maps, a whistle to attract ducks; print of Idaho deer; a pocket knife and maps.

Under the bureau's glass top, from left to right, starting with the corner near the waste basket, there are his calling cards; a prayer; a photograph of his friend Waldo Pierce with a marlin; a liquor license from Idaho; photos of Marlene Dietrich taken during the Second World War; photo of Lillian Ross, of *The New Yorker*, sitting between two of the actors from the film *Red Badge of Courage*; photo of his son Patrick and his wife at some Athens ruins; photos of Mary; photos from newspapers: Ernest at races, Paris; Ernest and his two younger sons and a friend; Scott Fitzgerald, his wife and daughter and Ernest; photograph of the sketch of a friend, Renata Borgitti; photo of Carmen Luz, a Spanish dancer, daughter of Pedro Herrera Sotolongo.

Closet: In it there are 6 guns and rifles, 1 pistol, different types of ammunition, 2 cases for guns, a Chinese hat, 2 pairs of old eyeglasses and several items of Ernest's clothing and shoes. On the bookcase in front of the window there is Hemingway's favorite weapon, the Mann-licher carbine, and the head of the African buffalo he shot on the plains of Serengetti, in January of 1934.

There was an air-conditioner in the room, but it was not used, because, according to Mary, Hemingway said that "other people were not as fortunate." In other words, he didn't operate the machine because others didn't have one like it. Mary swears this is true.

BATHROOM:        Weights; a bottle with a bat preserved in formalin (Hemingway called it "The Bottled Bat"); a small stand with books near the toilet, among the books a volume about Houdini; and on the wall, a wood carving of a *castero*, present from Mary, bought in Lima, Peru, in 1955.

VENETIAN ROOM:        On the wall beside the beds, from left to right; two Venetian landscapes; a small oil painting of the Bridge of Sighs, Venice; a view of Havana as seen from Finca Vigía by a British artist; a bullfight scene signed by Cane; a "Portrait of Papa" by Oscar Villarreal, brother of René, from San Francisco de Paula; a piece of the ceiba root taken from under the floor and placed on top of the cupboard.

The same wall, underneath the above: metal containers holding about 200 transparencies taken by Mary in Venice, France, Africa and Egypt; a small projector and a large one.

There is a bench from the Floridita bar and on it a roll of old maps and music, presents from a Venetian friend; a lamp and books on a night table.

A serving cart that holds books, magazines and galleys from books that other authors sent him for his comments. He bought the serving cart the winter of '50-'51. He meant to use it to transport hot dishes for the evening meal from the kitchen to the room when he wanted to dine informally. This plan was quickly rejected, inasmuch as trays are much easier to manage. There is a rush screen painted white.

On the shelves to the right of the door: a yellow umbrella used by visitors when it rained, to go from the door to the car. On the left, a seat with cushions; five sets of cushions for the living room, one for the library and several for Mary's room. Also, hats Mary and Ernest used in Africa. On top of the shelves, electric heaters and pictures of an Italian sculpture and postcards from Spain and Venice; a gift for Ernest Hemingway that has not been opened; two bottle holders and a leather corkscrew.

On the wall opposite the beds: a picture of Hemingway inscribed to Juan Duñabeitía, nicknamed "Sinsky"; an oil painting of a bullfight, given to Hemingway by person unknown. Underneath: bookcase, dressing table, seat and mirror.

Bookcase for paperback books: on top, African objects: ritual mask for Wakamba tribe ceremonies; carved wooden mask; tusk of a wild boar (the other tusk of the same animal was used to make the corkscrew that is on the table-bar in the living room); bead bracelet made and given to Mary by the Wakamba women near the camp in the swamps of Kimana, Kenya; doll made of fiber, a goddess used by an old witch doctor; ceremonial beaded headdress of the Masai tribe; decorated kidney-shaped receptacle made from a horn, used to carry fire in the rainy season or to carry water, also of the Masai tribe; and a basket used by the women of the Tanganyika tribes to store corn.

On top of the bookcase for paperbacks: A Chinese tempera painting, gift from Winston Guest and his wife.

MARY'S ROOM:     In the closet: The blue and white dress Mary was wearing at the time of the airplane accidents in Uganda, Africa on the 23rd and 24th, 1954. The belts are hanging on the door; there's a tempera painting by Dorothy Pound, wife of Ezra Pound; horns of a stag deer shot in Idaho, in 1948.

Bookcase: on the top corner of the bookcase an ashtray from Cabo Blanco Fishing Club of Peru; a pewter pitcher Mary bought in Holland in 1938; coral and shells from one of the keys north of Cárdenas. On the second shelf: Danish ashtray; an Italian pitcher; a ladybird and a deer. There are some initials in bronze, a gift from Alexander Calder. On the third shelf: a Van Gogh reproduction, a gift from Ernest; a match holder from Mary's father; a mechanical turtle from Hong Kong; an Italian elephant—all gifts. On the fourth shelf: Mary's jewelry box; a Victorian bracelet; insignias and service bars from the United States Army; a miniature bullfighter's cape.

Against the adjacent wall: a sofa with drawers that contain Christmas cards; maps; an African fly swatter; a fan; tail of a wild animal; tail of a Thompson gazelle; paper; cord.

Desk: Silver cup won by Hemingway; photograph of oldest son, John H. Hemingway, taken at his wedding to Byra Whittlesey Whitlock; a painting by Dorothy Pound; head of an Orix Beisa, shot by Mary in Kiwana Swamp, Kenya, 1953.

The other desk contains writing material, office effects and photos. In the top drawer there is an envelope containing instructions for the operation of several household appliances.

On the bed: A painting of ships at sea.

Adjacent wall: A picture of Hemingway by Kid Tunero's son; an early 19th Century Venetian mirror; a picture of Beatrice Ferguson Guck, cousin of Mary's, by Adams; a chest of drawers, and in it: an old clock and jewelry; a box for fishhooks made of mahogany, a gift from a friend, which was used to keep Christmas cards in.

The small table in the center of the room was made from a tray Mary bought in Havana. The legs were made at Finca Vigía. On top of the table are some foreign coins.

On top of the chest of drawers: A box for Mary's jewels, bought in Venice in 1951, and a small jewelry box to use on travels, and several objects from England, France, Spain, Italy and Mexico. The cigar case has a golden metal chain.

This was the first room modernized by Mary. She had the closet at the far side of the room removed and some large windows put in at the front and on the side facing the back of the house; she designed the night tables and the round benches, all made by Francisco Castro in the garage at Finca Vigía. The wood is mahogany.

FIRST FLOOR OF THE TOWER:      A home for the cats.

SECOND FLOOR OF THE TOWER:      Spears from the Masai tribe in Kenya, some given to Ernest Hemingway, some bought by him from the warriors of the tribe. (Ernest Hemingway learned spear hunting and practiced with quite good aim; he killed monkeys with spears near the Kimana Swamp west of Mount Kilimanjaro, Kenya.) There are some high boots to wear as protection from mosquitos, hunting boots and ski boots. There is a box that contains shells from the Cypraea family, brought by Mary from Africa. Hemingway found them in an island east of Shumoni, a fishing village south of Mombasa. They are the famous "money cowry" shells used as monetary exchange by the coastal tribes of Africa and which were accepted by them in the 18th Century in exchange for gold, ivory and slaves. There are also some African animal horns, covers for the windows in case of hurricane, and gift wrapping paper.

TOP FLOOR OF THE TOWER:      Ernest Hemingway's table, built according to Mary's specifications. He used it, but not very often. There are some books there and the head and skin of a lioness shot by Hemingway in the safari of 1933. Also, the chaise-longue where Ernest used to nap occasionally.

SWIMMING POOL:      There is a large bench poolside with movable top designed by Ernest in 1945. Mary designed the rest of the furniture and all of it was made at Finca Vigía. The cushions are kept in the dressing room. The pool's filter system was installed in 1950, the work done by R. Schmidt of Cia. de Purificadores de Cuba (Filter Company of Cuba), at a cost of $10,000, including the housing for the system. Hemingway liked the pool and he often worked or read in the shade of the pergola. Most of the time in the years he lived there, he would swim half a mile daily except in winter. Mary swam a mile a day. In the hot season, they would eat their lunch by the pool. The food was brought on trays from the house.

FILES:   In the late fifties, Hemingway bought a three-drawer filing cabinet. He had decided to organize his correspondence and certain documents. He called in his friend Roberto Herrera Sotolongo and asked him to put these papers in order. After Hemingway's death and with the Revolutionary government in power, the writer Fernando G. Campoamor became administrator of the Finca. Campoamor gathered all the documents found in the house and, together with those in the files, had them deposited at the Administration Council of Cuba, where they have been kept since then.

A look inside the filing cabinet reveals: the Nobel Prize accrediting diploma; necklaces made of seeds; insignias; a silver crucifix; foreign money, including francs, pesetas, pounds sterling, coins from the Belgian Congo, Egyptian piasters, liras; two Pan American diplomas dated 1941. There are also maps from France, China, Canada and Ethiopia.

Other objects: A medal with the inscription *Per Ardua ad Astra;* a metal plaque with this inscription: *Concurso de Pesca Hemingway* 1958 (Hemingway Fishing Contest 1958); another medal inscribed: CCC TO "GIGI'S" PAPA FOR HIS SPLENDID RECORD. July 21, 1942; a box of stationery with Finca Vigía letterhead; Prewi-Radio cable pad; small paper pad for messages; envelopes with Finca Vigía imprint; coin purse with seven francs; several loose coins of different value; and a bank check. A white wooden box with the initials MW containing Hemingway's war correspondent insignia; and an empty red velvet coffer.

## PERSONAL NOTE

Many friends provided encouragement, sustaining me in the hope that this book would one day be finished. Douglas Rudd devoted long days to it and Pablo Pacheco went beyond his duties as editor. Ramón Font Alvarez translated two hundred letters and Harold Spencer, Engracia Hernandez and Sandro and Joan Gandini lent their efforts. Lisandro Otero and José Gomez Fresquet were there at the beginning. Barbara Hutchinson, although she joined us at the end, also participated. Marilyn Bobes contributed time and knowledge and Bernardo Marques his boundless enthusiasm. Other helpful friends were: Vicente Dopico, Eliseo Diego, Jorge Rufinelli, Ramón Gonzalez, Waldo Valdés, Jorge Ramos, Rine Leal, Lourdes Casal, Marifeli Perez-Stable, Silvia Flamand, Mirta Miranda, Alberto Batista, Gladys Galindo, Alberto Korda, Anton Arrufat, Luis Baez, Rita M. Fernández, Juan Carlos Fernández, Enrique Román, Jesús Hernández, Alicia Llerena, Nicolás Perez Delgado, Hector Villaverde, Nancy Morejón, Pablo Armando Fernández, Radamas Giro and Alfredo Muñoz-Unsain.

The work was started in July, 1974, and took seven years to complete. At times it was like a fiesta. There were moments when I felt very close to the thunderous adventure. Now the book is finished, and *Hemingway in Cuba* is the result of the collaboration of many good companions.

# Index

## ABOUT THE AUTHOR

NORBERTO FUENTES is one of the most promising young Cuban writers to emerge since the revolution. Born in Havana in 1943, he studied art and sculpture before working as a journalist. Between 1961 and 1966 he was a front-line reporter in the Sierra de Escambray when government forces sought out counter-revolutionary bands.

Out of that experience came his collection of short stories, *Condenados de Condado*, which in 1968 won him the Casa de las Americas award, the most prestigious literary prize in Latin America. The book was translated into English, Italian and other languages.

Fuentes is a roving journalist, always ready to go on the march. For the past two years he has been with the Cuban troops in Angola, covering the conflict there. He has contributed to major Cuban publications—*Granma, Cuba International, Revolución y Cultura, La Gaceta*. His reportages are an invaluable testimony of the struggles, successes and shortcomings of a people building a revolution.

Fuentes graduated at Havana University in 1977, obtaining a degree in Cuban and Latin American literature.

In addition to his journalism, for the past seven years he has been engaged in writing *Hemingway in Cuba*, based on the novelist's long stay at Finca Vigía, now one of Cuba's most popular museums. Norberto Fuentes is the only person granted access by the Cuban government to all of Hemingway's papers, books and files.

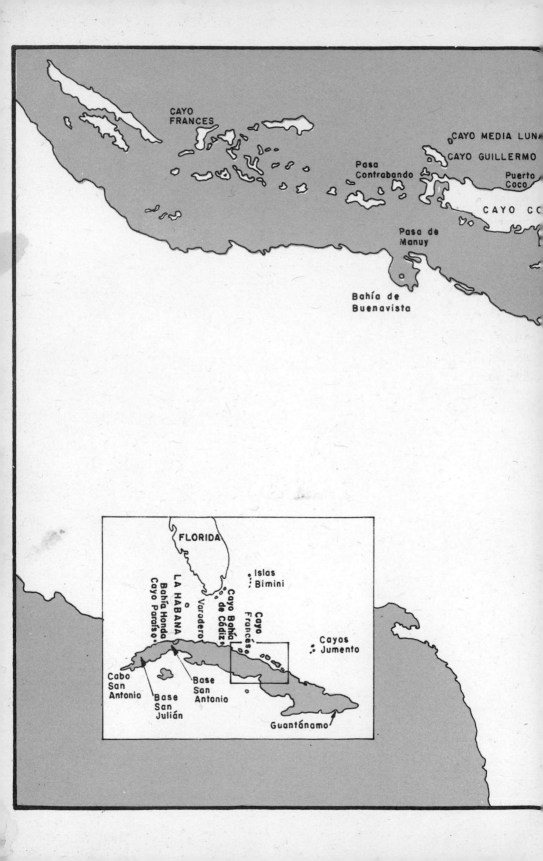